Praise for L. E. Modesitt's Saga of Recluce

"Modesitt has established himself with his Recluce series as one of the best 90s writers of fantasy." —*Vector*

"Reading any novel in the series invites the reader to fill in the picture of a tangible setting some critics have compared to Tolkien's *Middle-Earth*."—*Amarillo Sunday News-Globe*

"Already a landmark fantasy series." —*Romantic Times*

"L. E. Modesitt Jr. has been building a world that seems fantastic, with magic and feudalism rampant, but is riveted pretty thoroughly to the rigors of science fiction. There's a consistency across this universe that makes the magic, the science, the politics, and the economy seem plausibly well-integrated." —*San Diego Union-Tribune*

Scion of Cyador

"Modesitt's latest novel in the Recluce series portrays the transformation of a talented young man into a determined and deadly warrior who struggles to maintain his compassion in the face of war's horrors. The author displays a rare talent for portraying the day-to-day affairs of a vividly detailed world in which chaos and order form a dynamic duality." —*Library Journal*

"Modesitt once more spins a multilayered coming-of-age story that examines both a society and its use and misuse of power. . . . It offers an action-packed plot, with an involving cross-class love story and a thoughtful allegory of the price paid for exploitation." —*VOYA*

SCION OF CYADOR

L.E. Modesitt, Jr.

A TOM DOHERTY ASSOCIATES BOOK
NEW YORK

This is a work of fiction. All the characters and events portrayed in this book are either products of the author's imagination or are used fictitiously.

SCION OF CYADOR

Copyright © 2000 by L. E. Modesitt, Jr.

All rights reserved, including the right to reproduce this book, or portions thereof, in any form.

Edited by David G. Hartwell

A Tor Book
Published by Tom Doherty Associates, LLC
175 Fifth Avenue
New York, NY 10010

www.tor.com

Tor® is a registered trademark of Tom Doherty Associates, LLC.

ISBN: 0-812-58926-2
Library of Congress Catalog Card Number: 00-031517

First edition: September 2000
First mass market edition: December 2001

Printed in the United States of America

0 9 8 7 6 5 4 3 2 1

To Lee and Sheila:
may their house prosper

NORTHERN

CANDAR

GULF OF MURR

RECLUCE

EASTERN OCEAN

The WORLD

OCEAN

Gulf of Austra

AUSTRA

Blysta

Valmurl

WESTERN OCEAN

NORDLA

Swartheld

Luba

Cigoerne

Atla

AFRIT

South River

MEROWEY

HAMOR

NORTHERN OCEAN

Cape Devalin
Spidlaria
SPIDLAR
Kleth
Elparta East
Horns
Quend
Rytel
CERTIS
Jellico
Montgren
Vergren
Fenard Freetown
Telsen
Wevor
Hydlar
Telgya
Meltosta
Onpre
KYPHROS
Desiv
Telsen
Worana & Arastia
Haga
Fairhaven
RUZOR
Sunta
Worrak
Asula

Turkaven
SLIGO
Lavah
FREETOWN
(LYDIAR)
Renklaar
Ruzdya

HYDLEN

Gulf of Murr
Black Lands'
Holding End
Alberto Extina
Reflin
Lydkter

Alaren

Nylan
Matra Feyn
Wandernaught
Clarion
Sigil
Southpoint
Renstrm

RECLUCE

EASTERN OCEAN

CHibbell 1995

Characters

Kien	Magus, Senior Lector, "Fourth Magus"
Lorn	Son of the Magus Kien
Vernt	Younger son of Kien
Jerial	Eldest child and daughter of Kien
Myryan	Youngest child and daughter of Kien
Nyryah	Consort of Kien
Toziel'elth'alt'mer	Emperor of Cyador
Ryenyel	Consort-Empress of Cyador

MAGI'I

Chyenfel	First Magus and High Lector
Kharl	Second Magus and Senior Lector
Liataphi	Third Magus and Senior Lector
Abram	Senior Lector
Aleyar	Healer, daughter of Liataphi
Ciesrt	Magus
Jysnet	Lector
Hyrist	Senior Lector
Rustyl	Magus
Syreal	Daughter of Liataphi, consort of Veljan
Tyrsal	Magus

LANCERS

Rynst	Majer-Commander, Mirror Lancers
Luss	Captain-Commander, Mirror Lancers
Allyrn	Captain
Brevyl	Majer [commanding at Isahl]
Cheryk	Captain
Dettaur	Sub-Majer
Eghyr	Captain
Ikynd	Commander [commanding at Assyadt]

Lhary	Commander [Western Regional Commander, Cyad]
Maran	Majer [Patrol Commander, Geliendra]
Sypcal	Commander [Eastern Regional Commander, Cyad]

MERCHANTERS

Bluoyal	Merchanter Advisor to the Emperor [Bluyet Clan]
Denys	Merchanter [Bluyet Clan]
Eileyt	Enumerator [Ryalor House]
Fuyol	Merchanter [Head, Yuryan Clan]
Kernys	Merchanter [Head, Kysan Clan]
Neabyl	Emperor's Enumerator [Biehl]
Ryalth	Woman merchanter [consort to Lorn]
Sasyk	Chief of Guards [Dyjani House]
Tasjan	Merchanter [Head, Dyjani Clan]
Veljan	Merchanter Heir [Yuryan Clan]
Vyanat	Merchanter [Head, Hyshrah Clan]
Vyel	Merchanter, brother of Vyanat

Lorn'alt, Cyad Overcaptain, Mirror Lancers

I

If CYADOR BE the paradox of Candar, and supporting that paradox be indeed the duty of each of the Magi'i of the Quarter, then how must each magus approach that duty so as to support the way to the Steps of Paradise?

One scholar magus might say, "Support the Emperor of Light, for he is the one who must balance the Mirror Lancers and the Magi'i against each other, and against the growing might of the merchanter clans, who know but the greed for gold and the pleasures of the moment."

A magus who tends the chaos-towers might declare, "Take care that the chaos-towers endure while they may, for without the towers, Cyador is no more than any other land set upon our world."

Still another might claim, "Set forth rules for the Magi'i that they may lead all by their example and purity of devotion to chaos and the people who revere it."

For all that the Magi'i descended from those of the Rational Stars, the ways in which the duty of a magus could be set forth are myriad, and like unto chaos itself, often resembling itself, yet never the same and always changing. Each magus, from the most to the least devoted, will have a vision of that duty. Some will hold that by increasing their personal mastery of chaos, they will serve Cyador, the Magi'i, and chaos in the best fashion possible. Others will declare that mastery of chaos must always serve others first, for the magus who places himself before duty will always be corrupted into believing that what is good for him is good for all.

Yet neither be right, for a magus who serves only others will fly from one master to another, for each who asks of him becomes a master. A magus who elevates his mastery above all, would make all others his servant. Thus, a magus must be neither master nor servant, but one who walks the narrow path between. A magus without dedication to chaos will have no soul, and one who worships it blindly, no sense.

That dilemma sets forth the true paradox of the Magi'i, that we must master chaos without being mastered by it . . .

Paradox of Empire
Bern'elth, Magus First
Cyad, 157 A.F.

II

LORN OPENS THE door to the small upper-floor balcony, checking to see that the spring weather remains warm in the late afternoon. With a nod, he closes the door and turns to take in the main room of Ryalth's quarters—the low ebony table, the straight-backed black oak armchair that is Ryalth's favorite, the settee opposite it, and on the other side of the room, the green ceramic brick privacy screen that protects the main door from the inside. To his right is the alcove that contains the circular eating table and two armless chairs. To his left is the narrow archway to the bedchamber, and beyond that, the small bathing chamber.

He smiles as he looks at the portrait of Ryalth as a young girl. In it, she wears a high-necked green tunic, and a thin golden chain. The floor of the main room displays ancient blue wool carpet with a border of interlocked ropes, surrounding a woven image of a blue-hulled trading ship under full sail, the ill-fated ship once owned by Ryalth's merchanter father, and the one on which her parents had perished.

"Are you ready?" calls the redheaded lady who is his consort, as well as the head of the newly ascendant trading house—Ryalor House. Lorn sometimes still has trouble believing that she has incorporated his name into that of the trading concern she has established, even if he had helped her in the years before they were consorted.

"Yes. I was checking to see that it was still warm out." He crosses the room and steps into the bedchamber. There, he adjusts his sabre and the collar emblems on the new Mirror Lancer uniform that Ryalth had arranged to have waiting for him when he had returned from his previous duty station. His efforts in battling the Accursed Forest had destroyed all but one of his Mirror Lancer uniforms, and that one he had worn on the firewagon trip back to Cyad.

"Is it?"

"It's very pleasant." He smiles at her as he steps away from the narrow mirror set on a stand against the bedchamber wall. "Still . . . I almost wish that we were not going to my parents' for dinner again. I don't have that many days left before I have to leave for Biehl."

"They were charming the night before last." Ryalth eases past Lorn and before the mirror, touching her short red hair with the silver-backed and tortoiseshell comb. "And they don't keep us late. They do understand."

"That was because it was only them and Jerial. Vernt and his consort-to-be, and Ciesrt and Myryan will be there tonight." He steps forward and puts his arms around her waist, then kisses the back of her neck. "You smell so good."

"I'm glad you think so." For a moment, she leans her cheek against his. "You don't mind being here? In my quarters?"

"They're our quarters, and you are my consort, and I like being here with you."

"My rooms are so . . . modest, compared to your parents' dwelling."

"Nothing is modest when you're there."

"Such flattery."

"Not flattery. Truth," he insists.

"Truth is in the mind of the speaker," she counters. "The mirror reflects what is, and the image is of modest quarters."

Lorn laughs. "Are you ready?"

"It is not going to rain, is it, O magely one?"

"No . . . I checked, remember? It will be warm this evening. And I'm not that much of a magus."

"More than you admit."

Lorn does not answer, but hugs her and kisses her neck again.

"I like walking with you, knowing you can wear your uniform."

"Some may still think you my mistress," Lorn teases.

"Not if I wear the blue-and-green cloak."

Lorn laughs. "You can wear green, if you wish, now that we are consorted. Could not I wear blue, without subterfuge?"

"You could, but I like the cream-and-green better."

Lorn recalls a question he has failed to ask. "And how would the honored Bluoyal, the Merchanter Advisor, feel about a lancer wearing blue?"

"You didn't worry about that for years." She smiles. "Why now?"

"Because no one knew who we were." Lorn pauses. "What of Bluoyal? When Eileyt speaks of him, his mouth puckers, as with a sour fruit. Eileyt is usually so careful. Since he is the senior enumerator of Ryalor House, that is good. But he didn't conceal his distaste of Bluoyal to me, not at all."

"You are my consort," Ryalth points out.

"What of Bluoyal?" Lorn asks again.

"Bluoyal . . . I try to avoid him."

"Is he like Shevelt?" Lorn's eyes harden as he recalls the Yuryan Clan heir he had removed years earlier because of the man's attempts to use his position to force himself on Ryalth.

"No." She shakes her head. "No. Bluoyal is effective at telling the Emperor the problems the merchanters face, but he wishes all to pay him great homage for that effectiveness. He also was one of those who brokered the means for Liataphi's daughter to consort with Veljan."

"Oh . . . so, in a way, Veljan owes his position to Bluoyal and the Magi'i?"

"With some, that pearapple was hard to swallow."

"He has not bothered you?"

Ryalth smiles. "Save for collecting our—Ryalor's—scorth, no."

"A twentieth part of your revenues?"

She shakes her head. "It is called that, but it is but one part in fifty of the revenues after expenses." She drapes a light cotton cloak over her shoulders, blue with a green-and-cream border. "Best we go. I would not have your parents looking askance at me for delaying their son."

"They would blame me," Lorn points out. "Not you."

Ryalth shakes her head as she walks from the bedchamber and toward the privacy screen and the outer door. "They yet have that black angel–cursed Magi'i sense that all is their responsibility, and yours, as you are of the elthage blood. I can't even be responsible for delaying you."

Lorn opens his mouth, then closes it as he sees the sparkle in her eyes. "I'll hold you responsible . . . but just when you are." He opens the door for her.

"I hope so."

Once they have descended the stairs, they walk uphill along the Thirteenth Way, and then westward on the Road of Perpetual Light, in toward the center of Cyad for the three very long blocks before they reach the dwelling where Lorn was raised.

"We'll be first," Lorn says.

"Because your brother will wish to exert his superior position by later arrival, as will Myryan's consort?"

"I think Ciesrt just will wish he weren't coming, but he doesn't wish to offend father."

"Not Myryan?" Ryalth lifts her eyebrows.

"Ciesrt believes consorts are appurtenances."

"I am glad you do not believe such."

"You would scarce let me," he counters.

They laugh in the mild spring air, ignoring the carriages and wagons that pass along the Road of Perpetual Light. Lorn's eyes take in the Palace of Eternal Light to the west, and all the other white granite and sunstone structures that rise in the marvel that is Cyad, the shining city, the city beside which all others pale. The words of one of the verses from the silver-covered book come to mind, the book from Ryalth's heritage she had entrusted to him so many years before.

> The city, Cyad, lost light like a star,
> The dream, Cyad, guiding near and far.

He smiles to himself. Cyad is indeed a special city. Then he turns his eyes to the dwelling ahead.

Jerial meets Lorn and Ryalth at the door to Lorn's parents' dwelling. The healer wears a green tunic so dark it is almost black, and her black hair is cut short. "You always look so good, Ryalth." She studies her brother. "Did I tell you I like her?"

"I believe you have. Several times."

"You might as well go on up." Jerial shuts the door and steps around the inside privacy screen. "Mother and I thought we would eat on the upper portico tonight. It is warm, and the breeze is gentle."

"We're the first?" Lorn asks.

"Except for Father and Mother."

Lorn and Ryalth climb the three flights to the fourth and topmost level of the dwelling in which Lorn was raised.

Lorn's mother is waiting at the uppermost landing. "You look wonderful, Ryalth. I like the cloak."

"Thank you." The redhead inclines her head.

"I did persuade Myryan and Ciesrt to come tonight." Nyryah raises her eyebrows. "Ciesrt wanted to know if Vernt would be here. He was pleased to know that Vernt is bringing his consort-to-be. That's Mycela. I do not believe you have met her."

"I have not had that pleasure. In fact," Lorn adds dryly, "I had not had the pleasure of knowing he intended to take a consort until the other night when you told me."

"He has been seeing her since the turn of fall." Nyryah turns, and the three walk toward the southwest corner of the upper level, toward the roofed but open-air area flanked with columns that adjoins the warm-weather dining area.

They have barely taken their first steps when the door to the study opens behind them, and the white-haired Kien emerges. He walks toward them with the barest hint of a shuffle. "Greetings, Lorn, Ryalth. It's been such a long time since I've seen you two."

Lorn smiles.

Ryalth laughs gently.

"You'll have them here every moment, dear, if you aren't careful," cautions Nyryah.

"Not even an old magus like me could manage that," counters Kien. "Lorn will be gone again to his station in Biehl in less than an eightday."

The four walk slowly toward the portico dining area.

"The harbor always looks so beautiful from here," Ryalth observes. "You have such a wonderful view."

"We are fortunate," answers Nyryah. "At times, I sit here in the late afternoon and watch the clouds and the ships."

"Lorn!" Vernt appears behind them, accompanied by a blonde young woman who is laughing at something.

Lorn and Ryalth turn and step toward the two recent arrivals.

"Lorn, Ryalth, this is Mycela." Vernt smiles at the blonde. "This is my elder brother Lorn and his consort Ryalth. As you can see, Mycela, Lorn is an overcaptain in the Mirror Lancers, one of the youngest, I would venture, and Ryalth is the head of Ryalor House, one of the newly prominent trading houses in Cyad." Vernt smiles happily.

"How nice to meet you both." Mycela's smile is not quite simpering.

Lorn and Ryalth bow ever so slightly to the white-clad younger woman.

"Mycela is the daughter of Lector Abram'elth," Vernt explains.

Jerial slips by Vernt. "Ciesrt and Myryan are on their way up. She stopped to get something from her old room."

"You recall my sister Jerial," Vernt says.

"You wear green," Mycela says, wide-eyed, as she bows to Jerial.

"I am a senior healer, and without consort," Jerial says with a shrug. "The green is more appropriate."

"You *do* have such an unusual family, Vernt." Mycela giggles slightly. "They do so many things."

"Lorn!" calls Myryan as she appears behind Vernt, who steps back for Ciesrt and Myryan.

Ciesrt inclines his head to Vernt. "I am most glad to see you here." He bows slightly to Vernt's consort-to-be. "Greetings, Mycela."

Mycela giggles momentarily. "Greetings, Ciesrt."

"Perhaps we could sit down, now that Ciesrt and Myryan are here." Nyryah gestures to the dining table on the covered upper balcony, set as always, and as Lorn can recall from his childhood, so that all but Nyryah can look downhill and south directly at the harbor—and to the west and slightly uphill at the Palace of Eternal Light. Twilight lingers, and the sky remains the purple maroon that is beginning to fade, but the lamps set in brackets on the columns have already been lit. In the harbor, the white stone piers glimmer above the darkness of the water and before the Great Western Ocean farther to the south. The Palace remains an edifice of shimmering white, and light beams from its windows, from the innumerable lamps within its high-ceilinged corridors and halls.

Lorn and Ryalth are to be seated across from each other at the southern end of the table, with Nyryah at the end between them, and Jerial to Lorn's left and Ciesrt to Ryalth's right. Vernt and Mycela flank Kien, while Myryan sits between Jerial and Vernt. Lorn nods at Ryalth. "If you don't mind . . . could we change places?"

A faint smile crosses Jerial's face, but vanishes near-instantly, as the two consorts trade seats. A blank expression appears on Mycela's face.

As soon as Lorn takes the seat that had been Ryalth's, silence settles on the table, and all look to the north end.

"In the blessing and warmth of chaos, in the prosperity which it engenders, let us give thanks for what we receive." From the north end of the table, the white-haired Kien speaks clearly, then lifts his head and smiles. "It is so good of all of you to be here tonight."

The dining table around which the nine sit is covered with a pale green linen cloth, and set with glistening white porcelain plates. Quyal—the cook—appears with a large platter that holds fowl breasts covered in a thick cream sauce, and sets it before Kien. Kysia—the head of his parents' household, whose wages had been supplemented for years by Ryalth, secretly at first—follows a covered dish from which steam rises, and with a silver tray holding thin slices of dark sun-nut bread.

Lorn takes a sip of the wine—Alafraan—and glances at Ryalth, murmuring, "You had this sent here."

She smiles. "It was the least I could do, after all your parents have done."

"It was most thoughtful," Nyryah adds.

Lorn's lips curl into a rueful smile.

"You are not here long, are you, Lorn?" asks Ciesrt.

"No. I'm between duty assignments, and I'll be leaving on oneday."

"Where will you be going?" Ciesrt follows up.

"To head the port detachment in Biehl."

"You'll be the one in charge?" asks Mycela. "The head officer?"

"That's what my transfer orders say." Lorn smiles and passes the nut bread to his mother, after taking a slice for himself. "The port detachments protect trade and ensure that the tariffs are collected fairly."

"I imagine it will provide a respite after fighting the barbarians and the Accursed Forest," suggests Kien. "And it is somewhat closer to Cyad."

"What of the Accursed Forest?" asks Vernt. His brow furrows. "What exactly do lancer patrols do there?"

"We ride along the walls to see that no wild creatures escape. We also maintain order and guard the Mirror Engineers while they repair any walls that the Accursed Forest has damaged."

"The Forest damages walls?" asks the wide-eyed Mycela.

"Some of the trees that fall across the ward-walls are more than twenty cubits thick and nearly as hard as stone. They occasionally damage the wall and the wards that contain the Forest creatures." Lorn glances at Ciesrt. "I understand that the Forest project is coming along."

"I believe so, but that is not something that I do." Ciesrt shrugs. "There are rumors, but your father would know far better than I."

Vernt and Lorn glance at the oldest magus.

Kien smiles wryly. "I, too, must plead silence, except to say that there is a project, and if it works as it may, Cyad will need far fewer lancers to patrol the Accursed Forest."

After a moment of silence, Ciesrt looks across the table at Ryalth. "Myryan has said that you are head of a trading house."

"Ryalor House," Ryalth confirms.

"And you are truly the head of it?" Ciesrt asks. "Did you come to that because your parents had no sons?"

"Actually, Ciesrt," Lorn says smoothly, "she created it and built it from a clanless trading room into one that rivals many full houses. She is most skilled, and I was quite fortunate to prevail upon her to be my consort."

"Oh." Ciesrt frowns.

"There are not many lady merchanters who head houses, are there?" asks Myryan, her eyes twinkling.

"I know of only one other," Ryalth admits. "She is much older."

"Did she not inherit her position?" asks Jerial.

"I believe such, but I do not know for certain." Ryalth's words are cautious.

"So . . . Lorn is right," Jerial says. "You're the first woman in generations to head a trading house by your own ability, and perhaps the first to build one."

"I have had assistance. Those who work for me are good." Ryalth smiles. "And Lorn has been a great inspiration."

"He usually is," adds Kien, with a dry laugh, "even for those who have not wished such inspiration."

"Father!" Myryan mock-protests.

Kien finishes his fowl breast before looking at his younger daughter and raising his white eyebrows. "Your brother makes an impact wherever he goes. He always has. Talk to his friends, like Tyrsal and Dettaur."

"Where is Dettaur these days?" asks Ciesrt.

"The last we heard he was second-in-command or something at Assyadt," Jerial answers. "He writes occasionally, but he does not write of what he does."

"He still writes?" Lorn asks.

"He has hopes," Jerial says.

"He must be an important officer," offers Mycela. "If he is in charge of something, that is."

"He approaches women like a campaign," Jerial adds, "as if we were to be assaulted and captured. That is difficult." She smiles at Mycela. "At least for those who are healers."

Lorn looks across the table at Myryan. "How is the garden coming?"

"This year it's much better. Ciesrt powdered some limestone, and Ryalth had a cartload of stable manure delivered last fall. We still have jars and crocks of things, and I'm hoping that this year will be even better."

"She is wonderful with the garden." Ciesrt beams. "She coaxes the best vegetables and fruits from the land. I doubt any young magus has a consort so marvelous. And she cooks so well, too, and everything in the house is so neat, and clean."

"I will have to visit you, and learn your secrets," Mycela says. "I would not wish Vernt to lack for anything."

Lorn swallows and takes refuge in another sip of wine as the domestic conversation continues. Ryalth smiles at him gently, taking a sip from her own goblet as well.

"This time, we do have a proper dessert," Nyryah announces, after all have finished what they would eat, "the special creamed pearapple tarts." She looks at Lorn. "And there are enough for two apiece."

Lorn feels himself flush slightly in the dim light, hoping the others will not notice, and takes a sip of the Alafraan.

Nyryah gestures, and Kysia and Quyal appear beside the table to remove the dinner platters and to place a small plate before each of the diners. Her plate, and that of Jerial, have but one tart. All the others have two.

Lorn waits for all to be served and for Ryalth and his mother to begin before he takes a bite. He nods as he swallows. "They are good."

"You've always thought so."

"I think I'd best learn the recipe for this dessert," says Ryalth, with a laugh. "My cooking is far simpler, but . . . his favorite dessert . . ."

"Keep the cooking simple," suggests Jerial. "You haven't spoiled him yet. Don't start now."

"My own sister," Lorn laments, offering a sad face.

"Brush the crumbs from your chin, if you wish to look truly sad," Jerial counters.

Lorn laughs. So does Ryalth.

In time, the tarts vanish, and the conversation dies away.

Lorn nods to his mother, then his father. "I thank you both, and everyone else here for coming. I would that I could stay longer, but I have been traveling for days, and a few nights' sleep, I fear, has not made up for the travels and a long season with the Accursed Forest."

"It has been so good to have you and Ryalth here with everyone," Nyryah beams. "But we will see you more, won't we?"

"You will," Lorn promises. "As we can." He smiles and extends his hand to Ryalth.

The redhead stands, then bows to Nyryah, then to Kien. "Thank you both so much."

"I'll come down with you." Jerial slips away from the table and follows Lorn and Ryalth down from the table.

As the three walk down the steps to the front door, Jerial says, "I'm glad you got to meet Mycela."

"What do you think of her?" Ryalth asks quietly.

"She's perfect for Vernt," Jerial replies sweetly.

Lorn winces.

"I thought so, too," agrees Ryalth.

Both women smile.

After they are well clear of Lorn's parents' dwelling and Jerial has closed the door, Ryalth turns to Lorn. "I like Jerial."

"She likes you. That is most clear."

"You noticed that all the outside consorts were placed at first on one side of the table?" Ryalth says as they walk slowly eastward through the still-warm evening.

"I did what I could," Lorn says.

"I know." She reaches out and squeezes his hand. "Mycela didn't understand."

"Neither did Ciesrt. I'm not sure Vernt did. Jerial did. She smiled when we switched places."

"Was your mother displeased?"

"I'm not sure. There was no other way to set up the table, not by lineage, but I didn't like it."

"I'm glad you're the way you are."

Lorn squeezes her hand, and they continue eastward along the Road of Perpetual Light, back toward the quarters that have become his as well as hers.

III

IN THE LATE, late afternoon, just before twilight, the Emperor Toziel'elth'alt'mer and his Consort-Empress Ryenyel stand on the uppermost balcony of the Palace of Light, ten tall stories above the gardens. His tall but slender frame seems stooped under the silver robes he has worn to the last audience of the afternoon and not removed once he has departed the small audience chamber. Ryenyel wears a tunic of vivid green shimmercloth, and flowing trousers of a lighter shade, colors which enhance her mahogany hair and lightly freckled complexion.

The warm and moist spring breeze comes from the east, whispering past them and past the fluted bars on the grillwork with enough force that there is a trilling and humming from the bars—a sound both pleasant and loud enough to foil eavesdroppers, as intended by the builders of the Palace some eight generations previous. While cupridium flowers might have served the same function, the Palace of Light contains no such fripperies, nor any statuary. All lines are clean, elegant, and without decoration, almost totally without even carved inscriptions.

To the south, and downhill, beyond the trade quarter and the warehouses, are the white stone piers of the harbor of Cyad. Scaffolds rise around the two white-hulled fireships at the Mirror Lancer pier. One of the fireships the Emperor knows will never move again under its own power, and is being cannibalized to refit the second ship, the *Ocean Flame*. At the piers to the east of the scaffolds are tied two three-masted ocean traders, deep-sea vessels, neither of which is Cyadoran, and a pair of coasting schooners, one Sligan, one Spidlarian.

North of the piers and below the Palace, the sunstone walks and white-granite paved streets shimmer in the late-afternoon sun. The shops and scattered cafes to the west sport immaculate green-and-white awnings.

"Bluoyal'mer tells me that all is well with our trade," reflects Toziel, his right arm around the waist of the Empress. "Yet few ships in the harbor fly our ensign. And the Emperor's Enumerators report that tariff collections have declined each year."

"Perhaps not all the tariffs are being collected," suggests Ryenyel. "Can the Hand of the Emperor—"

"No. The Hand can send orders, but his effectiveness is lost once he leaves the shadows and is known."

"First Magus Chyenfel'elth must know who he is."

"He doubtless does, as we have discussed, but it is not to his advantage to reveal such." Toziel laughs. "Nor to ours." The Emperor shakes his head slowly, without taking his eyes from the City of Light spread out below him. "The chaos-towers are failing, and I am forced into supporting the plan of the First Magus to use all the chaos in those remaining around the Accursed Forest merely to confine the Forest so that it will not overrun eastern Cyador. That means those towers can no longer charge the lancer firelances or the chaos-cells of the firewagons." Toziel shrugs. "Is this the beginning of the last long afternoon of Cyad?"

"The chaos-towers in the Quarter of the Magi'i here in Cyad yet function," the mahogany-haired Empress points out, "and will for some years yet, according to the First Magus."

"Some years is not that many, as we know, and, while he would certainly wish it so, I have some doubts about Chyenfel's predictions."

"How could you choose otherwise, my love, even if he is too hopeful?"

"I could not, for the Forest is worse than the barbarians of the north. They can be contained with cupridium lances and blades, if with greater losses, but only some form of bound chaos will contain the Accursed Forest." A mirthless chuckle follows his words. "We know this, and yet, like a schoolboy, I must talk to soothe my soul over choices between evils. More Mirror Lancers will die. The merchants will lose more ships to pirates and raiders, and there will be unrest among the merchanters—"

"There is already, with Tasjan's plotting and his hiring of Sasyk to head his greenshirt guards," Ryenyel points out.

"Who could fault him for hiring a former Mirror Lancer officer?" Toziel's words are light, but his eyes are dark. "Especially in these times. Tasjan will turn any questions about Sasyk against me. And, amid all the changes, most in Cyad, and throughout Cyador, will fault me, for they have neither seen nor experienced the power of the Forest."

"That is always so," replies the Empress gently. "Folk care for but the removal of that which they know will harm them or for the addition of that which will benefit them. Few care for actions which benefit all, but slightly, if it means they receive less. Always it was so, and always will be. For that, there is an Emperor."

"Yet I must not seem to plan nor plot, for those who do are thought cold and calculating, no matter how they care for their peoples, no matter what benefits they bring, no matter how many lives they save."

Ryenyel nods. "That, too, is why there is an Emperor."

"Yet all these troubles would come to pass while I am Emperor?"

"The Magi'i have warned of such for many years, that the towers would fail, that what the ancients built would not last forever." Ryenyel places her hand over his—the one that rests on her right hip—and squeezes her fingers around his hand.

"At such times, I am almost glad we have no heirs," he muses. "For whoever follows me . . . whatever scion there may be . . . if there is one . . ."

"There will be . . . we have time," she reassures him.

"With a gaggle of Magi'i who plot, and a Majer-Commander of Lancers who believes them fools not to see the danger of the barbarians, and a Merchanter Advisor who doubtless abuses his knowledge and position to line his pockets and undermine Cyador, even as he protests that he maintains it?"

After a moment of silence, Ryenyel replies. "Your Majer-Commander, the most honorable Rynst, has come to understand that Bluoyal only wishes the towers and the lancers in order to support the merchanters' trading ships. Rynst also understands that while he cannot brook Chyenfel, the First Magus can be trusted far more than the Second. Or even Chyenfel's protégé, young Rustyl."

"Only because Rynst fears Bluoyal more than the Magi'i." Toziel snorts.

"Bluoyal treads a devious and deadly path. He would ensure that the Mirror Lancers and the Magi'i do not see that their interests are closer to each other's than to his."

"Rynst and Chyenfel have always seen such. We have talked of this before. Neither can afford to trust the other allied to Bluoyal. Yet they know that both Magi'i and Mirror Lancers are few indeed outside of the three cities. They cooperate like a pair of giant cats against a pack of night leopards. Most carefully."

"And when the towers do fail?"

"We will need far more lancers against the barbarians. Bluoyol's successors will find they still need lancers, but not until many perish, and more than a few vessels are lost."

"Thus, all will continue as today," she replies.

"It will not seem so, not to most. The emperors to come will either be powerful Magi'i or inspire loyalty within the Mirror Lancers, because it appears that either lancers or Magi'i can destroy an Emperor."

"Bluoyal believes that the merchanters will purchase the Palace of Light in years to come, perhaps sooner. We need to watch him, more closely, far more closely, for a merchanter rising would bring down Cyador more swiftly than the Accursed Forest or the barbarians."

"So has said the Hand, but he has also advised that we have time, and that Bluoyal will overreach himself before such can occur."

"Would that I could take comfort in that," says the Empress, leaning her head against his shoulder.

"Seldom is he wrong . . . most seldom."

"If he is . . . ?"

"If he is, if we fail, then blood will stain the sunstone of the Palace so deeply it cannot ever be lifted." He looks down and studies her drawn face. "I tell you this often, but . . . You give too much to me."

"What else would I do, dearest? We know there is no one else."

"Not yet."

As he speaks, her fingers lift to rest lightly on his cheek.

The orange glow of twilight floods from the hillside to the west, and the white stone piers of the harbor shimmer gold.

The Emperor and Empress stand on the balcony and watch the gold fade.

IV

SITTING AT ONE end of a long table in the corner of Ryalor House, in gray light of a stormy spring morning, Lorn reads through the stack of papers that Eileyt has set before him. The senior enumerator has assured Lorn that the papers have several examples of shady trading practices.

Outside of several clear errors in addition, Lorn has found nothing. He finally beckons to Eileyt, and when the gray-eyed man nears, says, "I don't think I'm seeing what I should be seeing."

Eileyt turns over the first three bills of lading, then points to an entry halfway down the fourth one. "Look at that closely."

Lorn looks at the entry: *Cotton, 20 bales, dun, Hamor.*

"Hamor grows dun cotton, but all they usually export is the good white. Look at the parchment—and it is parchment, which is another clue."

"It looks like it's smoother there, but just around the word *dun.*"

"There's more space around the word *dun,* too." Eileyt nods. "With parchment, you can use it like a palimpsest, take a sharp knife and scrape off the letters, then write in dun instead of white."

"But why? Why don't they just rewrite the bill of lading?"

"It's sealed below. A trader gets caught counterfeiting a seal, and he loses a hand. An 'error' in a bill of lading merely costs some golds in fines, but most of such 'errors' are never found. The tariff on white cotton is a gold a bale. It's a silver on dun cotton, and you can get that from Kyphros or Valmurl or even out of Worrak in Hydlen."

"But they all come from beyond Cyador," Lorn says.

"That is right," Eileyt says patiently. "But . . . if the Imperial tariff were a gold on Kyphran dun cotton, then people would use carts and smuggle it along the beaches below the lower Westhorns, and some dishonest merchanter in Fyrad would mix it with his real Kyphran stock and it would be hard to tell without counting every bale, and the Imperial Enumerators don't have the bodies or the days to do that. At a silver a bale, and the tariff is the same for a bolt of the finished cloth, it's cheaper and faster to ship the dun cotton, or any cotton from Kyphros, than smuggle it. Hamorian white cotton goes for five golds a bale these days . . . and dun for one. So . . . on this shipment, the trader could pocket nearly eighteen golds, just by changing one word on the lading bill. And he can claim, if he gets caught, that it was a mistake. If the Hamorian seal's intact, and a magus can see that, then all he'll get is a three-gold fine, maybe ten-. But most won't catch something like this."

"But the finished cotton . . . that's more like ten a bolt, and they're easier to carry," Lorn says, recalling his early trading adventures with Ryalth. "Why would anyone import the bales all the way from Hamor? They're bulky."

Eileyt nods. "Good. That's another reason to suspect this. Anyone can look at a bolt of finished cotton and see the difference between Hamorian white and Kyphran dun, but raw cotton—that's another story. Might even be something hidden in the bales, as well."

Lorn shakes his head, but he has asked Ryalth and her people to show him what they can about forbidden trading practices, even though it is unlikely he will be directly involved, except when called in by the Emperor's tariff enumerators, if he ever is. The more he learns, the more small references tell him how intertwined everything is—such as Bluoyal's involvement in the consorting between Syreal and Veljan that, because of Lorn's killing of Veljan's older brother Shevelt, has led to a greater possible influence by the

Magi'i in the affairs of one of the leading merchanter houses. That underscores why he would like to know enough to be able to ask his own questions should such arise. His experience with patrol tactics and the Accursed Forest was enough of an example of not knowing enough, to confirm his decision to learn what he can in the few days he has in Cyad. He is also coming to realize that it is far better—and less costly to all involved—to act before others act . . . rather than when it is obvious to all that one must act.

So he might as well learn what he can, since Ryalth cannot give up work, especially since spring is far busier for Ryalor House than Lorn ever would have imagined.

He looks back through the bills of lading again, looking for odd spacing, improbable goods, anything.

On the next to last, he finds something—or thinks he does.

"A hundred stone of zinc tools?" he asks. "Is this a cover for iron blades? It's a metal and almost the same number of letters."

"That's more dangerous, because iron-bladed weapons carry high tariffs, and selling them in Cyad or failing to declare them for shipment elsewhere can send a trader to prison," Eileyt says. "But some traders like to buy Hamorian blades and sell them elsewhere in Candar." The enumerator hands Lorn another set of lading bills.

It is nearly midday when Lorn walks into Ryalth's inner study. She looks up from a ledger.

"You have a nice study here," he observes.

"Merchanters call them 'offices,' dearest . . . remember?" She smiles. "But if you want traders to think you know less than you do, just call them 'studies.' "

"Thank you. That might be wiser. I can see why you're the trader, and I'm not." He shakes his head again.

"We work better together," she says.

"Do you have to work all day?"

"Zerlynk is coming in midafternoon. He had made an offer on cordage. I picked up some raw hemp from a Sligan trader last year, and got some peasants near Desahlya to turn it into rope. It's not top-line, and I'll not try to sell it as such, but we should make some silvers on it. After he goes, I can leave."

Lorn nods. "You're busy. I'll see what else I can learn."

"You might talk to Kutyr. He knows more than he'll tell me." Ryalth smiles again.

"He might not tell me, either."

"If you flatter him . . ."

Lorn shakes his head ruefully, then smiles, and turns.

V

BECAUSE THE CORE of a fully-functioning tower maintains an isochronic/ isotemporal barrier of approximately 1,000 nanoseconds, this temporal "dislocation" effectively provides not only the points of energy polarity which generate the raw power, as described above, and an insulation from the local temporality, but what can also be loosely described as a recharge impact on local spatio-temporal random-amplitude "chaotic" energy events. . . .

Observation indicates that proximity to the tower engenders a sensitivity to and an ability to impact and/or manipulate local spatio-temporal random amplitude events. . . . Such sensitivity, if not disciplined and trained, could adversely impact the continued operation of the towers.

. . . Oversensitization and disciplined training must be rigorously monitored in view of the macular cellular degeneration already observed among personnel with high exposure within the operating confines of the basic tower system. This is, as noted previously, in contravention of previously established principles and tolerances. . . .

In addition to degenerative effects caused by excessive proximity to the towers, similar effects have been observed in those individuals among the non-technical cadre with an aptitude for manipulating such local spatio-temporal random-amplitude events. It is recommended that such individuals be placed so that they also can be monitored, and, if necessary, disciplined, in order to assure maximum operating continuity for the remaining tower cores.

Establishment of a hierarchial social structure may prove necessary, should these effects persist, since the conditions and infrastructure for continued technical education and understanding may be limited . . .

> *Recommendations*
> *Personnel Manual [Revised]*
> Cyad, 15 A.F.

VI

TYRSAL AND LORN are seated in the garden at the rear of the sprawling and massive two-storied dwelling that overlooks the harbor from the western bluffs of Cyad. The air is cooler than in Cyad itself.

"You have a good view of the harbor here," Lorn says.

"Not so good as that of your parents," answers the red-headed mage. "And it was a long walk to the academy. Mother was not sympathetic to my riding or using the carriage. That's why I stay with my sister and her consort most nights these days—out of habit, I suppose." He shakes his head. "I dislike mornings."

"The house is yours, isn't it?" Lorn asks.

"I suppose so, but it's really Mother's, and it wouldn't be right to take it from her." Tyrsal smiles. "Besides, I can just claim I'm a poor junior magus, and that way, none of the Lectors will push me into consorting with someone I don't like."

"Like Aleyar or Syreal?" asks Lorn, with a grin.

"Syreal's sweet. What she sees in that block Veljan, I don't know. I don't know Aleyar."

"So you'd still consider her?" Lorn pursues. "They say she's sweet and pretty, too."

"Are you trying to complicate my life? Or just end it?" asks Tyrsal. "I don't think it would be good for my health to deal with Liataphi all the time."

"What about Ciesrt's younger sister?" Lorn's eyes twinkle.

"You want Ciesrt as . . ." Tyrsal shakes his head. "I'm sorry. It's hard to believe. Myryan is so nice. Ciesrt doesn't deserve her." He pauses. "Anyway, Rustyl has asked Ciesrt's sister, and she'll say yes to him. He's ambitious and a favorite of Chyenfel. So while she'll put him off for a time, in the end, she'll agree."

"Kharl'elth will give her no choice," Lorn suggests.

"You were so smart not to consort into a Magi'i family," Tyrsal says.

"As if I had much choice," Lorn points out.

"You could have had your pick of the lancer girls." Tyrsal grins. "But you did much better. Ryalth is beautiful, and she's smart."

"You've scarcely talked to her, except at dinner the other night, and I don't think you said a dozen words."

Tyrsal draws himself up in offended dignity. "I listened. You learn when you listen." His eyes smile, and then he laughs. "You haven't said much about your new duty. You don't like going to Biehl?"

"It's not the assignment. It's what's behind it. I'm too young to be an overcaptain, and I've too little service. Zandrey had almost eight years before they made him one, and I've had four, five if you count officer training."

"They're losing a lot of officers to the barbarians, Lorn."

"I'd bet I'll only be there until I get set up to make some mistake . . . or until I get promoted again and sent to an impossible assignment against the Jeranyi or some such."

Tyrsal laughs. "Nothing's impossible for you. You'll have it figured out before they send you. Didn't you say you were studying bills of lading and the tariff rules? Did anyone suggest that to you?"

"It's obvious. If you have to enforce trade rules, best you know something about them. I still won't know the local situation, and that could be a mess." Lorn takes a deep breath and holds up his hand. "I know. You're going to tell me that while it's obvious to me, it isn't obvious to other lancers." He offers a wry expression that is not exactly a smile. "I'm not other lancers."

"That's what I keep telling you. You're always thinking ahead."

"I try." He pauses. "But that's dangerous, too. People think you're a plotter or a schemer. Or cold and calculating, and they watch you twice as closely."

Trysal laughs again. "That's why you never tell anyone anything."

"Would you?" Lorn glances at the harbor and then stands. "I need to go. Ryalth should be almost done with the exchange—"

"And you don't want to miss a moment with her!"

The overcaptain grins at the second-level adept magus. "It doesn't take a chaos-glass to scree that."

VII

THE COOL SPRING rain patters on the roof tiles, collects there, and then flows in streams over the eaves, collecting in the rain gutters that line the structures and the white granite roads and ways of Cyad. Within Ryalth's rooms, Lorn and his trader lady sit side by side in the bedchamber, propped up on the bed with pillows. On the table beside the bed a single lamp is lit.

Lorn holds a narrow, green-tinted, silver-covered volume in his hands, the one Ryalth had given to him to keep for her, years before, and insisted he read. "I've carried it everywhere, and yet there's still not a mark on it." He turns the book in his hands. "I still wonder how it came to your mother."

"She never said. She just said it was special."

Lorn nods, wondering how special . . . and whether the book is another subtle indication of how unusual Ryalth is—and why.

"You read from it often?" Ryalth asks.

"Not every night. I couldn't when I was on patrol, and I didn't want to take it with me."

"Every eightday?"

"Usually." He smiles. "Sometimes more often."

"What do you think about the ancients now?"

"I don't know about the ancients." He frowns. "The writer was melancholy. They might not all have been like him."

"Wouldn't you have been, if you'd come from the Rational Stars to a wilderness? That's what Cyador was, back then."

"I'm not sure it still isn't." Lorn laughs.

"We have the prosperity of chaos, and the chaos-towers, and the roads and the harbor, all the things they built," she points out.

"People are still unhappy."

"Not all of them."

"Some . . ." he teases.

"Enough." She takes the book from his fingers, closes her eyes, and then opens it at random, handing it to Lorn. "Read this one."

"You haven't seen it."

"Read it, please."

Lorn clears his throat.

Chaos, and the promise of light,
Order, beckoning lady of night . . .
Should I again listen to which song?
We have listened oh so long.
Should I again fly on learning wings?
We have learned what yearning brings.

"That is melancholy," she says. "Let's try another one. You pick it."

"And you read it," he replies.

She nods.

Lorn closes his eyes and lets his fingers riffle through the smooth and heavy pages, finally stopping and handing her the open volume.

"This one always puzzled me," she says as she looks at the slanted and antique Anglorian characters.

"Read it," he suggests.

Ryalth's voice is low, almost husky as she brings forth the words.

Cyad is no home for souls of thought,
who doubt the promises they have bought,
for the Magi'i offer Chaos as a Step to all.
The lancers back with fire their call,
their faces of cupridium's silver-white
reflect each other's chaotic light.
Should Sampson pick this temple,
here too, he would be blind,
his eyes untouched,
his simple trust
lost in the reflections.

She closes the volume. "I always wondered who Sampson was. He had to be blind, but the words suggest he wasn't always, and yet, that he would be in Cyad, because everything reflects everything else, and gets lost in the reflections."

"And that doesn't happen?" Lorn laughs. "Think about the big dinner with my parents the other night, and the way Vernt and Ciesrt kept looking at each other. And Mycela, the way she just wanted to be a perfect consort, reflecting Vernt's every wish."

"That's somehow sad, too." After a moment, she adds, "You have to go the day after tomorrow. Would you read the one about pears now?" She hands him the volume.

He flips through the pages until he finds the words and begins, his voice soft in the dimness of the bedchamber.

> Like a dusk without a cloud,
> a leaf without a tree . . .
> . . . to hold the sun-hazed days,
> and wait for pears and praise
> . . . and wait for pears and praise.

After he sets the book on the table by the bed, he turns down the lamp wick, and lets darkness fill the room. His arms slip around her, and hers around him.

VIII

THE TWO MOST senior Mirror Lancer officers sit across a polished table desk from each other in the capacious study on the highest floor of the Mirror Lancer Court, two blocks west of the Palace of Eternal Light. A light drizzle falls outside the antique panes of the windows that date to the ancients, but the day is bright enough that none of the polished cupridium wall-lamps are lit.

His eyebrows lifting slightly, Rynst'alt looks at Luss'alt. "I understand that I as Majer-Commander of Mirror Lancers have transferred young Captain—pardon me, young Overcaptain Lorn—to the port detachment at Biehl, and that he is on his way there, or will be, most shortly."

"Yes, ser. He was assigned to the northeast ward-wall, and he saw more fallen trees and creatures in little more than a year than most patrol captains do in a full tour."

"So you decided he should be transferred to a duty with which he has no experience, not by his family, nor by his education?" Rynst smiles brightly at his Captain-Commander, then leans back in the chair upholstered and covered in green shimmercloth.

"The Emperor's Enumerators are the ones who apply the tariff and port laws, ser, and Overcaptain Lorn need only support them."

"An officer who has been commanding in combat and against the Accursed Forest will sit back on his mount or behind his table and accept their word? Do you think that likely?"

"Most officers would be pleased with such duty, ser."

"Pleased or not, is it wise? With Bluoyal's kin everywhere? How do we know that Bluoyal does not have some relative in Biehl?"

"I thought it wise, ser," Luss replies stiffly.

"You mean that the Second Magus thought it wise?"

Luss does not quite meet Rynst's eyes. "Overcaptain Lorn has also been seen walking with a lady merchanter—the head of Ryalor House," Luss says. "She has suddenly become most powerful. Out of nowhere, one might say, and that seems rather odd, especially for a woman."

"A woman who comes to power easily can be vanquished easily. Were he walking with the daughter of Liataphi, I would be concerned, Luss, but a merchanter? Even a wealthy merchanter cannot influence the Magi'i, and no merchanter can be more of an influence upon the Palace of Eternal Light than Bluoyal already is."

Luss looks impassively through the light rain at the gray

water of the harbor, and the darker water of the Great Western Ocean beyond.

Rynst points at the polished reflector of the lamp on the corner of the desk. "Cyad is like that reflector, Captain-Commander. Or like many reflectors set opposite each other. Each and every action is mirrored in every other. I know that you know what I do and plan, and you know the same of me, and each of us hides in the open behind those reflections." A cold smile crosses the Majer-Commander's mouth. "You are a good second-in-command, Luss, so long as you allow me to think for you. You allow Kharl to direct your thoughts . . . and there will be no one to protect you, for the Magi'i certainly will not. Nor will the merchanters. Especially Bluoyal."

"He seems most capable, ser."

"He is too capable for the merchanters, Luss." Rynst pauses. "Rather, he is seen as too capable. Being seen as such is more dangerous than being so. As for young Overcaptain Lorn, I would watch what Kharl wishes of him. You know that Kharl's son is the consort of the overcaptain's younger sister, of whom young Lorn is most fond?"

"I had heard such, ser."

"That other ambitious young magus to watch—Rustyl—he is pressing a suit for Kharl's daughter. Watch the honorable Second Magus far more than the overcaptain. Keep such in your thoughts when you meet with the Second Magus. Also keep in mind that the First Magus cares little for the Second, and that all the Magi'i respect the fourth magus far more than the three with titles. There is a reason why they call Kien'elth 'the Fourth Magus.' He is most capable—and also young Lorn's father. We are fortunate that he has no ambition to become First Magus." Rynst pauses. "Then, given the first three Magi'i, perhaps we are unfortunate."

"Yes, ser." Luss's brows lift ever so slightly.

Rynst gestures toward the door, suggesting that the meeting is at an end. "For all that, I could not have planned it better. I suggest that you consider why that is so before your next clandestine meeting with the Second Magus."

"As you suggest, ser." Luss's face is impassive as he stands and offers a perfunctory bow.

"I do look out for you, Luss, even though you do not see it as such. You might also ask whether my actions and advice have benefited you. Then ask the same of what others offer." Rynst returns Luss's bow with a curt nod.

IX

LORN STANDS ON the uppermost level of his parents' dwelling, looking to the south and out across the harbor of Cyad. The rains of the previous days have cleared, and the late-afternoon sky is a brilliant green-blue. The breeze is crisp, but not strong, and only scattered whitecaps dot the harbor to the south.

"I'll be leaving on the early firewagon tomorrow," Lorn tells his mother.

"I'm glad you came by this afternoon." Nyryah smiles warmly. "And so is your consort, I am sure."

Lorn flushes slightly.

The study door opens, and Kien stands there on the edge of the portico, blinking as if the light has momentarily blinded him. Still, his words are incisive. "Lorn, I would like a few words with you."

"You usually do, dear," observes Nyryah.

"Yes, I do." The magus smiles. "These days, I am given less and less time in which to deliver them."

Lorn grins and follows his father into the study. Kien closes the door, firmly, and gestures to the chairs before his table desk. Lorn settles into the chair on the left and waits as his father seats himself. For a time, Kien does not speak, but steeples his fingers together, and purses his lips.

"Lorn . . . you will be leaving tomorrow, I understand." The older man looks across the broad polished study desk. "For port duty in Biehl."

"Yes, ser."

"There are several matters we should discuss." Kien blinks, then nods. "First, I did wish you to know, as if I have not already made my feelings obvious, that you have picked most wisely in your choice of consort, far more wisely than many will understand until you are much older."

"Thank you. I was fortunate in finding her."

"You were fortunate in finding her, but wise to hold to her." Kien pauses. "There is far more to your consort than meets the eye. I would be most surprised if there is not a significant Magi'i heritage."

Lorn nods. "Nor I, although there is little overt evidence." He wonders about the silver volume of verse. Is that evidence? Or serendipity?

"Second," Kien continues, "I am going to request that you relinquish the claim of the firstborn to Vernt. I do not ask this for Vernt, but for Jerial."

Lorn nods. "I understand. You have a document?"

Kien points to the parchment on the front of the table desk. "You do not question that?"

"Ser . . . I will either be successful as a Mirror Lancer officer—and will not need the claim—or I will not, in which case, neither I nor Ryalth would need it."

The older man nods slowly. "You understand fully that you will have claim to but a quarter?"

"Yes, ser. But that will be many years from now."

"I certainly hope so," Kien says with an ironic twist to the words, "but one must make provisions."

Lorn notes the words, and wonders. But he stands and takes the pen, reading and then signing the document.

"I will register that in the Quarter tomorrow. And I do appreciate your thoughtfulness and consideration."

"Yes, ser."

Kien leans back and purses his lips. "Finally, I have one observation and a few questions I would like to pose to you. The observation is that while Cyad is indeed a marvelous city, its people are like those anywhere else. I ask you to consider that. The questions . . . well . . . I would prefer that you not answer them, but think upon them during your firewagon trip to Biehl—beyond that, if you feel the need."

Lorn finds his eyebrows lifting. Questions?

"There are but three questions. These are:

" 'What is it that allows Cyad to exist?'

" 'Could all the might of the Mirror Lancers here in Cyad, or all the might of the Iron Legions in Hamor, prevail against the will of those who live in such lands?'

" 'Are those who direct power or chaos the source of either?' "

Lorn concentrates on the questions, trying to hold them in mind.

Kien extends a single sheet of paper. "I have held this for a time, but you are old enough to ponder these."

Lorn takes the sheet, and sees that it holds the questions his father has just asked.

"My son . . . these are not idle questions. Nor are they the overly philosophical musings of an aging magus. They are not mine, by the way, and you may, in time, discover the source. That source is not important, but pondering the questions is most important for a Mirror Lancer who aspires to command beyond a patrol company. You are leaving for what may be your most dangerous duty."

Lorn frowns.

"Dangerous, because you will have time to think, because you will be flattered, and because you will discover, if you have not already, that the world is both far simpler than you have ever imagined, and far more complex." His father laughs. "Call the last my question. 'How can the world be more simple and yet more complex?' I leave that to you, for now."

The overcaptain nods slowly.

"I do not need to tell you to be most careful, and to listen more than you speak. You have learned that already. Remember that silence can be either a truth or a lie. Make certain your silence is taken as you mean it." Kien stands. "I could prattle on into the night, and your consort would be upset with me. So I will not, but know that I wish you well, and that no matter who you may have believed, I always have." He steps around the desk, awkwardly.

Lorn understands, and he hugs his father for the first time in years. "Thank you."

Kien nods, not speaking, and his eyes are bright. Finally, he says, "Best you go to Ryalth, and enjoy what time you have left."

As Lorn steps away from the study door, he can sense the cold chill of a screeing glass, and that chill is not that manifested by his father.

Keeping an pleasant expression, he hugs his mother a last time before he starts down the steps to the front door.

Again, Jerial is the one who stands by the door. "Be good to Ryalth tonight."

"I will."

"I know." Her smile is softer, not the professional expression of a healer.

He gives her a hug. "Thank you for being so good to her."

"She is good for you. Far better than any could imagine. She and I understand each other, and that is good." Jerial squeezes Lorn tightly. "You be most careful."

"I will."

Lorn finally releases his older sister and steps around the

privacy screen and down the steps to the Road of Perpetual Light.

How is the world simpler and yet more complex? His father's last question rolls through his mind.

X

HONORED SER, YOU summoned me." The tall man is slender, and his blond hair is both thick and fine, and shimmers as the light from the study window strikes it. His green eyes are pale, intent, as he straightens from his bow to the First Magus.

"Please be seated, Rustyl." Chyenfel's sun-gold eyes do not waver as he watches the handsome younger magus settle into the golden oak armchair across the table from him. "Being a discerning young magus," the First Magus finally adds with a deliberate emphasis on each word, "you have noticed that all is not as it once was in Cyador. I would have your thoughts on such."

"Honored ser, it would be presumptuous to assume that you have not already noted all I might say. So I will but touch on each matter. First, the chaos-towers are failing, yet all of Cyador depends on the energies of those towers. Few feel that the towers are failing, because they cannot imagine that. Instead, they feel as though the Magi'i are using the chaos-towers as a weapon to gain more influence over the Mirror Lancers and the Malachite Throne. Second, the outlanders have noticed that there are fewer fireships. We see more Hamorian traders and greater numbers of raids by the barbarians of the north. Third, the older merchanter houses and clans, those who have supported and understood Cyador, are being supplanted by newer houses, and, for the first time in memory, a trading house of note has been founded and operated by a lady trader." Rustyl smiles. "I have little against her, for she embodies the spirit of what once all merchanters in Cyad embodied, but it is disturbing that one of the newer and stronger houses must be created by a woman, when there are so many young men among the merchanters."

"Go on." The voice of the First Magus remains calm. "What else?"

"The Emperor is aging, rapidly, yet hides such, and has taken no steps to name a successor, perhaps for fear that such will disturb all of Cyad. He relies ever more on his consort, and turns from the main advisors—you, the honorable Majer-Commander of Mirror Lancers, and even from his once-favored Merchanter Advisor." Rustyl offers a far fainter smile. "Then there are those who have the skills to serve the Magi'i, but have placed themselves ahead of the calling of chaos." Rustyl shrugs. "I doubt not that there are many other manifestations that all is not well, and those may be beyond my knowledge and experience, but these are among those that I see."

"You see much of what others see and of which they will not speak." Chyenfel steeples his fingers before him, purses his lips, and pauses for a long moment, which stretches into silence before he finally speaks again. "There are also other cities in Cyador where your observations would be valuable. And where your presence would be noted, most quietly."

A pleasant smile remains on Rustyl's face as he waits.

"On threeday," Chyenfel says, "you will go to Fyrad to work with the Mirror Engineers."

Rustyl nods, if slightly. "I stand ready to carry out your wishes."

"You will be most helpful and most deferential, as you have been here. You will attempt to grant others any credit for what you accomplish. When you cannot do such, you will share such credit. If aught goes wrong, you will take the blame and find yet another solution, for which someone else will share the credit."

"Yes, ser."

"You will not proceed to the Accursed Forest, and you will disavow any knowledge of the sleep wards. You may note politely that such is the project and the work of the First Magus. Do you understand why?"

"Would that be because the chaos-towers surrounding the Forest will no longer be able to charge the firelances of the lancers and the entire project will be regarded less than favorably?"

"It would appear so." Chyenfel nods. "After several seasons, when it appears appropriate, you will be dispatched to Summerdock, where you will employ your skills and powers to assist the Mirror Engineers in improving the port facilities there. Throughout Cyador, over the few coming years, all must know of you, but only in passing, only as one who is experienced and trustworthy, as one who is young enough not to be totally bound to the old ways, but one who can use and help others with those ways in meeting the needs of the present."

Rustyl bows his head. "I understand and appreciate your foresight and wisdom."

Chyenfel laughs. "May you always do so, but old as I am, I do not see that you will. Remember that, should you reach my exalted age. The young always demur to power, even as they scheme to obtain it and consider how they could employ it in far better or more effective ways than their elders." A second laugh follows. "If we are successful, both in your work and your consorting, your turn will come, Rustyl. But mine is not over yet." The First Magus gestures. "You may go."

As the blond magus closes the study door, the smile fades from Chyenfel's lips.

XI

LORN PLACES THE bronze key in the lock of the upper-floor quarters that had been Ryalth's and are now theirs, but the door has already been unlocked. He steps inside. Ryalth stands just behind the privacy screen.

"You surprised me. You made your way here from Ryalor House earlier than I had thought," he admits.

"This is our last night together. I thought you would be awaiting me." Her smile is nervous, tentative. "I hastened from the Plaza."

"I am sorry. I was saying good-bye to my parents and Jerial, and before that, Myryan. She wasn't at their dwelling, and I had to find her at the infirmary. I returned as quickly as I could." He steps forward and hugs her, brushing her cheek with his lips and murmuring in her ear, "I'm glad you're here."

After a moment, she returns the embrace, and they remain pressed to each other for yet a time. Then she eases back, her hands holding his, his fingers cool around hers, her fine eyebrows lifting. "You took a while."

"My father had more than a few words of advice." He forces a wry smile. "And some questions. He gave me a sheet of them." Lorn raises the parchment. "He told me to consider them, to ponder them on the firewagon trip to Biehl."

"He accepts you for what you are, yet can offer but little assistance—unlike your brother, for whom he can do much," suggests the redhead.

"That may be." Lorn frowns. "He also offered an observation, almost as if I were a child, that while Cyad is a marvelous city, the people are as others. Why would they be otherwise?"

"Because, dearest, you still believe that a great city must come from great people." She offers a sad smile. "A great city can come from but a handful of great people, and the acceptance of the rest, who are grateful and pleased to benefit from the labors of the few. You have said as much yourself, yet I am not sure you believe it." Ryalth slips her hands from his and crosses the main chamber to the cooler, where she bends and searches, before lifting out an amber bottle of Alafraan. "I did save a few bottles for us here."

" 'Save'?"

"You will need some in Biehl." She grins. "Someone has to take care of those details." The grin fades. "You are worried."

"My father. He does not look strong . . . and he insisted on having a private talk with me." Lorn shakes his head. "Some of it, I don't understand. He practically threatened me years ago to stay away from you. He told me I must break off the relation with you, that it was not appropriate, and now he says I could not have picked a better consort anywhere, and my truth-reading shows that he means such."

"For that, for us, I am most glad." Ryalth uncorks the Alafraan and half fills two goblets, then recorks the bottle. "Perhaps the warning was to assure that you followed your heart and beliefs, and not custom."

"It has to be . . . but . . . that would mean . . ." Lorn shakes his head once more. "It would mean that he doubted from the first that I would be a magus. Yet he pressed me to excel in those studies and kept telling me how a magus must love the study and use of chaos above all."

"Is all that not true? Would you be what you are had you not done so well in those studies?"

"No," Lorn admits. "But that would mean he expected . . . all that from the beginning."

"He is your father. How could he not know?" Ryalth laughs gently. "We never expect the perception from our parents that we do from others who are wise."

"He has given me hints, but I seldom felt his use of the chaos-glass in following me."

"He knows you well enough that he needs no glass."

Lorn's smile is rueful. "And all these years, I thought I directed my own course."

"We never direct our courses solely, dearest of lancers." Ryalth extends a goblet to her consort. "Not even the highest do."

"We like to think so." He takes the goblet. "We like to think that the man—or the woman—makes the times, not that the times make them."

Ryalth's smile is gentle. "Thank you for including women. The original saying does not." She raises her goblet, then sips. "Much of what we think is illusion, dear consort, grasped for comfort."

Lorn lifts his goblet as she does, then sips the Alafraan. "I'm glad I didn't have to wait another year to see you. Or have you travel all the way to the Accursed Forest."

"As am I, but ... An eightday is scarce enough to greet, let alone part."

"Better an eightday than no time together at all."

She nods slowly, then looks at Lorn for a long time. "I can travel to Biehl more easily ... than to Jakaafra ... or someplace like Syadtar or Assyadt."

"Because it's a port city?"

"I can make a trading run. I know Fyrad, for I grew up there, but Biehl I do not know, and it would be best for Ryalor House that I do."

"Why Biehl?" he asks in spite of himself.

"Jera is the closest barbarian port, and many of the coasters run between the two. I would see what they trade that we know little of." She takes another swallow of the Alafraan, far larger than is her custom. Her deep blue eyes are large and near-luminous as she looks once more at Lorn. "I will write you of trade, for I can ensure my scrolls go but to you while you are in Biehl. I would not talk more of trade this evening. Nor of duty."

She sets the goblet on the table and moves around it toward him.

He sets down his goblet. As their arms go around each other, Lorn wonders at the sense of vulnerability he senses beneath her competent exterior . . . What is he missing?

But that wonder lasts but for a moment as their lips meet, and another type of marvel replaces the wonder.

Lorn'alt, Biehl

XII

As Lorn walks northward from the square in Biehl where the firewagon stops, within two blocks, he reaches the harbor area. To his right are the piers, and to his left—westward—is a short row of structures—their lower levels plastered and whitewashed. Both plaster and whitewash are worn away in places, exposing the old yellow brick beneath. The second stories of those buildings that have upper levels are of weathered planks, whose whitewash has mostly flaked away.

His eyes flick from the faded sign bearing the crossed candles of a chandlery, to a cooper's shop, and then to another building with no sign. Turning, his gear in hand, Lorn studies the three harbor piers—crude timber structures, weathered and splintered in places, not at all like the white stone piers of Cyad, Fyrad, or Summerdock. The piers jut out into the river that begins somewhere in the western reaches of the Hills of Endless Grass. Two schooners are tied at the middle pier, and an oceangoing brig at the outer one. The innermost, although empty, is more for smaller craft, Lorn suspects, and perhaps for fishing vessels unloading.

Both piers and the small city of Biehl lie on the western side of the River Behla. On the eastern side, there is a smaller town, and but what appears to be a dilapidated single pier, part of its shoreward side rising out of a mudbank or sandbar. From what the firewagon drivers had told him, the Mirror Lancer compound lies north of the piers and farther west on a low bluff overlooking the Northern Ocean, or that stretch of water where the Northern and Great Western Oceans meet.

The odors of dead fish, mud, and salt water mix in the

cool breeze blowing off the blue-black water north beyond the harbor. Streaks of white top the short and choppy waves in the harbor.

Since Biehl has no carriage for hire, not that the firewagon drivers knew, Lorn resumes walking, past the outermost pier, and the brig that bears a dark blue ensign—that of Spidlar, he thinks. Ahead the ground rises, and the uneven cobblestones of the road give way to granite paving stones, cracked and no longer set evenly but still more level than the stones of the road that flanks the harbor. The handful of trees yet bear winter-gray leaves, showing that spring comes later in Biehl.

The bluff is little more than a hill less than twenty cubits higher than the water of the harbor, and the Mirror Lancer port compound is small. That Lorn can tell even as he walks toward the gates. The yellow brick walls stand little more than five cubits, and extend less than eighty cubits on a side away from the gates—oiled golden oak, and open.

A single guard looks warily at the approaching Mirror Lancer officer. Finally, the stripling speaks. "Ser?" His voice squeaks.

"I'm Overcaptain Lorn." He shows the lancer the seal ring. "I couldn't find a carriage; so I walked."

"Ah . . . ser . . . there be none for hire here."

"I suspected such. Which is the headquarters building?"

"On the left, ser, but there be no one there but Squad Leader Helkyt, ser."

"That's fine." As he steps through the gates, Lorn realizes that the young guard doesn't equate him with an incoming detachment commander.

He studies the two weathered yellow-brick buildings in the middle of the compound, each long and narrow, and what appears to be a stable set against the rear wall. The roofs of all the structures are of a split gray slate, and there are patches of moss growing from between splits in the slate. Some moss also grows in the cracks between the ancient granite paving stones of the courtyard.

An open door beckons from the headquarters building to Lorn's left, and he walks toward it. There, he steps into the foyer and sets down his gear, then moves through the archway into a corridor. On the right-hand side of the corridor is another door, ajar, and Lorn peers in. The gloomy room is shallow and broad with a dais on which is a table desk with two chairs behind it. The space before the dais is vacant, and the stone tiles of the floor are dusty. Faint cobwebs adorn the closed window shutters.

The overcaptain turns to the door on the other side of the corridor, also ajar. He looks through the span-wide opening. Inside what appears to be a study, a senior squad leader leans back in the weathered oak chair, his boots propped on a footchest of the type that contains Mirror Lancer records. His eyes are closed, and he snores, intermittently. To his right is a closed door, presumably to the commander's inner study.

Lorn backs away from the doorway, wondering what else he may find. He leaves his gear in the foyer and walks slowly along the side of the building. Leaves have drifted into the corners between the courtyard paving stones and the bricks of the walls, scattered over dirt packed against the cracked and faded yellow bricks.

From the building across from the one containing the port-detachment studies, three lancers emerge. They stop and look at each other. Lorn can hear the murmurs.

". . . young officer . . ."

". . . overcaptain's bars . . ."

". . . some senior commander's son . . . think it's the new commander?"

". . . nah . . . too young . . . only send old dungblowers here."

As Lorn turns toward the three, the murmurs die away,

and they walk briskly toward the guard at the compound gate. Lorn turns back toward the door leading into the headquarters, but before he goes more than a halfscore of steps, the squad leader who had been snoring scurries from the building toward Lorn, fumbling a soiled green garrison cap into place over thinning gray hair.

"Ser?" The heavyset senior squad leader stops, then bows.

"I'm Overcaptain Lorn. I'm here to take over command of the port detachment. Is there a commanding officer here, or did he leave before I reported?"

"Ah, ser . . . Overcaptain Madlyr, he died of a flux . . . almost half a season ago. We'd been wondering when someone would come."

"I'm here." Lorn pulls forth the order scroll. "I didn't get your name, Squad Leader."

"Helkyt, ser. Helkyt." He takes the scroll.

Lorn shows the seal ring.

"Ah, yes, ser." Helkyt pauses. "That your gear in the headquarters foyer, ser?"

"It is. I thought I'd take a look around . . . while you were resting."

Helkyt flushes, but continues. "If you'd like, we can go to your quarters, and you can drop your gear there first."

"That would be fine."

Lorn steps past the squad leader with the thinning blond hair and the overround, jowled face, and walks into the headquarters foyer, where he reclaims his bags. He nods to Helkyt, who turns and walks northward along the side of the building.

The commander's quarters are on the second level of the headquarters building at the end away from the entrance Lorn had found first. There is a staircase directly up from the foyer, and the hollowed sunstone steps are dusty. The six-paneled door is of golden oak, and there are separations in the wood around the panels.

With the bronze key Helkyt has produced, Lorn unlocks and opens the door and steps into a small square foyer. The floor is of alternating green and cream diamond-shaped ceramic tiles. Lorn looks to the right. Through the archway is a small room, a study with a built-in bookcase, and a narrow desk. Before the desk is a straight-backed oak chair with a scrolled back—an ancient chair, or an old chair with an ancient design.

On the left is an open door that shows a small bedchamber with a narrow single bed.

Lorn steps ahead into the large main room, which contains two settees, upholstered in a green velvet, two armchairs and a low table, and several armless chairs set against the walks. Two of the chairs flank a sideboard.

On the left outer wall are four narrow windows. On the right inner wall is a set of open double doors that show a larger bedchamber. Lorn steps through the doors and sets the bags on the green-tiled floor. A modest double-sized bed without posts and with a low headboard is flanked by two tables with tarnished bronze lamps set on each. A faded green shimmer-cloth spread covers the bed. On one side of the small door that leads to a bathing chamber is a dressing table. On the other are two oversized armoires, set side by side. The bedchamber also has four narrow windows that match those in the main room.

"Ser . . . Some commanders, years back, ser, they brought their consorts."

"Mine might visit," Lorn says, "but she won't stay long."

"Ser?"

"She's the head of a trading house."

"Yes, ser."

Lorn turns and leaves the bedchamber.

"Ser . . . ah . . . I'll tell Daelya that you'll be needing the quarters cleaned."

Lorn nods. "If she could do that this afternoon while you and I talk over the situation here . . ."

"Yes, ser. She is your cook, also, ser."

The remaining rooms of the quarters consist of a dining room with a table large enough to seat a dozen, a kitchen with a huge ceramic stove that must be generations old, a breakfast room, and a back pantry, off which are service side stairs down to the courtyard.

Lorn nods to himself as he completes the quick tour and studies Helkyt. "I'd like to look at the barracks, and the stables, and everything else."

"Now . . . ser?"

"Now." Lorn smiles. "How will I know what you are talking about unless I see it?"

"Yes, ser." Helkyt's professional tone does not quite cover the dismay and resignation in his voice, but he turns and leads Lorn back down the steps. They cross the dusty paved courtyard to the other long building, entering through the double doors in the middle.

The odors of age, urine, and spoiled food assault Lorn before he has taken his second step into the barracks building. He glances around. The plan is similar to that of the barracks at Isahl, with two barracks areas flanking an open center mustering area.

Lorn turns left.

"Ah, ser . . . The north end has been closed for some time."

Lorn nods and keeps walking past the columns. While the bunk frames remain, it is almost impossible to discern them for the discarded materials scattered over and around them. Lorn can make out rotted timbers, empty and broken barrels, a twisted firelance shaft, several sets of shutters, and splotches of liquids on the tiles.

He turns and walks back through the mustering area, heading toward the area in use.

"Officer in the barracks!" Helkyt announces.

The first two bunks are unoccupied, bare horsehair mattresses sitting in frames, without even footchests at their base. Two lancers stand before footchests at the next set of bunks. Both are young, certainly younger than Lorn had been when he began lancer training. They wear but small-clothes. Lorn raises his eyebrows.

"They had guard duty at the gates last night, ser."

Lorn nods. "You can get some rest for now."

"Yes, ser," the two reply in near unison.

The remainder of the bunks are empty, but blankets lie strewn carelessly over mattresses, and dust has gathered in corners. Three of the footchests are open, and one lacks hinges and a lid.

Lorn's boots find sticky patches on the tiles as he walks along the barracks bay. He turns and walks back past the re-clining lancers and out through the mustering area. Finally, he stands in the clean air outside the barracks.

He looks at Helkyt. "Let's see the rest."

"Yes, ser."

As he follows the rotund squad leader, Lorn only hopes that the stables, the armory, the storerooms, and other sec-tions of the compound will prove less in need of cleaning and repair.

XIII

ON THE FIRST morning after his arrival in Biehl, Lorn sets the list he has written up on the wide desk in the administra-tive headquarters. Then he surveys the room more carefully than he had the day before. Like everything else in the Mir-ror Lancer compound at Biehl, the study Lorn has as a com-pound commander is larger than those he has seen elsewhere—and far older. None of the five manuals in the built-in oak bookcase has been opened in years, if not gener-ations, as Lorn discovers when lifting one and discovering that a thin strip of leather from the binding remains stuck to the wood of the shelves.

Fine cracks adorn the antique golden oak table desk, and he has never seen the like of either the ornate swirled bronze lamps or the wall sconces in which they rest. The chair behind the desk is large—and heavy. Dust puffs from the wide green cushion that covers the seat when Lorn plumps it. He rubs his nose, managing not to sneeze.

The window is stiff, but he eases it open enough to let in some of the moister and cleaner outside air. Then he reseats himself behind the desk, glancing toward the two chests filled with less than perfectly kept records, the study of which had occupied much of the previous evening.

After a deep breath, he clears his throat and calls, "Helkyt!"

The door opens, and the squad leader appears. "Yes, ser?"

Lorn motions for Helkyt to take one of the chairs on the other side of the table desk. He waits for the man to seat himself, and for a bit longer, before he begins. "We have more than a few matters to take care of around here, Helkyt," Lorn says with a cheer he scarcely feels.

"Yes, ser." Helkyt's voice is even, wary.

"First, best you know why I was sent here."

"That had puzzled me, ser, I must admit."

"You may have heard that the barbarians have been increasing their attacks to the east and the south of here. Isahl, Inividra, Assyadt—they've all had more and more attacks by larger and larger groups."

"I hadn't heard that, ser, but there's much we don't hear in Biehl."

"The Majer-Commander needs more trained lancers." Lorn waits.

"Ah . . . so . . ."

Lorn nods. "You understand that with the barbarians becoming more active . . . well . . . the Emperor does need more lancers in Assyadt . . . and we can either train them or find ourselves being transferred. All of us."

Helkyt tries to avoid swallowing.

"We both would rather recruit and train more lancers. That means we'll have to clean up the north wing of the barracks, and start acquiring more mounts, and sabres. We can only do a little of the firelance training here, because those lances are needed elsewhere, but I'll be seeing if we can be sent a few more, just in case the barbarians decide to come westward from Jera. It also means that we'll have to be ready to begin training no later than the turn of summer."

"The turn of summer, ser?"

The overcaptain gives the senior squad leader another smile. "I'm certain you can help me work this out, Helkyt. I'd much rather rely on someone of your experience in Biehl than to break in someone new."

"I am sure we can meet the Majer-Commander's requirements, ser. Ah . . . will there be other officers . . . company captains?"

"I was led to believe that I have the first opportunity here, Helkyt. I'd like to be able to work it out between us. If it proves to take too long, though, there could be several officers arriving, and the Majer-Commander would just bring in an entire new cadre."

"I am most sure we can work out matters, ser. Most sure."

Lorn leans back in his chair, but only slightly. "I am most pleased that you feel that way. Both the Majer-Commander and His Mightiness are known to reward success as surely as they punish failure. We would both prefer the rewards, I believe."

"Yes, ser. Yes, ser." Helkyt nods his head twice, quickly.

"Now . . . let's talk about what we can do immediately. The payroll first, because it affects how many new lancers we can train. I've been looking at those records."

Helkyt remains impassive in his chair, but his eyes flicker.

"The numbers don't add up." The overcaptain shrugs. "We cannot change the past, and I won't pass judgment on what has happened." He pauses. "But it won't keep happening. We have a payroll enough for two companies of lancers. We have less than one company. We aren't recruiting that many young lancers, and I would guess many of their skills are suspect. So . . . we'll have to make sure the lancers who aren't so good get retrained, as well. I'd like you to begin organizing the training program—both for recruits and for those who need more training. Pick the two best riding lancers for mount and formation training and the two best for sabres. They can be the same men, or they can be different. I may help out, as I can." Lorn frowns. "At first, with the sabre training, we'd best pad the blades to begin with, at least until the younger ones know which side has an edge and which does not."

Helkyt nods his head up and down slowly, then takes out a piece of squarish cloth and blots his forehead.

Lorn ignores the gesture and continues. "I'll meet with you and with the men you've chosen first thing tomorrow." He looks at the next item on his handwritten list. "The pay chest is the next thing. There's much of that payroll that seems to have disappeared. I'm sure that if you looked, you could find some of it. We're going to need it." Lorn smiles at Helkyt. "I'm also sure that if a good portion of the missing silvers and golds turn up and we accomplish what the Majer-Commander has in mind, he wouldn't want to bother himself with sending more officers here."

Helkyt nods slowly. "There are perhaps somewhat less than a hundred golds in the chest in the strong room, and some two hundred silvers. I might be able to find some others, placed elsewhere for safekeeping, now that we know what the Majer-Commander has in mind."

"I'm certain you will do your best." Lorn smiles briefly. "Now, how does our payroll get here?"

"We get a chest every other eightday," replies the senior squad leader. "I take the travel chest to the Emperor's Enumerators, and they fill it, and the guards and I bring it here and put it in the strongroom until we pay the men on sevenday."

"When you do next receive that payroll?"

"The day after tomorrow."

"Good. From now on, each time you do that, we'll count it here in the study, and we'll both sign a record showing how much we received."

"Yes, ser. I'll talk to the enumerators."

"That's a good idea. They should know what the Majer-Commander has in mind, too, especially before they provide the next payroll."

"I would think so, ser."

"I'll have to meet with them. Perhaps we should do it together."

"Ah . . . yes, ser."

Lorn smiles again. "I want to make sure that we're supplying them with the services they need."

"You said your consort was the head of a trading house, ser?"

"Yes. I've learned a great deal from her."

Helkyt smiles. "I am certain the enumerators will wish to learn that the commander has some understanding of trade and merchanters."

"You might send them a message to that effect, but I think we should meet with them tomorrow, as early as possible."

"Yes, ser."

Lorn glances at his handwritten list again. "The north wing of the barracks. We'll need to hire a cart or a wagon and carry all the junk off. Is there a rag-picker here in Biehl that might pay us something for the cloth and the wood?"

Helkyt's face blanks.

"You need to find out if there is. Also, we'll need to see about whether there is enough cuprite for the coppersmith to pay us . . ."

Lorn stops as Helkyt's eyes begin to glaze over. "I've offered enough for now. Why don't you start on working out who can do the training?" He stands. "We'll talk later."

Helkyt lurches to his feet. "I will have those names for you shortly, ser. Most shortly."

The smile does not leave Lorn's face until the senior squad leader closes the door behind him.

XIV

IN THE SPRING evening, sitting at the desk in his quarters' study, Lorn examines the payroll and expense-draw figures once more. He shakes his head. Without additional golds, he cannot afford both mounts and saddles for two full companies, even if he does not recruit the second new squad until midsummer. He may be able to draw upon the District Guards. He shakes his head once more, then jots an addition to his list. He needs to send a message to the District Guard Commander, and then visit the commander, for another aspect of his duties is to ascertain and verify the numbers and capabilities of those guards—something that has not been done in years. He sets aside his list and picks up the payroll figures again.

After yet another series of mental calculations, he sets aside the reckonings, knowing that unless he can obtain good horses more cheaply or saddles or . . . something . . . he will not reach his goals, and so many of those goals are but within his own mind. Knowing what he must do, he tries not to dwell on the audacity required. Yet, without audacity his future is dim indeed. And without knowledge as well, he reminds himself.

He laughs to himself. Still . . . he assumes that a man can make the times, when it is not at all clear that such is possible, or even that the times make the man. He will see; he must see.

He slips the chaos-glass from the single drawer and sets it on the polished wood. While Lorn knows that he must be successful in using the glass in order to survive and prosper, it has been difficult enough to follow those in the glass with whom he has little connection. Yet a chaos-glass would prove most useful as a battlefield tool—if only to see where the barbarians—or any enemy—might be riding.

Lorn concentrates. This time takes longer, far longer, than when he has sought individuals he has met or known about, before the silver mists clear and display a view of riders. The image displayed is that of a raider band. Lorn's only problem is that he has no idea where the barbarians might be, or what might be their destination.

After releasing the image, he takes a deep breath. Will he have to use the glass to map the northwest section of the Hills of Endless Grass? Or perhaps if he tries to call up an image of Jera?

He concentrates once more—and is rewarded with the vision of a town that appears much as Biehl must from above—except Jera appears to be on the north side of the River Jeranya. The sparkling in Lorn's eyes slowly turns into needles, then narrow stilettos that stab at the back of his eyes as he tries to make out individual sections of the town in the glass.

When he finally releases the image, his head is pounding, and tiny knives continue to jab through his eyes and into his skull. He sits with his eyes closed, well into the darkness, massaging his forehead, trying to rub away the throbbing that follows extensive use of the chaos-glass. Finally, Lorn opens his eyes, slips the glass into the drawer, stands, and lights the lamp. Then he takes out the pen and a fresh sheet of paper and begins to write, slowly, carefully. First come the letters to his parents and Jerial, then a shorter one to Myryan, and finally, the one with which he would have preferred to have begun. But had he started with it, the others might not have been written.

When he is finished with the last letter, the one to Ryalth, he looks over the scroll he has written—drafted most carefully, since he has no way to send a scroll through merchanters he can trust and thus must dispatch this scroll through the normal firewagon/courier system.

My dearest,

The trip to Biehl was itself most uneventful, but coming here has been far different from anything either of us could have imagined. To begin with, there was no one to relieve, since the previous overcaptain was an older officer who died over a season ago. As result of his untimely death, even more has been required than I had first thought because much has been neglected. The city, rather more of a large and old town, sits on the west side of the River Behla, to the south of the Northern Ocean . . . When the winds blow, it can be chill indeed . . .

It appears as though my duty here will also require recruiting and training young lancers so that I may provide trained men for service elsewhere, as required by the Majer-Commander. This is in addition to refurbishing the compound and providing lancers as necessary for the Emperor's Enumerators, who have done without such support and presence at least since the death of the previous overcaptain.

With quarters far larger than I ever could have imagined, and even suitable for a consort—at least to visit, although they are ornate in the old style, I do have some space in which to think, and to read in quiet. And I have a serving woman, consorted to one of the older lancers, who cleans and also cooks my evening meal. Although her meals are simple and plain, they are far

better than the food at my earlier duty assignments . . .
Because all has been so busy in dealing with the unsettled situation created by the untimely death of the previous overcaptain, I still have not had a chance to spend much time in the town itself or to determine what wares might be unique . . . but I have not forgotten that such is necessary . . .

I do miss you, and trust that all continues well with you.

He sets the scroll aside to dry, and sits back for a moment in the ancient and not terribly comfortable chair. Somehow, the quarters remind Lorn of the silver-covered book, almost as if they call up the time of the ancient writer. Biehl is an old town, and it is possible that the compound walls may date from the early years of Cyador, but the quarters date back perhaps three generations, certainly no longer.

With the scrolls still drying, Lorn picks up the slim silver volume, as unmarked as when Ryalth had first pressed it upon him, despite its being carried back and forth across Cyador. He opens it and fingers his way through the pages, until he reaches one of the more enigmatic verses.

I hear the lonely Magi'i
imprisoning their chaos-souls
in the corridors of their quarter,
forging firewagons, ships, and firespears
to ensure an old world never reappears.
I hear the altage souls lifting lances
against what the future past advances,
while time-towers hold at bay
the winters of another day,
what we would not face
what we could not erase . . .

until those towers crumble into sand
and Cyad can no longer stand.

Lorn frowns as he pages through the book and finds the
other verse, the one that shows Cyad as far more. He reads
the first two stanzas out loud.

In this season, the stones are sharp and clear,
from decisions once made in hope and fear,
those traditions grafted from stars long lost,
distant battles fought without thought of cost
lands wrenched from the grasp of order's dead hand,
that refugees could build a fruitful land.

Cyad, from your green and streets of white stone
will come the first peace this poor land has known.
From the Rational Stars and the three ways
will follow hope and justice for all days . . .

Lorn murmurs the rest of the poem's words to himself
once. The same writer, and in one case he has written of the
greatness of Cyad, and in the other, of its inevitable fall.
Lorn frowns. Cyad must not fall—not in his life.

He closes the book slowly. The writer had felt all those
years ago that the towers would fail, and yet he had persevered. Lorn frowns. Had he? The book offers no guarantee
of such. There are no verses saying what became of the
writer, nor any hints as to how the slim volume came into the
hands of Ryalth's mother.

Lorn glances out the window into the darkness that has
fallen on the compound. He is trying to rebuild the garrison
and compound. Can it be done? Can Cyad be re-formed to
retain its greatness without firewagons, without fireships,
without firelances? Will it remain Cyad?

And what is Cyad? He wonders, still without an answer to
his father's question, not one that satisfies him. All those

questions, and the melancholy words of the ancient writer, bring up once more the other question, simple enough, yet also without a simple answer. Do the times make a man, or can a man make the times? Was the ancient writer produced by the pressures of creating Cyador, merely reacting to those pressures? Or did he direct them? Since Lorn knows not who the man was, he has no answers, and the words of the writer offer no absolute assurances of either.

Lorn shakes his head, ruefully, yawning. Such philosophical speculations will not help in accomplishing what he must. He yawns once more, then stands and turns out the light. He has much to do on the morrow, as he does on every morrow.

XV

THE TWO MEN stand on the end of a white stone pier at which no vessels are tied. Under the heavy clouds of a chill spring day, the wind creates small whitecaps on the choppy gray-blue waters of the harbor of Cyad. Halfway toward the shore are two groups of guards, each by a separate bollard. One set of guards is clad in green uniforms, with gold trim, the second and smaller group in shapeless blue. All the guards watch the two merchanters who face each other.

Both men are beardless and wear blue shimmercloth. One is ponderous, tall, heavy, and his brown eyes seem almost hidden by heavy lids. His dark brown hair, though trimmed carefully, is thinning and lank and flops in the wind. The second merchanter is of average height, and trim. His hair is sandy-colored, tinged with silver-gray, and his eyes are hazel.

The heavy merchanter looks down at the smaller man. "Most honored Clan Head Tasjan, I have heard that there are those in the Dyjani Clan who murmur about the need for change among the merchanters."

"There are always those who wish change." Tasjan's voice is a mellow and deep bass, surprisingly for one so slender.

"The words are for more than change. There is talk about who will be Emperor."

"There have always been some who ask, 'Is it not time for a merchanter Emperor? Can we not support with our blades and golds someone who will live in the years to come? Can we not do away with those who revere the cracked and failing vase of the past?'" Tasjan laughs. "I have heard such questions since I was a boy. So have you."

"Such questions are dangerous now," Bluoyal observes.

"Because the Emperor is aging, Bluoyal? Or because he is less than satisfied with his Merchanter Advisor?"

"Remember, Tasjan, I was the one who calmed Fuyol when he would have hired blades to dismember you and your heirs, and the one who counseled patience."

"I appreciate your efforts, my old and valued friend." Tasjan shrugs. "Yet none would accept his golds, and now he is dying, and all look the other way."

"There was the matter of a Dyjani trade plaque," Bluoyal points out. "And a Brystan sabre refinished in cupridium. And the Dyjani are the ones who trade most in sabres from Brysta—the only ones, as I recall."

"Everyone knows we alone trade in such arms, excepting, of course, Bluyet House, which also does, but we know that the Emperor's Merchanter Advisor is far above suspicion," Tasjan replies. "That is why it was meaningless. It was an easy way to cast suspicion."

"And why," asks Bluoyal with a laugh, "would anyone wish to cast suspicion upon the most honorable Dyjani Clan? Because you are all so beloved?"

Tasjan returns the laugh. "We are most beloved, for we are the most successful at competing with the Hamorians in all that they do."

"Beloved or not, most honored and ancient friend, now is not the time for merchanters to raise questions. Time favors us more than action. Rynst grows older by the day, and without him, the Mirror Lancers will not know which way to point their blades. Chyenfel holds to life by sheer force of will against chaos, and when Kharl succeeds him, chaos will meet chaos, for the Second Magus will not support young Rustyl as a successor to the Malachite Throne—nor anyone supported by Rynst." Bluoyal shakes his head. "The Second Magus would be Emperor, and yet he cannot see that few even within the Quarter of the Magi'i will support him."

"He is a powerful mage, as is his son," Tasjan counters. "The fourth magus, who has balanced all, is failing, many say, and his daughter is consorted to Kharl's son. Many would support Kharl because he has a son, and for the sake of the daughter of the fourth magus, and to ensure that there would be an heir. The Empire cannot stand another Emperor without heirs, not in these times."

"And when the Second Magus fails . . . then what?" asks Bluoyal. "Will you then offer yourself as the man of the merchanters—or of the people?"

"I cannot imagine that happening," Tasjan replies.

Despite the cool wind, Bluoyal blots his forehead with a pale blue square of cloth that momentarily covers his entire visage. His brown eyes are hard as he studies the slender, sandy-haired merchanter. "You have talked of the failure of the Magi'i to others. Why will you not admit it to me?"

"Because you meet too often with Chyenfel and Kharl." Tasjan shrugs. "I will not admit such even now. I do believe, as do you, that there will come a time when a merchanter must sit upon the Malachite Throne. When that time will be, I do not know. Nor do you."

"You wager that time will be soon, and you are the merchanter, and your guards under Sasyk will make sure that at least some will make you such an offer."

Tasjan smiles. "While I would scarce refuse such, who would ever offer that to me—the head of the oh-so-beloved Dyjani Clan? As for Sasyk, you know that he is but to protect the interests of the House."

The older and heavier merchanter shakes his head ponderously. "You play with chaos-flame, my friend."

"You will be burned by such flames sooner than I, Bluoyal, for you are far closer to them, and Cyad is less than kind to those who cannot balance the chaos of chaos and the chaos of man."

"You seem most concerned for my welfare."

"I am, indeed, for if you fail, who will be Merchanter Advisor?" asks Tasjan. "I would not wish it to be Veljan, for reasons we all know. Nor Vyanat, who is all that you claim I am. And beloved as I am, who would wish me? Does that mean we would see someone like Kernys? Or the lady trader, the one who makes us look magnanimous in our petty revenges? No . . . I would much prefer you not fail."

"For now," suggests Bluoyal.

"But, of course." Tasjan laughs. "Would you have me lie outright?"

Bluoyal laughs as well, even as he lifts the wide blue cloth to blot his perspiring face once more.

XVI

IN THE EARLY-MORNING light that brightens his overcaptain's study, Lorn pores over the map of Biehl before him, trying to link what he has seen so far in the town with the old cartographic information. Some material he can see is outdated, for the map shows four piers in the harbor, and several structures that may have been warehouses that exist no longer.

His earlier perusal of the records in Helkyt's study also shows that at one time, the commandant of the compound had been a majer or sub-majer, and that there had been three companies quartered in the compound. He straightens and shakes his head, knowing he must act quickly and decisively, even before he knows enough to do so. He also knows that such actions must show as little as possible, for an intelligent officer who is young for his rank is already suspect.

"Ser?" Helkyt peers in the study door. "Have you been here long?"

"Since around dawn, I think." Lorn laughs. "Come on in and tell me about the Emperor's Enumerators. Close the door."

Helkyt closes the door and takes the seat nearest the wall. He brushes back a thin and long strand of blond hair, unconsciously swirling it over the top of his scalp where most of his hair has already vanished. "Mayhap . . . mayhap, ser, as you said, best you know about the Emperor's Enumerators here in Biehl, afore you visit such." Helkyt's brow is perspiring, despite the cool air in the study.

"Tell me," Lorn says easily.

"There be three enumerators—Flutak, Neabyl, and Comyr. Senior Enumerator Flutak," Helkyt says, "he is in charge of administering and collecting the tariffs here. Neabyl inspects the vessels to ensure they carry no contraband, and Comyr is the most junior. He will do whatever the elder enumerators request."

"How long has Flutak been the senior enumerator?"

Helkyt shrugs uneasily. "He has been such long before I was posted here."

"And you have been here?"

"Near-on eight years, ser."

"Does Flutak spend much time with the local traders and merchants? Or does he have relations among any merchant house?"

Helkyt moistens his lips. Finally, he speaks. "Not that I'd be knowing, ser, not for certain. Some say he has powerful relatives in Cyad. In Biehl, he is said to be close to the olive-grower Baryat . . . mayhap others, but those I've not heard."

Lorn nods. "What about Neabyl?"

"He came but five years ago, and Comyr three."

"Do any of them have consorts here?"

"Flutak has none, though it is said he has a mistress, the youngest daughter of Baryat. Baryat holds many lands to the south and west. There it is drier and more sunny."

"Are many barrels of olives shipped from Biehl?"

"More olives than most anything else, ser. Excepting clay, and that is worth far less."

What Lorn does not understand—or fears he does—is the most obvious nature of what Helkyt reveals.

"And Neabyl?"

"His consort lives in Summerdock, and it is said that she will not so much as visit Biehl. Comyr—he is young, and has none, none that any would know."

"I don't suppose you would know who those powerful relatives of Flutak might be, or whether they might be related to any in major trading houses?"

"That I would not, ser."

"You can return to whatever you were working on, Helkyt. We'll depart to see the enumerators in a bit. I have a few notes I would like to make."

"Yes, ser." Helkyt rises gingerly.

Lorn adds several items to the personal list that has gotten alarmingly long in less than the full day since he arrived in Biehl, then leaves his study.

In the outer study, Helkyt looks up from a stack of papers. "Ser?"

"I'll meet you at the stable."

"Be there in a moment, ser, if you will."

Lorn nods and slips out, past the door to the unused room across the corridor, the room that seems designed to be an audience chamber or some sort of official function space. Outside, the wind is stronger than earlier, but warmer and out of the south.

He is met at the stable by an ostler who, like many of those at Biehl, is older—white-haired and missing a good fraction of his teeth. "I be Chulhyr, ser." He looks at the uniform speculatively.

"I'm Lorn, the new overcaptain. I arrived yesterday, but you were not here, Helkyt said." Lorn smiles. "I need a mount. If you could recommend a good one . . ."

"You be wanting a stallion, ser?"

Lorn laughs. "I'd like a mount that will do as I wish and not argue about it."

The ostler laughs back. "Yes, ser."

As Chulhyr is leading out a chestnut mare, Helkyt hurries across the courtyard and arrives, breathing heavily. The ostler looks at Lorn. "She be having a will, but a firm hand be all you need."

"Thank you." Lorn studies the mare, then swings himself up into the saddle, where he checks the Brystan sabre. Then he and Helkyt ride across the courtyard.

"Have you found anyone to cart off the rubbish?" Lorn asks as they ride through the compound gates and past another too-young lancer guard.

"I'll be knowing that this afternoon, ser."

"And you'll have names for instructors?"

"Yes, ser."

Lorn nods. "Tell me about the places we pass, if you would."

"Yes, ser." Helkyt clears his throat. "There be the warehouse for the olive-growers, where they store the olives while they season, and beyond that be the potters, save that Aluyt casts but the large jars for seed oils and the like. . . ."

Lorn listens as they ride back toward the harbor, trying to fix the names and the structures in his mind, and match them to the map he has studied earlier. As when he had first entered Biehl, he sees few souls out and around the ancient town.

The enumerators' single-story building stands west of the piers, and slightly to the south of the chandlery, a square structure fifty cubits on a side, partly hidden from the rest of Biehl by a tall hedge. The green shutters are freshly painted, the panes of the windows clean of the salt that streaks the panes of the lancer barracks and, indeed, even of the windows of Lorn's quarters.

Lorn and Helkyt rein up at the side of the structure, where there are several stone hitching-posts, dismount, and tether their horses, before making their way to the square arched doorway. Inside is a narrow table, at which is seated a brown-haired young man in blue, whose tunic bears thin cream-and-green piping.

"Master Squad Leader," says the enumerator.

"Comyr," returns Helkyt, "this be Overcaptain Lorn. He is the new commander of the Mirror Lancers, and he has come to call on the senior enumerators."

"They had heard of such, and both will be glad to see you, Overcaptain." Comyr bows. "If you would but come with me." Comyr ushers them through a set of double doors into a large room, similar to the one in the lancers' headquarters building, except two men are seated at the table on the dais, with several stacks of paper between them.

The two rise. Both senior enumerators wear the same type of uniform: blue tunics over green trousers, with cream-colored web belts. On the forearms of their sleeves are two gold slashes.

"Senior Enumerators, this is Overcaptain Lorn," Helkyt announces. "Overcaptain, Flutak . . . and Neabyl."

Flutak bows. He is a broad man, almost totally bald, but with a muscular form that any barbarian might indeed admire. Although he is clean-shaven, his eyebrows are white and bushy, and white hairs straggle from his ears. "I am pleased to see that Biehl once more has a capable lancer officer." His voice is a mellow tenor.

"And I, too." Although Neabyl is small, black-haired, and wiry, he speaks with a deep baritone.

Lorn bows but slightly in response.

"And what might we be doing for you, Overcaptain?" asks Flutak.

"I was just here to tell you that I have been sent to Biehl by the Majer-Commander to train and rebuild the garrison, and to take a more active role in supporting the Emperor's Enumerators." Lorn smiles easily. "I thought it best you know that."

"Perhaps we should talk for a moment." Flutak moves gracefully toward the corner of the room and returns with two armless oak chairs. He sets one at each end of the oblong table. All four men seat themselves at the narrow oblong table.

Flutak looks at Lorn, as if suggesting he begin.

"As you may know," Lorn says slowly, "the barbarians have increased their attacks in many places on the northern borders of Cyad, and more trained lancers are needed to deal with these attacks. It was noted that Biehl has both the space and the facilities to recruit and train young lancers, and that the payroll is adequate to handle such." Lorn smiles. "So it is that I find myself here."

Flutak smiles easily, a smile that reminds Lorn of the late Majer Maran. "We have indeed heard of the depredations that the Mirror Lancers have faced in the field against the barbarians, and many had thought that the compound might even be closed, and its lancers sent elsewhere, for certainly lancers are scarce needed in Biehl itself. So I am most glad that is not the case, and so will those merchants who sell to the compound and the lancers."

"Yet, it is passing strange that more have not arrived with you," observes Neabyl.

Lorn shrugs. "It is scarcely strange. The Majer-Commander believes this task can be accomplished by an overcaptain. If it cannot, doubtless a majer and an undercaptain will follow. There may be an undercaptain before long, in any event, but it makes little sense for him to arrive until there are tasks for him to undertake."

The faintest flicker of a shared glance passes between the two senior enumerators.

"I understand that you inspect the cargos being ported here, and collect the imposts on such, and ensure that contraband, such as iron weapons and the like, does not makes its way from vessels trading here. What other duties do you perform that a lancer would be unlikely to have great knowledge of?"

"We provide the payroll for the compound," says Neabyl with a smile.

"That I understood, and for such we are grateful." After a moment, Lorn asks, "And I suppose you keep records of the ships that port so that one may compare from season to season and year to year?"

"That we do, and send the tariff revenues to Cyad."

"And perhaps with a stronger lancer presence, tariff revenues to the Emperor might indeed increase."

"The enumerators have never needed to rely on the lancers for that," suggests Flutak.

"Then, you are indeed fortunate here, for that is not so in all ports," Lorn replies evenly. "In any case, I did wish to inform you of that, and to assure you that, because of my deep and abiding interest in trade, I am indeed willing to support your efforts to carry out your duties to the Emperor and the Land of Light, as may be required by the Emperor and the Majer-Commander . . ." Lorn pauses, then adds, "and, of course, by you . . . as necessary."

"Overcaptain Madlyr had begun to take some interest in tariffs and trade . . . but he died rather suddenly after taking such an interest," observes Flutak smoothly.

"That was most unfortunate." Lorn smiles, his eyes cold.

He concentrates on fixing the man's face in his mind. "But perhaps it will be to everyone's advantage that the garrison here is restored with the protection of trade in mind."

"We would all look to the advantages of all," agrees Flutak.

"I see you do not maintain quarters here," Lorn observes before either enumerator can follow up on his last words.

"There is little reason to do such. Biehl has heretofore been such a peaceful port, with little need of lancers and guards."

"Of that I am certain, and certain it will continue as such," Lorn agrees, "for the lancers are being trained for their abilities against the barbarians, and there certainly are none here."

"No, indeed, Overcaptain."

Lorn rises. "I do thank you both, and I look forward to working with you as most necessary." He bows fractionally.

The enumerators rise more slowly.

"It is good to see you, a young and vigorous overcaptain here in Biehl, and we do hope that our experience will prove of assistance to you, Overcaptain," replies Flutak. "And that you will see fit to draw upon it."

"My thanks to you, and I am most certain that I will draw on your experience." The overcaptain inclines his head a last time before he turns and departs.

Lorn does not speak again until he has mounted the chestnut and they are passing the harbor piers on the return to the compound. "They have a new building, one of the few I have seen in Biehl."

"It is but four years since it was built."

Lorn studies the piers. The brig and one of the schooners have sailed, but a fishing boat is tied at the innermost wharf, where baskets of fish are being unloaded into a small cart.

"They did not seem pleased," suggests Helkyt.

"I doubt they are." Lorn laughs. "Lancer officers are never seen as totally welcome, but I am certain that they will be helpful and most supportive. I need to jot down several things, Helkyt, when we get back to the study. Then, after that, we may need the mounts again."

"Yes, ser." Helkyt remains silent as they continue riding, the expressions on his face varying from concern to puzzlement as he occasionally casts a sidelong glance at Lorn.

Two lancers are sparring almost desultorily in the shadowed northeast corner of the compound as Lorn and Helkyt ride to the stable. Lorn nods to himself.

"How she be, Overcaptain?" asks the ostler after Lorn reins up outside the stable and dismounts.

"Fine, but I will be needing her for a longer ride shortly."

"The exercise, that she can use."

"She will be getting more." Lorn smiles before turning and walking quickly across the courtyard. Helkyt scurries to keep pace with him.

Once back in his study, Lorn begins to jot down all his impressions, and where and about what the enumerators had lied. It seemed like almost every other sentence uttered by Flutak bore either a degree of untruth or a veiled threat, and Lorn has two sheets of paper before he is finished. He shakes his head before he calls the squad leader.

"Yes, ser?"

"Helkyt, we're going to take a ride in a few moments. It may take a large part of this afternoon as well. Do you know where Flutak and Neabyl maintain their quarters?"

"Ah . . . It is said . . ."

Lorn raises his eyebrows.

"Yes, ser."

"Good. We will take a ride, with several of the local lancers who may know about Biehl. You will point out all the places any overcaptain should know. Those will include the dwellings or quarters of the enumerators, prominent local merchanters, shipowners, factors . . . any crafters who might supply goods for the compound. It would be well for me to know such."

"Yes, ser. That I can see."

Lorn stands. "I will meet you in the stable in a few moments. I need to get something from my quarters."

Helkyt nods.

"And you need to find two lancers who were raised here and know the town and the gossip."

"Yes, ser."

Lorn ushers the senior squad leader out, then closes the door to his own study, and walks out into the courtyard, along the headquarters building until he reaches the main stairs to his own spaces at the north end. The dust has been swept from the quarters, and the aroma of baking bread comes from the antique oven, although Daelya is nowhere in sight.

Lorn reclaims the chaos-glass from its hiding place in the armoire under his smallclothes and carries it into the front study. There, he closes the door and slides the bolt in place before he takes out the chaos-glass and concentrates.

The silver mists appear, then fade, and a figure swims into view. Flutak sits alone at the oblong table. His brow furrows, and he glances out the window. The enumerator mutters something, but no one joins him while Lorn watches.

Lorn finally releases the image. Flutak definitely bears watching.

The overcaptain locks the door and hurries down the front steps to the courtyard and across to the stable where Helkyt and two lancers wait, already mounted. In the warm afternoon sunlight that pours through a clear green-blue sky, Chulhyr holds the reins to the chestnut.

"Thank you, Chulhyr. She's a good mount."

The ostler bows, and retreats.

Helkyt gestures to the two lancers. "This is Nayhul, and this Kurbyl." Nayhul is brown-haired and older, his face bearing a certain weathering, while Kurbyl is black-haired and fresh-faced.

"Good." Lorn mounts the chestnut. "You two and Squad Leader Helkyt are going to give me a tour of Biehl."

The three nod.

"I'd like to ride back along the harbor road, and the piers, and have you show me the crafters and important factors in town first, then the dwellings of the more noted local families," Lorn explains as the four ride out through the gates.

As they head down the slope, Nayhul coughs gently.

"What is it, Nayhul?"

The older lancer gestures to the right, to the west, at a large section dug out of the hillside that adjoins the one on which the compound sits. "There be the clay quarries of Jahlyr and his family. Fine clay for china, and crockery, so fine that the Spidlarians ship it all the way to Spidlaria," offers one of the young lancers. "And even some from Hamor."

"He is wealthy?" Lorn asks.

"Most so. Beyond, you see the villa?"

Lorn studies the brick structures on the far side of the hill, whose roofs and upper levels alone are visible from the road. "It looks large."

"They have many dwellings there, and stables, and a warehouse, and even a pool for bathing."

"Is there a large tariff on clay?" Lorn asks Helkyt.

"That . . . I would not know."

They pass the olive warehouse and then near the ocean piers. At the outermost pier in the harbor rides a two-masted deep-sea vessel, with an ensign of red and gold—Hamorian. "Do you know what the Hamorians come here for?" Lorn asks. "I cannot imagine that there is great enough wealth here for them to offload large cargoes."

"They buy most of all salted fish," offers Kurbyl. "My sire has sold some. And the china at times, and olives."

"I take it you didn't like being a fisherman," Lorn says.

"I much prefer a mount to a boat, ser. And a dry bunk."

The other riders laugh at the wry tone of the youngest.

"Anything else the Hamorians buy?"

"Mayhap some scented oils," ventures Helkyt.

The other piers are empty.

Lorn points to the crossed-candles sign, as if to ask about the chandlery.

"The chandler, he is Reycuh, but he is not much of a chandler," says Nayhul. "But Fuycyl, he is a most excellent cooper."

"Most excellent," adds Kurbyl. "My sire pays a copper more for his barrels for the salted fish he sells to the Hamor traders."

At the chandlery they turn southward, and Lorn listens as Nayhul offers explanations and names for almost every structure or dwelling they pass.

"The blue house . . . that be where the entertainer Fyella lived . . . old now, but my grandsire remembers her. . . . the yellow shutters . . . the cabinetmaker . . . and over there be Systyl, the chemist, with his powders and potions . . . The firewagon portico . . . that all lancers know . . ."

Before long they have left the center area of Biehl and follow a more winding road toward the southwest.

"Here be the dwellings of those of import, ser," offers Nayhul. "Over there, the reddish tower, that be the watchtower of Master Duplyr, above his mill."

In time, perhaps a kay more to the northwest, Lorn notes a long villa that sprawls across a low hill. "Whose dwelling might that be?"

Helkyt shifts in the saddle, but does not answer.

Nayhul finally answers. "That be the dwelling of one of the Emperor's Enumerators, the big one with no hair."

"Is that Enumerator Flutak's dwelling, Helkyt?"

"Ah . . . I believe so . . ."

"It is rather . . . substantial," suggests Lorn.

"It be the grandest in all of Biehl. So said my grandsire," adds Kurbyl, the younger lancer. "Near-on threescore builders worked on it for three seasons."

"And the villa on the next hill?" Lorn asks.

"That be the olive-grower Baryat," Helkyt says slowly.

"His daughter is Flutak's mistress?" Lorn asks.

"Ah . . . that is rumored . . ."

As he turns his head, Lorn catches the look between the two lancers, who clearly have not heard that rumor. A faint smile crosses the overcaptain's lips. "Rumors . . . one must be most careful with them . . . If they are untrue, then the innocent suffer, and if true . . ."—Lorn laughs gently—"then often the innocent also suffer."

Helkyt frowns.

"Ser?" asks Kurbyl, as Lorn has hoped he will.

"If a rumor is false, then those about whom it is told suffer. If it is true, then those about whom it is told often make those who tell the truth suffer." He shrugs. "That is why rumors are dangerous, especially about an Emperor's Enumerator."

Another look passes between the two lancers, and Helkyt shifts his weight in his saddle once more, most uneasily.

After the group has ridden almost another kay with more explanations of dwellings, and a sawmill, almost in relief, Helkyt gestures. "See! We have circled Biehl, and we ride toward the piers once more."

As they ride back through the compound gates, Lorn smiles, for he knows how to find Flutak's villa, and has accomplished a few more tasks.

"Thank you," he tells the two lancers as he dismounts. Then he turns to Helkyt. "And thank you, Helkyt. Before long, I will know my way around Biehl without guidance." Lorn looks at the late-afternoon sun, then adds, "I think I'll work on some things in the study in my quarters. I may not see you until tomorrow. Then, we'll need to go over the plans for getting the old barracks ready and setting up training sessions for the current lancers."

"Ah . . . yes, ser."

Lorn turns to the waiting Chulhyr. "Thank you."

"My pleasure, ser. My pleasure." The ostler takes the chestnut's reins and leads her back into the stable.

Lorn walks back to his quarters. In the small study, with the shutters closed to dim the strong, late-afternoon light, he tries the glass again, seeking the Emperor's Enumerator.

This time Flutak is not alone, but ushering a man from a room—and the room is not in the enumerators' building, but one of white stone—presumably the lavish villa Lorn has seen earlier in the day. The thin man who leaves bears twin daggers at his belt, and a coil of black rope. Lorn does not recognize the man personally, but there is little question what kind of profession he represents.

"So . . . more than a few rats in the granary." Lorn laughs harshly, then replaces the glass he knows he will be using more than he ever intended when Jerial had given it to him. He needs to make some preparations for the evening ahead, including using the glass to see how best to approach Flutak's villa, and in particular, his bedchamber.

XVII

DAELYA HAS LEFT a small stew in a pot, and a loaf of fresh bread, for Lorn's evening meal. Sitting in the breakfast room off the kitchen of his quarters, Lorn begins to eat both, wishing he had even Byrdyn to sip with it, but from what he can tell, there is no spirit factor at all in Biehl, unless the chandler or some other factor also trades in wine or spirits. Then, he has not had time to look, and wine is the least of his problems.

He is not sure whether his posting to Biehl is a test, or another attempt to remove his presence from the lancers—a presence apparently unwanted by some—or both, with different players trying to use him for differing purposes. His thoughts skitter to the questions his father had posed, particularly the first, for which he yet has no truly satisfactory answer: *What is it that allows Cyad to exist?* Other cities exist without chaos-towers, he knows, and without Magi'i. Other cities exist without emperors or harbors or without the riches that Cyad possesses. He snorts. Biehl exists, wretchedly, without any of those. All cities have people and structures, or they would not be cities, but those are answers far too simplistic, especially for his father.

The second question—"Could all the might of the Mirror Lancers here in Cyad, or all the might of the Iron Legions in Hamor, prevail against the will of those who live in such lands?"—suggests an equally simplistic answer. That answer is obviously no, and the answer is so obvious Lorn wonders why his father asked such a question. "Are those who direct power or chaos the source of either?" The answer to the third question is yet an equally obvious negative.

Yet Kien'elth is far from a stupid or obvious father and magus. So why has he posed such questions to Lorn? What does he wish Lorn to see beyond the questions? And the last unwritten question is so general the answer could be anything. How can the world be simpler and yet more complex than possibly imagined? The complexity is easy enough to see—in people like Maran and Flutak and even his father. The simplicity is something he has his doubts about.

Lorn still has no answers with which he is comfortable when he finishes eating. He washes out both pot and platter in the bucket of soapy water Daelya has left, then rinses them with the clean water in the pitcher and sets them in the rack on the table to dry. He walks slowly from the breakfast room where he has eaten alone, back to the study, where he looks down at the glass, concentrating once more.

Once the silvery mists clear, Lorn can see that the assassin now meets with two other men in a dim room. Lorn watches but for a moment, not wishing to spend energy on the glass when it will tell him little for the moment. As the image fades, he picks up the crude map he has drawn out, of the road and the best way to reach Flutak's villa. He hopes that Flutak remains alone, for the overcaptain knows he cannot afford to lurk and wait, or to dally.

Lorn also hopes that Flutak's assassins arrive relatively early in the night so that he can complete his own tasks before daybreak. He has few doubts that Flutak will act quickly, before Lorn can discover how much of the payroll is being diverted—and tell anyone else.

Lorn shakes his head as he considers what faces him. If he does not act against Flutak and the assassins quickly, then he will spend all too much time merely avoiding getting killed, and likely fail in his assigned duties, which will require all his efforts, so deplorable is the state of the post at Biehl. Yet if anyone can prove Lorn has acted to stop his own assassination, he will be considered inept if he fails and ruthless if he succeeds—and cold-blooded, either way.

His laugh is bitter. Why is it that people feel that revenge is justified, and acceptable, and that one is hot-blooded and human to undertake it, yet that to quietly prevent it is cold-blooded and ruthless—even if, in the end, far fewer souls suffer? Just from studying the payroll records, from looking at Flutak's villa, and from seeing the man immediately hiring an assassin, Lorn can tell the depth of corruption. But most would want greater proof. Greater proof will likely be Lorn's death, and he is unwilling to allow that. So he must act.

While he is uneasy about the decision, he cannot see any other option that will allow both his survival and his success at Biehl.

So . . . while he waits for the assassins he knows will come, he sits down in the twilight to consider again his sire's first question—the essence of what allows Cyad to exist. All cities exist because the people wish to live there, and can do so better than elsewhere. Why? Or how? Trade? But trade requires that people produce more of a good than they require, and they must have enough food and shelter to survive.

Finally, he nods, and dims the lamp in the study, then walks to his bedchamber, where he dims and then shuts off that light. Like most Magi'i, his night senses are excellent. Except for detail work such as writing or reading, he needs no illumination.

In the darkness, he studies again the firelance he has removed from the armory earlier in the afternoon, more fully charged now than then, and sets it against the molding of the double doors to the bedchamber.

Then he returns to the study, where he concentrates on the image of the man he had seen in the afternoon, and followed in the glass through the early evening. Three shadowy figures ride down a narrow lane, past what Lorn believes to be the clayworks to the south of the compound.

Lorn watches in the glass, then lets the image fade, nodding. He steps back to the breakfast room and eases the window open partway, enough to hear any sounds in the courtyard, should there be any. Then he waits, sitting in the chair where he had eaten.

When he believes yet enough time has passed, he slips back to the study and checks the glass again. The last of three figures is sliding down a rope from a brick wall—the compound wall. Lorn returns to the breakfast room, bringing the firelance with him, and sets it in the corner by the archway between kitchen and breakfast room. He unfastens the sabre scabbard and lays it on the table, after drawing the Brystan blade. Then he stands in the darkness that is like early twilight to him, waiting.

How long he waits, he is not certain, but he can sense the three men padding up the back service steps to his quarters, and the slight click of a brass key in a lock is confirmation enough for Lorn.

The three ease into the kitchen, and, without a word, two

slip through the side archway into the main room and across it to the closed double doors of the large bedchamber. A shorter figure remains in the kitchen by the door.

In the darkness, Lorn slides into the kitchen. The sentry peers forward, clearly expecting the return of his compatriots. Lorn moves, bringing the chaos-enhanced Brystan sabre across the other's throat, and knocking the heavy truncheon aside.

The gurgle is barely noticeable, but the dull thud of the man's body falling and the *clunk* of his weapon seem to echo through the kitchen.

Lorn ignores the sounds and retrieves the firelance in three steps, moving to the door between breakfast room and the main chamber.

"He's not there!" hisses a voice.

"The study!"

Lorn raises the firelance, using his chaos-senses to focus the firebeam tightly. *Hssst! Hsst!*

"Aeei!" One brief scream is the only sound that may leave Lorn's quarters.

He takes a deep breath, and moves to the two bodies, each sprawled with most of its skull burned away. Lorn swallows back the bile that has risen into his throat, standing there for a brief moment. Although the three had come to kill him, he dislikes becoming an assassin himself, save that he has little choice. He could not have captured them, and even had he, they would have said little, and he would have looked foolish trying to charge Flutak with hiring assassins. Then, he would have to kill the next set of assassins, if he could, and avoid other dangers—from possible poisoning to anything else Flutak could devise—each time with fewer advantages than the time before.

He finally bends down and searches the figures, but none bears anything that might prove useful, except for the gold and silver coins in their wallets, two daggers, a truncheon, and a short straight sword with a double edge. Lorn repeats the process with the dead sentry in the kitchen.

Then he drags all three figures out to the front, tiled foyer. There he lifts the firelance again, playing the chaos carefully across the bodies, trying not to burn the paneled walls or the woodwork. In a short time, nothing remains, except for a few metal items.

The worn broom from the kitchen is sufficient to sweep the ashes out onto the landing outside the door, and a rag removes most of the blackness from the tiles. It is also sufficient to wipe away the blood in the kitchen.

Lorn slips the weapons into the armoire he has not used, and then wraps the shoe nails in the soiled cloth, setting that in the back bottom corner of the armoire. After relocking both doors, he forces himself to the study, and despite his slight headache, focuses the glass on Flutak.

The silver mists swirl, revealing that Flutak is in his bedchamber, apparently alone, reading a scroll by the light of a lamp on the table beside the bedstead. Lorn lets the image lapse, then turns and leaves the study.

He reclaims the Brystan blade and scabbard, and the firelance, before he departs his quarters by the front door, which he locks as he leaves, not that locking seems to have had much effect. The courtyard remains quiet, as is the stable, and no one disturbs Lorn as he saddles the chestnut.

"Easy, girl . . . easy."

It takes him longer than it would the ostler, but before too much time has passed, he rides across the courtyard.

"Who goes?" comes the voice of a guard. "Show yourself."

"Overcaptain Lorn. I'm taking an evening ride."

"Ser?"

Lorn slows the chestnut so that the lancer can see his face. "I trust I will not be too long."

"Ah . . . yes, ser."

"Good evening, Lancer."

Lorn guides the mount out the gate and down toward the

harbor, toward the west road that will turn southward. The air is chill, a cold wind coming off the Northern Ocean with a dampness that promises a cold rain.

Once he is past the piers, Lorn turns westward, following the winding road, one hand ready to reach for the firelance in its holder, but the road remains dark and empty, and deserted as the chestnut carries him westward and south. While he does not know Biehl well, with the ride of the afternoon, his night vision, and his chaos-senses, he can find Flutak's villa—and the enumerator's bedchamber.

Still, in the darkness, the ride takes far longer than Lorn had recalled—or perhaps it seems but longer—until he is finally riding up a gentle slope toward the sprawling hillside villa. Below the villa on the south side of the slope is a stable, but Lorn guides the chestnut more to the north, where he finds a slender sapling beside the road. There he dismounts in the darkness and ties his mount to the tree.

Firelance in hand, he eases through the small olive orchard until he is less than a hundred cubits from the villa. For a time, he listens, and casts forth his chaos-senses, but he can sense only three figures moving—two sentries by the front door, and a third somewhere in the rear.

Lorn circles toward the rear of the villa, where he scales—slowly—a low brick wall in a spot shielded by what feels like a pearapple tree. Concealed by darkness and the tree limb, from the top of the wall Lorn studies the small courtyard.

The guard, who had appeared to be half-dozing on a stool, sits up abruptly as the Hamorian killer mastiff glides toward the wall beneath Lorn, growling softly.

"What is it? Another cat?" mumbles the guard.

The huge mastiff growls, again from below Lorn, then lunges upward.

Lorn levels the firelance, using it quickly on the guard, before the man can give an alarm, and then on the mastiff. He waits for a moment, but the faint thud of the guard's falling body goes unnoticed.

Lorn drops into the rear courtyard, where he uses more of the charge to ensure no trace of either guard or mastiff remains. He tosses the coins and metal nails over the wall before setting the guard's blade carefully on the stool and easing his way toward the rear door.

His senses can detect no one within the house who is moving, although there are servants or retainers sleeping in the south wing of the dwelling. The two guards in the front remain where they have been.

Is Flutak the noble and honest enumerator demanded by his position?

With significant portions of the Mirror Lancer payroll never delivered? With three guards and a deadly Hamorian mastiff? The largest villa in Biehl? Hiring three assassins to go after Lorn as soon as Lorn has suggested all is not as it should be?

The only sounds are those of the wind in the privacy hedges. Lorn's lips curl ruefully. Acting before anyone suspects such action has certain benefits, except that Flutak had also acted that way. Lorn hopes that he has foreseen more than has the enumerator.

The rear door, shielded by a token privacy hedge before which the sentry had been stationed, is barred from within. Lorn studies it for a moment with his chaos-senses, then lifts the lance and places it against the slight gap between the door and the frame. He triggers the lance, willing the chaos into a tight line.

His forehead is damp by the time the chaos has burned through the heavy bar, but the door remains closed. Lorn lets his chaos-senses touch the plate on the inside lock. His forehead is far warmer by the time the bronze bolt slides back under the pressure of focused chaos. Then, and only then, will the latch lift, allowing the door to swing wide, silently.

The wide tiled room he enters is empty.

Ignoring the intensification of his headache, Lorn slips

down the short corridor to the bedchamber, wondering if he will need to burn through another bar. He does not. Like most chambers within Cyadoran homes, the door has but a latch, and that lifts easily as he slides into the chamber, where the sole sounds are the loud snores of the sleeping enumerator.

Hssst! The firelance flares once.

From the far side of the bulky enumerator's body, a more slender figure bolts upright, her mouth opening.

Hsst! The firelance flares again, although Lorn's fingers are shaking as he lowers the weapon. He stands stock-still for a moment, swallowing silently. He knows he had no real choice, not after killing Flutak. Had Lorn not used the lance a second time, all would know what he has done, with a witness—and probably escaping servants who would also know, not to mention the guards in the front.

Nor can he afford to ride out, night after night, not after killing a mastiff and a guard. His lips tighten, even as his eyes burn momentarily. Why were there always innocents caught up with those who are less than honest?

Could he have done aught else? He knows that he will ask that question more than once as, slowly, he sets the firelance against the wall. Then, as he has done before in his own quarters, Lorn drags both figures onto a space of tile clear of rugs and upholstery, and plays the firelance across both, using his chaos mastery to direct and intensify the chaos-flames. There are no metal items to worry about. There are brown patches on the bed linens, but he can do nothing about those. Nor can he change what he has done, instantly reacting to kill the woman.

With another silent sigh, he eases back down the corridor and out the courtyard door, carrying the two pieces of the door bar. He climbs back over the wall, making a wide circuit of the villa.

The chestnut remains tied to the golden oak sapling.

"Easy there . . ." Lorn unties her and mounts quickly, still carrying the wooden bar.

He rides slowly and carefully away from the villa. Neither the glass nor his chaos-senses had revealed the woman's presence until he had killed the enumerator. Had he spared her, Lorn would likely have doomed himself. As it is, he treads a narrow and dangerous path.

He can tell himself that the woman was not totally innocent. The fact that she was probably the daughter of the olive-grower Baryat, who has doubtless been receiving special treatment from Flutak, suggests that the conspiracy to divert tariffs is not solely Flutak's doing. The elaborate luxury of the villa and the guards only testify to Flutak's corruption. Any woman who partook of the fruits of that corruption has made a choice.

But did she, really? Lorn knows his own sisters have few real choices. Was this woman any different?

Yet . . . what choices did Lorn have? If he had spared her, she would have given an alarm, and all too soon the trail would have pointed to Lorn.

Could Lorn have found some more clever way to deal with Flutak?

Perhaps his father could have, but Lorn has already found that his strengths do not lie in scheming, but in acting. With all the schemes already laid against him, he fears that not to act swiftly would have been his undoing.

And innocent men do not hire assassins immediately upon meeting a Mirror Lancer officer who only pledges to carry out his duty.

But . . . that does not change the sickening feeling that twists Lorn's guts. Nor the anger that goes with his sadness and regret. Anger that he is faced once more with situations where no choices are perfect, and anger at himself for not foreseeing the complications.

Lorn rides slowly along the road back toward the compound.

A kay farther along toward the harbor, he drops the door

bar's sections into a drainage ditch. His head throbs, and even in the darkness, he is seeing double images. He has drawn far more chaos from around him than is wise, and used it far more than he would have preferred, and partly in ways he regrets . . . and will always regret.

XVIII

LORN IS AT his study desk early the next morning—though not at dawn, not after the long night he has had, and the dreams about the young woman, who has appeared in them . . . pleading, her face taking on Myryan's countenance, perhaps because Lorn had never really seen her visage. For a time, he looks blankly in the direction of the open window.

Trying to push away the image of the pleading figure, he tries to draft the phrases that may prove useful in dealing with Neabyl, the remaining senior enumerator, when Helkyt appears.

"Ser?"

"Yes, Helkyt?"

"There be a problem, ser."

Lorn raises his eyebrows. He can think of several, though they seem trivial compared to his dreams of Flutak's mistress. "Yes?"

"Mayhap not a problem, but a matter most strange."

"What might it be?"

"You see, ser, there is a man. His name is Drakyt. None knows how he lives, but folk die, usually from blades stuck in them in the dead of night, and thereafter Drakyt has coin enough for good raiment and the best ale."

Lorn nods for Helkyt to continue.

"This morn, the guards heard mounts outside the walls, and when they went to see, there were three horses tethered there on the west side, well away from the gate. One of the mounts was a black that none but Drakyt can ride, or so 'tis said." The senior squad leader pauses, then continues as he sees that Lorn will not question. "There was also a hempen seaman's rope, tarred black, fastened over the wall. But none have seen any men within the compound."

Lorn shrugs. "Perhaps the guards scared them off. Until they show up to claim their mounts, all we can do is stable the mounts. When they return, we'll charge them for feeding their horses and put the charges in the payroll chest. Every copper will help. You might pass the word to the folk around the compound that's what we're doing."

"But . . . if they return not?"

"Say . . . in half a season, the mounts belong to the Mirror Lancers." Lorn looks at Helkyt. "Or do you think it should be longer?"

"I know not. . . ." Helkyt frowns. "This Drakyt is not one to anger."

Lorn laughs. "How would that anger this fellow? He leaves his mount, and the Emperor's Mirror Lancers feed it and take care of it? And we ask to be paid for the feed and care?"

"Ah . . . ser . . ."

"Yes?"

"It is said you went riding late last evening, and returned far later." Helkyt purses his lips. "You did not see or hear the mounts?"

"I didn't see a soul around the courtyard or outside the walls," Lorn replies most truthfully, if not with the entire truth. "If I had, I am certain all of the compound would have heard."

"Most strange." Helkyt bows, still frowning. "I will tell Tashqyt to have the mounts stabled."

"Tashqyt? He's one of the junior squad leaders? Dark-haired, with a square beard?"

"Yes, ser."

Lorn nods. "I'm trying to put faces to names. Is there anything else?"

"No, ser."

"Will we have a cart to carry off the rubbish from the north barracks?"

"This very morn, ser. Two." Helkyt smiles, an expression of relief.

"Good. I knew you could do that." Lorn rises. "All this talk about stray mounts reminded me. I need to talk to Chulhyr. I shouldn't be gone long."

"Yes, ser. I be going to the enumerators for the payroll, after I task Tashqyt with the stray mounts."

Lorn nods, and the two men separate as they leave the administrative building. Helkyt heads for the barracks, while Lorn crosses the courtyard through the light but cold rain that has turned the paving stones a darker sheen of gray. Despite the rain, Lorn nods, smiling, at the younger lancers who already are carrying debris from the north wing of the barracks into a nondescript cart. A worn and near-swaybacked mule stands in the harness.

At the stable, Lorn draws Chulhyr aside. "You know mounts well, do you not? Exceptionally well?"

"I might say so, ser, better than all but the farrier, and Spherl." Chulhyr frowns, waiting. "Have you found the chestnut wanting?"

"Dark angels, no," replies Lorn with a light laugh he does not feel. "We will be getting more lancers. We will be needing more mounts, and I would prefer it not be known yet. Can you scout around . . . ?"

"Ah . . . that I can do. And now is a good time, for last year's harvests and trading were not so good as in other years." The ostler pauses. "How many?"

"Enough for another company by autumn."

Helkyt and four other lancers enter the stable to find and

saddle their mounts. The senior squad leader inclines his head as he passes the overcaptain. The lancer following him carries a small chest.

"It might take that long unless you wished to pay more than such would be worth," Chulhyr replies slowly.

"We have some time, but that's why I wanted you to begin looking as you can."

"Yes, ser."

"Let me know when you have some you think we should purchase. You know where my study is."

Chulhyr nods. "I will bring you word, ser."

"Thank you."

The overcaptain walks back across the courtyard under gray clouds that appear lighter than before. Behind him, he hears the sound of hoofs on stone as Helkyt and the lancers set out to pick up the payroll.

Back in his study, Lorn writes several more thoughts on his list of items that need action. He had forgotten to ask Chulhyr about saddles and riding gear—whether there remained saddles from the time when two full companies had been quartered at Biehl and, if so, how usable they might be. Each idea begets more problems, and more work.

Then Lorn goes back to his plans for the enumerators.

He has finished what he can plan, drafted a scroll to the District Guard Commander in Ehlya suggesting that he will be visiting in the near future, and is working on the outline of a lancer training program at Biehl when the door from the outer study opens, then closes.

Thrap! Even before the sound of the knock dies away, Helkyt puffs into the inner study.

"Ser . . . ser . . ."

Lorn looks up from the draft of the training program.

"Ser . . . ah . . . there is a problem . . . with the pay chest. Senior Enumerator Flutak cannot be found."

"Cannot be found?"

"No, ser."

"Doesn't anyone know where he is?"

"All Neabyl would say is that he was missing from his villa and that no one knew where he had gone." Helkyt shrugs.

"Just because he's gone off on furlough or whatever doesn't mean we don't get paid," Lorn points out, forcing annoyance to creep into his voice.

"He is not on leave or furlough, ser. That is what Neabyl says."

"That shouldn't be a problem." Lorn frowns. "Isn't Neabyl a senior enumerator as well?"

"Yes, ser. But he does not wish to release the payroll without the assent of Flutak."

Lorn stands, then walks to the window, as if considering what Helkyt has conveyed. After a time, he turns. "Helkyt . . . this is a problem. We are entitled to a full draw of two companies, is that not true?"

"Yes, ser." There is the hint of a quaver in the squad leader's voice.

"Then, copy out that which we are entitled to. Underneath that, write that Overcaptain Lorn certifies that this is the payroll to which the Mirror Lancers in Biehl are entitled on this date, and that he has signed for its receipt." Lorn smiles. "We do not wish that our lancers not be paid, do we?"

"No, ser."

"And make two copies. On the second, place a line for Neabyl to sign, saying that he has received a copy and disbursed exactly these funds."

Helkyt nods slowly. "But he will not sign such or hand over the payroll."

"After you have drawn these up, we both will ride over to the enumerators' building, and I think we should take a full squad . . . say, in battle dress."

Helkyt swallows. "Ah . . ."

"The Emperor's Enumerators serve the Mirror Lancers, even as we support them." Lorn gestures. "Now, if you would send out word for the squad to be ready, and then draft those two statements . . ."

"Yes, ser." Helkyt nods twice, quickly.

It is nearing midmorning when the senior squad leader returns with the two drafts of the payroll account statements.

After he has read them closely, Lorn stands. "These will do. If the squad is ready, we will go visit Senior Enumerator Neabyl."

"Yes, ser. They await us in the courtyard."

"Good." Lorn slips on his winter jacket, waterproof at least, and follows Helkyt out.

Although he has not asked, the chestnut is saddled and waiting. As Lorn and Helkyt ride out through the gates, through a rain that is changing to a light drizzle, in the column behind them, Lorn can hear the murmurs.

". . . enumerators not like this . . ."

". . . think I'd worry more about the overcaptain not liking it . . ."

". . . first time . . . had a commander with a blade for a backbone . . ."

Lorn just hopes he won't cut himself too badly with that blade, or that he has not done just that already.

The waters of the harbor and the Northern Ocean beyond are flat and dark gray, and the piers are empty as the lancers ride past. At the enumerators' building, Lorn reins up, and the lancers do as well.

"Remain in formation, mounted," Lorn orders. "We will be a bit, but I'm sure you won't mind, since it is your pay we're getting."

There are a few smiles.

Lorn and Helkyt walk into the building, followed by an older lancer who carries the empty pay chest.

Neabyl comes out from the large room to meet them. He glances from Helkyt to Lorn, then past them to the squad of lancers remaining mounted in formation before the building.

He bows. "Overcaptain . . . I see that Squad Leader Helkyt has conveyed our difficulty."

Lorn nods at the doorway to the larger room with the dais, then walks past Neabyl and into the room. After a moment, the senior enumerator follows, an annoyed expression on his face. Behind him slips Helkyt. Lorn gestures for the squad leader to close the door, and Helkyt does.

"Overcaptain . . ."

"I see no great difficulty," Lorn says mildly. "We are owed a payroll. You are a senior enumerator of the Emperor, and you can provide such."

Neabyl shrugs. "I would not presume . . ."

"Are you not in charge here when Master Flutak is not?" Lorn asks.

"Ah, yes, Overcaptain."

"And do not the accounts for the payroll list what should be paid?"

"I do not have those . . ." Neabyl's voice is apologetic.

Lorn smiles. "I understand. I thought this might present a problem." He extends the first sheet of paper, drawing it from his jacket. "Here is our account for payroll and our draw for expenses for the eightday. I checked these against the original authorization for the garrison, the one signed by the Majer-Commander, and by the head of the Emperor's Enumerators in Cyad."

Neabyl studies the paper. "I would not know."

"I do. And the Majer-Commander would be most unhappy if his lancers were not paid. You do not have a record. So, if you will note, I will sign the paper so that all will know that you carried out your duty." Lorn pauses. "And you will sign an identical one saying that you disbursed these golds, and only these golds, to me as the payroll authorized on this date. In that fashion, when Master Flutak returns, he will have records, and there will be no question as to what funds were disbursed."

"Ah . . ."

"And you can use this as the basis for future accounts in the event that Master Flutak and your records cannot be found."

"That is true . . ." muses Neabyl. After a moment, he nods. "Yes, that indeed might prove beneficial to all, and I must say, I do like the idea of exchanging account statements for disbursals. It might remove any future . . . unpleasantnesses."

Lorn smiles. "One cannot undo the past, and change what has been, but one can change what will be."

"You have a persuasive way with words—and accounts, Overcaptain."

"Perhaps." Lorn continues to smile, adding, almost casually, "And . . . Neabyl . . . if by any chance there might be some shortages in the accounts, and if by chance Enumerator Flutak indeed does not return, it might be wise to report such . . . with the steps you have taken, such as this, to ensure they do not recur."

Neabyl's face blanks. After a long moment, a forced smile returns. "Your advice is not only persuasive, ser, but most wise, and should such eventualities be such, you can be assured that I will follow your words to the letter."

Lorn nods.

Neabyl returns the nod. "I will see that Comyr brings up a chest, and then we will count it, and sign your papers. I am sure none will fault our caution."

"None will fault it, I am sure," Lorn agrees.

As Neabyl leaves the large room, Helkyt glances at Lorn. "Ser . . . you talk as if Flutak will not return."

"That is because Master Neabyl acts as if he will not. Otherwise, there would have been no difficulty. Neabyl would be happy doing as Flutak has always done. That he would not, suggests that Flutak may have departed, not to return." Lorn adds in a lower voice, "Perhaps because all is not as well with the accounts as should be."

Helkyt swallows.

"As I told Senior Enumerator Neabyl, we cannot change what was—only what will be. And that we will do." Lorn continues to smile faintly as they wait for Neabyl to return. He knows he runs the risk of allowing Neabyl to seize golds and blame the shortage on Flutak, but there is nothing he can do about that, not without revealing more than he dares.

Nor can he ever reveal how he killed an innocent because he acted quickly against the guilty and the corrupt.

XIX

LORN YAWNS AS he leaves the kitchen in his quarters, after washing the dinner dishes. When he had been a mere lancer officer, under the command of others, he did not have to worry about dishes, but he had little space to himself, either. He yawns again as he walks toward the study. The day, and the previous night, have been long indeed, especially with the nightmare of the grower's daughter, whose face resembles Myryan's. Yet there is more that he must do . . . much more.

Even so, his thoughts drift back to Flutak . . . and the young woman. The woman was . . . is another matter, as his nightmares testify.

So far as Flutak was concerned, his mind is clear. While he may not have proof that would convince a justicer, he *knows* the depth of the enumerator's corruption. Neabyl's re-action was almost confirmation in itself. Lorn knows that, had he not acted against Flutak quickly, then any later action would be laid to his doorstep. One factor which removes him partly from suspicion is the unwillingness of most to believe a new officer would act so quickly and decisively . . . or that he would have the means so soon after arriving. Lorn takes a deep breath. For better and worse, he has acted, and cannot undo those actions. Nor has he yet discovered how better he might have acted.

Once in the study, he closes the inner shutters and slips the chaos-glass from the single drawer of the desk. After he sets it on the polished wood, he begins to concentrate, first on the name and image of Baryat, the olive-grower whose daughter Lorn has killed. The silver mists fill the glass, and then clear.

Baryat—gray-bearded and muscular—sits at a long table, flanked by three younger men, who appear to be his sons. The bearded man thumbs the edge of a knife, then speaks. While Lorn cannot hear the words, he can see the vehemence behind them. One of the sons brings a fist down on the table.

Lorn watches for but a short while, before letting the image lapse. Even so, his eyes are watering, and his head aches. For a time, he sits before the glass, his eyes closed, pondering. How much is the grower's vehemence based on the loss of his daughter, and how much upon fear of discovery of corruption? Will Lorn ever know?

As he tries to rest before he uses the glass once more, Lorn's thoughts skitter from Baryat to traders, to those in the Mirror Lancers like Maran who would see him dead and vanished.

Finally, he straightens, knowing that he must practice more, and become more adept at using the glass to see lands where he has not been, and to become able to translate those views into maps—and the other way around. He takes a deep breath, and concentrates once more upon the glass before him and upon controlling the silver mists.

XX

THE LATE SPRING afternoon is more like summer, damp and hot, as Lorn mounts in the courtyard of the Mirror Lancer compound. He studies the compound courtyard and buildings, quietly pleased that the leaves and dirt are gone, the stones are clean, the moss gone, even from between the pavement stones of the courtyard, and that the ancient windows now shine. Inside, more than a score of new recruits are housed in the north wing of the refurbished barracks.

A halfscore of recruits spar with padded blades in the open space to the west of the administration building, with Helkyt overseeing the training for the midday periods. Later, Lorn will return and take his rotation among the instructors.

The overcaptain urges the chestnut mare forward. As the six lancers ride through the gates, headed down to the harbor, beside Lorn rides the sharp-featured and black-haired Tashqyt, the more senior of the two junior squad leaders, and the one Lorn may consider for promotion to senior squad leader if and when he forms a second company at Biehl.

He stiffens in the saddle as the familiar chill of a screeing glass settles around him, and he wonders who might be watching. One of the Magi'i from Cyad—Ciesrt's father? Or the First Magus? Whoever it may be, he is strong, although the scrutiny is brief and quickly lifts, even before Lorn reaches the bottom of the slope.

A single ship is tied at the outer ocean pier—three-masted, and square-rigged, the largest vessel Lorn has seen at Biehl in the season he has been there. The plaque on the stern reads, *Lorava of Tyrhavven*, and a Sligan ensign hangs limply in the warm air.

"I don't think I've seen a Sligan vessel here before," Lorn says.

"Once they ported more often," suggests Tashqyt.

"Before the previous senior enumerator?"

"He was here when I was leaving childhood."

Lorn reins up the chestnut at the foot of the pier, then ties his mount to a timber supporting a railing. He waits as the five other lancers form up. Then, with Tashqyt beside him, and the four other lancers following, Lorn walks out the pier to the gangway of the Sligan vessel, and up the plank.

A bearded man with a single faded blue braid on a sleeveless tunic steps forward. Lorn's eyes are like chaos-fire, and the third officer backs away.

"... don't mess with them..."

"... white devils..."

Lorn ignores the murmurs.

Just beyond the quarterdeck, two older lancers from the original company stand behind Senior Enumerator Neabyl as he is returning the bills of lading apparently presented earlier by the vessel's master. Beside the lancers stands the junior enumerator, Comyr. The master—holding a leather wallet—looks up abruptly.

Neabyl turns, then frowns. "Overcaptain."

"Captain." Lorn bows slightly to the ship's master, then to Neabyl. "Senior Enumerator. It has been awhile since I have seen a Sligan vessel here, and I thought I might pay my respects." He offers a polite smile. "I'm Overcaptain Lorn, the commander of the port detachment and garrison here in Biehl."

"Pleased to see you, ser," offers the *Lorava*'s master. "It has been a time since we ported here."

"I hope we will see you more often in the seasons ahead." Lorn's smile is warmer than his first. His eyes go to Neabyl. "Have you assessed the tariffs yet?"

"Ah ... yes, ser."

"Are all the tariffs being collected as required?"

"Yes, ser."

"And only as required?" Lorn asks, watching and using his chaos-senses to truth-read the enumerator.

"Yes, ser. That is the job of an enumerator." Neabyl's eyes are chill.

Lorn smiles, a smile he means. "Good. Very good." He looks back at the captain. "Do you have any problems with the tariff collection?"

"Outside of paying 'em? No, can't say I do ... these days, Majer."

Lorn looks at Neabyl. "I think the master sees an improvement here. Perhaps he'll tell others." He looks at the captain. "After you finish with the enumerator, I would like a word with you." Lorn adds quickly, "There are no problems, and no extra tariffs."

"I'll be here, ser." The captain's voice is wary.

Lorn steps back and down the plank, followed by Tashqyt. The lancers wait.

Neabyl walks down shortly, accompanied by Comyr. His carriage is stiff, and his face cold. The two lancers detailed to him follow.

"Senior Enumerator?" Lorn steps forward and speaks before Neabyl can speak or walk by him.

"Yes."

"I trust you understand that my presence is not a reflection upon my lack of trust in you, but a necessity created by your predecessor."

Neabyl remains stone-faced.

"I also regret that I did not inform you in advance, but I did not know that this ship was porting until you had already boarded, and, in my capacity as port commander, I could not let the opportunity pass." He adds in a much lower voice, "And I have reported well of you to the Majer-Commander, for your efforts to improve the tariff collections here."

"I would that you had been able to tell me such earlier." Neabyl's voice is fractionally less cool.

"Were I more familiar with trade," Lorn continues, "I would create less awkwardness. I do appreciate your willingness to work with me to return Biehl to the port it was and should be again."

Neabyl's face relaxes a touch more. "I stand willing to do such."

"Thank you." Lorn pauses. "I am going to talk to the master about such matters as shipments of iron and weapons, and to see if he knows of such. The barbarians are raising larger forces."

Neabyl nods. "That . . . I can understand."

Lorn bows. "I will be meeting many ships, until we have convinced the traders that all has returned to what it should be, and I would ask your forbearance and your understanding that my presence is necessary not because of your conduct and actions."

"You have made that clear, Overcaptain." Neabyl pauses. "It is not an easy situation for either of us."

"No. I wish my actions were not necessary. I truly do."

Neabyl nods. "We should talk later."

"Thank you." Lorn bows.

So does Neabyl.

Once the enumerator has left the pier, Lorn turns to the junior squad leader. "Tashqyt . . . I shouldn't be too long, but I'd appreciate it if you and the men would wait here."

"Yes, ser."

As Lorn walks back up the gangway, he can hear the murmurs.

". . . *never* . . . heard an overcaptain take on an enumerator . . ."

"Overcaptain . . . wants things done right . . ."

". . . first time in years around here . . ."

If, *if* Ryalth sends him any Alafraan, several bottles will have to go to Neabyl, and Lorn will have to visit the enumerator more than once to praise him.

At the top of the plank, the captain is waiting. The weathered face wears a slight smile. "Overcaptain, you be a far braver man than I be, were I in your boots."

"Unlike you, Captain, I do not have my cargoes in the hands of the enumerators." Lorn's voice is wry.

"You wanted to talk."

"I do. About trade, and about what you are seeing." Lorn pauses. "I won't ask about coins and what cargoes are most profitable, Captain."

"Call me Svenyr."

"I'm Lorn."

Svenyr turns. "Might as well sit."

Lorn follows him to a small cabin in the upper rear deck, almost under the wheel.

The wiry master with the gold-and-silver hair and the square beard rummages in a built-in cabinet before bringing forth a bottle, which he pours into two mugs set on a table bolted to the deck. He nods to the pair of chairs. "Sit and sip, Majer."

Lorn takes one, and following Svenyr's lead, takes a sip of the red liquid that passes for wine, ignoring the promotion to a rank he sometimes wonders if he will ever live to make. He studies the weathered face.

"What be on your mind?"

"Several things. First, would you be willing to tell me if you know if more blades and iron are being shipped into Jera?"

"No secrets about that. Ultyn, master of the *Grenver*, was telling all he knew that he was carrying Brystan iron and shields there. Some local factors paying good coin for blades."

Lorn sips again. "This has been going on for the past three, four years?"

"Maybe longer. Jeranyi couldn't forge weapons iron if'n they sacrificed their firstborn and strongest cow. What else?"

"How long were the enumerators overtariffing here in Biehl?" Lorn concentrates again on truth-reading Svenyr.

"Truth be told, Biehl has not been the town it was once for near-on a halfscore years. I might be telling a few to give it another try. Be but one, though, less they see what I see."

Lorn smiles guilelessly. "Neabyl seems most capable, and we of the lancers have been able to work with him."

"Ha! Much as told the little sneak he was spitted on cold steel—or your cuprite blades—if he cheated a copper." Svenyr takes a long swallow of the vinegary wine.

"I believe he understands."

"You be meeting all the ships?"

"I told Neabyl that I would be . . . for a time, and when I can." Lorn pauses. "What cargoes would you like to carry that you cannot obtain?"

"Can't say as telling you that'd cause problems with the shareholders." The captain frowns, then worries his chin. "Always could use more dyestuffs, specially up along the northwest coast—Suthyans won't let us land anywhere but Armat, where they tariff high. Understand folk bring carts all the way from Rulyarth. Dyestuffs are welcome elsewhere, east of Armat, or going longhaul to Austra. Bright ones. Everyone's got brown."

"You know about the clay and china here?"

"Is old Kahlyr still doing that?"

"His son Jahlyr."

"Good to know." Svenyr swallows the last of the goblet. "Oh . . . the other thing is good spirits."

"You port in Cyad ever?"

"Times . . ." answers the captain, his voice wary.

"There's a newer house, Ryalor House—they have some good spirits you cannot find elsewhere."

"Hmmm . . ." Svenyr shrugs. "If I get there, I'll look."

Lorn stands. "You've been most patient, and I trust we will see you in Biehl again."

"One more time, anyways. Never promise more 'n once." The Sligan laughs as he rises.

The two walk out into the steamy heat of the afternoon. Lorn bows before he turns and leaves the *Lorava*.

He rides back to the compound silently, thinking over his mistakes, and what he can do to rectify them—if he can. Some, like the grower's daughter, he cannot.

He has little time for further thought, not after he rides in through the gates, because it is his turn to lead the sabre drills for the new recruits, and he must hasten into a training tunic and then take up a padded sabre.

By the time the drills are over, his brown training tunic is soaked, and his arms ache. So do his feet. He is so tired when he reaches his quarters that after he cleans up he can eat but half the emburhka that Daelya has prepared and left for him, and but a third of the fresh-baked bread.

After eating he makes his way to his study, and sinks into the chair, sitting in the twilight.

With a deep breath, he takes out the chaos-glass and concentrates, seeking out the olive-grower Baryat who, Lorn is convinced from his use of the chaos-glass, is hatching some plot against him. Baryat is still at table, stuffing in large quantities of some sort of casserole, and Lorn lets the image slip. He will try later.

He takes out paper, and dips the pen before he begins to write.

Dearest of Consorts—

I have not heard yet from you, but I trust all is well with you and with those around you . . .

We have recruited almost a squad of younger men for the lancers, and have begun training them . . . be a long summer, I fear, but many show skill already . . . and I hope to have them ready for duty elsewhere by fall, though that decision will be made by others . . .

. . . might consider the possibility of sending dyestuffs through coasters or those traders who are welcome in the Suthyan port of Rulyarth . . . understand that many there would purchase . . . but cannot obtain dyestuffs, because the Suthyans insist all dyes come through the larger port of Armat . . . while I know not how a trading house might avoid this proscription, save through landing at nearby ports . . . it would appear that those who could might profit. . . .

Lorn takes a deep breath and once more dips the pen. He can but hope that what he has gleaned from the ship's master and those factors he has visited around Biehl will prove useful to Ryalth.

After he finishes, he must again seek out Baryat—and perhaps Neabyl—with the glass. And tired as he is, he must continue to work on seeking out lands he has not seen before, either in the glass or in person.

XXI

CHYENFEL AND RYNST stand alone in the high-ceilinged audience chamber of the Palace of Eternal Light, waiting for the Emperor Toziel to appear. Bluoyal has yet to join them, as is often the case in recent eightdays.

The First Magus looks at Rynst and murmurs, "The sleep wards will be ready within less than half a season. At that time, but a few lancers will be needed around the Accursed Forest, as we had discussed earlier."

"What about patrolling the walls themselves?" asks the Majer-Commander in an equally muted voice. "Will not some protection be required for the new wards?"

Chyenfel shakes his head, smiling. "No. That is their beauty. These wards cannot be seen nor touched."

"While I would be most pleased to be able to send more lancers to the north, I must question this sudden announcement. Why did the ancients not attempt such? Did they not know of such?" Doubt colors Rynst's voice.

"They did." Chyenfel purses his lips, then tilts his head slightly, as if searching for an explanation. "Their words provided the knowledge and the keys to the sleep wards. Yet they feared that the wards would not work, and that the chaos-towers would be lost forever."

"And you know more than they?"

"We have learned some that they did not know, honored

Majer-Commander." Chyenfel smiles briefly. "They had less experience with chaos, for chaos works not the same in the worlds of the Rational Stars. That we do know from what they wrote."

"And," adds Rynst with a gentle laugh, "you will lose the towers shortly in any event if naught is done. So you of the Magi'i have little to lose."

"We lose more by providing the sleep wards, for we will not be able to provide as many charges for the firelances of your lancers, nor for the firewagons and the tow wagons of the Great Canal . . . and many will fault us for such. That alone should tell you that we act in the best interests of all Cyador, and not just of the Magi'i."

"That tells me that *you* have the best interests of Cyador at heart. You and the fourth magus." Rynst's words are low, careful.

"Is that why you watch the overcaptain in Biehl?" asks Chyenfel. "Do you think the son shares the honesty of the father?"

"He is more honest than most. Perhaps more honest than his peer Rustyl." Rynst smiles, watching for a reaction he does not get. "The overcaptain has begun to rebuild the garrison and the compound, without a word from me."

"He will face difficulties with the enumerators Bluoyal has suborned," suggests Chyenfel. "And with the golds our Merchanter Advisor does not receive."

"The senior enumerator has vanished, as I am certain you already know," Rynst points out. "And the overcaptain trains new lancers with his full payroll—or so I have heard."

"Bluoyal and the Emperor will not question such a 'disappearance'?"

"The Emperor may not discover such for a time, unless Bluoyal tells him or his consort, and that would lead to questions Bluoyal would best wish to avoid," replies Rynst.

"Yet you would let the overcaptain train his own Mirror Lancers? Would he dream of being . . . ?"

"He is young."

"That did not halt Alyiakal, as I recall."

"I think the overcaptain is not cast from that mold, but we shall see. Biehl provides a safe . . . distance for observation."

"And from Cyad," suggests Chyenfel.

"Have you not done the same with Rustyl?" asks Rynst.

"Like a good lancer officer, a good adept must see and do much throughout Cyador," replies Chyenfel. "Your overcaptain has seen little but fighting, and there is more to Cyador than fighting outlanders."

"And more than manipulating chaos," Rynst says smoothly. "He will learn trade in Biehl, as you well know."

"You'd best find him a consort," suggests Chyenfel.

"Although little has been said," says Rynst with a smile, "you know, as do I, that he has already found one. Not that he will have much leisure to enjoy such, with what he attempts."

"He is young," observes the First Magus, his eyes flicking to the harbor. "Very young, even for his years."

"You worry about his consort, though he is but a lancer?" Rynst watches the First Magus.

"Since he is a lancer, the worries are yours." Chyenfel's voice is firm and certain. He smiles. "You are rather fickle, are you not, Rynst? I thought that your favorite was the majer in Assyadt, the one your Captain-Commander has cultivated and placed so carefully."

"In the Mirror Lancers, an officer faces far more dangers. One must develop many successors. Then . . . one may survive who has the training and the talents. As you pointed out, not all of those possible successors have the same patrons or goals." Rynst closes his mouth as the rear doors of the chamber open and as Bluoyal hurries toward them to wait for the arrival of the Emperor and his consort.

XXII

LORN SITS AT the desk in his personal quarters, looking down at the glass as he has done so many evenings before. It has been nearly an eightday since the Sligan vessel ported and departed, and but a single coaster has shown up since—and no larger vessels.

Still . . . it will take time for the word to spread, and longer yet for masters and traders to take risks, for they tend to trust little that is not certain. Lorn frowns, thinking about trust. In the end, is trade based as much upon trust as the value of the goods? He laughs. Another simple question with a simple answer. Of course it is, for no trader can verify in advance the true value of all goods. They may be poorly made within; or good grain may surround poor, good cotton be wrapped over that of lesser quality.

With a deeper breath, Lorn looks back down at the glass, concentrating and seeking Baryat yet again.

When the silver mists swirl and part, the image shows the grower talking to a tall and thin man wearing gray and a black leather vest, who holds a bow. Lorn frowns. Archers—good archers—can kill without being visible.

Lorn understands the grower's concern or anger, but he wonders again how much is grief over a missing daughter and how much is anger and fear over the loss of golds and possible discovery of past bribes. While Lorn remains troubled over the woman's death, he has seen enough to know that all too many in Cyador do not value daughters over golds. Even that observation troubles him, true as he knows it to be.

Lorn's eyes drop as he considers the trade laws of Cyador that Baryat has already violated. It has taken Lorn almost the entire eightday to read the copy of the tariffs and laws he has borrowed from Neabyl and to find the sections which apply to Baryat. Those laws are most clear. One who bribes an enumerator can lose all his lands, and his life. Lorn's problem is simple, however. He cannot prove such bribery, nor who bribed whom. The reaction of the Sligan ship master, however, was yet another confirmation of Flutak's corruption.

As for the grower Baryat, Lorn may be able to prove that Baryat has hired a mercenary to kill him—a different offense, and also punished by death.

Finally, he shrugs. Tomorrow, he will act. There is little he can do at the moment that would further what he intends.

He takes a sip of the water in the mug, then shifts the larger sheets of paper so they are beside his right hand before he refocuses his concentration upon the chaos-glass once more.

When the image—that of a farm valley with a road along the ridge to the west—appears, Lorn looks from the image in the glass to the paper beside him on the quarters' desk, slowly drawing in the course of the stream, and the position of the hamlet that lies a good hundred kays west of Jera, nearly on the edge of the Hills of Endless Grass.

In nearly five eightdays of working with the glass daily— mainly in the evenings, he has developed both a series of maps, and a growing concern about the barbarian depredations. There are no Mirror Lancer outposts along the northwest coast of Cyador—not west of Biehl, in any case. Inividra is the closest main outpost to Biehl, and it lies a good two hundred kays east-southeast of Lorn's compound.

In the recent past, the Jeranyi barbarian attacks have been directed more at those sections of Cyador where the Grass Hills are narrow and more passable. The very ruggedness of that part of the Grass Hills that lies east of Biehl has been protection enough—that, and the fact that there is even less for raiders to seize that is close to the Grass Hills.

Lorn pushes away those thoughts for the moment, and concentrates on transferring what he is seeing to the map he is creating.

When the knives begin to jab into his eyes once more, he sets aside the glass, and stands, pacing around the small study of his quarters. As time has passed, he has become more adept, and can use the glass longer, but the end result is always the same. Or is that because he pushes until he reaches that point?

He pauses in his pacing to take yet another sip from the mug.

XXIII

IN THE EARLY morning light that fills the commander's study, as he waits for Helkyt to appear, Lorn reads through the Emperor's Code once more—the lines of the tariff and administrative laws. He shakes his head in wonderment. While he had known that Juist had acted as a justicer for the communities north of the Accursed Forest, he had not realized that the Emperor's Code bestowed that right upon the senior Mirror Lancer officer in any district. And Lorn is the senior—and only officer—within two hundred kays.

Could he have used the Code against Flutak? Hardly, because he would have needed hard evidence of the kind he didn't have, and wouldn't have had, assuming he had survived Flutak's attempts to kill him, since Lorn had no doubts that Flutak would have stopped with one attempt.

"Ser?" Helkyt peers into Lorn's study. "You ever sleep, ser?"

"Enough, Helkyt, enough." Lorn pauses. "We need to pay the olive-grower Baryat a visit."

"Baryat, ser? He be most respected here." The senior

squad leader shifts his weight from one foot to the other, not quite meeting Lorn's gaze.

"He's also bribed a few people, and done a few other acts against the Emperor's Code." Lorn lifts the volume he has borrowed from Neabyl.

"Doing and proving . . . those be different, ser," offers Helkyt.

"That is true. That's why we need to visit the fellow." Lorn smiles.

Helkyt shifts his weight again, looking down.

"You have a consort here in Biehl, do you not?" asks Lorn.

"Yes, ser. Dybnyt and I consorted sisters. My Gaelya is the sister to Daelya."

The overcaptain fingers his chin. "We'll take the first squad, and the lancers in training, but have them wear uniforms, and not training tunics. With firelances for the first squad, but not the training squad. And a firelance for me." Lorn frowns. "Best you remain here, in the event all does not go as it should. Tashqyt can be the squad leader, so long as I am there."

"Yes, ser. That might be best."

"I understand. Would you take care of telling Tashqyt and getting the squads ready? And let me know when they're almost ready to ride."

"Yes, ser." Helkyt bows and leaves the room.

Lorn shifts his reading from one section of the Code to another, the one dealing with the relationship of the District Guards to the Mirror Lancers. In training, the undercaptain candidates had been taught that even District Guard Commanders had to answer to the senior Mirror Lancer officer in a region, but Lorn wants to check the exact words and provisions.

"Blackest of angels . . ." he murmurs under his breath, for he had never thought he would be reading the laws of the land as a Mirror Lancer. Or using law like a sabre.

"More like a club or a truncheon," he mutters to himself.

He has found the words he sought and just slipped a leather marker into the pages when Helkyt returns.

"All are formed and waiting, ser."

"Thank you." Lorn stands, reattaches his sabre to his belt, and makes his way out into the courtyard, where a column is drawn up in twos, the senior squad riding before, and the training squad behind. Tashqyt holds the reins to the saddled chestnut.

"Thank you." Lorn takes them and mounts, touching the firelance, and then checking his sabre.

"Ser?" asks the squad leader.

"To the lands of the olive-grower and lawbreaker Baryat, on the road that leads south of the harbor and into the low hills west of Biehl."

"Yes, ser."

Lorn urges the mare forward and leads the column out through the gates and downhill. He scans the harbor as the mixed company rides southward, but the piers remain yet empty of any trading vessels, even of the more local coasting schooners.

"A lawbreaker?" asks Tashqyt, after the company has ridden nearly a kay west of the harbor, as though he has been mulling over what Lorn said for some time.

"Yes." Lorn moistens his lips. "Although it has been seldom required in recent years, whoever commands the Mirror Lancer garrison is responsible for enforcing the Emperor's Code. I have some reason to believe that Baryat has broken several laws." He smiles. "But we will talk to him and see."

Tashqyt glances back at the full company. "He has a large family, but . . . they are most law-abiding."

"I'd prefer that his family see the wisdom of not continuing the practices of the sire." Lorn's tone of voice is dry. "I also think they should understand that the force of His

Mightiness stands behind the trade rules of the Emperor's Code."

"Ah . . . yes, ser." Tashqyt is silent as they near the hill on which the grower's dwelling is set.

The slopes of the low hills are covered with trees—olive trees with the light-green of new leaves and the off-green of the winter leaves that have returned to their summer hues. Two stone posts mark the entrance to the villa and the houses along the crest of the hill above. A lane winds up the hill from the gate in sweeping turns.

Lorn turns to Tashqyt. "When we reach the villa, have the men remain mounted, with their lances and sabres ready."

"Firelances at the ready," Tashqyt announces.

A young man standing outside the front privacy screen of the villa stares at the company of lancers as they pass the last of the olive trees.

Lorn reins up the chestnut short of the youth and the green ceramic privacy screen. "I am Overcaptain Lorn, commander of the Mirror Lancers in Biehl and the Emperor's justicer of this district. I seek the grower Baryat. He is here. Tell him I seek him."

The youth gulps.

"Have him come forth."

"Yes, ser." After a second swallow, the youth turns and scurries, not into the house, but downhill to the south.

"Stand by to discharge firelances," Lorn orders quietly.

"Ready to discharge!" Tashqyt orders.

The lancers wait. Lorn remains mounted, studying the trees and the front of the villa.

A half-dozen men appear from the orchard area, led by the youth. Behind them, remaining at the edge of the olive trees, are several figures in gray, including a taller figure wearing a black vest. He remains behind the others, near the first of the olive trees. A broad-shouldered man, gray-haired and gray-bearded, muscular, and a half-head taller than Lorn, steps past the youth.

"My . . . my . . . an entire company to see an olive-grower. I am so flattered, Undercaptain." Baryat bows deeply, mockingly. He holds a long pruning knife, almost as long as a shortsword, whose edge glistens, as if newly sharpened.

Lorn dismounts. "As I told the young fellow, I am Overcaptain Lorn, commander of the Mirror Lancer garrison at Biehl, and justicer of the Emperor."

"For one carrying out justice, you bring many lancers."

"Justice is best served when it can be enforced," Lorn replies, watching the pruning knife.

"You'd not face me alone, Overcaptain. You're nothing without those lancers and that uniform."

Lorn steps forward until he is standing on the packed clay of the lane, less than three cubits from Baryat. He looks squarely at the grower. "I would be more than happy to face you alone, Baryat. You would die. You know that. But you are a cheat and a coward. You bribed the former enumerator with both golds and your daughter, and blame me for their failings and yours. I am not interested in being filled with shafts from hidden archers." Lorn stops, and his smile is cold.

Baryat sneers. "Words, Overcaptain."

"I am not interested in the past. I am also not interested in being assassinated in the dark. So I am here. Now . . . what do you choose? To keep lying and making plans to kill me when I am unaware? To fight me and die? Or to pay your tariffs fairly and forget the past?"

"I will . . . forget the past," Baryat says slowly, as if the words are choked from him. His fingers clench, one into a fist, the other tightening on the long knife.

Lorn looks at the grower levelly. "You lie." He glances at the tall man in the black vest who is slipping back toward the olive trees. "Tashqyt! Bring in those men in gray, especially the tall one. He's an archer, and there's probably a longbow nearby." Lorn draws the Brystan sabre.

Baryat pales, and his hands shake. In rage, Lorn suspects.

One of the archers runs, but the tallest does not. Instead, he walks forward, accompanied by another slighter figure, also in gray. That the lead archer does not run is another indication to Lorn that the man is a mercenary of sorts. Instead, the tall man walks toward the overcaptain and the lancers, and bows, then looks at the overcaptain and his extended sabre. "Your wish, ser?"

"I assume you have a bow concealed in the grove there?"

"It is behind the second tree. It is a good bow, and if you must kill me, at least ensure that my son or some archer who will appreciate it will receive it." The archer's gray eyes mirror both humor and concern.

"Are there any other archers around here?" Lorn asks. "Besides the three of you?"

"None of which I know, ser," answers the man.

"Or others paid to do so?"

"Again, none of which I know." The archer shrugs.

Lorn nods. "How much were you paid to kill me?"

"Ten golds, ser."

"And were you paid to kill anyone else?"

"The senior enumerator in Biehl—the new one."

"How much?"

"Five golds."

Lorn smiles ruefully. "I am most flattered to be considered worth ten golds."

"He lies!" Baryat exclaims. "He lies to save his own soul."

Lorn's eyes are like ice as he regards the grower. "No. He tells the truth in hopes of saving his life."

Lorn glances to the side as Tashqyt guides his mount toward Lorn, the third archer smiling sheepishly as he walks toward the overcaptain. His eyes return to Baryat. "Three archers?"

"You are no justicer. You kill in the dark."

Lorn wonders how to respond, for, truly, Baryat is correct

on one level. Lorn has killed in the dark. "Tell me, Baryat, how much Flutak reduced your tariffs for the use of your daughter. Two silvers a barrel?"

"Talk not to me of my daughter." Baryat snorts.

"Why not? You loved her so much you sold her to an enumerator for lower tariffs. Did you not?" Scorn fills Lorn's voice.

"I sold my daughter to no one," snaps Baryat, after a long silence.

The sense of untruth is so great that Lorn can see even Tashqyt offer a minute headshake.

"And I suppose you didn't accept lower tariffs, either?"

"If you had proof, you wouldn't be asking." Baryat offers a sneer.

"I'm not asking," Lorn replies quietly. "I'm telling you." The overcaptain looks from Baryat to the three younger men—the grower's sons, if his visions in the screeing glass have been accurate. "You are his sons. You can understand that the Mirror Lancers have a problem. If I kill him, you will find every possible excuse to avoid tariffs, and to have me killed or removed. If I don't, he will either kill me, or I'll kill him later."

"You . . . insufferable . . . little . . ." Baryat steps forward, his entire body trembling in anger, half-lifting the pruning knife.

Lorn's blade flashes, and a slash appears on the back of Baryat's knife hand. "That could have been your neck." He sighs . . . loudly.

Baryat continues to shake, but lowers the knife.

Lorn looks past the grower, but still watches the man. "Which of you is the eldest?"

A sandy-haired man, square-bearded, steps forward. "I be such."

"Listen most carefully. A man has cheated on his tariffs. He has used golds and his daughter to bribe a senior enumerator. The enumerator and the daughter have vanished. The man blames the Emperor's officials for their disappearance and vows revenge, even though the enumerator is guilty of accepting bribes. This man hires a mercenary archer to kill two officers of the Emperor who are looking into the bribery. Then he lies about doing so. He has cheated the Emperor and tried to kill two men for doing their duty." Lorn's eyes fix the eldest son. "Under the laws of Cyador, I could turn all your lands over to the Emperor. Should I?"

The sandy-haired and bearded son looks down at the packed clay of the cart road.

"Do your worst, and the black angels take you!" snaps Baryat. Blood continues to ooze from the slash on his hand.

Lorn looks at the son, then motions for the three archers to step aside. "You, archers, will return to Biehl with us. You must leave Biehl—either for the Grass Hills or the lands north of the Accursed Forest."

The tall archer bows his head. After a moment, so do the two others.

"And what of me, Overcaptain? Will you exile me?" Baryat's voice rises, fills with anger. "Will you turn your trained dogs on me?"

Lorn smiles sadly, ignoring the grower, and looking at his eldest son. "Should I turn your lands over to the Emperor, or will you keep his laws from henceforth?"

"Sybyn! Don't answer that. I'm the landholder," rages Baryat. "The Emperor will hear of this."

"Indeed he will," Lorn agrees. "He will receive a report of your bribery, your efforts to have two officials murdered, and your failure to pay proper tariffs. You no longer hold these lands. The question is whether your son will." Lorn looks at Sybyn. "You cannot lie to me. I will know, even as I know of your father's evils. If I allow these lands to pass to you, will you honor the laws of Cyador, and pay your just tariffs, and seek no further revenge against me or against any Mirror Lancer or enumerator?"

"You can't do this!" snaps Baryat. "Besides, you aren't man enough to do anything except threaten."

"I'd like your answer, Sybyn," Lorn continues, his eyes on the grower, rather than the son. "Will you obey the laws of Cyador and seek no revenge? If not for your sake, for the sake of your brothers, their consorts, and your children?"

"I . . . must . . ." stammers the younger grower.

"Coward! I disown you!" Baryat's eyes flash at Lorn. "You are a cowardly little man, also. You hide behind your bars and your uniform."

"You have hidden behind your lands and your golds," Lorn says quietly. "You bartered your daughter, and bribed enumerators. You have tried to buy my death, and you see nothing wrong with it."

"And I would have sooner than I did, the moment you arrived, had I known what you would do." Baryat glares at Lorn.

"All of you note his words," Lorn says. "He admits all of his lawbreaking."

Baryat's mouth closes abruptly. The three sons exchange glances.

"Prove it!" snaps the grower.

Lorn laughs. "I have seen Flutak's ledgers. They show more than—"

Abruptly, Baryat lunges forward with the glistening pruning knife slashing toward Lorn.

Lorn's blade flashes, with the smallest bit of chaos adding to its sharpness.

The grower's mouth is open, even as his head is separated from his neck.

"As justicer I have heard this man declare his guilt. Not only did he declare that guilt, but he attacked a Mirror Lancer officer. More than twoscore witnesses have also seen and heard this." Lorn lowers the sabre, but does not sheathe it, as his eyes seek out Sybyn. "I do not hold you or your brothers guilty of your father's misdeeds. Nor will aught in harm befall you or these lands—unless there are other misdeeds after this moment for which you are responsible. Do you hear and understand?"

"Yes . . . ser . . ." stumbles Sybyn, his face blank.

Lorn wipes the sabre clean with the square of cloth he takes from his belt, then sheathes the weapon. Then he mounts, and nods to Tashqyt.

For a time, the column rides silently, and they are nearing the harbor before Tashqyt, riding beside Lorn, clears his throat.

"Yes, Tashqyt?"

"You could have executed him even if he had not attacked you, could you not?" asks the squad leader.

"I could have," Lorn admits. "But I wanted as many lancers as possible to hear what he said."

"I thought as much, ser."

Lorn only hopes that the word spreads that he is fair as well as harsh, but he prefers to anticipate troubles, rather than react to such. While he has never seen Flutak's missing ledgers, and doubts anyone ever will, he has no doubts—not now—about Baryat's guilt.

But he wonders how long he will dream about the daughter.

XXIV

AT THE *THRAP* on the study door, Lorn glances up from the sheets that hold his calculations of the gear required for a lengthy ride by two full companies. While he would prefer to add another squad, he has no way at all to supply their gear, and many of the saddles his trainees use are barely serviceable. Two eightdays earlier, he had received a notice from the Majer-Commander, sealed by a Commander Inylt, that his provisions and equipment draw has been increased by five golds an eightday, and with that, he hopes, that he can upgrade the saddles and bridles, by summer's end, and purchase some replacement saddles. "Yes?"

"There is a ship flying the ensign of Cyad entering the harbor," Helkyt announces as he peers into the study.

"And you are here to tell me so that I may be at the piers before it lands to confer with the senior enumerator?" Lorn grins.

"You *had* said that you wished to avoid unnecessary unpleasantnesses, ser."

"I did say that." Lorn rises. "And I'd best be heading down there."

"Chulhyr is saddling the chestnut."

"Thank you." Lorn inclines his head as he departs the outer study and heads down the corridor and out across the courtyard, under high, hazy summer clouds. His forehead is damp by the time he reaches the stable, but, as Helkyt had promised, the chestnut is waiting. So is a squad of mixed lancers and trainees, with Tashqyt leading them.

The Cyadoran vessel has still not reached the pier, carefully tacking its way southward, when Lorn reins up in the harbor at the end of the pier, where Neabyl and Comyr stand in their enumerators' uniforms, with two linemen dressed in brown behind them.

Neabyl glances at Lorn and the lancers, but does not speak immediately.

"Greetings, Senior Enumerator," Lorn offers.

"And to you, Overcaptain."

Lorn dismounts and looks at Tashqyt. "Just have the men stand by here, except for those to accompany the senior enumerator." He turns to Neabyl. "I had thought I would announce to the master right away that we are both here to prevent the kind of misunderstandings that have occurred in the past about tariffs and their administration. Is that satisfactory to you?"

Neabyl offers a pleasant smile. "It is, and I appreciate your present thoughtfulness."

"And I apologize once more for the earlier awkwardness."

Neabyl steps along the pier, away from the lancers and Comyr, inclining his head. Lorn follows.

"I have received a scroll from the Hand of the Emperor," Neabyl begins. "I have been confirmed as the senior enumerator in charge of this station, and commended for my initiative in supporting your efforts to improve the port of Biehl." Neabyl smiles. "While this has not been easy, it is apparent that your ... initiative has been regarded favorably in Cyad, and I wanted to thank you for understanding the full extent of the previous circumstances."

"Hello there, the pier!" comes a call from the vessel.

The two linemen scurry toward the forward bollard, past the overcaptain and the enumerator.

Lorn bows his head, slightly. "I thank you for sharing such. After meeting Flutak, I had felt it could not have been otherwise." He pauses. "Did you ever have any success in locating the missing ledgers?"

Neabyl offers a crooked smile. "There were ledgers in Flutak's dwelling. They showed little resemblance to what they should have, but no entries that would establish anything beyond great irregularities. I took the precaution of sending them to the Hand of the Emperor, with copies to the senior enumerator. I have not heard about them."

Lorn nods.

"Lines out!" comes the order from the three-masted vessel.

"I appreciate your perception," adds Neabyl.

"Double up!"

Lorn and Neabyl study the vessel as it is being tied to the pier. *Red Lands* is the name carved into the plaque on the stern. Once the vessel is tied to the pier, Lorn follows Neabyl up the gangway, and Comyr and two lancers follow him.

"Senior Enumerator, Overcaptain." The ship's master, who wears a blue tunic with a double row of gold braid on his shoulder bows. "Captain Elvygg, at your service." He looks at Lorn. "You would be Overcaptain Lorn?"

"I am."

"Most excellent. Most excellent. Then I need not search you out."

Neabyl offers Lorn a sidelong glance.

"It is good to see you, Captain," Lorn says. "I might explain before you speak that both the senior enumerator and I are here, because, in the past, there have been . . . shall we say, some discrepancies in tariffs."

Elvygg smiles broadly. "Of that I had been appraised, and that, frankly, is why the *Red Lands* has risked a landing here. That, and the cargo, of course."

The captain extends the manifest and the supporting bills of lading to the enumerator. "Here you be, Enumerator. You will find them in order."

"Thank you." Neabyl takes the manifest and separates it from the bills of lading, which he hands to Comyr.

"Overcaptain." The man in the blue tunic bows once more to Lorn, and extends a scroll. "From your consort and Lady Trader. We also have a small cargo for you which we will offload once we have paid any tariffs due. Some wine, some baskets of goods . . ." He frowns, as if trying to recall the other items. "And also a halfscore of riding gear, saddles, and bridles in white leather."

Neabyl looks at Lorn. "You mentioned being related to traders and having an interest in trade, but not that your consort . . ."

"She is a merchant; I was not born such," Lorn explains. "I have tried to have her explain trade to me, but we have had little time together." He laughs ruefully. "Lancers see little of Cyad."

"That is so."

Lorn looks at Neabyl. "I would that you inspect any cargo due me with the utmost of care. I would not have it said that ever I escaped what was due."

"Ah . . . sers . . ."

Both look at the captain.

"The lady sent golds for the tariffs with me so that the overcaptain might not be troubled."

Neabyl smiles broadly. "Your lady is indeed thoughtful."

Lorn grins back, adding, "And wise."

While Neabyl and Comyr inspect the vessel and its documents, Lorn slips away to find Tashqyt.

"Do we have a cart at the compound?"

"Yes, ser."

"If you'd send for it . . . we're getting some riding gear, it appears."

"Yes, ser!" Tashqyt smiles for a moment. "Ser . . . we usually get gear on the firewagons."

"We have a different supplier, I think." Lorn's lips curl ironically.

A lancer is riding up to the compound by the time Lorn has walked back to the base of the gangway, where he waits for the enumerators to finish their work.

"How are the tariffs?" Lorn asks as Neabyl and Comyr come down the gangway.

"All is well, both in terms of our collections and his papers." Neabyl nods. "He is pleased, and the Emperor will be pleased. What more could any ask?"

"That the enumerators be pleased," Lorn suggests.

"We are pleased."

"Good."

Neabyl looks at Lorn. "You have quite a cargo there."

"There are a few items which I requested for you," Lorn admits.

Neabyl lifts his eyebrows.

"I am not suggesting anything improper," Lorn says, "but you have been supportive, and I did not think you would take amiss a few bottles of a good vintage."

The enumerator laughs. "Overcaptain . . . no one would take amiss such as that, and I will accept in the spirit in which you offer it."

"As soon as we have it offloaded," Lorn says, "you will have it." He pauses. "I would let it sit for an eightday. It will taste better."

"For such as you received, I will wait."

It is well into afternoon before the saddles and bridles have been carted back to the stable and the two cases of Alafraan, the case of Fhynyco, and the three large baskets which Lorn suspects contain uniforms and clothing, have been carried up to his quarters.

Lorn leaves them there and returns to his study in the administration building.

"Tashqyt said we got more saddles. That right, ser?"

"A halfscore, lancer-white."

Helkyt shakes his head. "First time since I been here."

Lorn just shrugs. "We do what we can."

Once he is back in his official study, Lorn opens the scroll from Ryalth.

My dearest of lancers—

I scarcely know how to begin. Your advice has proven its worth again and again, and Ryalor House is truly prospering. We have been accorded the rank of lower clan house, and so we have moved to the other side of the Plaza, with the smaller clan houses, but we have the topmost floor, once more, and some of the next floor down. I have three more junior traders, and Eileyt and two other enumerators, as well as those who act as our agents in other ports in Candar, Nordla, and Hamor.

You and I have also begun a clan of our own, and your sister Jerial insists the child will be a son . . .

Lorn swallows. Is he old enough, advanced enough in the lancers? He laughs. He could be penniless, not that he is, and Ryalor House would provide for the boy to come.

. . . and that he feels to be healthy and strong.

As you will know, I have also taken the liberty of sending some gear for your lancers, for an overcaptain cannot be at his best unless his men are well-equipped. If you need more, please do not be silent, for I would spend all I have to ensure your safety . . .

All she has . . . Lorn looks out the window until his eyes clear.

I dine perhaps twice an eightday with your parents, and your father will now even joke with me. Your mother asks if I would like more to eat, for she wants her grandchild to be healthy. Were I to eat as she would like, I could not walk . . .

I met the day before yesterday with Husdryt of the Dyjani Clan. I was reluctant at first, since I have doubts about Tasjan, especially with his guard chief Sasyk hiring yet more greenshirts—but your friend Tyrsal had suggested the meeting and vouches for Husdryt. Husdryt said he had learned all he knew from Tyrsal's father. We talked for some time, and some matters may come of it. . . .

Because of my condition, and for other reasons, I am reluctant to undertake a voyage at this time, and I trust you understand. Know that those are the reasons, for I would see you anywhere, were I the only one to consider . . .

All my love, my dearest.

Lorn considers the scroll, then shakes his head. Indeed he has been fortunate to find one such as Ryalth. He smiles briefly.

When he is alone, in his quarters, he will seek her in the glass, if but briefly, because, for all the warmth in Ryalth's words, there is also concern. Much concern.

While Lorn has often felt as though he may have some small hand in forging his future and destiny, on days such as this, with messages such as from Ryalth and Neabyl, he feels more like a ship at the mercy of the winds—and the winds of intrigue blow strong in Cyad, and may yet blow more forcefully, if he reads correctly between the graceful lines Ryalth has penned.

XXV

IN THE ORANGISH light of dawn, Lorn glances at the wide River Behla to his left, then at the scattered buildings of the town ahead. He and the squad that follows him have been riding since well before dawn, traveling upstream more than ten kays to reach the double bridges at Lower Island to cross to the eastern bank, and then traveling the east river road back toward Ehyla, the smaller sister town across the river from the port of Biehl. In Ehyla, at the guard station above the river, the District Guard Commander is supposed to meet with Lorn, according to the messages they have exchanged.

Lorn watches the river and the road, until he can at last see the single pier that juts into the river, a crooked and rickety structure whose upstream side appears blocked by a sandbar or mudbank. According to the messengers, the District Guard post is on a low hill directly east of the pier, halfway up the slope, and facing the river.

As they pass the kaystone that indicates Ehyla is but two kays away, Lorn studies the scattered dwellings, yellow brick affairs, most without privacy screens or hedges, some with the old-style thatched roofs instead of slate or tile, and the majority with unpainted and often sagging shutters.

A pack of four dogs appears from the low brush above the muddy river flats. The lead dog, a black-and-white mongrel, sniffs cautiously, then turns back into the brush. The others follow, although a smaller golden dog raises its nose for a last sniff before it, too, vanishes.

The guard post is indeed where the messengers have reported it to be, and Lorn and the second squad rein up outside the square two-story, and freshly whitewashed, plaster-walled building that dominates Ehyla.

Lorn looks to Whylyn, the other junior squad leader besides Tashqyt, and the one who leads the squad accompanying Lorn. "Have them stand down, but close enough to be ready to ride. See if you can find some water for the mounts."

"Yes, ser." The sandy-haired and beak-nosed squad leader nods.

Lorn dismounts, ties the chestnut to one of the hitching rings on the sunstone post below the steps to the stone-framed door, and checks his sabre. Then he walks up the steps and into the building.

In the small foyer sits a young, brown-clad guard. His eyes widen at the sight of the Mirror Lancer officer in cream and green standing before him. "Ser?"

"Overcaptain Lorn. I'm here to see the District Commander."

"Ah . . . yes, ser. He's expecting you."

If he is expected, Lorn wonders at the surprise. Or were they expecting an aging officer in the last stages of his career? His lips twist momentarily as he follows the young guard past one open door on the right—what appears to be a carelessly-kept armory of sorts—to the first open door on the left.

"Overcaptain Lorn, ser." The guard bows and backs away, letting Lorn enter the largish study alone.

The District Commander of the local guards stands. He is black-haired, small, with fierce black eyes, and a thin mustache that curves upward from the corners of his mouth. His crimson-trimmed brown uniform is immaculate, and the silver stars on his collar shimmer brightly.

"Commander Repyl, Overcaptain." Repyl gestures to a

wooden armchair across the polished wide desk from him. He does not wait for Lorn to sit before reseating himself.

Lorn glances around the study, taking in the bookcase, nearly empty, and the four footchests that appear to have been recently polished, before seating himself.

"Well, Overcaptain, the word is that you are beefing up the Mirror Lancers in Biehl." Repyl snorts. "Well past time for that."

"There is a time for everything," Lorn says mildly as he seats himself easily in the straight-backed chair. "The Majer-Commander has decided that much needed to be done at Biehl."

"You have ... what ... somewhat less than a company?" The commander pauses. "You have brought a full squad. What would happen if a ship ported in your absence, or pirates appeared?"

"The lancers under Senior Squad Leader Helkyt would do their duty. We now have almost two full companies. That is double what we had last winter." Lorn's eyes fix on the commander. "We recently received the equipment necessary to add another half-company."

"That is indeed a change." The commander smiles tolerantly.

"How many guards have you, Commander?" Lorn asks. "Those with full gear and weapons who could be called up and give an account of themselves?"

"No one has ever asked that." The District Commander draws himself up behind his ornate desk.

Lorn shrugs. "I am relatively new to the port detachment. I have spent most of my time in the Mirror Lancers as a fighting officer. Those questions come easily. Also, I was reviewing my statement of duties, and part of those duties is to inspect and verify the numbers and abilities of the District Guard forces. So I am here. That is why I sent that message to you."

"Ah ... yes." The commander nods. "One cannot fault

you for attention to duty. It has been long, I understand, since the full scope of those duties has been attempted. Tell me. How fares Senior Enumerator Flutak? A most imposing official." Repyl smiles.

"The senior enumerator was discovered to have been accepting bribes from traders and from one of the larger olive-growers. He vanished, as did most of the records. He has not been seen in a season. The grower, an arrogant fellow by the name of Baryat . . . he hired some assassins, and when I went to inquire, he not only admitted to bribery and hiring the assassins, but he attacked me with a pruning knife in front of an entire squad. The new senior enumerator in charge is Neabyl. He is most honest, most devoted to carrying out the provisions of the Emperor's Code. He has been commended by His Mightiness." Lorn smiles coolly. "We work well together, and Biehl is again beginning to receive more ships."

"Ah . . . yes . . . that is most interesting."

"You were about to tell me how many guards you had ready to ride," Lorn reminds the commander.

"The District Guard is near full-strength."

Lorn's eyes harden, and he waits.

"With two or three days' advance notice, I can raise two companies. We use cupridium lances—not firelances. Otherwise, our equipment is the same."

"I'm glad to hear that." Lorn stands. "You are busy; so am I. If you would show me the building—the armory, and the tackrooms . . ."

"I had not thought a man of your position . . ." the commander replies as he slowly stands.

"When one is sent to do a duty by the Majer-Commander," Lorn says evenly, "it is best that he carry it out."

"Yes . . . I can see that." Repyl fingers the right end of his waxed mustache. "Yes . . . I can certainly see that."

"The Majer-Commander has plans for Biehl," Lorn adds. "That much I do know." He gestures toward the door, then exits and crosses the hall to the armory he has seen earlier.

Someone has made a recent effort to organize the cupridium lances, and most have been polished, if hurriedly, and the sabres are racked as they should be. There is little in the way of supporting gear, such as small spades, water bottles, and saddlebags.

Lorn walks around the long and dim room without speaking until he is ready to leave. "The weapons are adequately cared for. More than half your guards would perish of thirst in any long ride—or you would have them scattered across the land seeking water. Best you find water bottles for them, and soon."

"Soon?"

Lorn ignores the question, posing one of his own. "Mounts and tack?"

"Each guard keeps his own mount. If it dies of a fault of his, he must replace it with one inspected by the guard ostler. Their mounts are in excellent shape."

Lorn senses the truth of the answer, both from Repyl and the system.

"The tackroom . . ." The commander leads Lorn to the north end of the building, where he unlocks a door with a simple brass key. "There is an outside door. It is barred except when we drill."

The tack is racked properly, and has been recently cleaned, although Lorn can see dirt in cracks in the leather, but the equipment is not nearly so bad as it could be—nor in as poor condition as some of what he had found at Biehl.

Lorn nods as they leave the tackroom, then turns to Repyl. "Matters appear solid here. Sometime in the late summer or early fall, I will be here to inspect all your guards, and their mounts." Lorn smiles. "I will require that they be equipped and provisioned for an eightday ride."

"That is not . . ."

"It is," Lorn says quietly. "I will give you an eightday's notice. If you find that difficult . . ." He leaves the implication unspoken.

"Ah . . . no. With an eightday's notice, we will be ready."

"Good. It has been a pleasure meeting you, and to learn that you understand that as the world changes so must what has been accepted in the past. I look forward to seeing you on my inspection."

"We will be ready, Overcaptain, when you arrive."

"Thank you." Lorn bows, then turns and walks past the nervous young guard and out to his waiting squad.

Without speaking, Lorn unties and mounts the chestnut. While Repyl is neither overtly dishonest nor hiding matters about the District Guards, the man is clearly upset by Lorn's visit and the changes taking place in Biehl. That means that he will bear watching, through the glass, and that means more work and headaches for Lorn.

"Form up!" orders Whylyn.

The lancers reform into a column two-abreast that rides south and back toward the bridges at Lower Island.

"If I might ask . . . ser?" ventures Whylyn after they have ridden a kay or so.

"The commander was quite pleasant," Lorn observes. "We'll be returning in half a season or so, perhaps a bit longer, to inspect the guards."

"They'll not be liking that," prophesies the squad leader.

They will like what Lorn has in mind even less, the overcaptain suspects.

XXVI

THE BREAKFAST ROOM is hot, even though the late-afternoon sun is dropping below the brick walls of the Mirror Lancer compound at Biehl. Despite the heat and still air, Lorn finishes his dinner—a breast of fowl smothered in sawdustlike slivers of quilla. The bread is a dry rye that is not much better than the quilla. The single glass of Fhynyco he allows himself makes the bread and quilla half-palatable.

After he washes and stacks the dishes, he walks slowly into his study, where he sits at the narrow desk and takes out the scroll he has received from his father earlier in the day. He unrolls it and begins to reads it once more, this time more carefully and slowly.

All remains well with us, although we are not quite so active as those younger . . . Kysia has continued to help in ways we had not anticipated, and I am certain that, whenever you do return to Cyad, she will wish to serve you and Ryalth . . .

We are pleased to have dinner with your lovely consort often, generally once or twice an eightday, if not more often. She and Jerial have gotten rather close, and at times, even Myryan will join them.

Myryan's garden prospers, and she often shares her bounty with us, and upon occasion Ciesrt will join us, although he and Vernt are most occupied, now that they are adepts of the full second level, with the growing and myriad challenges that face those of the Magi'i in these days . . . Your young friend Tyrsal, although a lower second, is beginning to show a certain promise, if delayed. I am glad to see that, given the attention that the First Magus has showered upon Rustyl, who shares some of the deportment of the lancer officer who continues to write your sister. It is said that an arrangement is close for consorting Rustyl to Ciesrt's younger sister, Ceyla. The older sister recently consorted with Zubyl . . .

More lancers are likely to be reassigned from the Accursed Forest in late summer or early fall . . . if all goes well.

Myryan and Jerial have been pressed into extra time

at the infirmary once more, as a result of the chaos-
tower failure on the *First Star* . . .

Lorn frowns. For his father to mention that chaos-tower
failure so openly must mean all of Cyad knows about the
failure, and that there were indeed many casualties. There is
also the hint that the ward-wall project, whatever it may be,
is about to be completed.

Will that have an effect on the barbarians? Will they find
out? Or will they mount attacks before lancers can be transferred? Or shift their attacks elsewhere? Lorn glances out
through the window at the growing twilight, a twilight that
has yet to bring coolness to the still air that enfolds the
lancer compound.

After a time, he lifts the scroll once more, frowning, as his
eyes drift back up to the lines about Tyrsal and Rustyl. His
father never mentions anything quite idly, and that means,
for some reason, he must keep Rustyl in mind in the seasons
and years ahead.

After he writes his reply, and another scroll to Ryalth, he
will take out the glass again, and make a greater effort to determine where the barbarians are gathering forces—if they
are—and to draw part of yet another map.

And he will have to plan how to best use the forces of the
District Commander . . .

He rubs his forehead, glancing out into the summer darkness he has not seen creep across the compound. The rest of
the summer will be long, and tiring, for he has much to do
with the lancers, his screeing of the barbarians, and his
maps—and with ensuring all ships that port in Biehl are
treated well and fairly. And with occasionally checking on
the olive-growers and other traders and factors.

None of these are exciting, nor glamorous. All are necessary, and the energy required leaves little for himself—or for
using the glass, if briefly, to view Ryalth.

XXVII

THE TWO MEN meet on the balcony on the north side of the fifth level of the Palace of Eternal Light. Even the lightest breeze whispers loudly across this balcony, making eavesdropping difficult. The Captain-Commander of the Mirror Lancers nods to the Second Magus.

"There will be changes in the coming year," Luss suggests.

"There are always changes," returns Kharl with a laugh. The breeze disarranges his reddish hair. He smoothes it back from his face. "Everything changes, and yet everything is the same, and that is how it has been, and how it will be. Do not deceive yourself, my valiant lancer officer."

"The Emperor's audiences are brief," Luss points out.

"There is nothing new to be said, and he waits for the results of the ward-wall effort of the First Magus."

"You opposed such; do you still?"

"I opposed that effort because I fear the loss of power for the Magi'i and for the Mirror Lancers, and because I had doubts that the plan would do little more than cost us the chaos-towers before they failed in their time. Chyenfel has convinced all, and there is now little merit in opposing what will be. It will be Chyenfel's last great accomplishment, and who am I to deny him such?" Kharl smiles. "It appears as though it may indeed succeed, and if it does, then the Accursed Forest will sleep for generations, and the Mirror Lancers will be free to send greater forces to the north. But your casualties will be much greater, I fear."

"Since we will have fewer firelances, we will need more lancers than even those stationed around the Accursed Forest," counters Luss. "Will you support such?"

"When you speak of the need for more lancers, I am reminded that your young overcaptain is most ambitious," Kharl observes.

"My overcaptain? I do not recall any being assigned to me recently."

"The young one who was dispatched to Biehl. I believe we had some discussion about the poor fellow," Kharl suggests, his green eyes seemingly laughing as he views both the harbor and the Captain-Commander of the Mirror Lancers.

"Ah . . . yes, that one, the one who is related by consorting to you, and who the Majer-Commander was kind enough to offer a less trying . . . position to." Luss smiles politely.

Kharl returns the smile with one equally bland. "I understand he has been quite successful in returning the outpost to some semblance of discipline, and even in beginning to recruit and train new lancers who can be used to replace those who have fallen to the barbarians." After the briefest of pauses, he adds, "And that the Majer-Commander was pleased with your initiative in sending him there."

"I am most gratified that my understanding of the officer's capabilities was recognized," Luss's eyes narrow slightly, "although I would expect nothing less of an officer so capable and of one related to you, even through consortship."

"I am pleased that my son's choice of a consort meets your approval. Although her brother is a lancer, and was not considered suitable to become one of the Magi'i, he comes from an old and worthy family, and it is clear he is a capable and hardworking lancer."

"He has risked his life for Cyador on many occasions, and any lancer who has done such is most suitable for reward and promotion," replies Luss.

"As you have ensured." Kharl nods politely. "You might also find some other information concerning him of slight interest. I have been informed by . . . certain sources. . . . that the tariff collections of Emperor's Enumerators in Biehl have nearly doubled in the past season." Kharl frowns. "Yet Bluoyal has informed me that the number of vessels porting in Biehl has changed little. He seemed rather amused when I suggested that perhaps matters had been amiss previously. It is interesting that the collections improved once the senior enumerator disappeared. He was a cousin to Bluoyal, I believe."

"That is a matter that *might* be of interest to the Majer-Commander."

"I thought it might be so. And to the Hand of the Emperor, should the Majer-Commander think it worthy to be carried so far."

"He will determine that. Of course, you could tell the Hand."

"Me? No Hand would scarce believe a word I said, were I even permitted to speak to him in the shadows."

"The wisdom of the Hand is legendary, I am told," Luss says. "I will pass on the information, and the powers above me will do as they please."

"As they always do." Kharl laughs so softly that the sound is lost in the breeze that rustles around the balcony of the Palace of Light.

XXVIII

DESPITE THE MIDDAY heat, after leaving the administration building, Lorn takes the steps to his quarters two at a time. There, he quickly eats some bread and cheese in the kitchen and then walks quickly to his study to use the chaos-glass.

He closes the shutters so that the silvered image will not pale against the bright summer light. After that, he pulls the old glass that had been his father's from the drawer and concentrates on its shimmering surface. He ignores the sweat that begins to form on his brow, from both the effort he makes and from the closeness of the study without any breeze from the shuttered windows. The silver mists form and vanish quickly, leaving a view of the port of Jera. There are two ships at the long rickety pier that winds out into the calm and nearly flat waters of the harbor. Both appear to have arrived recently, with carts on the pier, and goods being carried down the gangways.

Lorn concentrates on the vessel with the Hamorian lines. The pier seems to bow under the weight of the cart. Lorn tries to coax a better image of the long objects wrapped in cloth from his glass, but cannot. Still, they are wrapped separately; they are of iron, and there is little of value to be shipped from Hamor that would be handled such, except the large and heavy blades preferred by the barbarians.

He releases the image, and slips the glass into the drawer before opening the shutters. While he can draw maps in the late afternoon, and indeed, the shadows often make that task easier, he cannot follow ships and their trading in darkness. Nor, he reflects, at all, once they are at sea and beyond any harbor.

From his maps and his conversations with the captains of the trading vessels that have once again begun to frequent Biehl, Lorn can better understand the large image he is forming within his mind. That picture he likes not at all, although there is little he can do about it, and, at times, he wonders why he expends the effort. Yet he feels he must.

The barbarians trade tooled leather goods, often artistic; worked copper; and large baskets of some form of roasted nuts that must keep well. These reach Jera by the three branches of the river. In return, they purchase large amounts of iron blades better than they could forge. And those blades are used to kill Mirror Lancers.

More important to him, some of those blades are making their way west of Jera, with ever-increasing numbers of barbarians. So far, the barbarians have made no raids beyond the Grass Hills in the direction of Ehyla and Biehl. That also concerns Lorn, for when before have the barbarians failed to raid when they have had weapons and largely undefended hamlets?

True . . . the Grass Hills to the east of Biehl and to the west of Jera might better be termed "Stone Hills" for their steepness and for streams that are few and widely separated. And the barbarians have preferred to attack through the wider passes and vales of the southwest where grass and water are more abundant.

Lorn shakes his head. He can think about such later. For the moment, he needs to work with Tashqyt, Helkyt, and Whylyn on a better system for accustoming the trainees to firelances—without discharging the twoscore that are all that they hold in the compound.

After that, they will conduct more sabre drills . . . and Lorn will take up the padded heavy hand-and-a-half sword that he has had to learn to master in order to accustom the trainees to facing the barbarian blades.

XXIX

THE HOT LATE-SUMMER sun beats down on Lorn, and the sweat oozes from every pore, soaking the brown tunic he wears for training. Even after eightdays of training that he has made ever more rigorous, he still pours forth sweat. Now he can handle the big blade as easily as a sabre, though he prefers the smaller one for use while mounted.

"Break off!" he orders, glancing sideways at the two-on-three exercise on the flat sandy expanse of the beach to his left. He reins up the chestnut and lets the breeze off the Northern Ocean cool his fevered brow.

The squad leader—Tashqyt—reforms his squad before letting his lancers rest. Lorn nods.

Helkyt eases his mount up beside Lorn. "They are much improved, even the new lads from Vyun and those from Ehyla."

"They're getting there," Lorn says. "They're still not

ready to face the best of the barbarians, but most aren't that good."

"Ah . . . ser . . . no one's attacked a port detachment here in two-odd generations."

"That may be." Lorn's eyes fix on the squad leader. "And how many lancers end up back in the Grass Hills?"

"Less 'n a third, ser."

"Can you tell me which third?" Lorn feels another chill— the kind that provides no real cooling, but the mental coldness of a chaos-glass trained upon him. He ignores it.

"Ah . . . no ser."

"Do you want to condemn those men to die in the first skirmish they have with barbarian raiders?"

"No, ser." Helkyt's tone is resigned. "Just being that it is so hot . . ."

"The barbarians don't fight much when it's cool and comfortable, as I recall." Lorn pauses and blots his steaming forehead. "There's something else. Have you noticed the way the lancers act when they accompany Neabyl and Comyr and the new enumerator . . . Gyhl, that's it . . . on board vessels?"

Helkyt frowns.

"They're acting like lancers again. They're trained, and ready, and their carriage shows it. That makes the enumerators' tasks easier. It also tells the Hamorians and the other barbarians that Cyador is not to be a target."

"That be true, ser," the senior squad leader admits. "Neabyl be far cheerier these days, and even his consort came to see him."

Lorn suspects that has more to do with Flutak's disappearance than with the greater professionalism of the port-detachment lancers. "There are other reasons, as well."

Helkyt's eyebrows lift.

"The barbarian attacks have continued to increase, and we may be called upon. Or," Lorn smiles wryly, "I may find that my next duty will be there with some of these very same lancers."

Helkyt winces.

"You do your duty here, Helkyt, and after such a record of faithful service and a long career, I would doubt you will be transferred before you can claim your pension." Lorn blots his forehead again, aware that whoever used the chaos-glass has let the image lapse. Who could it be? It does not feel like Tyrsal, or his father, but Lorn has no sense of who the unknown magus might be.

"No offense, ser, but I'd be hoping your words be true." The senior squad leader laughs uneasily.

"They are not certain, but I'd wager that way." Lorn eases the chestnut toward Tashqyt's squad, lifting the huge padded hand-and-a-half blade that he will once again use one-on-one against the younger lancers to accustom them to fighting the long swords of the barbarians. "The one-on-one drills!"

Ignoring the sigh from Helkyt, Lorn hopes he can turn each of the recruits into at least a semblance of a lancer before too long. He has already sent a messenger to Commander Repyl, moving up the inspection date for the District Guards by two eightdays, and that means he and most of the Mirror Lancers will be leaving Biehl within three days.

From what he sees and has seen in his chaos-glass, he has less time than anyone else in Biehl knows, and his fate rests in large part on his judgments of what he has observed in his chaos-glass. Yet for all that his fate and the fates of many others rest on his calculations and observations, what he sees cannot be reported to anyone.

XXX

LORN LOOKS UP briefly and out the window of his first-floor administration-building study. The post-dawn air is still and warm, without too strong a breeze. He hopes the dry weather will hold, at least for a few days. Then he turns back to the papers before him. He is yet writing out the last of his scrolls, orders, and rough copies of maps when he hears Helkyt enter the outer study.

"Helkyt?"

"Yes, ser." The senior squad leader shakes his head as he steps into Lorn's study and sees the various stacks of papers. "You ever be sleeping, ser?"

"Not so much as I'd like, but that's not for trying." The overcaptain gestures to the chair across the table desk.

Helkyt sits down, almost gingerly.

"I'm going to impose some duties on you. I wish it could be otherwise, but you're the only one with the experience."

The senior squad leader's eyebrows lift.

"Tomorrow is when we go to inspect the District Guards, as you may recall."

"Yes, ser."

"I will be taking all the Mirror Lancers except for a half-score of senior lancers, and the halfscore of the most recent trainees."

"Ser?" Helkyt shifts his weight in the chair, uneasily.

"I have heard from some traders that there may be some barbarian raiders riding into the lands west of Ehyla. I thought that we might check that out while putting the District Guards through maneuvers."

"Best you take all the firelances, then, ser. Those we can do without—more so than you, if there be barbarians coming into Cyador."

"I appreciate your thought. I hope I am mistaken, but one never knows." Lorn shrugs. "My sources are usually good, but barbarians aren't always predictable, except in that they like to attack the lancers and people of Cyador."

"Ser . . . beggin' yer pardon, but in more 'n two seasons, I've yet to see you mistaken, and though I be no wagering man, were I one, I'd wager on what you know." He pauses. "And you be wanting me to keep things as you have?"

"That's right." Lorn leans forward. "We're before harvest,

and there shouldn't be too many ships porting, either to buy or sell, except for clay and china, and most traders won't come in just for that."

"The olive-grower Baryat's son—he been behaving himself?"

"So far as I can tell. But if he has any problems, they won't be with you." Lorn laughs ruefully. "We might get some orders transferring lancers to Assyadt or something," Lorn muses, "but don't transfer anyone until I get back. Or until it's clear I won't be back."

"Don't be talking that way, ser."

"I don't plan it that way, but I'd be a poor overcaptain if I didn't plan for the worst." Lorn points to the corner of the desk. "Those are the training plans for the next season, and some other papers that might be helpful."

"Yes, ser."

Lorn continues to brief Helkyt until nearly midmorning. He could have waited until later in the day, but he wants Helkyt to have some time to consider what he has told the senior squad leader so that if the older man has any questions, Lorn will still be in Biehl to answer them.

XXXI

AGAIN, BEHIND CLOSED shutters, in the late afternoon, Lorn studies the image in the glass. A long column of riders follows a narrow and dusty road—barely that—eastward through a long valley. Their destination is a narrow track through the most rugged and least hospitable section of the Grass Hills. At one time, from the look of the track, the way may have been more traveled, but its abandoned state and ruggedness are not likely to stop the barbarians.

Lorn shakes his head. As he has already determined, the destination has to be one of the towns west of the Grass Hills in Cyador, for there are no other Jeranyi towns west of the barbarian column. At their pace, they will enter the lands of Cyador in less than three days, perhaps four.

The Mirror Lancers leave to inspect the District Guards at Ehyla in the morning, and he has done what he can. His lancers know that they are headed out on maneuvers, and a possible scouting effort. Some of the older ones nodded knowingly. Several had already cached extra food, and the cooks have lodged a complaint with Helkyt.

Lorn smiles at that thought.

He lets the image fade, then calls up another image—this one of a trader in blue. Despite the lateness of the day, she remains in the large room he has come to recognize as her trading office. His lips curl as he recalls her lecture on the difference between studies and offices.

He lets that image fade quickly, for he does not wish to disturb her, although she glances up, her eyes narrowing, just before the image fades. As he sets the glass aside, Lorn wonders again what secrets lie in her ancestry—for she has sensed a chaos-glass searching when he was with her—and only those with abilities of the Magi'i can do such.

After a moment, Lorn reaches for paper and the pen he must substitute for being with Ryalth. In time, he writes slowly, trying to take care with each word.

My dearest,

When you receive this, it is likely I will be in the lands just east of the Grass Hills, east of Biehl and west of Jera. I have learned that a large group of barbarians may be massing and preparing to attack Cyador itself in an area where they have not attacked in generations, if ever.

There is no way to verify what I know, except by traders' words, and thus, we will be scouting, not knowing what we may find. If we do find barbarians, there will be no way to warn the Majer-Commander. What I attempt is a great risk, not only for me, but for you and for our son-to-be. Yet I fear the danger to Cyad and to us will be far greater if I do not act. I know you understand whereof I speak . . .

The barbarians have begun to attack in greater and greater numbers. It will not be long before the Majer-Commander requests that the young lancers I have trained be transferred to Assyadt or elsewhere, and then there will not be the forces necessary to turn away any attack through this, the most rugged section of the Grass Hills. So I must act while I have the forces to do so, and prevent the depredations that I fear will come if I do not.

I have heard from my parents that you have been kind to visit them and dine often with them and with Jerial, and for this latest kindness I am also grateful. When I will have furlough or home leave is most uncertain, and that I will not know until winter, at the earliest, if then.

He closes with the words, *My love,* and his signature, although it yet feels strange to be able to say such safely, for expressing love to one's consort is certainly acceptable, even in the Mirror Lancers.

The scroll will go to Helkyt in the morning, to be dispatched by firewagon. Even if it is read along the way, Lorn will have acted, and the results will be known, one way or the other, before any other officers can do anything to harm or assist.

He stands, and begins to roll the few maps he knows he will need. While he would like to take the glass, here in Biehl, unlike in a larger Mirror Lancer outpost, the glass will be safer left behind, for a camp is open to all, and lancer Magi'i are still most unwelcome to all too many Mirror Lancers—and especially to District Guards.

XXXII

IN THE LIGHT of early morning, on the flat below the District Guard headquarters at Ehyla, the First and Second Companies of the Mirror Lancer garrison at Biehl remain in near-perfect ranks as Lorn studies the lines of District Guards. He rides the chestnut mare down each line, occasionally stopping to check for riding rations and especially for water bottles. Only Tashqyt rides with him.

Commander Repyl remains on his own mount, before his two companies, and the partial squad of newer guards.

Lorn finishes the inspection, and nods to Tashqyt. "I will not be but a moment. While they are ready for maneuvers, I doubt Commander Repyl is ready to transfer his command." Lorn turns and rides toward the commander.

"And how do you find them, Overcaptain?" asks Repyl, even before Lorn reins up.

"In good order, Commander." Lorn gestures toward the guard building. "I have a matter of great importance to discuss with you. If you would accompany me?"

Commander Repyl's thin and perfect eyebrows lift. "This whole matter has been unusual."

"Perhaps unusual in recent years, but the requirement has been in the Emperor's Code for many, many years," Lorn says quietly, turning his mount eastward.

When they are a good hundred cubits from the nearest lancer, Repyl reins up. "I trust this will provide the . . . discretion . . . you wish?"

"For both of us." Lorn hands over a scroll. "I thought you would prefer to read this in a more private setting."

"Oh?" Repyl begins to flush even before he has finished the first section. Finally, the District Commander stares at the overcaptain. "You are within your rights, Overcaptain, but the Majer-Commander will hear of this."

"I am certain he will." A lazy smile crosses Lorn's lips. "Since I fully intend to tell him." Lorn waits. "I would suggest that you not be too hasty, Commander. If all goes well on these maneuvers, and your guards are as effective as they look, then you are likely to be well-regarded. If, somehow, I make pottage of the maneuvers, then you can claim you were being cooperative, as is your duty, and still appear fair and just."

The flush fades slowly. "I cannot say I am pleased."

"I wish it were otherwise," Lorn admits. "Do you wish to announce that your companies are being transferred to my command, and offer them your praise and support? Or would you rather that I do so?"

"I will do so—with grace, and I hope, skill." Repyl smiles tightly. "I trust you know what you are doing."

"I am trying to protect Biehl . . . and Cyador."

"With maneuvers?"

"I have received word that there is a large band of barbarians riding into the area east of here. We are the only forces available, and it will be better to stop them before they commit many depredations."

"You trust mere word?" Repyl's eyebrows lift.

"Commander, I could wait until I were absolutely sure. Then . . . if I wait, many will die, and much will be lost. If I am wrong, your guards obtain some riding and some training. If those who would have me wait are wrong, then the Mirror Lancers will be faulted for failing to protect the people." Lorn does not mention that the chaos-glass is seldom wrong, or that he has already seen the raiders massing to the northeast, moving along the narrow valleys into the Grass Hills and toward Biehl. His lips curl slightly. "I trust you understand."

"I fear I do, Overcaptain, and I fear even more that you

may be right than wrong." Repyl nods. "I shall do my duty with grace, and hope you are wrong, not because I wish you ill, but, as I have just said, because, if you are right, we, too, will soon face the continuing attacks that have so far graced Assyadt and Syadtar."

Not if I act swiftly. Lorn does not voice the thought. "Thank you."

The two turn their mounts back toward the assembled Mirror Lancers and District Guards.

XXXIII

THE SUN IS little more than a hand above the golden brown grasses of the rolling hills as Lorn finishes checking his map. After using the northern beaches as a highway, he and his force have headed inland. They now ride to the southeast, toward where he calculates the barbarians should be making their way out of the Grass Hills—along a narrow creek that meanders out of the rugged terrain and then dries up less than twenty kays from where it emerges. There may be scattered holds along the way, but small individual huts are hard to pick out using a chaos-glass—especially for Lorn when he is trying to map lands he has not seen. He hopes there are not too many such holds along the route the barbarians may take—or may have already taken.

Once off the beaches, the progress of Lorn's force has been slower than Lorn had thought, because the route he has chosen, while without gorges or larger barriers to travel, has no roads and no streams, just the kays of grass-covered plains set between distant higher hills.

"Ser," offers Tashqyt quietly. "Up ahead."

Lorn glances up from his efforts to roll his map and ride. He has to squint against the low and rising sun to make out the thinnest of lines of grayish smoke rising through the clear morning air. Its source is blocked by the low ridge before Lorn's force. He nods. "Let's see what the scouts report. Could be just an isolated holding, or herder's place."

They have ridden almost another kay up the gentle slope that is far longer than Lorn had thought, so gradual is its incline, and still have at least a kay to go before they reach the crest, when Lorn spies two lancers riding their mounts at a quicker walk than normal. He fears he knows what the smoke signifies, but he says nothing and keeps riding.

Swytyl rides up from the head of his squad and lets his mount flank Tashqyt's on the right as the three wait for the scouts to meet them.

When they near Lorn, the two lancer scouts swing their mounts around to ride parallel to Lorn on the left.

"Ser . . . there's a hamlet over the rise . . . along the stream," offers the scout closer to Lorn.

"The barbarians have already been there?" Lorn asks.

"Ah . . . yes, ser." The scout's quizzical look begs for an answer.

"The smoke," Lorn says, "and your haste in reporting. They aren't there now, though, or you would have been galloping back."

"No, ser. Didn't see none. Didn't see no one moving," answers the second scout.

"Just in case," Lorn glances at Tashqyt. "Four-abreast, firelances ready."

Tashqyt stands in his stirrups and half turns in the saddle. "Four-abreast! Firelances at the ready!"

The other squad leaders echo the orders, except that the District Guard squad leaders merely command, "Lances ready!"

The barbarians have moved faster than Lorn has thought, and his forces have been slower in coming across the grasslands south of the northern beaches, and the small hamlet may have been one of the first results of his miscalculations. His lips tighten, and his fingers brush the half of the firelance. He can feel sweat forming under his garrison cap and oozing down his sunburned neck and then his back.

As the chestnut carries Lorn over the crest of the grassy rise, he can make out the stream that he had tracked with the chaos-glass—and to his left, a gap in the rugged hills, from which the stream runs. Below them is a hamlet.

Lorn shakes his head. Thin lines of smoke and mist hug the ground around the hamlet. There are perhaps a dozen dwellings, if that, earth- or sod-walled. The roofs of most are caved in—burned out from within, as shown by the smoke that fills the hollow.

"Ser?" questions Tashqyt.

"Barbarians," Lorn affirms. "Yesterday, I'd guess. Everything's almost burned out."

Nothing moves in the hamlet, except the smoke, drifting on a breeze so light that Lorn cannot feel it as he leads the Mirror Lancers and District Guards down the grass-covered hillside and toward the stream.

The streambed is northwest of the hamlet and separates Lorn's force from the hamlet with a miniature gorge perhaps four cubits deep. Lorn turns the chestnut northwest and rides for almost half a kay before finding a place where livestock have crumbled the edges into a ford of sorts. The scouts cross first, and the water is less than a cubit deep on the legs of their mounts.

On the other side, Lorn sees a movement and turns to his right. There, a reddish-colored dog turns and slinks down the side of a dry irrigation ditch whose banks have been trampled down. A figure in brown lies sprawled facedown in the flattened grass beyond the ditch. The back of his tunic is covered in large splotches of darker brown. The flies buzz around the dead man.

Lorn gently urges the mare away from the body and rides parallel to the ditch, along the livestock path and toward the easternmost hut. The two scouts ride almost two hundred cubits ahead, but rein up by the hut, glancing back at Lorn and the main force.

Again, Lorn suspects he knows why. As the mare nears the dwelling—earth-walled, with a single window on the east side—Lorn swallows as he catches sight of another body. As he guides the chestnut onto the dirt lane that leads southwest toward the other dwellings, he moves his head slowly from the half-naked body of a woman, perhaps nearly as old as his mother, lying as if flung against the sod wall of the hut. He does not look closely to see exactly how she was killed. Nor does it matter, save that she suffered greatly and was slain in pain.

"Just follow the track past the dwellings," Lorn orders the two scouts. "Keep an ear for anything." He pauses, then turns to Swytyl. "Have your lancers check each dwelling, by pairs, just to see if there's a child or someone alive. And have different ones do each hut."

"Yes, ser." Swytyl turns to ride back to his squad, which is still on the livestock trail.

"You don't think anyone's alive, do you?" asks Tashqyt.

"No. But I wouldn't want to go off and leave a child or an infant to die because we didn't look." As Lorn speaks, once more, he senses the chill of a chaos-glass, a chill that lasts but moments before it vanishes.

The sharp-featured squad leader shakes his head as the four-abreast column, lances still ready, rides along the dirt lane that approximates a road through the hamlet.

There are bodies everywhere—far more than Lorn would have imagined for a hamlet so small—but the pattern is the same around each dwelling. The men have been slain quickly, as have small children. The women have been used and killed, even girls too small to be women and women who are grandmothers.

The overcaptain could have done without riding through the hamlet, having seen the work of the barbarians too often in years previous, but few of the Mirror Lancers he leads, and none of the District Guards, have seen such. So he rides slowly past each sod dwelling, letting the chestnut carry him back toward the southwest and away from the Grass Hills. Behind him, there are no murmurs from his force, none that he can hear.

In the grassy expanse to the south, Lorn sees scattered dark shapes, cattle that have scattered after the carnage, and some grayer forms—sheep.

As they pass the last dwelling, Lorn reins up. "We'll wait to hear from Swytyl."

"Halt!" orders Tashqyt.

Lorn sits on the mare, under the increasingly hot and bright harvest sun. "The stream goes along the road. We'll water farther on. The barbarians didn't mess it, and the locals kept their jakes away from it."

Tashqyt nods.

Shortly, Swytyl rides up. The squad leader is pale.

Lorn looks at Swytyl.

Swytyl shakes his head. "No, ser. There be not a soul living." He swallows hard. "Even . . . even babes."

"You see why . . ." Lorn does not finish the sentence.

"Yes, ser." After a moment, Swytyl adds, "Ser . . . there be many bodies . . ."

"We'll have to leave them," Lorn says. "We don't have the spades or the time, and if we delay here, what happens if they get to another hamlet?"

Tashqyt and Drayl, who has eased his mount forward to hear Swytyl's report, both nod.

"We'll follow this." Lorn points to the narrow road or track that heads southwest, generally following the stream. Hoofprints on hoofprints cover the dusty trail. "We'll stand down and water in a bit."

He urges the chestnut forward, after the barbarians, wondering how many more miscalculations he will make, hoping there will not be too many more.

XXXIV

THE SWEAT OOZES down the back of Lorn's neck, and the sun beats on the right side of his face as he rides southwest through the valley so wide and long that the Grass Hills that surround it on three sides are mere smudges on the horizon. Only to the southwest are no true hills visible, and that is where the river is.

Tashqyt rides to Lorn's left, as they make their way through the early afternoon, and as Swytyl rides up to join them.

"What did they find?" asks Lorn.

"Scouts say that the tracks ahead circle to the west, and that hill over there," the round-faced Swytyl reports. "There's a burned-out stead at the base of the rise. Bodies, too. Not pleasant. Like that hamlet."

"They were already there before we left the beaches. At the hamlet," Lorn adds, after a moment.

While the first hamlet that the Jeranyi had raided was little more than a group of dwellings and barns where herders grazed and raised cattle, so small that it had no name beyond its borders, Lorn still regrets that they had not been there when the raiders arrived. Now the nameless hamlet will remain so, since the Jeranyi had left no survivors. Had such a hamlet existed near Isahl, there would have been walls and berms, and frequent patrols by Mirror Lancers. East of Biehl, folk are not prepared for the raiders.

The trail that Lorn and the lancers and guards have followed southwest from the hamlet indicates that cattle or other livestock have been driven regularly toward a tributary of the River Behla, some forty kays southwest, where presumably they were added to those floated downstream on railed rafts for sale in Biehl and Ehyla. Intermittently, hides come with the cattle, according to Neabyl.

Taking such a small hamlet as the raiders have already would not have satisfied such a large group of Jeranyi, as Lorn is certain, and the raiders are following the livestock tracks and dirt roads to a larger town on the tributary—Nhais was once the name, although Lorn is far from certain that the name has continued, so old was the map he had found in the back room of the administration building. His glass-screed and hand-drafted maps have so far proven more accurate than those few surviving in the Biehl lancer compound.

Beyond Nhais to the south and west are other, and richer targets, such as the vintner's warehouses at Escadr and the cuprite mines at Dyeum. Whether the barbarians will dare to travel that far is yet another question. But if none stop them, Lorn fears the worst.

Lorn glances across the browning grass that reaches above the chestnut's knees. As if to underscore Swytyl's words about the barbarian atrocities, a thin line of smoke circles into a green-blue sky that holds but high and thin hazy clouds. The air is hot and still. "Did they see any signs of riders?"

"No, ser. Not even dust."

The dust would not rise high in the still air, but with no dust in sight, the barbarians are at least four or five kays west or southwest of Lorn's force.

Lorn nods. "We'll catch them."

He hopes to reach Nhais and the river before they do, circling around and in front of them. He also hopes he has not waited too long in setting forth, but he has pushed Commander Repyl as much as he had dared without revealing exactly what he had known beforehand.

XXXV

LORN HAS REINED up, turning the chestnut more to the south so that he is no longer squinting against the low afternoon sun that has been angling into his eyes from the right. His neck is red and raw, and burns from sun and sweat. The sweat that oozes from under his garrison cap keeps stinging the corners of his eyes. Yellowish dust coats his trousers and those of all the lancers, as well as the legs of all their mounts. The eight squad leaders and Lorn form a rough semicircle, listening to the sandy-haired and round-faced Swytyl.

"They are but little more than five kays before us, and they will be drawing up into their camp before long. We can reach them if we hasten—before they reach Nhais . . ." suggests Swytyl.

Several heads around the circle nod. The black-haired Tashqyt is not one of them. Nor is the grizzle-bearded senior squad leader of the District Guards.

"They ride slowly," Lorn says. "We have been hastening, and the day has been long. What if they turn, and what happens to our mounts and their riders?"

This time both the older District Guard squad leader and Tashqyt do nod.

"We are not looking for a battle a quickly as possible. We wish a great victory with few casualties," Lorn points out. "We will catch them on the morrow—when they reach the river there. The town is west, but the river winds. They will follow the river. So we will turn more westerly, and arrive at the town before they do."

"If they do not follow the river?" asks Swytyl.

"Then we are between them and the town, and the town

will not suffer, and there will be no heaps of bodies of the people of Cyador."

The other squad leaders nod.

"There is always the chance that they may find another hamlet," Lorn says slowly. "The maps do not show such, but it could happen. But we are the only force here, and we dare not let the barbarians by us to ravage a town such as Nhais, with scores of folk."

Tashqyt nods, then the other squad leaders.

Not for the first time does Lorn hope he is correct, but if he is wrong this time, the herders and the townspeople will suffer less. The last time, a hamlet suffered because his screeing had not picked out that the herding hamlet even existed—and because, he reminds himself, he had miscalculated his force's abilities and those of the raiders.

Still, while he would not have wished harm on the people, fighting there at the base of the Grass Hills would have been difficult, and impossible to contain the raiders.

Lorn looks around at the faces that study his. Is he putting too much trust in plans and maps? Doubtless he is, but the tracks across the grasslands show he faces more than ten-score barbarians, perhaps as many as fifteenscore, and his four companies could number little more than half the barbarians, and half his men have no firelances. Yet there is Nhais, undefended except for him, and Escadr and Dyeum beyond. So he must try to pick where and how he fights.

If he can.

XXXVI

LORN HAD FORGOTTEN what patrols are like in the heat of the Grass Hills—or the valleys nearby. Dust is everywhere, settling into boots, clothing, ears, eyes, and nose. His exposed skin is red, and his neck is peeling. Sweat burns his eyes, and they water much of the time. While the wind is welcome for its cooling, it brings more grit to his eyes and nostrils. Water must be rationed, and finding water for the mounts and then watering them in the scattered streams takes more time than he had recalled.

Even though it is harvest, and not the height of summer, heat rises in waves off the browned grasses by late afternoon. Then, by late at night, the air is chill, and Lorn and the lancers shiver under their single blankets.

In the hot early afternoon, he has reined up the chestnut mare on a low rise overlooking one of the few narrow streams feeding the river. Below him, the companies are finishing watering their mounts. While they do, Lorn studies the maps and the terrain around him, now becoming more hilly as they approach the river, and the town of Nhais. From what his maps show, Lorn judges that Nhais lies another twenty kays or so to the southwest, while the river is no more than ten to south. He and the lancers should be able to reach the town, or within five kays of it well before twilight—if his maps are accurate, and if the dirt track remains passable.

He looks up as three riders near—Swytyl and two of the lancers used as scouts. The lancers bear a look of concern, but Lorn waits until they rein up. Then he only says, "You have something new?"

"Ser . . . the barbarians have forded the river, and they have raided another small hamlet, perhaps of halfscore dwellings. They have halted . . ." Swytyl pauses, and Lorn understands all too well why the barbarians have halted.

"There is little we can do now." Lorn nods and keeps his sigh to himself. Another miscalculation, of sorts, but not one that would change his course, even had he known, for in the heat, he cannot push his men too hard and expect them to fight their best. And that they must do, outnumbered as his force is.

"They look to be traveling tomorrow along the south

side," Swytyl adds. "The hills are high, and the river narrower and deeper to the south. There are several hamlets on
that side, and none on this, not before Nhais. Not that we
can see."

"There is a way to cross the river at the town, a ford less
than a kay south," Lorn says. "We will ride longer tonight.
For if we cannot cross the river to attack them, neither can
they cross to attack us, even if they know we are here. We
will rise and move earlier in the morning, while it is cool,
and we will cross the ford and travel upstream. We will also
check to see where the river is deepest along a certain bend."

Swytyl raises his eyebrows.

"We will try to circle and attack them where they cannot
ford the river to retreat." Lorn offers a grim smile. "After all
their efforts, I believe we owe them that."

Swytyl nods. "Yes, ser."

"Have someone watch the river, though, as we ride toward
Nhais."

"Yes, ser."

Again . . . Lorn can but do his best, and hope. He does not
mention that, if he fails, the way lies open to Escadr and
Dyeum. It is enough that he knows.

XXXVII

THE SUN HAS not even risen when Lorn and his force ride in
along the dusty north road and into the center square of
Nhais, into a square consisting of little more than an open
dirt plaza, surrounded by low buildings, but the gray light is
bright enough to show the poverty of the place. On the west
side is an inn, with a front porch covered by a sagging roof
and supported by peeling, whitewashed timbers. The inn's
signboard depicts a brown bull. On the north side of the
square are a chandlery and a cooper's. On the east is a long

low building, with boards nailed across the windows and the door. The whitewash has peeled away from the shutters, and the wood is cracked and weathered. The south side of the square has three buildings of two stories each hunched together. The end two structures lean into the center one, but none bears a sign, and the shutters and doors of all three are closed.

The structures, except for the inn, show walls of a reddish brown brick. The inn has mud-plaster over the brick. That Lorn can tell from where the whitewashed plaster has broken away. All the roofs but that of the inn are of some form of woven withies, Lorn thinks, something he has not seen before in Cyador. The inn's roof is of ancient and cracked red tiles.

Nhais is not the kind of town that Lorn thinks of as Cyadoran. The dwellings are unkempt, without hedges or privacy screens. Many are without shutters. The streets are unpaved and dusty now, and will be muddy in rain and snow.

Lorn glances toward the inn once more, where three men stand under the sagging porch. Otherwise, the square is empty.

"Poor town," whispers Tashqyt.

"Poorer still if we don't stop the raiders," Lorn murmurs back.

As Lorn and the first squad of Mirror Lancers pass the inn porch, the murmurs of the three men drift toward the riders. Lorn listens, his hearing chaos-sense aided.

". . . Mirror Lancers . . . an overcaptain. What they doing here?"

". . . you want to ask?"

"Jerem said . . . raiders in the north . . ."

". . . let 'em go . . . less said the better."

"Better lancers 'n raiders . . ."

"Some choice . . ."

If they had seen what Lorn has seen, he reflects, they would not think such. But most folk do not reckon well what they have not seen.

Lorn and Tashqyt turn down the street leading southward, toward the ford, the dust-muted sounds of hoofs drowning out the murmurs of the men on the inn's porch. The houses by the square give way to huts, then a handful of hovels near the river.

The town is set on a low bluff, and less than twenty cubits above the river, and beyond the last poor hut, there is a slope down to the water. The river is lined with bushes and low willow trees, and the leaves of both are dust-covered. From bank to bank is less than a hundred and fifty cubits, and, in the dry time of early harvest, the river is low. Mudbanks protrude from the brownish water. Wagon tracks lead down the slope and up the far side a hundred cubits away.

Lorn turns in the saddle. "We'll cross in single-file by squads. Then we'll head back east along the river. Upstream of the town, we'll find a place to water the mounts."

"Well upstream," suggests Tashqyt.

Lorn nods.

"Cross by squads, single-file!"

"By squads, single-file," echo the squad leaders.

The chestnut sidesteps slightly as she takes a first step into the brownish water, but the river is so shallow at the ford that Lorn's boots never touch the water's surface. He reins up at the top of the bluff on the southern shore, scanning the river and the land and hills to the east. But he sees no one, not even animals or livestock, just a few scattered dwellings farther to the south and west.

Once the entire force has crossed, Lorn gestures to Swytyl, then waits for the squad leader to near before speaking. "Send out the scouts . . . at least five kays east of here. We'll ride along the river road here until we find a good place to water the mounts. Then, we'll keep moving north."

"Yes, ser." With a nod, the round-faced squad leader rides toward his squad and the lancers in it used as scouts.

"Forward, two-abreast, by columns!" Lorn orders.

Orange light is seeping over the low hills as the column begins to move eastward on the narrow and rutted dirt road that roughly parallels the river.

The sun stands just above the low trees and hills on the horizon when Lorn's force of Mirror Lancers and Guards halts on the south bank of the river, almost two kays east of Nhais. Lorn glances back, to the west, where the town is partly obscured by a slight haze, perhaps from a combination of moisture from the river and dust. To the east, low hills undulate beside the river, getting steeper more to the south. There are neither signs of the barbarians nor recent hoofprints in the dust of the road, except those placed there by Swytyl's scouts.

"Water by squads!" Tashqyt orders. "Keep the mounts out of the water."

After watering the chestnut, Lorn blots his face with a dampened cloth, then remounts and rides to the top of the low bluff that forms the southern bank of the river. So far as he can tell, as his maps had indicated, the river narrows and deepens as the hills steepen a kay or so east of where the force rests.

Shortly, he is joined by Tashqyt, Swytyl, Whylyn, and Drayl—the Mirror Lancer squad leaders, and by Wharalt—the grizzle-bearded senior squad leader of the District Guards.

Wharalt looks straight at Lorn. "Ser ... you been most careful in not pushing us. But you got scouts out, and we be heading toward where the raiders were going. We going to meet them soon?"

"Today or tomorrow," Lorn says. "Today, I would judge, but the scouts will tell us. I am hoping to circle south slightly, and then head northeast about five kays east of here."

"Ah ... ser, why not wait for them? If I might ask?"

"Because there is a bend in the river that has high bluffs, and we are going to trap them there, if at all possible."

Wharalt raises his eyebrows.

"Wharalt . . . we are the only force of lancers east of Biehl. If we allow any to escape, there will be more raids of the type we have seen. I cannot keep a large force here and leave the port unprotected, and I don't think you and the District Guards wish to spend the next several seasons chasing barbarians until the Majer-Commander can move more lancers here. So . . ." Lorn shrugs. ". . . we will attempt to remove them all at once. If that does not work, then we will be spending at least several more eightdays tracking and chasing those who escape." The overcaptain offers a wintry smile. "I would prefer none escape."

"When you put it that way . . . ser . . . there's more light on what we been doing." Wharalt nods slowly and evenly. "Mind if I pass that along?"

"No. They should know." Lorn pauses, then adds, "I'd also prefer that the raiders not know we're here or what we have in mind. The other thing you'd best tell your men, all of you, is that barbarians don't back down, and that they hate us all. What you saw in that hamlet and those steads is what all lancers find everywhere after a barbarian raid."

"What my brother said," adds Swytyl. "Came back without his arm. Said he was lucky. Said what they did to the women—"

"That's right." Lorn overrides the squad leader quietly. "You all saw that, and we don't want it to happen in Nhais. We need to move on now."

"Yes, ser." The assents are almost in unison.

The day continues to warm as they ride eastward along the river. By early midmorning, in the distance to the east, Lorn sees dark birds circling, but cannot make out whether they are vulcrows or smaller scavengers. Outside of the tracks of their own scouts, the road dust shows no signs of riders.

As they ride, once more the feel of a chaos-glass sweeps

across Lorn and is gone. The overcaptain purses his lips and keeps riding, silently.

They have ridden another five kays when the first of Swytyl's lancer scouts returns.

Lorn has the column stand down, and sends a handful of men down the steeper slope to the river to fill water bottles while he hears the scout report.

"You were right, ser. They're a-comin' down this road, slow-like, maybe another five kays, on the far side of the road."

"On the other side of this hill here—that's where the road and the river bend north, is it not?" asks Lorn. "And then here's another hill farther along?"

The scout looks at Swytyl, then at the overcaptain. "Yes, ser. Runs that way near-on two kays, maybe like three, 'cause there be another hill there."

"How far are they from that far hill, the one the road goes over?"

"Another six kays, mayhap."

Lorn nods and turns in his saddle. "Swytyl! Get me the squad leaders." While they gather, Lorn dismounts and checks his maps, and then hands the chestnut's reins to one of the younger new lancers. He glances up toward Tashqyt. "We'll need a few lancers to hold mounts. I want you all to look at a map."

"Yes, ser."

Once the four Mirror Lancer squad leaders and Wharalt are gathered, Lorn spreads the map on the dusty grass beside the road and outlines the geography. "Here we are . . . and that is about where the barbarians are. They probably are going to stay near the road here, and swing along the river like so . . . I can't see them climbing the hills there, as they're getting steeper, when there's a flatter and easier way to Nhais by the river road . . ." He pauses, and glances at the grizzled Wharalt. "Can your men hold a line until the barbarians are within a hundred cubits before you mount a charge against them?"

"Aye, we can do that."

Lorn nods and begins to outlines what he has in mind. "Wharalt . . . the barbarians have scouts, but they only ride about a kay or so ahead of the main body. They'll probably ride past the bend until where the road looks clear to Nhais. You wait behind that slope there, either until they turn back or until they're a good kay farther west . . ."

"Then we come up and block the space between the steep hill and the river, so they either charge us or turn into that space in the bend?"

Lorn nods. "If the scouts pass you, you'll have to have a man or two detailed to watch for them."

"We can do that."

The overcaptain gestures toward the river. "The road curves to follow the river, and because there's a hill to the south. We'll circle the back side of the hill, so there aren't any tracks on the road, and wait. Once they're past, we'll use the firelances to push them west, and they can either ride into the guards or draw up defensively on the flat ground of the bluff with their backs to the river—"

"If they don't push, ser . . . ?" asks Wharalt.

Lorn laughs. "Then we reverse the plan, and we hold the line and you charge."

"That be splitting our forces."

"We won't be that far apart," Lorn points out.

"They'll fight like black angels, you don't give them anywhere to go," suggests Drayl.

"They do anyway." Lorn points to the east where the vulcrows still circle. "That's another hamlet filled with bodies, I wager. We don't want them going anywhere."

"Yes, ser."

Lorn rolls up the map. "Get the water bottles filled, and the squads ready." He walks toward the chestnut, slips the map into the case behind his saddle.

". . . never seen maps like that . . ."

". . . around the overcaptain much, and there be much you never saw . . ."

Not too much, Lorn hopes, as he mounts.

He leads the two companies around the back side of the hill, far slower going as they dodge brush and patches of thorny green cacti that Lorn has not seen before.

Still . . . it is well before midday when they reach the back side of the slope that overlooks where the road turns north into the bend in the river. There, just below the crest of the hill, Lorn and Tashqyt wait, listening for hoofs, voices . . . anything. Below and behind them are the two companies of Mirror Lancers from Biehl.

The sun is more like that of late midsummer than of late summer or early fall, and sweat continues to collect under the brow of Lorn's garrison cap. The perspiration oozes toward his eyes, and he continues to blot it away with the back of his sleeve. Beside him, Tashqyt shifts his weight in the saddle.

The chestnut *whuffs*, and Lorn leans forward and pats her shoulder. "Easy . . . easy, there. Waiting is hard on all of us."

Lorn almost senses someone, something, and eases the chestnut uphill, just enough that he can peer eastward if he stands in his stirrups.

A pair of barbarians ride along the road, moving at a quick walk. Lorn ducks and eases the chestnut back farther downhill, out of sight.

As he and Tashqyt wait—as do the Mirror Lancers behind them—the sound of low voices carries over the crest of the hill, but not the meaning of whatever the two warriors are discussing. Tashqyt looks at Lorn. Lorn shakes his head, and gestures toward the east. "Not long," he murmurs, hoping he is correct.

The sun rises higher, and more sweat oozes down the back of Lorn's sunburned neck. He wishes there were trees or cliffs or some form of shelter, but the only types of vegetation that are more than shoulder-high are a very few straggly trees and the willows that intermittently flank the river.

A low murmuring drifts toward them, and Lorn straightens in the saddle. So does Tashqyt. Both wait until it is far louder, seemingly right below them.

Lorn continues to wait, then edges the chestnut forward up the slope.

The rough column of barbarians—riding three- and four-abreast—is more than halfway past Lorn. He ducks and eases his mount back downslope. From his single quick survey, he believes there are closer to fifteenscore riders.

Finally, he raises his arm—and drops it. Tashqyt does the same.

Behind them the squads, riding four-abreast in each squad, move up and over the crest of the hill, coming downhill at a quick trot before increasing their speed on the road and the flat that flanks it.

Three barbarian warriors trailing the main party look back and uphill at the charging lancers. All three wheel.

Lorn levels his firelance.

Hssst! Hsst! One of the men drops; the one on the far right twists in the saddle.

Hssst! Hsst!

"Short bursts! Short bursts!" Lorn orders.

"Short bursts!" echo Tashqyt, Swytyl, Whylyn, and Drayl.

Ahead, shouts come from the barbarian warriors.

As he rides toward the end of the barbarian column, Lorn watches as the barbarian force seems to separate—the leading riders spur their mounts and swing northward off the road, while perhaps twoscore of the trailing riders wheel to attempt to stop the Mirror Lancers.

With the Bristan sabre in his left hand, and firelance in his right, Lorn finds he is still leading the charge. He also senses the presence of a chaos-glass, then pushes that thought and feeling away.

Hssst! Hssst! The short bursts of lances flare through the already-hot midday air, and more than half the defenders are dead even before the first two squads of lancers plow through them—though not without casualties.

Lorn parries a big blade with the sabre, ducks, and back-hands the raider who has tried to bring the large blade to bear on the overcaptain.

Still, the defenders have created enough of a delay—as has another group farther westward along the road—that the barbarians have re-formed in a bowed semicircle in the bend area to the south of the road.

Lorn also doesn't like the ragged breaking-up of his own forces, and he barks out the orders. "Halt! Halt and re-form! Five-abreast! Five-abreast!"

His orders are echoed, and within moments . . . across a space of two hundred cubits, two forces face each other.

The sound of hoofs tells of the arrival of the brown-clad District Guards, their cupridium lances gleaming in the noonday sun.

Lorn—still in the front center of his re-forming Mirror Lancers—snaps, "Half the Guard on each flank! Half the Guard on each flank!"

Surprisingly, to Lorn, the barbarians do not charge, even as the red-trimmed brown tunics of the guards move into po-sition on each side of the two Mirror Lancer companies. That they do not charge bothers Lorn, but he waits, ready to order a charge at any moment, but wanting to make sure that the guards cover the flanks.

In the hot stillness, four barbarians ride forward, reining up a good hundred cubits from Lorn. The lead rider—a bearded blond giant—holds a figure before him in the sad-dle—that of a small girl. He holds a dull dark blade at the girl's throat.

"See, white demons! We have your women, more than a score. You let us return, white demon, and we will not harm these . . ."

Lorn stiffens inside. He glances to his left, then his right.

The guards to his right are not quite in position, but all his other forces look to be. "You have invaded our land, and I should let you leave untouched, after all those you have killed?" He calls back to the blond warrior, easing the chestnut forward as he does, so that he is a good twenty cubits forward of his forces, where he can be seen. He has not spied any archers, and he hopes there are none. He keeps his lance low, although he has raised it some.

"These lands you took from our forefathers. They are not your lands. They were never yours, and soon they will again be the lands of the Jeranyi." The Jeranyi leader jerks his head sideways. To his left is another rider holding a child, and Lorn can see women bound to mounts farther back in the barbarian forces. "We have your women, you see."

Lorn eases the chestnut farther forward.

"Do not raise your devil lance, or she will die. So will the others!"

Lorn forces himself and his lance swings up. *Hssst!*

The chaos-bolt drives through the bearded blond's chest. Almost as quickly, the big blade of the warrior beside the leader and the captive slashes through the girl's neck.

Hssst! The barbarian who has slain the woman slumps across his mount's mane.

"Charge! Discharge firelances at will!" Lorn orders. "Charge!" Lorn urges the chestnut forward, hoping the charge will force at least some of the barbarians to choose between fighting lancers and killing captives.

"Kill them!" shouts a barbarian, and the tall warriors charge to meet the Mirror Lancers.

Hssst! Hssst! Firelance bolts flash across the less-than-hundred cubits separating the two forces.

A high-pitched scream disabuses Lorn of the delusion that a few hostages might survive even before the firebolts from his lance rake across two barbarians. Then he is alternating slashes and parries with the sabre and triggering short blasts of chaos-fire on those few occasions when he can find enough space to take on a barbarian without striking a lancer or guard.

Dust swirls up, and horses scream. Men yell.

Lorn finds he is behind the barbarians, somehow alone for a moment. He lifts the lance.

Hssst! Hsst! Two bolts in succession drill through the back and neck of two barbarians.

Lorn turns to his right and looses another bolt, to bring down yet a third barbarian from behind. He gets in three more bolts before a giant of a figure with a blade nearly so long as Lorn's firelance comes charging past a dying lancer and toward the overcaptain.

Lorn barely manages to slide the other's blade off his sabre. The firelance crumples as he uses it to parry the barbarian's backswing, but the big blade remains caught in the thin cupridium of the lance long enough for Lorn to jab the point of the sabre through the other's neck, and wrench it back out. At times, the point he had added to the Brystan sabre has made the difference. He drops the lance and manages to yank clear the second sabre, smiling mirthlessly. Then he urges the chestnut toward a lancer beset by three barbarians.

Lorn takes the first from behind, and the second from the side with the official lancer sabre, and then he is past and fighting off another huge figure.

The dull sound of metal on metal becomes more common, and the *hsst*ing of firelances dies away.

Abruptly—or so it seems—there are, but lancers and guards looking blankly at each other, eyes darting this way and that, seeking another barbarian.

Lorn reins up, and looks across the grassy grass, grass now splashed with splotches of blood and other substances, and littered with bodies, some of horses, but mostly of men—and a handful of children and women. He tightens his lips and sheathes his lancer sabre, switching the Brystan one to his right hand. He is aware that whichever magus has been using a chaos-glass to view the battle is no longer doing so. "I hope you saw enough blood . . ." he murmurs under his breath.

After scanning the field, he reins up by a fallen barbarian, his eye caught by the shimmer of the blade beside the body, and dismounts. He takes the blade and studies it slowly.

"Ser! Ser!" Tashqyt guides his mount up beside the overcaptain's.

Lorn glances up at Tashqyt.

"It's over," the squad leader reports. "We even checked the edge of the bluff, but no one escaped that way."

"I know." Lorn lifts the big blade, Hamorian-forged and -ground, from the workmanship. "I want all the blades collected and saved. Put them on the spare and captured mounts. The Majer-Commander will need proof."

"Proof?"

"That Hamorian traders are sending blades to Jera, and that those blades are being used to kill lancers." Lorn mounts slowly. His legs are tired, and his eyes stab. Then he glances down at the body of a woman, sprawled on the grass. He does not see how she died, but she is barely younger than Ryalth or Myryan. Or the grower's daughter he had killed.

After a long moment, he looks up and meets Tashqyt's eyes. "This time . . . it's over." He clears his throat. "What about our men?"

"Ah . . . we took some losses, ser."

Lorn waits.

"A good score-and-a-half from the lancers, almost a score from the guards. And Whylyn, and two of the Guard squad leaders."

"Threescore . . ." Lorn's smile is tight. "Too many, but not bad for a first battle for most of them, and not at all bad against fifteenscore."

"Eighteenscore, ser. Ah . . . I thought we needed to know."

Tashqyt looks down. "They killed most of the captives, ser. Almost a score. Five survived."

Eighteenscore dead—more than in some small towns in Cyador. Lorn nods slowly. "Do we have any captive barbarians?"

"Halfscore, a bit more. They're all wounded."

"Where are they?" Lorn remounts the mare.

"Over by the bluff. There." The sharp-featured Tashqyt gestures.

In the late-afternoon light, Lorn rides toward the captives. He dismounts and hands the chestnut's reins to Tashqyt. He walks forward. There are fifteen men, all bearded, all with their hands bound behind them. One lies unconscious, on his side, in the dusty grass. The captives are surrounded by Drayl's squad—half dismounted with sabres drawn; the others mounted, also with blades drawn.

One of the captives lurches toward Lorn. "White demon!"

"You killed women and children who could not have harmed you." Lorn draws the Brystan sabre.

"You are all demons." The bound captive spits toward Lorn.

Lorn's face is like ice as he steps forward, and there is a dull *clunk* as the chaos-enhanced blade separates the barbarian's head from his torso. Both drop onto the blood-stained dust.

"My blood is on them all," Lorn looks up at Drayl, mounted. "Not yours. Kill the others."

"Ser?"

"If we release them, they'll think we're weak. Also, they killed those captives as certainly as if they had held the blades—and some probably did. We're not killing captives. We're killing the people who did." Lorn takes the chestnut's reins back from Tashqyt. "Do you want me to kill each of them myself?"

Drayl looks down. "No, ser."

"Then do your duty." Lorn mounts, then turns the chestnut

and leaves the squad leader and the lancers who had been guarding captives. He ignores the scattered curses and yells of the captives as they die.

His guts are tight, but his movements are graceful. His head throbs, and he can feel the tiredness in his arms and legs. Tiny knives stab at his eyes, a reminder that he has apparently used chaos in fighting, although he does not specifically remember doing so.

"... say one thing ... doesn't ask ... what he won't do ..."

"... butcher ..."

"... they any better? ... saw those steads ... what they did here ..."

Lorn has no answers, for every answer he had before the battle was wrong, and so is every one after it. He can but hope, once more, that he has chosen the lesser of evils, and the one that will cost Cyad the least in the years to come. But he knows that the wars with the Jeranyi have come to Biehl, fueled by old hatreds and new Hamorian blades, and before long, no matter what he could have done, there will be more raids and more destruction, and more deaths.

Is he but a puppet of the times? One reacting to old hatreds? Or is his evil worse, because he has the freedom to act, and has chosen to annihilate an entire force of barbarians in hopes of preserving Cyadoran lives, when he has no way of truly knowing whether his actions will? And whether he can make the times different from what they would have been without him?

XXXVIII

LORN'S MIRROR LANCERS and the District Guards ride along the north bank of the River Behla, westward toward Ehyla. They had traveled so far south and west in pursuing the raiders that the dusty river-road is a far shorter return than retracing their tracks to the northeast and along the beaches would have been.

Lorn studies the muddy river, a good hundred cubits across, but still not much deeper than four or five cubits in most places, except for the occasional narrows where the depths may reach twenty cubits. The willows are taller, and more abundant, and a scattering of other trees mixes with them along the bank. There are now some woodlots along the north bank, although the land beyond the south bank remains flat grassland interspersed with ever more frequent fields.

As he passes particular landmarks, he adds them to his maps, lightly and carefully with a charcoal stick, although he doubts he will use them again. While losing threescore-and-ten is not unreasonable against eighteenscore, the losses are more than have been seen in Biehl in generations. Despite the Hamorian-forged blades packed on the spare and captured mounts, he has no doubts that the outcry will be equally loud, and provide ample reason for his swift replacement. For if he is believed—that there is a true Jeranyi danger—the Majer-Commander must dispatch a more senior officer—and if Lorn is not, then he will be relieved to face some form of discipline.

Behind him the lancers still murmur, as they have for the last two days, almost as if they cannot believe what has happened, and must keep talking about it.

"... still don't believe ... overcaptain ... must have slaughtered more 'n score himself ..."

"... did all right yerself ..."

"Just let 'em kill her, he did. Pretty little thing ..."

Lorn winces, but continues to watch the river.

"Got 'em all, didn't he?"

"... know ... but don't seem right ..."

"... let 'em loose, and they'd kill more ... couldn'ta caught 'em all. You know that."

"... you saw that hamlet ... want 'em doing that to yer folk?"

"... still don't seem right..."

After a battle such as the last, Lorn doubts anything is right. He glances to the northwest. After two days of riding from Nhais, they still have more than a day's ride to reach Ehyla, if not two. And then his newest set of problems will begin.

XXXIX

AS THE MIRROR Lancers and the District Guards form up outside the guard building in Ehyla, a light drizzle falls from the low gray clouds moving in off the Northern Ocean and over the River Behla. While the clouds are dark, and getting blacker, so far, the rain has not even wet the dust on the road. Lorn rides to where the guard squads have reined up, and halts the chestnut before the grizzled Wharalt.

"Ser?" The senior guard looks steadily at the overcaptain.

"You and your men did a good job—a very good job, and we could not have stopped the barbarians without you. Some of them—and you—may ask in the future whether what we did was necessary." Lorn's eyes hold Wharalt's. "I spent three years in the Grass Hills, and I would judge so. I am returning your command to Commander Repyl, but I will also tell him how valiantly you all behaved. Also, under the Emperor's Code, death golds are paid to the families of District Guards who die under the command of the Mirror Lancers. It is not enough, and they will be slow in coming, but they will come, and that is why I asked for their names. I would not deny them what they paid for with their lives. I would that you would watch for such and ensure that the families receive those golds."

"That I will, ser." Wharalt bows his head. "Ser... even I can see what must be done. None like it, but none will gainsay it. Many would have cost us more, I fear. You and your lancers took the brunt of the attacks. And that I be telling all, ser."

"Thank you." Lorn returns the bow, then guides the chestnut toward the building entrance.

Commander Repyl waits on the steps as Lorn dismounts and ties his mount to a brass ring.

Lorn walks forward and bows to the commander. "Commander Repyl, I am pleased to return your companies to your command. They have performed valiantly and well, and your training and organization are to be commended."

Repyl's mouth tightens as he takes in the more than a score of missing mounts and empty saddles. For a time, he does not speak. "I am certain you did your very best, Overcaptain, valiant lancer officer that you are, but since I was not there, would you care to explain the casualties, Overcaptain?"

Lorn nods. "I will. I will also send you a copy of the report I will be dispatching to the Majer-Commander." He clears his throat. "We were fortunate enough to intercept a barbarian raiding force. There were about twentyscore. They were well inside Cyad, almost to Nhais when we were able to catch them on the south bank of the river. They had already burned at least three hamlets, a halfscore steads and holdings. They killed all but a score of the people living there."

"Three hamlets?"

"You can ask your guards. Those hamlets and steads were the ones we saw. There may have been other smaller places. We forced them into a corner, and they refused to surrender. In fact, they demanded that we give them all safe passage back to Jerans—or they would kill all the hostages." Lorn shrugs. "After all that they had killed already, I could not accede to that."

"You let them kill hostages?"

"We did save a handful, and those we left with friends and families in Nhais."

"You gave battle, and how many escaped?"

"None that we know of. We counted more than eighteen-score dead. I had your two remaining squad leaders verify that. We also returned with all their blades."

Repyl swallows. "You slaughtered eighteenscore?"

"I wouldn't call it a slaughter. We lost three-and-a-half score, and the lancers lost nearly twice what the Guard did," Lorn says mildly. "Nor had we much choice when the barbarians were headed west to sack Nhais."

"I . . . see."

Lorn doubts that the District Commander really does, but nods just the same.

Repyl lowers his voice as his eyes fix on Lorn. "You *knew* before you left."

"I did not know," Lorn says evenly. "I thought it highly likely, but I could not prove it. If I told anyone, people might have acted unwisely. There has not been a raid here in generations, and there will not be another soon."

"Acting such is dangerous."

"Not to act would have been more so, Commander. And in not acting, the danger was far greater to the people of Cyador." Lorn's eyes are flat as he adds, "I expect I will be relieved. Sooner or later, but most possibly sooner."

Repyl frowns. "Did you think of such before you left?"

"I did. But, after seeing what I saw in the Grass Hills for three years, I could see no other choice."

"Truly . . . truly amazing. An honest and effective over-captain in Biehl. One who serves his land before himself." Repyl shakes his head slowly. "You are right, Overcaptain. You not likely to remain here."

"I would expect not." Lorn smiles. "I wish you well with my successor if it should come to that. And . . . you did a good job training them. I meant that. I will also report that I exercised my power, and that you were most cooperative, and that our success would not have been possible without your work."

"I would appreciate such."

For a moment, the two look at each other. Then Lorn bows. "Good day, Commander."

"Good day, Overcaptain."

Lorn turns and walks down the steps to remount the chestnut for the long ride back to the compound at Biehl and the longer wait for his replacement—or transfer—or disciplinary hearing, although he will be taking steps to ensure that a punitive discipline is unlikely, including scrolls to his brother, parents, and Ryalth, as well as copies of his battle report to the commanders at Assyadt, Syadtar, and Isahl, warning them of the stepped-up barbarian attacks, and the growing prevalence of Hamorian weapons that he has found. He may seek other means to ensure he is merely transferred to a dangerous command, rather than disciplined publicly—if he can think of such.

Perhaps even a report to the Hand of the Emperor, although he knows not if one so addressed will reach the shadowy figure.

XL

IN THE QUIET of the twilight, two days after returning to Biehl and after writing scores of letters to families, drafting and dispatching battle reports, and persuading Neabyl and Comyr to authenticate the numbers and sources of captured weapons, Lorn sits at the desk in his personal quarters, sipping a glass of Alafraan and studying the chaos-glass. He finds no other raiders along the trails and tracks, but there is yet another Hamorian ship in the harbor at Jera.

Will all his efforts and all the deaths just fuel more hatred and allow the traders to sell more blades in Jera? Will the Majer-Commander have to establish outposts east of Biehl, or near Nhais, to protect the town and Escadr and the cuprite mines?

Releasing a deep breath, he lets that image of the harbor at Jera fade, for there is little he could do now, even were he to find another group of raiders riding through the Grass Hills or toward Nhais. There are none, he knows . . . not yet.

After another sip of Alafraan, and with a smile, he uses the glass to take a brief look at a lady trader, who dines on the upper portico of his parents' dwelling—alone except for Jerial. The two are laughing, but the laughs die away, as he realizes they—both of them—sense the chaos-glass.

Abruptly, Jerial smiles, and murmurs something, and Ryalth touches her fingers to her lips.

Hundreds of kays away, Lorn smiles, then releases the image, wondering again at his consort's sensitivity to the glass. His eyes stare, unfocused, into the twilight, as the momentary warmth the image of Ryalth has given him fades, and he considers again the past eightdays.

Perhaps fivescore Cyadoran men, women, and children have died. Nearly eighteenscore Jeranyi warrior raiders died because Lorn acted, and more than threescore Mirror Lancers and District Guards.

Why? Lorn can offer reasons, but the reasons make little sense. The Jeranyi feel that lands they have not lived upon for more than ten generations—if not longer—belong to them, and they wish to kill all those who now live there. Lorn has killed those Jeranyi, for they died because of his planning and tactics, to try to stop them from killing even greater numbers of Cyadorans innocent of anything but living where their ancestors lived.

After having seen the people who live east of Biehl, Lorn suspects many are of pure Jeranyi blood, yet they are considered white demons as much as he is, for all the years they and their families have been there.

Will those deaths change anything? Anything at all?

Without an answer, he picks up the silver-covered book and pages through it, slowly, scanning the lines. His lips curl ruefully as his eyes light on one of the verses that suddenly makes a great deal more sense to him. He reads the words, softly, but aloud.

> I wish that
> in this twisted land
> there existed a prayer
> as solid as my disbelief,
> or failing that,
> as solid as my
> > uncertainty.

Is that the job of a lancer or a magus of Cyad—to create certainty in an uncertain world? In a world where reasons seem distant, and insubstantial? Was that the purpose laid out by the refugees from the Rational Stars for the City of Eternal Light?

Lorn slowly closes the book and looks out into the darkness.

XLI

WITH THE INDIRECT light passing through the antique panes of the ancient windows, the polished white-oak table desk reflects the faces of Rynst and Luss as they sit across from each other in a long and windowed room on the fifth and highest floor of the Mirror Lancer Court, the room that is the inner study of the Majer-Commander.

Rynst looks at Luss, then speaks. "You are telling me that this overcaptain took the District Guards and two companies of barely equipped and half-trained Mirror Lancers and rode out for an eightday—leaving the port unprotected—and ambushed and somehow killed most-all of some barbarian raiders no one has ever seen or heard of? And he claims that they were planning to sack the town of Nhais, and then the vintners' warehouses at Escadr and the cuprite mines at Dyeum? And that they were doing this with fresh-forged Hamorian blades? Is that what you are telling me, Captain-Commander?"

"Yes, ser. Overcaptain Lorn insists that the barbarians were planning such. There was no proof, of course, on which he could base his actions."

Rynst frowns, and his eyes harden.

Luss's eyes drop. "He does say that he has fifteenscore of their blades in the armory at Biehl."

"Fifteenscore?" Rynst nods. "He has them, then, for he would not dare assert such, were it not so. Does he present any proof of such?"

"He sent a confirmation sealed by both of the Emperor's Enumerators in Biehl," Luss admits. "Fourteenscore-and-eleven, exactly, and all but five with recent forge markings."

"You did not mention that, Luss. Most amazing, most amazing, and you almost had me believing that he had fabricated it all. What else did he say?" Rynst pauses, before adding, "Not that I will not read his report myself, after all this."

"He wrote that there were more than eighteenscore barbarians, and that he and his forces killed them all, at the cost of three-and-a-halfscore in lancers and guards, ser." Luss smiles blandly. "That there were no survivors seems . . . unusual." Luss adds. "He did attach statements from all the surviving squad leaders, verifying the numbers and that there were no survivors."

"Does he say why there were no survivors?"

"There is a brief statement that survivors were not in the interest of Cyad, since there were no outposts nearby to deal with any follow-up raids that might occur."

"So he and his men killed eighteenscore barbarians, and he killed any captives. These barbarians were within the boundaries of Cyador?"

"That is what the overcaptain says."

"And what says the Second Magus?" Rynst's eyebrows lift. "I am certain you consulted him, since he is related to the overcaptain, albeit rather indirectly."

"He says that the battle took place well west of the Grass Hills, on a river east of Nhais. Overcaptain Lorn rode the beaches, then followed them down the valley, and struck them from behind, we believe. His glass indicates none of the barbarians survived."

"So . . . the honorable Kharl is so worried about the overcaptain that he took time to follow him in his chaos-glass." Rynst folds his hands together, then leans back in his chair. "Overcaptain Lorn left no survivors, and in the middle of nowhere, with no maps, no Magi'i, he managed to find them and kill six for every man he lost? Would that we had more like him."

"He did it without authorization of any sort, ser, and then he sent copies of his battle report to Assyadt, Inividra, Pemedra, Isahl, and Syadtar. His cover letter to those commanders suggested that they be wary as well, since he had discovered large numbers of Hamorian-forged weapons, and that as the commander of the port detachment he had heard reports from numerous captains that weapons were being shipped to Jera."

Rynst winces. "He is clever. One could not discipline an officer who kills barbarians and discovers from whence come their weapons, not without many officers questioning us."

"No, ser. That is why I thought you should know."

"So that the full responsibility will be mine, no doubt."

"It is always, ser."

"Perhaps we should transfer Overcaptain Lorn to a duty station where he can use his skills doing what he does best." Rynst glances at Luss. "What think you, Captain-Commander?"

"The overcaptain is rather good at killing barbarians, ser."

"And Biehl has become a worthy station, has it not?"

"Yes, ser."

"Perhaps Majer Brevyl should enjoy it . . . *Sub-Majer* Lorn will report immediately, without furlough or leave, to Assyadt and will be assigned command of the companies at Inividra. Oh . . . make it clear that our new sub-majer is to personally command at least some of the patrols. It is what he does best. You may go and ensure this occurs as swiftly as possible."

"Yes, ser." Luss smiles and stands.

Watching Luss depart, Rynst smiles as well.

XLII

As HE SITS at the desk in the administration-building study, in an midafternoon far too hot for harvest, Lorn dips the pen in the ink and forces himself to write yet another line in the revised training schedule he is developing for the late fall and early winter—if he is still in Biehl and if he can recruit more lancers to replace the two squads he has lost in the battle against the Jeranyi raiders. Almost two eightdays have passed since Lorn and the lancers have returned to Biehl, and the early-fall weather remains warm, almost sultry.

"Ser!" Helkyt opens the study door without knocking.

"Yes?" Lorn looks up from the sheets of paper spread across his desk.

"This just came on the firewagon, ser." Helkyt extends a narrow package wrapped in green shimmercloth—a cubit long and roughly cylindrical. "Said it had to go to you, urgent-like."

"Thank you." Lorn stands and takes the cloth-wrapped package, then sets it on the desk. He makes no effort to open it.

Helkyt remains standing opposite the desk.

"I'll let you know," Lorn says softly, adding once more, "Thank you."

"Ah . . . yes, ser." Helkyt bows and slips out, closing the door quietly.

Once alone inside his officer's study, Lorn stands and looks at the package. Finally, he unwraps it. He looks at the set of two heavy scrolls with their green seals and ribbons, and then at the green felt pouch as if it contains a serpent or coiled chaos.

He opens the first scroll, heavily sealed and with ornate gilt lettering at the top and the shield and lance emblem of the Mirror Lancers. There are few words, and while they would bring satisfaction to many lancer officers, they chill him.

. . . hereby convey upon Lorn'alt of Cyad the rank of Sub-Majer in the Mirror Lancers of Cyador, and the role of protector and defender of the Land of Eternal Light, the Steps of Paradise . . . and all benefits and duties associated therewith . . ."

In short, he is a sub-majer, a good three to five years ahead of the normal promotion patterns. He sets aside the first scroll and breaks the green seal on the second. The second scroll is worse, and he has to read it twice because his eyes skip from line to line.

Sub-Majer Lorn'alt of Cyad, you are hereby assigned as commander, and officer in charge of the Mirror Lancer outpost at Inividra . . . The urgency of this commission is such that you are ordered to take the next available firewagon from Biehl. You are to report to Assyadt immediately, and to present yourself to Commander Ikynd . . . As outpost commander, you will also take immediate command of those patrols to your choosing and lead each company under your command on a significant number of patrols . . . No home leave or furlough period is allowable in connection with your travel and transfer to this assignment. Furlough and home leave will apply as if your new assignment were a continuation of your present assignment . . .

A third and smaller scroll is attached to his orders, and Lorn reads it in turn.

Your relief will be Majer Brevyl, who has been detached and should already be in transit by the time you leave. He has been briefed on the arms situation with Jera and has received a copy of all reports you have transmitted to the Majer-Commander. It is strongly recommended that you take actual command of a specific company . . .

There is a scrawled signature beneath the message: *Luss'alt, Captain-Commander.*

Lorn nods to himself, then laughs humorlessly. Finally, he opens the green pouch and takes out the triple bars, laying them on the training schedule papers. He removes the arched double bars from his uniform collar and replaces them with the sub-majer's insignia. Then, he stands and walks to the door, opening it and stepping out. Tashqyt and Swytyl turn. The two have been talking to Helkyt. The senior squad leader's eyes catch the new insignia instantly, as if he had suspected.

"Ser! Congratulations!"

"Congratulations, ser!" echo both junior squad leaders.

"Thank you. Thank you all." He pauses. "Times . . . they are changing, and things are going to change more at Biehl. I've been transferred, immediately, to be the new commanding officer at Inividra . . ."

Tashqyt and Swytyl exchange glances, and the sharp-featured Tashqyt frowns.

Helkyt nods slowly, as if regretfully. "They want you back to fight the barbarians."

"Your new commanding officer is a full majer—Majer Brevyl. I served under him at Isahl, several years ago. He was a good man, and one who rewarded accomplishment, and punished failure.

"I have to leave on the next firewagon, and that will be the day after tomorrow." After a moment, the sub-majer adds, "I would like you to form up the men, first thing in the morning, so that I can address them."

"Yes, ser," Helkyt says.

"I'll leave the draft training schedule for Majer Brevyl. I think all the other records and reports are current. For now, I'm going over to talk to Neabyl. He and the other enumerators should know."

The squad leaders nod, and Lorn steps back into his study to claim his garrison cap before heading to the stable. Word travels faster than does Lorn, for Chulhyr has the chestnut saddled and waiting when Lorn reaches the stable.

"Ser . . . here she be." Chulhyr's eyes do not meet the new sub-majer's as he hands Lorn the reins. "So much . . . you been doing for the compound and Biehl . . . almost seems like a shame that you be going, but I'd be guessing others need you more."

"Thank you, Chulhyr." Lorn offers a smile. "That's certainly what the Majer-Commander thinks. Your new commander is Majer Brevyl, and I learned much from him. He can be hard, but he is fair."

" 'Fair' . . . good words from you, ser."

Lorn nods again and leads the chestnut out into the courtyard. He mounts and rides slowly out through the gates and down the hill to the harbor—and the enumerators' building.

Neabyl is in, and the two walk back into the large room with the dais, where Lorn sits down on the short side of the long table.

Neabyl takes his own place before a stack of bills of lading and manifests. "A new promotion, I see."

"Promotion and transfer," Lorn says. "I'm being sent to command the outpost at Inividra."

Neabyl laughs ruefully. "You had to be successful. With all the barbarian attacks, it's not a surprise." He pauses. "Do you know who your successor is?"

"Majer Brevyl—a good officer. I think the Majer-Commander is going to have to establish more outposts, in places like Nhais, I'd guess. He's gotten my reports, and he's likely to be cautious, but it will happen."

The wiry Neabyl brushes a hand through his fine black hair, smoothing it back off his forehead, then fingers his chin. "You *know* things, Overcaptain . . . I mean, Sub-Majer. Others have to discover them." He smiles. "What do you know that will affect me?"

"I'm not certain." Lorn frowns. "There will be more Hamorian traders going to Jera, and more ships here. I'd guess there will be more Mirror Lancers and outposts to the east, closer to Jerans and the northern part of the Grass Hills. Some factors and growers may protest to my successor that I was unfair, but that will come to little with the majer."

"All that I surmise. And what will happen in Cyad that may affect me? Do you know?"

Lorn smiles. "I can but guess. Why do you ask? What do you know that I should know?"

"I do not know for sure, but I received a command to provide copies of all remaining records involving Flutak. This came from the Hand of the Emperor."

Lorn frowns again. The Hand of the Emperor—the one Imperial functionary never mentioned by name—a shadow figure who issues orders in the name of His Mightiness, and whose power is seldom exercised. Yet . . .

Lorn shakes his head.

"Exactly," replies Neabyl. "I have sent those records which remained—those approved and signed by Flutak, especially those involving olives and a few other items." The dark-haired enumerator pauses. "You know that Flutak was a cousin of Bluoyal'mer, the Emperor's Merchanter Advisor, did you not?"

"I might have heard that, but that was years ago, and I hadn't even thought about it. I should have," Lorn says. "I wonder why the Hand is interested."

"I do not know, but I do not think I would be in Bluoyal's boots in this season."

"Nor I." Lorn laughs gently. "Would you like to ride up to my quarters so that I could present you with a few bottles of Alafraan?"

"I could not . . ."

"I have no way to take more than two or three with me," Lorn points out, "and while I will leave a few for my successor, we have been through much together, and a few bottles are little enough thanks." He stands.

Neabyl grins. "Put that way, I would not wish to see good wine wasted."

The two leave the dais room, Lorn for the last time.

XLIII

LORN SITS AT the desk in his quarters as twilight begins to fade. Once he has thought out and written down his remarks to the men he will leave, Lorn turns his pen to write the scroll to Ryalth. Write most carefully he must, since he has few doubts it runs the risk of being read somewhere along the way, and since he cannot wait for a trader ship.

> My dearest,
>   You may recall that when I wrote you last, after I returned from dealing with the barbarian invaders of Cyad, I thought that the Mirror Lancers would need to

create more outposts near Biehl. It would seem that the Majer-Commander of Mirror Lancers also views matters in a similar way, for I have been promoted and, when you receive this, may well be at my new duty station at Inividra, where I am to take command of the outpost . . .

Matters are such that I am not being granted furlough or home leave at this time, but I have been assured that I will receive home leave as would have applied had I remained at Biehl. Furlough, I fear, is likely to be deferred.

You have offered so much in helping to rebuild Biehl, in so many ways, and while I know that Majer Brevyl will be grateful for what he will receive, I wish that you had been able to travel here and see what good your efforts have brought. I hope you recall when I saw you with Jerial at the evening meal, and will understand my desire to see such again.

Lorn pauses. He feels as though there is more that he needs to say, but his mind wanders, as he considers the implications of the command in his orders to personally lead patrols—and the implication from the Captain-Commander that he take command of a specific company. For what reason? Just until he is overmatched and killed? Or can he find a way to use his orders to strike at the base of the raiders as he had at Nhais, instead of driving them away, raid after raid, as he had at Isahl? He forces his thoughts back to the scroll.

I cannot say how much I miss you, and how I will regret not being there for you and our child . . .

The words come more slowly as the evening darkens into night, and as his eyes blur for all too many reasons.

Lorn'alt, Inividra
Sub-Majer,
Mirror Lancers

XLIV

LORN STEPS OUT of the firewagon's front compartment, glancing back at the six-wheeled and chaos-propelled vehicle. The shimmering canopy that covers the drivers reflects his image, if bulbously. With a wry smile, Lorn passes through the columned portico at Assyadt. While the connecting firewagon from Chulbyn runs but twice an eightday, Lorn was fortunate or unfortunate enough to have had to wait a single day at the changing station. There he had written letters to his parents, Myryan, and another to Ryalth.

Under an intense afternoon sun, a hot fall wind gusts around him as he reclaims his two bags and looks for a carriage or some form of transport to the headquarters compound. There are no carriages, and a single wagon where two men in brown are already loading crates from the firewagon's freight compartment. Three lancers, one holding the reins to a riderless mount, are waiting on the far side of the firewagon platform.

The junior squad leader glances at Lorn, then at the shimmering insignia on his collar. He looks away, then back again. "Ser? Would you be Sub-Majer Lorn'alt?"

"I am." Lorn nods.

"Commander Ikynd has requested that we offer you a mount, ser."

"Thank you." Lorn crosses the platform and straps his gear behind the saddle. He mounts easily.

As he rides with the three lancers along the granite-paved street, far dryer and dustier than those of Biehl, he looks around the town. Assyadt is a smaller version of Syadtar, the headquarters town for his first assignment at Isahl under Majer Brevyl. Like Syadtar, Assyadt has clean and square stone or white-plastered buildings, green shutters, and tile roofs. He sees none of the slate roofs so prevalent in Biehl.

The compound is less than a kay from the firewagon portico, and yet is on the north edge of the town. As in Syadtar, the gates are open, with little sign that they have ever been closed. The lancers halt outside the first building inside the walls. "This be the commander's headquarters, ser."

Lorn dismounts, and unfastens his bags. "Thank you."

"No problem, ser. Best of luck, ser."

As Lorn turns and walks up the steps and through the square stone arch, with his chaos-heightened hearing, Lorn catches a few whispered remarks.

". . . young for a sub-majer . . . really young . . ."

". . . doesn't look like a butcher . . ."

The new sub-majer keeps a pleasant smile on his lips as he carries his gear through the open double doors and into the foyer.

"Ser!" The squad leader behind the foyer desk is on his feet. "You must be Sub-Majer Lorn."

"I am," Lorn admits.

"Both Commander Ikynd and Majer Dettaur would like to see you. If you would let me tell the commander you are here . . . ? Oh . . . you can set your gear on the bench there. I'll be just a moment, ser."

Lorn has barely set his bags on the golden oak bench and straightened his uniform as best he can when the lanky senior squad leader is back.

"This way, ser."

Lorn follows the squad leader down the short corridor and to the door on the left, and into a study smaller than the one Lorn had as commander at Biehl.

Ikynd stands as Lorn enters. He is a squarish man, clean-shaven, with short-cut salt-and-pepper hair and unruly and bushy eyebrows. His black eyes survey Lorn for a long moment, until the squad leader closes the study door. Then he grins and shakes his head. "Sub-Majer. . . . a pleasure to meet the Butcher of Nhais."

Lorn offers a rueful smile. "Ser, I cannot say I had heard the term before."

"Sit down." Ikynd gestures to the chairs before his wide table desk. "I'm sure that you haven't. Majer Dettaur coined it. We'll talk about that later."

Lorn seats himself, keeping a faint and pleasant smile on his lips.

"First . . . congratulations. You did what most thinking lancer officers are trying to do on every angel-cursed patrol." Ikynd raises his bushy eyebrows. "How did you manage it?"

Lorn shrugs self-deprecatingly. "Luck, having the right information at the right time, good lancers, and good District Guards . . ."

Ikynd smiles broadly, genially, before speaking. "That's a good line for Cyad. It's horsedung here. You want to try again?"

Lorn studies the commander for a long moment. "I exploited the rules of the Emperor's Code, invoked the authority of the Majer-Commander, found some old maps and updated them, used surplus payroll to recruit and train additional lancers, and gambled that the information I had was correct. I slaughtered every last raider because I knew no one would be sending any patrols after me. It cost me half my command, a third of the guards, and the lives of fivescore Cyadorans. Is that what you wanted to hear, Commander?"

Ikynd nods. "Almost." The smile returns. "How did you know the barbarians were even there?"

"I wasn't totally sure," Lorn lies, "but I knew that the Hamorians were landing scores and scores of blades, and the trading captains had heard that the raiders were going to strike where they never had before. To me, that meant the area east of Biehl. I told everyone that I needed the maneuvers for training and to test the District Guards. If I hadn't found the raiders, that's all that would have been known—and I'd have been able to recommend a company's worth of lancers for transfer to the Grass Hills." Another shrug follows. "Once we left the north beaches, the smoke was an obvious sign to anyone who'd done patrols in the Grass Hills, and we just followed them until I could trap them."

"Ingenious—and dangerous," observes the commander. "You were a captain under Brevyl, weren't you?"

"Yes, ser."

"You don't have to say, but what was his opinion of you?"

Lorn's eyes are hard as he fixes them on the senior officer. "Ser, he said I was one of the best captains he ever had, that I got more out of my men with fewer losses than anyone, and that he'd never liked me and probably never would."

Ikynd laughs, a deep rolling chuckle. Then he shakes his head. "Old Grind 'Em and Gut 'Em . . . always making sure a compliment has a thorn in it."

Lorn waits.

"You've got both kinds of guts, Lorn. The kind that'll risk telling the truth when people don't want to hear it, and the kind to take on a job everyone looks the other way on. My orders for you are simple. Give you Inividra, and make sure you lead a company as often as any buck captain. Give you adequate support, but nothing special, and keep you here until you do something stupid enough to get killed." The commander's lips curl. "And my second-in-command, the most honorable Dettaur'alt, with all his connections in Cyad, is sitting on his most esteemed rump, ready to report to the Captain-Commander if I deviate from those orders. Even if I'd never met you, I think I'd respect you for the class of your enemies. My respect won't help you much, not with everyone looking over my shoulder."

Lorn nods. "I think I understand."

"Do you?"

"Not so much as you do, I think, but enough." Lorn pauses. "What are the limits of what I can do?"

"You're the outpost commander. So long as you kill lots of barbarians, and you kill more than four for every man you lose, I can replace your lancers seasonally. If you lose a lot, regardless of the barbarian kills, that will depend on the Majer-Commander, though, because we only hold about a company here in Assyadt in reserve for the unexpected. You drop below three kills for every lost lancer, and the Captain-Commander, through your friend Dettaur, will have you out for some trumped-up disciplinary action."

All of what Ikynd says is the truth, but Lorn can sense, almost without truth-reading the officer, that there is more, far more, left unsaid.

"How far can I take patrols?" Lorn asks warily.

"The patrol jurisdictions are on the maps—so far as the lands of Cyador go. Stay out of the other outposts' Cyadoran patrol lands. If you want to risk going into Jeranyi territory, I don't care—just so long as you bring back your men, and there aren't too many lancer bodies left behind. And there aren't any District Guards to conscript."

"What about firelances and recharges?"

"We're down to three, perhaps four recharges a season."

Lorn winces visibly.

"It's tight and getting tighter, Sub-Majer."

"Mounts?"

"Those shouldn't be a problem. Before he left yesterday, Sub-Majer Kysken reported that he had twoscore extra from captures."

"Officers and companies?"

"You have five companies at full strength. Two undercaptains, and three captains. You rate an overcaptain, but you won't get him, not for several seasons, at least."

"What sort of raids is the area taking?"

"The numbers aren't much different than before. Say two

raids every three eightdays in your territories. The difference is that the raiding parties are larger."

"More blades," Lorn suggests.

"Could be. Could be anything."

Lorn catches the off-balance feel of the response, but merely nods. "Is there anything else of special importance to you that I should know, ser?"

The genial smile reappears. "I don't like reading long and puffed-up reports. I liked your battle report. Keep them like that, and we'll be on the same step."

"Yes, ser."

Abruptly, Ikynd stands. "Not much more to say. Dettaur's study is across the corridor. Good luck."

Lorn stands and bows. "Thank you, ser."

As Ikynd watches with an amused smile, Lorn opens the door and departs.

He crosses the corridor and steps into Dettaur's immaculate and smaller study. The taller man smiles and stands, slowly, from behind his study desk. Several stacks of papers are set on the left side, although Dettaur does not seem to have been reading them.

"You look good, Lorn."

"So do you." Lorn smiles. "And you've made Majer."

"Last season." Dettaur motions to a chair and reseats himself. "You've met with the commander. What did you think?"

"He's very direct," Lorn observes as he sits down.

Dettaur nods. "He hides as much as he reveals, but he never lies. You present a real problem for him. He likes officers who kill barbarians—he was born in Syadtar—and you are obviously quite good at that." The majer smiles. "You have also created a certain unrest, shall we say, in Mirror Lancer headquarters."

"By killing Jeranyi who were murdering people all across the countryside?" Lorn raises his eyebrows.

"No. By using the powers of a senior lancer commander to clean up the dirty little bribery games of the Emperor's Enumerators, to conscript the District Guards, and to call attention to how badly the Mirror Lancers had run the port compound by managing to double its size and turn it back into a fighting unit without costing Cyador a single additional gold." Dettaur shakes his head slowly. "There is such a thing as being too effective, Lorn. I haven't forgotten the lesson you gave me when we were in school. I know it was you." A smile follows. "That is history, and we have a job to do here."

"We do. What do you suggest?"

Dettaur purses his lips as if thinking, although Lorn knows that Dettaur has his response prepared. "Be careful. You're going to be here a long time. The commander can't give you any more support than any other outpost, and Inividra takes the most raids of all. We've also been told to expect fewer firelance recharges—something about the Accursed Forest chaos-towers."

Lorn nods.

"You were right about the Hamorian blades. At least, I think you were, and that's why the Jeranyi raiding parties will get bigger. When they get enough blades, more will go eastward, and Syadtar's outposts will see bigger raids then, too."

"While we have fewer firelances," Lorn says.

"Exactly. That's being a lancer."

Except Dettaur won't be out leading patrols, Lorn reflects silently.

"And don't expect any brilliant tactics to get you out of here. It won't happen."

The sub-major senses both the partial lie and the other's unease with the statement, but only replies, dryly, "I've noticed that already."

"You would. You're here. I've never seen you make the same mistake twice."

"I try to avoid that."

"Good." Dettaur gestures vaguely toward the open window. "You can have the senior officer's visiting quarters tonight, and your pick of any mount in the stable that's free. In the morning, you'll take your own replacements out to Inividra. It's a good two-day ride to the northwest."

Lorn laughs. "Like all outposts."

Dettaur stands.

So does Lorn.

"There's one other thing, Lorn."

"Yes, ser?"

"Ah, you anticipated me. That's right. But best you also remember that what you do reflects on the commander and me. So if you do well, so do we." Dettaur smiles.

"Then I'll have to do well, ser." Lorn understands that all too well. If he fails, it will be his fault, and if he succeeds, Dettaur will claim credit. And with Dettaur writing the final reports, and all couriers going through Assyadt, Lorn has yet another problem.

"I'm sure you will, and good luck, if I don't see you later." Dettaur flashes a last false smile, yet one more sincere to Lorn than many.

Lorn walks out of Dettaur's study and through the foyer to reclaim his gear. He has a long ride to Inividra, and a great deal to consider in an extremely short time, contrary to what Dettaur has urged. It is most clear that, if he does not act quickly—somehow—he will end up being slowly constricted into an impossible situation. Yet if he acts too quickly, he will not have the support of his men and enough knowledge to succeed.

It is also obvious that the commander and the majer dislike each other, that both lie in different ways, and that they can be trusted only so far as their own self-interests will take them. Nothing has changed with Dettaur since he left Cyad to become a Mirror Lancer officer years before, except that he has become more adept in using others.

As Lorn lifts the bags, before asking for directions to his temporary quarters, he laughs.

The senior squad leader looks up. "Ser?"

"Just thinking, Squad Leader. Which way to the senior-officer visiting quarters?"

"Third building back. The second set of steps. They're unlocked and the key hangs behind the door, ser."

"Thank you." Still smiling, Lorn turns toward the outer double doors of the headquarters building.

XLV

LORN RIDES BESIDE Yusaet, the senior squad leader being dispatched to Inividra as a replacement squad leader for the Fifth Company there. Yusaet is fair-haired, almost boyish-appearing, except for gray eyes that are as cold as the iron of a barbarian blade. The noontime post-harvest sun beats down on them as they lead the column through the narrow swale that enters the valley holding the outpost.

". . . still another five kays," notes Yusaet.

"They mostly herders in the valley?"

"Sheep . . . some goats, some cattle, and some do nothing except offer their daughters for the amusement of the lancers."

Lorn winces. "That is not good."

"What can one do, ser? The duty is hard; the men are lonely; most have no consorts, and many will not live to have such. As for the peasants, and they are such, their daughters are also livestock, for many are no different from the Jeranyi. They look the same, and they act the same, save our peasants obey the Emperor's Code, even if we must enforce it with a firelance or a cupridium blade."

"Years ago, I was told that the raids near Inividra were the worst in the fall. Do you know if this remains so?"

Yusaet gestures over his shoulder, at the column of three-score replacement lancers, and the five wagons behind that carry recharged firelances and rations.

Lorn laughs. "There could be that many going to Pemedra."

"Nearly so many, but not quite, ser."

"It's getting worse."

"I would judge that be so."

For a time, both men are silent, and the sounds that fill the valley are the murmurs of lancers, the hiss and whisper of the hot wind across browning grasses, the muffled clopping of hoofs on the hard and dusty road, and the creaking of the wagons.

As they near the outpost at the northeastern end of the valley, Lorn studies it with care. The compound at Inividra could have been a duplicate of that at Isahl, except that it is set upon a broader hill, rather than enclosing one with its walls, and that the valley in which the compound is set is narrower, with more rugged and drier-looking hills to north and east.

The outpost is at the east end of the long valley. The outer sunstone walls are a good eight cubits high and enclose corrals and barns. The inner wall contains, as at Isahl, the armory and several long barracks—all built of stone and roofed in tile. There is also a raised water cistern and a spring, with protective walls running from the spring to the armory.

Lorn guides the big white gelding northward onto the short road to the compound gates. As at Isahl, four guards hold the gates—two standing outside and two above them on the low parapets. All four watch as Yusaet, Lorn, and the replacement lancers approach.

With a nod to the senior squad leader, Lorn eases the gelding forward toward the two fresh-faced lancers who stand by the open gates. "Sub-Majer Lorn, reporting to take command."

"Yes, ser." Both stiffen at his words and at the sight of the triple bars on his uniform collar. So do the pair on the low parapets.

Once inside both the outer wall and, a third of a kay farther north, the inner one, Lorn guides the gelding to the right, toward the square tower he feels he knows, even though he has never seen it. He dismounts a dozen cubits from the square-arched doorway and ties the gelding to the unused hitching post. He leaves his gear on his mount for the moment.

The single guard standing in a narrow patch of shade inclines his head. "Ser!"

"Sub-Majer Lorn, Lancer."

"Lancer Weit, ser."

"Who is the senior staff squad leader here?"

"That be Nesmyl, ser. Inside, ser."

"Thank you."

"Yes, ser."

Lorn steps into the tower and takes several steps along the dimmer inner corridor as his eyes adjust.

A senior squad leader appears from the back corridor. His eyes widen.

"You're Nesmyl? I'm Sub-Majer Lorn."

"Yes, ser." Nesmyl is slender, brown-haired and balding. His brown eyes survey Lorn rapidly. "How would you like to proceed, ser?"

"Let's see the study, and get my gear and put it someplace, and then I'd like to meet some people."

Nesmyl nods and turns. Lorn follows a half-dozen steps past the narrow table that is Nesmyl's duty station.

The study is not large for an officer who commands an outpost as large as Inividra, for the room is less than fifteen cubits by ten, and contains but a table desk, a single scroll case, the wooden armchair behind the desk, and four armless straight-backed wooden chairs that face the desk. High windows on the wall behind the desk offer the sole source of outside light, although two wall sconces contain unlit oil lamps.

Lorn shakes his head, remembering how Majer Brevyl had pointed out that the most dangerous outpost was "Inividra in the fall."

"You can see, ser. Everything is ready for you."

"First, I'd like to meet all the officers who aren't on patrol."

"Ah . . . none are, ser. They were ordered to stand by for you."

"There are five, then, three captains and two undercaptains?"

"Yes, ser."

The sub-majer nods. "Where are my quarters?"

"Up above here. There's a back stair."

"All right. I'll unload my gear, and leave it there, while you summon the officers."

"As you wish, ser." Nesmyl follows Lorn down the corridor and out into the hot harvesttime afternoon.

The senior squad leader walks across the courtyard toward the barracks building that holds the officers' quarters and the large officers' study.

Lorn unfastens his bags from behind the gelding's saddle, and then carries them back past the sentry, into the tower, and along the short back corridor to the rear staircase. He has to put one bag in front of him and one behind him to make his way up to the next level.

As Nesmyl had said, the commander's quarters are in the upper level of the square tower, above his official study. They are also far smaller than those at Biehl, comprising but a small kitchen with an eating area, an equally small study, and a bedchamber barely large enough for the double-width bed and a narrow armoire.

Lorn sets his bags at the foot of the bed, extracts his orders and the few documents and reports he has brought, and heads back down the steps to his study.

He has barely set his orders and papers on the table desk when the senior squad leader returns.

"They will all be here shortly, ser." Nesmyl bows.

"Good. Once they're all here, show them in, if you would."

"Yes, ser."

Lorn looks around the study. The built-in shelves are mostly empty, except for a worn copy of the Emperor's Code, the thin Mirror Lancer manual, and several other volumes he does not recognize, including one entitled *The Navigator*. He picks it up, leafs through the pages, and sets it aside. Then he opens the first footchest on the left. It contains patrol reports—those of the First Company. He smiles. There are six footchests lined against the back wall, and he can guess the contents of five. He moves to the one at the right end. It contains accounts of supplies, mounts, provisions, firelances. Lorn closes it. Those records he will need to study.

Thrap.

Lorn looks up at the gentle knock. "Yes?"

"The officers are here."

"Have them come in." Lorn stands behind his desk as the five file in. Then he waits for Nesmyl to depart and close the study door. He remains standing. "I'm Sub-Majer Lorn. If you would each introduce yourself so that I can put a name to a face, I'd appreciate it."

"Captain Emsahl . . ."

"Captain Cheryk . . ."

"Captain Esfayl . . ."

"Undercaptain Rhalyt . . ."

"Undercaptain Quytyl . . ."

Lorn looks over the five. Two of the three captains—Emsahl and Cheryk—are veterans, older than he is, clearly. Esfayl looks to be newly promoted to captain, while Rhalyt and Quytyl are recent undercaptains. In short—two competent senior captains, one captain that might have promise, and two undercaptains who need watching.

"I'm not the kind who keeps much hidden," Lorn says. "So . . . since I'm sure there are rumors about me, I'll fill in the details. I'm from Cyad. My first three-year tour was at Isahl, under Majer Brevyl. Then came a tour on the northeast ward-wall of the Accursed Forest. We had the dubious distinction of handling more creatures and tree-falls than all the other three companies combined over that period. After that, I was commander of the port detachment at Biehl, and in charge of rebuilding it from less than a company to more than two. We were the ones who discovered the first Jeranyi raiding party trying to go through that part of the Grass Hills. They had eighteenscore. We had two lancer companies and two District Guard companies. They lost all eighteenscore, we lost a company and a half." Lorn smiles. "When the Majer-Commander found out, from what we captured, that Hamorian blades were being traded into Jera, I was transferred here."

Lorn looks over the five. The gray-bearded Emsahl nods. Cheryk fingers his long and pointed chin. The curly-haired Esfayl tries to conceal a frown. The red-haired Rhalyt and the whip-thin Quytyl merely look wide-eyed.

"Captain Esfayl," Lorn says quietly. "You look concerned."

"Ah . . . no, ser."

Lorn can sense the lie. "Don't lie to me. I won't pull it out of you, not here, but I can tell when you are."

The pale gray eyes of the veteran Cheryk narrow, and Lorn meets them—and smiles before speaking. "We're likely to receive the brunt of the attacks from the barbarians, and I'll be changing patrol assignments. You'll probably find yourself riding fewer patrols, but on those you do ride, you'll find more barbarians." His smile broadens slightly. "And I'm sure you'd want to know that I will be directing patrols in person, not from the safe confines of Inividra."

"Ser . . ." ventures Emsahl, his voice slow and almost drawling. "Some had said that you'd be relieving a patrol commander or shuffling us around so that the five of us commanded four companies and you handled the fifth."

Lorn shakes his head. "I don't feel that's a good idea. You know your companies, or you should, and you will"—his eyes fix on Rhalyt and Quytyl—"and I'll need that experience and knowledge if we're all to come through the next year with as few casualties as possible."

The two older captains exchange puzzled looks.

"Don't believe all the rumors. The truth is that I was brought here to be a hands-on field commander. That part is true. But I'm not taking over anyone's company. That's bad policy and worse tactics.

"Now . . . I'd like to meet with each of you individually, one at a time, in order of seniority. You're the most senior, Emsahl?"

"Yes, ser."

"Then you have the honor. If the rest of you would stand by out in the front foyer . . . ?"

Once the four others have left and the door shuts, Lorn motions for the gray-bearded captain to sit, then takes the chair behind the desk. It creaks as he sits. He laughs, softly, then looks at Emsahl. "Do you have any questions you didn't want to raise in front of the others?"

Emsahl looks stolidly at the front of the desk, his eyes not quite meeting Lorn's. Lorn waits.

"Ser . . . what they call you . . . lancers don't like to think they're blade fodder." The captain looks down.

"A few officers have called me 'the Butcher of Nhais' or some such. Is that the name you heard?"

Emsahl nods.

Lorn offers a wintry smile. "You can check anywhere, from Majer Brevyl on . . . I lose fewer lancers than any other officer for the number of kills and battles. I've lost a few more than some companies, but many other companies, facing the numbers my forces have, lost more—a great deal more. I slaughtered all eighteenscore barbarians. They'd already killed fivescore men, women, and children, and you know what they did to the girls and women in the hamlets they sacked before we got them. I had them all killed because I couldn't keep my forces that far from Biehl and I wanted to make sure that it was awhile before they could send another raiding party." Lorn pauses, sees the unspoken next question, and answers. "I fight. I don't command from the rear. You'll see."

Emsahl nods slowly. "Hoped it was something like that. You're not a lancer born, ser?"

"No, and my consort—I have one—is a merchanter." Before Emsahl can pursue those lines, Lorn asks, "What do you think our biggest problem will be?"

"Not enough firelance charges . . . and too many raiders attacking each company."

Lorn nods. "We may start using two companies on each patrol."

"With you in charge?"

"Yes. If the barbarians are raiding in larger groups, then they can't be in as many places, either."

"You make that work, ser . . . lot of lancers be glad to see it."

"We'll make it work." Lorn pauses. "Anything else?"

"No, ser."

"If you have things you see . . . or suggestions, I listen. Remember that." Lorn stands. "If you'd have Cheryk come in . . ."

Emsahl smiles briefly. "Yes, ser."

Lorn goes through a similar process with each of the officers, and the comments of the others are little different from those of Emsahl. They have obviously been sharing concerns and worries while waiting for him. At the end of the afternoon, for the most part, his initial assessments of each have changed little. He hopes that is because of the accuracy of those assessments, but only time will verify or disprove his judgment.

XLVI

THE EMPEROR SITS on the less massive malachite and silver throne that graces the smaller audience chamber. Behind his right shoulder, in her chair, sits his consort. Before him stands Bluoyal'mer, the Emperor's Merchanter Advisor. Save for the guards, and a senior Imperial Enumerator in blue and green, with the gold slashes on his sleeves, who stands by one of the guards by the door, no others grace the chamber.

"You summoned me, Your Mightiness?" The Merchanter Advisor's voice is clear and firm, and a faint smile follows his words.

"I did." The Emperor Toziel leans forward in the malachite-and-silver throne. "Did you not affirm that you would support the Emperor's Code, Bluoyal'mer?"

"Yes, Your Mightiness." Bluoyal's eyes do not meet the Emperor's.

"It has come to my attention . . . and to the attention of the Hand, as well . . . There is a relative of yours, some sort of cousin. I believe his name is Flutak . . ."

"I am not certain I could recall all those who claim me as cousin, Your Mightiness."

"Perhaps not, but you should recall this cousin. The Emperor's Enumerators visited your trading house this morning, at the request of the Hand." Toziel nods, and the senior enumerator in official blue and green, steps forward and hands several sheets of paper to the Emperor. The Emperor takes them with a faint smile, then continues. "These sections of ledgers offer that your house has paid a number of golds to a representative in Biehl." The Emperor nods, this time toward the guard by the rear door, who opens it.

The First Magus steps through the doors to the audience chamber and walks forward, to stand several paces to the left of the Merchanter Advisor.

A thin sheen of perspiration is beginning to form on Bluoyal's forehead.

"I trust you will not mind the observation of the First Magus," suggests Toziel mildly.

"No, sire."

"According to your own enumerators, your house does not have a representative in Biehl. Yet the ledgers show a number of payments to such a representative. Do you deny such?"

Bluoyal's eyes flicker from the Emperor to the First Magus before he speaks. "There may have been such payments, sire, if the ledgers show such."

"Did you know about these payments?"

"Yes, sire." The voice of the Merchanter Advisor is resigned, flat.

"Were those payments made to this cousin of yours, this Flutak?"

"Yes, sire."

"Were they made for the purpose of obtaining lower tariffs on goods landed at Biehl?"

"They were made for his services, sire."

Toziel frowns, pausing. "Precisely what services did you require of the senior Emperor's Enumerator in Biehl?"

"His assistance in assuring that cargoes were handled quickly and well, sire." Bluoyal's voice remains calm.

"Are you suggesting that the tariffing is not handled quickly and well without such gratuities? Or that your cousin is corrupt enough that he must be paid by the Emperor's Merchanter Advisor to do his duty most properly?"

"All is sometimes not as it should be, sire."

"That is most certainly true. Especially in this case."

Toziel's eyes, ringed with black, focus on the merchanter. "Do you deny that you bribed a senior enumerator, even while you serve as the Emperor's Merchanter Advisor?"

"I did not ask for special treatment for the house, sire." Sweat has begun to darken the armpits of Bluoyal's tunic, and the shimmering haze on his forehead is more pronounced.

"Did you bribe him, yes or no?"

Bluoyal glances sideways at Chyenfel, who continues to watch the Merchanter Advisor. "Yes, sire . . . but without ill intention."

"At times, Bluoyal," Toziel says quietly, "intention does not matter. You are hereby dismissed as the Emperor's Merchanter Advisor. Your dismissal will be conveyed to the Traders' Council, and to all the clanless traders as well, along with the reasons for my action. I will request three candidates from the Council to consider for the next Emperor's Merchanter Advisor."

Bluoyal drops his head.

"You may go." Toziel's words are like ice.

Toziel waits until both Chyenfel and Bluoyal have left the chamber before rising. The Empress follows him back to her salon, where he sits, carefully and slowly, upon the white divan. For a time, he does not speak.

"You disliked replacing Bluoyal," Ryenyel finally says.

"I would that I had not been required to do such," he replies. "Not at this time."

"All the merchanter houses have such arrangements somewhere, my dear," offers Ryenyel.

"I know. . . . the larger ones, at least, and were I to act against all who do such, I would have no merchanters, or rebellion and chaos upon my hands." Toziel shrugs tiredly. "Yet . . . when it is spread all over the Palace of Eternal Light . . . and across Cyad, that my own merchanter advisor has corrupted the senior enumerator of a port . . . ?"

"You must act. And you did." Ryenyel smiles sadly. "I liked Bluoyal, but unless he flees quickly, he will perish in the dark. He has made enemies, and he has no protection now."

The Emperor lowers his head, and massages the tight muscles in his neck with his left hand. "Who will they send me as candidates?"

"Vyanat'mer, Veljan'mer, and either Tasjan'mer, or more probably, one of the lesser clan heads, perhaps Kernys'mer or another."

"The lady trader?"

Ryenyel shakes her head. "Ryalor House is far too recent, too small, and too untested. And the traders would not advance a woman."

"If those be the candidates ..." Toziel shakes his head. "Vyanat'mer is the one I must choose."

"That is why those will be the candidates," prophesies the Empress. "After this and all the scheming, none of the merchanters will trust Bluoyal's clan, especially if Denys'mer is his successor. Few outside the merchanters will trust Tasjan and the Dyjani, not with the greenshirts Sasyk trains. The Jekseng and Kysan are too weak ..."

"Vyanat's house will also act with more care."

"One trusts so. For a time."

Toziel nods slowly. "Is it not always so?"

The Empress smiles sadly.

XLVII

THIRD COMPANY, WITH Emsahl and Lorn riding in the van, makes its way through a warm drizzle more like summer than of fall, and along a narrow track that turns northwest as it rises out of a wide flat valley. A good two kays behind the column, and behind the last riders of Quytyl's Fifth Company, lie the berms and barns of another small hamlet, and scattered fields already harvested.

The scouts ride a good three kays ahead, over the crest of the low pass between hills.

"Do you think we'll see barbarians?" asks Emsahl. "With a force this large?"

"We'll see them," replies Lorn. "They're less and less afraid of Mirror Lancers. That could be because they're getting more and better blades from Hamor."

Lorn is careful not to comment directly on what he knows, although he has studied the chaos-glass, in his private quarters, and has found two raiding parties in the Grass Hills. One was angling more toward the territories protecting Pemedra, the other clearly headed for a hamlet to the northwest of Inividra—one with lower berms—and more cattle—and farther from the normal raiding patterns. And that is the one toward which he and the two companies ride.

"You brought back such blades, it is said."

"Over fourteenscore. I left them in the armory at Biehl, but I had the Emperor's Enumerator there attest to their numbers. Most had Hamorian forge marks. A few were Brystan."

"You have reduced the number of patrols in each eight-day," Emsahl probes gently.

"I think you'll find that we will be just as effective with the newer patrol patterns and larger forces." While Lorn is using the chaos-glass to target his patrols, he dares not explain, but one advantage of being commander is that he does not have to explain—except to Ikynd and Dettaur—and neither can ask that often or that directly unless they come to Inividra, and Lorn suspects that will be highly unlikely in the near future.

"That is true," observes Emsahl, lapsing into silence.

Lorn blots the damp rain from his forehead and readjusts his garrison cap. Tomorrow—and the barbarians—will come soon enough.

XLVIII

AHEAD OF THE column of lancers is a long, low rise that leads to the next of the endless valleys in the southwestern reaches of the Grass Hills. The drizzle of the previous day has been replaced with a clear green-blue sky and a chill breeze out of the north that reflects the season. Lorn touches the fully charged firelance in the holder before his right knee, just to ensure it remains charged for the task ahead. They should be nearing the raider force, but the scouts have not seen anything yet.

As he straightens, he looks to his left at Captain Emsahl. "How have you been facing the barbarians?" Lorn asks. "How wide a front?"

"Four-abreast."

"Staggered or in columns?"

"Usually in columns."

"When it's right, we'll try a staggered approach that's five-abreast, and I'd like each lancer in the second and fourth lines with his mount's nose almost to the rump of the lancers in the first and third lines. I want them to use the shortest firelance bursts they can. If they don't hit a raider, then they need to aim again."

Emsahl frowns.

"I know . . . they're used to swinging the lance . . . but if they swing lances now, they won't have any chaos left in their lances by the end of this patrol." Lorn smiles ruefully. "And they'll say that they'll be dead so that it won't matter."

Emsahl laughs, the ironic sound of one veteran to another.

"Tell them to try it on the first burst," Lorn suggests. "Then they can swing the lance, but try to do it in bursts."

"That . . . that they might try . . . especially if I tell them that anyone who exhausts his lance before the battle is over will be in the first rank for the rest of the season."

Both officers look up as a scout rides up from the trail on the right side of the column, then turns his mount toward them.

Lorn keeps riding as the messenger guides his mount around and up beside the sub-majer.

"You were right, ser. Barbarians . . . they be entering the valley ahead. Eightscore, mayhap nine-," says the scout. "They carry the large blades in their shoulder harnesses, and blades like sabres at their waist."

Eightscore—and Lorn has tenscore Mirror Lancers in all of Inividra. He smiles. "How are they riding. What sort of column?"

"Two-abreast, ser. Must run back near-on a quarter-kay. They be riding slow-like, real steady."

Lorn nods to the lancer scout. "Fall in behind us for a bit."

"Yes, ser."

"Let's try something." Lorn smiles grimly at Emsahl. "They don't know we're sending out two companies to-gether yet."

"No, ser."

"Quytyl and I will lead Fifth Company over the ridge— the way the scout came. There's a woods along the other side. . . . scrub oaks, but enough for cover . . ."

Emsahl frowns. "There be that, as I recall, but . . ."

"I have good maps," Lorn says quickly. "We'll sweep out of the oaks as they come by and hit them on the run with the firelances. Then we'll come charging back along the road. You have Third Company lined up on the upper slope right about there . . ." Lorn gestures toward the right side of the slope ahead. "First, people forget to look up, and even if they do, they have to come uphill."

Emsahl nods. "That might work."

"If they have scouts, you'll have to make sure they don't escape to warn them." Lorn shrugs. "And if the ones we attack don't follow, we don't lose anyone because we'll only come close enough to be in lance range. We're bound to kill or wound some of them. If they do follow, your men will be steady enough to get more, and the hill will allow you to charge down if you have to."

That gets a second nod from the veteran. "Might get 'em mad enough to ride hard."

"Let's hope so. You set up your men, and I'll take care of Fifth Company."

"Yes, ser."

Lorn rides back along the column to Quytyl. Several lancers watch carefully as he passes.

". . . got that look. . . . barbarians somewhere near . . ."

". . . hope he's as good as they say . . ."

Quytyl looks up from talking with his senior squad leader, Yusaet, as the undercaptain sees Lorn approach.

"Ser." The undercaptain bows his head.

Yusaet starts to rein back his mount.

Lorn gestures for him to remain. "I need both of you and your other squad leader, Undercaptain. There's a column of barbarians entering the next valley. We're going to attack and set up an ambush. Call in your squad leaders."

"I'll get Syldn," Yusaet offers, and eases his mount away.

"Halt the company. We won't be taking the road much farther anyway."

"Fifth Company! Halt! Column halt!" Quytyl raises his arm.

As the lancers rein up, the painfully-thin undercaptain again turns to Lorn and asks, "How many?"

"Eightscore, maybe nine-."

"Yes, ser." Despite his affirmation, the undercaptain's eyes carry much doubt.

"Don't worry, Quytyl. That's my task. Yours is to get your company where it kills barbarians."

Yusaet returns with Syldn, the junior squad leader, and Lorn motions them into a mounted semicircle facing him on the road, and begins to explain once more, ending with, ". . . we don't want anyone to slow down or use a sabre. Use quick bursts on the lances, and then ride like the black angels were chasing you . . . just over the hill. Then we'll reform five-abreast blocking the road."

"Will we have time, ser?" questions Yusaet.

"We'll have time, because Third Company will be on the hillside, waiting for the raiders after we ride by." Or so Lorn hopes.

He motions to the trail that winds up the slope and turns the bay gelding toward it.

"Follow the majer!" Quytyl orders.

"Up the trail, after the officers!"

As Lorn leads the Fifth Company, he cannot help but wonder if he will ever survive to be a full majer, but he pushes the thought away, glancing back to his left to watch as Emsahl moves his lancers along the road to set up the ambush.

The gelding steps sideways, jolting Lorn, and he is forced to concentrate on the goat path that he has chosen. While he *thinks* they are headed where his maps show they can mount a flying attack, screeing from a distance and riding over rough hillsides are not the same thing. Not at all.

The company winds its way up along the trail taken by the scout, and Lorn worries about the slow progress through the creosote bushes. When they near the ridgeline, and the first scattered scrub oaks, he listens, and tries to use his chaos-senses to detect any thing before them, but the ridge area remains quiet.

The scrub oaks—some of their leaves red and ready to drop, the rest showing signs of winter-gray—cover the top of the ridge, beginning near the top of the goat path that the lancers follow. Once they are on the side, Lorn leads the company along the ridgeline until he finds the streambed he has seen in the glass, and they follow that dry stream downhill another kay.

The scrub oaks are thinning, and the road is in sight—no

more than half a kay away across the browning grass—but not the raiders. Despite a trip that has seemed interminably long to Lorn, Fifth Company appears to have reached the end of the valley before the raiders.

Lorn holds up his arm and reins up where they remain slightly higher than the narrow trail that is perhaps a half a kay downhill. The lancers are shielded by the scrub oaks, so much so that only the portion of the road leading south and to Lorn's left is visible. Slowly, the lancers halt.

The sub-major turns to Quytyl. "Have them re-form two-abreast. We'll wait until the barbarians have ridden just past us." He pauses, then adds, "And tell the men to be quiet."

Quytyl eases his mount back and offers orders in a low voice. Shortly, he returns, reining up beside Lorn. Slowly, the murmurs die away, and the only sounds are those of the breeze ruffling drying leaves on the oaks and whispering through the knee-high grass around the low trees. An occasional *whuff*ing comes from one mount or another.

The breeze picks up, and then dies away, and still the lancers wait.

Then there is the faintest of sounds, and Lorn watches as two scouts—or what pass for such—ride past the scrub oaks, continuing southwest without looking back, and starting up the slope toward the low pass beyond which are stationed Emsahl and his Third Company.

The lancers wait once more, until the muffled sound of hoofs and voices rises over the sounds of the light wind, and the few insect and bird calls.

As Lorn's scout had said, the barbarians ride two-abreast, and their voices are loud in the midday air.

Quytyl touches Lorn's arm.

Lorn shakes his head and murmurs, "Not quite yet." He wants the barbarians far enough ahead so that his lancers can rake the column with firelances, but not so far that they run the risk of being cut off.

Then he raises his arm, and drops it, hissing, "Now!"

As he has instructed, and not totally expected, the lancers begin to ride past the scrub oaks, and down the slope, picking up speed. He hears a horse scream, and fears he has already lost a man, but even so, the barbarians do not turn, not until Lorn is within two hundred cubits, and the surprise stretched across their bearded faces holds for yet another fifty cubits.

Lorn aims the firelance, not with sight, but with chaos.

Hsssst! Hst! Hsst! Two of the three bursts strike raiders, and one tumbles from his saddle immediately.

Lorn tries again. *Hsst! Hst!*

Because he has to turn the gelding to stay on the road, and to avoid the rougher ground on the far side, he is not certain about the results, as his mount carries him past the head of the column. Behind him, he can hear other firelance bursts, and he risks a quick glance over his shoulder once he has the gelding running on the road.

So far as he can see, most all his men are still riding, and the barbarians are riding after them, if not so quickly as Lorn would like.

"Keep them moving!" he snaps at Quytyl.

"Keep moving!"

With the dust rising everywhere and the hissing snaps of firelances dying away, Lorn has no idea how successful his hit-and-run attack has been, beyond the three or four raiders he knows he personally wounded or killed. He glances back over his shoulder once more, then slows the gelding as it is clear, despite the settling dust, that there is a growing separation between the barbarians and the lancers.

Rather than stop just beyond the rise in the road, as he had planned, Lorn does not rein up until he is several hundred cubits beyond, nearly a third of a kay.

"Re-form on me! Re-form—five-abreast."

"Re-form on the majer!" Quytyl's voice joins Lorn's.

With the jostling and confusion, Lorn fears that the five-abreast rank will not be in place when the barbarians arrive.

Again, Lorn's worries are unfounded, for the lancers are formed, and even the mounts' breathing has settled down before he sees even the dust on the road from the approaching riders.

The barbarians do reach the crest of the hill.

"Discharge at will!" commands Emsahl, his voice drifting to Lorn on the light breeze. "Discharge at will."

Firelance bolts *hsst* from the right, down into the blade-wielding warriors, but the raiders have re-formed into a wall across and beside the road more like eight-abreast—and that will clearly reduce the impact of the Third Company's firelance crossfire.

"Charge!" Lorn raises his firelance, then lowers it, urging the big white gelding forward. He forces himself to wait on discharging his own firelance until he is within fifty cubits of the raiders, some of whom have turned eastward and are starting to charge uphill.

Hsst! Hssst!

Then Lorn is far too close to use the lance, and he struggles with the sabre even as he uses the lance more like a shield—a most unwieldy one.

In time, he finds that he has surged through the barbarians, somehow, and he wheels the gelding, then stops. Several raiders, their backs to him, are surging toward a lone lancer, whose lance has been wrenched free.

Lorn lifts his own firelance. *Hsst! Hsst! Hsst!*

Barely has he released the third bolt when a pair of raiders with their barlike blades are riding down on him.

Hhstt! Without thinking, Lorn throws a Magi'i firebolt at the first, and swings up his Brystan sabre to parry/slide the big blade of the other away.

Dust, blades on blades, and scattered firelance bolts fill the afternoon, and Lorn circles the field, picking off raider after raider, trying to avoid getting involved in direct group melees.

At some point, there are no more raiders—except for a

score or more who have scattered and ride downhill and northward, back toward Jerans.

Lorn sits on the gelding. He has been cut somewhere on his scalp—blood runs down his cheek. His arms ache, and there is blood splattered everywhere on his uniform. He looks dumbly around.

"Fifth Company, first squad! Re-form on me!" Yusaet's voice rings through the slowly settling dust, as, following his example, do the voices of other squad leaders.

Lorn's head throbs, and the knives that have become too familiar stab through his eyes, so that they water and burn. He stiffens in the saddle as he makes out the blurry figure of a bearded officer riding slowly toward him.

"You all right, Majer?" asks Emsahl.

"Right as anyone after . . . something like this."

Another officer rides slowly toward them. Quytyl has his left arm strapped to him, and his face is white.

"How are you?" Lorn asks.

"Arm's broken . . . I'd guess. Fine . . . other than that." The undercaptain forces a smile. "Bastard broke my lance and arm. He forgot I had a sabre."

"How did we do?" Lorn asks Emsahl.

"We didn't lose many—maybe not even a halfscore. Fifth Company lost more."

Lorn looks to Quytyl. "Three-quarter score, last count, ser. Another halfscore wounded, but most'll ride again."

"Need to see to things." Emsahl nods to Lorn and turns his mount.

So does Quytyl.

Lorn rides slowly to the crest of the hill, looking northward, but the barbarians are halfway through the valley, well past the scrub oaks from which Lorn had attacked.

By late afternoon, the column rides slowly southeast, back toward Inividra. Lorn hears a few voices, but they pass over and around him.

". . . mean bastard . . . the majer . . . saw him kill halfscore anyway—behind, front . . ."

". . . didn't even stop when they came different . . ."

". . . never seen an officer . . . killer like that . . ."

Lorn holds in a sigh. The killer, the butcher . . . is that all he is good for?

"Ser?" asks Emsahl, riding to his left.

"Yes." Lorn's voice is hoarse and tired.

"They didn't come like you thought."

"No. Things never work quite the way you think. Someone has been thinking about firelances," Lorn admits. "That's why we had to come back and charge. I'd thought we could hold a line, but it wouldn't have worked."

"You did it so fast."

"We had to," Lorn points out.

"Most wouldn't have acted so quick." Emsahl pauses. "That why the commander wants you on the patrols?"

"It's one reason, I'd like to think, but he didn't tell me."

"We killed almost eightscore, ser, and I had the company gather the blades they could. Some Brystan sabres there, and a bunch of the big ones from Hamor, like you said."

"I was afraid of that," Lorn replies.

"Put them on the captured mounts," Emsahl continues. "We got another twoscore of those." He laughs. "Peasants are going to find some plow and cart horses."

"They'll never know how costly those beasts are. They probably won't care, either." Lorn laughs, once.

Emsahl is silent as they ride southward, back toward Inividra.

Lorn still wonders. A score of the barbarians did escape, despite his efforts, and his forces still lost almost a score themselves—one a casualty of a rodent hole on the first charge from behind the scrub oaks. His comparative success may mean larger and larger forces on both sides. The glass will tell—the glass he cannot reveal—but he can only hope that it will take time before the barbarians react that way.

He will also need to figure a counter to their new use of the broad front—one that will cost him even fewer lancers.

The weary sub-majer takes a deep breath.

XLIX

LORN SITS AT the head of the single table in the officers' dining area. Emsahl is on his right, Cheryk on his left, then Esfayl beside Emsahl, and the two undercaptains at the end across from each other. Quytyl's arm remains in a splint, but he can move his hand, if gingerly.

The sub-majer looks at the large casserole dish, from which emanates the odor of very strong and very heavily seasoned mutton emburhka. He raises his eyebrows and takes a ladleful, easing it onto the battered brown platter before him, then leaves the ladle in the dish for Emsahl, and breaks off a large chunk of warm and crusty bread.

A cold rain outside pelts on the tile roof, and a thin line of water wends its way down one wall near the corner of the room.

Lorn waits for Quytyl to serve himself before starting to eat.

The six officers eat silently for several moments.

"Ser?" asks Cheryk. "Do you have any idea what the patrol schedule will be like next eightday?"

"Not for sure. I'll have it ready in the next day or so. I was hoping for some dispatches on what's happened at Pemedra and the other outposts." Lorn smiles wryly. "If there's a large raider group there, we're less likely to get one. They all fit together."

"Ser . . . it seems strange, but we haven't missed a single raider party," Esfayl says between bites. "Last eightday, we didn't get to that valley until they were already there . . . but they didn't get away, either. And we're not riding as many patrols."

Emsahl and Cheryk both nod their agreement.

"I think that's because the raiders have more weapons, and they're riding in bigger groups. They have to raid larger hamlets, or there's not enough loot for them. That makes it easier to figure where they'll go." Lorn laughs. "If they go back to smaller groups, then I'm not sure how we'll do."

"They'll have to, won't they?" asks the curly-haired junior captain. "When we can use two companies, they lose a lot more."

"I'd think so," Lorn says, "but I'm not going to tell them that. This way is easier on us."

"I heard that we might get another company," ventures Cheryk.

Lorn nods and swallows the tough mutton in the emburhka. "That's very likely. The Magi'i have some project with the Accursed Forest, and they say that, if it works, they won't need as many Mirror Lancers." He frowns. "But we'll need them, especially if they keep cutting back on firelance recharges." His eyes go to Emsahl. "How is the training on shorter bursts with the lances going?"

"They're getting it." Emsahl offers a slow, sardonic smile. "Some of them finally figured out that if they have more chaos charges left, they don't have to spend as much time using a sabre against one of those iron bars."

"Even when they don't hit square, those big blades hurt," affirms Quytyl, glancing down at his arm.

"You can't block them. You have to parry or slide," points out Esfayl. "The newer blades the raiders are carrying hold an edge longer, too."

"Why can't the fireships do something about those traders, ser?" asks Rhalyt. "It doesn't seem right that we let them sail right past our ports and ship those blades to the Jeranyi."

"The fireships don't know which ships are carrying blades, and they can't stop all the traders," Lorn says. "So long as the Jeranyi will pay golds for blades, and there's a place to land them, some trader from somewhere is going to do it. We don't have enough fireships to cover our own ports, let alone the Eastern and Western Oceans."

"Still seems wrong . . ."

Lorn nods, and lets the other officers carry the conversation.

After the meal, Lorn walks back through the rain that is beginning to dwindle into splatters on the stone pavement, and then slowly up the narrow steps from the corridor behind the first level study.

He has been at Inividra five eightdays, and he has made patrols with all the companies. One of the patrols was without incident; the other five encountered barbarians, although one raider group was less than a score—perhaps scouting—and turned back north well before Lorn's forces could pursue.

Once he is in his small quarters' study, Lorn extracts the screeing glass, knowing that trying to use it in the rain will tire him more and leave him with a headache, but he wishes to see another scene, one not of valleys, and roads, and rivers, and barbarians, but one of more immediate need.

Looking at the glass, Lorn concentrates, ignoring the immediate headache as the silver mists form and then swirl aside.

Ryalth is propped in a large and ornate bed, an infant at her breast. She glances around, then her eyes narrow. Abruptly, she smiles and briefly lifts the fingers of her left hand to her lips.

Lorn smiles, then, after another long look, releases the image. He frowns, for although Ryalth looks healthy, Lorn recognizes neither the bed nor the room, and yet she has not written him about moving quarters. Then, perhaps because she senses when he can see her and knows that others may well read what she writes, she may have chosen not to convey such information.

As for Lorn, he must spare chaos-energy for more screeing of lands and barbarians—while it is yet light in the late
afternoon and early evening, and in the morning, before he
goes down for the day—and for maps, and all that he can to
kill barbarians while losing as few lancers as possible.

After a time, he puts the glass away, then descends the
stairs once more, and crosses the rain-slicked stones of the
courtyard. Above him the clouds are beginning to part and to
show stars.

He walks along the corridor and then into the officers'
study, noting that the only officer there is Rhalyt and that he
has a bottle of Byrdyn set beside the mug at his elbow. As
Rhalyt sees Lorn, he slips something under his patrol report
and stands.

Lorn smiles, recalling that he had often done the same. He
walks toward the red-haired undercaptain.

"Ser."

"Undercaptain . . . if you want to hide something, don't
call attention to it by moving it as soon as a senior officer
appears."

Rhalyt flushes.

"I used to hide scrolls I was writing to my consort that
way," Lorn continues. "That was before we were consorted."
He smiles. "So long as you get your reports done, you can
write whoever you wish . . . and don't be afraid or ashamed
of it."

"Yes, ser."

"You have a couple of lancers who are spraying their
lances all over the place. Have your squad leaders talk to
them. And talk to Emsahl about the training he's doing. You
need to follow his example once he has it worked out. We
may need that chaos-energy later this season."

"Yes, ser." Rhalyt nods.

Lorn half-turns, then adds, "And don't let me stop you
from writing scrolls. They're important, too." He smiles to

himself as he leaves the study, and walks toward the north lancer barracks.

There, he has not taken one step inside before someone calls, "Majer in the barracks!"

Lorn shakes his head, and walks the north wing, then the south, saying little, just looking, before leaving. He finds nothing he should not, and has not since his second informal inspection. While he does not wish to intrude or interfere too much, he also knows that his presence shows he wants to maintain order and discipline, and that he cares.

He walks slowly back to the study, and the maps, except he pushes them aside as he seats himself at the narrow desk. Instead, he pulls out and rereads Ryalth's last scroll.

My dearest lancer,

We are well, as I know you know, but still must I write you such. Your son Kerial is healthy and strong, and I believe he looks more like you, with his brown hair and amber eyes. . . .

I do not know that you would have heard, but the Emperor now has a new Merchanter Advisor. That is Vyanat'mer, of the Hyshrah Clan, a house nearly as strong as the Dyjani. Veljan was also considered. Bluoyal was dismissed because he had been discovered paying bribes to a senior enumerator in the port of Biehl. As you know, the enumerator has vanished, but not the record of the payments. Bluoyal has also vanished, but none can say whether by flight or by his many enemies. When one falls from power, enemies multiply . . .

Ryalor House has had some profitable commerce with the Hyshrah traders, and have found them to be most careful folk, and I trust that Vyanat'mer will prove like them. . . .

We had once talked about iron trade, but Ryalor

House has never engaged in such, although I have heard of those who have, particularly in northern ports, but after your adventures, it is most certain that we will not follow that course, even were it profitable. As poor Bluoyal has discovered, there are always records somewhere, for a trader cannot determine whether he profits or fails without such.

Lorn frowns for a moment, then smiles at Ryalth's observations and indirect advice. There are always records—somewhere. He finishes the scroll, and then takes out paper and his own pen.

Dearest,
    As well you know, patience is scarcely my greatest virtue, yet all I do in these days requires such, for the barbarians seem endless at times, and, as in all new situations, there is much I must learn . . .
    Winter is coming, with the cold rains, and chill winds, and with it, I would hope, fewer attacks by the barbarians, and more time to plan and consider how to deal with these changing times, times that change even as most turn their eyes from the change . . .
    From what I can calculate and have seen, in your words, as well, you and Kerial must be doing well. I cannot tell you how much I miss not being with you in these times . . . but I am glad that Jerial and Myryan were there to help you, and while I have also written them to express my deep gratitude, would you also again convey it for me?
    Would that I could be there in person, but you know you are always in my mind and thoughts.

He rereads his scroll once more, then rolls it and seals it, heating the wax with a touch of chaos.

Then he takes out the silver volume and pages through it, settling on the verse he selects for reasons he cannot articulate.

I look to the hills whence cometh no aid;
my god is not divine, for he is made—
made of man, made of fire, filled with salt.
His eyes are a single star long since set.
He does not praise the lame and halt.
He judges not, nor yet does he forget.

Is there such? A great being presiding over the Steps of Paradise? The ancient writer certainly had doubts about such—and more than a slight suggestion that mankind makes its own gods and images to worship.

When he sets aside the volume and finally slips into his cool bed, he does not sleep well.

L

THE EMPEROR AND his Consort-Empress sit upon the white divan in the Empress's salon. A cool fall wind sifts into the salon through a window open but a finger-width. Toziel massages his forehead with his left hand, then drops it and turns to Ryenyel. "The days are long . . . yet you have something upon your mind."

"Do you recall Ryalor House, my dear?" asks Ryenyel.

"Is not that the one headed by the mistress of Kien'elth's eldest son?"

"Not precisely. That is, she is not his mistress. You sent an inquiry through your Merchanter Advisor."

"Vyanat'mer? Why would . . . ?" Toziel smiles. "I did not. You did. Perhaps I should hear before I speak. What did Vyanat's merchanter find—and where?"

"In the small town of Jakaafra . . . in the recording book of consortships."

"The lancer took her as his consort, you're telling me?"

"Quietly . . . but he did, and not even his family knew in advance, from what we can tell."

"Good for him."

"Wise, as well."

Toziel blots his forehead. "Angels . . . I'm tired . . . I just talk to people, and I'm tired."

"I know."

He smiles sadly. "Of course you do. How much longer?"

She shrugs.

"A year? Two? Three? Not more than that, I would wager. Is that why you mentioned Ryalor House? They're young."

"Not any younger than we were, those long years back. They have just had a child, a son."

"Is he . . . ?"

"Who would know? But both parents are most intelligent, as are the grandparents, and seldom does such a union produce a dullard. And it may be that there is magus blood on both sides."

"How would you know that?" Toziel raises his eyebrows.

"Her mother's mother's mother . . . let us just say that she was not unfamiliar with the Palace of Light . . . and consorted in haste."

Toziel laughs, then shakes his head. "That will matter little unless . . . What of the sub-majer?" He pauses. "You have more to say. That I can see. I should listen."

"He had been on port detail in Biehl—watching ships, and talking to their captains and officers, I would gather. Then he conscripted the District Guards . . ." She smiles.

"He is *that* overcaptain?" Toziel shakes his head. "I think not so well as I should these days. Did not Rynst send him to Assyadt?"

"He did, after the Majer-Commander discovered that every lancer commander was apprised of the details of what happened at Biehl. He was directed, even as a sub-majer, to command company patrols."

"I imagine the barbarians will attack in force there." Toziel's voice is simultaneously hoarse and wry.

Ryenyel smiles. "We shall see. We have some seasons." She adds, almost as if it were an afterthought, "Ryalor House has been recognized as a clan house. That was one of Bluoyal's last acts. It takes all of the uppermost level of the plaza building on the clan side. Do you not find that interesting?"

"Rather. So she is very sharp ... and effective, I would judge, somewhat like someone else I know."

The Empress smiles. "You are kind."

"No. I know what I know." Toziel massages his forehead before he speaks. "Do you think he can survive and prosper in—is it Inividra?"

"I would judge so, but he must do so against the opposition of almost all the senior Mirror Lancer officers."

"If he can manage such over the next year or two, and is not discredited, suggest to Rynst that he would be a good assistant, you think?" Toziel leans back on the white divan and closes his eyes.

"If he can survive, our suggestion may not be necessary," Ryenyel replies. "As for us, there are no others, save Rustyl and Dettaur, and neither has a consort, although it is likely that Rustyl will take the daughter of the Second Magus for a consort."

"That will make matters difficult for Chyenfel." Toziel laughs. "Or perhaps more so for Kharl."

"I think not. The Second Magus will promise to both his son and to Rustyl, and then do as he pleases with the support of both."

"They are both of the Magi'i."

"Chyenfel thinks that times may change."

"Not that quickly," the Emperor says.

"One would hope Rustyl will see that, but he is like a shadow cast by a man none can see. As for Ciesrt, he is but a cipher for his sire. Dettaur, on the other hand, is a cipher for no one, but he has courted many ladies, and none will have him. For an esteemed lancer, that is a message one cannot ignore."

"He seems to be ignoring such a message rather easily," suggests Toziel.

"For now." Ryenyel coughs, several times, then finally clears her throat. "Like you, I find the days are getting longer."

"That is because you support me."

She waves off the comment, then adds, "Dettaur dislikes this Lorn, and will attempt to place him where he cannot survive."

"If one of them does not succeed, or Rustyl or Tasjan does, black order will follow us and raze Cyad . . . within a generation if not sooner. But you cannot give either anything, else he will not be strong enough to hold it." Toziel sighs. "There have been possible scions . . . most with magus blood, Dymytri, Eghyr, Volynt . . . and something happened to each, and now we are not so young as we were or as we appear. And now the Magi'i, and even the merchanters, are seeking to advance their own to force me to acknowledge one."

"Luss and Kharl arranged for the failure of most of those in the lancers." Ryenyel shrugs wearily. "Yet how could any hold Cyad if they could not hold themselves against that pair?"

"You did not find this Lorn?"

"No. I would that I could say such, but until Maran disappeared I did not even consider him as a possibility. Nor his consort."

"Many did not consider you." Toziel laughs gently, but the laugh dies away. "I wonder if we see such worries as do those who have children."

"Is there any question, my love? You are the father of Cyador."

"A father without an heir." Toziel's voice is low and tired, and his eyes drift closed.

Ryenyel touches his forehead lightly, gently.

LI

LORN LOOKS OUT the commander's study window at the heavy snow pelting the ancient panes of glass. The stones of the courtyard have turned white, and rime has formed on the inner corners of his windows. Winter has begun to settle in, and his chaos-glass shows little trace of raiders, only a few scouting and foraging parties, small enough that Lorn has reverted to single-company patrols, spacing them as far apart as he dares.

He finally picks up the scroll from Dettaur—the one that arrived with the replacement lancers at the turn of winter an eightday previously—and the one to which he has yet to reply, since he has no intention of sending a courier just for Dettaur.

> Your reports have been well-received by the Commander, and, we understand, by the Captain-Commander on behalf of the Majer-Commander. Much credit is due you for your efforts carrying out the policies and strategies implemented by Commander Ikynd . . . The number of barbarian deaths as compared to Mirror Lancer losses remains acceptable, although the Commander would hope that you could improve those numbers by the time of the spring raids, as by then you will have become more familiar with the procedures and terrain around Inividra . . .

Good old Dettaur, Lorn reflects, always throwing in a dig and a suggestion of inadequacy. Some things hadn't changed in more than ten years.

> So long as you do not use an excess of patrols requiring two companies, occasional multi-company pa-

trols are acceptable to keep the barbarians off-guard, but the Commander wishes to remind you that continual use of such is an unacceptable gamble with the safety of the herders and people of Cyador. . . .

We also regret to inform you, and all other outpost commanders, that the Magi'i can but supply three firelance recharges for each lancer each season. In compensation, you will receive another company of lancers at Inividra at the turn of spring, before full barbarian raiding activities resume.

Lorn snorts. Another temptation for him to spend himself. If he does not use his abilities to recharge firelances—quietly—more lancers will die. Yet one lancer-magus can recharge comparatively few firelances for five companies, and he cannot afford to exhaust himself in that fashion, not with the amount of chaos-energy he must spend using the chaos-glass. As in everything, the higher he rises, the more demands there are that he has neither time nor energy to fulfill.

After a long slow breath, Lorn looks out at the snow once more. Well before spring he had best decide what he can do, and what he will need to do, for Jera is a port that remains ice-free throughout the winter, and trading vessels continue to tie to the piers there—and to bring in ever greater numbers of higher quality iron blades.

LII

IN THE LATE-WINTER afternoon, Lorn stares into the chaos-glass, painstakingly transferring details of the image he has called up onto the maps on his personal study desk, as he tries to trace the geography of where the Jeranyi raiders travel. After he finishes drawing in a section of river, and the low hills around it, he releases the image, sets the pen in its holder and closes his eyes. He massages his temples for a moment, then leans back, his eyes still closed.

His thoughts do not cease, and he has to wonder, even with his maps, how he can continue to fight against a seemingly endless enemy. How many new strategies will he be able to develop come spring and summer when the barbarians flood southward once again? How can he direct his patrols under such conditions without giving away the secret of his ability to find the barbarians?

His abilities, mighty as they might seem to some, are limited. If he concentrates greatly, he can summon images in a chaos-glass, or charge a firelance or so, or move a door latch from the other side of the door, or throw a handful of firebolts. He cannot do all at once, or even in succession. His abilities can only change the edges of what may be—so far as he can tell.

After a moment, he opens his eyes, and shakes his head.

Why had he been so successful in Biehl? Because he had not waited for the enemy to come to him, but moved to take the fight to them. Was that the overall problem with Cyador?

Why had no one taken the fight to the Jeranyi?

He fingers his chin, looking blankly through the window into the cold and gray afternoon, out at patches of snow and frozen and thawed and frozen ground beyond the walls of the compound.

Cyador is far from crowded. Its people do not use all the lands they have, not really. So the Mirror Lancers are not attacking, but merely defending. Lorn shakes his head. Had the ancients established the Land of Light with all their force in the belief it would grow to fill those borders? Or to use the border areas as buffers?

He ponders, considering the discussion he had years earlier with his mother, before he was sent to Jakaafra to patrol the Accursed Forest, where she had pointed out that Lancers and Magi'i were few indeed. Cyador has expanded, and those who have been expanding their numbers have not been the lancer officers and the Magi'i, but merchanters, crafters, working folk, peasants, and others. Even so, Cyador has not expanded to fill its lands to overflowing.

Is that because its people are prosperous? What is prosperity? Is prosperity the answer to the first of his father's questions? A frown follows that. Cyad would exist without prosperity, and without the Magi'i, but it would not be Cyad as he has known it.

His mind skips to the third question, and he laughs as he thinks of Dettaur, realizing that Dettaur does not understand that a lancer officer's power comes only from the acceptance by his men of the officer's authority. A single officer can be killed by a misaimed firelance from behind, or by one deliberately misaimed.

Therefore, as his father's second question intimates, the lancer officers maintain power because the people accept their handling of it. The barbarians do not accept the power of the Mirror Lancers, and so, the struggle is between the beliefs of the people of Cyad and those of the Jeranyi and Cerlynyi.

And that conclusion helps little at all in determining how he will face the spring and summer raids.

His lips twist, and, slowly he reaches for the silver volume, opening it and paging through, stopping and reading the last lines of the verses about recalling the Rational Stars.

I had a tower once, across heavens from here. . . .
Oh . . . take these new lake isles and green green seas;
take these sylvan ponds and soaring trees;
take these desert dunes and sunswept sands,
and pour them through your empty hands.

Those are not the words of an empire builder, Lorn feels, or of a man seeking to conquer lands. He pages farther into the book, reading another section.

> . . . I hear the altage souls lifting lances
> against what the future past advances,
> while time-towers hold at bay
> the winters of another day,
> what we would not face
> what we could not erase . . .
> until those towers crumble into sand
> and Cyad can no longer stand.

Those, too, are the words of a defender. He shakes his head. Everything his father has stood for, and the Mirror Lancers—all are the roles of defenders. And while Cyad—and her people—are well worth defending, defenders always lose in the end . . . *if* they always fight on their own territory.

His eyes look into the gray afternoon, an afternoon that somehow does not appear quite so gray, quite so forbidding. He needs to find a way to take the fight to the Jeranyi.

Yet how can he? With five companies, six at the turn of spring?

Does he have to defeat the barbarians? What about the question Rhalyt had raised? He had no fleet, no fireships to stop the traders going to Jera.

Then he nods. Perhaps there is a way. Perhaps . . . but it will require much more screeing, and time, and then . . . he will see.

LIII

THE WINTER LIGHT coming through the ancient window-panes of the low Tower of the Magi'i is supplemented by that of the wall lamps and their polished cupridium reflectors. The First Magus does not stand, but remains seated behind the desk in the austere study on the topmost level of the tower as the Second Magus bows and makes his way to the golden oak armchair opposite Chyenfel.

The Second Magus bows once more before seating himself. Had he looked directly at the First Magus, he would not have seen his reflection in the eyes of the older magus, but only the blank sun-gold of an aging and powerful magus.

"You are so mannerly, Kharl," offers Chyenfel. "It is one of your virtues, and I do most appreciate that."

"You wished to see me? In private?"

"I did. The inner tower of the Magi'i will fail at any time. It could last a year, two at the outside, but it could collapse within a season. I thought you had best know this, for the Captain-Commander will doubtless press you when I announce that we will again be cutting back on the recharging of firelances and firewagon chaos-cells."

The green eyes of the Second Magus flicker but once. "Can we not suggest that it is merely weakened?"

"You would have me lie to the Emperor and the Mirror Lancers? When the Hand of the Emperor will know, and when he will ask such of the Hand?"

"Neither the Hand nor the Emperor will long last, ser."

"Nor will I, you are thinking."

"I cannot deceive you." Kharl shrugs. "Yet . . . in public I would counsel prudence. Any chaos-tower but that one can fail. That one, it must not be seen to fail."

"And when the word is out, what then?" Chyenfel's tone is mild. "We will have lied, and failed."

"By then, ser, it will matter not. I warned you of this, years ago. I told you that we would need every chaos-tower. You assured me that the Accursed Forest was a greater danger. Now you have taken the towers of the ward-walls, and hidden them in the mists of time. Half the fireships are without chaos-towers, and we cannot hide that. We have but a handful left. Without the towers, Cyad as we know it will perish. Without the power of the firelances, for no magus can recharge but a handful a day, not and do aught else, without the speed of the firewagons, and without the might of the fireships . . ." Kharl tilts his head and raises his eyebrows. "What will we have?"

"We still have the cupridium blades, and lances such as are used by the District Guards. We have great roads and canals that none can match. We have a people of talent and wisdom."

"For how long? Cupridium cannot be forged without the towers."

"Kharl, that is not so. Tools of cupridium can be forged with the residual chaos of the world—and there is much of that."

"It will take a magus for each blade, and each will have to be hand-forged—if there is anyone with the technique."

Chyenfel leans back and smiles. "You surprise me, Second Magus. I would not have thought you so. What message are you conveying? That we pretend all is well?"

"I find it preferable to the flux chaos of the alternative." The red-haired and green-eyed Second Magus pauses, then adds, "Then, the inner chaos-tower may last a few years."

"Long enough for me to have returned to chaos, so that you may do as you see fit, I am sure."

"I would not offend you, nor cross you, honored First Magus."

"Not while I live." Chyenfel smiles. "I may yet retain my vitality longer than you suppose. I did wish to tell you, in the event that your most creative mind might seek a more . . . encouraging approach."

"I thank you, and I will think upon it." Kharl inclines his head. "If you have no further requirement of me . . . ?"

"Not at the moment. Not at the moment. But . . . Kharl . . . what if the next Emperor is as Toziel, and not as, shall we say, the Captain-Commander? Or even a younger magus?"

"Such as Rustyl, you mean?"

"I know you would follow Toziel, but that will not and cannot happen. Content yourself with following me. For all your deviousness, you would make an effective First Magus. I suggest you consider such."

"I will consider much, honored First Magus."

"With more than polite lip service, I would suggest. While Toziel is far older than he appears, he is not yet failing, and he searches for an heir to the Malachite Throne—an heir who is not of the Magi'i."

"He will search far, for there are none among the lancers, that he will ever find, and certainly, to elevate a merchanter would stain the sunstone of the Palace of Eternal Light with so much blood that it could never be scrubbed away."

"I have learned, as you must have—or will—that 'never' and 'none' are most dangerous words, and that those who utter them often must swallow them most often."

"I bow to your wisdom." The Second Magus inclines his head, as if waiting.

"You may go." A weariness infuses Chyenfel's words, and he nods at the younger magus.

"I thank you, and wish you a pleasant rest." Kharl stands and bows, before turning and easing his way from the austerity of the study.

The sungold eyes of the First Magus follow him out with the power of still-banked and massive chaos. A faint smile lingers on his lips.

LIV

IN THE LATE afternoon, Lorn steps into the front corridor and foyer of the square tower at Inividra, his saddlebags over his shoulder, sabre at his belt, and his winter jacket still fastened. He nods to Nesmyl. "We're back."

"Yes, ser. Were there any barbarians?"

"No. They know it's winter. Only lancers are out now." Lorn laughs ruefully. "Any dispatches from Assyadt?"

"No, ser. Captain Esfayl would like to see you. One of his men deserted, and was found in the local hamlet—with a local . . . entertainer."

Lorn nods. "We'll have to do something." Since Esfayl's Second Company wasn't actually on patrol, Lorn may be able to just have the man given a few lashes, and have his pay docked for a season, but he will need to speak to Esfayl first. "Is there anything else?"

"No, ser."

"Good." Lorn gestures toward the narrow back stairs. "I'll be in my quarters until dinner."

"Yes, ser. If you do not need me . . ."

"Go." Lorn laughs. "You'll be doing long days come spring."

Nesmyl smiles, as if reluctantly, then bows.

Lorn carries his gear up the narrow stairs. His legs ache from riding in the chill. Although the patrol from which he and the Fourth Company have just returned to Inividra has been short, the cold makes such patrols seem far longer. They had found no barbarians, as Lorn had known, and no tracks of such, but he will be able to report to Dettaur that he has indeed taken another patrol, for all must seem in accord with Dettaur's wishes, and those of Commander Ikynd.

Once in his quarters, Lorn pulls off the winter jacket, glad that one of the lancers has at least kept the stove stoked so that Lorn's rooms are passably warm. Then he puts away his gear and unclips the sabre, setting it by the armoire.

The tired sub-majer stands for a moment at the foot of the bed and tries to stretch his legs. Then he walks to the small study, pausing behind the chair and desk to glance out through the half-frosted ancient panes. Outside, the gray clouds make it difficult to tell whether the flat and dim light is because of the clouds or the coming twilight.

With a wry twist to his lips, Lorn seats himself once more at the desk in the upper study of the square tower and takes out the maps. He has almost a bell before dinner, and he might as well accomplish something more fruitful than empty patrols required by a vengeful superior.

He pauses. In some ways . . . are the Jeranyi like Dettaur? Dettaur has forgotten that Lorn broke his fingers for a reason—because Dettaur had been bullying all the younger boys at the school. Yet all Dett recalls is that Lorn broke his fingers, not all the injuries and humiliations he had foisted upon others. All the Jeranyi recall is an ancient humiliation, and not all the endless deaths and mutilations that they have inflicted over the generations.

The sub-majer pushes those thoughts away, applicable as they may be, and concentrates on the maps and his ideas for dealing with the barbarians. On those maps before him on the desk, Lorn follows the track of the south branch of the Jeryna River, using the map calipers to check the distances, trusting that he has managed to keep the scales relatively consistent. He adds up the figures. Then he does the same for the west branch.

Finally, he nods. If it does not snow too late, and if the Sixth Company arrives as scheduled . . . then the travel aspects of what he is considering may work. Unhappily, that is only part of what he needs.

There are also twoscore extra firelances in the armory, and those will help.

Yet he must find exactly what he seeks, or all that he plans will be of little use to him—or to the Mirror Lancers. And even after two full eightdays of using the glass, he has not found what he needs.

Slowly, he pulls out the chaos-glass and sets it on the desk, half dreading the headache he will have before he is done. He squares his shoulders, and concentrates on the glass, letting the silver mists gather, and then give way to images, one after the other, until he has the building he wishes in view. He takes a deep breath and focuses his attention on the entry doors.

The image that appears is of two heavy, dark-stained doors, nothing more.

He tries again, focusing on a window that seems brighter

than the others, and is rewarded with a view through a half-open shutter of a man in maroon and blue sitting at small table with a chest of some sort before him.

Lorn tries to catch and hold the image of the trader—or factor—and to focus on the room.

In time, he is rewarded, although his eyes are burning, and his headache is intensifying, but the scenes are indeed clear. The building does have chests with ledgers, and warehouse space, largely empty at the moment.

Lorn nods and sketches it in on the larger map he is drawing. He almost blurs the lines, for his hand has begun to tremble. He sets aside the pen and closes his eyes for a few moments, before he resumes drawing.

Then he halts, for he cannot afford to spoil the work he has done.

Yet his efforts are slow . . . so slow that some days he feels he will never accomplish what must be done before spring—not with patrols, and reports, and training, and inspections. Intensive use of the chaos-glass is far harder than merely raising chaos—at least for Lorn.

He shakes his head and closes his eyes once more, before opening them again. Before long he must descend and cross the courtyard for dinner, and he must not appear tired, or less than encouraging.

LV

THE SNOW THAT had fallen in the more northern valleys and plagued Lorn and Esfayl on their return ride has barely left a dusting around Inividra, and the paving stones in the courtyard are clear, with but small drifted piles of white in the corners of the walls and buildings, as the two officers rein up outside the stable at the outpost in the winter twilight.

Lorn turns to Esfayl. "Captain, remember . . . fighting the weather gains nothing. The storms always win."

"Yes, ser."

Lorn dismounts and leads the gelding toward the stable door, but Hasmyr the ostler has already started forward to take the white's reins.

"Good to see you, ser, and with all your lancers and mounts," offers the gray-bearded ostler. "Seen too many young captains lose men in the winter." He winks at Lorn, then looks up at Esfayl. "I can take your mount, too, ser."

"Oh, thank you," replies the captain.

"Thank you, Hasmyr," Lorn says as he quickly unfastens his gear from behind the saddle, as well as the spare sabre he has made it a habit to carry.

"Not being a problem, sers."

Esfayl grins sheepishly at Lorn as the two officers step away from their mounts and the ostler. "I suppose I still think of the Mirror Lancer words about carrying on through the storms of life and the battles with the eternal forces of darkness."

Lorn laughs. "I learned that it's hard to fight nature when I was patrolling the Accursed Forest. It's better when you can avoid it. With the Forest, we couldn't, but there's little point in it out here."

"Ser . . . you didn't say a word to Hasmyr."

"He's probably seen scores of captains here, and a half-score sub-majers, I'd wager," Lorn points out. "He likes the horses, and he doesn't want them lost when they don't have to be." Lorn pauses. "I'll see you and the others at table in a few moments."

"Yes, ser." Esfayl nods and bows his head. "Thank you, ser."

As Lorn walks across the damp stones of the courtyard toward the square tower, he refrains from shaking his head. Duty . . . duty—as either a student magus or as a lancer, he'd never felt that blind obedience to the past or to some absolute belief was wise. Yet . . . why did so few see it that way?

He laughs, gently and ironically, to himself, noting that

his ignoring such traditions has him walking a narrow path between two kinds of disasters, with Dettaur and, apparently, Captain-Commander Luss'alt waiting for some sort of transgression that will allow them to find an excuse to disgrace or discipline him.

His saddlebags on his shoulder, he walks past the duty sentry and into the square tower.

Nesmyl is waiting, and steps forward. "Ser, there were several dispatches and scrolls with the supply wagons. I put them all on your study desk."

"Thank you. I'll get to them after I eat." Lorn shakes his head. "I think the officers are waiting for me."

"That might be." Nesmyl smiles. "I doubt they would wish to start when their commander has just returned from patrol."

Lorn ducks into the study and glances at the desk, looking over the three scrolls. There are two official dispatchs, doubtless from Dettaur in Commander Ikynd's name, and a scroll with the green seal of his father. While he is not surprised to find one from his father, he is equally surprised not to find one from Ryalth. He fingers his chin and nods. Just because he has not received such a scroll does not mean it does not exist. Her reactions to his use of the chaos-glass are proof enough for Lorn, both of her devotion and that she is more than even his father has seen.

He takes the scrolls in his free hand and slips back out of the study and up the narrow stairs, trying not to scrape the walls with saddlebags and sabres. Again . . . Nesmyl has made sure the stove is stoked, and that his quarters are warming. Some smoke has drifted into his quarters, for he can smell the smoky odor of peat, as though the stove had been opened and checked recently. Clearly he had not been expected to return early, but someone had seen them and hurried to refire the stove.

Lorn laughs. There are some benefits to being commander. He leaves the three scrolls on his upper study desk—to read after dinner—and carries the gear to his bedchamber where he leaves the saddlebags on the footchest and the sabres leaning against the wall in their scabbards. He will need to clean and oil the blades later.

Leaving his winter jacket on, Lorn washes his face and hands, then hurries back down the narrow steps, out of the square tower, and across the courtyard. He is the last to reach the officers' dining area, but then, he has no doubts that dinner was held after Nesmyl—or Emsahl or someone—had seen them coming down the road from the north.

"Good evening," Lorn offers as he nears the end of the table at which the five other officers are standing. "Esfayl and I appreciate your waiting for us." He seats himself quickly, and then serves himself a large helping of the mutton stew, wrinkling his nose at the heavy pepper scent, and hoping that the carrots and roots are neither too stringy nor too mushy. "At least it's hot," he says, nodding at Esfayl.

"Been warm here, ser," says Cheryk. "Warm for winter, anyway."

"It's going to get colder." Lorn passes the big casserole dish to Emsahl, then breaks off a chunk of the bread and passes the basket.

"When it's cold," Cheryk points out, "there aren't any barbarians out. We'd be lucky if it stayed cold."

"We'd still have to patrol," Lorn says. "The commander and the assistant commander in Assyadt think that the barbarians will attack immediately if we don't."

"That's true only in summer," says Emsahl. "Or late spring, after they've done most of their planting."

A moment of silence follows, and Lorn eats several mouthfuls, ignoring the softness of the vegetables and the toughness of the mutton.

"Ser . . . ?" ventures Rhalyt from the end of the table, "one of the squad leaders said that you'd known Majer Dettaur for a long time."

Cheryk and Emsahl both frown. Esfayl winces almost imperceptibly. Quytyl, his arm still bound in a light splint, looks down at the table.

"Actually, that's true. We went to the same school, and my mother knew his. He was two years or so ahead of me." Lorn takes a mouthful of the peppered stew, then adds, into the silence, "He was much then as he is now."

"You will run across officers you know, Rhalyt," Emsahl suggests. "There aren't that many officers in the Mirror Lancers."

Lorn nods. "I went through officer training with the captain who relieved me at Jakaafra."

"Just wondered, ser," says Rhalyt. "You know . . . with rumors . . ."

"Most rumors have a grain of truth in them," Lorn observes wryly, "but sometimes it's like a single grain of rye in a whole loaf of white."

"Like the rumors of giant serpents along the ward-wall," suggests Emsahl.

Lorn clears his throat.

Emsahl looks up, surprised.

"They do exist. They're rare. We only came across one in the years I was there. But it was large, almost two cubits in breadth and close to forty in length." Lorn laughs. "They're not nearly so dangerous as the stun lizards or the giant cats . . . but seeing one was a shock."

"Which was more dangerous?" asks Rhalyt, as if wanting to make sure the subject stays changed.

"The large stun lizards . . . if you're facing only one. But the giant cats usually come in pairs or double pairs, and the night leopards in packs." Lorn shrugs. "So . . . it's hard to say."

"How do they compare to barbarians?" asks Quytyl.

Cheryk, Emsahl, and Lorn all laugh. Quytyl flushes, and this time Rhalyt is the one to look down at the table.

After the last chuckles die away, Lorn says, "The northeast ward-wall is the only one that has casualties anywhere close to a barbarian patrol company, and they ran about half what I had at Isahl. The southwest ward-wall company lost perhaps a quarter- to a halfscore of lancers a year."

"Why the northeast wall, ser?" asks Esfayl.

"No one ever gave a good answer," Lorn replies. "Some say it was the winds, some the way the wall was designed, some the fact that it is closest to the Westhorns . . ." He shrugs.

Cheryk shakes his head. "You were assigned to Isahl, there, and here?"

"And Biehl," Lorn points out.

"But those three are the toughest duty stations in each area, ser."

"I'm just lucky." Lorn looks at Esfayl. "You're from Summerdock, aren't you?"

"Yes, ser."

"Does it get as hot as here in the summer?"

"No, ser. There's always an ocean breeze . . ."

Lorn nods for the young captain to continue. The rest of the dinner conversation will be uneventful. He can assure that much.

After dinner, Lorn walks back across the courtyard, through a night wind that is considerably colder than earlier, and past the duty sentry at the tower. "Good evening."

"Evening, ser."

The lower level of the tower is dim, with but one lamp lit, and Lorn stops and turns down the wick to put it out before starting up the stairs. Although he would like to read the dispatches and scrolls, he forces himself to hang out his damp gear on the wall pegs by the stove first. Then he checks the sabres, drying and oiling them, before he returns to the study and the scrolls.

He looks at the two official dispatches, then shrugs and breaks the seal on the one that looks shorter. He unrolls it and begins to read.

. . . hereby inform all officers bearing commands throughout the Mirror Lancers that losses of provisions and other supplies have been reaching unacceptably high levels ... strongly recommend that all commanders review the use and storage of such, and that the use of local supplies be adopted whenever possible ...

The seal and signature are those of Luss'alt, Captain-Commander of the Mirror Lancers.

Lorn nods to himself as he sets the scroll aside and picks up the second one with a Mirror Lancer seal. It is addressed to him as, *Commanding, Inividra.*

As noted in the scroll which you are receiving from the Captain-Commander of Mirror Lancers, the handling and storage of provisions has become a problem at many isolated stations, such as Inividra. Therefore, individual commanding officers must take a greater role in assuring that such provisions are stored and used with care and are not wasted ...

The commander has noted that your last request for supplies is somewhat higher than that of previous submajers, and has requested that you explain such.

Lorn snorts. The answer is simple. He has more men still alive than did Sub-Majer Kysken, and more men require more food.

... and request that you send a response with the next scheduled courier to Assyadt.

The signature and seal are Dettaur's, as Lorn has known even without reading them, for Dettaur is clearly trying to establish any possible grounds for proving Lorn is less than competent. Moreover, the odds are good that, sooner or later, Lorn will be out on a patrol when some request for something comes in, and Lorn's response will be late, thus giving Dettaur yet another example of Lorn's unresponsiveness. Dettaur is clearly very good at setting up officers to be discredited.

The sub-major looks out into the darkness beyond his study window and the inner shutters that he has not closed, despite the chill coming off the ancient panes of glass. He half stands and, shaking his head, closes the shutters. He reseats himself and opens his father's scroll, reading slowly.

We trust all is well with you at Inividra. Life continues here much as it has throughout the winter, and for those of us for whom the cooler weather is not such a joy as once it was . . .

Although Mycela is expecting a child this summer, young Kerial is our first grandchild, and a delight he is. All of us can but hope you will be able to see him while he is still young. I can recall when you were that young, dark-haired and smiling as well, and it seems not that long ago. Life is fleeting and fragile, and we forget that when we are young and strong.

Your consort continues to amaze all, and Ryalor House prospers. Her enumerators are known both for their probity and loyalty, and in these days, after the revelations about the former Merchanter Advisor to the Emperor, those qualities are more greatly respected than in recent years. It is interesting to note that none recall or have mentioned the events that led up to the disclosures, and for that we can be grateful, although it is said that the Emperor knows far more than any but those directly involved.

Lorn frowns slightly. While he had sent a copy of his battle report to the Hand of the Emperor, with its references to Hamorian blades, he does not recall that he made any reports about the sorry state of the Emperor's Enumerators in Biehl. Did Neabyl report more? He continues to read.

Myryan is already planning for improvements to her garden for next year. Ciesrt and Vernt continue to work together, although I understand this may not continue when Vernt is advanced to a lower first. Your brother works hard, and that has made his understanding of chaos far deeper in some ways than those who are more facile. His understanding of the fundamentals of chaos application may prove most useful to the Mirror Lancers and to you in the years ahead.

I trust you will be prepared for the spring with the barbarians and all that may ensue, and we both wish you well . . .

Lorn finds himself frowning once more as he looks over the scroll. The words and the script are those of his father, yet there is a hint of shakiness about the characters that he does not recall, and that bothers him. Perhaps because of that shakiness, he recalls the questions his father had given him, questions to which he has yet to find satisfactory answers.

Then . . . each day, he finds more questions for which he has no answers which satisfy him.

Although he is tired, and it has been all too long a day, he eases aside his father's scroll and slips out the chaos-glass. He will allow himself a quick screeing in the glass.

He concentrates, and the silver mists form, and then part, to reveal two figures sleeping side by side in an ornate bed he recognizes only from the glass, and in the room he also has determined, but only through screeing, that is a part of newer and larger quarters for his consort. While Kerial does not move, Ryalth turns, almost as if she senses the chill of the glass, and Lorn releases the image.

For a time, he sits in the dimness, his eyes closed, massaging the back of his neck and head with his left hand, then dropping his chin against his chest to stretch tight muscles in his neck and upper back.

Finally, he stands, and twists down the lamp wick. Tomorrow promises another long day in catching up on reports from his last patrol and in composing a polite reply to Dettaur, yet one which will refute the hidden allegations, he hopes without angering his old schoolmate, at least not any more than Dettaur is already angered.

LVI

AT THE SOUND of the door opening, Kharl turns, a welcoming smile upon his face as he advances across the fourth-floor balcony of the west wing of the Palace of Eternal Light.

The man who steps onto the sunstone floor tiles of the balcony is muscularly wiry, with black hair streaked with gray. His eyes, a pale and piercing blue, fix on the dancing green orbs of the Second Magus. He wears shimmercloth blues and bows. "Honored Second Magus."

"Honored Merchanter Advisor," returns Kharl.

"You suggested that it might be better to meet informally." Vyanat gestures around the empty balcony and smiles. "Most informal. Neither furnishings, nor obvious eavesdroppers. You will pardon me, honored Kharl'elth, if I lack the polish and the obscuring language of my predecessor. I am a plain-spoken trader. What do you wish?" He slips toward the chest-high cupridium railing, where he leans forward into the slight breeze. "It is rather pleasant here. The air is not only warm, but fresh."

"Fresh, it is, and sometimes there is much to be said for forthrightness," replies the red-haired Second Magus. "This may be such a time." He smiles. "As with many in Cyad, there are certain aspects of my life over which I have no control, yet about which I must confess that I have certain . . . concerns."

"As you say, most of us find that to be true. In what particular does this concern me? You would not have requested a meeting with me if it were not a matter of intrigue or trade." Vyanat smiles. "And if you did, you are wasting time for both of us."

"As you may know," Kharl begins, looking out across the winter-gray waters of the harbor, his eyes looking into the distance, "my eldest son is consorted to a healer, and she is from a most distinguished family. Her father is Kien'elth, of whom you are likely to have heard."

Vyanat nods, waiting.

"And one of her brothers is likely to become a first-level adept magus in a season or two, if not sooner. The other was not destined for the life of a magus, but has become quite well-known as a most effective Mirror Lancer battle commander."

"And the one who inadvertently revealed my predecessor's bribery schemes," Vyanat observes. "For which the good Majer-Commander decided to reward him by assigning him as commanding officer of the most-attacked lancer outpost in the Grass Hills."

"That appears to be true, as you say," Kharl continues, "if a Mirror Lancer matter. This young officer consorted himself to a young merchanter, and did so without the knowledge and consent of his family. A true love match, one might say. I have the smallest of requests, you understand, just that I would appreciate anything you might do to ensure that nothing that the lady merchanter does might be construed to reflect, shall we say, adversely, upon her family."

"Or upon you and your son, or your daughter and her new consort-to-be, by extension," Vyanat replies. "I think I understand your position absolutely, most honored Second Magus."

"You understand, honored Merchanter Advisor, that with the growing . . . link with chaos effected by Kien, and the comparative inexperience of young Vernt, his magus son, I feel a certain responsibility . . ."

"I am most certain you do, honored Second Magus, and I will assuredly do what I can to ensure that Ryalor House abides fully with the Emperor's Code."

"One must look out for the consorts in one's family . . ."

"I do appreciate your feeling for family and your concerns. You need say no more." Vyanat bows slightly. "And since I am, as I said, a plain-spoken trader, unless you have other concerns, I must, alas, return to the Plaza, for being an advisor to His Mightiness does little to ensure that one's business continues as it should." He pauses. "Especially since His Mightiness and the Hand have made it most clear that merchanters must earn their golds in trading goods and not favors." Vyanat bows once more, then steps away.

Kharl does not frown until much later, well after the balcony door closes.

LVII

AT THE HEAD of Fourth Company, with Cheryk to his left, Lorn rides through the light swirls of heavy snowflakes that have replaced the late-winter rain. The road is wet, but without snow or ice. Beyond the bare ground, the snow does not melt, but builds where it strikes the grasses in the fields on each side of the lane leading up to the outer gates of the outpost at Inividra.

"Be glad to get dry again," Cheryk says. "Sometimes, I'd rather have snow than rain."

"Especially if there's a hard freeze coming." Lorn nods in agreement as the two officers ride through the open outer gates, passing guards bundled in winter jackets.

"Didn't have to use any firelance charges."

"So far." Lorn still worries about having enough firelances, as it is clear that the number of lances and recharges will be decreasing every year.

Beyond the inner gate at Inividra, the stones of the courtyard are warm enough that the fat snowflakes have melted, and left the stones damp and not slushy or icy.

"Not a bad patrol," Lorn notes to Cheryk.

"Any patrol without raiders is a good patrol, ser."

Lorn laughs. "We could hope for a long winter."

"Don't know as which is worse."

"Raiders, as we both know." Lorn reins up outside the stable.

Before he dismounts, Hasmyr is standing by the stable door. "How be the mounts, sers?"

"There's a mare lame in the second squad," Cheryk says.

"I'll be looking at her, then."

"Thank you, Hasmyr." Lorn hands the gelding's reins to the ostler, then unstraps his second sabre and his gear. After a nod to Cheryk, he crosses the courtyard to the square tower, and the sentry. "Good afternoon, Wyett."

"Afternoon, ser."

"Let's hope it doesn't freeze after all this wet snow."

"No, ser. Rather not see that."

After a nod, Lorn slips into the door to the square tower, where his senior squad leader and administrative aide is standing by his desk, waiting.

"A Captain Gyraet reported," Nesmyl says. "With a full company of lancers. They're in the old south bay. And there is a dispatch on your desk."

"Thank you." Lorn nods as he walks back toward the rear staircase. "If you can find the captain, I'd like to talk to him before the evening meal. I'll be down as soon as I unload my gear."

"Yes, ser."

Lorn slips up the stairs, where he stops but long enough to leave his gear and sabres in the bedchamber before descending to the commander's study. There, he takes off the winter jacket and hangs it on the wall peg. For a moment, Lorn looks at the dispatch, sealed, and doubtless from Dettaur. His lips curl, and he lifts the scroll and breaks the seal, beginning to read.

Now that the new Magi'i barrier is in place around the Accursed Forest, the Majer-Commander is sending an extra company to each outpost that is expected to receive heavy barbarian attacks. Captain Gyraet and his company are one of the first to arrive. I would caution you that because their mounts could not travel by Mirror Lancer firewagon, there are few spare mounts, and there will not be many for several eightdays.

Lorn frowns. Inividra has close to a score-and-a-half spare mounts, mainly from those lost by the raiders in the fall. How many does Dettaur expect Lorn to lose in the next few eightdays?

I have already cautioned Captain Gyraet about this as well.

The sub-majer laughs. Trust Dettaur to find creative new ways to undermine Lorn, and trust him to tell Lorn as well. Dettaur has great skill at positioning himself. That is clear.

Commander Ikynd and I look forward to the reports of your accomplishments once spring turns, and the barbarians begin their raids.

"I wager you do, Dett. I wager you do," Lorn murmurs to himself.

Thrap.

At the rap on the door, he turns. "Yes?"

"Captain Gyraet, reporting for duty, ser."

"Come in." Lorn motions for the officer to enter the study.

Gyraet is the image of the popular lancer officer, slender but muscular, dark-haired, with a strong but not protruding squarish chin, and piercing green eyes. He bows to show just the proper amount of deference. "Sub-Majer."

Lorn gestures to the chairs on the other side of his desk. "Please sit down." As he seats himself, he studies the officer and can sense the doubt buried behind the pleasant smile. Doubt—that is something Lorn would rather deal with than hostility. "I take it that your ride here was more damp than snowy."

"Yes, ser." Gyraet offers a rueful smile. "I think I'd prefer the snow, were it not too deep."

"Most lancers would." Lorn pauses. "Did you come from the Accursed Forest?"

"Eastend, ser."

"Is Majer Weylt still there?"

"He is. The word is that he may be going to Fyrad to be in charge of maintaining the southern part of the Great Canal."

"He was most helpful to me when I was at Jakaafra," Lorn says.

Gyraet frowns for a moment, then smiles. "You were that Captain Lorn."

Lorn laughs slightly. "I think I was the only Lorn assigned to Northpoint."

Gyraet nods. "Majer Weylt talked about the giant serpent you killed, and the time you killed a stun lizard by hurling a blade into its eye."

"Those are accomplishments I'd rather not have been remembered for, a combination of unwise audacity and ill chance."

Gyraet adds, more levelly, "It's also said that you dealt with more tree-falls than any captain ever, and that you lost fewer lancers for the number of wild creatures killed."

"That is possible. I don't know about *ever* . . . but in the five years before and the years I was there that was true."

Gyraet moistens his lips.

"Is Sub-Majer Hybyl still there?" Lorn asks, almost idly.

"Yes, ser."

Lorn wonders how much he dares say or intimate. After a moment, he decides on another approach. "You've doubtless been briefed by Commander Ikynd and Majer Dettaur?"

"Commander Ikynd was rather short."

"He probably said that I had a good record killing barbarians, and that was what you were being sent here to do."

"Something like that," concedes Gyraet.

"And he said it bluntly, and perhaps added a few words about the fact that you'd best be careful because I've been known to be hard on officers who don't agree with me."

Gyraet remains silent, but Lorn can sense through truthreading that he has been accurate enough.

"Majer Dettaur, on the other hand, was doubtless more detailed, and suggested rather indirectly that while everyone is pleased with the results of what I do, that you be most careful in how you deal with me."

"Ah . . . something like that." Gyraet tries not to shift his weight in the chair, and his eyes do not meet Lorn's.

"I could be most charming and welcoming," Lorn goes on, "and mislead you, and cast doubts about the characterizations that have been made. I don't think I will, because you're obviously perceptive, and feel you're in a most difficult situation, being assigned to command a company under the Butcher of Nhais." He smiles. "Have you read the battle report about Nhais?"

"Ah . . . no, ser."

Lorn walks to the end chest, which he opens, and from which he extracts one of the copies he has brought to Inividra with him. He closes the chest and then tenders the report to Gyraet. "Read it. Now. I'll wait."

"Yes, ser." Gyraet doesn't conceal his puzzlement, but takes the report.

As Gyraet begins to read, Lorn scans Dettaur's scroll

again, then sets it aside and glances toward the window. While his old acquaintance's tone bothers Lorn, he has to ask himself whether Dettaur is so bent on revenge that he will take any opportunity to goad Lorn, or whether his missives are designed to push Lorn into early and unwise action.

Lorn frowns. Dettaur certainly had been unable to see·Jerial's disgust with him, but bright enough to understand exactly how Lorn had managed the Biehl situation. Then, Lorn reflects, does he have any choice but earlier action when firelance charges are becoming ever scarcer and the numbers of barbarian raiders growing?

"Ser?"

Lorn glances up. "I'm sorry. I was thinking." He pauses. "You've finished it?"

"Yes, ser."

"As you can see, many of the details of the report were authenticated by others, including various officers and enumerators. I wanted you to read it so that you would have some idea of what is happening north of the Grass Hills and why you've been assigned here."

"Majer Dettaur did not mention the Hamorian blades."

"He probably didn't mention the fivescore herders and women and children they slaughtered, either."

"Ah . . . no, ser."

"And I doubt he mentioned that we usually have plenty of spare mounts here—close to twoscore at the moment."

"No, ser."

Lorn smiles once more, then nods. "That's all for now, Captain. You might want to talk to the other officers, especially the more senior ones. I'm sure each has his own view of matters." He stands. "I'll see you shortly, at dinner."

"Yes, ser." Gyraet stands, then bows before he departs.

Lorn walks to the study window and looks out at the intermittent fat flakes that drift by the ancient panes of glass.

Did the ancients have to deal with the same kind of in-fighting? Or had they pulled together more because they had been required to in carving a land out of the wilderness and in fighting against the Accursed Forest?

Somehow, Lorn suspects that what he sees in the Mirror Lancers, and with Dettaur, is scarcely new. The melancholy tone of the silver volume of ancient verse attests to that.

And yet . . . the melancholy ancient was one of those who built the City of Light, of which there is no equal.

LVIII

LORN WATCHES FROM the study window as two provisions wagons roll through the light rain and across the courtyard to the storerooms beside the stables. With the rain, he is glad that he has not dispatched any patrols. While the snow beyond the Grass Hills is melting, his use of the chaos-glass has shown Lorn that the barbarians remain within their hamlets and that they have not yet begun to gather.

Unhappily, the unknown magus or Magi'i continue to follow him, clearly trying to determine what he is doing. Also unhappily, more traders have docked at Jera, and more Hamorian blades have been unloaded and stored in the warehouses there. Before long, the blades will make their way up the branches of the River Jeryna to an even greater number of barbarians.

Lorn turns, frowning, as there is a knock on his study door. "Yes?"

"Ser . . . there is a dispatch." Nesmyl bows, then extends the scroll.

"Thank you." Lorn nods and takes it.

As he leaves the study, Nesmyl closes the door. Lorn breaks the green lancer seal and begins to read.

Sub-Majer Lorn, Mirror Lancers, Commanding at Inivdra,

Winter is about to end, and at the turn of spring, you can anticipate an increased number of barbarian raids. Commander Ikynd wishes to convey once more his concerns about the tactics you have used in the past. He would emphasize that regular single-company patrols are to be used. Multi-company patrols offer far too great a risk of allowing the barbarians to attack an unpatrolled area, especially now.

Furthermore, your field expertise will be needed, and therefore you are strongly urged to take command of the company of your choice, preferably one commanded by an undercaptain. In such circumstances, it should be noted that using multi-company patrols might be seen as preferential treatment for those lancers you command personally, and this is another reason why multi-company patrols should be minimized . . .

Assyadt has yet to receive additional mounts to support those companies transferred from the Accursed Forest. Large losses of mounts, as may occur with patrols involving more than one company, cannot be replaced . . .

These are trying times for all Mirror Lancers, and their commanding officers should and must rely on the practices and tactics that have served so well for so long, and to that end Commander Ikynd strongly urges that you turn your energies and talents.

for Commander Ikynd, Majer Dettaur,
Assistant Commander, Assyadt

Lorn sets down the scroll and walks to the window once more, looking into the gray day and drizzle for a time. Finally, he turns and crosses back to the door where he peers out. Nesmyl glances up.

"Nesmyl . . . if you would send word for the officers to gather in the officers' study . . . I'd like to meet with them there."

"Yes, ser."

"Thank you."

Lorn turns back to the study, and walks to the footchest against the wall that holds dispatches and other communications to the outpost, generally from Assyadt, but at times from Mirror Lancer headquarters in Cyad. He begins to sort through the dispatches, pulling some, leaving others, until he has close to a halfscore. He arranges them, then rolls them up, with the latest scroll from Dettaur around them.

He nods, hoping his instincts are correct. Finally, he tucks the scrolls under his arm and steps from the study.

"They should be ready, ser." Nesmyl is standing by the desk with Yusaet beside him. The more-junior senior squad leader had either been the one to convey the message, or to hold the desk while Nesmyl did. "Thank you, Nesmyl. Or you, Yusaet, whoever passed the word."

"Thank you, ser." Yusaet bows.

". . . got that cold look . . . wouldn't want to be whoever's he angry with . . ."

Lorn takes a breath as he leaves the square tower. He doesn't need to show his anger with Dettaur to the officers. The drizzle seeps around him as he crosses the courtyard to the barracks building that holds the officers' study. Under his arm is the large roll of scrolls.

As he enters the officers' study, Lorn looks at the six officers who rise from where they have been sitting around two adjoining tables. "Please sit down."

He looks around the room as he unrolls the scrolls and sets the pile before him. He realizes he is wagering much on what he is about to do, but he needs to know how they will react. After a long moment of silence, he says, "Most of you have asked about the patrol schedule for the spring. For the moment, I'm not going to post one."

He waits again, noting the faint frown on Quytyl's face, and the eyebrows that Esfayl raises momentarily. "Instead, I'd like to read you all something." He pauses. "These are all dispatches I have received from Assyadt over the past several eightdays." He picks up the first scroll.

We regret to inform you that you can expect no more than three firelance recharges, as the Commander has conveyed earlier in the year . . .

Then he reads from the second.

We cannot supply any spare mounts, and will not be able to do so until at least sometime in late spring or early summer . . .

And the third.

We must also insist that you refrain from the practice of using multi-company patrols. Mirror Lancers must be able to take on significantly larger barbarian forces without needing to rely on additional lancers . . .

Emsahl snorts . . . loudly.
Lorn picks up the last scroll and reads.

Further, it is most strongly suggested that you relieve your least effective company commander and take personal command of that company . . .

Lorn waits, letting the words sink in before he speaks again. "Those all came over the course of the winter. This morning, I received yet another such scroll, which repeats all of those messages and adds another. I'd like to read that as well." Lorn clears his throat and reads Dettaur's latest scroll in its entirety. As he reads, he surveys the room, and from what he can sense, most of the officers are disturbed.

As he finishes reading the last scroll, Lorn sets it down on the table before him. He looks across the six faces, again studying them before he speaks. "I'll leave these here for each of you to read so that you can see for yourself that I have not made up or distorted the language." He pauses and lets the silence draw out. The room remains still for a long time.

"Ser . . . were those all from either Majer Dettaur or Commander Ikynd?" asks Esfayl.

Lorn nods.

"We lost fewer lancers last fall than any time since I've been here," Emsahl says slowly. "And you tell us that—"

"No. I'm not saying that. Those were dispatches from Majer Dettaur on behalf of Commander Ikynd."

"Never was much of a patrol commander . . ." suggests the normally silent Cheryk. "Worse than Sasyk, and he was a sour pearapple . . ."

Gyraet's eyebrows lift.

"Well, he wasn't. He'd always take on the biggest barbarian, and forget about the rest of the lancers."

Lorn clears his throat, loudly. Cheryk's words will be more effective later, when Lorn is not around. "I wanted you all to know the kind of suggestions I've been receiving." He smiles. "I'd like you all to consider that I have not yet been forbidden to use multi-company patrols. And I have not been ordered to relieve one of you. 'Strongly recommended,' but not ordered."

"It sounds like that won't be long," suggests Emsahl.

"If we keep doing things the way we have been, I'm sure that's true. If each of you patrols by yourself, we're going to take some heavy losses." Lorn pauses.

Emsahl smiles. "I'm thinking, ser, that you got an idea. Elsewise, you wouldn't be having us here."

"I do." Lorn nods. "It's something different. Commander Ikynd told me we could go where we wanted once we were in Jeranyi territory. I think it might be a good idea to put a stop to some of these raids where they ought to be stopped—over in Jerans—and I believe we can do it. We'll have to do it before I get any more dispatches." Lorn lifts the most recent scroll. "I got this one today, and it will probably be two eightdays before we're sent any more provisions, and dispatches."

"You're thinking of going into Jerans?" asks Gyraet.

Lorn nods. "We had better odds when I tracked down the raiders in Biehl and hit them when they didn't expect it. If we wait . . . they'll just gather more and more barbarians."

"Pretty risky . . ." offers Gyraet.

"Not so risky as fighting eightscore with one company," suggests Cheryk. "That's what it's coming to, these days, if the sub-majer follows those directives."

"What if they attack here?" asks Esfayl.

"That's a good question." Lorn smiles. "But if we strike first, what barbarian will dare leave his homeland to attack Cyador while we white devils are in Jerans?"

"No . . . they'd not be doing that," affirms Emsahl. After a moment, he grins. "When do we start, Majer?"

"How about next twoday?" Lorn smiles grimly.

LIX

In the glow of his quarters' study lamp, Lorn looks over the maps yet again, checking the routes, the planned stops, the possible points of conflict—and the places that must be destroyed. He has not told any of the captains his exact plans, only that an unnamed town on the South Branch of the River Jeryna is their first goal. That much is true, for it is one of the towns where the raiders gather, and not all have yet gathered, but enough have, and so have their mounts.

Slowly, he puts the maps in the order he wishes, then rolls them up and ties them into a single bundle.

Tomorrow all six companies of Mirror Lancers will pull

out of Inividra, something that has never been done before. So far as the stories and the records tell, no one has ever combined more than two companies of Mirror Lancers in making an attack, not in recent generations.

His lips curl. He may find out why that is so, but he can only do what he feels is best, for the older tactics are less and less effective, and the chaos-towers are failing. And Lorn, child of Cyad, will not stand and watch.

He laughs softly, mirthlessly. He also has no real choices, for to follow Dettaur's instructions will mean either death or disgrace in slow increments, for Dett is most excellent in political maneuverings—far, far better than Lorn.

In the darkness, Lorn takes out the chaos-glass and sets it on the desk before him. His head still aches slightly from the use of the glass in the late afternoon, but he would see Ryalth and Kerial a last time before he casts his fate to chaos.

When the silver mists part, he watches the sleeping pair only for a few moments before he releases the image. He would not disturb their sleep.

While the chaos-glass will be in its wooden case in his saddlebags, he doubts he will have either the time or privacy to use it—but for an extended campaign he dares not leave it behind, either, not with Dettaur watching everything he does.

There is one more thing that will accompany him— Ryalth's ancient silver-covered book. He holds the volume for a time before opening it, wondering not for the first time how her mother came to have it, and whether it means, as he believes, that she is nearly as much of a child of the Magi'i as he is. He laughs, softly, for the Magi'i will claim neither of them.

Then he pages through to see if any of the ancient verses call up echoes of what he feels, looking out at darkness and an uncertain future. He finds one, whose words strike him in a different way, as they often do, when his choices and circumstances have changed. He reads aloud, softly, to himself.

We stand in a world we did not know
reaping lives and deaths we did not sow.
Some reach for roses of another place,
a world beyond chaos in time and space.
Some raise copper blades, strangely graced,
to destroy new truths that cannot be faced.

Chaos is, as the river and the hills,
and I will live my life as chaos wills,
for Mirror Towers have fallen from the skies,
and venerated truths become but lies
when held as orders from our ill-starred past,
talismans to recall what cannot last.

To build what must be built, and raise new halls,
to guard what must be held in shining walls,
to slay the demons of unreasoning hate—
all those, and more, have come to be my fate.

Do I regret the stars that cast me here?
No more than knowing life is fragile, dear
and fleeting, or that my words die unread,
for words cannot contain what souls have said.

" 'Words cannot contain what souls have said . . . ' " Lorn
muses, nodding to himself.

His eyes drift back up to another phrase—"demons of unreasoning hate." There are so many who hate so fiercely that
it is beyond reason, from the barbarians to Dettaur to those
Lorn does not even know. The ancient writer had said his
fate was to slay such. But the other poems had revealed the
man's sensitivity—and Lorn is not unaware of the irony of
slaying demons of hate. Where each demon is slain, more
hate is raised, yet hate unchecked also multiplies, and love
alone will not brook hatred that holds a blade.

"So you will raise a greater blade?" Yet he has searched and can find no other choices, not that are open to him, in this world, at this time, for doing what others will is death indeed. And doing what others will is not the way to save Cyad so that what it stands for will continue to shine out. He finds another page and reads the concluding stanza.

> Merage, altage, elthage, all bow to thee,
> from Rational unity come these three,
> and neither chaos, nor the lance, nor gold
> shall seize this city of the stars foretold,
> for Cyad holds the fate of all this earth,
> and all of soul and skill that is of worth.
> So shine forth both in sun and into night
> bright city of prosperity and light.

He looks into the darkness for a long time before he stands and then walks to his bedchamber where he places both the silver-covered book and the chaos-glass in the saddlebags he will carry in the morning.

LX

WITH HIS SADDLEBAGS over his left shoulder, Brystan sabre at his belt, lancer sabre and map scrolls in his left hand, Lorn looks at Nesmyl. "You have a half-squad, and the cooks and other staff. I wish it could be more, but we will need every man."

"Many be the lancers who would have given much to see what I see, ser. It be long past time that the raiders be bearded in their lands. I'd almost be wishing I be with you, ser," replies the slightly bent senior lancer. His smile is crooked. "Almost."

"Times have changed, Nesmyl, and we must change with

them." Lorn gestures toward the study. "If Majer Dettaur should arrive here, not that I expect him, you can tell him that, in accord with his wishes, I have all the companies on patrol in order to better protect the lands and people of Cyador."

"That I will, ser. That I will."

"I suggest closing at least the inner gates, once we ride out."

"That I had considered already, ser."

"Do you have any last questions?"

"This be not a question . . . but . . . ser . . . should you bring back much booty and success, best you take it and lay it at the feet of the commander at Assyadt."

"If . . . if we are so fortunate . . ." Lorn nods a last time and walks to the door, and then out into the gray light of a sunless morning just after dawn. His boots carry him across the courtyard to the stable, where Hasmyr has the white gelding waiting for him.

"There be a small pouch of grain there, ser. Most you dare carry. Try to find such for all the mounts, as you can."

"I will," says Lorn as he fastens his gear behind the saddle, then checks the firelance and his water bottles. His eyes go to the spare mounts, which carry another score of spare firelances, few enough for the forces he has mustered.

He mounts and then rides across the paving stones of the courtyard toward the most junior undercaptain, Quytyl.

"Ser?"

"How's the arm?"

"Still a touch stiff, ser, but strong."

"Good," Lorn says, even as he doubts the young officer's words. "Fifth Company will be second for now, behind Third Company." While he had given the order the day before, he wants to reemphasize it.

"Yes, ser."

Lorn checks with each of the other officers, then rides to the front of the column where Emsahl and Third Company are formed up. "Let's go."

"Yes, ser." Emsahl raises his arm, then drops it.

The sound of hoofs on stone fills the courtyard, and the road to the inner gates, as six companies ride out from Inividra.

The early morning remains gray, with high thin clouds and a light but warm breeze out of the southwest, as the column turns toward the road to Jerans. Lorn looks backward at Inividra, where two older lancers close the inner gates—an outpost empty except for Nesmyl, the cooks, and less than a halfscore of lancers.

Neither for the first time, nor the last, Lorn suspects, he wonders if he can manage to accomplish what he plans.

From what he had seen in the glass the afternoon before, and again early in the morning, the only barbarians stirring are those to the northeast, far closer to Syadtar. That makes some sense, because the later snows, the spring snows, had fallen more to the west, but the roads are muddy in only a handful of places, and the barbarians appear involved either in planting or dealing with their flocks and other spring farming or herding tasks.

Lorn squares his shoulders and studies the road ahead.

LXI

LORN CONTINUES TO wear his oiled white-leather winter jacket, but leaves it open for the hint of breeze that occasionally rises. He is warm, but not quite sweating, as he rides northwest on the narrow trail-like road that leads out of the Grass Hills. The high clouds have remained with the Cyadoran forces for all three days since they have ridden out of Inividra, but the rain has been light and intermittent. None has fallen on the Cyadoran forces since shortly after dawn, but mist rises off the hills to the northwest, where the warmish rain has been melting the last of the snows. Roughly five kays beyond those hills, if his maps are correct, lies the first barbarian town on his route through Jerans.

Lorn rides at the head of the column, beside Emsahl, on a road which is damp clay, but with few puddles or muddy sections. Directly behind them is Emsahl's senior squad leader, and the junior squad leader for Third Company's first squad.

"We're headed away from Clynya, are we not, ser?" asks Emsahl.

"The raiders who strike Assyadt come from the northwest, mostly from the towns along the branches of the River Jeryna," Lorn says. "That's where we're headed."

"You've been planning this for a time, ser." Emsahl's words are a statement.

"At least since Rhalyt asked why we just sat and watched." Lorn frowns as he studies the hills. "The first town ought to be on the far side over there, through that odd-looking pass. There's a stream on the other side, the first real one north of the Grass Hills."

"You know you were coming to Inividra, ser?" asks the older captain.

"I knew I'd be sent somewhere to fight barbarians," Lorn answers.

"You've been collecting maps and stuff on the barbarians for a long time. Have to be, with all you know."

"When you're not born a Mirror Lancer, you know you'll fight barbarians," Lorn points out. "It makes sense to learn as much as you can."

"Folks don't always do what makes sense."

"True enough." Lorn laughs. "Let's hope that what the scouts find makes sense as well."

The bearded Emsahl grunts an assent.

Still, it is midmorning before Lorn sees the scouts riding toward them. He turns toward the captain. "Emsahl, would you have one of your lancers summon the officers?"

"Yes, ser." The older captain turns in the saddle. "Dwyt, send a messenger. Majer wants the officers quick-like."

"We'll rein up here, and let the men stand down for a bit." Lorn turns in the saddle. "Companies! Halt!"

"Companies halt!" The orders echo back down the long column while Lorn rides forward another fifty cubits or so to wait for the scouts.

Emsahl rides up to join him, followed by the other officers, one by one, coming as they do from farther back in the column. Gyraet, bringing up the rear with Sixth Company, is the last to rein in his mount with the others, only moments before the two scouts arrive.

"Go ahead and report," Lorn says.

"Yes, ser," offers the square-bearded and older lancer scout. "We took the back side of the hills, ser, like you ordered, and looked down. There be no one even looking at the roads. Men in the fields are plowing, and others be doing ditchwork and such."

"How many people?"

"Twentyscore, I'd judge, from the dwellings, but that be including women and children."

"Probably eightscore men of all ages," Lorn muses aloud. "The ditchwork is along the river?"

"Yes, ser."

"The far side?"

The younger scout nods. "Mayhap a halfscore there, could be a few more."

"Are there many herders or others farther out in the fields?"

"Could be some. Didn't see any, ser."

"What about flocks or herds?"

"None more 'n kay from the town, then, ser."

"Thank you. If you'd stand down for a few moments . . ." As the scouts move away, Lorn dismounts, almost slipping on the damp clay, and waits for the others to do likewise, and for the scouts and two other lancers to hold their mounts. Then he unrolls the map and hands one side to Rhalyt to hold while he points out the landmarks and begins to explain. "Here's the town. The road comes in here. There are the ditches, and here's the center of the town. Rhalyt—your company crosses the stream at the ford here, and heads east. Your task is to take out all the men working on the ditch. Use sabres or short bursts, and make it quick. Then come back down the road to the north of the ditches. You can kill any man old enough to bear a blade, but don't touch the women or the children."

"Yes, ser."

"We'll also send one company around the town to the road that leads northwest. That company will be Second Company." Lorn looks at the young captain Esfayl. "Your task is to make sure no one rides out of the town—no one. We don't want word being spread that we're here—at least not if we can help it. You ride west on this side of the river—there's a lane ahead, I think, and then cross the stream and hold the road west out of the town."

"Yes, ser."

Lorn looks at Gyraet. "Captain—you'll stay with the main body until we reach the crossroads here on the other side of the ford. Then you take the lane out this way, to the north, and sweep through that area."

"Yes, ser."

Lorn looks around the officers. "Our tasks are simple. We want to kill any of the barbarians who might ride against us, but no women unless they take up arms. Once we've removed anyone who can raise a blade and we hold the town, we want to take all the blades, and all the mounts, and we'll need supplies to get to the next town and mounts to carry them."

"All the mounts, ser?" asks Esfayl.

"If they have no mounts, they can't ride after us or send word somewhere else quickly after we leave."

Cheryk nods, and he and Emsahl exchange glances.

"It sounds simple, and something will probably go wrong," Lorn says, "but keep in mind that you want to make sure that this town won't be able to attack Cyador for a good long time. This is only the first town, not the last . . . so have your men use sabres when they can—but only when they can safely." Lorn rolls up the map. "Do you have any questions?"

Glances flick back and forth between the officers.

"Guess I'll ask, ser," offers Cheryk. "You're planning a campaign, ser, not just a few raids?"

"If we can do it," Lorn admits. "If things don't work, then we change. The more towns and blades and mounts we can take out, though, the fewer barbarians you'll face this year, maybe for a few years."

Cheryk nods. "Best we take as many as we can, losing as few as we can."

When no one else volunteers a question, Lorn steps to the side and slips the map into the long pouch behind his saddle. "Let's form up. We'll try a four-abreast front once we get to the other side of the stream."

"Yes, ser."

Lorn swings back into the gelding's saddle, then waits for the officers to rejoin their companies and pass the orders. His eyes keep looking down the empty road, then back along the column that holds six companies.

"Ser?" Emsahl's voice is polite. "Third Company's ready."

"Thank you. We'd better wait a few more moments."

Lorn turns the gelding and stands in the stirrups. He watches as Gyraet rides out to the shoulder of the road and lifts his arm. "They're ready in the rear. Column forward!"

The orders ripple back, and, as the Mirror Lancers ride to the northwest, Lorn wonders once more about what he plans. He is no better, and perhaps worse than the barbarians, for although they slaughter innocents, they were not born in Cyad.

The Cyadoran forces ride a kay or so farther, before the

road swings more northward and toward the stream, but the road remains empty.

Esfayl lifts a hand in salute as his Second Company passes Lorn, and turns due west on the lane or animal track that parallels the stream on the south side. Lorn returns the salute.

"No one ahead, ser," reports the scout who has pulled his mount around and beside the sub-major.

"Still?"

"No, ser."

The road curves out from behind the hills and slopes down for a hundred cubits, before twisting back around a hillock with trees spaced across it, clearly an orchard of some sort, although the limbs are near empty except for scattered and furled gray winter-leaves. As the column nears the orchard, a figure—a lanky youth in a matted sheepskin jacket—stares from behind a tree where he has been emptying a sweetsap bucket. After a moment of silence, his mouth open, his eyes taking in the lancers in their winter jackets and uniforms, he runs, yelling, around the hillside toward the small hut partway around its base, perhaps three hundred cubits to the west. Whitish smoke rises from the chimney of the hut. As he runs, the youth yells, "Demons! White demons!"

"Let him go," Lorn says. "We need to get across the stream." He urges the gelding into a fast walk, aware as he speaks of a sweet odor in the air. Something from boiling down the sweetsap?

He concentrates on the road, as it slopes downhill and curves back to the ford. There, the brownish water is almost fifty cubits wide, and runs swiftly, nearly knee-deep on the mounts, as the lancers cross in pairs. The water is higher than normal, running through leafless bushes on both sides. The slope on the north side bears several sets of ruts and two or three sets of hoofprints, not even recent.

The gelding sidesteps and *whuff*s at the top of the rise before the road resumes, and Lorn glances around, but the crossroads is empty. Lorn leads the column to the left, westward toward the town.

The first dwelling west of the crossroads and toward the center of the small town is a single-story hovel on the left side of the road, less than twenty cubits back from the rutted track. It has mud-brick walls and a thatched roof that is dark with age. A bearded man, about Lorn's age, peers from the window as if he cannot believe what he sees.

Hsst! Lorn's single firebolt goes through the man's neck, and there is a scream from within the house.

"Frig!"

"Majer means to wipe 'em out . . ."

". . . what they been doing to our folk for years . . ."

Lorn presses his lips together. He glances over his shoulder, but Gyraet and his Sixth Company have already veered off from the main body and quick-trot northward on the narrow farm lane. The dust farther east and behind the column shows that Rhalyt's First Company is moving east toward the ditchworkers.

"Quick-trot! Now!" Lorn orders, and the three captains behind him echo the orders, which are relayed by the squad leaders.

As they ride westward, toward the town, even from a half-kay away, Lorn can see that the houses are not set square to the road, or to the lanes, but almost haphazardly, with ramshackle outbuildings, and often piles of rubbish within kays of the dwellings. An odor, both rancid and acrid, hangs over the place.

Lorn unsheathes the sabre, holding it in his left hand with the reins, for the moment, the firelance out and leveled in his right, as they ride toward the first clumps of dwellings.

"Get the demons!"

From the right, charging from behind an abandoned and roofless hovel, rides a group of barbarians, perhaps a half-score bearing the long and dark iron blades of Hamor. Ignoring the superior numbers of the lancers, they spur their mounts toward the four-abreast front of Mirror Lancers that is all the road permits.

"Short bursts!" Lorn says. "Short bursts!" He follows his orders with two quick *hsss*ing blasts. One barbarian topples from his saddle, and another lurches sideways into the mount of the rider beside him.

Hsst! Hssst!

Lorn ducks a wildly-swung blade, then triggers a quick fireblast at a figure under a sagging porch who is drawing a longbow. The man drops, and a small fire begins in the wooden planks around his feet.

Lorn sees several figures running down a lane to the left and turns the gelding. "Third Company . . . first squad! Follow me!"

"First squad! Follow the majer!" Emsahl echoes.

Lorn urges the gelding forward, and within a hundred cubits he sweeps up on a running figure, using the Brystan sabre and a hint of chaos as the man tries to throw himself aside—too late. Another man tries to duck behind a low tree, but Lorn directs a chaos-bolt from the firelance through his shoulder.

"Demons! They're everywhere!" screams a girl or a woman.

Lorn reins up to the side of the lane, glancing past the house to his left where three lancers are riding down a pair of barbarians. A gray-haired woman throws herself from a raised porch, a long dagger in hand, but the nearest lancer twists away, and levels his lance. *Hssst!*

The woman staggers, and his mate slashes down with a sabre.

Lorn turns. Two younger men, barely old enough to hold blades, charge from behind the side of the porch.

Hsst! The first goes down with a bolt from Lorn's firelance. The second lifts his blade as if to hurl it toward Lorn, but another lancer rides by and cuts through the youth's shoulder with a sabre.

Lorn leads the first squad along the lane, catching sight of three men running from what appears to be a smithy. "Get them!" He gestures for three lancers to ride them down, before turning the gelding to his right to face a gray-bearded rider with a long and ancient blade. Lorn does not attempt swordplay, but drills a chaos-bolt through the man's chest, and rides past.

A woman screams and runs from a hut to grab a child, scooping him up in her arms and then scrambling back through a door that she slams shut.

Lorn passes the hutlike dwelling and turns to the left, paralleling the main street, the first squad riders following him. They sweep the back lane, finding and slaying perhaps another six or seven men, before Lorn regathers the scattered squad, and rides back to the main street or road that parallels the stream, where he reins up. The main road in the town has not even a square, just several buildings clumped together, on both sides. Scattered along the roadside are bodies. One is that of a woman, a blade lying by her outstretched arm. The others are all men.

Flames are already crackling from several buildings.

At the sound of mounts, Lorn turns and looks through the growing smoke as Emsahl brings in the second squad of Third Company. "We cleared out the houses along the left side, ser. Quytyl and Fifth Company did the right side."

Lorn glances at Emsahl. "Did you lose anyone?"

"No, ser. Few slashes, nothing serious."

Lorn nods, and the air is silent except for the orders of officers and squad leaders, and the sound of flames. The submajer glances up as another set of riders approaches from the west. Esfayl reins up with perhaps a halfsquad.

Lorn waits.

"We're holding the east road, ser. About a halfscore tried to escape or send word. One tried to go through the fields." After a moment, the curly-haired young captain adds, "We killed them all."

"Good." Lorn nods almost reluctantly. "It's hard that way, but they won't be killing our women and children."

In time, Rhalyt appears, leaving his company halted in a four-abreast formation. "We took out the ones on the ditch, ser. Close to a score. A bunch of herders saw us, and got their mounts. Almost another score. We killed most of them, but one rode east, and we couldn't get him."

"That can happen." Lorn pauses. "Did you lose any lancers?"

"Two wounded, ser. Not bad."

As Cheryk rides up, Lorn glances to the two undercaptains. "Rhalyt—you need to patrol the lanes on the river side. Don't go into any more houses. If someone tries to use a bow, just use a firelance. If they hide, use the lance on something around the house that will burn it.

"Quytyl, you do the same thing on the side of the main street here away from the river."

"Cheryk will be gathering supplies and blades." Lorn gestures to the normally taciturn older captain. "You know what supplies we'll need."

"Yes, ser."

"Take what food you can find quickly and put in on the captured mounts." Lorn swallows. "Water all the mounts, and make sure everyone eats something. Don't let anyone go off alone. Then burn the barns and granaries."

"Ser?"

"We're not coming back this way, and if they don't have food, they'll not be riding south into Cyador."

Cheryk nods. Lorn can also see the nod from Emsahl.

Mounted on the gelding, the Third Company's first squad behind him, Lorn waits and watches as Cheryk's men set to work and as another set of buildings begins to flare into flame. He tries not to look at the scattered bodies, mostly bearded, that are strewn along the main street, and not at that of the woman.

He and the first squad slowly patrol the main street, waiting for Cheryk to gather supplies, but they see no one, and hear no one, although at one point, Lorn thinks he hears sobs from a shuttered dwelling. He does not stop.

The sun is into early afternoon when Cheryk reports. "We've got three captured mounts strapped with blades, and ten with provisions we can use. Also ran into a few more men with blades."

"Did you lose any lancers?"

"No, ser. Nasty slash, but clean, for one. They weren't expecting us."

"No. There hasn't been an attack into Jerans in more than a generation. They've forgotten what our holders and herders face every year." Lorn pauses. "We need to tell the men that it will get tougher with each town."

"Yes, ser." Cheryk pauses, the glances across at Emsahl who has ridden up and waits. "Each town?"

"Each town we can manage, as I said earlier. We're going as far as we can. We need to remove not just the barbarians, but their blades and where they get them. And no matter how fast we move, sooner or later, someone is going to discover we're coming. We'll take the west road, following the stream. There's another town there, a good forty kays along. We'll stop short, and then strike there tomorrow." Lorn looks at the two older officers, first Emsahl, then Cheryk. "Are we ready to move out?"

"Yes, ser."

"You, Cheryk?"

"Yes, ser."

"Companies! Forward."

The column of Mirror Lancers starts out the west road, riding through the swirling smoke and the odor of death and charcoal.

"White demons . . ." hisses a woman from the shuttered windows of the house twenty cubits to Lorn's right.

Without slowing, Lorn looks at her and levels the firelance.

She does not move from the window, nor does she wince. "Go ahead. Turn me to ashes, brave demon."

"We don't kill children. Unlike your brave warriors, who gut women and small children."

"You took our lands."

Lorn does not answer. He has no answer, for there is none. His hands bear unseen blood, from the old woman just killed by his lancers to the olive-grower's daughter in Biehl, yet he doubts that any course he would take that might be effective would not shed some innocents' blood. The only real question is how he can shed the least. He also doubts that the ancients had many choices, except dying or turning into barbarians, and the barbarians will always think the lands of Cyador are theirs.

"Demons . . ." hisses the woman from the window he has passed.

Lorn does not look back at the smoke curling into the sky, but keeps his eyes fixed ahead, looking for men with blades, and for Esfayl's Second Company on the road before them.

LXII

BY LATE AFTERNOON the clouds have thinned into a high haze, and the day has warmed considerably, enough that Lorn has taken off the winter jacket. The stream to the left of the road is running deeper and faster, perhaps because the last of the snow is melting.

Yet neither Lorn nor the scouts can see any signs of recent travel on the road itself, no new tracks that would signify someone fleeing them—only cart tracks several days old and a few hoofprints. Have those who escaped the carnage at the first town fled eastward? Does no one expect him to be heading northwest? Has he done something so unexpected that none know how to react?

The road is a good ten cubits above the water almost on a bluff overlooking a bend where the current has dug a deep pool. Lorn glances at the stream, now almost a river, and the deep pool in the bend.

Then he glances at Emsahl, riding to his right. "You think that's deep enough down there to cover fivescore blades?"

Emsahl smiles. "Deep enough, ser. Good idea, too. Don't want to carry 'em, and they'll likely rust before they're found. If they're found."

"If you'd send a messenger back to Cheryk?"

Emsahl turns in the saddle. "Dwyt . . . the majer'd like to see Captain Cheryk up here for a few moments."

"Yes, ser."

Lorn looks down at the river bend ahead. While he'd wanted to carry the blades, it is a waste of horses and can only slow them down. He wonders what some future peasant will think when the river changes course and his plow runs into iron . . . or will the plow just turn up red dust as it cuts through the clay deposited over the years?

He shakes his head, riding northwest and waiting for Cheryk to join them.

LXIII

FROM THE LOW hillside to the east of the second river town, Lorn studies the approach, from the saddle of the white gelding, his eyes flicking from the map to the town and back. He is flanked by Emsahl, Cheryk, and Esfayl, whose eyes follow Lorn's in the early-morning light. Mounted behind them are the other company officers.

Unlike the first town, the second town is more regular. Some of the dwellings are white-plastered, and some have tile roofs. Lorn can see a small square and what appears to be an inn, and beyond the town, fields with evenly lines of recently-turned dark soil.

"What do you think?" Lorn finally asks Emsahl.

"Sweep through . . . slay those we can get. Fire the warehouses and the barns. Don't go house to house."

"And get the supplies and mounts we can," Cheryk suggests.

"And the blades." Lorn rolls the map and nods slowly. "Third and Fifth Companies come down the main road." He glances to his left. "Esfayl, can you circle ahead and block the road to the west?"

"Yes, ser."

"Go ahead and get your company moving. We'll give you some time to circle out to the west."

Esfayl nods as he guides his mount away from the others.

"Cheryk and Gyraet—you'll take the river wharfs and warehouses. You head around the front of the hill, and then take the old road by the river." Lorn looks over his shoulder. "Rhalyt . . . your company will follow me, and we'll go where we're needed. We'll start with Third Company."

"Yes, ser."

Lorn and the officers turn and ride back down the narrow trail past the herder's cottage where five lancers watch over the herder and his family to ensure that none escape to warn the town. The bearded man looks impassively at Lorn and the officers, then drops his eyes abruptly. The boy, whose head does not quite reach his father's shoulders, stares at Lorn. The graying woman watches her son. All three project an air of disbelief, as if Mirror Lancers could not possibly be attacking so far inside Jerans.

Lorn looks toward the road below, almost wishing he had not undertaken the whole campaign, yet he knows of no other way open to him to stop the increasing attacks of the Jeranyi. His lips twist. Then, he knows of no one else in Cyador who wishes the attacks to stop, or who wishes such enough to do something. If there were no attacks, many in the Mirror Lancers would feel that they had no purpose. And the traders who supply the blades do not wish the attacks to cease, for they would lose golds. It seems that the only ones who wish the attacks to stop are the lancers who die and the poor folk of northern Cyador who are the victims.

Esfayl already has Second Company moving along the trail that circles the northern backside of the ridgelike hill by the time Lorn reins up at the head of the column of waiting Mirror Lancers.

Rhalyt reins in behind Lorn, then turns in his saddle and addresses the two waiting squad leaders. "We're to follow the majer. Our task is to deal with any problems. Keep your lances ready and use short bursts."

Once Rhalyt finishes, Lorn nods and says, "We need to wait for a bit to let the others pass the orders and get ready. Cheryk and Gyraet will be turning south once their companies clear the hill." He cocks his head, listening for the orders from the other officers.

". . . taking the river wharfs and warehouses . . . turn left at the first crossroads . . ."

". . . short bursts! Really short bursts."

The sub-majer and Rhalyt wait for Emsahl and Quytyl to join their forces.

"Ser . . . do you think they'll have a force waiting somewhere?"

"I don't know. We didn't see anyone, and the town is open enough, without much in the way of trees. So it will be hard to hide a large group of armsmen."

"Ser!" Emsahl calls forward. "Third and Fifth Companies are ready!"

"Fourth and Sixth stand ready!"

"Column forward!" Lorn raises his arm, then lowers it, and urges the white gelding forward.

Again, the road eastward between the narrow river and the hill is empty, and the dampish clay shows but a few wagon tracks and scattered and older hoofprints. A low fence of rails set between piles of stone flanks the road on the right and uphill side, then ends a hundred cubits short of the first crossroads, distinguished mainly by the lack of bushes or trees, merely a flat area, with a lane winding around the west side of the hill on the right side of the road, and a rutted way on the left.

As he and First Company near the crossroads, Lorn looks over his shoulder and can see Cheryk and Gyraet lead their companies southward, splitting the Cyadoran forces. He turns to Rhalyt, "Have them go to four-abreast. The road is wide enough now."

"Four-abreast. Four-abreast!"

Just past the crossroads, a kaystone on the right shoulder notes: *Disfek, 2 k.* A single thatched dwelling is nestled in a hollow to the right of the road a half-kay or so beyond the road marker. Behind it is a long and low building around which are gathered a handful of chickens that begin to scatter as the column of riders approaches. Someone slams the gap-planked front door of the thatched house, and then the shutters are closed from inside, long before Lorn and Rhalyt reach the eastern end of the stone and rail fence that separates the unkempt brown grass from the damp clay of the road.

Less than two hundred cubits beyond the house with the chickens, a thin white-haired man turns toward the sound of hoofs, gawks for a moment, and then runs, spindly-legged, toward a white-plastered dwelling on the north side of the road that leads toward the central square. "White demons! White demons! Run! Hide! White demons!"

"Demons . . . !"

Shutters and doors close along the wide road, and shouts echo between and beyond the houses, rising well over the sound of hoofs.

Somewhere a bell begins to ring, clanging loudly and discordantly. From where, Lorn cannot say, for he remembers no belltowers or, indeed, any form of tower from viewing the town either from the hillside or earlier in his chaos-glass.

Lorn studies the makeshift lanes between the houses that they pass. Abruptly, he catches sight of barbarian warriors—nearly a score—trotting northward away from the center of the town and away from the Third and Fifth Companies.

"Follow me!" Lorn wheels the gelding down the lane parallel to the road and urges his mount forward into a pace faster than that of the barbarians.

"Follow the majer!" Rhalyt orders.

If Lorn can get enough ahead, then he can slow the barbarians with his firelance, enough for First Company to catch up and attack. He also would far rather deal with armed warriors than unarmed men who *might* be such.

Lorn can see the Jeranyi riders only intermittently, over gardens and between scattered trees, houses, and outbuildings. The riders appear to be looking backward, but not to the lane a hundred or so cubits east, where Lorn and First Company are paralleling their progress and slowly moving up.

After almost a kay, he turns the gelding westward down another track that slants to the northwest, angling toward the road carrying the barbarians. He is perhaps fifty cubits from the road on which they ride when the first riders appear.

Lorn levels the firelance and triggers it at the barbarian on the side of the column closest to him, a fresh-faced rider barely a man. *Hssst!*

The young rider's upper shoulder flares into blackness, and he falls away from Lorn, his mount shying into the rider to the west of him. At the attack from the side, the bearded barbarian beside the man who fell, yanks the huge broadsword from his shoulder harness and turns his mount toward Lorn. So do two other riders.

"Leave them!" bellows a voice.

The Jeranyi riders turn toward Lorn, ignoring the orders. Behind him, Lorn can hear First Company nearing. Lorn triggers the firelance and lets fly with two more short bursts.

Hsst! Hsst! One strikes the rider beside the warrior with the enormous broadsword who bears down on Lorn.

Hhssst! A longer burst fells the big rider, and the broadsword tumbles into the clay, but the riders following are so close that he is suddenly using the lance more as a shield, and the sabre to slide away the heavier and longer iron blades, absently wishing he had both sabres out.

Still, he cuts through the Jeranyi force, then sees two men starting to ride northward, away from the battle.

Hssst! The lance blast drops one, but the second man guides his mount to the side of the road, where he is shielded by a spreading, broad-branched tree. Lorn turns the gelding, and drops another rider from behind.

Then he is blade-to-blade with a wiry and bearded man. As a dagger knifes toward him, Lorn desperately throws pure mage-fire at the man, who collapses as his dagger slashes the leather of Lorn's jacket.

The sub-majer wants to wipe his forehead, but concentrates on the swirling mass of mounts and men, except that the swirls subside, and all the riders who remain are Mirror Lancers. Two or three other Jeranyi riders have slipped away from the melee, but most of the Jeranyi are dead.

Lorn blots his forehead, then looks down at the slash in his jacket, and the red on his tunic. The slash across his ribs has barely broken the skin, but has resulted in enough blood to give the impression of a more severe wound.

"Are you all right, ser?" asks Rhalyt.

"I'm fine. Careless and stupid, but fine." Lorn pauses. "How many did we lose?"

"Two, ser, looks to be," the undercaptain says. "Two others wounded."

"Strap the dead to their mounts for now. We'll have to bury them tonight. We can't carry them all the way back to Inividra. Gather the blades, and any other weapons. We don't want to leave any around."

Lorn finds a clean rag, gathers a touch of the black order,

ignoring the headache it creates, and lets it suffuse his scratchlike wound, then slips the cloth under his tunic to absorb any last drops of blood.

The Jeranyi living farther from the borders do not appear nearly so good with weapons as those who raid Cyador regularly, or they do not do as well when surprised, and if either is so, he indeed has a chance to complete his campaign.

Once First Company has gathered the fallen blades and lancers, Lorn rides back toward the center of the town at a fast walk, Rhalyt and his company following, with perhaps fifteen blades strapped to a captured barbarian mount. Lorn glances from dwelling to dwelling, but most are barred and shuttered, as if to resist a siege or the like. Most are single-storied with plastered walls, plaster over withies in many cases, although one or two of the larger structures are of whitewashed bricks.

Emsahl and Quytyl hold the square, with three of the four squads stationed at intervals, firelances out and leveled. Several lancers are carrying out food from the chandlery, and loading it on packs fastened to a halfscore of horses commandeered, Lorn suspects, from the stable adjoining the inn.

"Ser?" Emsahl looks at the sub-majer as he reins up.

"There were some raiders—a squad's worth or so—trying to escape. We got most of them."

"Riding away?" asks Emsahl.

Lorn nods.

"Almost a shame you have to run them down," ventures Quytyl from thirty cubits away.

Lorn laughs bitterly. "Amazing how brave they are when they're killing people in our lands and when they have more blades and mounts, and how they aren't interested in fighting when they're outnumbered."

"Most people are like that," Emsahl suggests.

"Is everything going all right here?" asks Lorn.

"Locals cleared out almost before we got here. Might have been that bell."

"Load up as quickly as you can. I'm going to check the wharf area."

"Yes, ser."

The river is less than half a kay from the square, and, once more, Lorn passes shuttered houses, wondering how many men who might bear arms are hidden within. Yet there are too many houses for his men to break into each, not without risking losses he can well do without.

Lorn reins up by the river wharf, where five bodies of men in gray-and-brown tunics lie across the wharf, as if they had died trying to stop the lancers from reaching the single flatboat tied there. As Lorn surveys the wharf, Cheryk rides forward.

"What's in the flatboat?" Lorn asks.

"Bundles of wool, some tanned hides, two boxes of scented candles, a dozen amphorae with some sort of oil, and a strongbox with a hundred or so golds in it."

"We'll need to keep the golds." Lorn laughs. "We might need them to pay the men."

"Best we hope not." Cheryk grimaces.

"Ser!" calls another voice.

Lorn turns in the saddle.

"I think you'll be interested in this, ser." Gyraet rides toward Lorn, gesturing toward the leather-wrapped package strapped behind his saddle. "We found fivescore blades in the second warehouse. Fourscore, maybe five-, were from Hamor. A score or so were cupridium sabres. No lancer markings, either, so that I'd say they were forged for trade."

"Where's the trader?"

"Ah . . . he tried to escape. With those. I had to use a firelance."

"Are those his trading records?"

"Look to be, ser." Gyraet offers a grim smile. "If I read 'em right, some of the blades being used against us were forged in Summerdock."

"We need to keep those," Lorn says. "Very safe."

"You ought to carry them—once we get the blades loaded and the stuff we want from the warehouses."

"Which warehouse had the blades?"

"That one there—blades, some of those polished iron shields that'll block a firelance, and those axes with hooks." Gyraet gestures to the westernmost structure—smaller and older than the one from which the lancers are loading provisions.

"Make sure it's burned to the ground," Lorn says quietly, "both of them."

"Aye, ser."

"We shouldn't be staying here too long."

"What about the flatboat there?" asks Cheryk who rides out from behind the back of the warehouse.

"Burn it. Use the oils," Lorn says. "Are you almost through here?"

"Yes, ser."

"Set everything afire and join the other companies in the square. We'll form up there, and ride out." Lorn turns the gelding.

". . . you hear that? . . . friggin' traders in Summerdock . . ."

". . . do anything for a gold . . ."

". . . our blood . . . their golds . . ."

As Lorn rides toward the square, Rhalyt and his First Company following, again past houses with shutters fastened, and some few with doors flapping in the light wind, Lorn can sense a brief chill of a chaos-glass, which fades almost as quickly as it passes over him. The glass reminds him, once more, that his efforts to protect Cyador are going to cause more disruptions he had not foreseen, as if everything in Cyador and Candar is twined together in a web where the slightest tug on one side ripples the entire world.

Still, he wants to get out of Disfek and on the road toward Jera, for that is where he can do the most damage, and perhaps find the greatest support for what he feels, but cannot prove.

As he nears the square, he can hear the crackle of flames and see dark smoke beginning to rise into the sky, and the odor of burning wood and oils fills his nostrils. The Third and Fifth Companies are re-forming into four-abreast columns in a square empty except for bodies and lancers.

Lorn squares his shoulders. They have barely begun to do what must be accomplished, and more than a hundred kays still lie before them.

LXIV

LORN SITS ON a flat section of a stone wall by the side of the river road, under an oak that has barely begun to show new spring leaves and whose winter leaves remain mostly gray. He reads through the sheets of paper and parchment and bills of lading that Gyraet had discovered in the river town of Disfek. He has to squint in the early twilight to make out some of the words and figures. A few insects chirp in the low grass sprouting from under the brown stalks left from the previous year, and the occasional *twirrp* of a traitor bird berating some lancer drifts to Lorn as he reads.

"Ten sabres from Bluyet House, Summerdock . . ." Lorn shakes his head. After his experiences with Flutak or Baryat the olive-grower, he cannot say he is totally surprised. Some traders and functionaries will clearly sell anyone or anything to make golds. He takes a deep breath, recalling the grower's daughter, and wondering how many other innocents will die as a result of his efforts to make things right.

"Right as you see them," he murmurs to himself, before checking the dates on the records. The sabres were purchased recently—well after Lorn left Biehl, and after the

Emperor's Merchanter Advisor was replaced, Lorn thinks, although he is not certain about when that had occurred.

"Ser?"

Lorn looks up to see Emsahl, Gyraet, and Cheryk standing in the road. "Yes? I wanted to read these . . . in case there was something in there about blade sales in other towns."

"Ah, ser . . ." Gyraet begins. "I said I thought there were traders from Cyad selling blades to the barbarians . . . and . . ." The captain shrugs.

"These two good captains had their doubts?" asks Lorn.

"Yes, ser," answers Emsahl.

Lorn flips back through the pages, then proffers a sheet to the senior captain. "This is the first. There are about five . . . so far. I'm not quite through them all."

Emsahl reads slowly, then hands the sheet to Cheryk. He looks at Lorn. "I'd be asking whether we might be better heading back."

"A line of retreat?" Lorn raises his eyebrows.

"No lancer company has been this deep into barbarian lands."

"That's true, and if we have to, we can cross the river and take the south side back. Right now that would be most unwise."

"Unwise?" asks Emsahl.

Lorn smiles, almost bitterly. "Captain, surely you don't think that a few blades like this mean anything? Any trader could make a mistake. Besides, what difference does a half-score or even a score of blades make when there are so many barbarians?"

"Ser!" Then Emsahl catches himself.

"That is what I'd be told right now if we returned," Lorn says. "A halfscore of blades forged in Summerdock mean nothing."

"He's right," Gyraet says. "They don't care if we lose another score of lancers because there aren't enough firelance recharges. Why would a halfscore of sabres forged in Summerdock change anything?"

"You knew this, ser?" asks Emsahl.

"I had a good idea. All the barbarians we killed east of Biehl had Hamorian blades, but they were new, and the traders were telling me everyone was trading blades in Jera. I'd seen a few Brystan sabres earlier, and I thought there would probably be others." Lorn stands and shrugs, taking back the sheet from Cheryk after the older captain reads it. "Tales don't mean much to lancer headquarters. The only thing they accepted was fifteenscore blades in the strongroom of the compound, attested to by two enumerators."

"So . . . we're hunting blades as well as Jeranyi, ser?" asks Emsahl.

"Both," replies Lorn wearily. "Both."

LXV

ALTHOUGH A COOL breeze blows out of the north, the morning sun that foreshadows summer beats down onto Lorn's back and neck, heating his whole body, and he continually blots his forehead and face as the Cyadoran force rides westward along the rutted river road toward the river town that the older maps had named as Berlitos. Since leaving the town of Disfek, they have swept through a handful of hamlets and smaller towns, but have found neither armsmen nor blades, and only a few score warriors, and they have been able to avoid using firelances, relying on torches and sabres.

Still, Lorn reflects, if they remove a few score warriors here and a few score there, before long, the Jeranyi will not be nearly so able or eager to invade Cyador.

The trees are far thicker now, particularly on the north side of the river where the Cyadoran force rides, and even farther north Lorn can see heavily wooded hills, with fields hewn from the forests. The fields do not show signs of sprouts, and even the roadside grasses are mostly brown, with few green shoots beneath. Because of all the trees and hedgerows even in the cleared fields, Lorn has sent out more scouts to assure they are not surprised, but the reports he receives have shown no signs of armed Jeranyi. The relative scarcity of people tends to confirm the idea that the Jeranyi do not attack Cyador from poverty or from having too many mouths and too little land, but for reasons unrelated to golds or food.

Ahead on the right shoulder is a kaystone—a large kaystone that Lorn can read from more than fifty cubits away: *Berlitos, 10 k.* From his maps, Berlitos is the only large town between his force and Jera—and it lies on the eastern triangle of land between the North and the South Branches of the River Jeryna.

"Must be a big town," suggests Emsahl.

"The maps and the traders say almost fiftyscore," Lorn says. "Some don't live in the town, but nearby."

"Could raise a force there—a large one."

"We'll have to see what the scouts discover and report," Lorn replies.

At the second kaystone, one that says—*Berlitos, 5 k.*— Lorn gathers the officers. They all dismount and he unrolls one of his maps to brief them under the shade of a tree that resembles an oak, but is not, while he waits for the scouts to return.

"There is a long gradual slope ahead, a giant ridge that ends in line of hills ahead, and the town is on the flat below the hills. There is but one bridge, and that goes over the North Branch of the river almost as soon as you ride down into the town. Esfayl, I'd like you and Second Company to hold the bridge. We'll all be there to take it, if necessary. Then we'll take the main road right to the town square and then to the warehouse and trade district. We're not going to try to slay anyone who doesn't attack us. Berlitos is far enough from Cyador that there aren't that many barbarians from it who ride against us. Here, we have a different task." He pauses. "We're going to destroy the three traders' warehouses behind the river piers, and then burn them and the piers." He looks at Esfayl. "We'll have to leave the bridge because we'll need that to get to Jera."

"We're going on?" asks Rhalyt.

Esfayl winces.

Lorn looks around. "I wasn't sure we could make it, but if we can take Berlitos without heavy losses, we're going to Jera. That's where all the blades are being ported, and on the way back we can follow the West Branch of the River Jeryna to within thirty kays of Inividra." Lorn pauses. "If we're in good shape we can even take out a few more raiders from behind on our way back home."

"Ser," says Cheryk, "here come the scouts."

Lorn turns and waits.

The lancer scout reins up before Lorn. "Ser . . . on the end of the long ridge, mayhap four kays west—that's where the road starts to go down into the town—there be a good fivescore barbarians formed up."

"Did you see any others?" Lorn looks up at the lancer.

"No, ser."

"What sort of arms?"

"Mostly the big blades—some with the poleaxes that have the hooks on 'em. And they're wearing gray uniforms."

Lorn nods, even though he likes the idea of uniforms not at all. "Is it open ground there?"

"Fields in front of them, but lots of trees on both sides of the road east and toward the hills."

"So we can't circle them?"

"Be hard, ser. Have to go through the trees."

Lorn glances at the map, then frowns. He looks at the

scout. "Is there enough room for a squad to ride by at an angle—say fifty cubits out, and then turn back westward?"

The scout frowns, and his eyes glaze, as if he is trying to visualize what he has seen. After a moment, he clears his throat. "Might be, ser."

Lorn motions for the scout to move his mount back. He turns to the officers. "What do we have left in the firelances?"

"Maybe . . . three, four charges in each," suggests Gyraet. "Some without any, some pretty close to fully charged."

"We'll form up . . . say a third of a kay back from them . . . and if they don't charge, we send the squads in one at a time . . . have them ride in at an angle and discharge their lances across the front . . ."

Emsahl smiles. "And if they break ranks, the squad comes back, and we take the barbarians on the front?"

"If they charge," Lorn says. "I don't think they will at first. They've picked the best spot to defend the approach to the town. The road narrows into a pass of sorts behind them. There are trees, and we can't bring all our lancers into the fight there. We'd get picked off if we try to go through the woods. But if our lancers ride by, at around forty cubits, they can blast the front rank of their armsmen. If they have those polished shields, then have them aim lower, and take out the mounts. We'll keep sending a squad at a time, until they attack, retreat, or until we destroy them."

"You think they'll just stand there?" Cheryk frowns.

"They won't know what we're trying at first. I'd guess they won't charge for the first squad or two." Lorn shrugs. "Then, who knows? If we can pick off a score or so, if they charge, we can cut them up in wider fields beyond the trees. If they hold or retreat, we'll keep using the firelances of a squad at a time. At some point, if we're careful, they'll either charge blindly or break." He stops and studies the faces of his officers. "Any questions?"

"What sort of formation?"

"We'll ride there in columns of two, and form up that way,

each company beside the next starting on the right with First Company. Leave enough space so that, when they charge, if they do, you can shift into four-abreast before we meet the charge."

After another glance around, Lorn shrugs. "We might as well mount up and see what we face." With a wry smile that he feels he is wearing too often, he walks to the gelding and swings up into the saddle.

The officers also mount, and, shortly, the Cyadoran force rides eastward.

It is slightly before midday when the Cyadoran forces reach the eastern end of the open spaces and look westward along the road that is flanked by near-solid forest. The road itself is blocked by almost fivescore Jeranyi wearing gray-ish blue tunics—uniforms of sorts—and some bear long Hamorian blades. Others bear the long-handed billhooked axes that Captain Akytol had mentioned years before when he had relieved Lorn at Jakaafra. They are mounted in a line running from about twenty cubits from the woods on the north side of the road, to twenty cubits from those on the south side, a line almost seventy cubits wide and two rid-ers deep.

Lorn watches as the Cyadoran forces form up by com-pany, the squads side by side, so that each company presents a four-abreast front. The Jeranyi still do not move, but wait.

"First Company, first squad, forward and discharge lances at will!" orders Lorn.

Lorn can almost sense the Jeranyi puzzlement as a single squad rides out from the Cyadoran forces, then angles to-ward the center of the Jeranyi line.

Hsst! Hsst! . . . Perhaps twoscore firebolts rake the front riders of the Jeranyi. Lorn watches carefully, and he sees no more than half a score of those bolts hit before the first squad from Rhalyt's company rides back to its position on the right flank.

"First Company, second squad!"

Lorn watches closely as more firebolts slash the Jeranyi. This time, close to a score hit the defenders, and he can sense the movement among the barbarian riders. "Emsahl . . . Cheryk . . . Third and Fourth Companies—squads to four-abreast. Stand ready to charge."

"Third Company . . ."

"Fourth Company . . .

Esfayl's voice rises above those of the senior captains. "Second Company, first squad, forward!"

"Fifth and Sixth Companies! Four-abreast! Stand ready to charge!" Lorn orders.

Esfayl's first squad has no more than begun to discharge firebolts when the entire Jeranyi line begins to move forward, slowly, then into a full gallop. After but a few steps, the Jeranyi have become a ragged line with no cohesion.

Even before the movement is readily apparent, the veteran Cyadoran captains are issuing their orders. "Forward! Discharge at will!"

"Concentrate the firelances on the riders with the axes!" Lorn orders. "Firelances on the axes!"

"Firelances on the axes!"

Dust lifts from the road and from the recently-tilled narrow fields flanking it, as the larger Cyadoran force knifes toward the outnumbered Jeranyi.

Lorn forces himself to hold back slightly, not to be in the absolute front of the line, but he still drops two Jeranyi with his firelances, and easily ducks under a clumsy blade to dispatch a third Jeranyi with his Brystan sabre. As he wheels the gelding, he realizes that the battle, if it could be called such, is almost over.

Half the Jeranyi have been wounded or downed before they reached the Cyadoran lancers, and half of those remaining are felled by the more experienced Mirror Lancers within moments. The others are so outnumbered that is not long before they, too, lie across the road and fields.

As he rides through the dust already settling in the early

afternoon, toward his captains, Lorn frowns. Are the only barbarians who can fight, those who live on the edge of the Grass Hills?

"More like a slaughter." Cheryk is shaking his head as he watches the sub-majer ride up.

"Send out the scouts. Let's make sure it's not a trap," Lorn orders. "And set up two of the companies for attack in case another force arrives. Third and Fourth!"

"Yes, ser."

"Sixth Company, guard the road behind us!"

"Quytyl! Have your men collect the blades and dispatch their wounded."

"Yes, ser."

Lorn remains mounted, studying the road and the areas beyond, but the only riders who finally near the Cyadorans are the scouts, riding along the road from the pass that leads down into Berlitos.

Lorn gestures for Emsahl, Cheryk, Esfayl, and Gyraet to join him, and the four captains ride over and rein up beside Lorn.

"Go ahead," Lorn tells the lancer scout.

"There be a few folk on the bridge, ser, but it be like no one even knew we fought. We looked down, and the wagons are moving by the river, and a rider or two be on the roads, mayhap a carriage."

Lorn shakes his head and looks over the captains. "Let's take the town as we planned. Esfayl . . . the bridge. Third and Fifth Companies—the square, Fourth and Sixth—the wharf area. First Company on me."

With a wry smile, Lorn realizes that Rhalyt and his men are assisting Quytyl. "I think we need to tell the undercaptains." He turns the gelding and rides northward toward what had been the right flank of the Cyadoran formation.

"Ser?" asks Rhalyt.

"You lose anyone?"

"One man, ser. One of those axes."

"What about their weapons?"

"There aren't any sabres. A few axes, but most are the big iron blades."

"All right. The scouts say the town is undefended. We're going down, and First Company will follow me."

"Yes, ser."

"I'm going to tell Quytyl his orders, and then I'll be back."

Rhalyt nods as Lorn eases the gelding more northward until he reins up beside the other undercaptain who is watching as two lancers fasten blades to a captured mount.

"We didn't lose anyone, ser," Quytyl announces. "Two wounded, though."

"Badly?"

"One won't be fighting."

"Can he ride and watch the pack animals? They both should."

Quytyl nods.

"You'll be working with Emsahl to take the square—same as the last big town, Disfek or whatever it was. So, as soon as you're finished, form up your men in column behind Third Company."

"Yes, ser."

Lorn turns, then rides back toward Rhalyt and First Company. He blots his forehead and under his eyes. Each day seems hotter, as if they were nearing midsummer, even though it is but early spring.

"Ready to ride, ser," announces Rhalyt as Lorn nears.

A lancer rides up almost simultaneously and announces, "Captain Gyraet says Sixth Company is ready to ride, ser."

"We'll be riding shortly," Lorn temporizes, his eyes and chaos-senses still surveying the field and the trees beyond. While nothing feels exactly wrong, it does not feel right, either, and Lorn finds himself pursing his lips.

Once the Cyadorans have re-formed and ride along the road that winds between two forested hills, and then down the steeper grade toward Berlitos itself, Lorn continues to survey the hills, both with his eyes and chaos-senses, despite the double number of scouts before the main force. Neither he nor the scouts find any armsmen on the descent.

The first dwelling the Mirror Lancers reach on the outskirts of Berlitos, not quite before the road levels out, is set in a grove of sweetsap trees, and is long and narrow, with ancient and heavy crosstimbers framing and bracing the door. The shutters are equally heavy, and old, and fastened tight. What looks to be a small stable is barred equally firmly.

"Be hard to break in there," observes Rhalyt.

Lorn does not comment, but wonders why a town with houses built so sturdily has armsmen so inept. Or are the houses sturdy for that reason? He suspects he will never know.

At the base of the hill, Esfayl takes Second Company northward to secure the bridge—a long and narrow stone-and-brick structure that angles from one island in the placid North Branch to another, and then to a stone pylon set in shallower water, before turning again and rising slightly to a low bluff on the northwest side.

The bridge is empty so far as Lorn can see.

The remaining five companies ride westward along the wide dirt road, leaving the empty bridge for Esfayl.

Unlike the dwellings they have seen elsewhere, those in Berlitos are all of wood, timbered dwellings painted bright colors and resting under more trees than Lorn has seen since he had been assigned to the Accursed Forest years before.

"Sturdy dwellings," observes Rhalyt.

"We might be able to burn this town, but I don't think we want to take it house by house," Lorn says.

"If that's the way they fight, do we need to burn it?" asks Rhalyt.

Lorn does not answer as he urges the gelding in the direction of the town square, past more of the barricaded dwellings and outbuildings. All the noise, all the dust, comes from the lancers. The dwellings are silent.

As the companies enter the town square, Lorn gestures to Cheryk. "Go on to the warehouses and the wharf! First Company and I will meet you there."

"Yes, ser."

Lorn reins up and surveys the town square. In the center of the square is a six-sided brick-faced platform roughly fifty cubits on a side. The sides are a cubit-and-a-half above the dirt and clay of the road that circles the platform. There is no railing, and no discernible purpose for the platform. The buildings around the square are all heavy, two-story timbered structures—like the rest of Berlitos, seemingly impregnable without the Mirror Lancers spending forever battering their way in.

"Have the company hold here," Lorn tells Rhalyt before riding toward Emsahl. The sub-majer can see a chandlery, a cooper's shop, a weaver's, perhaps a fuller's, before he reaches the senior captain. Lorn reins up and glances at Emsahl.

Emsahl shrugs.

"The wood here is old," Lorn ventures.

"It will burn."

"Burn it. Use torches," Lorn commands. "As much of the square as you can, then ride your companies to the bridge." Part of Lorn's command is out of pique, and part is out of a feeling that the Jeranyi must not be allowed to think they can hide behind heavy walls and mock Cyador.

"Yes, ser. Probably the best way to handle this place."

"I'm taking First Company to the wharfs. We'll meet you at the bridge."

"Torches!" Emsahl orders as Lorn turns back to Rhalyt and First Company.

"Ser?" asks the undercaptain.

"We'll ride to the wharfs—it's only a half a kay south."

"First Company!" Rhalyt orders. "Forward . . ."

Lorn looks at the buildings beyond the square. They, too, are massive timber structures—massive and old.

Unlike the buildings in the town square, the doors to the

three warehouses that stand behind the river wharfs are all open, and lancers are carting out some provisions—and blades.

Gyraet rides to meet Lorn. "The warehouses here are mostly empty, ser. Doors were open. Not a soul here. Some wool, some hides, some barrels of oils, a halfscore of barrels of salted meat."

"And no traders?"

Gyraet shakes his head. "They left some blades—almost tenscore, but there are no records, and it doesn't look like there were any."

"Any more cupridium sabres?"

"A score, perhaps."

"We'll keep those, and I want you and the captains to sign a paper saying that we found and dumped into the river the other ninescore blades. Actually, we'd better list all the blades we've dumped, from the first town onward." Lorn's lips twist. "Then . . . have a half-squad ride over to the bridge—Esfayl should have it in hand—and one of the lancers should use a weighted rope to find the deepest point off the bridge."

"Yes, ser."

This time there were blades, but no records.

"Emsahl is firing the square, and the buildings around it will catch fire soon. Can you finish here quickly?" asks Lorn. "Use torches to fire the warehouses."

Gyraet laughs. "We're near finished already. Not that much here."

"Good. Let me know when your company and Cheryk's are ready to ride."

Lorn turns his mount, back toward the town square. As he looks northward, in the direction of thin lines of black smoke and the fires that will rage before long, and toward the bridge he cannot see, the bridge that will lead to Jera, Lorn is not even sure they have taken Berlitos so much as killed some inept armsmen, ridden through the place, looted and burned a few warehouses and the center of the town and ridden on. He wonders whether he is making an enormous mistake in pushing on toward Jera.

Yet the weapons have to come from somewhere, and go to someone who can use them, and he has to stop the easy flow of blades. If he can.

He shakes his head.

LXVI

To THE SOUTH of the bivouac, the River Jeryna runs smoothly, its now-deep waters dark in the twilight. Somewhere out in the camp, Lorn can hear the *twirrrp . . .* of another of the ubiquitous traitor birds scolding some lancer. A few spring insects chirp down by the river bank, and in the greenish purple sky, stars are beginning to appear.

Lorn opens his saddlebags, and his fingers slide over the cool surface of the silver-covered book of verse. Even in the warm evening, after a hot day's ride, with the sun pounding down on the saddlebags, the book is cool. For a moment, his fingers rest on the cool surface, and he thinks of Ryalth—and Kerial.

A faint smile comes to his lips.

Then, with a long slow breath, he extracts the soap he will take down to the river, and closes the saddlebag. His eyes lift into the clear night sky, seeking stars he cannot identify, for there is no chart of which are—or were—the Rational Stars.

Had the ancient writer felt as Lorn did, looking back as the smoke and flames engulfed the forested town of Berlitos? Had that ancient wondered why he had to do what he did? Had he asked himself what difference his actions would make?

Lorn drops his eyes from the faint stars of twilight and laughs, a soft bitter sound, but loud enough for himself.

Of course the ancient writer had wondered. That is why so

many of the verses are melancholy, why so many convey a sense of futility.

Lorn shakes his head. He can but do what he feels best, and he knows that blades coming from elsewhere to Jera are killing lancers for no good reason except to fuel and justify ancient hates—and perhaps to fatten the purses of traders who care little for the men whom their trades kill.

LXVII

IN THE MORNING light, the brown waters of the River Jeryna swirl through the bushes half-submerged at the water's edge. Farther offshore, the currents occasionally show eddies and whirlpools that appear and disappear, but there is no white water on the lower reaches of the river, just a muddy expanse of brown a good two hundred kays wide and thirty deep. By looking along the river that flows to his left, Lorn can see touches of gray-blue on the horizon—the Northern Ocean.

If his maps and calculations are correct, they are within ten kays of Jera, and before long they should be seeing increasing numbers of steads and dwellings. He shifts his weight in the gelding's saddle and glances back along the river road at the column of Mirror Lancers, then back at the road before him. A grassy swale drops away on the right side, then rises into a long grassy slope for grazing—but there are no sheep or cattle anywhere to be seen.

As Lorn rides around the sweeping curve that brings the road to the right and more northward, he sees another of the stone-and-rail fences to the right of the river road, but all is still as the Cyadoran column rides toward the fence and the buildings behind it.

"Another empty stead," observes Gyraet, whose Sixth Company rides in the van with Lorn for the day. The captain inclines his head to the right toward the slab-timbered farm dwelling on the low slope north of the river road. There are three outbuildings of various sizes, but even the chicken shed seems to have been emptied.

Behind the buildings, the spreading trees, and the low slope are rolling hills, and then, perhaps five kays northward, the steeper but still-forested slopes that mark the boundary of the High Steppes.

"All of them have been empty for the last day," Lorn replies.

Word of the Cyadoran force has spread throughout Jerans—or at least along the river. The dwellings near the road are all abandoned. Lorn can see thin lines of chimney smoke rising into the green-blue sky from those houses on more distant hillsides, but the scouts have reported that every holding is either empty or shuttered and barred. Yet the scouts have seen no evidence of regular armsmen or barbarians, nor any tracks in the lanes and roads.

Lorn stretches as best he can in the saddle and takes a deep breath.

Midmorning still finds Lorn and the Cyadorans on the river road, but Lorn can see a distant outline of several ships in the harbor and the gray-blue of the Northern Ocean beyond. The road has also carried them closer to the steep hills that border the port city to the north—and to a kaystone, whose inscription is clear enough: *Jera, 5 k.*

"Seems like the last five kays have been ten," Gyraet says.

"Or fifteen," Lorn says with a laugh. He glances ahead toward two figures in white riding around the curve of the road. "Send a messenger to summon the officers." He and Gyraet keep riding, leading the column toward Jera along the dusty road that holds few tracks, and those mainly of heavy wagons.

Emsahl and Cheryk arrive within moments. Both glance at Lorn.

"We'll keep riding until the scouts and the other officers arrive," Lorn says.

Esfayl and Rhalyt are next, followed by Quytyl, who has barely reined his mount into a walk behind the more senior captains when the scouts ride in and turn their mounts to ride alongside Lorn and Gyraet.

"What did you find?" asks the sub-majer.

The gray-bearded older lancer speaks first. "Roads are clear, ser, like everyone's fled. No tracks like armsmen or barbarians. More wagon tracks than we've seen before."

"You think traders are trying to pack their goods and flee?"

"Could be . . ."

"What about the city?"

"Less smoke from the chimneys than you'd see most days," answers the ginger-bearded scout. "Didn't see no folk or mounts about, except around the wharfs—that was from the hill a couple kays from there, and it was hard to tell, but the port part seemed busy, ser."

"No armsmen?" Lorn wants to be sure.

"None we saw."

The sub-majer turns in the saddle. "This time we're going straight for the ocean piers and the warehouses." He glances across the faces of the captains. "We'll worry about the city later." At the puzzled expression that crosses Quytyl's face, and Cheryk's worried frown, he adds, "We're after all the blades and the traders. They're trying to escape. The city will still be there, but they may not."

"And their records won't be, either," suggests Gyraet. "Sub-majers need things like records to take back to commanders who haven't been in the field. Without proof, in a year, they'll forget, and we'll be facing more cupridium blades from Summerdock—with fewer firelance charges."

Emsahl nods slowly.

"The river road runs straight to the piers, right along the

river," Lorn explains, "and once we get close, we'll go to four-abreast. First Company, move up. You'll follow me." Lorn reflects that on this campaign he has effectively followed Dettaur's directive, by alternating his own command between the First and Fifth Companies. Then, Dettaur will be furious when he discovers what Lorn has done—if Lorn survives to report his actions.

"Once we get closer, I'll give more orders, but, remember, we want to take the harbor and the warehouses first."

"Yes, ser."

Lorn looks at the scouts. "You need to head back out and see if there are any armsmen or barbarians forming up to attack—or defend."

As the scouts ride off, Lorn still wonders at the lack of resistance. Or will the Jeranyi wait until he has almost returned to Inividra, without firelance charges, before they mount a final attack? He shrugs to himself.

Roughly a kay later, the road sweeps upward perhaps twenty cubits over the distance of half a kay and northward. At the top of the low rise, the harbor and Northern Ocean stretch out before Lorn, with the city's buildings and dwellings set on an incline to his right, and the warehouse and harbor directly before the riders. To the left, the river widens so that it is difficult to tell exactly where the river ends and the harbor begins

Less than a kay ahead is the first section of the stone riprap of the seawall, and there two redstone pillars flank the road. The pillars are without gates or a gatehouse. Riding up the incline from the seawall are the two scouts, moving at almost a gallop.

As Lorn starts down the incline toward the approaching scouts, he can feel the wind shift from barely a flutter to a strong breeze out of the northwest, bearing the scent of salt air and the less appetizing odor of dead fish. He glances upward, but the sky remains hazy, a white film covering the clear green-blue that he had seen earlier in the morning.

The scouts ride in beside Lorn and begin to report, even without waiting for an order. "Armsmen ahead, ser. Maybe twoscore—with boards and blades."

"How far?"

"A kay, mayhap, beyond the pillars, but afore the warehouses, it looks to be."

"Shields? What kind?"

"Sort of look like Mirror Shields."

Lorn glances at Rhalyt. "Send a messenger to have the captains join me here again for a few moments. We aren't stopping."

"Yes, ser." The undercaptain turns and relays the message.

Lorn studies the road and the harbor. While he cannot be sure, there appear to be two vessels still tied up at the long spindly pier that juts well out into the harbor. There are carts and people jostling toward the pier, and a reddish block of figures that must be the armsmen the scouts have reported. The sub-majer keeps riding.

Emsahl and Cheryk arrive first. Then come Esfayl and Gyraet, and finally, once more, Quytyl.

They are less than a hundred cubits from the redstone pillars when Lorn begins to talk. "There's a company or more of armsmen trying to block us from the harbor. They've got polished mirror shields and armor. Who has the most firelances working?"

"We do, I think," ventures Cheryk.

"I'd like you to take the lead. Have your men aim the firelances for the mounts. Bring them down quickly. I'm going to take First Company and Second Company and get behind them if we can." Lorn glances toward Esfayl, then Rhalyt. "You ready for that?"

"Yes, ser."

"Fourth Company to the fore! Fourth Company to the fore!" Cheryk's deep voice rises over the sound of hoofs and mounts and lancers murmuring.

Lorn turns to Rhalyt and Esfayl. "Once we pass the pillars, move your men to the right shoulder. When I signal, have them follow me."

"Yes, ser."

"Gyraet and Emsahl . . . you support Cheryk."

"Yes, ser," reply the other two captains.

Lorn eases the gelding to the right to pass through the stone pillars. To his left is a long line of rose-thorns covering a brick wall of almost five cubits. Behind the wall is a short open space, and behind that, the brick-walled backs of older buildings, few with windows, some shuttered, others boarded.

As the Mirror Lancers ride toward the harbor wharfs and warehouses ahead, along the uneven cobblestones that have replaced the dirt and clay of the roadbed beyond the pillar gates, the echoes of their mounts' hoofs clatter into the pale midday. The high thin clouds of morning have thickened just enough more to blunt the sun's light into a bright haze.

Ahead is a line of armsmen, mounted, and three-deep. As the scouts have reported, each wears a breastplate, armored gauntlets, and a crimson tunic. All bear shimmering mirror shields and iron blades longer than sabres, but shorter than the massive barbarian blades.

"Lancers!" calls a voice. "You let the merchants depart, and we'll leave the city to you!"

"You surrender and let us have the merchants, and the ships, and we'll spare you!" Lorn counters.

"Prepare to die!" calls back the voice.

Lorn turns to the senior captains. "Cheryk! Remember! Use the firelances we have left on the mounts! Bring them down!"

"Fourth Company! Prepare to discharge firelances. Aim at the mounts! At the mounts!"

As Cheryk orders his men, and Gyraet and Quytyl move up their lancers, beyond the massed armsmen, along the wharf, Lorn can see figures scurrying out of one of the ware-houses. "First Company! Second Company! Follow me!" He turns the white gelding back along the first lane to the north, past the side of what appears to be a tannery, away from the barrels and the stench, and he wonders why the Jer-anyi ever allowed a tannery in the city itself. Beyond the tan-nery, he turns the gelding westward on the empty street, half mud and half ancient cobblestones, past a large cooper's shop, and then past a building that is but half-built.

Some five hundred cubits farther westward, almost to where the street ends in a brick wall, he finds a side lane, be-tween a cabinet-maker's and an unmarked structure, and rides through it. As the gelding quick-trots out of the alley-like lane, a gray-haired woman dashes to escape, but the gelding knocks her to one side. Lorn hopes she can get clear of the riders that follow.

He turns the gelding to his right, toward the first of the warehouses and the long and angled pier beyond that which he has seen so often in his chaos-glass. Figures are moving, some running toward the pier and the ship beyond. The three-masted ship at the end of the pier is red-hulled—Hamorian.

"Rhalyt—take the second squad and block the pier—don't let anyone on it—if you can. Keep anyone from boarding that ship! First squad, stand by me!"

As Rhalyt rides up with the first squad of first company, the undercaptain starts to separate out the second squad, and Lorn quickly surveys the seawall and the harbor. A blue-hulled vessel has left the pier and, in the darker water be-yond the immediate harbor, spread its sails.

Lorn waits until he sees the first part of Second Company. "Esfayl, attack the armsmen from the rear!"

"The armsmen from the rear. Second Company!" orders Esfayl, turning his mount back toward the battle.

"First Company, first squad!" Lorn rides toward the pier and toward the end warehouse where a figure in gray runs with a torch toward the building. Lorn lifts the firelance, and triggers it. The man who had been running toward the warehouse with the torch, pitches forward into the clay, and the torch drops on the cobblestones.

Lorn keeps riding toward the pier, his squad almost up to Rhalyt's as they pass the end warehouse. Behind him, he hears shouts, the *hsst* of firelances, and the sound of metal on metal.

"Frig! Bastards are behind us!" yells someone.

"Quarter! Quarter!"

"No quarter! No quarter!" Lorn yells, turning and trying to send his voice back toward the pitched fight. "They'll be sending blades to kill you in a year! No quarter!"

He hopes his words are heeded, but he rides toward the merchant or factor running beside a heavy-laden handcart filled with wooden footchests. The cart and merchant have almost reached the foot of the pier, when the bearded man looks back. The factor or trader—in a gold-trimmed crimson tunic—then begins to sprint toward the pier, leaving the handcart. Two guards scramble after him.

The two porters in gray abandon the cart and scramble off the cobblestones of the wharf road toward the gap in the brick wall beside the last warehouse. For the first time, Lorn spurs the gelding, and the white responds, his hoofs clattering on the stones.

Lorn lifts the firelance, aiming it toward the fleeing merchant.

One of the guards stops and turns, then lifts his big blade. He sees the firelance and jumps off the side of the seawall into waist-deep water. The second guard sprints onto the single long pier, past the slower and heavier merchant, his legs pumping as he dashes around abandoned handcarts and shoves an older man in maroon into a bollard. The man totters, then plummets into the gray water of the harbor.

Lorn triggers the firelance. *Hssst!* The bolt strikes the

wooden planks of the pier seaward of the merchant. "Trader! Halt or die!"

The trader looks to the end of the pier, where his former guard jumps across the widening gap between the Hamorian ship and the pier, grabbing a dangling line which has been cut, for the other end of the line dangles from the last bollard on the pier. Then the trader stops and shrugs, helplessly, lifting his arms.

Lorn watches for a moment, then shakes his head. He can do nothing about the trading vessels that have escaped. Slowly as the last ship pulls away from the end of the long and narrow pier, it will be beyond the range of his firelance by the time he can reach the pier's end. He can only hope that what he needs is among the abandoned bags, bales, and handcarts on the pier, and the street that borders the pier and seawall. He turns the gelding.

"Rhalyt! Take the pier, and make sure that no one makes off with any of the bags or carts! And guard that trader in crimson. Don't let him escape or kill himself."

"Yes, ser."

Lorn turns the gelding, and the first squad follows him as he rides back toward where the armsmen and the lancers had been fighting. He winces as he sees the number of mounts lying across the street. As he nears, the last armsman in crimson falls to an attack of three lancers.

Lorn reins up, looking around. Except for the dead Hamorian armsmen, all those remaining at the eastern end of the street flanking the seawall are Cyadoran lancers.

Cheryk rides forward. "Lost near-on a halfscore, ser. They were better than any we've faced."

Lorn nods. "I'm sorry. But we couldn't leave them here to provide a guard for more shipments of blades."

"No, ser. Not after all we've done."

Esfayl eases his mount toward Lorn. "Ser?"

"Are your men in order?"

"Yes, ser."

"I'd like you to find as much lamp oil as you can," Lorn orders. "Around here, if you can. Bring some of it to the long pier out there, and some to the warehouses."

Esfayl raises his eyebrows.

"We're going to burn the piers before we leave." Lorn mouth twists into the smile he dislikes. "It's harder to land blades if you have to bring them in by boat. And the warehouses, once we take anything we need."

Gyraet rides up. "We're going through the nearer warehouse, ser. Spidlarian, looks like."

"See what you can find, quickly, and records, if you can." Lorn looks back at Emsahl. "Can you and Fifth Company stand guard while we do what has to be done?"

"Yes, ser."

"We'll try to be quick."

Lorn rides back along the seawall. In a way, he feels ineffectual, for it seems as though all he has done is ride back and forth.

Rhalyt's lancers are escorting a bearded figure in crimson from the foot of the pier toward the front of the last warehouse, a three-story timber structure that still flies the ensign of Hamor. The trader's hands are bound behind him, and there is a slash across his cheek.

"We got him, ser, and some others who might be traders."

"Hold him there, and don't let him near the warehouse." Lorn rides toward the foot of the pier, and the abandoned handcart filled with footchests, where he dismounts, absently handing the gelding's reins to the nearest lancer. He steps to the handcart, and the chests, then notes the heavy leather bags beneath the footchests. He leans forward and manages to wrench one free. The weight and sound of coins confirm his suspicions. He motions to Rhalyt, who has remained mounted.

"Ser?"

"We'll need a guard here. Several."

Lorn looks back at the four chests, then lifts the top one and opens it, running through the papers. He shakes his head. They will need a wagon. It will take more time than he dares take in Jera to sort through the records.

"Rhalyt," he calls again. "We need to find a wagon to carry this, and any supplies we can use. See if you can have one of the squad leaders round up one and some team horses."

Rhalyt nods.

Lorn remounts the gelding and looks out into the harbor, where the Hamorian trader has also spread its sails. He shakes his head again, then rides the short distance to the end warehouse, the Hamorian one. He dismounts and ties the gelding to a post by the door. Rhalyt also dismounts and follows him.

In the front room are open wooden cases, one is half-filled with long dark iron blades, coated with oil and wax. The other nine cases have not been opened.

Lorn counts the blades in the open case—over a score. "It looks like there are over twentyscore blades just here."

Two lancers slip in, and Rhalyt motions to the door. "Best you check the rooms before the majer."

The graying veteran nods and steps through the doorway. After several moments, he returns. "No one there, ser."

Lorn and Rhalyt enter the storage section of the warehouse. Some of the racks are empty, but most of the goods have been left in the warehouse. Lorn sees bolts of cotton, amphorae which may contain olives or oils, barrels of dried fish, dried fruits, even some barrels of clay from Biehl.

"Ser!" Rhalyt gestures.

Lorn rejoins the undercaptain, before whom are two wooden cases, each lettered in a grayish greaselike paint: *sabres, cup., 2 sc., Smdck.*

"Fourscore lancer-type sabres—made from cupridium,"

Lorn says. "We'll need to take these back. We'll have to cart them and the other blades out front."

Lorn steps back out from the storage area into the side room where his glass had shown that records had been kept, but the room is bare except for a flat table and a chair. Marks in the floor dust show where chests had been.

"Ser," calls one of the lancers, "Captain Esfayl is here with a wagon."

Lorn hurries out into the still-hazy afternoon sun. Two lancers stand by the bound trader, and beyond them, Esfayl is mounted beside a four-horse team. The large wagon behind the team carries eight huge barrels of lamp oil. Esfayl grins at Lorn. "We got the oil, ser."

Lorn grins back, momentarily. "We'll use six on the pier, and one each for the two large warehouses. There's oil in this one, anyway. Have your men space the barrels evenly along the piers—one at the outermost end. Put a small hole in each and roll them in so that the oil spreads over the wood. Then, I'll go out and set them afire."

Esfayl nods.

"We'll use the wagon for the blades and the coins and supplies—and the records we've gathered. Leave it here so Rhalyt's men can load it."

As the lancers begin to unload the barrels and roll them along the rough cobblestones toward the pier, Lorn turns to the Hamorian trader. "You seem to have a prosperous warehouse here—especially in blades."

The Hamorian trader, his hands tied behind him, spits on the cobblestones. "You are a worthless piece of dung . . . a man whose mind is as narrow as the lance you carry."

"If I didn't need you to deliver a message. . . . you'd be dead," Lorn says quietly. "I might burn off your right hand, though, if you aren't silent."

The trader closes his mouth, and his eyes radiate hate.

"Cyador doesn't like Hamorian traders making golds off blades that kill its lancers." Lorn fixes his eyes on the trader.

"Think long about why we're here. We're going to leave you here. Someone will find you, I'm sure, and you can explain everything."

The bearded trader looks down.

"Oh, I know you won't explain it to the locals." Lorn laughs. "They might cut your throat. But you're going to have to explain it to your backers, and perhaps to the Emperor of Hamor." He shrugs. "You might get away with not telling them . . . until the Majer-Commander of Mirror Lancers conveys the same message to the Hamorian traders in Cyad. He might even mention that you'd been told." Lorn offers a nasty smile.

"I will convey your message, but you are but an impetuous young majer, and you will change nothing," the trader says slowly. "Lancers come, and lancers go, and nothing changes."

"I won't change the hearts of traders," Lorn admits. "You'll always place a gold above a life . . . but I just might change where you trade for those golds."

The bearded trader looks down.

"Tie up his legs and leave him on the edge of the seawall, out of the way. And have someone check all those bags, for golds or trading records." Lorn walks to the gelding, where he pulls out the firelance. Then, carrying it carefully, he makes his way out to the end of the long and spindly pier . . . setting his boots carefully on the slippery wood. At the end, he looks out to the Northern Ocean, but both trading vessels have vanished into the limitless gray-blue expanse.

He turns and lowers the lance. *Hssst!* From the small firelance-bolt flames lick upward and across the wooden planks. Lorn walks back toward the shore. He uses the firelance nearly a halfscore of times, although much of the chaos comes from what he draws as a magus, and his head aches, and his eyes water by the time he steps off the end of the pier. The seaward end is already a raging blaze, and the sea breeze carries the heat inward.

"The warehouses . . . they're ready," Rhalyt calls. "We've also got the chests and bags in the wagon, and some dried meat and hard cheese—and the boxes of sabres. We can't fit all those blades in the first wagon."

"Let's see if your squad leaders can find another." Lorn tilts his head. "Did your men make sure they got oil on the wall timbers as well? And everyone's out of the warehouse?"

"Yes, ser."

After three firelance-bolts, one side of the warehouse is in flames, and the crackling orange flames and black smoke rise into the hazy afternoon sky.

Lorn has Rhalyt repeat the process with the warehouse of the Spidlarian traders.

Then he gathers the captains. "Now we'll move toward the city square closest and up the hill. Bring torches. Keep saving the firelances. We're going to burn anything else that will burn as we leave," Lorn orders the captains. "I want it to be a long, long time before traders can make golds bringing blades here."

He remounts the gelding and waits as the Mirror Lancers re-form, and as the three wagons that they have gathered are lined up. Behind him the flames mount—because the traders will stop at nothing to gain golds, and he has but one chance to halt their killing trade.

LXVIII

In the late afternoon, Lorn glances downriver and back at the clouds of black-and-gray smoke that have drifted across both the river and the harbor, the result of the flames that continue to consume the city that had been Jera. With all the trees and the old wooden structures, with few of stone or brick, Lorn doubts much will remain by morning. The decaying port town had been little more than a collection point for Hamorian and Spidlarian traders to drop off arms. . . . but it doubtless had been home to many, who will suffer from his actions. Some are innocent, insofar as anyone who benefits from living in a city that prospers from trade in killing implements is innocent.

His eyes go to the rear of the column and the wagons that creak after the Mirror Lancers. The first wagon is filled with chests containing golds and silvers, more than five thousand golds at rough count, and all sorts of trading records that Lorn must read. The second holds weapons—Hamorian longswords and Brystan sabres—as well as the cases of unused and recently-forged cupridium sabres clearly forged in Cyad—without lancer markings. The third holds provisions, as do the packhorses that bring up the rear.

Once he returns to Inividra, Lorn will recommend that the fireships of Cyad—those remaining—land lancers, and rebuild the town as a Cyadoran colony. Controlling the River Jeryna will choke off an easy supply of weapons to the Jeranyi, and holding one town will be far less costly than facing endless lines of barbarians across the north of Cyad.

He smiles to himself. Again, he is thinking as though he had real power to do or recommend such. While his efforts have been somewhat successful, he has no doubts that he will face severe disciplinary action—assuming he can even return to Inividra with most of his forces. Yet, as always, his real choices have been limited.

"Strange city," ventures Quytyl, riding beside him.

"In many ways," muses Lorn. "The warehouses near the pier were new, built over the ruins of older buildings. There were abandoned buildings, and the armsmen were Hamorian." He shakes his head.

"Why were the Hamorians there?" asks Quytyl.

"Trade, golds . . . it's almost as if they were starting to take over the city."

"Could they? It's a long voyage from Swartheld to Jera, isn't it?"

"They held part of it," Lorn points out. "Those records will tell. I'll have to read through them before we get back."

After several moments of silence, he glances back once more at the gray-and-black smoke that still rises from the burning city.

They have another eightday, at least, of riding, and fighting, to return to Inividra. While Lorn can "inspect" a few firelances, and add some chaos, his energies are limited, compared to the number of lances. As with everything, what he can do is limited.

Lorn shakes his head slowly.

LXIX

TO THE WEST of the road are two fields—the first Lorn has seen in almost half a day of riding along the West Branch of the Jeryna River. The neatly tilled fields, with but shoots of green appearing, are separated by a hedgerow of thorny roses, with irrigation ditches running from the river to the fields. On a low hill on the far side of the southernmost field is a dwelling, its walls of odd-shaped rocks mortared together. Both fields and ditchworks are empty under the hot spring sun that blisters through the green-blue sky of midday.

Lorn glances from the fields to the dusty road and then to the narrow river to his left, really a large stream that is no more than fifty cubits wide and perhaps five deep, just deep enough to make easy crossing difficult.

He squints as he sees the dust on the road ahead—the scouts returning, and returning in haste, a good sign that trouble lies ahead. With a long, slow deep breath he waits.

"Trouble, looks like," offers Cheryk, who leads the Cyadoran forces with Fourth Company.

"The last few days have been too calm," Lorn agrees.

"We're getting closer to the Grass Hills, and if there's going to be a real attack, here's where it's likely to be."

"Jerans is a strange place," Cheryk observes. "It's almost like the barbarians aren't a part of it. But the Jeranyi are sending weapons."

"Someone is," Lorn temporizes.

The two officers ride in silence, waiting for the pair of scouts.

"Ser! Barbarians ahead!" calls the lead scout from a good fifty cubits away.

Lorn motions for them to ride beside him, then waits until they turn and draw abreast.

"There's a raiding party of sorts riding up from the east on the other side of the river, ser, like they knew we were here," reports the balding scout. "They be heading toward the ford."

"How many?"

"Fourscore. Could be a bit less."

"We're back in true barbarian territory." Lorn smiles.

"About how far to the ford?"

"Four kays, I'd say." Those words come from the younger, ginger-bearded scout. "Could be a bit more."

"We'll probably stand down and water the mounts here, then ride on. Go on back to where you can watch the ford. Let us know if they cross early or if they don't cross."

"Yes, ser."

Lorn looks at Cheryk. "I'll need all the officers. Tell everyone to stand down and water the mounts now. We may not get a chance later."

Lorn and Cheryk rein up, then wait in the still heat of the day while Semdyl passes the word and the other officers ride forward to join them.

This time Gyraet is the last to pull his mount alongside. "Sorry, ser, but we were having trouble with the rear wagon."

"How much trouble?"

"Wheel's beginning to split under the rim. We brought spare wheels, and that won't be a problem, except I don't know as it will last until we stop tonight."

"We have more trouble—fourscore Jeranyi raiders ahead. The kind we see in the Grass Hills." Lorn surveys the faces. "We don't have many firelance charges left, do we?"

"My second squad has a few," offers Gyraet.

"I'd like to put them up front, and have them use the fire-lances on the first charge."

"We'll be ready."

"Good."

"Esfayl . . . your men ride well, I've noticed. I'd like to pull them out and have them strike the barbarians on the flank. Which flank, we'll see as we get nearer . . ." Lorn continues to outline his simple battle plan.

Once everyone is briefed, Lorn waters his gelding in the brownish waters of the West Branch of the Jeryna, water that does not appear too dirty, although he does not drink himself, but samples the last of his water bottle. Then he leads the gelding the score or so of cubits from the riverbank to the road, where he waits until he has word that all the mounts have been watered.

Finally, a messenger from Quytyl arrives, "Fifth Company and wagons are ready, ser."

Lorn nods at Gyraet. "Let's go." He raises his arm, then drops it. "Column forward!"

"Column forward!" The order echoes back along the lancers.

The Cyadoran force has ridden another two kays or so when the younger, ginger-bearded scout rides up. "They're across the ford, ser, and watering their mounts. Still a good two kays from here. Lyrsen's watching from the rise . . . not much of one, but he'll be riding out if they head this way."

"Good. Did you notice any different weapons?"

"Didn't see any of the axes with hooks. Don't think

they're that good on a mount. With a longer pole, be good for a footman."

Lorn studies the road ahead, then turns in the white leather saddle that has become more dun under the rigors of the past seasons. The road is wide enough and the shoulder even enough. He glances at Gyraet, who heads his second squad. "Have them go to four-abreast. Pass it along."

"Four-abreast! Four-abreast!"

Behind him, the column widens and shortens, and Lorn coughs as the following wind swirls more dust into his face and lungs. Then he blots the combination of sweat and dirt off his face, and studies the road before them as it slowly rises as it heads southeast, so that there is a four-cubit bluff above the water on the south side of the river. If the scout is correct, the ford and the barbarians lie another kay beyond the top of the gradual rise up which the Cyadoran force rides.

At the top of the hill, the other scout rides to meet Lorn and Gyraet. Lorn signals for the column to halt.

"See, sers . . . They're forming-up there, keep us from the ford."

Lorn nods. According his maps, the road swings back to the north side of the river for at least forty kays farther, and the south side is almost impassable because it verges on one of the more rugged sections of the Grass Hills. Then, he does not understand why the raiders do not remain on the north side and force the Mirror Lancers to attack from the ford—unless they regard that as somehow cowardly. He shakes his head.

"Ser?" asks Gyraet.

"I don't say I understand why they crossed the ford."

"Ah . . . ," offers the scout. "Look there on the other side . . . see that shimmery white? That's sand . . . once you get off the road, it's sand, and it be soft, like powder."

Lorn hopes the road is firm enough for the wagons, even as he understands the logic of the barbarians' positioning.

Emsahl, Esfayl, and Cheryk ride forward, and all the officers look down the gradual slope.

"Now . . . sers . . . the river side of the road," the scout goes on, "it be sand like the other shore. The grass and dirt is firm on the south side."

"Esfayl . . . you'll have to swing out from the right, then," Lorn says.

"Yes, ser."

Lorn looks down at the barbarian force. "We'll have to go to a two companyfour-abreast front . . . probably by those bushes where the slope levels out. I wouldn't ride uphill against us before that."

"Yes, ser."

"Gyraet, put your first squad on the river side, your second squad on the right shoulder. Cheryk . . . if the ground is firm, can you flank Sixth Company on the right?"

The older captain nods.

"First and Fifth Companies, follow until you're on the flat . . . then, Rhalyt . . . you put your company behind Sixth Company, and see if you can come in from the left. You'll have to feel that out."

"Yes, ser."

Lorn looks downhill. "We'll have to do what we can." He leans forward to touch his firelance. "I've got a few charges left, so I'll stay with Sixth Company."

As the Cyadoran force begins moving down the slope of the road at a walk, Lorn keeps watching the barbarians, but they hold ranks, waiting.

No sooner than has Sixth Company passed the bushes, and Third Company moved up beside them, than the Jeranyi riders charge.

"Wait until they close!" orders Gyraet. "Discharge at thirty cubits! *Thirty cubits*. Short bursts!"

"Now . . . charge!" Lorn orders, raising and dropping his arm.

The ground shivers under the impact of tenscore sets of hoofs.

Hsst! Hssst! Lorn tries to keep his lance level and moves from barbarian to barbarian as the raiders dash toward the Cyadorans. From the corner of his eye, he can see white-clad figures swinging southward, but he forces his attention onto the oncoming riders, who have begun to spread.

Hsst! Hsst!

"Short bursts!" Gyraet insists.

Even before the raiders are within twenty cubits, the sound of firelances dies away, except for an occasional burst from those few with more than a charge or two. Although the raiders have lost almost a score of riders to the lances, those remaining hold their big blades ready to beat through the shorter and lighter sabres of the Mirror Lancers.

Lorn uses the last charge in the firelance—the last of those he had put there the night before through his own efforts as a magus—on a rider who seems to be a leader, then drops the weapon and pulls out his second sabre, half ducking, half sliding the blade of a barbarian, then offering a backslash to another as he passes.

Dust swirls around the riders, and air is filled with the dull clanging of metal on metal, the muffled *thud*s of metal on flesh or bone. Lorn finds himself through the three-deep line of the barbarians, and turns, riding back to pick off a dazed younger barbarian who can barely raise his blade.

A graybeard turns toward Lorn, and his big blade whistles. While Lorn manages a half-parry, half-slide, his left arm is numb even from the glancing impact. His right is not, and he twists and brings the Brystan sabre across the graybeard's upper arm. The blade drops, and Lorn forces his left arm into a slash-thrust, then ducks and rides clear as the older warrior slowly topples out of the saddle.

Two of the big barbarians charge out of the pack toward

Lorn. He cannot quite bring the gelding around quickly enough, and barely can slide the first big blade.

A glittering lancer-sabre slashes down across the shoulder of Lorn's second attacker, and the first barbarian turns toward Quytyl—who has wheeled his mount to help Lorn. Lorn leans forward, almost off-balance, but manages a thrust to the giant's throat. The sabre catches, and Lorn has to jerk to free it, then almost loses his seat as the blade abruptly comes free.

The dead barbarian's mount slams into Lorn's leg, even as he tries to get the gelding past it to help Quytyl, who has been engaged by yet another pair of Jeranyi.

Desperately, Lorn throws the firebolt of a magus at one of the barbarians, whose chest flares into flame, but before he can use either blade or form another firebolt, the big blade of the remaining barbarian slams through Quytyl's guard.

All Lorn can do is flame the last barbarian after Quytyl slumps in the saddle, then turn his mount to seek out others, his blades slicing almost without thought, as he becomes a butchering machine, his blades edged with rage and chaos.

Again, as in so many battles, one moment Lorn is fighting, and the next, the field is empty, except for Mirror Lancers. He glances toward the river, where less than half a score of raiders ride eastward on the far shore, then back around him, where scores of mounts are riderless.

"Ser!" calls a voice.

Lorn turns the gelding and rides toward Yusaet, Quytyl's senior squad leader. He wipes the sabres and sheathes them as he does. He is abruptly aware that he is seeing in double images, and that his skull is being pounded like an anvil by an unseen hammer.

"Ser . . ." Yusaet looks at the sub-major. "I saw . . . you tried to get to the undercaptain."

"I wasn't quite fast enough," Lorn admits. "I got one, but . . ."

"I saw you kill three, right there, ser. No one could have tried harder."

"Thank you. He would have been a good captain." Lorn straightens. "For now, you're in charge of Fifth Company."

"Yes, ser."

"See about what wounded you have, and gather any stray mounts. You know what to do."

Yusaet nods. "Yes, ser."

Lorn eases the gelding toward the depression where the road turns and drops toward the river, where Cheryk, Gyraet, and Esfayl have gathered momentarily. Behind him, there are the murmurs.

". . . sub-major . . . see the way he used those sabres?"

". . . saw him cut four out of the saddle, got another four with his lance . . ."

". . . maybe more . . ."

". . . never saw a senior officer fight like that . . ."

"Never will again, either. Keep it in the Company."

The last voice is Yusaet's.

". . . but . . ."

"Keep it in the Company," Yusaet repeats.

A quick and bitter smile crosses Lorn's face, one he erases as he nears the three officers.

"Are you all right, ser?" asks Esfayl, an expression that is half frown, half of concern.

As Lorn reins up, he looks down at his trousers, then at his sleeves. His uniform is smeared and splattered with blood, and everything around him seems to pulse, because his double vision wavers. He moves his arms, stands slightly in the stirrups. His arms ache, and his head still throbs, but he can find no wounds. "I'm all right." He looks at the three. "Do we have any idea . . . how many we lost?"

"Almost a score, ser," Gyraet reports. "And Emsahl."

Lorn winces.

"Some bastard got him from behind." Gyraet pauses. "And you know about Quytyl?"

"I was there, but I couldn't reach him. I'm not sure his arm healed right, but he never said anything about it." Lorn's words feel slow on his tongue.

"Not having the firelances hurts," Cheryk adds.

"That's one reason why we did this," Lorn points out. "We'll have fewer and fewer firelances every year. Next year I'm not sure anyone will be able to do what we did. Not without more lancers and greater losses."

"Most commanders worry about this year's losses," Gyraet says slowly.

"It is not a comfort to me," Lorn says, "to save a score of men for a year so that threescore will die next spring." He laughs harshly and bitterly. "It's not a comfort to lose a score on the way home, either."

"That is why you are a majer—"

"Sub-majer," Lorn corrects with a laugh.

". . . and you will go on to be a commander or more," Gyraet finishes.

"If I survive being a sub-majer." Lorn looks over the three, trying to focus his vision, and failing. "I'm sorry, captains. I'd hoped we could do this with a few less casualties." He pauses. "Let me know when you're ready to move across the ford."

"Yes, ser."

Lorn eases his mount a hundred cubits or so uphill, where he looks out over the site of the brief and bloody battle. Threescore barbarians dead, and a score of lancers, the lancers because a sub-majer had an idea for reducing casualties, and the barbarians because. . . . Lorn still is not sure he knows. Is it hatred too deep to wash away with either blood or water? Or the needs of the barbarian culture fueled by the greed of the traders?

He shakes his head and studies the West Branch, whose

waters have dwindled into a stream barely ten cubits across, and then at the northern side of the Grass Hills.

He doubts they will face more attacks before returning to Inividra. That is where his real problems will begin.

LXX

ON THE NIGHT of the day after the battle on the West Branch ford, Lorn sits in the twilight, on the side of a slope above one of the few springs in the Grass Hills. He reads slowly through the papers in the second footchest carried by the wagon back from Jera. There are two piles of paper and parchment before him. Most sheets go in one pile, but every so often he sets one in the second pile, the one with but a handful of sheets in it.

The wind off the hill is light, but Lorn has to use stones to keep the papers in their piles.

He looks up at a cough to see Gyraet standing there. "Yes?"

"Might be as I could help some," offers the captain. "Don't tell many people, but I do have some traders in my family."

"So do I," Lorn says. "It's still hard." He grins and gestures to the third chest, still closed and set behind the second one. "I'd appreciate the help. I really would. You know what we're looking for—anything that shows traders sending weapons to Jera." He pauses, then adds, "And anything that might show that Hamor is trying to get a foothold there."

"Like the Hamorian armsmen?"

"Didn't you think it was strange that we didn't see many armsmen once we left the Grass Hills—and those we did see were from Hamor?"

Gyraet bobs his head. "Well-trained, too, and that's a bother."

Lorn understands. Is the Emperor of Hamor supplying blades to the barbarians to weaken both the barbarians and Cyador? He glances down at the papers, and takes a deep breath.

Gyraet opens the third chest. "Lots of invoices here, too many for an old and dying port like Jera. Makes you wonder."

"It does." Then, Lorn wonders about so many things—how Ryalth and Kerial are doing, the health of his parents, and what new schemes Dettaur is hatching. But he cannot deal with any of those until he returns to Inividra.

By then, he must know what the traders' papers show, and what he will do with what they show.

LXXI

THE TWO MEN stand in the shade of a fourth-floor eastern balcony of the Palace of Eternal Light. The light sea breeze gusts around them, removing the heat that oozes outward from the stone walls.

"How do you find Vyanat'mer?" asks Luss.

"He is a merchanter of much intelligence," replies the Second Magus. "He takes great pains to hide it behind a facade of simple honesty and bluntness, although he is, for a merchanter, both honest and blunt."

"But not simple," replies the Captain-Commander with a laugh.

"He is simple in what he believes. He is not simple in how he moves to support those beliefs."

"What does he believe?" questions Luss, almost idly, as if he cares little for the answer, but feels he should ask the question.

"That traders should be fair, and so should the Mirror Lancers and the Magi'i." Kharl smiles. "He knows this is unlikely, yet he believes it, and will scheme and support those who come closest to those ideals."

"He might prove more dangerous than Bluoyal."

"Far more . . . especially when we do not know who will be the next Hand of the Emperor."

Luss raises his eyebrows. "I had not heard."

"It is never announced. There is but one Hand, and none know him . . . save some guess."

"I would not have guessed."

"Good."

"That may change matters . . . in Inividra."

"It may, but not to make matters for you better, Captain-Commander. The Hand tempered matters."

"When will . . . ?"

"There may not be one appointed soon."

"No Hand?" questions Luss. "Is this because Toziel becomes more tired, and his thoughts wander? What will you do?"

"Captain-Commander . . . there is little any of the Magi'i can do. Not at this moment. The Emperor appoints the Hand, not the First Magus, and even if the First Magus were to press for young Rustyl, he is far too young and too direct to be a Hand, and far too well-known because of Chyenfel's favors. And Chyenfel has groomed him to succeed Toziel, if necessary, not himself or the Hand."

"If you . . . once Toziel . . ."

Kharl shakes his head, and laughs. "Would any accept a magus known to have been one of the Three on the Malachite Throne?"

"They might accept you."

The Second Magus laughs. "Your flattery is welcome and most obvious."

"Yet the Empress . . . Toziel listens to her more and more."

Kharl laughs again. "He has always listened to her. As he has aged in these last seasons, he has become less able to conceal that he does. Do not worry about dear Ryenyel. She is sensible, and she will not long survive the Emperor."

Luss frowns.

"It is not like that," explains the red-haired Second Magus. "None of any sensibility would, I think, plot for her death. She can neither hold the Malachite Throne nor advise an heir of her body. And she understands Cyad, perhaps better than Toziel. They have been . . . so close . . . that she will follow him within eightdays, perhaps a season or so, but no longer. So . . . the Emperor will do without a Hand. None love the Hand, and so, none will complain. All will advance their candidates to be Toziel's successor, but he likes none of them. So we wait, and hope that blood does not stain the sunstones of the Palace of Eternal Light. Or that what blood falls is but a few droplets and not a storm."

Luss frowns, but does not speak.

LXXII

AS THE MIRROR Lancers ride toward the stables at Inividra, under the clear green-blue sky and hot sun of a late-spring day, Lorn reins up outside the square tower.

The older sentry stiffens as his eyes take in Lorn's blood-splattered uniform, "Ser!"

"We're back, Duytyl," Lorn says.

Before Lorn can make his way to the door to the tower, Nesmyl steps outside. "Ser. It's been near-on five eightdays." His eyes flick back toward the tower. "Much has happened."

"A great deal. We had a lot of ground to cover." Lorn looks at the senior squad leader. "Did the commander send any replacement firelances?"

"Yes, but just one set—not even that—fivescore."

"That will do. Have there been any raids anywhere, that you know of?"

"No, ser. Not a one."

"Good."

"Ser . . . there is another sub-majer here." Nesmyl coughs. "I . . . believe Majer Dettaur sent him . . . with orders."

"I'm not surprised. Majer Dettaur would do something like that." Lorn smiles wryly. "I'll go in and pay my respects."

Nesmyl glances at Lorn's sabre and nods.

"I doubt it will come to that." Lorn steps toward the door and opens it. He blinks for several moments in the comparative gloom of the tower, then glances around. The foyer is empty. He walks easily toward the door to his official study and steps inside.

A dark-haired officer, somewhat older than either Dettaur or Lorn, gracefully stands from behind Lorn's desk. "You must be the errant Sub-Majer Lorn." He has flat brown eyes similar to those of Majer Maran, and the unconscious arrogance of Dettaur.

"I'm Lorn." He steps forward. "I see that you've made yourself at home."

"I thought I might as well, since you were nowhere to be found, and I was sent to relieve you."

"I was out patrolling—as requested by both the Captain-Commander and Majer Dettaur."

"It matters not. Oh, I'm Sub-Majer Uflet, and your orders are there." Uflet points to a green-ribboned scroll on the corner of the table desk.

Lorn picks it up, breaks the seal, and begins to read, but without taking his attention away from Uflet.

Sub-Majer Lorn, Mirror Lancers of Cyador, Commanding, Inividra,

You are hereby relieved of your command, and of all rights and privileges associated therewith. This action is taken in accord with the previous directives of the Captain-Commander of Mirror Lancers for your failure to comply with directives, particularly those involving the use and deployment of lancers in the protection of the people of Cyador. You are to report immediately to Assyadt for reassignment.

The signature and seal are those of Dettaur, Majer, Mirror Lancers.

"It all seems pretty clear," Lorn observes. "Dett's usual approach."

"Majer Dettaur understands the traditions of the Mirror Lancers," Uflet says stiffly. "I have found him to be honorable and trustworthy."

"Then you don't know him very well." Lorn laughs once. "Relieving a post commander for doing his duty is honorable?"

Uflet smiles. "Major Dettaur would certainly not act so without a very good reason."

"That is certainly so." Lorn nods, then looks at the dark-haired sub-majer. "I'd appreciate it if you'd wait here. I'll tell the officers, those who are left. They, and I, deserve that courtesy."

"But . . . of course." Uflet's smile is as false as Dettaur's or Maran's. "I imagine those losses could have been avoided with the use of more traditional patrolling."

"With more traditional patrolling, we wouldn't have lost more than a handful so far this year. I would have lost twice as many by the end of the year. As it is, I lost a captain and an undercaptain, along with a company of lancers." Lorn smiles faintly. "We accomplished a great deal. We killed somewhere around twentyscore barbarians. More, probably, but those numbers we can attest to with great certainty. But, as you know, the numbers don't matter. Especially not to Dett. He never could count." Lorn pauses. "I'll be back in a few moments, and we can take care of the formalities."

"Of course." Uflet offers another smile, both false and smug.

Lorn closes the study door as he leaves.

Nesmyl glances at Lorn.

"We're working things out, Nesmyl. I need to tell the officers a few things. Then I'll be back."

"They're . . . waiting in the officers' study. I thought that might be best."

"Thank you."

Lorn leaves the square tower and crosses the courtyard, his boots light on the paving stones, his brow wrinkled in thought. Then, he shrugs.

The four officers stand as he enters the study.

Lorn stops and looks at the four remaining officers, wishing that Emsahl were among them. Then he begins to speak. "Some of you may already have guessed that my approach to dealing with the barbarians has not found favor in Assyadt. Those of you who have guessed such were right. Majer Dettaur has decided—without even hearing the results of our efforts—that I should be relieved and disciplined. Of course, there haven't been any raids in all of the northwest section of the Grass Hills—and that's the first time in a generation that spring has passed without raids. We did lose a company and two officers. That's also the fewest casualties in the spring in a score of years. But I am to be relieved." Lorn smiles, wryly, then adds, "I'd like to go to Assyadt and present my case to the commander, since all the directives have come from Majer Dettaur. I'd also like to live through it." Lorn grins. "Anyone like to come with me and bring a company or two?"

Gyraet nods. "I would."

"Might be interesting," suggests Cheryk.

"That's a rebellion," ventures Esfayl.

Rhalyt glances from Esfayl to Gyraet.

"You don't have to come, none of you," Lorn says, "but I'll put orders in writing that I ordered you all to come. That might work better anyway."

"If I'm ordered," Esfayl suggests, with a wry smile, "what can I do?"

"We'll leave in the morning . . . oh . . . there are fivescore firelances in the armory. That's all the commander could spare for the summer."

Esfayl glances at Cheryk. "I don't know as I need orders, then. Patrolling under the old system with that few charges is suicide anyway."

"Like I said," Cheryk observes, "going to Assyadt might be interesting."

"I need to deal with a few other problems, rather immediately," Lorn says. "I'll check with all of you before dinner."

"Yes, ser," says Gyraet. "We'll make sure the men are ready."

"Thank you."

Lorn bows his head, briefly, then turns and walks back out and across the courtyard and back into the square tower.

Nesmyl leans forward as if to inquire.

"I told them." Lorn smiles. "I need to talk to Sub-Majer Uflet. Matters may change somewhat. So . . . if you would stand by?"

"Ah . . . yes, ser." Nesmyl's eyebrows lift.

Lorn makes sure the door is closed as he steps back into the study. "I've talked over matters with my officers, and they understand the situation."

"Then perhaps we should have Nesmyl draft the change-of-command letter," suggests Uflet.

Lorn smiles. "It seems, Sub-Majer Uflet, that I've been ordered to Assyadt, with my lancers. I would strongly suggest you remain here for their return."

"That's rebellion. Major Dettaur would hardly be pleased." Uflet eases around the side of the table desk with a serpentlike grace. "Then, he would not be surprised, either."

Gathering chaos around him, Lorn picks up Dettaur's scroll. "Majer Dettaur decided that before I even returned. I'm sure you're rather good with a sabre."

As if to prove the point, Uflet already has his sabre out

and is moving toward Lorn before the younger sub-majer has even finished his words.

Hssst! Uflet's mouth is open, before his upper body flares into chaos-fire, and then ashes. The sabre clunks dully on the stones of the floor.

Lorn looks at the headless corpse lying on the study floor and shakes his head. He wonders how many more there will be.

Then he summons more chaos.

When he is done, his head throbs, and his eyes are watering, but the only traces of the sub-majer are his sabre, some buckles, a small dagger, and a few coins—and dark marks and ashes on the stone floor. Lorn leans the sabre—warm to his touch—in the corner behind the desk, and then pockets the other warm metal items.

He rubs his nose, trying not to sneeze at the fine ashes circulating in the room, before he walks to the windows and opens them. As an afterthought, he uses a touch of chaos to incinerate Dettaur's scroll.

He lets the fresher air from outside circulate through the room before he goes to the door and opens it.

Nesmyl steps forward. "Ser?"

"We'll be leaving in the morning for Assyadt. The officers already know."

"Ah . . . 'we'?"

"All the lancers and I will be."

"What happened to the sub-majer?" asks Nesmyl, looking past Lorn to the apparently empty study.

"He decided that he didn't want to get involved quite yet," Lorn says. "It's possible that you won't see him again. Then, you may. It is highly unlikely that you will see me again, one way or another."

"I didn't see him come out."

Lorn shrugs. "You can imagine that I'm not terribly interested in the sub-majer at this point."

"No, ser." Nesmyl tries to conceal an expression of bewilderment. "But Commander Ikynd and Majer Dettaur. . . ."

"Don't worry, Nesmyl. The lancers and I are going to Assyadt, and I'll be seeing both the Commander and the Majer. I wouldn't have it any other way. If Sub-Majer Uflet doesn't return, a new officer will come back with the lancers to take over Inividra."

"But the barbarians—"

"I doubt very seriously if enough are left alive to consider riding into Cyador without starving their clans." Lorn turns. "At the moment, I'm going to clean up and change uniforms. Then I'll be down to start writing my report, at least until dinner."

"Very good, ser." Nesmyl's eyes stray toward the open study door.

"You won't find Uflet in there, but you can certainly look," Lorn says with a lopsided grin.

"Ah, no, ser. That's all right."

Lorn walks to the front of the square tower, where he reclaims his saddlebags and extra sabre, and then carries his gear to the narrow rear stairs. As he climbs up to his quarters—his for one last night, he knows he can wash the blood from his uniforms—at least mostly—but he wonders what will wash the blood from his soul.

LXXIII

LORN LOOKS FROM the study window of the personal quarters at Inividra out into the purple twilight of a late-spring evening. He still has a trace of a headache, and every so often he has to blot his eyes.

He has finally completed a short version of his report, since there is little point in a longer version, which contains enough—the numbers of barbarians slain, towns sacked, blades seized, some six thousands golds recovered and being returned and, of course, a summary of the blade trade in Jera, and the profits going to Hamorian, Spidlarian, and, unfortunately, Cyadoran traders.

He takes out the chaos-glass and lays it on the desk. Then he pulls out the chair and sits down, concentrating. The silver mists form, then swirl aside into revealing an image—Ryalth is breast-feeding Kerial at a table—the lower inner dining area of Lorn's parents' dwelling, and Jerial, wearing a dark green or black tunic, is seated across the table from her.

Both women look up. Jerial says something, and Lorn swallows as he sees the tears roll down Ryalth's cheeks. Jerial smiles, and Ryalth frees a hand and touches her fingers to her lips, as if to send a kiss across the hundreds of kays that separate them.

Lorn watches for several moments, wishing he could convey more than his presence or existence, before he finally releases the image.

They and Kerial are well, it appears, and at least, at least, they know he is alive.

He stands and walks nearer the open window, looking out and down at the courtyard.

"The Butcher of Nhais . . . and now the butcher of Jerans . . ." He shakes his head. Flutak and Baryat would have left Nhais defenseless, and Dettaur would have condemned three times as many lancers to die—and for what?

So that, in the first case, a corrupt enumerator and grower could gather more golds, and in the second, so that all the older lancer officers could rest assured that time-honored traditions did not change, even as the world did? Or so that traders in Summerdock and Swartheld could make more golds off those lancers' deaths?

Even if the traders and cupritors of Cyad did make golds from selling blades, training more lancers and arming them would raise their tariffs, or shift the cost in golds to someone else's tariffs. For those in Cyad, it makes no sense. Yet, is he the only one who sees such? Or the only one who is stupid enough to act on what he sees?

"The only one stupid enough . . ."

He turns from the window. He doubts he will sleep well, for all his self-justifications.

LXXIV

THE GUARDS OUTSIDE the open gates of Assyadt look up as the Sixth Company of Mirror Lancers approaches, followed by a long column of lancers. The younger one's eyes widen as he sees that the firelances are out and leveled.

"Sub-Majer Lorn. I'm here to see Majer Dettaur." Lorn smiles coldly.

"Ah . . ." The younger guard swallows as the gray haired ranker elbows him.

"I'm sure you're welcome, ser," the older guard speaks firmly and quickly.

"Thank you." Lorn inclines his head, then looks to Gyraet. "The first building is the commander's. Go four-abreast at each door with the lances."

"Rhalyt! Secure the stables!"

"Yes, ser."

In the momentary silence that follows, as Lorn rides slowly across the stones of the courtyard, he catches the hard words of the senior guard.

"Near-on killed us! Don't say a word to man like that . . . he be the butcher, they say . . . only officer brought the Accursed Forest to its knees, slaughtered threescore raiders himself in Nhais . . . Black angels know why he be here . . . but that be for the commander and the majer . . ."

Lorn half winces, half smiles as he nears the first white-stone building, and then reins up. Reputations have their advantages, and disadvantages. He doubts his troubles will be with lower officers or rank-and-file lancers. Then, they never have been.

"You want a few lancers with you?" asks Gyraet.

Lorn pauses, then reluctantly nods. "It might make things . . . quieter." After a moment, he looks up at Gyraet and Cheryk. "I shouldn't have to say it, but anyone who attacks you is an enemy of all those lancers who have died."

"Yes, ser," affirms Cheryk.

"First half, first squad," orders Gyraet. "Follow the majer . . . with lances. Use the lances against anyone who lifts a blade against him. Anyone, officer or ranker."

"Yes, ser."

Gryal is the squad leader who dismounts—a burly man with a slash that goes from ear to cheek. "Time we had a field commander lettin' 'em know, ser."

"Thank you."

Lorn gathers chaos around him as he steps through the square-arched door.

The three senior squad leaders in the open foyer freeze as Lorn walks in, followed by the armed lancers.

"Ser . . . ah . . . lances . . . not . . . here . . ." stumbles the older squad leader.

Lorn does not recall his name. "They are now. Is Majer Dettaur here?"

"I'm here, Sub-Majer Lorn." As he draws out Lorn's title and name almost contemptuously, Dettaur moves from his open study door into the corridor. "I see you did bring a few lancers."

"Gryal . . . I'd appreciate it if everyone else remained in their places," Lorn says. "We'll be finished with any unpleasantness much more quickly."

"Yes, ser."

"Dett . . ." Lorn replies, "we have some matters to discuss." He lets his chaos-senses range toward Dettaur's study, but can feel it is empty. "Majer Dettaur's study is empty. We'll be discussing the problems his ill-advised orders caused." Lorn smiles, then inclines his head toward the open door. "Gryal . . . if the commander should appear, I'm sure you'll find a way to keep him in his study."

"Yes, ser!"

Dettaur winces, if almost imperceptibly. "I suppose a private talk would be better."

Lorn understands Dettaur's hopes, but merely replies, "I think so. You first."

Dettaur walks into the study, moving quickly as if to separate himself from Lorn. Lorn closes the door, his eyes on the majer.

"You were relieved of command by Sub-Majer Uflet . . ." Dettaur begins.

"He never got around to that, but then, we didn't stay long in Inividra. I can honestly say that he never had a resignation ready for me to sign. To my knowledge, there are no orders in Inividra ordering my resignation."

Dettaur's lips tighten. "You . . . you think you can get away with anything. You always have. You think the rules don't apply to you. You won't. Not this time."

"Dett . . . there are six companies of lancers that hold this outpost. They've seen the trading records. They've seen your stupid orders. They've seen how you sent them out to die by requiring tactics that were idiotic. You honestly don't think I could force tenscore lancers to come here against their will, do you? They're here because they know they'll be dead unless things change. They wagering their lives on it."

"Bad wager, Lorn. You'll all die."

"I don't think so, Dett. Assyadt never has more than a company of lancers here, if that."

"You know everything. You always did." Dettaur smirks, and his hand edges toward the hilt of his sabre, oh so slowly.

"Dett, one question. Why did you block all Ryalth's scrolls to me?"

"I never did a thing."

"That's the wrong answer. You can't lie to me."

Dettaur laughs, drawing his sabre and stepping forward. "You never were as good as I with a blade."

"You're wrong—twice, Dett." Lorn lifts his own sabre, but as he does so he gathers chaos from around him, and there is more than enough, fueled by anger and hatred as well, to extend his blade so that it knocks aside Dettaur's sabre and slices through his neck like a razor.

Dettaur does not even have time to look surprised.

Lorn leaves the body on the study floor and steps out into the corridor. He glances toward Gryal. "I think Majer Dettaur understands the problem. Finally." With a crooked smile, Lorn steps ᴧcross the corridor and into Commander Ikynd's study.

The commander looks up from where he has been sitting behind his table desk. "When I saw the mounts and lances, I thought it might be you, Lorn." Ikynd offers his genial smile, but remains seated behind the desk. "I didn't expect you to return here in such force. I thought you would be patrolling. You're dead, now. You just don't know it. You couldn't wait . . ."

"I almost waited too long, Commander. Another season, and most of those men would have been dead. They know it, too. Why else would they be here?"

"It really doesn't matter, you know. Lancers and lancer officers are supposed to die. Don't you know that? Anyway, Dettaur will come in and kill you, if I can't. He's very good at that."

Lorn smiles lazily but does not lower the sabre. "Not good enough. Dett's already had his say. He's dead. You can be a hero, or you can be dead. Which?"

The genial expression drops. "If you can deliver, butcher boy, I'd prefer the hero. Wouldn't any self-respecting lancer?"

"Of course. Especially if other people do the work and die," Lorn replies, an indolent tone to his words.

"You're rather insubordinate. That's rebellion. The Majer-Commander won't hesitate a moment to have you executed."

"I don't think so. He might have you executed, though. He'll need someone to blame, and you'll be more convenient." Lorn smiles. "It might be best if you blamed Dettaur first, and commended me for bringing the problem to your attention."

"Problem?" Ikynd raises his eyebrows theatrically. "What problem?"

"The port of Jera no longer exists. They'll rebuild it—but that will take time. Outside, there are three wagons and a halfscore of packhorses. Almost fiftyscore Hamorian blades. That doesn't count those we had to dump in the river. We took them from the warehouses in Jera. Then we burned the—the warehouses." Lorn's smile is humorless. "We also razed and burned somewhere around a halfscore other towns. And I brought back some trading records, along with fivescore cupridium blades—without lancer markings. The records show that they came from Summerdock—and I have the records and the weapons to prove that several Cyadoran trading houses helped transfer those weapons to the Jeranyi traders. Oh, and more than six thousand golds from those traders."

"So . . . our corrupt traders . . . you know and the Emperor knows they've always been corrupt . . . they made a few golds. It's been going on for generations. Our task isn't to enforce the trade provisions of the Emperor's Code. It's to protect the people. Have you forgotten that?" The genial tone returns to Ikynd's voice.

"Six thousand are more than a few golds." Lorn laughs. "And I've saved more Cyadoran peasants than all the officers in Mirror Lancers combined, and you have the gall to suggest I've forgotten my duty?"

"It's not what you do, Sub-Majer. It's how you do it, and neither the Captain-Commander nor the Majer-Commander will like what you did."

"You did it, too," Lorn points out. "If you want to be a

hero . . . that is. We're going to compose scrolls, a great number. We report on the campaign, the results, and the proof—and the scrolls go to every lancer commander in Cyador." Lorn smiles. "And to the Captain-Commander, the Majer-Commander, the First Three Magi'i, the Hand of the Emperor, the Merchanter Advisor, and to the head of every trading house in Cyador. And then we wait. And I'll act in poor Dett's place until we see what happens."

"You'll leave Inividra unprotected?"

"There won't any raiding parties for a long time, Commander. That, you can be sure of."

"Oh . . . you seem most sure of that."

Lorn is, for his glass has shown him that no Jeranyi raiders are riding anywhere in the northwest Grass Hills— then, there are but a handful of raiders left alive in that area. "Without mounts and without weapons, the Jeranyi will have some problems. Besides, it's spring, and if they don't gather their scattered herds and plant—they'll starve, and they know it."

"A bigger wider blade . . ." Ikynd shakes his head. "Black-angel death . . . Alyiakal had nothing on you. He murdered half of Cerlyn, you know?"

"We had peace for a generation, then," Lorn suggests.

"Do you really think that you'll be promoted after this?" A note of curiosity infuses the commander's voice.

"No. I think I'll be summoned to Cyad. I'll be offered a position advising the Majer-Commander. It's too dangerous to leave me with lancers, and I've eliminated any immediate danger from the Jeranyi, and there are more lancers that can be brought from the Accursed Forest." Lorn shrugs. "It's dangerous to overtly kill a hero who eliminates a threat—not immediately, anyway, and a lancer who discovers the complicity and corruption of leading trading houses. The Majer-Commander will wish to ensure that all is well with the traders, and that, or something else not involving lancers

344 ◊ L. E. Modesitt, Jr.

will be my job—which will give them all an incentive to have me assassinated after I am in Cyad and safely forgotten." Lorn smiles coldly. "After all, I'm merely a butcher. I can't possibly understand the intrigue."

"I'd offer you my job, were I the Captain-Commander. I wouldn't want you in Cyad."

"He might, but the Majer-Commander won't. Who would want me with twenty companies loyal to me?"

"You have a high opinion of yourself."

Lorn shakes his head. "Your picked captain went with me to prove me wrong. He was one of those who urged me to come here. You forget one thing, Commander. Lancer officers don't like being used as counters in a wagering game, and when they find out that's happening, they want to put a stop to it. Without firelances, and without a change in lancer orders, they're all dead, and they know it."

Ikynd winces.

"You see?" Lorn waits. "Now . . . we have a number of scrolls to write—after you see the blades and the records. You're going to write that you gave me the leeway to stop the raids, and I did, and you're going to report that there hasn't been a raid in all the northwest in almost a season . . . and there hasn't. Then you're going to suggest that, now that Sub-Majer Lorn has accomplished the task set forth by the Captain-Commander, that he be returned to Cyad for duty there."

Lorn gestures toward the door with the sabre. "We're going to look at what's in the wagons we brought."

Ikynd stands. "You'd kill me, without blinking an eye, wouldn't you?"

"If necessary."

"The sabre's in your left hand. All lancers . . ." Ikynd shakes his head. "You can use the sabre with either hand, can't you?"

"Yes. Dettaur never saw that."

"There was much he didn't see." Ikynd shakes his head, and the genial tone returns to his voice. "I will indeed recommend you return to Cyad. You won't even have to force me."

"You might even mean it, after you see how many cupridium sabres the traders from Summerdock sold to the Jeranyi."

"The Captain-Commander is going to have trouble with someone like you who really cares for Cyad."

"Let's go look at the wagons, and then we'll have the lancers unload the records and invoices into Dettaur's study. You'll have to explain that poor Dett didn't want to have this revealed."

"He didn't, I imagine, because if it came out you discovered it, he'd never be promoted back to Cyad. He was always a city lancer." Ikynd laughs. "You're a true lancer, and you'll never be happy in Cyad. You just don't know it."

"You could be right." Lorn smiles and steps back as Ikynd moves toward the door.

LXXV

IN THE LATE afternoon, Lorn sits in Dettaur's study, although it is temporarily, if not technically, his for the moment. A light and pleasant spring breeze sifts through the window that is but partly ajar and brings a faint odor of a flower he does not recognize.

His lips quirk, and he looks down at the copy of the report on his campaign and of the scroll he has sent to Cyad—and across Cyad. Then he looks up, blankly, at the ancient golden wooden panels of the wall.

Outside, in the foyer, are a pair of lancers from Gyraet's Sixth Company, detailed by the captain to protect Lorn. With them in the foyer are the senior squad leaders who continue the administrative work for the compound and the out-posts it serves. The sub-major shakes his head. The waiting is the hardest part, as if he were sitting on a chaos-tower that could flare at any moment. Yet he has done all that he can do.

He stands and walks to the window, checking the lancers who patrol the compound, wondering how long he can command them and whether they will see scores upon scores of lancers arriving, or whether he will simply receive a scroll dispatching him to Cyad—or back to Biehl . . . or some other out-of-the-way place.

He walks back to the desk and lifts the small bag he carries with him everywhere—along with the Brystan sabre. In the bag are the chaos-glass that had once been his father's, and the silver-covered book, and the originals of the most incriminating of the trading papers taken from Jera.

Lorn slips out the chaos-glass and sets it on the desk. He concentrates. The silver mists part, and reveal Ikynd standing by the window in his personal quarters looking out over the courtyard. The commander shakes his head and turns from the window. Lorn releases the image.

Although he has kept a close watch on the commander, he still worries about the man, particularly since he knows Ikynd is true to only the principle of self-interest. At the moment, Lorn serves his self-interest, but anything could change that, nearly instantly.

After a moment, Lorn slips the glass back into its wooden case, and the case back into the bag. Finally, he begins to write, although he has no idea whether this scroll will reach its destination.

My dearest,

There have been some difficulties with couriers and messages, and I have not received any of your scrolls, if there have been such, since the turn of winter. Nor have I received any others. So I know little of what may have happened to you or in Cyad.

I trust that you and Kerial are well, and that your efforts with Ryalor House have been rewarded. We have been through an arduous campaign, and rode all the way to Jera, where we discovered that many of the blades that have been slaying lancers have come from not just Hamorian traders, but even from cupritors and traders in Summerdock. This was a shock, and when we returned to Inividra, I faced a greater shock, since there were some indications I might be relieved of command because of my efforts in the field.

I came to Assyadt where Dettaur attempted to kill me. For reasons that are unclear, he did not want my report on the blades to go to the Majer-Commander. Much remains unclear, but Commander Ikynd and I have sent a report to the Majer-Commander, and to others, detailing my campaign and the blade-trading in Jera. The campaign was successful enough that for the season so far, there have been no raids from the northwest Grass Hills by barbarians. We also know of none in the areas of outposts controlled from Syadtar, but we would not receive such reports until much later.

At the moment, I am acting as the deputy to Commander Ikynd in Assyadt, waiting to find out what my next assignment may be.

You and Kerial are well, I trust, and I can but hope it will not be that long before I can see you both under pleasant circumstances.

Lorn sets the scroll aside to dry. He reaches for another sheet of parchment for the one he will write to his parents. Then he pauses and looks out the narrow window and watches one of his lancers—mounted and riding a post. He can but hope that at least some of his dispatches have found their way beyond Captain-Commander Luss and that Majer-Commander Rynst will act as Lorn has predicted.

With a deep breath, he smoothes the parchment and begins to write.

Later, after he reviews the status reports from Pemedra and drafts a response for the commander's seal, he will inspect the lancers and meet, once more, with his captains . . . and wait.

LXXVI

AN EIGHTDAY HAS passed since Lorn has sent out his dispatches. The headquarters compound at Assyadt has heard nothing, except standard dispatches about such matters as procurement of mounts, sent before Lorn's report could have been received, and another caution about the declining number of firelances and recharges available—somewhat concerned-sounding reports from the outpost at Pemedra that there have been no barbarian attacks and no barbarians sighted.

Lorn has been acting as Ikynd's deputy, drafting dispatch scrolls for provisions, inspecting the compound, drafting the request for replacement officers for Inividra, spending some time directing the arms drills he had scheduled for his lancers, and even, hard as it had been, drafting a letter to Dettaur's family informing them of his death in the line of duty. Yet, still he has time to worry about what may come, and his eyes go from the study door to the window and back again.

Thrap!

Lorn looks up as Commander Ikynd steps into his temporary study, then stands. "Yes, ser?"

"You are so formal." Ikynd laughs, before his voice returns to its genial tone. "You're the one in command."

"No, ser. You're in command. I'm just not letting you do

anything that will hurt the lancers in the outpost or the field until we hear from the Majer-Commander."

Ikynd shakes his head. "First, my command is run by a scheming city lancer who is favored by the Captain-Commander, and now by a Cyad-raised, magus-born, patrol commander who's the opposite. You'd think you'd been raised in Assyadt and not Cyad."

Lorn shrugs, waiting for the commander to continue.

"What will you do if the Majer-Commander sends ten companies?" asks Ikynd, still standing by the open door.

"Walk out and surrender," Lorn admits.

"You wouldn't try to go out in a blaze of glory or some such?"

"That wouldn't be fair to the men. I've tried to take the risks myself. They've done their tasks. I just didn't want to get killed and have them die because someone like Dettaur was determined to put me in a position where I had to die or they did." Lorn frowns and adds, "When it was totally unnecessary."

The commander laughs. "If no one had bothered you, I'd wager you'd have died somewhere doing your duty."

"I wasn't looking for trouble," Lorn admits, "but I couldn't let lancers die when they didn't have to. And I couldn't let Dettaur keep doing what he was doing. If it hadn't been me, sooner or later, it would have been someone else."

Ikynd turns back toward the door. "One way or another, it won't be long. The Captain-Commander doesn't look from hand to hand." He pauses. "Now that you've made me hero," offers Ikynd, "how long will you dare to leave Inividra and the poor peasants without protection?"

Lorn fingers his chin. "Not long. I have been considering it. I think you should detail a company to stay here, and the rest should return to duty at Inividra, with an experienced captain promoted to overcaptain until the Captain-Commander decides."

"Besides Sub-Majer Uflet?"

"I doubt that the Sub-Majer will return to Inividra. We've heard nothing from Nesmyl."

"He's the second senior officer to disappear around you."

Lorn offers a faint smile. "Just a coincidence, I'm sure. I'll draft an order for you to promote a captain to overcaptain."

"I can't do that."

"The Code says commanders can make temporary promotions and recommend them to the Captain-Commander. There's no overcaptain at Inividra anyway."

Ikynd shrugs. "I had forgotten that. Who do you have in mind?"

"I would have recommended Emsahl, but Gyraet would be a good choice. Or Cheryk."

"I'd prefer Gyraet, if it's all the same to you," suggests Ikynd.

"I'll talk to them about leaving, and let them know."

"It would be easier, one way or another, if most were gone before this is resolved," Ikynd points out.

"You are right about that," Lorn says.

"I am sometimes," suggests Ikynd. "Commanders do learn something over the years."

"You were wrong only in allowing Dettaur his head." Lorn smiles.

"Was I?" Ikynd lifts his eyebrows. "If you are correct, I will be a hero, and he'll be disgraced and forgotten, despite your kind words in that letter."

Lorn bows.

Ikynd returns the bow. "I won't keep you from meeting with the officers." He pauses. "I'd like to be able to report that most left after the matter was brought to my attention. It would be better for you as well, either way."

"I'll talk to them now."

Ikynd slips back to his study, and Lorn walks into the corridor and then out through the foyer. He stops just outside the building to let his eyes adjust to the bright sun. As he looks up, a after a few moments, he sees Rhalyt riding toward him.

"Good day, ser," offers the undercaptain, reining up his mount before Lorn, who recalls that First Company is the duty Company for the afternoon.

"No word yet," Lorn says easily with a grin, "as I'm sure you know, but we'll be sending five companies back to Inividra shortly."

The undercaptain nods. "I thought that might happen."

"I'm going to talk to the others."

"Yes, ser." Rhalyt inclines his head.

"I think you should be among those to return. You're only an undercaptain, and could have a fine career. The Majer-Commander is short of experienced lancers and officers, and he's not about to waste talent and experience."

"Yes, ser. Thank you, ser." Rhalyt inclines his head.

"Thank you," Lorn says with a smile, before turning and walking across the sun-splashed main courtyard toward the north barracks and the shadowed courtyard where he has ordered his captains to drill the men in sabres.

As he steps past the corner of the barracks, the order rings out, "Stand down!"

The three captains walk quickly toward Lorn, who waits until they have gathered around him. "There's nothing new. Not right now. I've been thinking things over. We've done what we can do here," Lorn says slowly. "The Majer-Commander and the Emperor know what they need to know. I'll need one company to remain here for a while, but it's time for the other five to return to Inividra . . . before the barbarians resume their raids. For the company to stay here, Commander Ikynd will sign the orders . . . but I'd prefer a volunteer."

Esfayl grins. "Well . . . my sister does live in the hamlet next from Assyadt." He looks at Cheryk and then at Gyraet.

"You can have it." Cheryk looks at Lorn. "What of you, ser?"

"We've either gotten the Majer-Commander to see the problem with the traders, or we haven't. I'll be staying here to see what happens. The commander will appoint a temporary over-captain for Inividra. The outpost has been short one, anyway."

"Best be one of us," suggests Esfayl. "One of you two."

"The commander would prefer Gyraet," Lorn says, looking at Cheryk. "It could be either of you two."

Cheryk nods. "Not that I wouldn't like the rank, but Gy-raet'd be better for now."

Gyraet flushes. "I have not been at Inividra long."

"You'll do," says Cheryk. "And you have to write all the reports."

"Ser . . ." Gyraet begins. "This . . . I did not . . ."

"I know." Lorn looks at Gyraet. "I hope you can handle it. I think it's better this way, and I think you two and Rhalyt need to prepare to leave first thing in the morning. I'll arrange for as many firelances as I can find for you. I've already drafted and the commander has signed a request for replacement officers. There will be raids by late summer, I think. Not much before, and they'll be small raids on isolated hamlets. So you will need to go back to one-company patrols." Lorn grins. "I'm not saying that to make the commander happy. If nothing happens, by a year or two from now, you may need to resume larger patrols, but I don't think the barbarians have enough men for large raids now."

"I'll wager they don't," says Esfayl.

"You'll have to rotate taking Second and Fifth Companies," Lorn says, "until you get the replacement officers."

"We've done worse, and there won't be raids for a time," Cheryk says. "Are you sure matters here are settled?"

"As settled as we can make them." Lorn shrugs. "And I wouldn't want any peasants—or lancers—to suffer. If everyone is under proper orders, then I doubt there will be many problems."

"Yes, ser."

"I'll make sure you all have orders by this evening."

As he turns and recrosses the courtyard, he hears the low voices.

"... doesn't look good ..."

"... always looked out for his men ..."

"... angel-fire few officers like that ..."

Lorn has no more than returned to the study and reseated himself at the desk he occupies when there is a knock on the door, and a squad leader—Gryal—peers in.

"Ser?"

"Come on in."

Gryal steps forward and hands Lorn a scroll, one with a blue seal and bound in a blue ribbon. "This came in for you with the couriers. Thought you ought to get it personal."

"Thank you. I suspect it's from my consort. Her earlier scrolls never reached Inividra."

"There was word about that ..."

"Were there any other dispatches?"

"No, ser. But word is that you get everything first." Gryal grins. "Way it ought to be."

"Thank you."

"Not a problem, ser. The squad leader bows and backs out. Lorn lifts the scroll, then breaks the seal and begins to read.

My dearest lancer,

I have received the first scroll from you in seasons, but I knew, as you know, that you care, and now I know why there were no scrolls.

Jerial says that she is not surprised by your former classmate, nor am I surprised at what you discovered in Jera, or that you have found yourself in Assyadt. In my own poor way, I have passed on the information you have sent, and spoken, if briefly, to Vyanat'mer. He already knew and had read your official report, and he appreciated that you had seen fit to inform him so that he was not surprised in meeting with His Mightiness.

I do not know what will come of your actions and report. Much is in turmoil here, with your family, as you know . . .

Lorn swallows. His family? His parents? Myryan? It could not be Jerial. Later, when he is truly alone, he will have to search with the chaos-glass.

. . . and with the death of the Hand of the Emperor. No one knows who the Hand was, as always, but word of his death still did get out. The Emperor himself was ailing for a time. So no one knows about many matters and may not for several days yet, and it may take longer for you to find out.

Whatever may happen, I love you and know that you have done the best you could, with your destiny and your talents, and we hope you will be safe and in Cyad before too long.

Lorn looks at the scroll. Safe and in Cyad? Those two do not go together. That he knows all too well.

He takes a deep breath. He needs to draft the orders for the five companies and their lancers. That is one problem he can resolve . . . and one he should have handled earlier, or at least considered before he did.

LXXVII

IN THE DARKNESS and quiet of the quarters for visiting senior officers, Lorn sets the chaos-glass on the narrow desk. He takes a long slow breath, and then concentrates. The silver mists fill the glass, then swirl and finally part. But the glass is blank, an opaque and silvered shimmering blankness.

He lets go of the image he has sought, and tries a second time, this time thinking about his mother, about the conversation that they had had on the portico in a cold wind so many years before. But once more, the mists reveal only the silver blankness.

Lorn can feel the perspiration on his forehead, despite the warmth of the late-spring evening. For a time longer, he sits in the dimness, wondering if he has lost the ability to control the image in the glass, because of his fears or the strains upon him.

Then he tries again, and this time the mists reveal Ryalth and Kerial—asleep on the ornate bed. Ryalth turns, as if restlessly, and Lorn releases the image, reluctantly, but glad that she and Kerial appear well.

He tries once more for the first image . . . and is rewarded again with the silvered blankness that fills the circular glass. When he stops concentrating and the glass clears, his eyes burn. That blankness must mean that his parents are dead, and they have been dead for at least a time, because of the tone of Ryalth's letter. She had written as if their deaths had occurred eightdays in the past.

That is yet another reason for Dettaur's death—except Lorn almost wishes he had made Dettaur's end far more painful. Why had Dettaur been so petty? He still could have sought to discredit Lorn without such smallness.

Lorn shakes his head. Even as he understands, he does not.

Finally, in the dimness of the single oil lamp, he picks up the silver-covered book, leafing through it until his eyes find a verse.

Ashes to ashes
and dust to dust . . .
Chaos to order and back to flame
brings back no songs without name . . .

Except . . . except Lorn will remember, remember words of concern, words of advice, guidance he had not known his parents had even exerted or offered.

He looks sightlessly into the darkness.

LXXVIII

LORN LOOKS OUT into the gray late afternoon. While it has rained earlier, the clouds have lifted some, and the heavy rain has subsided into a light mist. A fog rises from the stones of the courtyard.

Three days earlier, Gyraet and five of the six lancer companies from Inividra had left on their return. The officers had been both concerned about Lorn and relieved to be heading back. Lorn can understand both sets of feelings, and remains grateful for their concern. Surprisingly, at least to Lorn, after all those chill touches on the Jeran campaign, he has not felt the touch of a single chaos-glass. Does that mean that the Majer-Commander does not trust the Magi'i in dealing with Lorn? Lorn is not certain whether that is to his benefit or not. His eyes take in the gray clouds once more. Is the delay because of the delicate situation with the Emperor? Or because the Captain-Commander or the Majer-Commander is gathering Mirror Lancer companies to send to Assyadt? That would seem unlikely, yet Dettaur's pettiness in destroying personal scrolls to Lorn also had been unlikely, for such destruction had done nothing to advance Dettaur.

Lorn shakes his head, reminding himself that he has certainly not been above pettiness.

Thrap.

The worried sub-majer's head snaps up at the knock. "Yes? Come in."

"Majer . . . ?" Esfayl steps into the study with a lancer.

The lancer, who bears the green braid of a special messenger from the Majer-Commander, carries a dispatch pack and glances nervously from Lorn to the dark-haired captain, and then back to Lorn.

"He just got here from Cyad," Esfayl explains. "I

thought he ought to see you first. He has dispatches from the Majer-Commander."

"Ser, there are two for you, but one is for Commander Ikynd."

Lorn looks at Esfayl. "Is the commander in his study?"

"I think so."

"We'll all go there. That might be best." Lorn smiles wryly. "I could be wrong, but if the Majer-Commander is sending two scrolls to me, then I can hope for the best."

A puzzled look crosses the messenger's face, but Lorn does not elaborate as he stands and steps toward the door. "Come on."

The messenger follows Lorn across the corridor and into the second study.

Lorn nods to the messenger. "That's Commander Ikynd. He can read his scroll first."

The messenger steps forward and hands one scroll to Ikynd, then steps back and hands two to Lorn. He eases back beside Esfayl by the half-open study door.

"You aren't reading them all first?" asks Ikynd.

"That one is for you."

"They're sending you somewhere else." Ikynd laughs. "Otherwise, there would have been companies of lancers here."

"Unless they're insisting I take Dettaur's place," Lorn suggests.

"I could do worse," the commander says dryly. "You actually ask what I think." He breaks the seal and begins to scan the lines, then looks up. "You can read yours, Sub-Majer. I won't spoil the surprise." A look of both ruefulness and interest appears on his face.

Lorn opens the first scroll. The message is brief, curt.

Sub-Majer Lorn, Mirror Lancers, Assyadt/Inividra,

You are hereby detached from your present assignment immediately upon receipt of these orders and ordered to report to the Majer-Commander, Cyad, personally, for assignment at his discretion.

The only unusual feature is that the orders are signed and sealed by Rynst, the Majer-Commander, himself.

Lorn opens the second scroll.

Sub-Majer Lorn, Mirror Lancers, Commanding, Inividra,
This is to commend you for your actions in undertaking a campaign to ensure the safety of the northern borders of Cyador, the Empire of Eternal Light. Your actions in destroying barbarian staging areas and confiscating and destroying large quantities of Hamorian-forged blades have resulted in the saving of untold lives of the Mirror Lancers and in resolving a potentially serious situation before it could worsen. Your immediate superior, Commander Ikynd, will also be commended by separate notice, for his wisdom in allowing you the latitude necessary to undertake this dangerous campaign. A copy of this commendation has been placed in your file at Mirror Lancer headquarters.

The second scroll is also signed by Rynst.

Esfayl looks from Lorn to Ikynd and back again.

"It's all right," Lorn finally says. "The commander and I have been commended, and I'm being transferred to Mirror Lancer headquarters in Cyad."

"Congratulations, sers," says Esfayl.

"I think you'll probably be leaving tomorrow, when I do," Lorn tells the young captain, then looks at Ikynd, "if you agree, Commander."

"He can take the provisions wagons an eightday early," Ikynd says.

Lorn nods toward the door. "The commander and I have a few matters to discuss."

"Ah . . . yes, ser."

Both the lancer messenger and Esfayl step out of the commander's study. Esfayl closes the door behind him.

"You know what that commendation says, don't you?" Ikynd's genial tone returns.

"I'd assume that it says that you authorized me to undertake a dangerous and foolhardy campaign, on the verge of breaking every Mirror Lancer regulation, but that, since it was successful beyond anyone's expectations, we are to be commended—and watched most carefully in the future. That's why I'm going to Cyad to report to the Majer-Commander personally."

"That is the way I would read it." Ikynd shrugs. "It doesn't matter much to me. They'd never have promoted me again anyway, and I've but one tour left after this before I can get a pension-stipend. Rynst doesn't know what to do with you, but you're too valuable to have killed, and too dangerous to let loose for a while. I'd guess he wants you around him, the way some men want trained giant cats."

Lorn smiles wryly. "So that everyone watches me, instead of him?"

"Something like that." Ikynd tilts his head. "Dettaur was dangerous because he was too self-centered, you know?"

"I know. If he'd been successful in getting me and my lancers killed, he would have found himself before a discipline hearing—or something would have happened to him."

"Now . . . I'm short something like four officers." Ikynd smiles ruefully. "I'll have to draft my own orders."

"You'll have four more officers within the eightday. With the moving of the lancers out of the Accursed Forest posts, headquarters will be happy to have openings for a majer, sub-majer, and two captains or undercaptains." Lorn adds, "And they'll all be good, traditional lancer officers."

Ikynd nods. "We could use more tradition for a while."

Lorn steps toward the door. "By your leave, Commander?"

"I appreciate the courtesy, Sub-Majer." Ikynd shakes his head as Lorn steps out and closes the door behind him.

LXXIX

IN THE EARLY-MORNING light, Lorn rides toward the firewagon portico in the center of Assyadt, followed by the two lancers from Esfayl's Second Company. The two will return the white gelding to the stable at Assyadt before leaving with Esfayl to ride back to Inividra.

As the three lancers pass the south side of the square in the early-morning light, Lorn can see a number of people under the porch of the Cuprite Kettle, the largest inn in Assyadt. Most of those on the porch seem to be watching him. His chaos-trained ears pick up the low words he should not be able to hear.

"Sure enough . . . that's him, the one they call the Butcher."

"Looks young . . ."

". . . rode all the way to Jera . . . sacked every town . . . killed scores and scores."

". . . say he took over the compound here . . . made the head of the lancers in Cyad meet his terms."

". . . can't be . . . just a sub-majer."

"That's what they say."

". . . looks like a nice young officer . . ."

". . . what's a real killer look like? No different from anyone else . . ."

Lorn keeps his shoulders square, and a smile on his face, even as he wonders how the whole town knows. Then, how could they not know, not when six companies of lancers held the compound for an eightday?

The three ride through the square and toward the white sunstone portico that lies another three hundred kays ahead.

"We'll wait, ser, until the firewagon pulls up," offers one of the lancers.

"Thank you. I think it will be awhile before Captain Esfayl is ready, anyway."

"Rather wait here than help load wagons," suggests the second lancer.

"Ser . . . how long 'fore the barbarians start raiding again?" asks the first.

"Midsummer, I'd judge. The raids will be small ones. I'd be surprised if you saw any large raids until next year. It might be longer if the Majer-Commander does something about Jera."

The two lancers look at each other. Lorn understands the look. Neither ranker believes anyone will do anything. The three ride in silence to the smaller square that holds the firewagon portico. There, Lorn reins up on the far side of the paved way, in the shade of a weaver's shop, waiting for the firewagon.

At the low rumbling of wheels on the stone pavement, Lorn turns, but he only watches as the firewagon comes to a stop under the portico. A handful of incoming passengers, which includes a young undercaptain, disembarks before Lorn dismounts and begins to unfasten his gear.

"Undercaptain!" he calls to the thin red-haired young officer.

"Yes, ser?" The undercaptain glances toward Lorn.

Lorn looks up at the lancers. "If you'd let him ride the gelding back . . . ?"

"Be a pleasure, ser."

"Ser?" asks the undercaptain.

"I'm leaving. Rather than walk, you can ride my mount back to the compound. That's where you going, isn't it?"

"Yes, ser. That is, I'm going there on the way to Inividra."

"You're in luck," Lorn says. "Second Company is leaving this morning with Captain Esfayl. He and Commander

Ikynd will be very happy to see you." He looks to the lancers. "Best you be getting the undercaptain to the compound. I'll be fine."

"Yes, ser."

Lorn takes his bags and crosses the pavement to the portico and the waiting firewagon. He nods as he passes the undercaptain. "Have a good trip."

"Yes, ser. Thank you, ser."

"You're welcome."

Lorn steps onto the sunstone platform, catching the undercaptain's words to the lancers.

". . . was that?"

"Sub-Majer Lorn."

"*The* Sub-Majer Lorn?"

"Yes, ser."

Lorn manages not to wince as he crosses the raised portico and turns toward the front compartment of the firewagon.

The driver glances at the insignia on Lorn's collar. "Sub-Majer . . . ser . . . you wouldn't be the one . . . ?"

" 'The one'?" Lorn asks.

"The one who put the barbarians in their place, I mean, ser?"

"I'm Sub-Majer Lorn," he admits. "The Butcher of Nhais, the Butcher of Jerans, I suppose, too."

"Much obliged to you, ser," the driver says. "Shoulda been done years ago. Used to be at Isahl years ago, when Majer Brevyl first got there. Sub-majer, he was then. Not bad, he was, but we just rode out and chased 'em away. Never hit 'em where it woulda done some good." The driver smiles. "Long past time, you ask me."

"I thought so," Lorn replies. "Not all officers agreed."

"They're not . . . ?"

"No. I did get a sort of a commendation, and a transfer to work for the Majer-Commander."

"Good thing, ser. Way folks were talkin', the drivers, we were fearin' they'd lock you away for doing what oughta been done generations back." The driver grins. "Sorry, ser. Just the way we feel." He pauses. "You need anything, ser, you let us know."

"I will . . . and thank you."

As Lorn places his gear under the seat, he can feel how much lighter it is—by at least three uniforms—than when he had left Cyad more than a year before. It is difficult to believe that it is only a little more than a year and a season since he had left.

Yet everything has changed. He has a son, and no parents. He has become the first Mirror Lancer officer in generations to undertake a campaign outside Cyador, even if it had been a relatively short campaign, and he has slain two senior officers on this tour, even if but one can be confirmed, and made both enemies and admirers throughout the Mirror Lancers—and, apparently, throughout at least some of Cyador.

He slips into the front compartment and unfastens the Brystan sabre, setting it against the outside wall of the coach before seating himself on the far left side, in the seat facing forward.

"Last call for outbound passengers! Last call!" comes the voice of one of the drivers.

A portly figure in purple scrambles into the front compartment. "Hurry . . . hurry . . . act like Mirror Lancers, order folks around . . ." The white-bearded man sees Lorn's uniform as he looks up, and swallows. "Begging your pardon, ser." His eyes catch sight of the sub-majer's insignia, and he swallows again. "I truly do, ser."

Lorn smiles politely. "I'm sure you meant no offense, and I took none."

"Thank you, ser. Thank you."

Lorn wants to sigh. At least, once he gets away from Assyadt, he will be just another sub-majer, and not *the* sub-majer.

LXXX

IN THE DARK-PANELED office that is scarcely more than ten cubits by ten, Vyanat looks up from the antique ebony Hamorian desk at the sandy-haired man who steps into the room and slides into the equally antique ebon armchair.

"You requested I visit you, Vyanat," Tasjan says pleasantly. "I could have refused, but I did not see the value in that. So I am here. What do you wish?"

"You are continuing to purchase blades from the cupritors in Summerdock," Vyanat observes.

"I am. Every blade has remained in Cyador, I am sure you will be pleased to know."

"For now."

"For quite some time, I believe," Tasjan says, his tone almost indolent. "Or aboard my vessels. I am training a somewhat larger number of guards for all vessels under the Dyjani ensign. With the decline in the number of fireships, and their voyages, this is but prudent, do you not think?"

"Were it any merchanter but you, Tasjan, I would have little difficulty believing that there would be a need for an additional fivescore guards. But you . . . and Sasyk . . . already, you have that many under arms, and that is in addition to the arms for the seamen on your vessels." Vyanat'mer smiles, coldly.

"What can I say?" Tasjan laughs. "The warships being built by the Mirror Lancers will not be completed for yet several seasons, if then, and they look less than sufficient to protect our ships and cargoes. We of the Dyjani must look to our own interests in these days."

"Yes, you must. That is why I hoped you would come."

Tasjan's eyes narrow. "You are being devious. What

happened to the honest and straightforward Merchanter Advisor?"

"He occasionally has to use a devious phrase to get your attention." The dark-haired merchanter's smile is off-center. He waits, letting the silence fill the small study, before he finally speaks again. "Tasjan . . . do you want Rynst to bring the Mirror Lancers into Cyad and turn the harbor red with blood?"

"And leave the north unprotected? He won't do that."

"He can do exactly that. Don't you listen? Don't you read? Did you read that battle report from that sub-majer?"

"He razes Jera and kills a few score barbarians. It's about time. The Hamorians will think twice about trading so close to Cyador."

"He destroyed every town of any size close to the Grass Hills, and he slaughtered most of the barbarians. And he also brought back some six thousand golds, all too many of them coined in Cyador. For the next season or two, perhaps longer, there won't be that many raids. There won't be any, I'd wager, for a year."

"And that will free Rynst to bring in more lancers and provide the coins to pay them—without raising our tariffs." Tasjan smiles. "Who will command them? There's not a decent field commander in Cyad. They've all been sitting at desks so long most couldn't find the release on a firelance— if there are even any left in working order in a season. There haven't been that many good field commanders anyway. Not in years—except perhaps for this fellow, and they'll get him killed one way or another. Quickly, I'd wager."

Vyanat nods. "I thought you might find it interesting that Sub-Majer Lorn is being ordered to Cyad to work for Rynst directly. Over the Captain-Commander's objections."

Tasjan smiles broadly. "That . . . that . . . my friend, is worth my honoring your request." He nods. "Indeed. Indeed, it is."

"So . . . now what will you do?" inquires Vyanat.

"What everyone else will do. Wait . . . and watch."

LXXXI

LORN PACES BACK and forth in the small room at the waystation at Chulbyn, an ancient stone-walled room with a polished granite floor without any covering, a single bed, a low table, and a row of golden-oak pegs set shoulder-high in the stone for garments. There is one oil lamp in a bronze sconce, from which a low light suffuses the cramped space.

Lorn reaches out and slides closed the oak beam that is the bar for the door, then opens one of the two bags he has carried from Inividra. From it, he takes the wooden case that holds the chaos-glass. He places the glass on the low table.

He concentrates, and watches as the silver mists swirl and dissipate to reveal Ryalth and Kerial in the ornate bad he has not ever seen, except through the glass. He notes, for the first time, a smaller bed in the background, but both his consort and his son are sleeping, as they seem to, side by side, and they are safe. Lorn smiles as he releases that image.

For a long moment he waits, before trying to call forth a second image, and then a third. He still obtains but a silver blankness in trying to call up images of either parent—and a faint throbbing in his skull and dampness across his brow.

Finally, he releases the glass, shaking his head. He replaces the glass in its wooden case, and the case in the bag. From the other bag, he pulls forth the green-tinged and silver-covered volume that he has carried for so long across Cyador—and even across Jerans.

He opens the book, reading and paging slowly, seeking a verse, one that somehow seems right for the night, right for a journey whose end could be indeed anything. A verse that he might read in a new way, one that offers that melancholy insight of the ancient writer. There is a short verse, vaguely comforting, and he smiles.

Virtues of old hold fast.
Morning's blaze cannot last;
and rose petals soon part.
Not so a steadfast heart.

" 'Not so a steadfast heart . . . ' " Lorn murmurs. But how difficult it is to maintain a steadfast heart in a world where chaos reigns and the only thing steadfast seems the dark order of death.

He continues to turn the pages until he finds a poem he must have read, but does not recall.

Though some will find their fears in depths of night,
noon's pitiless sun brings the deepest fright.
While they who sing of good and truth, and praise
bright chaos for the coming light of days,
then cite the Mirror Towers of a distant earth,
yet forget their children's and their gardens' worth,
I strive in this strange sun's chaotic light,
to lift from souls war's endless bitter blight.
So elthage men turn their eyes to glasses,
blank silver for the future as it passes;
those of chaos hold altage high above
as though alone white fire kindled love.
Yet their white-lit chaos will bring with rue,
but destruction to those whose way is true.
Like sunstone walls, the truth will also fall,
for the future lies beyond any wall
in the green skies, open fields and dreaming nights,
where unfettered thoughts are free for endless flights.

I can but strive, and act with flame and blade,
to break down bitter truths that time has made,

and striving, lay my soul before the fire,
in hopes of exceeding mere vain desire.

Lorn shakes his head. The ancient writer had few illusions about Cyad, about men and women, or about himself—and yet, whoever he had been, he had persevered in the hope that what he strove for in building and strengthening Cyad would prove greater than he had been. Can Lorn attempt less?

He closes the book, replaces it in the bag.

In time . . . in time, he will sleep.

Lorn'alt, Cyad
Sub-Majer,
Mirror Lancers

LXXXII

LORN SHIFTS HIS weight on the hard seat of the firewagon, his eyes going out the window as the vehicle rumbles downhill along the smooth stones of the granite way that will pass west of the Palace of Eternal Light. Outside, a light warm mist filters out of gray clouds, leaving a shimmering sheen over the white granite and sunstone buildings and streets of Cyad. The trees are full-leaved, and the green-and-white awnings are spread.

Lorn smiles as he beholds each facet of the City of Eternal Light as the firewagon carries him past the upper merchanters' quarter, as the Palace of Eternal Light appears, and as he can see the blue-gray waters of the harbor. For all its intrigue and problems, Cyad is truly a city of light and one of hope for the world. He finally leans back from the window.

Inside the firewagon, on the right side of the compartment, is a round-faced magus, at least a second-level adept, for he wears the lightning emblem on the breast of his tunic. The magus is older, with gray at his temples and the hint of the sungold eyes that distinguishes many of those Magi'i who work heavily with chaos. His eyes and chaos-senses have lighted upon Lorn occasionally, and more than once in the past hundred kays of the journey has puzzlement crossed his face.

The sole other occupant of the front compartment is a silver-haired merchanter who continues to sleep quietly in the corner opposite Lorn's, directly across from the magus. Abruptly, he sits up—when the firewagon begins to slow as it approaches its final stop at the harbor portico. After a moment, he looks around, then out into the mist, nodding as he catches sight of the larger merchanter mansions on the hill.

He turns to his travel companions. "Majer, Magus . . . I wish you both well." His eyes twinkle as he looks at Lorn. "You will find much has changed, Majer."

"I imagine it has," Lorn responds, wondering exactly how much the merchanter knows, for the man has scarcely spoken to him since they boarded at Chulbyn the day before, and Lorn has only given his name and his previous duty station.

"The essentials of Cyad change but little," replies the magus.

There is the slightest of lurches as the firewagon brakes to a complete stop under the portico.

"They will change more than even the Magi'i can know, honored ser," suggests the older merchanter. "My best to you both." With a sprightliness that belies his appearance, the merchanter is the first to leave the firewagon.

Although Lorn reaches for his sabre immediately, he waits for the older magus to depart the firewagon before he extracts his bags from under the seat and slips out into the warm moist air of Cyad. Once outside on the platform portico, he sets down the bags and clips his sabre to his green web belt before looking toward the carriage-hire lane across the narrow way from him. Since there are several carriages, he lifts his bags and crosses to the first, addressing the driver. "The Traders' Plaza."

"Yes, ser."

The driver leans back and opens the carriage door for Lorn, who sets the two duffels that hold his gear—and his chaos-glass and Ryalth's book—on the floor of the covered carriage. The carriage feels confined and stuffy, yet damp, and Lorn is glad when the short ride ends and he can step out into the misty warmth outside the Traders' Plaza, where he tenders three coppers, before making his way across the outside Plaza toward the clan side.

Once again, he has no idea of what to expect, except that Ryalor House is on the uppermost level. Figures in shimmercloth blue glance at him, then glance away at the sight of the cream-and-green Mirror Lancer uniform.

"... don't see many senior lancers here ..."

"... family, probably ..."

Family indeed. Lorn smiles as he walks up the steps— wider and older than those on the clanless side of the Plaza, with depressions in the center of the granite risers. On the uppermost level he finds the doorway with the Ryalor House emblem above it—the inverted triangle with the intertwined *R* and *L*—and steps through the open doors of ancient and polished golden oak.

He does not even quite make three steps into the open space inside the door before Eileyt has two junior enumerators taking his bags and ushering him toward the private study—or office, as Ryalth calls it—that is his consort's. As he walks toward the rear corner, he can see that Ryalor House now occupies several rooms.

"She's here, Majer, and told us to be watching for you," Eileyt says. "She has been for several days."

"I see." Lorn laughs gently. From the reception he is getting, he has the impression that Ryalth has been most forceful.

Ryalth stands in the open door of her office, in her blue tunic and trousers, her hair shorter, but with a wide and warm smile on her face. As Lorn nears, she steps back into the office, and Lorn finds himself standing before her, his bags being deposited beside him. Then the door is closed, and Lorn is not sure who holds whom, only that they do.

"You're back," she finally says, leaning away enough to speak, but leaving her arms around him.

"I'm back. It's so good to hold you."

"It's good to hold you." She glances sideways at him. "You're worried."

He nods. "I'm not sure I should be here. I'm supposed to report to the Majer-Commander as soon as I arrive. But it's been so long."

"The Majer-Commander can spare us these few moments."

Lorn agrees, and they embrace again.

After a time, Lorn glances around, then sees the small high-sided bed in the corner.

"He's sleeping," Ryalth says. "I'm glad you looked."

He puts his arms back around her. "I've looked so many nights."

"I know. I could feel it. That's why . . . how . . . I knew you were all right and that you cared when there weren't any scrolls."

"There were," Lorn says. "Dettaur intercepted them all, and all yours to me."

"Jerial never liked him. Neither did your mother."

"I never got the scrolls about that, either," Lorn says.

Ryalth shakes her head. "Why would he do that?"

"Some people are like that. He's always wanted to bully people, and I've stopped him several times."

Ryalth frowns. "But if you got no scrolls . . ."

"Your last scroll, the only one I received after the first two seasons ago . . . it said something about the family problems . . . and the glass . . . it came up blank."

"I'm sorry. Jerial wrote, too, and I think Myryan did."

"I never got them."

"Do you have to go? Right away?"

"I can't stay too long. I probably should have gone straight to the Mirror Lancer Court, but . . ." Lorn shrugs, then grins. "It has been so long, and I love you, and I've missed you." He also has wanted to at least see Ryalth before he sees the Majer-Commander, for he knows not what lies ahead. "And I've never seen Kerial, either."

Ryalth takes his hand and leads him toward the small bed. "He's beautiful."

Lorn looks down at Kerial, his skin fair and clear, his fine hair reddish. After a moment, as if aware he is being studied, the infant opens his eyes, already amber, and gazes back, lifting a chubby hand as if to touch Lorn's face. Lorn bends and brushes the boy's cheeks with his lips.

"I'm glad you came here first. It's the first time you have."

"You're the most important one. Both of you."

"I'm glad." She touches his cheek. "Will you come back here?"

"As soon as I can." He draws her close for a last embrace. "As soon as I can."

It remains a while before Lorn finally reclaims his bags, straightens his uniform, and steps back out into the main space of Ryalor House.

". . . doesn't look so dangerous . . ."

Eileyt's laugh is loud enough for Lorn to recognize. "You don't think her consort would be dangerous?"

As Lorn manages to cross to the outer double doors, he can sense the silence of recognition behind his back. At the doors he looks back. He and Ryalth smile at each other. After a long moment, he turns once more and carries his bags toward the stairs. He hopes he can find a carriage to the Lancers' Tower. While he knows where the building is, he realizes that he has never been inside the structure. Nor has he ever met either of the men whose names are so familiar.

LXXXIII

THE TWO MEN pause in the third-floor corridor, outside the main and empty audience hall of the Palace of Eternal Light. Fifty cubits behind them are a pair of guards. Otherwise, the corridor is vacant.

"Greetings, most honored Second Magus," offers Luss.

"Greetings to you, Captain-Commander." Kharl inclines his head. "I have not seen you often recently."

"With fewer audiences being held by His Mightiness . . . I have been occupied in the Mirror Lancer Court."

"Ah, yes, I understand. The difficulties in Jerans . . . rather embarrassing, I would imagine. It must be difficult to persuade the Emperor of the necessity of more lancers in the north when a sub-majer is able to ravage the land and take a major port with less than six companies, and then bring back more golds than his expedition cost."

"He moved quickly, and raided effectively," Luss counters. "He took nothing . . . except, of course, a number of blades, including quite a few that were shipped to the barbarians by the house of the former Merchanter Advisor . . . and one other house. The Mirror Lancers remain astounded, of course, that the farseeing Magi'i were unaware of this." The Captain-Commander bows slightly. "There is talk, I also have heard, that Vyanat'mer may move to strip clan status from Bluyet House."

"There is always talk, but we have not heard such from Vyanat himself, and he is most direct."

"Oh, most honored and devious of Magi'i, you suggest that some plant the rumors so that Vyanat will seem weak when he does not do such."

"That has been known to happen," replies Kharl smoothly. "And when will your young sub-majer who caused this . . . unsettling . . . return to Cyad?"

"He should be here shortly." Luss glances to the west, toward the lower building that holds the headquarters of the Mirror Lancers.

"Today?" presses the Second Magus.

"That is possible." The Captain-Commander smiles, and his bushy black eyebrows lift. "You seem most interested in a mere sub-majer. But then you do have a certain . . . interest."

"I do," admits Kharl. "He is a former student magus, and all such reflect on the Magi'i, although to date he has reflected most credibly upon the Mirror Lancers. You act as though you are worried about him coming forth to present himself. Will he? Or does he indeed need to worry?"

"You would know better than I, honored Second Magus, for he is related to you, if somewhat indirectly."

"Were he my son, or a full magus, I would have no

doubts. But since he is not, and since he is a lancer..."
Kharl shrugs. "That is why I inquire of you. I also must admit that I am curious to see how you and the Majer-Commander receive him. And scarcely for—as you put it—for personal interests."

"Oh?"

"His actions have pointed out weaknesses in the Mirror Lancers and corruption in the merchanters. Were anything to happen to him, particularly immediately, more questions would be raised about the Mirror Lancers being some-how... indebted to the merchanters." Kharl laughs. "I know that such could never happen, but the perception would be there, nonetheless. It would not affect the less-senior officers, for young Lorn's actions would be taken as more... representative... of their abilities and motivations."

"The Majer-Commander is most aware of the subtleties of the situation."

"As I am most certain you are, Captain-Commander," Kharl suggests. "You have always placed the reputation of the Mirror Lancers high in your priorities."

"As have you the reputation of the Magi'i in yours." Luss bows. "If you will but excuse me, honored Second Magus, the Majer-Commander expects me most shortly."

"I am most certain that he does, and I wish you well."

LXXXIV

LORN STEPS INTO the front foyer of the five-story white granite building, a structure larger than any in the compounds and outposts where he has served, but one not terribly large—less than a hundred cubits long and sixty deep at the base, with each floor having a terrace, so that the structure narrows with each floor. The foyer itself is perhaps thirty cubits on a side with a set of wide white granite steps at the back, just behind a square stone arch that contains no ornamentation. The stone walls are also plain white sunstone, while the floor is a slightly pinkish white granite that has been polished into a shimmering finish. The only decoration in the foyer are the two green tapestries on the rear wall flanking the archway to the stairs. Each silver-bordered tapestry shows a silver sabre crossed by silver firelance.

A single senior squad leader sits behind a golden-oak table desk on a sunstone dais in the middle of the foyer, flanked by two Mirror Lancers in spotless cream uniforms, each with a sabre and a short firelance.

Lorn steps forward.

The squad leader glances at Lorn's insignia. "Ser?"

"Sub-Majer Lorn. I have orders to report to the Majer-Commander personally." Lorn extends the scroll.

The squad leader takes the scroll and reads. His eyes linger on the last lines and the signature. "Yes, ser. It's rather unusual. His study is on the fifth floor. You will need to present your orders to him. Ah . . . that is, squad leader Tygyl will present them."

Lorn smiles as he takes back the order roll. "I understand. The steps there?" He inclines his head to the wide steps at the back of the foyer.

"Yes, ser."

Lorn lifts his bags. He had debated leaving the bags with Ryalth, but that would have made it clear that he had not come directly to the Mirror Lancer Court.

The sub-majer crosses the foyer and walks through the square arch to begin ascending the steps, which rise a half-flight to a landing. From each end of the landing, another set rises a half-flight to the next floor. The pattern continues for four flights. Lorn pauses at each landing and takes several deep breaths. He scarcely wants to arrive at the Majer-Commander's study panting and puffing, although he expects he will be waiting for a while.

At the open space of the topmost floor, there is another

senior squad leader seated behind yet another golden-oak table desk. There are three doorways from the foyerlike space—one to the right, one to the left, and one directly behind the squad. The doorways to the left and right are closed and each guarded by a pair of Mirror Lancers, again with sabres and the short firelances. The double doors behind the table desk are open and unguarded.

Lorn steps forward and extends the order scroll. "Sub-Majer Lorn. As ordered, I am reporting personally to the Majer-Commander." As an afterthought, he also extends the hand with the Mirror Lancer seal ring.

"Yes, ser. They've been expecting you." The squad leader studies Lorn for the briefest of moments. "You came directly, I see."

"As directly as I could," Lorn says.

"The Captain-Commander will see you first, and then the Majer-Commander." The staffer turns in his chair and gestures toward the open doors behind him. "If you would wait in the anteroom there . . . ? There is water and some fruit and cheese there, if you haven't had a chance to eat recently. And, ser . . . I'll be giving your orders to the Majer-Commander."

"Thank you." Lorn inclines his head.

"Not at all, ser." The senior squad leader rises and walks toward the door to the left—on the north side of the open foyer.

Lorn lifts the bags and walks toward the receiving area. The room beyond the double doors is small, no more than ten cubits by fifteen, with a settee against the oak-paneled wall opposite the doors. The settee is flanked by two narrow and open windows. Set out from the settee and at right angles are two wooden armchairs, each with a green cushion. Against the wall at the right end of the room is a golden-oak sideboard with several trays upon it.

Lorn sets his bags beside the wooden chair closest to the door, and makes his way to the sideboard, where he pours water from the crystal carafe into a matching crystal mug. He studies the water and the trays of bread crackers and cheese, and the fruit bowl with his chaos-senses, but can detect nothing untoward. He lifts the mug and drains it almost immediately. After refilling the mug, he then takes several hard crackers and a drying wedge of cheese, and eats them. He will need his senses about him, and it has been awhile since he has eaten. He takes a second round of crackers and cheese, and finishes those.

"Ser?"

Lorn turns.

"The Majer-Commander has requested that you meet with the Captain-Commander first." The squad leader gestures toward Lorn's gear. "You can leave those there."

"Thank you." Lorn stops by the bag and extracts a rolled bundle before he follows the staffer out of the receiving area and toward the door on the south side of the foyer.

The squad leader opens it for Lorn, but does not enter.

Lorn steps into the study, a space roughly fifteen cubits wide and thirty long. To his right is an oblong table, with eight armless chairs. The entire wall on the right side of the room is comprised of golden-oak bookshelves, and most of the shelves are filled with volumes. Lorn conceals his interest as he catches sight of several shimmering silver book spines.

The left wall is mostly of narrow windows, although but two are open. The south end of the room contains a wide and polished table desk, set before two wide widows that overlook the south end of Cyad. The man who stands behind the table desk has black hair and bushy black eyebrows and wears a silver sunburst crossed by a sabre on the collar of his cream-and-green uniform.

Lorn bows. "Captain-Commander."

"Sub-Majer Lorn. It's good to see you." Captain-Commander Luss gestures to the chairs before his table desk, waiting a moment before reseating himself.

Lorn steps forward, past the conference table, and takes

the chair on the right side. He does not offer the rolled scrolls, keeping them loosely in his left hand.

The Captain-Commander looks full at Lorn and smiles. "You do not look half so deadly as the legends which already surround you."

"Legends are made by those with other goals, I fear, ser," Lorn says smoothly. "I have always served Cyad and the Mirror Lancers."

"Indeed you have, and that is something that all too many of your commanders seem to have forgotten." Luss's smile fades into a faint professional shadow of the one which welcomed Lorn. "The problem the Majer-Commander faces is that all senior officers feel that they serve Cyad and the Mirror Lancers . . . if you understand what I mean."

"You suggest, ser," Lorn says slowly, "that there are as many visions of the Mirror Lancers as there are senior officers."

"Not quite that many," Luss says with a laugh. "Not near that many . . . but enough."

"Which vision do you and the Majer-Commander serve? It would be best that I know that if I am to carry out my duties."

Luss laughs again. "Were it that simple. Were it that simple."

Lorn waits, knowing that Luss is watching for a commitment of sorts.

After a time, Luss begins to speak, deliberately. "You have been most diligent in reporting your actions, from the time you first served at Isahl. I have reviewed those reports. You have always reported clearly, and so far as any can tell, with great accuracy. Your reports from Biehl showed even greater detail and accuracy. Yet there were no reports from Inividra until the last report that you wrote for Commander Ikynd. You did write that report, did you not?" Luss lifts his eyebrows.

"I wrote a number of reports while I was commanding at Inividra. As commanded, I sent them all to Majer Dettaur.

There were no reports in the files at Assyadt when I reported there after the Jeran campaign." Lorn shrugs. "I had suggested that duplicates be sent from Inividra to Assyadt, but I was detached, so that I have no idea if that was carried out."

"You suggest that Majer Dettaur destroyed such reports."

"Ser . . . I have no idea what occurred. I can only say that the reports I sent were not in the records chests at Assyadt. I know the reports were written and delivered. Beyond that, only Commander Ikynd and Majer Dettaur would know."

"You killed Majer Dettaur."

"He attacked me without warning or reason. I defended myself. I imagine, although one can only surmise, that he feared that my presence would reveal that he had been distorting the records of my actions and that he would be disgraced."

"Yet, you merely reported that he had died in the line of duty," Luss says.

"Would there have been any point in revealing that he had distorted the records? Would it have helped the Mirror Lancers?"

"No." Luss shakes his head. "Most sub-majers who found their actions debased by a superior would not have acted in such a fashion."

"I cannot say I enjoyed letting Majer Dettaur have an honorable death," Lorn admits. "But my satisfaction would have served the lancers ill."

Luss nods. "Indeed it would. Your restraint there was impressive. Because of the difficulties that might have occurred, Majer Dettaur's reports to lancer headquarters have also been destroyed, and, as you had apparently already suggested, I have requested that Commander Ikynd have duplicates of your reports copied and sent here for the records."

"I think you will find them thorough and accurate," Lorn replies.

"Of that, I am most certain." Luss smiles. "I have little else to add. I did wish to meet you, but the Majer-Commander will be detailing your duties. He was most particular that you would be working directly for him. You should feel flattered. He seldom takes such an interest in a sub-majer."

"I feel most fortunate," Lorn replies. "In working for the Majer-Commander, and in having your interest and advice, ser."

"I am glad you feel so, and trust you will always do so." Luss rises and steps around the table. "We need to bring you to the Majer-Commander."

Lorn stands and follows the senior officer back past the conference table and out into the foyer area, past the staffer's table and to the double doors on the north end of the foyer.

Luss opens the door and motions for Lorn to enter. The sub-majer does so, and Luss follows him inside, closing the door.

The study is the same length as that of the Captain-Commander, but wider, close to thirty cubits, and there are windowed doors that open onto a roof terrace that, Lorn can see through all the windows on each of the three walls before him, surrounds the study.

The gray-eyed, gray-haired Mirror Lancer officer who stands beside his table desk is not so tall as either Lorn or Luss, and more slender, yet there is the strength of a tested sabre in his frame, and in the gray eyes that seem to take in everything.

"Ser . . . Sub-Majer Lorn," offers Luss.

"Greetings." Rynst looks at Luss. "And thank you, Luss. I will be talking to you later about the deployments."

"Yes, ser." Luss inclines his head and slips back out of the study.

Lorn stands waiting.

"Come on . . . have a seat. It's more comfortable than a firewagon. Tygyl said that you came almost directly here."

"Yes, ser." Lorn steps forward, past the conference table that is more than twice the size of the one in the Captain-Commander's office, and takes the seat opposite the left-hand corner of the polished table desk. Through the window before which Rynst sits, Lorn can see both the gray-blue waters of the harbor and the Palace of Eternal Light, the outlines of both blurred by the mist of the late-spring day.

Rynst'alt surveys Lorn slowly. "You are indeed your father's son. It's too bad that he didn't live to see it. I'm sorry for his death."

Lorn forces his himself to swallow and his face to turn blank. "His death?"

Rynst frowns. "You didn't know?"

"No, ser. I did not know. I worried because there was no response to my scrolls home, and I have feared, but I did not know. I did fear the worst."

"You were sent scrolls."

Lorn offers a tight smile. "Majer Dettaur thought it best I should not be troubled by scrolls from my consort or from my family—only from my sire."

Rynst's face tightens. "Those are harsh words about a fellow officer, and someone who has been close to your family."

Lorn meets the older officer's eyes. "I do not trouble myself to lie, ser. He would have destroyed the outpost at Inividra to ensure my death. He put my men at risk with every order he issued in the name of Commander Ikynd."

Rynst raises his eyebrows. "If that be so . . . it might explain much. Yet I cannot see why he would do such. He had a bright future."

"Mine looked brighter to him, ser. That, he could not abide."

"You will have to deal with this . . ."

"I already have. When I reported to Commander Ikynd, Dettaur attacked me with a sabre. I was forced to defend myself." Lorn smiles. "I took the liberty of bringing his orders for you to examine." The sub-majer extends the rolled bundle.

As he takes the scrolls, Rynst sighs. "You are indeed your father's son. Act quickly, and support your actions." He pauses. "Your father was more than any knew, as you will discover."

Lorn lowers his eyes for a moment, trying to control the burning in them, even though his father's death is not the sudden shock he has expressed. He swallows. "I'm sorry, ser. Even though I suspected . . ."

"I can understand that." Rynst nods. He reads through the scrolls, cursorily, then looks at Lorn. "You did not protest Dettaur's actions?"

"How?" Lorn's lips twist. "By dispatching a lancer messenger for a three-day ride to post a scroll that would be read by the Captain-Commander?"

Rynst frowns. "Do you really think you can wear Alyiakal's mantle?"

"No, ser. No man can wear another's."

"That sounds like Kien." The Majer-Commander shakes his head. "Such honesty is most dangerous in Cyad, young Lorn."

"Ser . . . dishonesty with you is far more dangerous."

Rynst laughs, a low rueful sound, shaking his head. "Chaos-light . . . you sound so much like your sire. The dry honesty . . ." He shakes his head again. After a long moment, the Majer-Commander pulls a pouch from his desk drawer and extends it. "You've been promoted. You're a majer. I can't afford to have aides who are less than majers. No one listens to them. Most don't listen to majers, but you've enough background and a reputation for action that being a majer should be enough. Besides, too much rank right now would not be wise."

"Yes, ser." Lorn takes the soft shimmercloth pouch.

Rynst leans forward. "Your tasks are very simple. You do what I ask. You do nothing for anyone else, unless you are certain it is to accomplish what I have set before you."

"Yes, ser."

"You have not had any furlough or leave in close to two years. Is that not correct?"

"Yes, ser."

"You need to see your consort and your family, especially after learning of your father's death. You have the rest of this eightday, and all of the next. When you return, in addition to your normal reporting duties, your first task is straightforward enough. You write well, and swiftly. That is clear." Rynst's lips twist into a smile that is near-ironic. "Not all appreciate that. You know that the chaos-towers are failing. Otherwise you would not have gone to Jera. Draft a plan for dealing with the Jeranyi. For the first draft, do not consider the factions in Cyad. Once you return, you will draft what you believe to be the best lancer solution. Do not put a line to paper until you return. Is that clear?"

"Yes, ser."

"I will see you an eightday from oneday." Rynst smiles slightly as he stands, "And Majer . . . two matters: First, put on the insignia before you leave the outer study. And, second, it might be best if no other officers and enumerators disappeared—at least for a while. I don't have officers to waste, even bad ones, and I've suggested, even to the Captain-Commander, that you'll refrain from such if he will. Now . . . go and spend some time with your consort and family."

"Yes, ser." Lorn stands.

Rynst's smile is fatherly—almost—as he watches Lorn leave his study.

LXXXV

LORN WANTS TO touch the emblem on his collar—the miniature crossed lances—as he sits in the carriage that conveys him back down to the Traders' Plaza. The short trip seems almost a metaphor for his recent life, as he feels he moves from point to point with nothing exactly being settled, each action somehow not quite finished.

He glances through the carriage window. A patch of blue sky has finally appeared over the harbor, spreading slowly as he watches, and mist begins to rise off the white sunstone piers where the warm sun strikes them.

Lorn leaves the carriage driver with half a silver, and walks quickly across the Plaza. His steps are less deliberate as he climbs to the topmost floor of the building holding Ryalor House.

This time, unlike others when he has arrived, his consort is not meeting with other factors or traders, and her smile is even warmer—and more relieved—as he opens the door to her private office. He closes the door behind him.

Kerial in her arms, Ryalth steps forward. "What happened?"

"I met with the Captain-Commander, and then the Majer-Commander. The Majer-Commander promoted me right there and said I had furlough until an eightday from next oneday."

"You have time to spend with your family?"

"I was ordered to spend it with you."

"Maybe you should bend the rules more often."

"This is the first time I have ended up with more time with you," he points out.

"Let's go home. We can talk there," she says. "For once, I don't have anyone coming by, and I don't want anyone to show up." She eases back toward her table desk and scoops up a blue leather bag. "Kerial's things."

Then she opens the door and beckons to Eileyt, who sits at a small table a halfscore of cubits from her door.

The senior enumerator stands and slips toward the three. "Yes, Lady?"

"Eileyt, we're leaving," Ryalth says quietly. "If I come in tomorrow, it won't be for long. I'll be in on fourday to meet with the Austran."

"Yes, Lady."

"You know where to send a messenger if it's urgent, but it had best be most urgent."

The senior enumerator smiles and bows his head. "I trust it will not be necessary."

"So do I." Ryalth shifts Kerial—whose arms and pudgy fists have begun to windmill—from one shoulder to the other.

As the couple and their son cross the front room of Ryalor House, Lorn is aware that all the merchanters watch them, if covertly, and he wonders exactly what has been said about him, for they see Ryalth every day.

Several merchanters from other houses step aside as Lorn, Ryalth, and Kerial make their way down the steps and out onto the Plaza whose eastern side, in the late afternoon, is finally bathed in sunlight.

On the lower level, another pair of younger enumerators freeze and watch. Lorn catches the words after they pass.

"See . . . he's real . . . Majer now . . . too."

". . . better not offend Vyanat'mer, then. It's too short a trip."

Lorn wonders about the last words.

Ryalth smiles. "You are the subject of some many rumors among the merchanters. Vyanat copied parts of the report you sent him. He suggested that he would send any traders who sold weapons to the Jeranyi to see you personally."

"I suppose he called me the Butcher of Nhais, or Jera?"

Ryalth frowns. "No . . . he was more complimentary than that."

"That's what Dettaur called me."

"From what I have heard from Jerial, I'm not surprised." Ryalth says, turning westward as they leave the Plaza.

"She liked Dettaur less than I did." Lorn looks along the Road of Benevolent Commerce. "Where are we headed?"

"Home."

"You have a better place?" He smiles. "I knew that from the glass, but I never got any scrolls . . ."

Ryalth frowns. "Those were in the ones—"

"—that Dettaur intercepted and destroyed." Lorn laughs.

"For that alone he should have been slain."

"It wasn't just for that," Lorn says quietly. "I killed him because what he was doing would have killed more lancers and because he would have done anything to destroy me—and you." He shakes his head. "And mostly because he attacked me rather than explain."

"You had said he had tried to kill you."

"He still thought he was better with a sabre."

"Your brother Vernt—he said your friend Tyrsal told him that you could use a blade with either hand, and that no one in the lancers could match you."

"I doubt that," Lorn protests. "There are probably a number."

"Zero is a number, too, my dear, and closer to the truth. After all, Dettaur was among the best, and he is dead."

Lorn cannot dispute that, although Dettaur's death was aided by Lorn's control of chaos-energies, and that, he cannot mention anywhere. "Why did you decide to move? Kerial?"

"For that reason, and because this location is much better, and closer." An amused expression crosses her lips.

They turn down a narrow side way—narrow for Cyad, perhaps only twenty cubits wide—that was perhaps once intended as a service way for the larger mansions that front the Fourth and Fifth Harbor Ways. Halfway down the road is a wall that runs between two carriage stables. In the center of that alabaster wall is a heavy iron gate—a rarity in Cyad.

"The gate came from Hamor. I felt it would prove . . . useful." Ryalth's lips curl, but the expression is not quite a smile. After extracting a key from her belt wallet, she unlocks the gate, then locks it behind them after they step around the privacy hedge of thornroses that blocks any view from beyond the gate. Beyond the hedge is a garden, with a fountain shaped like the trunk of a pearapple tree. Flanking the fountain are two teardrop-shaped flower gardens, each backed by a shoulder-high boxwood hedge. The green marble walk leads to the fountain basin, circles it, and then melds back into a single pathway leading to the dwelling beyond.

"When it's warmer and the water sprays, the fountain has the shape of a true pearapple—almost, anyway," the redhead explains.

Lorn takes in the dwelling on the far side of the garden. It is low, merely two stories, with a covered veranda supported by fluted green marble pillars. The house itself is also of marble, a shade of white, lightly tinted green. He can see the wide windows and the double doors. "It's lovely."

"It should be." Her words are light. "Let me show you."

Lorn follows her around the fountain basin and up the three wide marble steps. A polished wooden settee sits before the wide window on the left side of the doors, and is flanked by two low tables.

"The cushions are inside. I don't sit out here in the winter, and I've been so busy that somehow, the cushions never got out here." Ryalth unlocks the heavy white-oak door and motions for Lorn to enter.

He does, but once he moves around the inner ceramic privacy screen, he stops cold in the entry foyer.

There are four steps down, so that the ceilings are far higher than they had looked from outside. The walls are a pale green stone, half-covered with gold-trimmed green hangings, and covering more than half the pale green marble floor is a six-sided woven green carpet, bordered in blue and edged in gold. Two archways lead from the foyer.

"Kysia . . . Ayleha, I'm home!" Ryalth calls, shifting Kerial from her right to her left arm.

A heavyset gray-haired woman appears in the left-hand archway and nods. She wears a tunic and trousers of pale green, and a darker green scarf covers her throat, almost to her chin.

"Ayleha, this is Lorn . . . my consort, the one I have talked about. He is Kerial's father. He hasn't been able come to Cyad very often." Ryalth waits for a moment. "Lorn is the only one who is welcome here when I am not. The *only* one. We owe him everything. Everything."

Ayleha bobs her head twice. Another figure appears in the archway behind Ayleha—Kysia, Lorn suspects, who had served in his parents' house.

"I'm going to show him around. We'll have dinner when we usually do. Lorn and I have much to talk over."

The silent serving woman nods once, then smiles.

Lorn realizes she has no teeth, but he smiles and says, "I'm pleased to meet you, Ayleha."

The woman nods, first to Ryalth, then to Lorn, before slipping back through the archway.

"She doesn't speak."

"She can't. She was a slave in Hamor. To one of the merchant princes. They don't like their secrets spread. She tried to escape. She finally succeeded, and someone who owed me a favor thought I might find her useful." Ryalth sighs. "She is, and she's grateful, and she cooks well, and it still bothers me."

Lorn touches her arm. "You can only do what you can do."

"Sometimes . . . that's not enough."

Lorn is the one to allow himself to sigh. "I know."

Ryalth gestures to the short, muscular, gray-eyed woman who remains in the archway. "And you remember Kysia?"

Lorn laughs as he recalls the servant whom Ryalth had paid surreptitiously to help his family and report to her. "I'm glad to meet you closely, and face-to-face."

"And I you, ser." A mischievous smile appears. "You are difficult to avoid."

"You won't have to, not anymore."

Kysia bows, the smile still on her face.

"He hasn't seen the house."

The gray-eyed young woman bows and slips back through the archway.

Still wrestling with a squirming Kerial, Ryalth turns to Lorn. "We have much to talk about. But let me show you the house, first." A smile dances across her lips as she moves toward the right archway from the foyer.

"You didn't have to tell Ayleha you owed me everything. You don't."

"But I do." Her thin eyebrows lift. "You deceived me, dear lancer. I thought there were but a few hundred golds in that chest you gave me, oh so long ago. There were also rubies and emeralds and close to another thousand golds beneath the lining." She laughs. "So I deceived you, and used them." She draws Lorn from the central foyer through the wide arch into the front sitting room. "A small portion of our ill-gotten gains."

The sitting room contains the bordered carpet that depicts the trading ship that had sunk with Ryalth's parents aboard so many years before, and the settee from her earlier quarters, and a great deal more, including a tall and polished golden-oak bookcase and a matching sideboard set under one of the wide windows.

From the sitting room, Ryalth leads Lorn into a dining room with a table that will seat almost a score easily.

"For when we invite your family," she explains.

"Will Ciesrt even come?" asks Lorn.

"Now that you are working for the Majer-Commander, I imagine he will be most ready to sup with us," Ryalth says dryly. "If only to see what he can discover."

"Wahh!" interjects Kerial.

"Hush, sweetheart, we'll be just a bit, but your father hasn't even seen the house yet."

Kerial sniffs, loudly.

The kitchen, where both Kysia and Ayleha are laboring, chopping onions and other vegetables, is as large as the entire quarters Ryalth had occupied on the east side of Cyad.

With Kerial squirming more and more, Ryalth hurries up

the center stairs and toward the heavy oak door in the middle of the south side of the house. The master chamber—with a small balcony beyond—stretches a good thirty cubits along the middle of the front of the house, and is almost fifteen cubits deep.

Lorn looks at the ornate, triple-width bed. "I've seen this so many times in the glass. I'm glad I'm here to see it in person."

"So am I."

"Wahh!" adds Kerial.

"He's hungry . . . and . . ."

"That's all right. I've been traveling for days. I can clean up while you feed him."

"By then, dinner for us will be ready, and, after that," Ryalth says, "Kerial is usually tired enough to sleep."

"When did you get that?" Lorn asks, inclining his head toward the little bed.

"About three eightdays ago. I hoped you would be coming home."

Lorn bends toward her, dodging Kerial's flailing arm, and brushes her cheek with his lips. "I'm very glad."

"You get cleaned up, and I'll get your very insistent son fed." Ryalth smiles again. "The armoire on the left is yours. It's empty."

Lorn returns the smile and sets his bags beside the armoire.

LXXXVI

WHAAA . . ."

Kerial's protest is the first sound Lorn hears, as the barest tinge of gray seeps through the shutters. The tired majer winces, then suppresses a sigh as Ryalth slips from the large bed to the smaller one.

"There, there...Mother's right here." She lifts the reddish-haired boy and cradles him in her arms, then one-handedly readjusts the pillows on her bed before slipping back beside Lorn, and easing Kerial's hungry mouth to her breast.

For a time, Lorn just watches his consort and their son.

"You're quiet," Ryalth says.

"It's strange, almost amazing, to be here," he admits. "And to think that we have a child."

"You were amazing last night." Ryalth shifts her weight slightly to brush a strand of short red hair off her forehead.

Kerial sucks loudly.

Lorn flushes. "I missed you."

"I've missed you." She smiles. "Couldn't you tell?"

Lorn finds himself flushing more.

"I like it when you do that."

"What? Turn red?" he asks wryly.

"You're always so composed when anyone sees you," she points out. "Someone who doesn't know you would think you feel nothing. I even wondered at first. It made more sense once I began to understand the Magi'i."

"That nothing is hidden, you mean?"

Ryalth sits up and lifts Kerial to her shoulder, patting him on the back gently. She is rewarded with a small burp, and she eases him down and lets him nurse from the other breast. "It's more subtle than that," she muses. "Watching people through a glass and using your senses to listen when no one thinks you can—I've seen you do that—doing that takes time and effort. No one can watch anyone all the time. So you never know what someone knows, only that they could know."

"I can sense when someone uses a glass," Lorn points out. "So can you."

"Sometimes, but mostly when it's you. It's hard, otherwise."

"Unless it's a strong magus," Lorn suggests, then adds, "There must be some Magi'i in your background."

Ryalth offers a gentle laugh. "I've wondered that, lately, and if that's where the book came from. But there's no way to find out now."

"I suppose not. But Father would be very happy to know it . . . and pleased."

"I have funny feelings about that. I don't feel like a magus or a healer."

"You weren't trained that way . . . but you're certainly as perceptive as my sisters, and you can sense things. That's one reason why you're a good trader."

"I don't know." Ryalth shakes her head. "The whole bit about the chaos-glasses—you told me that most Magi'i can't feel anyone using a glass. That's why they have to act as though everything they do could be watched or heard. It's still hard to deal with. You were that way to begin with. Your brother still is."

"I suppose that's why manners and customs are important." Lorn frowns. "Everyone expects them, and their sameness makes meeting and greeting someone safer."

"That's the impression, but I can tell when they're genuine and when they are just a formality. Most people can."

"You're saying that the more adept of the Magi'i can use that to their advantage?"

"Don't you?"

Lorn laughs. "You know me too well."

"You'd better keep using it, now that you're back in Cyad."

"You're right. I'm still worried."

"Why?" Ryalth's blue eyes are warm as they study him.

"The Majer-Commander has something in mind for me, and the Captain-Commander isn't exactly that fond of me."

"Neither is Bluyet Clan," Ryalth says dryly. "You're lucky that Vyanat'mer is the Merchanter Advisor to the Emperor. The Hyshrah Clan have never been fond of those of Bluyet. And Denys—he's Bluoyal's successor—was close to Bluoyal."

"What's Vyanat'mer like?"

"He seems very direct. He speaks but the truth, and his words are blunt." Ryalth shakes her head. "Behind the bluntness and the use of truth, there is great subtlety. Like Bluoyal, and like Tasjan, he believes that the days of the Mirror Lancers, and especially of the Magi'i, are passing."

"They won't pass entirely," Lorn replies. "The better Magi'i can draw chaos from the world around them. It's not spoken of widely, but they can."

"How many? One out of ten?" asks Ryalth. "If the towers fail . . ."

"*When* the towers fail," Lorn says.

"Then, most of the Magi'i will be powerless, or have but a fraction of their former power," Ryalth notes. "Vyanat knows that. Golds won't lose their power, but the Mirror Lancers will be less powerful without firelances . . ."

"Not necessarily. We could raise more lancers."

"And how will you pay them and arm them?"

"I bow to you, my lady," Lorn says. "Both will take more golds, and that will lead to greater power for the merchanters."

"You can think about that later." Ryalth disengages Kerial's mouth and lifts him to her shoulder. "What would you like to do today?"

Lorn offers a wide smile.

"Besides that. That will have to wait until later."

"I need to see Jerial and Myryan and Vernt."

"I had thought they could come here for dinner in a few days," suggests Ryalth.

"We still need to see Jerial and Myryan before that."

"Today would be better. We can hire a carriage for the day," suggests Ryalth.

"You could afford one all the time," Lorn says, "from what I've seen, you prosperous trader." He grins.

"There's no point in that. Most of the time, I don't need it. Besides, that would draw attention." Ryalth moistens her lips. "When we get up, I'll have Kysia find a messenger to let them know we'll be dropping by. Jerial might be gone, otherwise. Myryan gets home in the late afternoon tò prepare dinner for Ciesrt."

Lorn nods. "Would you like me to hold Kerial while you get washed and dressed?"

She smiles. "That would be nice. He usually has to stay in his bed and fuss."

The majer slowly takes his son, who is beginning to squirm, and lifts the infant boy to his shoulder.

"Keep your hand behind his neck. He's not that strong there yet," Ryalth cautions.

Lorn eases his fingers up Kerial's back. "How are you this morning, young man?"

A slight burp is followed by, "Aaaaa . . ."

Lorn smiles crookedly as he feels the dampness on his shoulder. There is much he will have to get used to in Cyad—both in the Mirror Lancers and at home.

LXXXVII

IT IS NEARLY late midmorning when Kysia comes to the top of the stairs and announces, "Lady, ser . . . the carriage is here."

"Thank you," Lorn calls, clipping the Brystan sabre in place.

"I'll carry Kerial. You don't have that many uniforms left," Ryalth says.

"Again," notes Lorn. "I'll need to have some more tailored."

"Very stylishly."

"No . . . not too stylishly."

After a moment, Ryalth nods. "Well-fitted, but not dandy-ish." She slips Kerial, who wears a cream-colored tunic above green trousers that look baggy, into the crook of her left arm.

Then the two descend to the main floor of the dwelling that still amazes Lorn in its deceptive size and luxury. Outside, the sun shines brightly, although there is a slight haze that lightens the green-blue sky.

The carriage that waits outside the iron gate is older, although the polished golden-oak and spruce of the closed body have been kept oiled and clean.

As Lorn and Ryalth step outside the iron gate, Lorn looks at the gray-haired coachman. "The Road of Perpetual Light, at the crossing of the Tenth Way." He opens the carriage door and extends an arm to help Ryalth inside.

"Yes, ser." The coachman smiles. "Handsome young-'un, there."

"Thank you," Ryalth says as she steps up and inside the carriage.

"You be needing me all day?" asks the coachman.

"Most of it, I'd think," Lorn replies. "You'll be paid for the whole day."

"Thank you, ser."

With a nod, Lorn follows Ryalth into the coach and closes the door.

As the carriage passes the Fourth Harbor Way East, Lorn can sense the chill of a chaos-glass, and he looks at Ryalth. Her lips quirk.

"Did Kysia find a messenger to send to Jerial?"

"Of course. Otherwise Jerial might have been at the infirmary, but she's not. She's packing up her things."

Lorn winces. "I hadn't thought about that."

"She'll be fine, dear," Ryalth says. "Unlike some."

He forces himself not to take a deep breath when the unseen chill of the chaos-glass passes.

Ryalth raises her eyebrows.

"I don't know." He answers the unspoken question. "A magus, but . . ." He shrugs. "It could be any first-level adept."

"There will be more," Ryalth says, patting Kerial on the back.

"I fear so—now that I am back in Cyad."

When the coach pulls up outside the dwelling that had been Lorn's parents', he steps out quickly, holding the door and offering a hand to Ryalth.

"You can wait in the shade here," Lorn tells the coachman. "And there's water in the lower garden there."

The driver nods.

"I don't know how long we'll be."

"We'll be here, ser."

Lorn and Ryalth walk toward the door, but before they have even started up the steps, Jerial opens the door and steps beyond the privacy screen. Lorn's older sister is clad in a deep black, and there are circles around her eyes.

Lorn steps forward and hugs her.

"I'd hoped it would be you." She steps back and gestures. "Come on in. Things are messy . . . I'm packing."

Lorn holds back a frown and waits for Ryalth to carry Kerial past the tiled privacy screen, then nods to Jerial, and follows the women into the house.

"Kerial just keeps getting bigger," Jerial notes as she closes the door.

As they walk up to the second level, Lorn looks at Jerial. "I'm sorry. I was never told. I didn't get any scrolls from you or Ryalth."

Jerial nods. "I feared that when I didn't hear, and when I realized that Dettaur was at Assyadt. I could feel it when you looked for Ryalth when we were together."

The three take seats in the sitting room.

"Gaaaa . . ." Kerial announces, waving a chubby fist. "Gaaaa!" He lurches in Ryalth's arms toward the dark-haired healer.

"He's being social," Jerial says with a smile.

"He knows his aunt," Ryalth counters.

"He's like his father." Jerial grins at her brother. "Or like you were before you met Ryalth."

"Thank you for the last phrase," Lorn says.

Kerial lurches once more, and Ryalth stands and carries her son to Jerial, who takes him easily.

"You're getting to be such a big boy," Jerial coos at the infant.

"About Father . . . Mother?" Lorn asks. "How long has it been?"

"Father died on twoday of the third eightday of winter. Mother did not last three eightdays beyond. I don't think she wanted to . . . and she had spent so much energy keeping him alive."

"I'm sorry . . . you know I didn't know."

"What could you have done?" Jerial shakes her head. "I think I'm angriest that Dettaur took your scrolls to Father. At the end . . . Father would reread the older ones, and he would talk to me about when we were young."

"How was he . . . at the end?" Lorn ventures.

"The same as always, except weaker. He was still sometimes saying the usual platitudes, except that they weren't for him—and sometimes the unexpected. He told Vernt that there would come a time when Vernt would need your help, and that Vernt had better not tilt his nose too far back to see it."

"He said that?"

Jerial laughs. "And he told me that there was life beyond Cyad, and not to forget it when the time came. He didn't say much to Myryan that way, except to enjoy her garden, 'for gardens are worlds.' "

Lorn swallows, fearing his father's foresight. "You said you were packing . . ."

"The house is actually Vernt's, you know, but he suffers me to live here for the moment, although his consort will probably change that." Jerial laughs. "They've already moved into the master bedchamber, and brought in one of the servants from her family, now that she's expecting."

Lorn raises his eyebrows.

"You met her. Vernt's consort."

"I know. Mycela—she's the daughter of Lector Abram'elth. One of the last scrolls I got from Father said she was expecting this summer."

"She is. She does dote on Vernt, but the cream and simpering can get heavy at times, especially now that she's already planning the child's entire life."

Lorn glances at Ryalth.

"I already told Jerial she was welcome to stay with us," Ryalth says.

"A merchanter I know has consented to let me live in his dwelling," Jerial says, with a faint smile.

"Someone who once was a dissolute gambler?" Lorn asks, almost idly.

"Exactly. It's an arrangement of convenience."

Ryalth nods.

Lorn turns to his consort. "I don't suppose that Ryalor House made those arrangements?"

Ryalth smiles brightly. "How could I have done otherwise?"

Lorn shakes his head, then looks at his sister. "You'll be close to us?"

"Only about three blocks to the northwest. It's a small place. It used to be a carriage house." Jerial smiles. "That way, at times, I can take care of Kerial."

"You two . . ." Lorn shakes his head, then glances toward his consort.

Kerial has begun to windmill his arms, and Jerial glances at Ryalth.

"He's hungry, I think," Ryalth says.

Jerial stands and carries the boy to his mother, and Ryalth takes him, then unfastens several buttons on her tunic and eases her son to her breast. "He is hungry—again."

"Father left some things for you," Jerial looks at her brother. "Vernt got most everything to do with the Magi'i, but there are several stacks of books for you . . . and some papers he gave to me that he asked that you read as soon as you returned to Cyad."

"We can send some of the warehouse workers from Ryalor House with Lorn to get the books later in the eight-day," Ryalth suggests, shifting Kerial slightly as he feeds.

"Don't make it too long . . . and I need to get that box for you, while I'm thinking about it." Jerial rises. "I'll be right back."

After Jerial takes the stairs, lightly and quickly, Lorn glances at Ryalth. "She seems to be all right."

"She is." The lady trader studies her son fondly. "You are a little piglet." She looks up. "I'll wager you were, too."

Lorn shrugs helplessly. "I don't recall."

"I've heard about you and the pearapple tarts."

"I was older then."

"And probably more restrained," the red-haired woman counters.

Lorn is still laughing as Jerial comes back down the stairs from the fourth level. The carved wooden box that Jerial carries had rested on one of the lower shelves in his father's study, Lorn recalls, although he has never seen the box open. It is perhaps a third the size of a lancer footchest, and made of a dark and shimmering wood, inlaid with spirals of intertwined shimmering white cupridium and green lacquered cupridium.

"The box was Grandfather's, Father said." Jerial extends the box. "It's filled with papers, and there's a folded and sealed letter to you there."

Lorn swallows and takes the box.

"Oh . . . and Vernt has made the arrangements with the registry to have the shares of the bond transferred to you and to me and Myryan."

Lorn frowns.

"Father and Mother had set aside enough in golds," Jerial explains, "and some in a trading account, so that the house wouldn't have to be sold. Vernt will even have some golds, as well as the house." The dark-haired healer looks at her brother. "You were kind to relinquish the elderclaim."

"I'm not even the oldest, and I couldn't see you and Myryan suffering."

"You think I'd suffer?" Jerial arches her eyebrows.

"Well . . ."

"I'm doing fine, but I thank you."

"Whhaaaaa!" Kerial interjects as Ryalth shifts her son to her shoulder to burp him.

"Now . . . in a moment, you can have some more, you little piglet."

Kerial's burp is loud, and Lorn winces. Ryalth smiles as she lowers Kerial to her other breast.

"You'll get used to it," Jerial predicts.

"I'm sure I will." Lorn looks down at the heavy box in his lap once more. "Did Father say . . . anything?"

Jerial shakes her head. "Just that you would understand."

"For a while, I think he despaired of my ever understanding anything."

"He just wanted you to think that," suggests the dark-haired healer.

"Ryalth has said as much," Lorn admits. "You two think alike . . . too much, at times, I fear." He grins.

"Poor . . . poor lancer officer," Jerial coos at her brother.

"It's a good thing you're my older sister," Lorn mock-grumps, "and that I respect you."

"Very good, because you still don't know everything," Jerial responds. "Ryalth and I have to make sure you listen to us." She grins.

"I'm outnumbered." Lorn looks from side to side.

"You're overdramatizing, too, dearest," suggests Ryalth.

Lorn shrugs.

"How long will you be free?" asks Jerial.

"I have furlough until an eightday from oneday, but I'll be

reporting directly to the Majer-Commander to work here in Cyad."

"That's quite an honor," Jerial says evenly.

"A dangerous honor," he admits. "More dangerous as the seasons turn."

The healer nods slowly. "What else are you doing . . . today?"

"We also need to see Myryan," Lorn says.

"Yes, you do." Jerial's words are firm.

Lorn tilts his head at the tone of her words.

"She doesn't talk to me—not really talk—and I don't think she's that happy. She will talk to you."

"We'll go there from here."

"I'm glad."

Ryalth disengages Kerial. "No. No biting." She closes her shirt and tunic before burping her son.

Jerial stands. "You two need to see Myryan, and I need to finish packing before Mycela's simpering turns to whining."

"She whines?"

"Most politely," Jerial says dryly. "It's still whining."

Lorn stands, then helps Ryalth. The three walk down to the front door, Lorn with the ornate wooden box under his arm.

"I'm looking forward to your dinner," Jerial says. "I've been eating too much of my own cooking lately."

Lorn raises his eyebrows.

"Mycela's cook's and my tastes aren't exactly the same. That's another reason to finish the packing." Jerial grins as she opens the door.

The coachman has the carriage door open before Lorn and Ryalth have descended the steps out to the Road of Benevolent Light.

"Out to the Twenty-third Way," Lorn tells the coachman. "East," he adds as an afterthought.

"Yes, ser."

Lorn assists his consort into the coach, then follows and settles himself on the seat beside her. "Kerial is doing well."

"We'll see how he lasts," Ryalth replies.

Lorn glances at her, seeing the weariness in her eyes. "You're tired."

"It isn't always easy, being the mother and the lady trader, even with a bed for Kerial in my trading office. And trading now is more dangerous than ever."

"Why now?"

"The Emperor has lost three fireships, and there were never enough to protect all the traders. Piracy is increasing, particularly in the Gulf of Candar. They say that the pirates have built a small base on Recluce." Ryalth shrugs. "The Emperor's Enumerators are getting stricter, and since there's no Hand to appeal to . . ."

"You wrote about that. The Emperor hasn't appointed a new Hand?"

"Not yet. There are rumors that he's ill, as well. That means prices go up and down with the latest rumors, and that makes merchanting even harder—without the sleep I lose to my little friend here."

"Gaaa . . ." Kerial says.

"Yes, you, piglet," Ryalth replies.

The carriage slows.

"Twenty-third Way, ser and Lady!"

Lorn waits until the coach comes to a halt before opening the door and then helping his consort out. Still holding on to the box from his father, he glances up. "I don't know how long . . ."

"That be fine, ser. You're paying, and waiting is easier than traveling."

"Thank you." Lorn glances toward the small house.

Perhaps because of the strong midday sun, the blue tile roof of the two-story dwelling seems more vivid than when Lorn had visited Myryan before, and the green-glazed brick walls more faded. The blue-and-green-tiled outside privacy screen retains the time-faded golden lily inset in its center.

The two walk to the front entrance, and Lorn knocks once. There is no response. He knocks again.

"Hello!" he finally calls when there is no answer to his knocking.

"Lorn! Ryalth! I was out in back!" calls Myryan as she hurries from the side gate toward the couple at the front door. "In the garden."

"Always in the garden," Lorn says as he hugs his younger sister.

As had been the case when he had last seen Myryan, Lorn notes how frail she seems, although there is no sickness or chaos surrounding her. Even in the nondescript gray shirt and trousers she has been wearing in the garden, the slightest scent of trilia and erhenflower enfolds her. Myryan—never anything but slender—looks almost painfully thin to Lorn, despite the broad and welcoming smile and the thick and short-cut unruly black hair curling out around her face.

"Come on!" Myryan says as she opens the front door. The black-haired healer leads them through the front door and the small, tile-floored foyer into the front sitting room, with its pleasing green-tinted, off-white walls. After she flips open the three narrow and shuttered windows and gestures toward the settee upholstered in faded blue, Myryan steps to the windows, and one after the other, opens the shutters to let in the light, then waits until they sit before taking the straight-backed oak chair.

"I wrote you scrolls from Assyadt," Lorn says, "but I found out later that Dettaur destroyed most of the scrolls I wrote or that were written to me."

"I didn't write much because you didn't write back."

"I did write. Dettaur intercepted the scrolls going both ways."

"Dettaur? Your old schoolmate? You never liked him that much."

"For good reasons."

"I didn't know him that well. Jerial despised him."

"He wanted her to be his consort," Lorn said.

Myryan shakes her head. "That box . . ."

"It was Father's. He left it to me, with a letter."

"Somehow . . . it should be yours." She pauses. "Are you going to be in Cyad long?"

"Quite a while. I've been transferred to work for the Majer-Commander in the headquarters at Mirror Lancer Court. I have a little more than an eightday of furlough."

Myryan bounds up from the chair. "Ryalth is hungry. She's almost white. You have to have some lunch with me. It would be better later in the year, because I'd have fresh vegetables, but the spiced pearapples I put up last fall are still wonderful—"

Ryalth laughs. "Pearapples! I should have guessed."

Almost in moments, Myryan has the table off the kitchen set with all manner of food—two sets of cheese wedges, dark and rye bread, heavy square crackers, pickled roots . . . and the spiced pearapples. "I got some ale, because there aren't any juices yet—if that's all right. And there's never any coffee anymore."

"Fine. Ale is fine," Lorn reassures her.

Myryan pours three mugs full and hovers over the side of the table.

"You can sit down," Lorn says with a laugh as he starts with the white cheese that is so scarce at the Mirror Lancer outposts and munches it with a heavy cracker, also something he has seen few of over the past years.

"Is there anything else . . ."

"It's fine."

Myryan eases onto the edge of her chair.

Ryalth slowly eats a small wedge of the yellow cheese with what Lorn suspects is a pickled turnip, a combination far too bitter for him. Kerial's chubby figures grasp toward the cheese. "This is Mother's food. You can have some before long."

"Gaaa . . ."

"Not now. Later," the mother tells her son.

"We're going to dinner with Ciesrt's parents tonight," Myryan volunteers.

"How are they?" Lorn asks.

"They always ask when they can expect a grandchild. Lately, the questions are getting more pointed." Myryan shakes her head. "I'm not ready for that." She looks at Kerial. "Now . . . if they were all as happy as he is . . . I might think about it." Abruptly, she turns to Lorn. "Kharl is quite close to the Captain-Commander of Mirror Lancers. They talk a lot. I've picked that up."

"I'm sure I'm too lowly to be of concern to such well-placed men," Lorn says with the hint of a laugh.

Myryan shakes her head. "There's something going on. Whenever Kharl sees me coming, he smiles, and he doesn't mean it. Sometimes, he'll change what he's talking about so quickly that the person he's with looks confused."

"Probably Magi'i things," Lorn replies.

"Listen to your sister," Ryalth says. "Healers can sense those things." She looks at Myryan. "What do you think is going on?"

"I don't know. Kharl schemes a lot. He always smiles, and he never means it, and there's always chaos swirling around him."

"Does Ciesrt know?" pursues Ryalth.

"Not much . . . he sometimes looks bewildered, and then Kharl gets this patronizing look on his face. I feel sorry for him then, but there's not much I can do." Myryan takes a small nibble of white cheese.

"No, you can't," Ryalth says gently.

"Are you sure there's enough?" Myryan glances from Ryalth to Lorn and back again.

"There's more than enough," Lorn says firmly. "Enough for three times this many." He pauses. "How's the garden coming?"

"I already have sprouts for the beans and the melons."

Myryan smiles, tossing her head slightly. "And you'll be here this year, so you can have fresh melons. They were really good last fall."

"I'll look forward to that," Lorn promises.

"Do you know how long you'll be in Cyad?"

"A year or more, I'd guess, but no one has said. The Majer-Commander said I'd been away from my consort and family too long, and sent me off on furlough as soon as I arrived."

"You actually met him?" asks Myryan.

"I'll be working for him directly," Lorn says.

"Ciesrt said that everyone in Mirror Lancer Court is ordered to work for him, but most never see him." The black-haired healer smiles. "He'll be surprised."

"Just tell him that I met the Majer-Commander. I'll have to actually report for work before I know if what he said is what he meant. I'd look a little foolish," Lorn points out, "if Ciesrt's right. And he might be."

Myryan nods. "He'll still be impressed that you met Rynst'alt. His father is always talking about him."

"He is?" asks Ryalth.

"Waaa . . . waaa . . . gaa!" interjects Kerial.

"They keep saying that he's been there forever. Most senior lancer officers don't even remember the Majer-Commander before him."

Lorn nods. "That's good to remember. He's gray-haired, but he doesn't look that old."

Ryalth glances at Lorn, her eyes going down to the squirming child.

"Ah . . . I think Kerial's getting fussy," Lorn says.

"You don't have to go yet, do you?"

"He won't be much fun before long. It's time for his afternoon nap," Ryalth says, as she stands. "Past time."

Lorn rises also.

"Now . . . you're coming to dinner on sixday," Ryalth turns to Myryan. "You and Ciesrt, and Ayleha will be looking after Kerial, so that we'll have more time to talk."

"We'll be there. Even Ciesrt seems pleased. He's looking forward to it."

"Good," say Ryalth and Lorn, nearly simultaneously.

"And," Lorn says, "you could come over next eightday and have a midday meal with us. Or me . . . if Ryalth has to go back to being the merchanter."

"I'd like that."

"Waaa!" Kerial yells.

The two parents slip toward the door, with Myryan following. Lorn reclaims the ornate wooden box on the way out.

Myryan waves from beside the privacy screen as they enter the coach.

"She's nervous," Lorn says as the coach lurches forward.

"Wouldn't you be? Her consort's father is plotting, possibly against her brother. Her consort doesn't understand half of what's occurring, and both her consort's parents are looking at her and demanding that she produce an heir."

"I'd be very nervous."

"She is," Ryalth points out, rocking Kerial, and looking down at him. "We'll be home before too long, and you'll be in your little bed."

Lorn glances back through the carriage window, but Myryan has vanished into the house or garden.

LXXXVIII

LORN SITS DOWN on the settee Ryalth has brought from her old quarters on the east side of Cyad and looks at the ornate box, the box he had seen so often in his father's study, with its almost ebony finish, and the inlaid metal spirals that almost seem to stand out from the wood, even though they are set so flush to the wood that Lorn's fingers can detect no edge or roughness. A box . . . and questions, and perhaps a hundred golds, those are his tangible heritage.

From upstairs, the sound of a lullaby drifts downward, and the murmurings of Kerial's protests die away.

Lorn looks down at the woven image of the ship on the carpet, then at the box. Their heritages . . . so different on the surface, and yet not so different.

Ryalth slips down the steps and into the sitting room. She slides onto the settee beside Lorn. "I'm sorry."

"For what?"

"It doesn't seem like much. From your father, I mean."

"He couldn't do otherwise. Vernt's the magus, and he gets the dwelling, and six-tenths of everything else above the bond. I get half of the remainder, and Jerial and Ciesrt split the rest."

"It's not fair for your sisters, either."

"Cyad isn't that fair to women, especially those of the elthage."

"I have more than they do . . . it's strange."

"I told you that a long time ago. You didn't believe me. The Magi'i need their healers. There are so few Mirror Lancers and Magi'i."

"So they are kept in chains of custom, thinking they are privileged and pampered."

"Not all believe that. Jerial doesn't. She never has," Lorn points out.

"She is not usual."

"No." Lorn smiles. "She's not, and neither are you. How many lady traders have created houses?"

"You helped—greatly."

"Even if I did, there had to have been others with coins, yet they did not do as you have done. Is that not true?"

"It is hard for me to admit such."

Lorn shakes his head. "I don't see why. You are the one who did it."

Ryalth gestures toward the inlaid box. "Best you look through that. Jerial made sure you had it as soon as you arrived."

Lorn nods and opens the wooden box, frowning, looking slowly through it, for, under the letter, are stacks and stacks of paper. Some contain diagrams, and others, what appear to be closely spaced words, almost as if they were parts of a book or a manual. He slowly eases those back into the box, then finally breaks the seal on the folded letter. He begins to read the precise handwriting that bears the hint of shakiness in each character he had seen but in the last few scrolls he had received from his father.

My dear son,

You may have already begun to see what necessary cruelty has been visited upon you, for you are one of the few hopes of Cyad and Cyador. If you have not, this will offer a few more keys to the lock of the future.

First, I must say that for your wisdom and fortune in finding your consort, I cannot tell you how thankful I am. For without her, I am not certain you would have the future you may. She is a treasure greater than any other, and I regret that I could not say such in the early years, when you would have looked askance had I expressed favor for her. You had to discover that for yourself, against my wishes, if necessary, although I would ask that you recall that I did not persist in my opposition, as I did in other matters.

Lorn cocks his head, then laughs. Beside him, Ryalth lifts her eyebrows. Lorn hands her the first sheet of the letter. "You should read this."
She takes it and begins to read.
Lorn continues with his father's words.

Second, the papers that accompany this missive are for your use. Some are for you to use with Magi'i of your choice, but of those I know who are close to you, I would suggest but Tyrsal and your brother. For all the rumors about him, I can also say that Liataphi is far more trustworthy than those immediately above him, although the First Magus under whom I have served can generally be trusted to think about the well-being of Cyador.

Lorn pauses and looks at Ryalth. "What do you think?"

"After I came to know your father, I liked him." She smiles. "He understood just how rebellious you were."

"Me?"

"You," she affirms. "You'd best keep reading while Kerial sleeps."

Lorn looks back at the parchment sheet he holds.

Third, I have not been fully responsive in revealing the truth about my duties, for my association with Toziel is far closer than I have indicated. This may come to light. It may not. As I once remarked, unguardedly, you are far closer in temperament to him, I think, than most would ever realize. For all our past closeness, do not presume upon it or approach him or his consort unless you are approached. This I cannot emphasize too strongly.

"Didn't the Hand of the Emperor die about the same time as my father?" Lorn asks Ryalth.

"A little later, I think . . ." Her mouth opens. "Of course . . . of course . . ."

Lorn nods. "It makes a great deal of sense." He hands her the second sheet of the letter. "Especially if you read this."

Ryalth scans the letter and then looks at her consort. "Best you be most careful, dearest, for he will have had enemies, careful as he was."

"I doubt he had as many as I already have," Lorn says dryly. "He was far more cautious."

"A Hand must be silent and cautious. Had you been such, would you now yet live?"

"I think not." Lorn glances back down at the letter.

Fourth and finally, I would that you remember that, while fear motivates most men far more than hope or justice, fear seldom sets their feet to moving forward. One can paralyze one's opponents with fear, but one must stand forth to lead. I was never one much for standing forth, or perhaps my skills did not lie in such. Yours do, and you must lead through your talents. Do not let your talents lead you. I did not wish you to be of the Magi'i, for your skills would have led you away from yourself.

My blessing and my curse, alas, are the same. Go forth and do great deeds. You may succeed. You may not, but a life lived in betrayal of what one is cannot be considered a life lived, and already you have lived more of a life than most twice your years.

Lorn looks blankly at the signature for a time, then silently hands the last sheet to Ryalth. She takes it and reads, this time more slowly, finally looking up at him.

"Do men make the times, or times the man?" he asks quietly.

"Your father was a man of his times, and you are one of your times."

"That's true," Lorn says. "But . . . are we what we are because of those times, or because we simply *are*—regardless of the times?"

"He was a man of his time. You could be one for all times."

"You're kind, but I don't know about that."

Ryalth smiles—an amused expression. She only says, "Perhaps you should read the rest of the papers—at least some of them—to see why he wanted you to have them."

"Yes, honored Lady Trader."

"And don't humor me, most honored Majer and Mirror Lancer."

Lorn winces. "I'm sorry."

"Read them."

Lorn sets aside the letter and begins with the first sheet.

In the days to come, for any man who would wish to inhabit the Palace of Eternal Light, he must assure himself first of the support of the Mirror Lancers, then of the merchanters, and lastly of the Magi'i . . .

Many have claimed that the Magi'i hold the key to power in Cyad, and thus in Cyador. This illusion has proven useful to the Magi'i, and to those who sit upon the Malachite Throne, for the Magi'i can be said to recommend and require that which is necessary, yet not popular.

Lorn flips to another section, then a third, before another set of words catches his attention.

When the chaos-towers fail, and fail they will, he who would be leader of Cyad must know what will serve to replace them and the devices which now they power. For a vast land must have means of moving people and goods that are faster and carry more goods than mere horse- or ox-drawn wagons. . . .

. . . what is often forgotten is that there remain the lesser forces of chaos within the world, such as that released when burn wood or the hardest of coals. These I have detailed in the pages which follow, and the means by which they may yet be implemented before all the chaos-towers fail.

Lorn sits back. He can only look at the papers.

"What's the matter, dearest?" asks Ryalth.

"He knew it all. He knew everything, and he never told me. He never told me."

"But he did. He told you when you could use what he knew. Could you have done aught with it before now?"

Lorn shakes his head. "But he knew, and he left it all to me."

"The times were not right."

Lorn frowns, but says nothing, his eyes going to the box in his lap, and the papers that he knows must hold far more than he had ever imagined his father would have considered, papers he must read, and read soon.

His eyes burn, and Ryalth reaches out and takes his hand.

LXXXIX

THE CAPTAIN-COMMANDER OF Mirror Lancers sees a figure in shimmering merchanter blues and angles across the wide corridor before the vacant Great Hall of the Palace of Eternal Light, his steps gauged so that his path intercepts that of the shorter man. "Greetings, honored Merchanter Advisor."

"Greetings to you, Captain-Commander," returns Vyanat'mer. "How go matters in Lancer Court?"

"As well as can be expected." Luss bows his head slightly. "I wish to commend you on your dispatch. You were most quick to ensure that the battle report on the Jeran . . . campaign was circulated to all trading houses."

"We would not wish to unwittingly cause greater casualties for the Mirror Lancers. So all the large clan houses needed to know, as well as others trading to the north."

"Including Ryalor House?"

"Ryalor House is a clan house, and larger than many," replies Vyanat'mer. "The house trades widely, as do several."

"And Lady Ryalth was not perturbed?"

"The lady is well-aware of her responsibilities to the Empire, as are all the most perceptive house chiefs."

"I would hope so, especially now."

The wiry but muscular Merchanter Advisor laughs. "What you hope, Captain-Commander, is for anything you can use to discredit the young majer who made you look like a donkey in a fancy uniform. Failing that, you will seek to make me resemble that same animal. I have also made *that* clear to all the clan heads. The merchanters do not intend to take sides in a struggle that will take place either within the Mirror Lancer Court, or the Quarter of the Magi'i. Nor do we wish to be forced to side with one faction or another."

"Brave words, Vyanat. I recall that the majer also brought back some six thousand golds, many coined in Cyador, and it might be most interesting to discover how those reached the hands of the Jeranyi."

"They reached them because people everywhere hold good coins and spend the poor. Now . . . if you had found clan houses with Hamorian-minted golds or Suthyan coins . . . then I would be concerned—and rightfully so." Vyanat'mer shakes his head, but not a strand of the gray-streaked black hair moves. "As for my words, they are not brave. They are accurate. Chyenfel cannot live that much longer. The old Hand of the Emperor is dead; there is no new Hand. Rynst will live long enough to ensure that you will not succeed him unless you can have him murdered, and then all will look to you. If you can discredit Majer Lorn, then you hope to discredit Rynst, for you dare not kill him."

"That is a most interesting set of observations."

Vyanat smiles coolly. "What I do not see is why you need to discredit young Lorn. He is far too young to threaten your position or Rynst's. It is clear that the Majer-Commander only wishes him to remain in Cyad for a year or two, so that he understands how matters are. He can also be used, if necessary, to command any lancers Rynst may need to bring into Cyad. He is clearly ruthless enough for that, and Rynst can disclaim responsibility. Then he will go back out to Syadtar or Assyadt as a commander for several tours, and only then, if he succeeds, will he be considered as a possible Captain-Commander. You will either have consolidated your position as Majer-Commander, or you will be dead, long before that can possibly occur."

Luss frowns.

"Is that not true? So why do you worry?" Vyanat laughs. "Perhaps you are concerned for the Second Magus? Rynst cares little for Kharl'elth, and would do all he could do to keep him from succeeding Chyenfel. Have you noticed how carefully the clever Kharl has suggested problems with both the Third Magus and with the late Kien'elth? And with what Rynst does?" A second laugh follows. "And who would that leave for First Magus?"

"And you, of course, have no ambitions at all?" asks the Captain-Commander.

"I make no secrets of my ambitions, and I have several. The first is to ensure that my head and my body both remain healthy and attached to each other. I have no desire to follow the example of my predecessor. The second is to ensure that the Magi'i and the Mirror Lancers do not meddle excessively in each other's affairs, because the merchanters will be the ones who suffer from such. I do not delude myself into thinking that we will ever have the esteem accorded to either the Mirror Lancers or the Magi'i. Look at Bluoyal. He actually thought he could use intrigue to fill the chests of his house. And where are those of his house now? Fearing that I will take away their clan status, cowering in the corners of their warehouses, and watching every shadow cast by every lamp on every corner of the merchanter quarter of Cyad."

"Those are fine words," Luss replies.

"Fine words are but as fine as the truth they portray," counters Vyanat. "I do not ask you to believe my words, Captain-Commander. Test them yourself. Ask who would benefit from any action to discredit each of those men. How does young Lorn benefit? He has a consort and a young son, and he is recently consorted enough that he would like to enjoy both. He knows that he must support Rynst, or perish. Rynst has doubtless told him not to anger you. If he angers you, he angers Rynst. He will try not to anger Kharl, for his sister is consorted to Kharl's son. His consort is a merchanter. Thus, everywhere he turns, he must tread with care. So why is he a danger? Who uses him to divert prying gazes? And why do we never hear of the other young man favored by the First Magus? Is it because Kharl wishes him to be thought of less? Or to be unseen until it is too late? Or does Chyenfel position the other?"

"You seem to have the answers, honored Merchanter Advisor."

"I have the questions. You must find the answers that satisfy you, not the ones that satisfy me." Vyanat smiles gently. "You might also ask why the honored Second Magus says little about the lesser number of firelances that your lancers receive, and why he opposed the sleep barrier for the Accursed Forest. Or perhaps why young Majer Lorn relinquished his elderclaim to his younger brother before he returned to Biehl and then to Inividra. Such an action could not benefit him."

"It is most intriguing that you know so much."

"Merchanters must traffic in information as much as golds, or we would perish, Captain-Commander. Would you like me to recall that in your first posting, in Pemedra, you were commended for bravery?"

Luss shakes his head. "And what other tidbits would you pull forth?"

"That you discouraged your eldest—your daughter— from consorting with a young magus, perhaps on the advice of the honored Kharl'elth." Vyanat smiles almost sympathetically. "About that, I have learned, Kharl was doubtless correct. The young magus was demoted and sent to the Mirror Engineers in Fyrad, where he will doubtless supervise the repair of the Great Canal for many years to come." The Merchanter Advisor nods. "Now . . . if you will pardon me ... I am already perilously close to being late to meet with several clan heads to resolve a dispute over the classification of cottons. And I do not seek to give you false information. As I said, I but pose the questions. You must find those answers which satisfy you." A last smile follows his words.

Luss nods, belatedly, then frowns after he turns and begins to walk toward the staircase that will carry him to the lower level and the walkway to the west, and toward the Mirror Lancer Court.

XC

THE LONG TABLE in the dining room of Ryalth's house—and Lorn's, too, he supposes—is set for seven. The linen is cream, trimmed in green-and-blue, and the cutlery is an antique silver. The light comes from the antique bronze wall lamps with their recently and brightly polished reflectors. Lorn sits at one end of the table, with Mycela at his left and Jerial at his right, and Ryalth at the other end, with Ciesrt at her left and Vernt at her right. Myryan sits between Ciesrt and Jerial.

"Beautiful silver," Myryan says to Ryalth, although she avoids touching the knife.

"It's one of the few family heirlooms I was able to keep," the trader replies. "That, and a few pieces of furniture and the carpet in the sitting room.

"Family things are important," announces Mycela.

As she speaks, Lorn pours another two fingers of Alafraan into her glass, keeping it below a third full. He takes a last bite of the marinated and spiced fowl dumpling, then smiles at his consort.

"They are," Ryalth agrees. "Would anyone like more—of anything?"

"I could stand another of those dumplings, thank you," Ciesrt says.

Ryalth passes the casserole dish.

"A bit more bread for the sauce," Vernt adds.

"Lorn, what will you be doing for the Majer-Commander?" asks Ciesrt as he serves himself two more dumplings. "Are you working directly for him, or for one of the commanders who reports to him?"

Lorn laughs. "I don't know. He told me to spend time with my consort and family, and to report back an eightday from next oneday. He said I'd be doing some writing, since I wrote well and quickly. So I could just be another junior majer acting as a scrivener. I'll find out then, I suppose."

"You couldn't ask him?" asks Mycela, sweetly. "You are a hero, they say."

"I'm not a hero," Lorn says politely, "but even if I were, heroes don't question the Majer-Commander, not that way." He smiles. "Just as Vernt wouldn't ask the First Magus why he was picked to do"—Lorn looks at his younger brother—"whatever you're doing now."

"Oh . . . I didn't think of it that way." Mycela smiles sweetly at Vernt.

"That makes sense," Ciesrt announces. "I certainly wouldn't ask any of the three Magi'i why I was tasked with something."

"Even your father?" asks Jerial, a glint in her eye.

"I might say something bland, to see if he'd offer an explanation, but I wouldn't ask. We learned that as children." Ciesrt shakes his head.

"Do you ever run across any of those I was student with?" Lorn asks, not caring whether Ciesrt or Vernt provides an answer. "Like Tyrsal or Rustyl?"

"I see Tyrsal sometimes," Vernt answers. "He works in the chaos-cell section for Lector Stumlyt. I haven't seen Rustyl, except in the corridors, in years, I don't think. The First Magus sent him to Fyrad to work with the Mirror Engineers, they said, and then to Summerdock to work on the harbor. He was gone for a while. He just got back, maybe three eightdays ago."

"He was on the Great Canal," Ciesrt mumbles as he finishes a dumpling. "Thought he was something special, working with the highest of the Mirror Engineers and then the older first-level adepts when he got back. Still tilts his nose."

"He always did," Vernt adds. "Ever since he discovered he could draw chaos out of the natural world. He's not the only one, but he thinks he is."

"Maybe someone is encouraging him," suggests Myryan.

"Why? So they can make him First Magus in another halfscore of years?" sneers Ciesrt.

"I thought he was going to be Ceyla's consort," offers Jerial.

"It is most likely," Ciesrt admits. "He is handsome in his way, and she finds him most intriguing. Father has also suggested that she has few-enough choices left among the Magi'i."

"You do not sound pleased," Jerial adds.

"He can be all right at times, and I suppose we'll get used to him." Ciesrt shrugs. "He is talented. There is little question of that."

"Maybe he wants to be Emperor," says Mycela. "You know, the Empress can't have children. They don't have any."

"Dear, Magi'i can't take the Malachite Throne," Vernt says gently.

"But . . . the Emperor has an elthage title," Mycela protests.

"His Mightiness also has a merage and an altage title," Jerial points out. "They're all honors."

"Not totally," Ryalth says. "His mother was merchanter, his father a Mirror Lancer before he became Emperor, and one of his grandsires was from the Magi'i."

Lorn keeps a straight face, letting the silence drag out before turning to Ciesrt. "Whatever the Magi'i did with the Accursed Forest, it did free up more lancers to fight against the barbarians. And the lancers are grateful. I thought you'd like to know."

"I thought you defeated them all." Mycela's voice is puzzled. "Or killed them all."

"Those in the northwest," Lorn explains. "There are still the Cerlyni in the northeast, and unless someone else follows up on what I did, in a few years the Jeranyi will be back to raiding south of the Grass Hills again."

"Didn't you sack the port where they were getting their blades?" asks Ciesrt.

"We did, and we burned the warehouses and took all the blades and brought them back. But trading blades is profitable for the Hamorians, and I wouldn't be surprised if there were traders back there by fall, or next spring at the latest."

"Do you trade blades?" Mycela looks wide-eyed at Ryalth.

Myryan looks down, and Jerial covers her mouth for a moment.

"No. I'd rather not sell something that could kill my consort," Ryalth says politely. "Or any other lancer."

"Oh, I guess that would not be a good idea." Mycela smiles.

"I'm glad she doesn't, for many reasons," Lorn says quickly, and with a laugh. He can sense that Myryan is having trouble not rolling her eyes or giving some outward sign of her feelings. He glances at Vernt, then at Ciesrt. "Since it's done, can either of you tell me what the Magi'i did in the Accursed Forest?"

The two lower, first-level adepts exchange glances. Then Vernt nods. "I shouldn't say how it was done, but the result was a combining of order and chaos to put the Forest to sleep, so that it is like any other forest, or mostly so. Some large animals will escape, I imagine, but they won't be as big as the ones in the past, and they'll get smaller, more like the ones in the swamps along the river and the forests above the delta. That's why some lancers are still patrolling. And it's really not safe to enter it. So the walls will have to be maintained."

Lorn nods. "The growers will complain for a time, I'm sure."

"The peasants always complain about everything," Ciesrt notes. "If it's not the Magi'i or the Mirror Lancers, it's the merchanters or the weather."

"Usually the merchanters," Ryalth says lightly. "We're grasping and greedy, and few think about how much it costs to bring anything from anywhere."

"But they always say there would be nothing without food," Ciesrt answers with a laugh.

Lorn sits stock-still for an instant, thinking about one of the questions posed by his father over a year earlier.

"You look surprised, Lorn," Jerial says.

"I was just recalling something Father said along those lines years ago."

"I don't recall him talking about peasants," Vernt muses.

"Not peasants," Lorn replies. "About what allows Cyad to exist. And that's food . . . except I think what he meant was that the lands of Cyador have to produce not only enough food for the peasants who grow it, but enough for the people of the cities. And there has to be enough that the peasants will sell it willingly."

"They never sell anything willingly, do they?" asks Mycela.

"I think I see what Father meant," Vernt says. "There are not that many Magi'i or Mirror Lancers . . ."

"Exactly," Jerial adds. "Nor healers. Nor Mirror Engineers."

"Nor gardens," finishes Myryan.

Ryalth merely nods, a knowing smile on her lips.

Ciesrt frowns, and Mycela smiles blankly.

Lorn lifts the bottle of Alafraan. "Would anyone like any more? Before we start on dessert?"

Jerial grins at Ryalth, and, after a moment, so does Myryan. Vernt shakes his head ruefully.

XCI

LORN HAS FOUND the cushions to the wooden-framed settee that is on the front veranda of the house, a dwelling that is somehow both new and yet familiar to him, and has set them out. In the late afternoon of early summer, he sits there on the veranda, holding Kerial in his lap. He wears a stained pair of uniform trousers and an old undertunic—both more suited to caring for an infant than to a lancer's study.

"Your mother will be home before long."

"Gaa . . . ooo . . ." A chubby hand gropes toward Lorn's mouth, and Lorn lets the boy touch his cheek and jaw.

A dull *clunk* echoes across the front garden and past the fountain.

Lorn smiles. "I think that's her." He lifts the boy to his shoulder and stands as the iron gate opens.

Ryalth steps through it and out from behind the privacy screen.

Lorn moves down the walkway and past the fountain and the mist of cool spray that fans from it in the hot afternoon sun.

Ryalth smiles as she nears father and son. "Were you a good boy?" She bends forward and brushes Kerial's cheek with her lips. "Were you good for your father?"

"Gaaa . . . waaa . . ."

"Yes," Lorn translates.

"I'm glad."

The two walk side by side past the fountain and then under the veranda roof. Lorn and Kerial follow Ryalth through the doorway and down the steps into the front foyer.

"I need something to drink. I'm thirsty. But we can go back out on the veranda." She smiles again. "I'm glad you found the cushions. That's something I've been meaning to do."

Kysia appears as they step into the kitchen.

"Do we have any juice?" asks Ryalth.

"All we have is wine and ale—or water," Kysia apologizes. "I've been looking for juices, but they're all vinegar or wine right now. The peaches are late this year, and even the greenberries . . ."

"Ale." Ryalth says. "If you don't mind."

"Ah . . . two, please," Lorn adds.

The gray-eyed Kysia grins, then scurries through the big kitchen, before returning with two beakers nearly filled with amber liquid.

"Thank you."

"And supper?" asks Kysia.

"Whenever it's ready. I'm hungry, but not starving," Ryalth says. "Don't you and Ayleha hurry it and spoil anything. We'll be on the front veranda."

The red-haired trader carries the two glass beakers and their amber contents back through the house and foyer, up the steps, and out to the veranda, where she settles onto one side of the settee. Lorn settles onto the other side, shifting Kerial so that the boy is on his lap, half facing his mother, held by Lorn's right arm.

With his left, Lorn takes the beaker Ryalth offers. "Thank you."

"Thank you for taking Kerial. It made the day much easier."

"Waa . . ." offers Kerial tentatively.

"In a moment," Ryalth says. "Let your mother have a sip of her drink. You can wait, you little piglet." She takes a long swallow of the ale.

"How did it go with the Austrans?"

"Not that well." Ryalth sighs after another swallow of the

amber ale. "They're talking about larger guarantees on the inbound cargoes, and unless we open a warehouse in Valmurl or send someone there . . . or unless I buy another longhaul ship or even two, which we don't have the golds for . . ."

"You'll start losing coins one way or the other?" Lorn gives Kerial a gentle squeeze.

"I fear so. Now that there are fewer fireships, we can see the lack of respect growing."

"I don't think there ever was any in Hamor," Lorn says.

"There wasn't anywhere, but people behaved as though there was."

"Whaa . . . ?" asks Kerial.

"A few more moments, dear." Ryalth takes another swallow of the ale.

"Respect is always based on power, I think," Lorn replies. "From the scrolls I did get, I thought we had lost the towers on four fireships, and other lands know that."

"Five, at least. They're hiding them in a cove near Dellash—the end of the island away from Summerdock."

"We'll start losing the towers in Cyad before long."

"Why the fireships first? Because the salt is harder on them?"

"That, and the ships move. Over the years, even with the temporal barriers, that puts more strain on them. There won't be one left in another five years, I would guess."

"No one is saying much, but they've laid the keels for warships with sail and cannon."

Lorn shakes his head. "We could build chaos-fired steamships. We should."

"Is that . . . ?"

"It's all in my father's papers, even the plans he took from the forbidden archives. I'll need to make copies . . . maybe for Vernt and Tyrsal, when the time comes."

"He thought you could make it happen."

"As a junior majer?"

"You'll be more than that," she predicts.

"That doesn't look likely."

"It will happen. It has to."

"I won't argue with you. I usually lose." He grins, then adds, "If it does, I hope it's in time to prevent the worst."

"You think it will be that bad?"

"What do you think? You saw the way Ciesrt and Mycela reacted at dinner the other night. They don't understand, and too many of the Magi'i and Mirror Lancer families are like that."

"Can you make the stone real?" she asks.

He smiles at her reference to the first time he had told her his ambitions, but the smile fades. "I don't know. I'm not sure I know how. I know what to do if I could get there, but getting there . . ." He shrugs. "The papers will help, if I can figure out how to apply what he's given me . . . If I get the opportunity."

"See what you learn working for the Majer-Commander." Ryalth shakes her head. "Your furlough has gone by so quickly. You'll have to go back on duty in three days. Almost two eightdays doesn't seem very much after all you did and all the time you were away."

"This time, it's not so bad," he points out. "I'm not leaving for someplace like Jakaafra or Biehl."

"I wish I could have come to Biehl."

"I do, too, but you would have been upset. The town was old, and slowly falling to ruin."

"I'll wager what you did changed matters."

"I don't know. I would hope so."

"We've brought back some of the china you recommended. It's sold well, and I've commissioned some silver-and-black sets for the Austrans."

"Whhh*aaa*!" Kerial interjects.

"I know. I know." Ryalth swallows the last of the ale in her beaker and sets it on the stone tiles of the veranda beside the settee, then takes Kerial from Lorn. "You always get fed before we do."

"Mmmm . . ."

Lorn shakes his head as he watches Kerial begin to suck.

"When he's hungry . . ." Ryalth says with a laugh. "But he won't be protesting when we eat."

"Or later," Lorn says.

"You are very hopeful, dearest."

Lorn flushes.

After a moment, so does Ryalth.

XCII

LORN AND RYALTH sit, propped up with pillows, in the triple-width bed with the headboard with the ornately-carved edges and the smooth and curved bedposts. Ryalth cradles Kerial in the crook of her arm. The sole light in the room is the wall lamp on Lorn's side of the bed, which casts a golden glow.

"What will you do tomorrow when you report?" she asks.

"I'll probably have to write reports and orders for outposts and things like that. Someone has to, and it won't be the Majer-Commander. The one definite thing he said was that I'm supposed to develop a strategy for dealing with the Jeranyi. The only way I think we can deal with them is if Cyador takes over the port of Jera, but with the fireships failing, I have my doubts as to whether anyone will support that." He chuckles. "The Majer-Commander said not to worry about that for my first draft. I don't. It's the second draft that I worry about."

"You'll think of something. You always do."

Lorn raises his eyebrows.

"Is the book nearby?" she asks.

Lorn leans toward the bedside table, then straightens and flourishes the green-tinged silver-covered volume. "Right here. I left it here after we read last night."

"Read me something . . . please."

Lorn flips through the pages to find the verse that is their favorite. He smiles as he smooths the pages and begins to read.

Like a dusk without a cloud,
a leaf without a tree,
a shell without a sea . . .
the greening of the pear
slips by . . .

. . . to hold the sun-hazed days,
and wait for pears and praise
. . . and wait for pears and praise.

"I like that," she says quietly, easing Kerial from her arms to her shoulder where she gently burps him. "I think he's going to sleep."

"Good," murmurs Lorn. "He was supposed to have gone to sleep after dinner. And then after we walked him around the garden."

"Now . . . he is your son." Her low and soft voice cannot disguise the hint of laughter.

"Difficult, you mean?"

"You said it. I didn't." With an innocent smile, Ryalth slides to her feet, crosses the few cubits between the large bed and Kerial's, and eases their son into his bed. After a moment, she slips back beside Lorn.

They both look toward the smaller bed.

Lorn stiffens as he hears a snuffling sort of snore. They both wait, but Kerial does not stir.

"Read me something else. I'd just like to lie her for a moment and listen. If you don't mind . . ."

"I'll read softly." Lorn opens the book once more and turns until he finds the page for which he searches. "It's not as cheerful as the one about the pear, but whenever I read it, it always made me think of you." Lorn clears his throat gently.

Virtues of old hold fast.
Morning's blaze cannot last;

and rose petals soon part.
Not so a steadfast heart.

" 'A steadfast heart'—I've always liked that. I'd forgotten it, though." She leans her head against his shoulder. "I worry about you being here."

"You worried about me being near the Accursed Forest and fighting barbarians," Lorn points out.

"It's not the same. Cyad can be even more dangerous."

About that, Lorn knows, she is certainly right. The dangers are not at all the same, for those of the Forest and the barbarians could be seen, and fought with a blade or a firelance.

XCIII

LORN BARELY HAS been assigned a table desk in a small study on the floor below the Majer-Commander—and been introduced to the squad leaders and senior squad leaders who will do his copying and other clerical tasks, and is looking out the single narrow window, uphill and away from the harbor—when there is a knock on his open door.

A young-faced squad leader—one of those whose name Lorn has not caught—stands there. "Ser . . . the Majer-Commander wishes you in his study for the meeting."

"Thank you." Lorn grabs the small inkstand and a pen and a stack of paper and hurries up the stairs. He has no idea to what meeting he has been summoned.

As he reaches the open foyer outside Rynst's study, Tygyl—the senior squad leader at the desk—says, "Go on in, ser. He's expecting you."

Lorn steps into the Majer-Commander's large study, cautiously. "Ser." He bows to Rynst, who stands by his table desk looking eastward at the Palace of Eternal Light, which stands out against the hillside and surrounding structures despite the overcast day.

Rynst glances at Lorn, then smiles. "I see you understand." He points to the conference table. "I sit at this end, with my back to the Palace. It's symbolic, but the Emperor does stand behind me. You sit at my left. You are to take notes on who says what, and why—unless I tell you that there will be no notes."

"Yes, ser."

"You are to sit. Because you are not officially part of any meeting, you do not stand when the Captain-Commander or the commanders enter. Once the meeting is dismissed, you are an officer and will behave according to protocol."

"Yes, ser." Lorn slips toward the conference table and takes the straight-backed and armless chair to the left of the larger, armed chair. All the other chairs except the one in which he sits have arms.

"You are not to speak unless addressed directly, and only to return pleasantries or if I tell you to speak." Rynst moves toward the conference table, but halts a few cubits back from his chair.

"Yes, ser."

"I will introduce all the commanders this time. Remember them. After this morning, I will only introduce officers you have not met."

Lorn nods, then checks the cupridium-tipped pen. He makes a mental note to bring two for any future meetings.

The first commander to enter the Majer-Commander's study is a spare and tall man, with thinning brown hair that has almost disappeared from his skull except around his ears.

"Commander Inylt is the supply commander, in charge of allocating provisions," Rynst says. "Inylt, this is Majer Lorn. He is my new strategic adjutant and aide."

Inylt is wiry, even thinner than Rynst, and squints as he looks toward the younger majer. "Lorn . . ." He laughs as he says the name. "Fine report on blades and trade. Wish more field commanders understood that. Glad to see you."

"Thank you, ser. I recall your name on provision draw orders. When I was at Biehl."

Inylt nods and takes a seat near the foot of the table on the south side, spreading out his papers into three stacks.

Luss is the next officer to enter, and takes the position at the foot of the table, opposite Rynst, without addressing Lorn. As the other four commanders enter, Lorn notes each name, and puts a phrase about each next to the name on a separate sheet. He hopes he can keep the names straight.

When five commanders have entered and seated themselves, Rynst clears his throat.

Lorn glances at his list:

Inylt—Supply [thin, bald]
Sypcal—Eastern Region [red-haired]
Shykt—Ports and Facilities [thin face, curly brown
    hair]
Muyro—Mirror Engineers [dark, bearded]
Lhary—Western Region [blond, tall]

"Part of this meeting is for you to meet Majer Lorn. He will be working for me, directly, on a strategic plan we will be developing to deal with the barbarians to the north under the new conditions we face. He will also be my aide and adjutant for meetings."

"I presume this plan will address fewer firelances and fewer firewagon transports?" asks Luss, although his question is almost more of a statement.

"Don't forget the higher costs of provisions," adds Inylt. "And more spoilage if they go by horse team."

"If you have direct suggestions, submit them in writing to me, and I will pass those which are appropriate to the Majer." Rynst smiles and glances down at a list that has appeared as if from nowhere. "What do the Mirror Engineers think can be done with the fireships with failed towers—if anything? Commander Muyro?"

Muyro fingers his square black beard before answering. "The hulls are too heavy for conversion to sailing vessels, ones that would have the speed necessary to protect trading vessels. They could be fitted with old-style cannon, either using a cammabark propellant or black powder or some hybrid, and stationed at the main harbors as stationary batteries."

Rynst glances at the thin-faced and curly-haired man. "Commander Shykt?"

"I have discussed this with the Third Magus, as you suggested. Although chaos can be removed from the world itself and stored in cells such as those used for the firewagons, it would take the majority of the first-level adepts perhaps a year to amass enough chaos to power a single ship on a voyage from Cyad to Fyrad. Those are rough calculations, but adequate to prove that the Quarter of the Magi'i cannot offer a feasible solution."

"Did he have any other suggestions?"

"He thought that use of chaos-cells might be possible on several vessels to power one firecannon on each of those vessels. It would still require much effort, and fabrication of the cells as older ones fail would likely not be possible without the equipment in the Quarter of the Magi'i."

"That equipment is powered by the chaos-towers in the Quarter?" asks Luss.

"Yes, ser," replies Shykt.

"There is no way to replicate it?"

"No, ser. Not according to Senior Lector Liataphi."

"You might wish to confirm that, Captain-Commander, say, with the Second Magus. I will bring up the matter with the First Magus." Rynst pauses. "While we have suspected this, the failure of the chaos-cell replicating equipment will mean that, within a halfscore of years, the last firelances will be exhausted." He turns to Inylt. "We had talked of this earlier. Have you any other thoughts?"

"The District Guards already use cupridium lances. They are two cubits longer than firelances, but lighter and stronger than iron or any combination of wood and iron. It appears likely that we will have operating chaos-towers for several years yet. The cupridium, once transformed from cuprite, is stable. I would suggest ordering and stocking a minimum of five hundred score cupridium lances over the next two to five years. The Magi'i can still form cupridium without the chaos-towers, but it is a laborious process—"

"And there will be many demands on those few Magi'i who can amass and manipulate natural chaos-forces," adds Commander Muyro. "That will be most true in the first years."

"We will need more Mirror Lancers," Luss observes, "once the firelances are gone. Perhaps we should start to increase those forces now."

Rynst nods. "We have discussed this before." He tilts his head to the side. "Captain-Commander . . . perhaps you and Commander Lhary and Commander Sypcal could provide a short paper estimating the increased losses arising from using cupridium lances, and showing how many more Mirror Lancers and officers we will need once the firelances all fail."

"Ser . . . that would be but a judgment," Luss replies.

"We all make judgments, and offer opinions," says Rynst mildly. "I wish no more opinions or discussion on the subject of the need for more lancers or foot until you have put your best judgment in writing and presented it to me."

"Yes, ser."

The red-haired Sypcal and the blond Lhary exchange glances, but neither speaks.

"Commander Inylt, have you a report on the progress in converting the captured Hamorian blades into golds in a way that will not have those blades being used against our lancers in less than a season?"

"Yes, ser. It cannot be done. The best we can do is break the blades and sell them for high-grade iron, preferably in Lydiar. That will net us perhaps the equivalent of fifty golds."

"Fifty?" asks Sypcal. "Those would bring over a thousand as blades."

"True," replies Inylt. "But if we contract to have a trader ship them to Hamor, no one will bid on them for more than five hundred, and they will be shipped back to Jera or Rulyarth and sold for a thousand or fifteen hundred, and we will have our lancers dying by fall or next spring. Each lancer undercaptain costs us twenty golds to train, and another twenty to equip and send to his first station. If we lose a score of them over two years to those blades, we lose both the golds we gain and the experience of the officers. The training for a ranker is less costly—say, two to five golds—but I would judge that those blades might kill another hundred rankers."

"Break the blades and take what you can get," Rynst orders quietly. "Now . . . what about the reports about food spoilage for the outposts around the Accursed Forest?"

"Spoilage is higher," Inylt admits. "That is because the Mirror Engineers were required to turn to the use of oxen for the barges on the Great Canal, and grain and flour are too bulky and heavy to load on the remaining firewagons . . ."

Lorn conceals a frown. "Remaining firewagons"? The term implies that there are fewer firewagons, not just less chaos-cells for them.

". . . there are not enough ox teams, and the oxen are slower than the chaos-powered boat tows that were used before. The air is damp along the Canal, and the delays mean that there is more mold and spoilage. More oxen are being bred and trained, but it will be another year before there are enough."

Rynst merely nods, his eyes moving to Shykt. "When will you finish the report on the possible need for Mirror Foot or Lancers as detachments on long-haul Cyadoran traders?"

"At least two eightdays, ser. We need to meet with more of the masters of the vessels, and that means we must wait until they port."

Rynst looks across the table. "Does anyone have anything new to mention?"

"No, ser."

"If not, I'll see Lhary and Sypcal tomorrow afternoon." The Majer-Commander nods and stands.

Lorn waits, then stands as well, and waits until the Captain-Commander and the five commanders depart. Then he gathers his papers together.

"Majer?" says Rynst. "I expect those notes in report form on my desk in the morning. Have your clerk make a copy for the Captain-Commander as well."

"Yes, ser." Lorn bows.

"There will be another meeting tomorrow afternoon. There is every twoday afternoon. That is when the Captain-Commander and I review the actions of the field commands. Only Commanders Sypcal and Lhary will be with us. If you have time after doing the notes, I would suggest that you begin to consider the strategic plan for the north."

"Yes, ser."

Rynst turns, as if to dismiss Lorn.

The majer slips from the study and makes his way down to his own study on the floor below. He pauses as Fayrken—the senior squad leader assigned to Lorn—looks up from his narrow desk outside Lorn's door.

"Yes, Fayrken?"

"There are all the reports for tomorrow's meeting in the left box on your desk, ser."

"Thank you. I'll have another report that will need to be copied for the Majer-Commander and the Captain-Commander. I hope I'll have it before long. Oh . . . and I'd better have a third copy for us."

"Yes, ser. They sometimes misplace reports." The hint of a smile lurks in Fayrken's green eyes.

"Especially if there are no copies?" asks Lorn.

"It would seem that way, ser."

Lorn shakes his head slightly, then steps into his study and sets the papers and inkwell and pen on the freshly-polished but battered golden-oak surface. As Fayrken had told him, there is a stack of papers in the box in the corner. He picks up the first and reads: *Reports from the Accursed Forest Company Patrols, Eightdays four through twelve, Winter, 205* A.F.

He replaces it in the box and sits down at the table desk. His eyes go to the narrow window and the gray day outside. He had wondered if he were the only one thinking about the failure of the chaos-towers. He was not, it is more than clear; yet for all the concerns, only Inylt appears to consider what might be workable alternatives.

Lorn fingers his chin. Or is Inylt simply more direct? Information can be power. Yet information of that sort becomes useless if it does not lead to a solution, and those who hoard such information for personal gain may rule or command the forces of a failing land. He shakes his head. That is not quite accurate, either.

Again . . . again . . . he has much to learn, and he fears he has less time in which to learn it than it once seemed.

XCIV

SITTING AT HIS table desk, the afternoon sun pouring through the narrow window, Lorn holds the rough list of possible options for dealing with the Jeranyi. Somehow, matters seem less clear when viewed from Mirror Lancer Court than they had from his outpost at Inividra. There, he had only had to worry about keeping casualties low, killing the Jeranyi raiders, and seizing blades and other weapons to reduce the Jeranyi ability to attack Cyador.

He takes a deep breath and looks down at what he has written.

Under the first option, the Mirror Lancers can take the

port city of Jera and establish an outpost there. That will require at least ten companies, plus a heavily-walled compound and regular shipments of supplies and provisions. It will probably require periodic raids or sweeps of the surrounding countryside, and the policing of any and all traders and goods shipped into the city. In effect, it would also transfer many of the casualties from the Mirror Lancers in and around the Grass Hills to those in Jera, and it will cost more golds than the other options. Over time it is possible that Jera could become part of Cyador, and that might lower costs and the numbers of lancers required, but not for many years. Still, the first option will probably have the lowest total number of casualties for the Mirror Lancers.

Under the second option, the Mirror Lancers can request that a magus use a chaos-glass to keep track of the ships going in and out of Jera, and conduct periodic raids . . . or attempt to board or sink vessels which bring weapons.

Lorn shakes his head. Although the golds required are probably less, that option is unworkable, not without a warship permanently stationed in Biehl and tasked only to patrol that section of the Northern Ocean. With the number of fireships dwindling rapidly, stationing one in the north all the time is highly unlikely. Lorn also doubts that any of the Magi'i would relish or handle the task in the detail necessary, but that is something best not put to ink.

The third option would be to continue what the Mirror Lancers have been doing—at least before the current year, and Lorn's raid. Even with more innovative patrolling, with multiple-company patrols and more lancers, over time casualties will increase, especially after the firelances fail.

Lorn glances at the stack of reports filling most of the top shelf of the bookcase set against the inner wall. He has read them all and gathered the numbers. In the previous year, from turn of spring to turn of spring, the Mirror Lancers in the compounds and outposts along the Grass Hills had lost nearly fortyscore lancers and twoscore undercaptains and captains. Those figures did not include the casualties who had recovered to fight again. Ten years earlier the numbers had been half that. The figures will go down for the current year, even with his own loss of two officers and more than a company of lancers, but they will not stay down for long unless something changes.

What about more raids into Jeranyi territory? As a fourth option?

Lorn fingers his chin. It is one thing to conduct a single campaign to stop the flow of blades and to deliver a message. It is another to keep raiding another land, for if he recommends that, how is he any different from them? Another consideration is that Mirror Lancer casualties will rise on such raids if they come more often because the Mirror Lancers will lose the advantage of surprise and the Jeranyi will expect such campaigns and will be far more prepared.

He shakes his head. The strategic plan requested by the Majer-Commander is looking more and more difficult . . . and he has yet to consider the operational, logistical, and tactical considerations of any of the options.

He massages his forehead, then looks blankly toward the half-open window.

XCV

LORN'S RAPIER SEEMS to flicker, weaving a wall between him and Tyrsal, as the shorter redhead dances away from the young majer.

"Enough!" Tyrsal jumps back, not lowering his blade for several moments.

Lorn lowers his practice rapier immediately, glancing toward the pair of older majers who continue to practice at the far side of the hall.

Tyrsal also lowers his practice blade and wipes his forehead with the back of the sleeve of his padded practice tunic. "There's no point to this. Even with you blindfolded and left-handed, I'd still get skewered. You can sense where you are better than most first-level adepts."

"Me? No." Lorn shakes his head.

"I'm not blind, my friend," says the second-level adept wearily. "You had your eyes closed on that last round. You were relying on your chaos-senses, not your eyes."

"I can't hide that from you, I see." Lorn grins.

"Most wouldn't notice—except maybe Rustyl or the three top Magi'i. They wouldn't expect it from a senior lancer."

"I'm not that senior."

Tyrsal sighs, loudly. "Lorn, I can count. There are perhaps a score-and-a-quarter outposts across Cyador that require majers. There are less than a halfscore that require commanders outside of Cyad."

"How do you know that?"

"All I had to do was list all the places where lancers go, and see roughly how big they are." Tyrsal shrugs. "Then I asked a few questions and listened. I might be off by a bit, but that's not my point. From what I can tell, there are less than threescore Mirror Lancer officers who are majers and commanders. There could be less than that. That makes you a senior officer, like a first-level adept in the Magi'i."

"So why don't I feel so senior?" asks Lorn with a laugh. "I'm like the wood panels on the wall. Everyone knows they're there, but no one pays much attention."

"That's because," Tyrsal says, half-dramatically, "you've been able to act before, without having to persuade everyone. If you figured out how to fight the Accursed Forest better, everyone was happy . . ."

Lorn can recall a few officers who were not, but he continues to listen.

". . . and when you found out how to stop the Jeranyi raids, you only had to kill Dett, who deserved it years before, anyway, to get the Majer-Commander to listen. But you were doing what you were ordered to do—if in a different way. Now . . . you assist someone who makes the decisions, and no one asks for your advice, and no one gives you any real actions to take." The redheaded magus laughs. "So you ask me to spar and take it out on me."

"I'm sorry."

Tyrsal shifts his weight as he walks toward the rack that holds the practice weapons. "I'm going to have bruises on my bruises. That's what I get for sparring with a professional." He grins. "You'd do better against other lancers."

Lorn shakes his head. "You're better than most of them."

After racking his practice blade, Tyrsal looks long at Lorn. "You're honestly telling the truth. You are." He shakes his head. "No wonder so many fear you."

In turn, Lorn racks his blade and pauses. "You're good with truth-reading, aren't you?"

The redheaded magus nods, then grins almost boyishly. "Why?"

Lorn shakes his head, mimicking Tyrsal's abrupt gesture. "No wonder they keep you away from the senior Magi'i." He grins in return.

"I'd tell you to go home to your consort, except that it's the middle of the day, and we both have to get back to work."

"I'd tell you the same, except you don't have a consort."

Tyrsal looks down.

"Don't tell me there is someone?" Lorn grins again. "After all those years of telling me you'd never find anyone?"

"Perchance . . . I don't know."

"Do I know her?" Lorn waits.

"You know of her . . . but don't ask. If it works, you'll be the second to know."

"After your mother?"

"I have to tell her first." Tyrsal smiles boyishly once more.

Lorn nods, asking, "Do you want to bring her to dinner

next sixday? The only one who I might ask is Jerial, and she won't say anything."

Tyrsal frowns, then smiles. "Why not?"

"I'll check on the day with Ryalth. I might have to move it one day or so." Lorn frowns to himself. "Best I let you know tomorrow."

"That's fine." Tyrsal blots his forehead. "If we want to get anything to eat . . . we'd better hurry."

"According to the outside board, there's a stew at the Kettle."

"It's better than going hungry . . ."

"But not much?" asks Lorn as he follows Tyrsal toward the washroom.

"Not much at all." Tyrsal laughs.

XCVI

COMMANDER SHYKT AND Commander Muyro sit across the Majer-Commander's conference table from each other, Muyro on the north side, Shykt on the south. Each has a document before him. Lorn is seated in the armless chair to Rynst's left.

The door to the study opens, and a commander unfamiliar to Lorn steps inside. He has rugged features, a pockmarked face, and iron-gray hair. He also carries some form of document under his left arm. "Greetings, Majer-Commander."

"Commander Dhynt," Rynst announces. "Majer Lorn is my new adjutant and assistant." He remains seated as he continues. "Commander Dhynt is in charge of the fireships . . . such as they are."

Dhynt nods brusquely in Lorn's direction and sits down in the chair beside the brown-haired Shykt, inclining his head to the swarthy Muyro and then to Shykt. He places the thick set of papers on the polished table before him.

Rynst studies the iron-haired and square-faced commander. "This is the fifth meeting we have had over the last year about the problems with the chaos-towers. Each of you is supposed to have a report for me."

A round of nods follows the words of the Majer-Commander.

"I will study the documents, but I expect a summary from each of you." Rynst glances at the most recent arrival. "You may begin, Dhynt."

The gray-haired commander clears his throat. "The chaos-towers which provide the power systems for the fire-ships came from the Rational Stars, somewhere beyond chaos itself, and cannot be built on our world. In the more than tenscore years since the creation of Cyador, no chaos-tower has ever been successfully restored, even when it appeared identical to those still functioning. Further, the power projection systems employed by the Magi'i and Mirror Engineers cannot be used except with the concentrated chaos-power supplied by a tower. The Magi'i have attempted to use a number of the most powerful Magi'i in concentrating naturally-occurring chaos, but that chaos was either somehow different or not powerful enough to make the projection equipment work. Since the projection equipment is required to fabricate new chaos-cells, such as those used in the fire-wagons, and those used in the firecannon, while firecannon could be mounted on sailing warships, the Magi'i estimate that such cells will last only for one- to twoscore years after the failure of the last chaos-tower."

Lorn writes as quickly as he can, hoping that he can convert his notes into a credible report without forgetting anything important.

Dhynt clears his throat and glances at Rynst.

Rynst nods for him to continue.

"That means we can neither repair nor replace the fire-ships and the firecannon. The most feasible option would appear to be the immediate construction of a fleet of fast sailing vessels of comparatively narrow beam, with deep keels, and extensive sails, capable of carrying conventional cannon powered by cammabark or some form of black powder."

"I understand we now have but a quarterscore fireships left with full function. How long before we have none?" asks Rynst.

"As I have told you before, ser, ten years at the longest, more probably five, I would say. The Magi'i and the Mirror Engineers tell me one of the ships might last a score of years. I think not. Each firecannon must be disassembled and cleaned and the arming cells and the cables replaced almost every voyage. The strength of the firebolts varies from discharge to discharge even so, and that variation is increasing with each voyage."

Rynst nods evenly and turns to the swarthy commander. "Commander Muyro?"

"Yes, ser. I am not so eloquent as Dhynt, ser. You asked the Mirror Engineers what new devices we could develop to replace the firelances. As Commander Shykt has already noted, the most feasible replacements for the firelances are cupridium lances, such as those already used by the District Guards. We are also looking into the fabrication of cupridium mirror shields. They have a more advantageous strength to weight proportion, so that a lancer will have greater protection but carry a lighter burden than with either a wooden or iron-sheathed shield. Also, the smooth surface will deflect an iron blade . . ."

As he continues to take his notes, Lorn represses a frown. Mere deflection might not always be good, since it could easily send one of the Jeranyi edged bars into a mount, or a lancer's legs.

"You might wish to make several of those shields and see how they work," suggests Rynst. "In actual combat."

"We will have a score ready in an eightday, and they could be issued to a squad in one of the companies along the Grass Hills."

Rynst glances at Lorn. "Majer, you have had the most recent combat experience. Where would you suggest that the shields be tested?"

"I would suggest at Isahl or one of the outposts in the northeast out of Syadtar, ser. There are likely to be more raids there this summer."

Rynst nods. "Do you have any observations on the lances and the shields?"

"When I was at Biehl, I did command some District Guards against the barbarians. The cupridium lances worked fairly well, but some of the lancers had trouble knowing when to drop the lances and switch to their sabres. There might need to be some training on that. The shields could be useful, but I don't know whether the entire surface should be polished. If they are designed to deflect a blade down, lancers could lose their legs or their mounts. Perhaps several designs should be tested."

"Those are good thoughts. Have you considered them, Commander?" asks the Majer-Commander.

"The deflection had been raised, ser."

"And? Did anyone determine whether it was a possibility?"

"No, ser."

"Before our next meeting, you are to have someone conduct trials to see if the design you are using will deflect a blade into the lancer and the mount. If this is a possibility, you are to develop alternative designs."

"Yes, ser." Muyro nods, his face impassive.

"Commander Shykt?"

"We were tasked with determining whether the defenses of the ports, compounds, and outposts would need to be changed if firelances and firecannon were no longer available to the Mirror Lancers. In simple terms, the answer is no. All the facilities were initially designed so that they could be defended without the use of chaos-powered weapons. We did discover one weakness, but that is not with the defenses. Because horse-drawn supply wagons are both slower and more vulnerable to attack, and with all provisions coming by such teams, it might be prudent to increase food and supply storage areas in some of the more exposed outposts, and to schedule somewhat more frequent reprovisioning." Shykt nods that he is finished.

"Do any of you have any questions?" Rynst looks from face to face. "If not, the meeting is over. I will take your reports and read them. Then they will go to Majer Lorn, who will keep them for my use in developing strategic plans." The Majer-Commander stands.

Lorn stands with the other officers, stepping back ever so slightly, and waiting until the others leave, each handing the documents he brought to Rynst as each leaves the study.

When the study is empty, Rynst turns to Lorn. "That is one function of having a junior commander at these meetings. Few of us have recently fought. Thank you."

"You are welcome, ser. I tried to ask it as a question."

"I noticed that." Rynst smiles. "Muyro will still be irked, and the Mirror Engineers will doubtless have little good to say of either of us for the next few eightdays. And the lancers whose legs you have considered will never know someone was looking out for them. That is one of the difficulties of being in Mirror Lancer Court. All are angered at your questions, and when you point out defects, but seldom is any credit offered." He shakes his head. "You have several days for the report of this meeting." After a pause, he asks, "How is your draft of the plan for dealing with the Jeranyi coming?"

"Slower than I had thought, ser. I have developed a list of options, and I am working out the costs and the advantages of each."

Rynst laughs. "Just remember that costs mean nothing if we lose too many lancers or the Jeranyi take our lands."

"Yes, ser. I understand."

"You do, but some of my commanders do not." Rynst looks down at the stack of documents he holds. "You can take these in the morning." With a smile, he adds, "I must go to the Palace of Eternal Light for the afternoon audience with His Mightiness. Have you ever been in the Palace?"

"No, ser."

"In a season or so, once people start to think of you as merely my tool, I'll take you." The Majer-Commander nods. "Until tomorrow."

"Yes, ser." Lorn bows, then gathers his notes, and slips from the study.

Outside, he sees Commander Shykt, standing beyond the table desk, and Senior Squad Leader Tygyl. Shykt beckons, and Lorn walks toward the curly-haired and thin-faced commander.

"Ser?"

"Interesting point you made about the shape and design of the shields, Majer. You've had a great deal of combat experience, have you not?"

"Yes, ser."

"How would you compare your experience in actual skirmishes or battles to that of most majers?"

Lorn frowns, then replies carefully. "I have probably had less combat experience than some majers because I was promoted more rapidly than many, but I have had more combat experience than perhaps half, and more recent combat experience than almost any."

"A fair and accurate answer." Shykt nods. "I would suggest that you write a short note to Commander Muyro, apologizing—very indirectly—for the suggestion about the shields, but noting that the Majer-Commander knew of your recent combat experience and that you had no choice."

"Thank you, ser."

"Muyro's an idiot, Majer, but he's also a cousin of both Rustyl and the Second Magus. He is one of those officers who forgets nothing, but learns little."

"I think I understand, ser."

"You don't, not yet. My son's an undercaptain at Peme-

dra. I'd like to see him live to become a majer someday."
Shykt nods. "Good day, Majer."

"Good day, ser."

Lorn walks slowly back down to his study. Shykt scarcely
looks old enough to have a son old enough to be a Mirror
Lancer officer, but every word the commander had said had
been the truth, without equivocation and without evasion,
and that bothered Lorn as much as if there had been some
deception in Shykt's words.

Then . . . truth can also be deception.

Lorn shakes his head.

XCVII

LORN AND RYALTH sit across from each other at one end of
the long table that can hold nearly a score. Their meal is simple, a fowl casserole, with early peaches, and fresh dark
bread.

Lorn looks up from his platter. "This is good."

"Ayleha is a good cook. So is Kysia. At times, the combi-
nations are strange." Ryalth laughs, holding Kerial in her left
arm as she eats right-handed. "You will see."

"Anything would be better than outpost fare," he replies.
"I hadn't realized how much I missed good food."

"I have. I just watch you eat."

"I've missed a lot. Mostly you."

The red-haired trader smiles. "I know, and I'm glad of
that. I had hoped it would turn this way, but I never counted
on it."

Lorn returns the smile, but his expression fades quickly.

"Something's bothering you," Ryalth says slowly. "You
keep sighing and hesitating, as if you want to talk about it,
and you don't. You've been like that for several days."

Lorn tilts his head. "I can't keep much from you."

"I can't keep anything from you," she points out. "Is it something from the Mirror Lancer Court?"

"In a way." He frowns. "It's stupid, and I didn't realize that it was bothering me." Lorn offers a lopsided grin.

As she chews a mouthful of the casserole, she nods her head for him to continue, and bounces Kerial on her knee in an effort to keep their son content.

"In my campaigns in Biehl and in Jerans, we came across more than fiftyscore well-forged iron blades and probably threescore cupridium sabres. I have no doubts that the traders of Hamor will be back with scores more. Possibly they are already. There seems to be no scarcity of blades in Jerans, and Jerans is a far poorer land than Cyador." He takes a sip of the amber ale before continuing. "Yet . . . there is great concern that the Mirror Lancers will not have weapons, and the Majer-Commander is trying to plan for matters that will not come to pass for years." Lorn shrugs. "That, I would ask you keep to yourself."

"Gaaaa . . . waa . . . dah . . ." Kerial windmills both arms.

"I will, my dear." Ryalth shifts the increasingly restless Kerial to her other leg before continuing. "Traders supply what folk want. The barbarians dislike Cyador, and will pay for blades to attack us. To allow such trade is to Hamor's advantage, and to the traders' advantage."

Lorn purses his lips. "I can see the advantage to the traders."

"Dearest . . . how does the Emperor raise the golds to support the Mirror Lancers and fight the barbarians?"

Lorn wants to strike his forehead, for the answer is so obvious. "By tariffs, mostly on trade, but he cannot tariff goods coming in as heavily as goods going out because, if the import tariffs are too high, no outsiders will trade."

"He cannot tariff outgoing goods heavily, either, or we cannot sell as cheaply as others can, and if that is so, we will not send goods out from Cyador, and there will be fewer tariffs," Ryalth says. "The lands across the Eastern Ocean have more traders, and the profits are great. They do not protect their traders, but simply let those who trade well, prosper."

"So does the Empire of Eternal Light," Lorn points out.

"But those across the Eastern Ocean don't have any lands adjoining them. We do. So they need fewer lancers, and only ships to protect their ports."

Lorn reflects. All of the continent of Hamor is under the Hamorian emperor, and no one can attack any of Hamor except by sea. The same is true of both Austra and Nordla, although it is but a short voyage across the Gulf of Austra that separates the two island continents.

"And Cyador is richer than Jerans or Cerlyn or Gallos or Spidlar," Ryalth adds. "So the barbarians to our north can see a reason to raid us, if and when they can."

"They hate us as well, and will pay for blades to exercise that hatred," Lorn muses, "while we do not hate them, but merely wish to hold what we have."

"They will continue to purchase blades, and Hamor will allow the trade in blades to continue." Ryalth lifts Kerial. "Now . . . don't hit your mother," she admonishes her son, taking a chubby fist and redirecting it.

"And," Lorn continues, "because lands of the Eastern Ocean must support only a few warships, the tariffs on traders are low."

Ryalth nods. "But the fireships are less costly to operate because they have smaller crews and can travel faster, and against the wind."

"Now that will not be true," Lorn points out. "Matters will get worse. Sailing warships are more costly." He frowns. "That is why—"

"Gaaa!" Kerial interjects.

"The papers your father provided?" Ryalth guesses.

"He wrote that the chaos of coal-burning could be harnessed to create steam. There are even plans . . ."

"Has anyone suggested such?"

"No."

"There must be a reason. I would not bring that idea forth until you know why." She lifts Kerial to her shoulder. "Yet I cannot see why. Traders need protection, but Ryalor House cannot afford a single warship. I can provide arms so that pirates will think again, but no trading clan can afford to outfit a ship that will not turn a profit, and warships do not turn profits. Perhaps Vyanat'mer fears that tariffs will go up—and Bluoyal did worry about such, as you know."

"The plans are from the Archives of the Quarter—I think that is what my father wrote. Vyanat might not even know," Lorn says slowly. "Such engines would require much chaos-force to create and would need to be forged by an iron-worker and a mage together."

"But they would continue the power of the Magi'i," Ryalth says.

"Then why has Chyenfel not brought forth such a plan?"

"Perhaps he has, or perhaps he would wait to offer such until he feels others would support the effort. Would not the chaos-fired steam vessels cost much more to build and require larger crews?"

Lorn nods. "But they would be faster than sailing ships and could go against the wind."

"Whhaaa . . . gaaa . . . whaaa!" Kerial flails in his mother's arms.

"How could the Empire raise the golds for them? And how could the merchanters pay such tariffs?" Ryalth stands, struggling with Kerial. "Our friend is ready for bed, and I cannot delay or he will be restless for all too long. Best you think about this while I put him down. I will be back when he sleeps."

"Go." Lorn laughs softly.

As Ryalth carries Kerial from the dining area and up the stairs, Lorn stands and picks up the platters. He considers the questions his father had posed, what seems so long ago, as he carries the platters to the kitchen. *Are those who direct power the source of either?* That had been the third question, and he is beginning to understand the reasoning behind the question. The First Magus can direct the power of chaos, but is not its source; the chaos-towers and the world itself are. The Majer-Commander controls the Mirror Lancers, but their weapons come from the skills of the cupritors and the Magi'i and their pay from the tariffs on the merchanters. While the fireships effectively are controlled by the Magi'i, once their towers fail, the Magi'i, too, will become more dependent upon the merchanters.

"I'll take those, ser," Kysia offers as Lorn enters the kitchen.

"Oh, thank you, Kysia. I'll bring in the other dishes."

"You don't have to, ser."

"It's no problem. Ryalth is putting Kerial to bed." Lorn turns, his thoughts still churning, turning to the last question posed by his father. *How can the world be more simple, and yet more complex?*

He laughs as he picks up the casserole dish, the dish that had held the peaches, and the empty basket that had held bread. The world is governed by power. It may be the power of golds, of chaos, of weapons in the hands of trained men, even of love, or of words well-spoken. The simplicity is that power governs. The complexity is that no man, no group of men, can possibly track all the sources of power and their impacts. Power is like chaos—while it can be used for good or evil at the moment, it is essentially unpredictable over time.

With a headshake, Lorn hands the dish and basket to Kysia. "Strange thoughts," is all he says as he walks back through the house and out onto the veranda, where he stands at the edge of the stone, looking up at the night sky. Somewhere out there are the Rational Stars. He smiles at the contradition of the two terms. For a star is concentrated chaos, which cannot be rational and predictable, not over time, even as it is, for were the flow of chaos from each star not relatively stable, life would not exist.

His father was indeed right, not that Lorn has yet figured out any way to turn those observations into use. Lorn has yet to determine how to accomplish the far more simple task of reducing the raids from Jerans with fewer golds and less Mirror Lancer casualties.

XCVIII

LORN STEPS FROM his study and out to the table desk in the wide fourth-floor corridor of Mirror Lancer Court. There he hands the three sheets which summarize the meeting dealing with the failure of the chaos-towers and the impact on the Mirror Lancers, to Fayrken. "I'll need two copies."

"I can copy these immediately, ser," answers the sandy-haired senior squad leader. "Majer Hrenk is still in Fyrad."

"Thank you." Lorn smiles. After nearly two eightdays at the Mirror Lancer Court, he has yet to meet or even see Hrenk, the Mirror Lancer majer who is an aide to Commander Muyro. "Do you know when he'll be back?"

"No, ser. He's inspecting the spring flood damage to the Great Canal. There were more giant stun lizards and more runoff. A message to Commander Muyro about that came yesterday." Fayrken smiles. "Glad he's not back yet. If it is like last spring he'll have a huge report for me to copy."

Lorn nods.

"Majer Lorn."

Lorn turns to see the Captain-Commander standing in the fourth-floor foyer. Lorn bows. "Yes, ser?"

The bushy-browed Luss approaches and halts perhaps

three cubits from Lorn. "I was reading your latest report. You write clearly and well, Majer."

"Thank you, ser."

"I do not think I understood how clearly and well. And you understand much."

"I do my best to listen, ser. There's much I need to learn."

"I have noticed that. You also hear what is not said. That, too, is a most valuable talent, particularly when allied with prudence and caution." Luss smiles with his mouth, but not his eyes. "How are you finding Mirror Lancer Court?"

"I'm finding that everyone here is most perceptive and intelligent, and that matters are far more complicated than they seemed when I was a field commander," Lorn answers with total truthfulness.

Luss laughs once, not quite harshly. "Do not let the apparent complexity deceive you. In the end, there is often but one choice."

"Yes, ser."

With a nod as much to himself as Lorn, Luss turns and walks back toward the steps and begins to walk up to the fifth floor.

"He must think you've done something right, ser," says Fayrken.

"I'd never met him before I came here, and I've only talked with him once—that was very short. I've taken notes at perhaps a handful of meetings where he spoke," Lorn replies.

"He once told a commander that he'd best fall on his sabre while he had enough brains left to complete the job."

Lorn raises his eyebrows.

"Yes, ser. I heard it myself."

"I'd better be quite careful." Lorn already knows that.

"You are, ser. I can tell that from how you write."

"How come you aren't an officer?" Lorn asks. "You're brighter than many captains."

Fayrken shakes his head. "My da was a weaver in Summerdock. Barely learned my letters, but I didn't want to be a weaver. So I became a lancer. Then I saw that I'd die one day somewhere in the Grass Hills if I didn't get to be a squad leader. So I buttered up one of the older fellows and got him to help me with my letters. After I made junior squad leader, almost lost my leg in a Jeranyi raid, and while I was healing, I was a clerk in at the headquarters in Syadtar. Commander Ryuk brought me here, five years ago." Fayrken grins. "Now . . . ser . . . if I got myself to be an undercaptain, now . . . where would I find myself?"

Lorn grins back. "Probably in Inividra or Pemedra or Isahl."

"I need but another few years for a pension, if a short-coin one, and I've a consort and two young boys."

"In your boots, I'd do the same," Lorn says. "There's not much point in traveling the same ground twice, first as a ranker and then as an officer."

"Ser?"

"Yes, Fayrken?"

"Is it true that you are the first officer in ten generations to invade Jerans?"

"I don't know about the ten generations . . . but the first in many."

"Some say . . . you've killed more barbarians by yourself than some whole squads . . ."

Lorn frowns slightly, then tilts his head before answering. "I've had the fortune—or misfortune—to be in more battles and fights than almost all officers near my age and rank. When you fight more, if you survive, you'll kill more of your enemy. I'm not sure that killing measures much more than surviving." He straightens and shrugs. "I've tried to do what I thought was right. Looking back, I'm sure it wasn't in some cases. But if you don't decide quickly, you don't get a chance to think it over later." For some reason the image of a young woman in an enumerator's bedchamber flashes through his mind—another quick decision, perhaps good for him, but hardly for her, and yet at that moment, had Lorn had any real choice? He offers a lopsided smile. "I'm sorry . . . that's a long answer to a short question."

Fayrken nods. "Best I get on with the copying. Majer Hrenk will not stay in Fyrad forever."

"Thank you." Lorn turns back toward his study, and the strategic plan he has yet to complete.

XCVIX

THE BELL ON the iron gate rings, and Lorn hurries forward from the veranda, down the green marble walk to and around the fountain, and past the privacy hedge to open the gate.

"An iron gate, Lorn?" Tyrsal stands there in the whites of a magus with a petite blonde woman dressed in a shimmering green tunic and trousers. She is no taller than Lorn's shoulder.

"Ryalth thought it might be useful. Please come in." Lorn steps back and pulls the gate wide. "She's waiting on the veranda."

After the couple steps around the tightly-grown conifer privacy hedge, Lorn relocks the iron gate, and follows them up the green marble walk to the veranda, where Ryalth waits.

"This is Aleyar," Tyrsal announces, almost embarrassed, grinning slightly at Lorn as he rejoins them.

Lorn manages not to raise his eyebrows, recalling how, years before, Tyrsal had said that the blonde and poised young healer standing on the veranda was too young—and then, she probably had been.

"You are amused?" asks Aleyar with a gentle voice.

"I am indeed, but for reasons you would not find unpleasant, Lady Healer," Lorn says.

"I can sense that. I look forward to hearing them."

Tyrsal flushes. So does Lorn.

Ryalth and Aleyar exchange glances, and amused smiles.

Aleyar glances at Tyrsal and begins to laugh. "I think I'll enjoy this far more than I'd thought."

"Oh . . ." Lorn says. "This is Ryalth, my far better self."

Ryalth shakes her head. "Perhaps we could sit out here for a bit and have something to drink," she suggests, gesturing toward the wooden-framed settee and the two armchairs. "We have some early redberry juice and some Alafraan, and amber ale."

The red-haired Tyrsal glances at Aleyar.

"The redberry, if you please." Aleyar seats herself in one of the two armchairs.

"The ale," Tyrsal says, taking the other chair.

"I'll get the drinks," Ryalth says before Lorn speaks. "You want ale, don't you? I'll be back in a moment."

"Yes, thank you." After a moment, Lorn settles onto the settee.

"As I told you, Lorn is my oldest and dearest friend," Tyrsal tells Aleyar. "He made my life easier when we were in school, and it cost him dearly later. He could have been a first-level adept if he'd been able to stay in the Magi'i."

"We both survived," Lorn replies mildly.

Aleyar casts a quizzical look at Tyrsal and then at Lorn. "You both agree that is the truth." She shakes her head.

"Tyrsal is being kind," Lorn says.

"I think not," Aleyar replies.

"Here is the redberry." Ryalth reappears with a tray on which are four glass beakers, two of redberry and two of ale. She extends the tray to Aleyar, who takes one of the redberry beakers, and then to Tyrsal.

Lorn takes the other ale, and Ryalth sets the tray on the

small table beside the settee, where she seats herself, before taking the last beaker.

"How did you two meet?" Ryalth asks as she looks at Aleyar.

"Because of Lorn, actually," Tyrsal says. "In a way. I saw her at the infirmary when Lorn didn't answer my scrolls and I'd gone to see Jerial to see if his duty station had been changed again."

"I didn't know you'd written." Lorn shifts his weight on the settee. "You never said."

"Well, after all the other problems Dett caused, I didn't see much point in making you any angrier at him." Tyrsal takes a sip of ale. "That day, Aleyar was talking to Jerial. So I waited until she left to talk to your sister." He grins. "I did ask Jerial who she was, but I didn't do anything for several eightdays."

"Almost a season." Aleyar laughs.

"But I didn't forget."

"No . . . you asked everyone who might know me about me, though."

Tyrsal flushes. "Anyway . . . I finally asked her father for permission to call on her. He was very kind and said I could." The red-haired magus shrugs. "That's how it happened."

"How did you meet Lorn?" Aleyar asks, her gaze on Ryalth.

Ryalth smiles mischievously. "It happened a long time ago. He was a student, and I was a very junior trader. He was walking, looking for a willing woman, when a man attacked me and the trader I was with. Lorn saved us both, and me from a truly deplorable fate. Somehow, we found we belonged together, and he defied his father to make me his consort. That was many years later, of course."

"Except," Lorn adds, "my father had such a high opinion of Ryalth that he forced me to defy him for her because he feared I wouldn't value her enough otherwise."

A faint flush suffuses Ryalth's face and neck.

"You didn't tell me that," Tyrsal says.

"I didn't find that out until after we were consorted," Lorn admits.

"A love match, across backgrounds." Aleyar holds her beaker of redberry, then takes another tiny sip. "You were fortunate that your parents saw her worth."

"Didn't that happen with your sister?" asks Lorn.

"You mean Syreal?" Aleyar nods. "It did. I can't say I understand exactly how. Veljan is the sweetest man. He is a good trader, and he'd do anything for her, but Syreal is so bright. Compared to her, he's a sweet dumb ox, but he adores her, and she's happy. She really is. It's for the best for everyone. That became clear after Fuyol's death. Shevelt was a lizard of a man, and the clan owes a debt to whoever killed him. The entire Yuryan Clan loves Veljan, because he is honest and does the right thing. He's so honest by nature, and Syreal tells him what to do . . . and if she doesn't know, she asks Father." Aleyar laughs. "Between the three of them, the Clan has prospered greatly, and what's funny is that all of them know it, and so does most of Cyad—and everyone's still pleased."

"It makes sense," Lorn says. "Veljan is honest. That means he won't do anything he feels is wrong. Your father is shrewd, and he will give the best advice for his daughter and her consort, and Syreal loves Veljan and won't accept any advice that would hurt him. And everyone else understands that, which means that they can trust Veljan to be honorable, and they all know why."

"That is rare indeed in Cyad," Ryalth says dryly.

"Father is honest, too," Aleyar points out. "That's why he was a friend of your father, Lorn."

"And why he keeps his distance from the Second Magus?" Lorn probes.

Aleyar looks down at her half-full beaker of redberry.

"I know," Lorn says quickly. "Kharl'elth is the father of

Myryan's consort, but he is known to be less than straight-forward."

"That is a most polite way of putting it," Tyrsal says quickly. "And the less said the better, if you please."

"I am sorry," Lorn apologizes. "I did not mean to offend."

Ryalth rises. "I think this is a good time to go inside for dinner. I just saw Kysia hovering in the archway."

Tyrsal and Lorn also stand, quickly, and the four make their way to the table in the dining area where Lorn stands waiting on one side of the table, across from Ryalth, and then seats Aleyar to his right, while Tyrsal—after seating Ryalth—sits to her left.

Kysia and Ayleha appear with platters and serving bowls and then two baskets of bread, followed by a silver tray on which there are slices of sun-nut bread.

"Sun-nut bread, I see. Your family always served that," Tyrsal says.

"The emburhka recipe comes from Lorn's family," Ryalth replies.

"I thought I recognized the aroma," Tyrsal says as he takes the serving bowl that Ryalth hands to him.

"The wine is Alafraan," Lorn says. "Would you like some?"

"Just half, please," answers the blonde healer. "I like it, but much wine does not like me."

"That's true of many healers," Lorn says as he pours the requested amount into her goblet. "Myryan never has more than a goblet, and usually only half." He fills the other three goblets three-quarters full, then sets the bottle down and offers the emburhka to Aleyar.

She takes the dish, and then asks, smiling almost mischievously, "Will you tell me why you were so amused when Tyrsal introduced me?"

Lorn glances at Tyrsal, who flushes once more.

"Go ahead, Lorn." A wry smile crosses the lips of the red-headed magus. "Try to be kind to me."

"It goes back many years, before I left the Quarter of the Magi'i," Lorn begins slowly. "It really begins with me, on the night I met Ryalth, as I recall."

Ryalth raises her eyebrows. "I have not heard this."

"My father was talking about the need for suitable consorts, and he asked if I had ever taken the trouble to talk to you." He inclines his head to Aleyar. "He made some comment like, 'It would not harm you to talk to her to see if you would like her.' I thought that I might, except later that evening I met Ryalth and that changed everything."

"Good thing for me that you did," Tyrsal says, smiling at Aleyar.

The blonde healer returns the smile, warmly.

"But . . ." Lorn draws out the word, grinning at Tyrsal, "I remembered what my father had said, and several years later, I mentioned your name to my dear friend, and he made some comment to the effect that while you were sweet, beautiful, and charming-looking, he worried much about presenting himself to the great Third Magus." Lorn inclines his head to Tyrsal. "I'm glad he decided to anyway."

"So am I," replies Aleyar. "Even if it did take him a season to get his courage up."

"Prudence, that's all," mumbles Tyrsal, flushing once more, and partly hiding behind the goblet of Alafraan that he holds.

"You didn't need that much prudence with Father," the healer says gently. "He likes you."

"I didn't know that he would," Tyrsal points out. "I don't come from a long line of Magi'i, like Lorn or Rustyl."

Aleyar shivers, if slightly.

Ryalth glances at Lorn, then says gently, "You don't seem that fond of Rustyl."

"He called several times . . . before Tyrsal. I put him off. Father let me, thank the Rational Stars," Aleyar says. "His eyes and heart are cold, and he's even colder deep within."

Her eyes go to Lorn. "You ... and Tyrsal ... both of you have a warmth inside."

Lorn nods. "Tyrsal is warmer, I think."

"It would appear that way," Aleyar admits, "but you hide what you are well, as well as any of the senior Magi'i." She looks at Ryalth. "He's warmer than he will admit, is he not?"

"Yes," replies the red-haired trader, with a smile. "I thought so from the first, but it took years to find it so."

"And he is terrible to his foes," Aleyar adds. "A healer can see that as well."

Lorn shrugs and offers a lopsided smile. "You both have seen through me."

After setting down her goblet, Aleyar laughs, softly but warmly. "No one sees through you, Lorn. We can judge you by what we do not sense."

"Enough ... enough," protests Tyrsal. "You'll have the two of us apart like a pair of roosters for stewing."

"Definitely roosters," Ryalth says.

Lorn barely manages not to choke on the mouthful of emburhka he is swallowing.

"I won't pursue it." Aleyar turns to Ryalth. "What is it like, being a lady trader? Syreal has told me about some of it, but do you think people treat you differently because you're a lady?"

Ryalth gives the slightest of shrugs. "At first, it was difficult." Her face hardens. "I learned a great deal." A brief smile flits across her face. "Some of it from Lorn. I don't think he understands how much, or about what."

Lorn understands—now. He manages to keep an interested smile on his face.

Tyrsal glances from Ryalth to Lorn. He swallows.

Aleyar nods. "Now they all accept you, even defer to you. That's what Syreal says. There was talk of your name being put forward as a possible Merchanter Advisor."

"That would have been a gesture. Some gestures are useful. That would have served no useful purpose," Ryalth replies, passing the basket of still-warm bread to Tyrsal.

"She sounds like someone else I know," Tyrsal says with a laugh, taking the bread, and glancing at Lorn before turning his attention back to Ryalth. "How is trading these days?"

"It's getting harder," Ryalth admits. "Not because of Kerial, but because of the tariffs. We saw another one-gold increase at the turn of summer." She glances at her consort. "From what Lorn tells me, I fear that there will be more."

"Syreal says the same thing," Aleyar says.

"Why?" asks Tyrsal. "Just because we've lost a few fireships?"

"It's not just the loss of the fireships, but the failure of the chaos-towers," Lorn says. "Without firelances, it will take more lancers to hold back the barbarians, and more lancers—"

"I see," Tyrsal interrupts. "I'm slow, but not stupid. More lancers cost more golds, with their horses and blades and stipends. More horse teams will be needed on the roads, and that will make transport slower and more costly . . . It affects everything."

"Unless the Magi'i can find another way to use chaos, perhaps the natural chaos of the world," Lorn suggests.

"Some have been working on that. Most Magi'i aren't that strong," Tyrsal points out.

"Or . . ." Lorn says slowly, "unless there is some way to use natural chaos with machines of some sort." He glances at Tyrsal. "Is anyone working on something like that?"

"I wouldn't know that. I'm a very lowly second-level adept."

"You could be a first-level," Aleyar says. "You're good enough. You will be soon."

"I'm not sure I want to work that hard," Tyrsal parries.

"You worry too much," counters the blonde healer. "Father thinks you're better than many of the Firsts."

"There's much to worry about in Cyad these days." Tyrsal makes a vague gesture.

"Does anyone want more of the emburhka?" asks Ryalth.

"No . . . I'm full," Lorn admits.

"Except for the pearapple tarts?"

He laughs. "Except for the pearapple tarts."

Ryalth gestures, and Kysia and Ayleha appear to remove the platters and serving dishes.

Lorn pours a half-goblet more wine for Ryalth and Tyrsal.

Tyrsal frowns. "There's something I've been meaning to ask."

"Oh?"

"There were rumors . . . about your father . . ." Tyrsal suggests.

"I heard them," Lorn says. "That he was the Hand of the Emperor. He never told me anything like that, and there wasn't a thing in his papers or his letters that mentioned it, even indirectly." He shrugs. "That doesn't mean he wasn't, but I'd guess that the Emperor would be the only one who could say, and he's said nothing. Not that I know, anyway."

"He hasn't named a new Hand, either, from what I've overheard," Tyrsal says.

"Father says he should, but will not, not until he names a successor," Aleyar volunteers.

"A successor?" Ryalth frowns.

"The Emperor looks young, but he is not. This is something all healers know, though we say little," Aleyar replies. "The Empress is a healer, and tends him constantly, so that he looks young. They have no children, not even any nieces or nephews, and both have outlived their siblings. There was a nephew, but he was a lancer officer who was killed years ago."

A nephew killed years ago—that alone indicates an old Emperor to Lorn. "No one speaks about a successor."

"No one will," says Ryalth. "Not openly. The Magi'i and

the lancers do not want to lose their powers, and the merchanters do not want Cyador to be seen as any weaker or as in turmoil, because we will lose golds."

"There must be some in Cyad who could turn that to a profit," suggests Lorn.

"There are, and they will, and the clans will let them, so long as it is done quietly."

"And if not?" questions Tyrsal.

"Several warehouses burned, and some ships never returned to port before the lancers and the Magi'i agreed on Toziel's sire. And the Captain-Commander of Mirror Lancers was killed by the old Third Magus, and the Second Magus vanished."

"That's not in the history scrolls," Tyrsal says dryly.

Aleyar laughs softly.

"I know. I know," replies the redheaded magus. "I am hopeless in my desires for openness and truth."

"You never told me that Lorn had suggested you meet me," Aleyar points out sweetly. "That was not in your personal-history scroll."

Tyrsal shakes his head so ruefully that the other three laugh. "Best I talk of some other matters. Quickly. How is Myryan doing?"

"She says she's fine." Lorn shrugs. "I still worry about her. She's so sweet, but her eyes are sad, like Mother's were the last time I saw her."

"We choose to be healers," Aleyar says quietly.

"But your choices are limited," Ryalth points out. "As the daughter of a magus, you can keep the house of your consort, or become a healer, or do both . . ."

"Or leave Cyador," Aleyar says. "Before I met Tyrsal, I was thinking about that. Healers are welcome elsewhere in Candar, especially in the east. Lydiar, especially."

"You would have done that?" asks Tyrsal.

"Rather than accept someone like Rustyl? Certainly. Father can protect me now . . . but he is not so young as he thinks."

Lorn holds back a frown. The Emperor is old. So are Rynst and Liataphi.

"Here are the tarts!" Ryalth announces as Kysia appears with a platter.

Lorn smiles. He can do little else this evening, except enjoy Ryalth and the company of Tyrsal and Aleyar—and he is happy for his friend.

Besides, the pearapple tarts are good. He has already sampled one in the kitchen earlier.

C

His Mightiness Toziel'elth'alt'mer leans forward in the smaller malachite and silver throne of the Lesser Audience Hall. "We now have but four fireships capable of protecting our interests." His eyes go to Rynst. "How goes the construction of the three sailing warships?"

"The first will be completed by late fall, the others thereafter." Rynst nods slightly.

"And the cannon?"

"We have tested one. More work will be required."

"And how many golds?" asks Vyanat'mer.

Toziel's head turns slowly from Rynst to Vyanat. "You question the need for such weapons and vessels?"

"The need for such vessels? And more armament?" Vyanat'mer shakes his head. "The need, never. I question how we can afford such. Already the Empire of Eternal Light tariffs those of us who are merchanters at nearly ten golds on every hundred we take in."

"The tariffs of Hamor are higher than that," Chyenfel points out.

The gray-haired Rynst glances from Toziel to the First Magus, then to the blue-eyed Merchanter Advisor.

In her smaller seat behind Toziel's shoulder, Ryenyel appears disinterested, her eyes absently ranging from one advisor to another.

The merchanter laughs ruefully. "The tariffs levied by the Hamorians are high on parchment, but their enumerators are not so well-trained, and can be bribed by those of Hamor. I would even guess that bribery is encouraged. Were I to attempt such, I would lose a ship or a hand or both. So we pay golds there, and those are golds they do not pay, while they but pay ours. That can mean that our traders often pay twice as much in tariffs as do the Hamorians."

"Without fireships and a larger fleet . . ." Rynst says quietly.

"You wish that we should go to war against Hamor?" asks Toziel. "Or bar our ports to the Hamorians, so that they will bar theirs to us?"

"No, sire." Rynst shakes his head. "No, sire, but the Hamorians know we cannot do such."

"Why can we not require the Hamorians to pay greater tariffs than do our traders?" asks Chyenfel.

"Then they will do the same," counters Vyanat, "and we will find ourselves in an even worse position."

"How then, honored Merchanter Advisor, would you counsel me?"

"I would counsel you to reduce the tariffs on all goods."

"And how are we to support the Mirror Lancers and keep the barbarians from pouring across the Grass Hills?" Toziel raises his eyebrows. "With fewer firelances and recharges available, we need more lancers, not fewer."

"Lower their stipends," Vyanat says genially. "By increasing tariffs, you have lowered what we make and can pay our seamen and workers."

"They will be risking their lives more," Rynst says, "and you suggest we pay them less?"

"You cannot pay what you do not have," Vyanat counters.

"If tariffs are raised, fewer goods will pass through Cyad. We already trade fewer goods than generations earlier. One has but to look at the empty warehouses and piers to see that. Fewer goods provide fewer golds in tariffs. That is true even with higher tariffs."

Toziel frowns, then fingers his chin. "Let me say what you all have said: Because we have fewer warships, our traders pay higher tariffs elsewhere in the world. To build more warships will require golds. To get the golds one must raise tariffs on something. Raising tariffs will lower the golds we gather because fewer goods will come to Cyad and fewer will leave. Without more golds we cannot pay for more Mirror Lancers, but we will need more lancers because we have fewer firelances and firewagons." The Emperor pauses. "If you are all correct, then Cyador is doomed. Yet we are prosperous. So there must be a fault in this reasoning." He smiles. "I would that each of you reflect on this and bring me your thoughts the day after tomorrow." He stands.

The three advisors bow as the Emperor of Cyador, Land of Eternal Light, turns and makes his way from the audience hall, followed by Ryenyel.

CI

LORN LEANS FORWARD in his study chair, ignoring the warm afternoon breeze of full summer that scarcely cools Mirror Lancer Court at all. He forces himself to read slowly over the summary and conclusion page of his draft plan for dealing with the Jeranyi—the paragraphs that matter the most, in a way, since he doubts anyone but the Majer-Commander will ever see more than the summaries. Perhaps even Rynst will not read more than the summary.

As he has drafted the plan, Lorn has included everything he can think of, from the costs of carrying blades from

Hamor—figures Eileyt and Ryalth had helped him calculate—to distances between the planned stops of a campaign to take Jera, and even the supplies necessary in the event that the Mirror Lancers were not to raid the storehouses of the Jeranyi.

He forces his eyes back to the lines that feel so tired, because they are the result of far too many drafts, and far too many revisions.

. . . Cliffs form most of the coastline from Biehl to a point roughly one hundred kays west of Rulyarth. Jera is the only port with practical access to the lands of Jerans. Control of the port, therefore, controls the majority of trade . . . The Jeranyi do not have supplies of iron or metal-working skills. That is true especially for finely-wrought metals and weapons. If Cyador holds Jera, then Cyador can limit the easy flow of blades to the Jeranyi . . .

Any campaign to take the port of Jera can be accomplished with tenscore lancers, although a larger force would limit any uncertainty. . . .

. . . The geography of Jera is such that a fortified wall can be placed on the highlands west of the port to limit access and to control the trade along the River Jeryna . . . With the growing possibility of the lack of chaos-powered tools in the future, such a fortification should be started immediately after the port is taken.

The harbor waters are shallow. Deeper draft vessels must be moored at the end of long piers necessary to reach deeper water. To build piers closer to the port's seawall will require extensive dredging. In either case, once the port is taken by land, it would be difficult, if not impossible, for any enemy to land armsmen or lancers by ship inside the fortifications. . . .

This plan may well have defects, and is not without

its costs. It will not eliminate all future losses by the Mirror Lancers to Jeranyi and Cerlynyi barbarians in the Grass Hills. Any other plan is highly unlikely to prove either effective or workable, as detailed above.

Lorn takes a deep breath. The last sentence is the dangerous one, because it is impossible to prove another plan will not work without implementing it—and failing.

Finally, he stands and carries the plan out to Fayrken for the senior squad leader to copy before Lorn takes it upstairs to Tygyl for delivery to the Majer-Commander.

"Ser?" inquires the squad leader as Lorn approaches his table.

Lorn hands the report to Fayrken. "This is the report that the Majer-Commander requested. I need just one copy."

Fayrken takes the sheets, and studies them. "Lot of writing here, ser. Late tomorrow, I'd say."

"When you can." Lorn smiles faintly.

"Be starting it now, ser. With the firewagons running less often, I'd guess, Commander Hrenk is still in Fyrad."

"Thank you."

"Yes, ser." Fayrken nods.

After Lorn walks back into his study, closing the door behind him, he looks down at the polished surface of the desk, then out through the open window at the clouds to the north that promise a late-afternoon thundershower. He has already spent almost half a season in Cyad, going to meetings, taking notes, and writing reports, and he feels as though he has accomplished almost nothing, except learning how—in his sparring with Tyrsal—to handle a sabre in either hand without using his eyes at all.

The best thing about his assignment in Cyad is that he and Ryalth have had much more time together, and that he has had a chance to get to know his son. Yet that happiness is tinged with the certainty that times are changing in

Cyador—emphasized by the fact that he is being followed by more than one magus in more than one chaos-glass—and that such change is likely to become more and more swift as the seasons pass.

The chaos-tower in yet another fireship has failed. There is no word on the appointment of a new Hand of the Emperor. The number and frequency of firewagons traveling the Great Eastern and Great North Highways has been reduced twice. The number of recharges for firelances has been reduced to an average of one per season per lancer, and the cupritors are beginning to fashion cupridium lances destined for not just District Guards, but for the Mirror Lancers as well, though none have said such openly.

In the shipyards at Fyrad, the keels have been laid on two new warships—sailing warships. And although Lorn has the plans for better vessels, he dares not bring them forth, not when every gold spent by the lancers is grudged by the merchanters and questioned by the Magi'i, and not when the basis of such plans comes from hidden Magi'i sources.

CII

LORN SITS IN the armless chair at the conference table to the left of the Majer-Commander, as Captain-Commander Luss seats himself at the far end of the table. The redheaded Commander Sypcal, the Eastern Regional Commander, sits on the left side. Across from him is the tall and blond Commander Lhary, the Western Regional Commander.

Rynst lifts the thin stack of papers and then sets them on the conference table before him. "I have read your report, Commanders, but I would like your views on what is most important." The Majer-Commander's eyes focus on the red-haired Sypcal. "First, your thoughts, Sypcal."

"Yes, ser." Sypcal glances down at the report before him,

then squares his shoulders slightly. "As you know, ser, fire-lances have been the most important tactical weapon of the Mirror Lancers against the barbarians of the north since the beginning of Cyad. Our tactics have been based on their use, and replacement with cupridium lances will require extensive retraining of both officers and lancers. New tactics will need to be developed and implemented, and casualties will certainly be higher initially, and perhaps always." Sypcal pauses. "I could offer more details, but those are the considerations I see."

Rynst nods. Luss does not.

"Commander Lhary?" asks Rynst, his voice level. "Can you add anything?"

"Yẹs, ser." The blond commander looks directly at Rynst. "You requested that we address what would happen if the long cupridium lances replaced the firelances. The first impact would be on tactics. We would lose the ability to kill barbarians at a distance. While a firelance is not accurate beyond thirty to forty cubits for the average lancer, that distance accounts for roughly one-quarter of barbarian deaths in a battle. We have been killing three to four barbarians for every lancer killed. If the cupridium lances and the sabres remain as effective as the firelances and the sabres in close combat, the loss of stand-away killing power will mean that we will lose almost one lancer for every two barbarians killed. In the first assault, when forces actually meet, the cupridium lances, because of their length, will be slightly more effective, but become almost useless in a melee, whereas firelances retain some effectiveness." Lhary smiles politely and clears his throat gently before continuing. "We have studied the battle reports of the past two years. We estimate that we will lose another three to four lancers in each melee involving a full lancer company.

"... In effect, to compensate for the total loss of fire-lances, each outpost which had five companies before this year, and which now has six as a result of the transfers from the companies that were patrolling the Accursed Forest, will require at least one additional company."

Luss nods, ever so slightly.

"I see," Rynst says. "Together you are suggesting that we will need more training and more lancers, and that our casualties will be higher. This will cost more golds, and those costs do not include the golds required to pay for obtaining the cupridium lances." Rynst leans forward.

Sypcal nods.

"That is true, Majer-Commander," Lhary replies smoothly. "We felt that you should know fully what the costs would be before you supported or opposed any changes in the placement and numbers of Mirror Lancer companies in the north."

Lorn tries to keep taking notes as quietly as possible, while still studying the faces of the officers and trying to truth-read them.

"What do you think, Luss?" asks Rynst.

"I would suggest that you study the report most carefully and become most familiar with the calculations before you discuss matters in any meeting with the Merchanter Advisor. Commander Lhary can be asked about the calculations, Commander Sypcal about the tactical questions."

Rynst offers a faint smile. "It appears as though none of our choices are to our favor. To control the barbarians we cannot use the tactics and weapons we have favored. Nor is it likely that the Emperor will favor spending the golds necessary to maintain the northern outposts in the way suggested by your report, Commanders." He looks at Luss. "Do you think so, Captain-Commander?"

"At present, it would seem unlikely, ser." Luss's voice is cautious.

"I would have all of you consider what other approaches to dealing with the barbarians might be possible, and at what costs." Rynst looks first at Lhary, then at Sypcal. He does not actually look at Luss.

"Yes, ser," replies the redheaded commander.

"Ser," adds Lhary.

"We will meet again in an eightday." Rynst stands. "Until next twoday."

Lorn stands with the other officers, waiting until Luss and the two commanders depart before gathering his notes.

"I would like your report on this meeting by midday tomorrow, Majer."

"Yes, ser."

"It will be interesting to see what happens at the next meeting on this matter." Rynst offers a broad smile.

"Ser." Lorn bows.

"You may go, Majer."

Lorn bows again, and makes his way from the long study out into the fifth-floor foyer, nodding to Tygyl as he passes the desk where the senior squad leader sits.

"Majer?"

Lorn looks to the top of the open stone staircase where the Captain-Commander waits. "Yes, ser?"

"Have you finished your report to the Majer-Commander, Majer?" Luss offers an ingratiating smile.

"I have submitted a draft, ser." Lorn shrugs apologetically. "I do not know if the Majer-Commander has read it. He has not spoken about it. He has not asked for changes or revisions."

"I am most certain he will, in his own time, Majer. The Majer-Commander always acts when he wishes."

Lorn nods.

"And he uses what will benefit him and the Mirror Lancers, in whatever fashion may best serve both," Luss adds. "Serving in Mirror Lancer Court is not the place for those who wish to be known in Cyad or Cyador."

"I had not thought it otherwise, ser," Lorn says politely.

"Best you should remember that in the seasons to come, Majer. Good day." With the same unvarying and warm smile, Luss turns and walks toward the door to his own study.

Lorn starts down the steps to his own study, and the report on a meeting he must have ready for copying before the afternoon is out.

CIII

As HE WALKS around the bedchamber, carrying Kerial and patting his son on the back, Lorn yawns. The sole light in the room is a single bronze lamp on the bedside table, its wick turned low enough that only a faint glow extends beyond the table.

"You don't have to do that." The tired-eyed mother looks up from the ornate bed, trying not to yawn. "You really don't."

"You're so tired your eyes are black, and you almost fell over into the armoire," Lorn says. "You need some rest." He shifts Kerial higher on his shoulder and pats his son's back again, continually and gently. "Jerial says there's no chaos here, and I don't sense any, but his tummy still bothers him."

Ryalth laughs. "It's strange to hear you talk about his tummy."

"Children don't have stomachs; they have tummies," Lorn offers in a falsely arch tone. "Now turn over and go to sleep."

"I'm tired, but I'm not sleepy." Ryalth yawns.

Lorn shakes his head. "Not sleepy?"

"You need sleep, too. You won't think very well tomorrow," she counters.

"It doesn't matter right now. I can't do anything, except write reports on meetings." As Kerial half cries, half whimpers, Lorn concentrates and pats his son on the back and circles in the space between the bed and the armoires. After another two circles, he looks at Ryalth.

Her eyes are still open.

"Do you have any idea how the Emperor could raise more coins from tariffs?" Lorn asks.

"Why do you ask?"

"Because it seems impossible," Lorn replies, stifling another yawn and patting the unhappy Kerial, who continues to whimper every time his father stops walking. "No one respects our traders unless we have warships and lancers, and we need more of each, with the chaos-towers failing. That takes more coins, but if tariffs go up, there is less trade and fewer coins."

"Lower the tariffs on trade and tariff something else—like the dwellings of the Magi'i." Ryalth shakes her head. "That won't work. There aren't enough Magi'i. I'm too tired to think."

"Just close your eyes and try to sleep. You need it more than I do." Lorn slips toward the single lamp by the bed and turns down the wick. With his night vision, he doesn't need the light, and Ryalth needs the darkness and the sleep.

Then he continues to walk in circles, patting Kerial and humming softly.

CIV

LORN LOOKS AT the stack of reports on the corner of his desk—most of them copies of requests for provisions and weapons. Finally, he picks up the first one—from a Majer Kuyn at Pemedra—and begins to read.

He is on the second page when there is a knock on the door of his Mirror Court study. He looks up. "Yes?"

"Majer, if you have a moment?" A red-haired commander

steps inside—Commander Sypcal, the Eastern Regional commander of Mirror Lancers.

Lorn stands quickly. "Of course, ser."

Sypcal closes the study door and glances at the chair across the table desk from Lorn. "If you don't mind . . . ?"

"Oh . . . please." Lorn waits until the commander sits before reseating himself and waiting for the other to offer his reason for calling on a junior majer.

Sypcal's green eyes take in the room, then focus on Lorn. "You have a pleasant study, Majer, and very little showing your personal side. I would not have expected otherwise. You are wise to do that." A rueful expression crosses his lips. "Especially in Cyad, where everyone seems to know everything."

"Cyad is known to be like that."

"You would know that, having been raised here." Sypcal glances toward the window, slightly ajar, then back at Lorn. "I am going to be honest with you, Majer Lorn. I am not a city lancer. As all can tell you, I come from Geliendra, and my father was a cooper."

As he sits closer to Sypcal than he has at the formal meetings in the study of the Majer-Commander, Lorn can see the silver streaks in the red hair, and the fine lines radiating from around the commander's green eyes.

"No one was more surprised than I was when Rynst—he was Captain-Commander then—asked me to come from Assyadt to Cyad. I've been here seven years."

"All speak highly of you, ser," Lorn says.

"Everyone speaks highly of everyone in Cyad. How could it be otherwise?" A smile crinkles the corners of Sypcal's mouth.

"You suggest that it is only a question of how highly one is spoken?"

"And about what one is praised. I am praised for my grasp of tactics, Inylt for his grasp of logistics, Muyro for his understanding of the operations of the Mirror Engineers . . ." Sypcal shrugs. "My tactics mean little in Mirror Lancer Court."

"They mean much in the field," Lorn replies.

"You are kind," Sypcal says. "And we may speak of that later. I do have one question. You may choose not to answer it, but I would prefer to ask."

Lorn smiles wryly. "That sounds like a dangerous question."

Sypcal laughs, once. "Not that dangerous." He pauses. "Would you care to tell me why the Captain-Commander fears you?"

Lorn forces a laugh, one he hopes is genial enough. "I wasn't aware that I created fear, except perhaps among the Jeranyi and some of the junior lancers I commanded." He lets the smile that follows the laugh fade. "If what you say is true, I could hazard a guess, but it would only be such."

"Would you?" Sypcal raises his eyebrows.

Lorn decides to gamble, although it is not really that great a gamble. "Several officers have been sent to kill me under questionable circumstances. They failed."

"So it is said." Sypcal nods. "Will you indulge another question?"

Lorn nods.

"Do you know why you are in Cyad? You are arguably the best junior field commander in the Mirror Lancers. Had you been given command in Syadtar, we might not even have a problem with the barbarians, or certainly far less of one. The Majer-Commander, for all his faults, and he has many to accompany his strengths, has always been known to favor good field commanders in the field."

"But you are here," Lorn points out.

Sypcal shakes his head. "I was a good field commander. I know what it requires to be a great one, but I am older than I look, and tired, Majer. I suggested to Rynst that you be given the command at Syadtar—or the assistant command and then promoted. He refused, without giving a reason."

Lorn does not conceal the frown. "That, I cannot say. Commander Ikynd at Assyadt recommended that I be assigned to Cyad."

"And you doubtless drafted that recommendation?"

Lorn smiles. "Let us say that it was a mutual decision. I felt that I had too little experience to take on a large field command, and certainly not enough rank. I did not want another immediate assignment fighting, and it appeared likely that staying in the field would require that." He shrugs.

"And you had already had a port detachment." Sypcal nods. "From your viewpoint, it makes much sense. You could see your consort and family, and you could learn more about the lancers." He smiles again, openly and warmly. "Have you?"

Lorn nods. "A great deal. Enough to discover that there is much more to learn."

"There always is." Sypcal stands.

Lorn does as well.

"Thank you for indulging my curiosity. I'm pleased to know that you are capable of dealing with the unexpected. One can never be too careful in Cyad." Sypcal takes a step toward the door, and then turns back. "Oh . . . you might wish to know that Commander Lhary and the Captain-Commander were most pleased that you were assigned to Cyad, rather than a larger field command." Sypcal smiles once more, but only with his mouth. "I trust you will find use for that observation."

"I cannot say I am surprised by the preferences of the Captain-Commander. I had not known of Commander Lhary's preferences."

"Commander Lhary is most circumspect about both his preferences and his life. Circumspection is often necessary in Cyad. Good day, Majer."

"Good day, ser." Lorn bows slightly.

Once the door is closed, Lorn frowns. Has he waited too long? Has he been reacting too much to events? He laughs, half-bitterly. All he has done in Cyad is react.

Yet . . . what can he do? What should he do? Everything that Sypcal said bore the feel of truth, and Lorn could sense that the commander offered no barriers.

Action would be far more to his preference than to wait, but there is a time for action, and that time has not come, nor does Lorn yet know of any way to hasten it.

His eyes flick to the reports he must read, but he raises his eyes and glances out the window once more, for a long moment, before returning to the reading at hand.

CV

AFTER TAKING A last sip of the Alafraan, Lorn looks across the dining table at Ryalth, then at Jerial, who sits to Ryalth's right. Outside the open windows, the sky is darkening into purple, and a cooler breeze blows off the harbor from the south, strong enough to stir the air in the house, despite the walls that surround house and garden.

"You've been wanting to say something all through dinner," Jerial says. "I recognize that pose."

"It's serious," Ryalth adds. "You didn't want to spoil dinner, but that's why you asked Jerial."

"You both know me too well," Lorn admits with a rueful laugh. "I have no secrets from either of you."

"What is it, dear brother?" Jerial arches her dark eyebrows.

"Something is about to happen. Not immediately, but I think someone, or more than one person, has decided that my notoriety has faded enough." Lorn glances across the table from Jerial to Ryalth. "Can you have someone in-quire—very discreetly—about Commander Lhary?" he asks. "And a commander named Sypcal. I've been given hints that Lhary has contacts of the kind one must treat with great care. Sypcal seems to be what he is, but I'd like to know."

Ryalth and Jerial exchange glances.

"I can ask," Ryalth says.

"So can I," Jerial says. "It will take an eightday or so if you want none to know."

"The fewer know, the better. There is time . . . now." Lorn hopes there is time. "Also . . . I hate to say this . . . but I'd feel happier if we had some guards."

Ryalth laughs. "I could see your concerns rising over the past eightday, and Eileyt has reported more curiosity, especially from certain Austran traders. I've already taken certain steps."

"Austran traders?" Lorn frowns. "I thought the problem was from the Nordlans."

"It depends on which problem. Tasjan is associated with the Austrans."

"He's the Dyjani Clan head," Lorn says. "What does he have to do with the Mirror Lancers?"

"Nothing that one can see, save that he believes that the Mirror Lancers and the Magi'i bleed the merchanters. Eileyt told me yesterday that Tasjan has been hiring and training guards, supposedly for his ships, but he has four times the number of armsmen he needs for the ships, and yet he looks for more."

"Does he believe that, if there is too much unrest in Cyad, the merchanters will demand that a merchanter succeed Toziel in years to come?" asks Lorn.

"A merchanter on the Malachite Throne?" Jerial's mouth opens for a moment.

Lorn shrugs. "My suspicions are always raised by those who raise arms where there are none. Cyad is held not by the lancers, but by fear of the Magi'i and their firebolts and powers. If the chaos-towers fail, and in years to come, when the Emperor dies and there are no lancers in the city . . . ?"

Ryalth nods. "Some have suggested that."

"That would destroy Cyador," Jerial protests. "The Emperor—"

"—is far older than he looks," Lorn says. "You might discuss it with Aleyar sometime. That is what she said, and I felt she was telling the truth."

The dark-haired healer shivers. "No wonder you worry. This will all happen within a few years, will it not?"

"It may," Lorn says. "That is why I feel confounded. If I act too quickly, I will fail. Too late, and the same will happen."

"We cannot decide that tonight," Ryalth says firmly. "And with all of that to be considered, I have done a few things to make matters safer without being so obvious."

Lorn raises his eyebrows.

"We're getting several geese. A small flock, almost."

"Geese?"

"They are very good at warning of intruders, and they do multiply, so that we can occasionally have roast goose. They're also not as obvious as guards, and they can't be bribed."

"I've also noticed that there are thornbushes under all the lower-floor windows," Jerial says.

"Those were planted when I purchased the dwelling."

"Like the gate, and the bars on the doors to the bedchamber?" Lorn asks.

"I had this feeling . . ."

Lorn shakes his head. Again, he is reminded that there is more in Ryalth's background than any outsider might ever guess.

"We'll also be getting a second set of iron locks on the doors. Just the kind that you lock from the inside, not with keys. I have told the ironworker that while they may not be necessary today, tomorrow you could be sent back to the Grass Hills if they need a field commander." Ryalth looks at her consort. "I have made inquiries, and we will be taking on as houseman a lancer who recently received his stipend.

He's a cousin of Kysia, and most trustworthy. He also likes to garden. Everyone knows this. His children are grown, and his consort is a seamstress. They will have the lower rear quarters."

"You anticipate me well, my dear." Lorn shakes his head.

"Cyad is not like Inividra, where the enemy is known," the redhead replies. "Everything must be done in the open and yet without people suspecting. Someone I know and hold dear showed me this years ago."

"And forgot . . . I've been in the field too long," Lorn says with a snort.

"You can no longer forget," Jerial says. "Matters are indeed getting serious. I had not understood fully. Something else bears on this. I received a short scroll at the infirmary. It was from Rustyl, begging for permission to call upon me."

"You are the highest of the healers left without consort." Lorn winces, then frowns. "But he has as much as asked for Ciesrt's younger sister Ceyla as consort. You were there . . ."

"What he wants, I do not know, but I did grant him permission to call. I will let you know what I discover. Or if I discover nothing—that is most likely."

Ryalth shakes her head. "I could not live that way."

Both Lorn and Jerial smile and look at her.

The lady trader flushes. "That was a foolish statement. We are living that way, are we not?"

Lorn nods, sadly.

CVI

LORN GLANCES DOWN the white granite walls of the public corridor that leads from the section of the Quarter of the Magi'i where parents can bring their children to be tested for chaos-order talents, to the adjoining doorway. Beyond the door is a second corridor, one that leads to the building where the older student Magi'i receive their instruction.

Lorn steps through the doorway with confidence, and into the corridor that is usually empty in midmorning. A good hundred cubits farther, he steps through a side door, whose chaos-lock he slides aside. He smiles, briefly, noting to himself that sliding a chaos-lock is far easier than sliding a bronze or cupridium bolt. He hopes his order-chaos abilities have been long since disregarded by the Magi'i, or at least undervalued, as he closes the door behind him and walks along another, far less public way to a narrow set of white granite steps.

Lorn takes the side stairs, the ones he has scouted with his chaos-glass, and the ones that are used only by the Magi'i—not that there is any overt prohibition on use by others, since it requires the skills of a first- or second-level adept, or a renegade lancer magus, to unlock the doors.

At the top of the steps is a foyer, far smaller than those in Mirror Lancer Court, with a single table desk set on the shimmering polished-sunstone floor.

The fourth-level adept, painfully young-faced, glances up from his table, then looks again as he takes in the formal cream-and-green Mirror Lancer uniform and the insignia of a majer. His mouth works, then finally offers a question. "Ser?"

"Majer Lorn of the Mirror Lancers, son of Kien'elth. I am here to see the Third Magus." Lorn smiles pleasantly.

"I . . . I'm not sure . . ."

"Spare me the lie," Lorn says gently. "He is in. He may choose to see me; he may not; but let us keep that part honest. Just ask him if he will spare me a few moments."

"Ah, yes, ser. I'll see." The very junior magus scurries down the corridor his desk blocks, knocking at the second door on the left, and then stepping inside.

Lorn waits, a half-amused smile on his face.

Almost immediately, the fourth-level adept returns, trying not to shake his head. He looks at Lorn, the surprise evident on his young face. "He . . . he said he would see you, ser."

"Thank you." Lorn inclines his head slightly. "I appreciate your assistance."

"It's the second door, ser."

Conscious of the wondering gaze of the junior adept on his back, Lorn walks to the indicated door, which had been left ajar, and steps inside.

Liataphi stands as Lorn closes the door behind him. Lorn bows and straightens, waiting.

The fourth-floor study, like that of the Majer-Commander, has a view of the Palace of Eternal Light, save that the Palace is to the northwest, rather than to the east. The study is also smaller even than that of the Captain-Commander, and not all that much larger than the study Lorn had used as commander in Biehl. The furnishings are simple, ancient, but polished and unmarred, consisting of a wide table desk, four golden-oak bookcases set against the granite of the inner wall, and three wooden armchairs set before the desk and one behind it.

Liataphi himself looks at Lorn with dark circles under pale gray eyes that are nearly colorless, except for the hint of sun-gold that seems to come and go. His blond hair is thin, short and wispy, yet he is broad-shouldered and muscular, and half a head taller than Lorn. After a moment, he smiles, faintly, yet not coldly. "I must say that your appearance here does not totally surprise me. You are your father's son." He gestures to the chairs and reseats himself.

"Thank you for seeing me." Lorn takes the chair closest to the door.

"I must remind you, Majer, that for a junior member of the Majer-Commander's personal staff to seek out the Third Magus would be considered . . . unusual."

"Possibly, I should have done so earlier. My father left me a letter which suggested that I should pay my respects to you. I was transferred back to Cyad, as you may know, rather quickly, and I have not done this kind of work before . . ." Lorn lets the words drag out slightly.

"All that you say is true. As was all that your father said. But I suspect that there is far more there, or you would not be here."

Lorn smiles and nods. "My father also suggested that I would need to make contacts outside the Mirror Lancer Court, and he felt that you are and have always been trustworthy."

"That does not mean that I will agree with you—or with the Mirror Lancers," the Third Magus points out.

"No, ser, it does not."

"Might I ask why you would not seek out the father of your sister's consort?" A smile lightens Liataphi's eyes, but does not move his mouth.

"You could, ser, and I would respond that most times it has been unwise to go against my father's advice."

Liataphi laughs, a booming sound that fills the study. "Would that my daughters felt that way."

"Your third daughter respects and accepts your advice. I have never met the others, except Syreal, and that was but in passing."

"You and your consort have impressed Aleyar. Her judgment is usually sound, I have found, like that of her mother." Liataphi nods. "I am not unaware that you are a friend of young Tyrsal. Most times I would not pry, but . . . this time I will. Is he a good match for my daughter?"

Lorn considers for a moment. "I would think so. He is a good person. He is the most honest and the most thoughtful of all those I knew as a student mage. I do not know your daughter well, for I have had dinner with her and Tyrsal but several times, and that is why I could not venture more. I would that my sisters had shown interest in him."

"You believe that." Liataphi nods.

"Yes, ser. But I would not suggest that Tyrsal be considered a likely candidate for one of the Three Magi'i."

"You feel he is somehow deficient?" Liataphi's eyebrows lift.

"No. He is perceptive, intelligent, and trustworthy. He can discern plots and schemes from the slightest hint. I do not believe he is devious enough."

"Another fourth magus—like your sire?"

"He is much like my father in those ways," Lorn admits.

Liataphi laughs. "When I listen to you, Lorn, I almost wish I had had a son."

"You can talk to Tyrsal. He will listen and consider."

"From you . . . from your family, those are high words." Liataphi pauses. "Why did your sisters not choose him?"

"Jerial will choose none. Myryan cares too much to deceive Tyrsal about what she does not feel." Lorn feels that he must be honest and direct, but the revelations are dangerous. Still, he can no longer wait and react. He may have waited too long already.

Liataphi nods slowly. "You risk much in seeing me. Especially so directly."

"I risk less in coming directly. Often the Majer-Commander has members of his staff discuss matters with Magi'i, and I am very junior."

"Not so junior as you think. Still . . ." Liataphi's sad, pale eyes focus directly on Lorn. "What do you seek from me?"

"Your advice, and, if you feel so inclined, your support in the future."

Another of the booming laughs fills the study. When the sound dies away, Liataphi shakes his head. "In that . . . In that, you are most unlike your sire."

"I lack his ability to convince indirectly, ser. I can but ask."

"That you have. That you have." There is a pause. "I will do what I can, but I will not act against the spirit of the Magi'i. I will not oppose your efforts unless they threaten the Magi'i."

"I can ask for no more."

"You could, but you know I could not give it." Liataphi smiles. "And what of Tyrsal?"

"He understands, and . . . he is like my sire."

"I thought as much." Liataphi stands. "I think we should take a brief walk, if you do not mind. I would like to have you see an old acquaintance of yours. He is an assistant to the First Magus, and a cousin through consortship to the Second Magus, and he may be yet related through his own consortship of the Second Magus's daughter. I suppose that would make him a relative of yours as well, in more than one way." The Third Magus shrugs. "Then, most of us are related somehow."

"That must be Rustyl," Lorn says as he rises.

"He has risen quickly within the hidden side of the Quarter, and some say that Chyenfel is grooming him to be one of the Three." Liataphi walks to the door and opens it, turning down the corridor and away from the foyer.

"The hidden side? Would there not be more support for him were he more visible?" asks Lorn openly as he hurries to stay with the taller and long-legged Third Magus.

"I do not question the First Magus about some matters," Liataphi says lightly. "Neither does the Third Magus, although it is likely our reasons are somewhat different."

"The Second Magus . . . it's strange, but I've never actually met him," Lorn says.

"I am sure you will in time, especially with your sister as his son's consort."

"That may be. I'm told that Ciesrt has become more and more capable as a magus, and that he applies himself with great diligence."

"His diligence would be a credit to any magus, and his devotion to chaos, I would judge, even outstrips that of his sire." Liataphi slows as he takes another corridor that branches off to the left. He stops at a half-open door and knocks on the heavy golden-oak door itself, then pushes it open and steps into the small study that holds little more than a table desk, several bookcases, and three chairs, one behind the desk. A light warm breeze blows from the single narrow window.

"Ser!" Rustyl stands, his deep-set eyes flicking from Liataphi to Lorn, his narrow features impassive.

"Majer Lorn, I believe, was once a student with you." Liataphi offers a pleasant and superficial smile. "He is now on the staff of the Majer-Commander, and I found him quite unexpectedly, and thought I would bring him by to see you before he returns to Mirror Lancer Court."

"It's been quite some time, Rustyl," Lorn says easily. He gestures. "I see that you are a full first-level adept. That's quite an honor and accomplishment."

"Oh . . . thank you. I've been fortunate in what I've been able to do in the Magi'i."

"Were you involved in the Accursed Forest ward project? If so, I'd like to thank you," Lorn goes on. "Its success has made possible the transfer of more lancers to deal with the threat of the barbarians."

"That was an effort by the First Magus, and my part was minor," Rustyl admits. "At the time, I was assisting the Mirror Engineers in Fyrad."

Lorn detects the shading of truth in the response, but merely nods. "And now?"

"I do whatever the First Magus requires."

"As do we all," Liataphi says dryly.

"Well . . . whatever you do, I'm sure it is for the good of Cyador, and I know that you will continue that work. It's good to see you." Lorn smiles and nods.

"I'd best be escorting the Majer out of the Quarter, Rustyl, but I thought it would be a shame if I did not bring him by."

"Thank you, ser." Rustyl inclines his head. "It was good to see you again, Lorn."

"And you, too." Lorn can easily detect the lack of truth in Rustyl's parting words, and the dislike beneath their pleasant tone.

Liataphi and Lorn walk back down the corridor.

"I thought you should see Rustyl, if briefly," offers the older magus.

"Your kindness and perception are much appreciated," Lorn replies.

"In these times that verge on great change," Liataphi continues, "it is best to know how those who may affect you feel, and not how they are presented by yet others. For that reason alone, I am most pleased that you followed your father's suggestions." The Third Magus walks past his own doorway and toward the foyer. He does not halt until he has passed the desk and the fourth-level adept who sits there. "It has been good to see you, Majer. Convey my best to the Majer-Commander, and assure him that the Magi'i will do their best."

"That I will, ser."

"And perhaps my consort and I could host you and your consort at a dinner with your friend Tyrsal and Aleyar."

"I would like that, and I think Ryalth would as well. I have been out of Cyad so long that I fear she had thought we would never be able to meet people together."

"I will send an invitation from my consort to yours. That will make it more social."

"Thank you, ser."

"You are welcome. I imagine you can find your own way from the Quarter."

"That I can, ser."

Liataphi smiles, then nods for Lorn to depart.

Once again conscious of eyes on his back, Lorn turns and walks down the steps. Will his meeting with Liataphi lead to more? That, Lorn cannot say, except that Liataphi has offered as much encouragement as any of the Three Magi'i could, and Lorn senses neither deception nor malice in the man. He wishes he could say the same for Rustyl.

CVII

IN THE FULL light of a late afternoon in midsummer, Lorn unlocks the iron gate to the dwelling, steps inside, and locks it behind him. Once inside, he pauses to blot his forehead with the back of his hand. Then he steps around the privacy hedge and starts toward the cooling spray of the fountain, already savoring the cooler air inside the walls that surround the garden.

Sssssssss!!! Two white objects flutter out of the shade to his right. Lorn staggers as a dull blow slams into his right thigh. Something else jabs at his left calf.

His sabre is in his hand before he realizes the attackers are two large grayish white geese. He steps back, using the flat of the blade to blunt the jabbing beaks, although the cacophony of hisses and squawklike noises continues as he edges around the big birds and toward the veranda, and as the geese pursue him with darting bills and an occasional blow from a cocked wing.

He laughs as he climbs the steps onto the polished tiles under the veranda roof and turns to see Ryalth emerging from the foyer, also laughing.

"Dearest! How do you like our guards?" Ryalth straightens up, still laughing as she speaks.

"I doubt any will enter the house without their presence being well and fully announced."

"We will have to pen them, I fear, when we have company for dinner."

"That might be wise." Lorn glances back at the two hissing birds, who remain on the walk, their small eyes fixed on him.

"I'd like you to meet Pheryk." The redhead turns to the figure who has followed her.

A muscular man with iron-gray hair and a short square beard stands just beyond the door to the foyer under the roof of the veranda. Behind him is a slender white-haired woman, who continues to smile.

"Most would have run or slashed up the geese," Pheryk observes with a smile on his mouth and in the dark brown eyes.

"I was surprised," Lorn admits. "I didn't expect the geese so soon."

"You told me that sooner was better," Ryalth points out.

"Indeed I did." Lorn laughs once more.

Ryalth turns to the white-haired woman. "This is Ghrety. She's Pheryk's consort."

"We're most pleased that we can be of service," Ghrety says, bowing. "Never thought that little Ryalth would ever be a mighty trader lady."

"I take it that you've known Ghrety before." Lorn looks to his consort.

"Of course, dear. She was my nursemaid's sister, and I knew she'd consorted with a Mirror Lancer. Actually, that was how I found Kysia to begin with, because Ghrety recommended her. Kysia's Pheryk's cousin."

Lorn nods. Ryalth will not bring anyone into the household whom she cannot trust. "I'm am glad you are both here. I am sure Ryalth has already told you of my concerns."

"Yes, ser." Pheryk smiles. "Be good for us, as well. For now, young Phelyt and his consort can have our place without the old folk to worry about, and we'll have the pleasure of a young one about—and folk who need what we do."

"Young Kerial—he'll be needing clothes, too," adds Ghrety.

"All the time," Ryalth says. "He's growing so fast."

There is a moment of silence.

"Not that I'd be meaning to put sweetsap in your mouth, ser," offers Pheryk, "but when word got round about what you did to the barbarians, many were the plain lancers who cheered under their breath. More of that been done years back, never would we have had the troubles of the past years."

"That's what I thought," Lorn says. "I was fortunate enough to be where I could do something about it."

Pheryk smiles. "Once, ser, that be a happy accident. Twice be not."

Lorn shrugs. "Best I still claim fortune and such in Cyad."

"Aye." The gray-bearded man nods. "That I understand."

Lorn glances back at the geese, who have reduced their clamor to an occasional hiss, and half smiles, before turning to his consort. "Have you all any more surprises for me?"

"Well . . . we now have iron bolts, and Pheryk has put them in place on most of the doors."

"My da—he was a journeyman cabinet-maker, and I learned a thing or two before I joined the lancers," explains the gray-haired veteran. "Be a shame to scar the doors more than you must."

Lorn nods. Once more, Ryalth has done far better than he could have.

CVIII

IN THE FADING light of a late-summer afternoon, the first-level adept steps into the study of the High Lector and First Magus of Cyador. He bows. "Thank you for allowing me to intrude, ser."

"You seldom intrude, Rustyl. Or not without reason. You may sit." Chyenfel brushes back his silvering black hair. "What did you wish?"

The tall and blond Rustyl looks at the First Magus for several moments, as if deciding how to begin. "Did you know that Majer Lorn was in the Quarter the other day? He was meeting with the Third Magus."

"That is not surprising. The Third Magus often meets with the officers serving the Majer-Commander to advise them on matters such as the availability of firewagons and the services we provide them. Those are part of his duties."

"A mere majer?" Rustyl sneers, his deep-set eyes cold in his narrow face.

"Majer Lorn is perhaps the most effective field commander the Mirror Lancers have had in generations. The Majer-Commander knows that the lancers will soon have to do without firelances. Why would he not have such a commander talk to Liataphi?" Chyenfel smiles coolly. "The Majer-Commander is not unaware of the majer's background as a student magus. Do you think he would not employ such?"

"I had thought of that, ser. Yet . . ." Rustyl leaves the words hanging.

" 'Yet'? You believe there is more?" Chyenfel's voice offers a tone of mild curiosity. "What might that be?"

"That . . . I thought you might know, ser. The Third Magus did make a point of bringing Lorn to see me." Rustyl looks directly at the First Magus.

"To upset you, Rustyl. And he has clearly done that."

Rustyl smooths away the momentary frown on his face. "Yes, ser. Yet I do not see what purpose that served."

"Liataphi knows that I have given you duties to prepare you for greater responsibilities. Perhaps he wished to show you that there are others in Cyad to whom equivalent responsibilities have also been given. While Majer Lorn was not suitable for the Magi'i, that does not mean he lacks ability, and the Majer-Commander has recognized that ability."

Rustyl nods.

"And I have no doubts whatsoever that Liataphi wanted to

reintroduce you to Lorn not only to suggest that you are not so special as you believe yourself, but to use you to deliver the same message to me." Chyenfel smiles coldly. "And you have done so."

"I beg your pardon and indulgence, ser."

"That is acceptable, Rustyl. Liataphi has suggested that he does not wish to be First Magus. He has even hinted that he may not wish even to be Second Magus. He does not wish, however, that whoever may follow me be excessively arrogant, and this little stratagem was designed to call my attention to your stratagems." The First Magus steeples his fingers together above the polished golden-oak surface of his desk table. "You dislike Majer Lorn. The Third Magus knows this. Lorn is perceptive enough to sense this dislike. Now . . . Liataphi has been able to convey to the Majer-Commander, with little beyond a polite greeting, that you are arrogant and to be watched with care. You are one of my protégés. Therefore, I must be watched as well."

Rustyl is silent for a long time.

"You have a question, yet you have concerns about voicing it," Chyenfel finally says.

"Yes, ser. I honestly do not understand what the Third Magus would gain from this."

"I should not have to explain, Rustyl. Think." Chyenfel leans back and waits.

Rustyl pauses, and the quiet in the study draws out before he finally speaks. "Yes, ser. He makes it known that I am not worthy or ready of greater responsibilities. He casts doubt upon your judgment. He gains greater trust from the Mirror Lancers. But he is Third Magus, and not Second."

"And who of the Mirror Lancers is close to the Second Magus?"

"The Captain-Commander." Rustyl's face clears, and he nods.

"Exactly. Rynst will never trust the Second, and whom does that leave?" asks Chyenfel.

"What would you have me do, then, ser?"

"Nothing different, not for now. For if you change what you do, it will validate what the actions of the Third Magus have suggested."

"I see."

"I believe you do." Chyenfel smiles once more, if coolly. "Think upon this incident, Rustyl. Think upon it with great care."

"Yes, ser."

"You may go." Chyenfel looks blankly out upon the Palace of Eternal Light for some long moments after the first-level adept has left the study. Then he takes a deep breath.

CIX

IN THE DIMNESS of the upstairs study in the dwelling, Lorn rubs his forehead, then concentrates once more on the chaos-glass before him, trying to bring up the image of Rustyl. He smiles to himself. At least one advantage of using the glass in Cyad is that any of the upper-level adepts of the Magi'i might be suspect, and since none have felt his use of the glass, Lorn wagers that they will not know who follows them.

The silver mists appear, and then clear.

The blond figure of the first-level adept appears, in the same study where Lorn had seen him with Liataphi. Rustyl glances up from the study desk—and the glass before him—an annoyed expression on his narrow features. Even through the glass Lorn can see the hardness in the other's deep-set eyes. Rustyl looks down at the glass, clearly concentrating.

Hoping that Rustyl cannot use his glass to see who is screeing him, Lorn quickly releases the image. Then he almost casually slides the wooden cover across the glass, so that there appears before him but a wooden box, before leaning back and massaging his forehead with his left hand, then the back of his neck. Even after several moments, there is no feeling of the chill which accompanies a glass looking at him, and he slowly releases the breath he had not quite realized he was holding.

After blotting his forehead, for the evening is warm despite the ocean breeze that helps to cool the upper level of their dwelling, Lorn takes several more deep breaths before he leans forward and returns to the chaos-glass.

He concentrates again, and the silver mists part to reveal the red-haired Commander Sypcal sitting on the edge of a bed in a modest bedchamber. Sypcal is bare-legged and wears but an undertunic. The woman to whom he is talking is gray-haired. She is propped up with pillows and wears a high-necked white cotton gown. She smiles as the commander speaks.

Lorn releases that image quickly as well, but with a more cheerful feeling.

The next image he attempts is that of Rynst, but the gray-haired commander sleeps on his back in a bed next to a figure Lorn suspects is the Majer-Commander's consort.

The following image he calls up is that of the Captain-Commander. Luss sits alone at a table in a dwelling, with a bottle of wine before him. Lorn almost feels sorry for the man, even though he knows Luss has plotted for Lorn's failure more than once.

At last, Lorn slides the chaos-glass into the compartment at the back of the drawer, and stands. He has learned little, as he does most nights and afternoons, but he knows more of those with whom he deals, and those insights gain more value with each passing day.

He walks down the hall to the bedchamber, remembering to slide the iron bolt in place as he steps inside.

Ryalth looks up from the bed, where Kerial nurses at her breast. "Did you discover aught?"

"Very little new. Rustyl is using his glass—almost every night, I think, but I have not sensed him seeking us, and I wonder if he is so discreet that I cannot sense him."

Ryalth shakes her head. "He is of the Magi'i. A fallen student magus who is but a majer is no threat to a high first-level adept."

Lorn laughs. "That could be." He shakes his head, and his eyes go to the silver volume beside the bed. He picks it up, and flips through the pages until he finds the lines. He reads softly.

> There is no Cyad for souls of thought,
> who doubt the promises they have bought . . .
> . . . their faces of cupridium's silver-white
> reflect each other's chaotic light.
>
> Should Sampson pick this temple,
> here too, he would be blind,
> his eyes untouched,
> his simple trust
> lost in the reflections.

"I wonder yet about that verse," Ryalth says softly, easing Kerial into a different position for nursing.

"I don't even know who this Sampson was," Lorn says, "but I feel like he must have faced what we do."

"You are wise enough not to have simple trust, dear lancer," Ryalth says. "Not in Cyad." After a moment, she adds, "Even if you do want to think of Cyad as something special."

"It is. There's never been a city in the world like it."

"That is true," Ryalth concedes, "but it was created by people like any other."

Not quite, Lorn reflects, or Cyad would not exist.

Ryalth eases Kerial to her shoulder and pats his back. He burps softly, then yawns.

Lorn smiles at his consort.

"He's sleepy," she says softly.

"Good," murmurs Lorn. "Good."

"So am I," she says with a faint smile as she rises to slip their son into his bed. "Sleepy, I mean."

Lorn manages not to roll his eyes. He *can* use the sleep.

CX

LORN BOWS AFTER he closes the door and enters the study of the Majer-Commander. "Here are the reports of the last meetings, ser. You requested that I deliver them personally."

Without looking up from the scroll he peruses, Rynst gestures for Lorn to seat himself on the far side of the wide table desk. Lorn does so, his eyes momentarily taking in the cloudy morning, and the Palace of Eternal Light framed by the window behind the senior lancer officer.

Rynst finally sets down the scroll and shakes his head. "What did you find out when you met with the Third Magus?"

Although he had not mentioned the meeting to anyone, Lorn is scarcely surprised that Rynst has discovered that it took place. "Not that much, ser. He is troubled by the confidence that the First Magus places in Rustyl, and he expressed a certain lack of surprise that I had never met the father of my sister's consort."

"Why did you go?"

"My father's last letter to me, the one he left in his papers, requested that I pay my—and his—respects."

Rynst nods. "Do you intend to visit him again?"

"No, ser. Not in his study. Not unless you have a duty for me."

"I note a careful phrasing there."

"My best friend is likely to become the consort of his daughter. If this happens, I may see the Third Magus again."

"Ah . . ." Rynst smiles, somewhat more warmly. "He is the one with whom you spar."

"Yes, ser. He is very good."

"That is what Commander Lhary said. In fact, the commander suggested that the young man might have made a good lancer officer."

"I told Tyrsal that, ser, but he did not believe me. If I might relay the commander's observation . . . ?"

"You certainly may." The Majer-Commander pauses, as if to signify his desire to change subjects. "Majer . . ." Rynst draws out the title.

"Yes, ser?"

"I have not spoken to you about your report. Nor will I for a time."

"Yes, ser." Lorn waits.

"The Captain-Commander has expressed some interest. Has he inquired of you?"

"He asked if I had completed it. I told him I had submitted a draft and that you had made no comments."

"A draft. Very good phrasing, Majer. And what did he say then?"

"He said that you would read it, and that you would use it in the best fashion to benefit the Mirror Lancers."

"Anything more?"

"Only that I should not expect recognition for my work, that the Mirror Lancer Court was not the place for such. I told him that such was what I expected."

Rynst glances at the reports Lorn has set on the desk.

Lorn eases them across the polished wood.

"Luss is right. For that you can be thankful." Rynst nods brusquely. "You may go."

"Yes, ser." Lorn rises and bows before turning and departing the study.

CXI

RYALTH PATS HER hair into place as the hired carriage rolls eastward along the Road of Perpetual Light, past the Sixth Harbor Way East. "I still wonder why the invitation was sent to Ryalor House."

"First, because it is a social occasion, and second," Lorn continues, "because a lady trader who heads a house is more important than a mere junior majer in the Mirror Lancers."

"You will turn my head with such words." She puts out a hand to steady herself as the carriage turns uphill.

"I do hope so."

"You don't think Jerial minds taking care—"

"If Jerial minded," Lorn says dryly, "we'd both know it."

"Yes. We would." Ryalth laughs. She shakes her head. "I still can't believe that Rustyl had the nerve to ask her if she would be his consort when he had already asked Ceyla."

"He didn't ask that seriously. He did it to try to upset her, and me."

"He picked the wrong healer for that," Ryalth says. "If it had been Myryan . . ."

Lorn nods. "I'm glad it wasn't."

"I can see why you don't care for him."

"He still could be dangerous with Chyenfel supporting him."

"Only because his mistakes will hurt innocent people." Ryalth snorts.

Lorn isn't sure. Rustyl is far from stupid, and what appears to be a stupid maneuver must have a deeper purpose. Lorn just can't figure out what it might be, unless it's a blunt attempt to force Lorn to act against Rustyl. Or one designed to show utter contempt . . . which may be the most likely explanation of all, Lorn reflects.

The hired carriage rolls to a stop opposite the gate of sunstone sculpted into the semblance of a bower wreath. Behind and to the west of the stone flowers of the gate-wreath rises a three-story dwelling. Gate and house are just west of the corner where the Ninth Way East meets the Road of Prosperity. Liataphi's three-story house is but two blocks from the one Lorn had grown up in—now inhabited by Vernt and Mycela.

As she steps from the carriage, Ryalth looks down at the wide blue shimmercloth trousers, the white shirt, and the green-trimmed blue vest and blue boots she wears. Then she glances at Lorn. "How do I look?"

"Wonderful."

"You say that because you love me."

"I love you, but you still look wonderful." Lorn looks to the coachman. "It will doubtless be well after dark."

"You've paid handsomely, ser," replies the balding driver. "I'll be here. Be much easier on me than driving all over Cyad."

The two step through the gate and up the halfscore of steps to the outside privacy screen, where Lorn rings the bell.

Almost immediately, Lorn hears the door open, and the broad-shouldered Liataphi steps around the screen and bows. "Welcome. Do come in. Tyrsal and Aleyar are already up in the sitting room." He bows again to Ryalth. "Lady trader, all have remarked upon your abilities, but none have mentioned your beauty."

"Thank you." Ryalth flushes slightly.

Lorn smiles.

"You are most fortunate, Lorn, to have a consort of talent and beauty."

"I am, and even more fortunate that she was kind enough to accept me as a consort when I asked."

"As I recall, your father was surprised. Pleasantly so, but surprised." Liataphi nods. "We should not be talking down here. Do come along."

As they follow the Third Magus up the circular stone staircase, Lorn murmurs, "I said that you looked wonderful."

"You were right, but it's pleasant to hear it from someone else."

The redheaded Tyrsal rises from the settee as Lorn and Ryalth step through the archway. "Greetings."

Aleyar rises and bows to Ryalth, then to Lorn. The older and white-haired woman, wearing a white-and-green shimmercloth tunic and trousers and sitting in the armchair to the right of the healer, nods pleasantly.

"This is my consort Lleya," Liataphi says. "You know Tyrsal and Aleyar, of course."

"We're pleased to meet you, Lady Lleya," offers Ryalth.

"I would appreciate it greatly if you would do away with honorifics," Lleya says warmly. "We must deal with them all too much away from home."

Lorn and Ryalth seat themselves on the second settee, upholstered in white and green.

"You are a healer?" Lorn asks Lleya.

"I no longer go to the infirmary, for there are others, like Aleyar and your sisters, who are far better than I."

"She's still good," Aleyar affirms.

"My most loyal daughter."

"Most accurate," Liataphi says. "Were you a poor healer, she would have said nothing."

"Healing takes more energy as one ages." Lleya touches her snow-white hair. "So I work with the herbs in my garden. I do have a special kind of brinn. I've managed twenty generations of it, and each more powerful than the last."

"Your astra is also good," Aleyar adds.

"Before we have dinner, Lorn, Ryalth . . . there is one thing." Tyrsal turns slightly red. "Outside of the families, you should be the first to know. Aleyar has consented to be my consort."

"That's wonderful," Lorn says, feeling fully the warm smile that spreads across his face.

"I'm so glad for you two," Ryalth adds.

Tyrsal glances at Lorn, but Lorn just smiles.

Tyrsal still flushes.

"You two!" Ryalth chides the younger men.

Lorn flushes and manages to swallow a laugh. "My apologies, my dear. And to you, Aleyar."

"Whatever it is, you two rascals should bury it," Lleya mock-scolds.

"If we don't," Lorn replies, "my lady trader is likely to bury me."

Tyrsal laughs. "She's the only one ever to get the better of you."

"And I hope I'm wise enough to remember that," Lorn counters.

"On those words, perhaps we should move to the dining area," suggests Lleya, rising from her chair.

"Excellent idea," seconds Liataphi.

Lorn and Ryalth sit together on one side of the table, with Aleyar and Tyrsal on the other side, and Liataphi and Lleya on each end.

"This is a mild and traditional lamb loaf in lemon citron sauce," Lleya says, "with grass-rice and chopped quilla."

Lorn has never been that fond of quilla, but he helps himself to the rice and quilla, as well as the lamb, and is surprised to find that however the normally oily root has been prepared, has left it merely tangy and mild and a complement to the slight bitterness of the dark grass-rice. "This is excellent."

"Very good," Tyrsal adds.

"If the recipe is not a family secret . . . ?" Ryalth ventures.

"Oh . . . I'd be happy to share it with you," Lleya says. "Or Aleyar can show you. She prepares it as well as I do—perhaps better."

"As well . . . if I am fortunate," says the blonde healer.

Lorn takes another chunk of the sun-nut bread, ignoring Ryalth's knowing smile. "I cannot say how much we appreciate the invitation. After so many years of being away from Cyad, it is so good to be able to dine with friends and their family. I was always here such a short time, that we scarcely saw more than my family."

"I was so sorry to hear about your parents," Lleya says. "They were such good people, and both will be missed far more than most will ever know."

"Thank you," Lorn says. "I miss them. I was lucky to have them." He inclines his head to Ryalth. "My lady was not so fortunate. Her parents perished in a shipwreck when she was a child."

Lleya nods. "That is hard."

"I wondered . . ." Tyrsal says, "but I didn't wish to intrude."

"My father was a merchanter in Fyrad," Ryalth says. "Then I came here to live with my aunt. She died the year before I met Lorn."

"You two have known each other for a long time, have you not?" asks Lleya. "You act that way. Or are you so well-known to each other by closeness of spirit?"

"Both," Lorn says quickly. "I met Ryalth when I was still a student magus. It took me a time to appreciate her as fully as I now do."

Lleya glances at Ryalth, as if asking for the redhead's view.

Ryalth laughs, gently. "I fear it also took me much time to appreciate him. I also did not think it appropriate to encourage a magus. Or even a Mirror Lancer."

"But he obviously persisted," replies Lleya.

"There was no one else to compare to her. For me, there still is not," Lorn says.

"That's true," Tyrsal says. "I didn't know who she was when we were students, and later, but he never looked at anyone else."

After a moment of silence, Lleya glances at Lorn. "Isn't it rather strange for you to be on the personal staff of the Majer-Commander . . ." The older woman shakes her head. "I am afraid that did not come out the way I intended. What I meant is that you have accomplished a great deal very young, and most of those with whom you work in Mirror Lancer Court are far older. Does that not seem strange?"

"I can't say that I've had the time to think of that," Lorn says. "I knew I would probably be the youngest officer there, and the most junior, and what I do is basically make matters easier for the Majer-Commander. I take notes at meetings and follow up with the other officers to make sure that the material the Majer-Commander wants is supplied." He shrugs. "It's a job for a junior majer. You have to know enough to understand what he needs and wants, and be young enough not to worry about running errands."

Liataphi chuckles. "Would that some first- and second-level adepts—not you, Tyrsal—understood such."

Lleya turns to Ryalth. "I am sure everyone asks you what it is like to be a lady trader, when there are and have been so few. I would rather ask, if I might, what advantages being a woman provides."

"No one has asked that." Ryalth tilts her head, as if pondering. "I would judge several. Caution is one, for a woman can make fewer errors, and so, I learned caution early. That I am a woman allows me greater caution, when often, were I a man, others might question my resolve." Ryalth smiles. "Thus, I can plead caution where a trade is unwise, and still be bold where boldness is necessary."

"Do you think more caution is needed in these days?" asks Liataphi.

"Greater care, I would judge," Ryalth says.

"In trade or in dealing with other traders?" The eyes of the Third Magus betray a slight twinkle.

"Both." Ryalth takes a sip of the wine. "The fortunes of

trade are changing, and that means some houses will benefit, and others will not."

"How is trade changing?" asks Tyrsal. "Cyador produces the same goods it always has, and is not that true of other lands?"

"Hydlen has had a most dry year, but last year they had a surplus of crops when there was a blight in Hamor. So coins are plentiful in Hydlen. Many factors are scurrying to purchase contracts on the exchange, knowing that grains and dried fruits will bring more. The larger growers know this as well, and they will not sell at last year's prices. But the Emperor raised the tariffs on goods and grains leaving Cyador." Ryalth shakes her head. "Many will lose on such wagers."

"What would you do?"

"I already purchased some few contracts on foods that will not ship well, such as pearapples and the softer white corn-wheat."

Tyrsal laughs. "Because everyone will be shipping the other to Hydlen, and the prices of what remains will rise?"

"One wagers so." Ryalth shrugs. "I doubt I will lose, but there could be storms, or floods, or eightdays of hot dry winds from tomorrow until harvest. That is why I have been more cautious than some."

"Is Tasjan one of those who would trade in Hydlen?" inquires Liataphi.

"He might. The Dyjani trade everywhere, and he has many ships, both for the coastal trade and the long-haul ocean vessels."

"He is said to plan for years into the future," says Liataphi. "Or so I have heard. Unlike those of Bluyet House, who apparently rely upon the use of golds where golds should not be used."

"That trait has served them ill in the past several years," Ryalth says.

"Will Vyanat'mer take clan status from them?"

"I doubt he will do such," Ryalth replies. "He has not spoken to me or any I know about such. The Dyjani continue to strengthen their ships and coffers, as do the Yuryan Clan, as you must know. Because Vyanat'mer is of the Hyshrah, all that his house does is watched most closely. So he would not wish to strengthen his rivals by casting down Bluyet House." Ryalth shrugs. "That could happen, but I would not wager my golds on that."

Liataphi nods. "Nor I. A wise observation."

Ryalth looks to Aleyar. "Have you two set a date for the consorting ceremony?"

"The fourth eightday after the turn of fall, we think. We will know in a day or two. Mother wanted to see if her sisters will be able to travel from Summerdock then."

"Aleyar was always their favorite, and this will be the first formal consorting we've seen."

Lorn nods, understanding all too well the events hidden behind those words.

"You will be coming, will you not?" asks Aleyar, looking at Ryalth.

"We will be there," Ryalth says.

"If . . . if the Majer-Commander does not send me somewhere," Lorn adds. "He hasn't said anything, but I am a Mirror Lancer."

"Ryalth will be there," Aleyar says. "And Jerial and Myryan will be at the dinner."

Lorn smiles. "I will do my best."

"You had better," Tyrsal says with a laugh.

Ryalth smiles.

"Now . . . for dessert," Lleya announces, as two serving girls begin to remove the platters and dishes from the table, "we are having peach cake with a special glaze."

Ryalth glances at Lorn and smiles.

He smiles back sheepishly.

CXII

THE SPARE AND slender Toziel walks slowly into the robing
room that adjoins his and the Empress's bedchamber. There
he slips off his outer robe of silver, carefully hanging it on
the carved golden-oak frame that has served such a purpose
for generations of Emperors. Then he removes his boots and
walks toward the high bed. He uses the bed step to climb up.

He stretches out slowly, then murmurs. "Chaos-light, I'm
tired."

Leaning back on the pillows that are arranged to support
him in a half-sitting, half-reclining position, he closes his eyes.

Ryenyel pulls a chair around to his side of the bed, and
seats herself. "The audience was long. You should have
stopped it sooner."

"I know. I heard your cough."

"I coughed but once," she says. "That was a risk itself. I
cannot help you, my dearest, if you will not heed my signals."

"I dared not leave then, not when Chyenfel had just suggested that I might consider candidates for a new Hand,"
Toziel ventures.

"Nor when Rynst asked for more Mirror Lancers? Nor
when Vyanat questioned once more the source of the golds
for those lancers . . . ?" The Empress sighs. "There will always be such questions. They will last long after we are
gone."

"Long after I am, certainly." Toziel's voice reveals a self-
deprecating dryness. "Yet still I must act as though I will be
on the Malachite Throne longer than my advisors will be
there to advise me."

"You may have to be."

"Why do you say such?" Toziel is the one to cough, almost doubling up in agony before he slowly leans back on the pillows once more.

Ryenyel waits until his breathing returns to a steady rhythm before she speaks. "Rustyl grows impatient. So does Luss, and Tasjan is gathering and paying armsmen, and his chief guard is developing his own contacts. Tasjan will soon have more trained armsmen near Cyad than there are lancers within two days' travel."

"And I should do nothing?"

"Dearest, you can but tell others. You have no Hand."

"If I tell the Majer-Commander, then . . ." Toziel's words fade.

"He will order in two companies of Mirror Lancers and put them under Majer Lorn, and the piers will run red with blood."

"So . . . how can we get word to the lady trader who is the head of Ryalor House, and how do we make sure that the lancers are on their way?"

"Majer Lorn does not like to kill, but he will not hesitate if he thinks it necessary," Ryenyel states.

"You have proof?" Toziel smiles wanly.

"My dear . . . what I know and what I can prove are not the same. It is most difficult to prove someone died with no body. The only killing he admits to is that of Majer Dettaur, and most would admit that was justified. The dead majer left too much in writing, and too many orders designed to kill young lancers in order to discredit Lorn. It has taken years to amass what I know, and there is nothing of substance to that, only rumors and words. There is no proof that Lorn killed a trader named Halthor when he was but a student, or Shevelt, or Majer Maran, or Sub-Majer Uflet, yet in all cases, except that of Shevelt, he was among the last to see each alive."

"And Shevelt—I thought he was killed because he knew that Bluoyal was behind the sale of sabres to the Jeranyi . . . the plated sabre?"

Ryenyel shrugs. "It could be. It could also be that Shevelt had talked openly of forcing himself on Lady Ryalth to humble her, and that Shevelt died while young Lorn was in Cyad."

"Or it could be that Kernys, or one of the smaller clan heads, made certain that young Lorn knew such . . ." Toziel coughs, then winces.

"Kernys . . . or others . . ."

"Can Lorn be persuaded that Tasjan offers a similar threat to her?" asks Toziel. "Can that persuasion not come from the Palace, even indirectly?"

"Little persuasion will be needed. Tasjan dislikes women in any position of power. We will think on how to encourage him to make his dislike of Ryalor House somewhat more well-known. I do not think it will be difficult to avoid any trails." Ryenyel shrugs.

"What if I suggested that the Majer-Commander bring two companies of lancers to Cyad as a demonstration of might for the outland traders—perhaps conduct maneuvers near the piers somewhere, using firelances?"

"And have Majer Lorn set up the demonstrations?" Ryenyel arches her eyebrows.

"It is most transparent, yet who could fault it with the failure of the fireships?"

"Would Rynst balk at Majer Lorn?" asks the Empress.

"I would merely ask him who he would place in charge of the forces."

"And ask questions?"

"Again . . . it could be transparent, but we might not have to. Would he want a senior commander or the Captain-Commander in direct command? Or someone who owes their position to him?"

"Perhaps you should bring that up . . . tomorrow. I will find a way to get word about Tasjan to the majer."

Toziel nods. After a moment, he closes his eyes.

Only then does the Empress frown, but she stands, and moves toward the bed, her fingers touching the Emperor's temples lightly. In time, she seats herself, nearly as pale as the Emperor had been, but his breathing is stronger, and the worst of the pallor has left his face.

CXIII

ON THE LATE-SUMMER day, Lorn glances up from the Majer-Commander's conference table. Through the windows on the north side of the study, he can see dark clouds rolling out of the north and toward the harbor. To his left sit three commanders, Shykt on the north side of the table, with Muyro and Dhynt on the south, the same side as Lorn, who studies the three from the armless chair to Rynst's left.

Rynst clears his throat. "Commander Dhynt?"

The older commander with the rugged features and pock-marked face looks toward the senior Mirror Lancer officer. "We have four fireships operating, but the tower on the *Firestar* is showing signs that it may fail at any time."

The swarthy Muyro raises his eyebrows. "I was not aware that any but the Magi'i would make such predictions, and they seldom are that accurate."

"We keep records, and with six fireships having failed over the past five years or so, we have some idea of what occurs. The amount of chaos-energy produced by the chaos-tower within the ship shows changes, often from moment to moment, far more than in previous operations. Occasionally, there are bursts of power that destroy the storage cells. This chaotic chaos, if you will, becomes more and more prevalent." Dhynt offers Muyro a cold smile. "Then the tower fails, and we have a ship good for little more than scrap."

"After having fireships that no one could match for near-on tenscore years, we now must resort to sailing vessels with cannon? Is that what you are all telling me?" asks Rynst.

"There may be other possibilities," offers Muyro.

"What are those possibilities?" counters the Majer-Commander. "Why have I heard nothing of them? If they are possible, why are we building three sail-propelled warships?"

"Golds," replies the curly-haired and thin-faced Commander Shykt.

"It is true. The Emperor has said that he will not commit more golds to any other warships until the first one is completed and tested," Rynst says.

"Then it will be next summer—or fall a year from now before we have more than three of the new vessels," replies Commander Dhynt.

"Longer," suggests Shykt. "The hulls are narrow, the keels deep, and the masts tall. No one is sailing a ship such as that. There will be difficulties. It is unwise to build many of an untested vessel."

"It is unwise to have no way to protect our merchanter vessels," says Rynst. "Or so the Merchanter Advisor says."

"Of course, he would want to invoke the power of warships," Shykt replies. "But I would note that the Hamorians send long-haul vessels across the Eastern Ocean, and their traders do well without warships."

"I beg to you to explain what you mean, Commander," says Muyro smoothly. "Surely, you are not suggesting we need no protection."

Shykt shakes his head. "I did not say that. I suggested we need no protection against the Hamorians, at least not directly."

Rynst nods. "We need protection against those nearer—the barbarians, the Gallosians, even perhaps the Hydlenese. There, sailing vessels will suffice—if they sail as planned, if the powder cannon discharge as designed."

"Still, those are many *if*'s, ser," suggests the iron-haired Dhynt.

"Indeed." Rynst studies the three commanders in turn, beginning with Shykt and ending with Muyro. "You three are here to provide answers and strategies which will reduce uncertainty. You are not here to offer ways to increase uncertainty."

Shykt looks evenly at Rynst. "I cannot provide certainty in a land where every gold for certainty and security is grudged. I can offer strategies, and I have done so. To make a strategy work requires golds—or greater mastery of chaos and order. We are losing the devices which allowed us to use chaos. We must either accept greater uncertainty or greater costs. Or find another way in which we can employ chaos. It must be a way that others cannot use." Shykt pauses. When no one else speaks, he adds, "I am not a magus or a Mirror Engineer. I do not know the ways of chaos. So I have proposed what I do know." He nods to Muyro. "You know something about chaos and engineering. What do you propose, Commander of the Mirror Engineers?"

Muyro's eyes smolder. He clears his throat. "As I have said for the past two years, no one has been able to rebuild or to operate a chaos-tower that has failed. Never. We have looked through all the ancient archives and found nothing that the Magi'i can employ."

Lorn holds back a frown, and glances from Muyro to Shykt, and then to Dhynt.

Dhynt nods. Shykt frowns.

"You have some question of that, Commander Shykt?" asks Rynst, his voice almost lazy in its gentleness of tone.

"Nothing that the Magi'i can use—or nothing that they will use?" asks Shykt.

"What do you mean by that?" asks Muyro.

Shykt turns to Rynst. "If I might . . . Majer Lorn successfully eliminated the threat of Jeranyi raids. He did so, if I read his reports correctly, by first using multicompany patrols to reduce the number of raiders near the Grass Hills. He then combined his forces and raided Jerans, and destroyed the port of Jera to stop the flow of iron blades to the barbarians. All of these were tactics available to his predecessors. No one else attempted such, because such actions were counter to accepted practices. I do not know the secrets of the Magi'i, but I must question, because I am the sort who does so, whether there are not other means to harness chaos to our benefit. Perhaps these techniques are also counter to Magi'i custom and practice." Shykt smiles ruefully. "From what little I understand, even the First Magus faced great opposition within the Magi'i for his project to put the Accursed Forest to sleep, and from what little I know, that project employed traditional manipulation of chaos." The curly-haired commander shrugs.

"It is a fair question," Rynst acknowledges. "Do you have an answer, Commander Muyro?"

"I am sure that the Magi'i have investigated every possibility."

"Just as you had looked into the deflection of blades with the new shields?" asks Rynst, his tone of voice between sarcasm and irony.

Muyro flushes, a dark unhealthy color suffusing his swarthy face.

"I trust you will consult with the Mirror Engineers and the Magi'i about this." Rynst smiles gently. "We must adopt new weapons and doubtless suffer higher casualties. I think it only just that the Magi'i consider that which might do the same for them. If they do not, then the barbarians will pour in, and as the Magi'i should know, the first to go under those iron blades will be those in white."

"Yes, ser." Muyro's voice is level, but his face remains flushed in anger.

"That will do for this meeting." Rynst rises. "Good day."

Lorn rises, waits for the commanders to leave, then gathers his papers, and bows to the Majer-Commander before he turns to go. "By your leave, ser?"

"I saw your eyes, Majer. You were of the Magi'i. Know you of any such possible ways to better harness chaos?"

"I do not know how such might be accomplished today, ser. I do know that there were rumors of other ways of using chaos among the Magi'i, but I never became an adept, nor did I ever hear more than rumors as a student." Every word Lorn says is true.

Rynst nods. "Perhaps Majer Muyro can find something. I have my doubts, but he will raise the question. Over time, even that will help." The Majer-Commander laughs, once. "One hopes. You may go."

Lorn is thankful that none of the commanders remain on the fifth-floor open foyer, and he hurries down to his own study, nodding to Fayrken as he passes.

"Another meeting report, ser?"

"Another report, Fayrken. This one will be short."

"That be good, ser. Majer Hrenk has a long report about the piers at Fyrad."

Lorn steps into his own study and sets his notes on the desk.

At the low roll of thunder, he turns to the window, where the first fat drops of rain strike the ancient panes—the large droplets hitting almost with the force of hail.

What can he do? It is clear from the indirect signs he sees that the Cyad he has known is changing. The merchanters are having trouble trading against the outlanders and want lower tariffs. The barbarians will threaten again, unless action is taken. The Emperor is failing, perhaps dying. The Magi'i are not changing, nor do the Mirror Lancers—except for perhaps Commander Shykt and the Majer-Commander—wish to offer anything new to the Emperor or the others who advise Toziel.

He has to do something, but what he can do is little enough ... for now. He stands in his small study, a floor below the Majer-Commander, feeling that he could do more. Yet his father advised against approaching the Emperor. Even if he goes against his father's wishes, he has no way to gain access to the Palace of Eternal Light—except as an intruder, and that is not exactly to his benefit.

Equally dangerous is the implication that there are reasons why the Magi'i have not offered another way to use chaos to replace the fireships and firewagons. Now it is clear that he must study his father's papers once more, even more carefully, to see how he might advance the plans and suggestions contained therein. The papers offer solutions, yet his father could not advance them, even as Hand of the Emperor. Is there any way Lorn can?

He looks at the stack of notes and takes a deep breath, then pulls out the chair and seats himself. First, he must write the report of the meeting.

CXIV

ONCE IN HIS dwelling study, Lorn sets the box from his father on his desk and leafs through the stack of papers, his fingers fumbling as he scans the sheets, looking for a section he has read several times, hoping that the section says what he has recalled.

"What are you doing?" asks Ryalth from the doorway, juggling Kerial on her shoulder. "You didn't even try to find me. I was bathing Kerial. He'd spit up and made a mess."

Lorn lowers the papers. "I'm sorry. I've been thinking about this all afternoon. We had a meeting today. Maybe I have an answer. These papers. You remember we talked about the engines—the iron chaos-heat–transfer steam engines—they talked about it . . ." Lorn finds his words trying to tumble out faster than he can think about them.

Ryalth laughs. "Wait . . . the papers will be there in a moment. I've never seen you trying to talk so fast."

Lorn takes a deep breath. "You remember we talked about why no one had tried to build the chaos-fired steamships?

Why no one ever talked about them? At the meeting today, Commander Shykt asked a strange question. The others thought it was strange. He asked whether the Magi'i could use chaos to build a better warship or weapons. He wasn't that direct, but that was what he was hinting at . . ."

"Do you think he knows?"

"No. He knows something else. What he understands is that the Magi'i don't want to do things that might limit their power."

"That's hardly strange. No one does. Traders don't do trades that will cost them more than they make."

"There's a difference," Lorn points out. "Cyador will become far poorer, perhaps even fall to the barbarians, if the Magi'i do not use their powers. Shykt was suggesting that they would rather see Cyador fall than use their powers in a new way."

Ryalth laughs, still patting Kerial on the back, but the sound is ironic. "You are remarkable. You were thrown out of the Magi'i because you would not put their ways above everything. You are surprised that they will not change?"

Lorn shakes his head. "I had hoped for better."

"Your father tried to make things better in his own way, and he was powerful. He could not even keep you in the Magi'i."

"Not safely," Lorn admits. "When you put it that way . . . Still, it is hard to believe that they would let the land die." He crooks his lips. "I should know better. It took the First Magus years, from all accounts, to get the Magi'i to agree to his plan for the Accursed Forest, and they only agreed to that when it was clear that nothing else would work and that they would lose those towers anyway."

"What did your father say?"

"That was what I was looking for."

"You look, and I'll tell Kysia to ready dinner. Then you can tell me. I *think* Kerial is going to go to sleep."

"I hope so." Lorn smiles.

The redhead shakes her head again, ruefully and lovingly.

As Ryalth leaves the small upstairs study, Lorn returns to paging through the sheets in the old carved wooden box, slowly and more methodically, forcing himself to read at least enough of each page to ensure that it does not deal with the material he seeks.

Roughly a third of the way through the material he stops.

As it is described on the pages which follow, once the chaos-towers fail, all is not lost. Those senior in the Magi'i will claim that no other devices, such as chaos-steam transfer engines, can be constructed, because iron and chaos are not compatible. Too great a closeness between iron, order, and Magi'i is not desirable, but it is not necessary. . . .

. . . to fabricate such a device requires the extraction of order from the natural world, and its infusion into the iron as it is being forged. When I was young, I worked with a smith. He is long since dead, and he knew little beyond what his forebears had taught him, and yet we did indeed forge a blade out of iron—darker than most, and of inordinate strength.

I could not touch the blade, not without suffering ferric poisoning, but there was no need to do so . . .

Lorn continues to read, nodding as he does.

The First Magus—the one two before Chyenfel—did not wish to consider such a means of finding an alternative to the chaos-towers, for none of the chaos-towers had failed, and there was seen no need to do such. He was also concerned about use of such a method when it could be used to forge blades and shields that might well prove a useful shield against chaos-bolts. Once the method was used, he said, all the barbarians would learn, and then Cyador would have defenses far less effective against the northerners.

Now . . . the towers are failing, and so am I. Perhaps worse, because I once looked into the matter, the reference material was removed from the archives of the Quarter and burned. Most of it I had copied previously, and that is what follows this explanation . . .

The Mirror Lancer majer shakes his head. "The idiots. . . ."

. . . do not attempt to bring this to light directly, but find one among the Magi'i who will see it for the salvation of the Magi'i, and not as a threat. For, if the Magi'i retain this as a secret, then they will retain a manner of power that they would not otherwise do . . .

A voice calls from below. "Lorn . . . dinner is almost ready." "I'll be down." Lorn looks at the notes, half smiling.

He has some copying to do . . . a great deal . . . because he cannot let the originals into anyone else's hands. Not when they are all that remain.

Copying his father's "memoirs" will be time-consuming, but certainly less risky than using a chaos-glass, for anyone who uses a glass to observe him will but see him writing, and that is certainly expected of a junior majer.

He shakes his head once more as he thinks of Muyro and the First Magus his father had confronted. Then he closes the box and stands.

CXV

LORN GLANCES AT the polished blond wood of Vernt's table desk, the same desk that had been their father's. Vernt has even left it in the same place in the study, and most of the books are the same. The chaos-glass is Vernt's, larger and more prominently·displayed on the left side of the desk. On one of the side tables, there is also a frame that contains a drawing of Vernt wearing the whites of a first-level adept. Where Vernt found an artist, Lorn has to wonder, unless perhaps that is one of Mycela's hidden talents. Lorn feels the woman must have some.

"I hear you are doing well over in Mirror Lancer Court," Vernt says conversationally.

"I'm very quiet." Lorn laughs. "How are things going for you?"

"As expected, I suppose." Vernt frowns.

"In short, everyone's worried about the chaos-towers failing, especially the one in the Quarter, and no one has an answer."

Vernt shakes his head. "You know I shouldn't say anything."

"You didn't. I did, and it's true. We have meeting after meeting. All too many deal with how we will handle the barbarians without firelances and firewagons, and what kind of ships can replace the fireships. I can't imagine all those meetings with the Majer-Commander, the Captain-Commander, and all the senior commanders, not unless things are getting serious."

"Should you be saying that?"

Lorn shrugs. "It's a problem that concerns both the lancers and the Magi'i. I'm a lancer; you're of the Magi'i. I'm not telling you anything those above you don't know, and you're not about to tell anyone else."

"I know," Vernt replies. "Still . . ." He frowns.

Lorn takes out the pouch with the papers inside, those it has taken him more than an eightday to copy—although he has taken the precaution of making two extra sets. "Here's something that you'll need."

"That *I'll* need?" The taller man's eyebrows rise.

"A long time ago, at Father's suggestion, I went through the Archives," Lorn lies, offering a chuckle. "Except I didn't tell him, because . . . well . . . you know . . . I didn't want to admit he might be right." The smile fades. "Then, of course, I couldn't tell him."

"There's always something I remember that I would have liked to tell him," Vernt agrees.

"I copied these." That is absolute truth, a truth even Vernt can sense. "I think now is the time, or it will be shortly, for them to reappear."

" 'Reappear'?" asks Vernt.

"I asked Tyrsal to see if these were still in the Archives. He says they're not."

Vernt frowns.

"They're the plans and the methodology for building a coal-fired, chaos-steam transfer engine."

"They say it can't be done."

Lorn shakes his head. "Like many things, that's a partial truth. Read through the pages and you'll understand. A magus cannot build that engine, nor touch it, but a magus is necessary, and the engine can be built, and it will operate. Heat transfer isn't that much different from chaos transfer when you look at it. It's far simpler, in fact, on a practical basis."

"They'll laugh at me—proposing a steam-chaos engine when we have chaos-powered firewagons that will do much more."

Lorn shook his head. "You don't understand. You don't propose anything. You wait."

"What good will that do?"

"The Quarter chaos-tower will fail, sometime in the next year." A lazy smile crosses Lorn's face. "Six fireships have already had their towers fail."

"How do you know anything about the Quarter tower?"

"Even a former student magus can sense that—I do visit Tyrsal now and again, and the tower's not that far away."

"I can't do anything, Lorn."

Lorn smiles again. "All right. You can't do anything. Then you won't need those." He gestures toward the stack of papers he has left on the desk. "I would like to leave you with one thought."

"What is that?" Vernt frowns. "I know you. There's more to this than a thought."

"No. There really isn't. Not now." Lorn pauses. "Right now, the Magi'i have power. While a few Magi'i—like Chyenfel and Rustyl—have the power to draw chaos from the natural world, most don't. They have to draw and direct stored chaos. Once the towers are all gone, there's no more stored chaos. Therefore, there's much less need for the Magi'i, and their power in Cyador will be far less. The merchanters will gain power; the lancers will perhaps hold their power. If . . . if the Magi'i have a way of building engines such as these, there will be another form of fireship upon the oceans, and another form of firewagon upon the great highways—and the Magi'i will hold power."

"No one will believe me." Vernt shakes his head.

"First . . . you wait until matters are more desperate. Second, you say that the papers are something that your father developed, and that you have carried on his work. That's true enough, in a way."

"Lorn . . ."

"And don't tell Ciesrt or Kharl. If this works, Kharl will take the credit. If it doesn't, he'll steal it and then blame you and Father. If you want someone higher to talk to, you might try either the First Magus or the Third."

"You don't like Kharl, do you?"

"I don't like Ciesrt, and Kharl raised Ciesrt. For what it's worth, most in Cyad outside the Quarter do not trust the Second Magus. They praise his intelligence, but do not turn their backs." Lorn pauses. "If matters look desperate, and the Magi'i are looking for an answer, any answer . . . then, if the others do not listen, you can try Kharl."

"That's the most persuasive thing you've said." Vernt laughs. "When you would give something you believe to someone you dislike . . . you feel strongly."

"What can I say?" Lorn shrugs. "In the meantime . . . if you would humor me . . . brother . . . you might keep those in a safe place. If anything *should* happen, it might be wise for someone among the Magi'i to have a plan."

"I'll read them, and keep them safe. I might even look in the Archives."

"You won't find anything."

"I might find traces of what was removed."

"You might," Lorn agrees.

Vernt leans back in the chair, in a way that reminds Lorn of their father. "What is in this for you?"

"I'd like to see Father proven right. I'd like to see Cyador remain strong." Lorn purses his lips. "I've seen some of the rest of Candar, and I've seen how the barbarians treat innocents, and how they hate us. And there's nothing like Cyad anywhere."

"You were the one who defended the barbarians, as I recall," Vernt says.

"You were right. I was wrong." Lorn stands. "One way or another, I hope you find those useful."

"We'll see. But none will know whence came these. That, I will promise." Vernt stands. "I don't know as I believe your dire predictions, but none can gainsay your devotion to Cyador." Vernt glances. "Did you bring a mount?"

"I walked. It's not that far." Lorn touches the hilt of the sabre. "Cyador is still safe at night, but . . . if not . . . I'm prepared."

"I'm sure you are."

The two brothers walk from the study and down the steps.

CXVI

ENOUGH ... THAT'S MORE than enough." Tyrsal puffs out the words, backing out of the roughened stone of the sparring circle.

"That's fine. I didn't get that much sleep last night. Kerial is teething."

"You couldn't . . . ?" asks Tyrsal.

"I know enough about healing, but Jerial says it's not good to use it on infants for normal things like teething—something about upsetting their chaos-order balance too early. It's different if they're really ill." Lorn takes a deep breath and blots his forehead on the back of the sleeve of the exercise tunic.

"You're doing it all without vision, aren't you? The sabre? No matter which hand you have the blade in?"

"Most of the time," Lorn admits.

"Ha! I thought so."

"You're getting better," Lorn points out. "I have to work harder these days."

"I have to, sparring with you."

"So do I, working against you." Lorn places the practice sabre in the rack. "You must have something on your mind." He smiles. "A certain young lady, perchance?"

"Aleyar does occupy my thoughts—more than I'd ever thought." Tyrsal lowers his voice, his eyes going to the pair of merchanters sparring in the background. "Why don't you walk partway back toward the Quarter with me?"

Lorn nods. "All right. Then I'd better get washed up quickly. I do have to finish another meeting report."

The two walk toward the shower room adjoining the exercise hall. Lorn washes quickly, but Tyrsal is quicker yet, and waiting as Lorn finishes smoothing his tunic in place and clipping his cupridium-plated Brystan sabre to his green web belt. He feels safer with that particular sabre, especially in Cyad, and the cupridium shields the ordered iron beneath . . . enough so that only a very accomplished magus who is very close to Lorn would even have a chance of noting it, for order is far less obvious than chaos.

Lorn's hair is still wet as they walk along the paved walkway beside the road of Perpetual Light in the warm early-fall afternoon. He looks at the shorter, redheaded mage. "You have that worried look. Is it about being consorted?"

"Chaos, no!" Tyrsal takes a deep breath, then glances over his shoulder, then lowers his voice. "Last night . . . Mother had asked if I would drop by. She asks so seldom that I hired a coach."

Lorn nods.

"She had a message for you."

"For me?" The taller man frowns.

"She wouldn't tell me where it came from, and begged me not to ask. She did say that the person who sent it had never lied, and about that she was telling the truth."

Lorn feels his stomach churning, and a chill coming down his back, and a chill from premonition, not from being watched in a chaos-glass, although he has experienced more of that in the last few eightdays as well. His voice is even as he says, "That seems strange."

"The message wasn't about lancers or Magi'i, either."

"Your mother was from a merchanter background, and so was your grandsire, though, didn't you say?" Lorn asks.

"I did say that." Tyrsal glances back again before continuing. "The message was a request for you to inquire about what Tasjan has said about the lady head of Ryalor House, and his plans for the more than tenscore armsmen he is assembling." Tyrsal glances at Lorn. "That was all."

Lorn suppresses a swallow. "That is more than enough. More than enough."

"When you sound like that . . . I wouldn't wish to be Tasjan—or you." Tyrsal's voice is bleak.

"We'll have to inquire. That's all." Lorn offers a shrug he does not feel.

"There's always been something about you. You know . . . did it bother you to break Dett's fingers all those years ago?"

Lorn frowns. "I hadn't thought about that in a long time. I didn't want to, you know, but he wouldn't listen to anyone. He kept bullying people whenever there weren't any proctors around, as if he were allowed to do anything he could get away with." He shrugs, almost sadly. "Dett was always like that. Some people are."

"And some people, like you, feel that they have to do something about it."

"If someone doesn't, even more people get hurt," Lorn says.

"I suppose that's true, but I've never had the certainty of being as right as you feel you are."

Lorn's laugh is harsh. "I've never been that certain. You could ask Ryalth about that. But I guess I'd rather act on what I feel, than reproach myself later for not acting. Sometimes, I shouldn't have acted. And sometimes I should have, but probably did the wrong thing."

"Not very often, from what I've seen." Tyrsal sighs. "There . . . you can go. That's what I wanted to tell you." The redheaded mage stops. "I know you have to get back to Mirror Lancer Court."

"I'm glad you did. You know how I feel about Ryalth."

"I know. That's why I hope you don't find too much wrong."

"Would you have been told if I didn't have to worry?" asks Lorn.

Both glance at each other as a chill—the chill of a chaosglass—falls across them.

"That's why I worry. Another reason," Tyrsal says.

Lorn catches Tyrsal's eyes with his own. "Thank you. I mean it. And don't worry. At least not too much. Give Aleyar our best. And you two are coming to dinner on fiveday, remember?"

"We'll be there."

With a smile—one he does not feel—Lorn inclines his head to his friend, and then turns, walking swiftly, but not too swiftly, into the sun toward Mirror Lancer Court and his small study, and the meeting report he has not finished.

CXVII

LORN HAS JUST arrived at the dwelling, and stands on the veranda, blotting his forehead from the heat of the late-fall afternoon, when he hears the gate open and close. He turns to see Ryalth and Ayleha walking around the privacy hedge. Ryalth carries Kerial, whose whimpers rise over the splash and spray of the fountain.

Lorn hurries toward them.

"Are you all right?" Lorn asks, taking Kerial. His son's whimpers immediately increase into an intermittent wailing as Lorn walks beside Ryalth past the cooling spray of the fountain.

"We've all been better." Ryalth's voice holds an edge.

"I'm sorry. Can I do anything?"

"Keep holding him. I know he's teething. At least, I hope it's just teeth."

Belatedly, as he steps into the shade of the veranda, Lorn uses his chaos-order senses to study Kerial, but he finds nothing except the faint redness around the boy's teeth. "It's just his teeth."

"I hope he gets the rest of them soon." She shakes her head. "Maybe I don't. He's starting to bite."

Lorn pauses at the door to the foyer. "Why don't you just go upstairs, and wash up and lie down or just spend some time by yourself?"

"You don't want to see me?"

Lorn holds back a sigh. "Everyone has been asking things of you all day. Kerial has probably been unpleasant and whimpering all day. I gather trading wasn't good, and you had problems there. I do like to see you, but the way you've been talking, I only thought you might like some time when no one was asking or demanding."

"Maybe I do."

"I'll stay out here with Kerial."

"You just got here, didn't you?" asks Ryalth.

"Just before you."

"I shouldn't leave him with you. You've had a day, too."

Lorn laughs. "Just take care of yourself for a while. We'll be fine."

"Are you sure?"

"You deserve a rest."

"Thank you." Ryalth's voice softens, and she smiles for the first time since she stepped through the iron gate. "I won't be that long."

"However long it takes, and then take some more time for yourself."

She nods and steps into the foyer.

Lorn walks around the veranda, patting Kerial on the back. After what seems like tenscore circles in one direction, he turns and walks the other way. He can feel the dampness on his shoulder where his son half gnaws, half slobbers on his uniform in between whimpers.

The sun has dropped behind the larger dwellings and the hillside to the northwest, and Lorn has circled the veranda more than a score of scores before Kerial finally begins to snore on Lorn's shoulder. He walks another score of circles and then makes his way slowly through the dwelling and up the stairs. He meets Ryalth at the top.

Her eyes widen.

"He's asleep," Lorn mouths as he walks as softly as he can toward their bedchamber, and Kerial's bed. Kerial does not wake as Lorn eases him down on his back, then backs away slowly.

Outside their chamber in the corridor, Ryalth smiles.

"Thank you. I know I shouldn't get cross." She points to his shoulder. "You're wet."

"I think the uniform felt good to chew on." Lorn starts down the stairs, then looks at her. "I'm sorry. I didn't ask about dinner."

"Kysia says it's about ready."

"Good. I am hungry." Lorn continues down the stairs to the main floor.

"You should be. It's late. You walked him for a long time."

"You were upset."

"I was. Immilhar's *Western Wind* is lost, in a storm in the Gulf of Austra. That was a good ship, a good captain, and we had a good hundred golds in the cargo, and a chance for double that. I'd finally gotten them to take the golden-melon brandy, and this was the first real order." Ryalth shakes her head. "Let's go eat, before Kerial wakes up."

"He might sleep awhile."

"I'm not counting on it." She turns toward the dining area.

Lorn follows her, and almost as soon as they sit, Kysia arrives to set a platter, a covered dish, and a basket of dark bread on the table.

"Ale is all we have," announces the gray-eyed server.

"That will be wonderful," Lorn says.

After Kysia returns to the kitchen, Lorn gestures to Ryalth to help herself, then serves himself two slices of the rolled and stuffed pork covered with a brown sauce. Then he takes some of the nutted beans, and a chunk of dark bread.

Kysia returns with a pitcher and pours the ale into their glasses, then vanishes once more.

"Have you found out anything about those commanders—Sypcal and Lhary?"

Ryalth looks abashed. "I'm sorry. I did. Days ago . . . and somehow, every time I meant to tell you, something happened or Kerial was fussy . . . or something. I'm really sorry. I know it was important . . . I guess I'm trying to do too much."

Lorn finishes chewing a mouthful of the stuffed pork, and then swallows. "I understand. You are trying to run a trading house, look after a son, and please a consort, and each is more of a task than it should be." He pauses. "About Sypcal?"

"He comes from Geliendra. His father was a tradesman. He was considered a good field commander, but he cashiered a captain by the name of Sasyk." Ryalth raises her eyebrows.

"Sasyk . . . I've heard the name somewhere, but I don't recall right now."

"Sasyk is some relative of Tasjan, and he's the one in charge of Tasjan's guards."

"Why did cashiering an officer cause a problem for Sypcal? That's what you're hinting."

"A tradesman in Assyadt made a charge that Sypcal had ordered some wine and not paid for it, and then threatened to kill the tradesman if he insisted on payment. Sypcal had a receipt. The tradesman said Sypcal forged it. Sypcal brought in two captains who had witnessed the transaction. The tradesman claimed they all lied. Sypcal did lose his temper, and killed the man. The justicer said it was allowable because the man had committed fraud and tried to disgrace an officer. The merchanters in Syadtar were less than happy."

"Let me guess," Lorn says. "The tradesman was either a relative or in debt to Tasjan, or something."

"His daughter was his mistress—one of them—for a time."

Lorn takes a sip of ale. "So then Rynst ordered Sypcal to Cyad and put Ikynd in charge at Assyadt?"

"Not quite. Rynst had selected Sypcal as commander in Assyadt, and the town was upset . . ."

"So Rynst had Luss pick the commander to succeed Sypcal?"

Ryalth nods.

Lorn shakes his head. "What about Lhary?"

"No one knows much of anything, except that he was considered a good company officer at Pemedra. Since then, he's always been someone's assistant, except for a short tour when he was the commander of the outposts around the Accursed Forest. He's very close to Luss, and he has no consort."

None of that surprises Lorn.

"Anything new about Tasjan?" he asks after several mouthfuls of the stuffed pork.

"There's always some gossip." She wrinkles her brow, then frowns. "What was it? Oh, he sent a scroll to Vyanat. This time he asked the Merchanter Advisor to request that the Mirror Engineers build more of the new warships to protect the traders. He said that with the changes in the Accursed Forest and the sack of Jera and all the golds you brought back, the lancers didn't need as many arms and men, and that between your loot and the golds saved the lancers could build the ships without increasing tariffs."

"Hmm . . . does anyone know what Vyanat said?"

"No."

"He's forgetting that the lancers are also losing their fire-lances, and we'll need more Lancers to do the same task. He should know that."

Ryalth laughs.

"I know," Lorn says. "Knowing something, and conveniently forgetting it when it serves your purpose, is nothing new in Cyad. Still, I have to wonder."

"Why are you interested in Tasjan?"

"Rumors," Lorn says. "I was sparring with Tyrsal, and he's heard from his mother that Tasjan was up to something. She didn't know what, and neither did Tyrsal."

"You're not telling me everything."

"No. The rumor also indicated that Tasjan wanted to cause trouble for you and Ryalor House." Lorn shakes his head. "Are you sure that Magi'i blood doesn't run in your family?" He takes a swallow of the ale, then another serving of the stuffed pork from the platter.

"That's not something that would have been mentioned when I was that young, and..." Her mouth twists into a awkward smile, "I'm certain that Mother wasn't about to say anything, not until I was older. Then, she couldn't."

"You're more Magi'i than some Magi'i."

"You're kind . . . I think."

"Accurate." He frowns. "I need to see if I can find Tasjan in the glass. Would you watch and see if what I call up is Tasjan—if I can?"

"When you do that . . . it's so strange," Ryalth says. "I know others can scree, too, but it's different, to me, anyway, when it's your own consort."

"You didn't mind it when I used it to see you."

"No . . . but it was still strange . . . to feel your presence and know you were hundreds and hundreds of kays away."

Lorn stands. "I'd like to do this now, just in case Kerial wakes later."

"You *are* worried. Usually . . . in the evening . . . if he's sleeping . . ."

Lorn flushes. "I am. Worried, I mean." Then he grins sheepishly before he walks softly from the dining area and up the stairs to the study.

With Ryalth standing behind him, the small study's shutters drawn, Lorn seats himself and looks down at his own reflection in the chaos-glass. "What does Tasjan look like?"

"He's about as tall as you are. He's slender. His hair is sandy-blond, and there's some silver in it. He doesn't have a beard. His eyes are light-brown and green mixed together. Oh, and there's a pockmark, just one, below his left eye."

Lorn tries to concentrate on both the appearance and the essences of Tasjan. For a long time, the silver mists swirl across the glass. Perspiration beads Lorn's forehead.

Finally, an image appears—one of a sandy-haired man

sitting at the end of a long table, a wine goblet before him. The only other figure at the table is a bearded man wearing a uniform of off-green who sits to his right, with gold epaulets.

"That's Tasjan," Ryalth affirms. "And the other one wears the uniform of his guards. It might be Sasyk, but I don't know."

"He has special uniforms for his armsmen?"

"Oh, yes. Some of the other traders think he's putting on airs."

Lorn concentrates, trying to fix Tasjan's image in his mind, before he finally lets the chaos- glass turn blank once more. He blots his forehead, then massages his neck. For a moment or so, he sits before the glass with his eyes closed.

"That's hard work, isn't it?" Ryalth says softly.

"Especially when I don't know what exactly I'm seeking."

She frowns. "I thought Magi'i couldn't use the glass if they didn't . . ."

"Most can't, I found out later. I had to learn on my own." His laugh is ragged. "I guess I didn't know any better."

"That image didn't show much."

"Usually they don't," Lorn says. "You see people talking, working, eating, all the things we all do. It's more useful for things like making maps, or for finding forces when you know the terrain. I want to look at a few other people—quickly."

Lorn decides to try to seek Luss, and concentrates. After the silver mists clear, the glass reveals the image of the black-haired and bushy-eyebrowed Captain-Commander sitting at a table covered in green linen. To the right of the Captain-Commander is the blond commander Lhary. They are deep in conversation, and Lorn immediately releases the image.

"Who are they?"

"The Captain-Commander and Commander Lhary."

"They're plotting something. They just looked that way."

"I'm sure they are, except Lhary is brighter than Luss."

"That's worse."

Lorn agrees silently. "Watch the next image."

The figure of Rustyl appears once the mists dissipate. The image of the first-level adept is blurred, and wavers, but Lorn can make out that the magus stands in a corridor looking through a window in solid granite. He lets the mirror blank.

"He's studying the chaos-tower of the Magi'i. Much good it will do." Lorn frowns. "At least, I hope it won't do him much good."

"But . . . if he could repair it . . . or make it last longer . . . ?" asks Ryalth.

"I'd have to praise him for it, and mean it." Lorn sighs. "And watch him even more closely." He closes his eyes and rubs his forehead.

Ryalth steps up behind him and massages his shoulders.

Lorn sighs. "That feels good." For a time, he just sits there, enjoying the feel of her fingers on his shoulders and neck.

Ryalth's fingers run through his hair, stroke his neck, and then her lips brush the back of his neck. "Kerial's still asleep," she whispers softly.

He flushes, but he eases from the chair and takes her in his arms.

CXVIII

THE TWO WOMEN—one a trader and one a healer—sit across the dinner table from each other. Beside the trader sits a Mirror Lancer officer in his working uniform of cream-and-green. The trader wears shimmercloth blue, and holds an infant dressed in a green shirt in her lap. The healer wears green, and pushes a lock of curly black hair off her forehead. The gentle scent of erhenflower emanates from her.

Lorn looks across the dinner table at his younger sister. "We're glad you could come this time."

"So am I. Ciesrt doesn't like to come to family things unless Vernt's there." Myryan shrugs. "But Ciesrt's in Summerdock for an eightday or so."

"What's he doing there?" asks Lorn.

"Something to do with reclaiming the chaos-storage cells on the fireships—the ones whose towers failed. Some can be used on the firewagons, and some for firelances, I guess." Myryan takes a last bite of the glazed fowl. "I shouldn't have eaten so much."

"You brought the squash and lentils," Ryalth said. "We don't get vegetables like you grow. Neither of us has time to garden, and Pheryk and Grehty came too late this year to plant one. Pheryk says he knows just where he'll put the garden next year." She smiles. "That's next year."

"We haven't asked, and you haven't said," Lorn says, "but how is Ciesrt?"

"As always." Myryan takes a long swallow of the Alafraan.

"What's the matter?" Lorn asks gently.

"Nothing . . . or nothing you can do anything about." The black-haired healer shakes her head. Her fingers twine around the stem of the goblet.

"Is it Ciesrt?" asks Ryalth. "Something we should know?"

"It's not Ciesrt. It's his father." Myryan looks to Ryalth, and then at the softly babbling Kerial in her lap. "He's so sweet."

"Tonight," Lorn says with a laugh. "Tonight, he's sweet."

"The other day Lorn had to walk him in circles for forever. I was so worn-out that when Lorn saw me, I just snapped at him." Ryalth smiles. "He took Kerial and sent me upstairs for a bath and a nap."

"I'm still amazed." Myryan smiles, if but momentarily. "I never thought of Lorn as a father."

"Neither did I," Lorn admits.

"What about Kharl?" asks Ryalth gently.

"He's pushing Ciesrt. He wants us to have a child. He's talking about having me see some other healer besides Jerial."

Lorn manages not to frown.

Myryan turns to him. "You know something about this, don't you? And you didn't tell me . . ."

"No . . . I didn't know a thing, but I have to wonder." Lorn purses his lips.

Both women look at him and wait.

"Kharl is the Second Magus. There's no great respect or affection between him and the other high lectors. Everyone knows that."

Myryan nods.

"It's also common knowledge in the Mirror Lancer Court that Kharl has been courting the Captain-Commander of Mirror Lancers."

"But . . . old as Chyenfel is . . . he is still strong, and he keeps chaos at bay," Myryan says.

"Exactly," Lorn says. "Who is not keeping chaos at bay, or will not be able to for long?"

Myryan and Ryalth look at each other, then at Lorn.

Lorn waits. He does not want to offer any suggestion, because he wants to see if the connection is logical.

"Rynst is old . . ." says Myryan.

"He looks older than he is. He will outlive Chyenfel," Lorn says.

"Vyanat'mer is the youngest of the advisors to the Emperor," Ryalth says.

Myryan's hand goes to her mouth. "You aren't serious . . . a Magi'i . . . the Malachite Throne . . . the lancers . . . oh . . . that's why you mentioned Luss."

"I don't *know* that," Lorn says. "But you had mentioned that they had been pushing for a child before. And you are the daughter of the most respected magus of the generation."

"If Myryan has a child, then there are two generations of heirs . . . is that what you're suggesting?" asks Ryalth.

"I don't know. They just could want grandchildren . . ."

"Ciesrt's older sister consorted with Zubyl almost two years ago, and she's finally expecting in midwinter." Myryan snorts. "They haven't said so much as a word about it. Kharl hasn't, anyway."

Lorn takes a small sip of the Alafraan. His guts are churning.

"This upsets you, doesn't it?" asks his sister.

"Yes. Not as much as it's upsetting you, though." He offers a crooked smile. "I was just guessing."

"No one wagers against your guesses," Myryan says. "Not if they know you, and I've known you too long." She pauses. "I still can't believe it. How could he possibly think . . . ? And Ciesrt, he's never said a word. Not a word."

"Would he know?" asks Ryalth.

A bitter smile crosses Myryan's face. "He wouldn't even think of it. He hopes he'll make lector someday. He's knows he's not as bright as his father, and in that way, he'd do whatever he could to please Kharl." She looks at Lorn. "Whatever made you think of that?"

He shrugs helplessly. "I couldn't say. The pieces were there, and . . ." He shrugs again.

"Do you want a child?" asks Ryalth.

"No . . ." Myryan shakes her head slowly. "Not like this . . . not . . . I can accept being a consort. I can support Ciesrt, and make him happy. I'm not strong enough, not like Jerial. I couldn't take having everyone look at me, and judge me, or say no one wanted me . . ." She swallows. "I'll be all right. Really . . . I will be."

Ryalth reaches across the table with her one free hand and places it on Myryan's. "We're here. You can stay here . . ."

"Everyone would know."

"Healers are respected elsewhere," Ryalth says. "I could get you passage anywhere in Candar—even find you a patron in some ports."

Myryan shakes her head once more. "I'll be fine. Sometimes . . . I just pity myself too much. I have a consort who wants me, and he's gentle, and kind in his own way. I have a house and a garden. I'm respected as a healer. I've never had to make my own way, the way you have, Ryalth. Or fight people like Lorn has." She swallows. "I'll be fine."

"You can stay here tonight," Ryalth says.

"I'll do that, but that's all. Tomorrow . . . I'll be fine. It's just . . . Who could I tell? Jerial's so strong. She doesn't understand. Mother understood . . . I miss her so much. I wish I could talk to her." Twin streaks of tears ooze down her cheeks. "I miss her . . ."

"I miss them both," Lorn says.

"Gaaaa. . . ." Kerial says, softly, a chubby hand extending toward the sobbing healer.

"She would have understood . . . she would have . . ." Myryan blots her eyes with a shimmercloth handkerchief.

Lorn and Ryalth exchange a brief glance.

"I'll be fine," Myryan says, more emphatically, wiping away the last trace of tears. "I just need a cry now and then. I didn't expect . . . not here, but I'll be fine."

"You'll stay here tonight," Ryalth says, and her words are not a question.

"In the morning," Lorn adds, "you can talk to Pheryk about where he ought to put the garden. Neither Ryalth nor I would have the faintest idea."

"I can do that." Myryan offers a faint smile. "Thank you for listening . . . both of you."

"What is family for?" says Lorn.

"You've always been there, Lorn. I remember that. No one else knew . . . except Mother. And you went to Father when he was mad at you for other things, and you gave me time." She shakes her head. "Sometimes, I wish I were the one giving."

"You do. Healers give all the time." Lorn grins. "And you give things like fruits and vegetables we couldn't get elsewhere."

"I mean . . . big things, like you and Father have done," replies the healer.

"Right now, all I do is read reports and go to meetings and write reports on them to the Majer-Commander. That's not very big."

Myryan looks at him, her eyes unwavering. "You know what I mean. You're sweet, dear brother, but please don't humor me."

"The vegetables were to cheer you up," he replies, "but I meant it about the healing."

Myryan laughs, and there is but a slight edge to the sound. "You're still the big brother."

"I always will be." He gives an exaggerated and sheepish shrug. "For better or worse—mostly worse, I fear."

"You two . . ." Ryalth's tone is half scolding, half mock-exasperation. "If you keep this up, Kerial will get cranky, and I won't get to eat any pearapple tarts because I'll be putting him to bed, and Lorn. . . ."

". . . will eat them all," finishes Myryan.

"What can I say?" asks Lorn.

"Not too much," suggests Ryalth, gesturing toward Kysia, who has peered out from the archway from the kitchen. "If we could have the tarts?"

"Right away, Lady."

"I'll never live down the tarts," Lorn complains.

"Never," Myryan agrees.

Lorn only hopes that Myryan is as fine as she says she is, even as he knows she is not, and as he knows he does not know how to resolve her problem, not as quickly as it needs to be resolved.

CXIX

IN THE GOLDEN glow of the single lamp, Lorn sits on the edge of the ornate bed, his eyes focused nowhere. He can hear Kerial's gentle breathing from the small bed against the wall.

"You're worried about Myryan." Ryalth sits up, propping a pillow behind her against the headboard.

"Wouldn't you be?" asks Lorn. "I've thought about it, but I can't think of anything that would help." He frowns. "Not that wouldn't hurt you and Kerial worse."

"You've thought about that before."

"I debated killing Kharl'elth just before I became a lancer officer, when it was clear Father would consort Myryan to Ciesrt. I didn't try. Instead, I pleaded to Father. He waited almost two years, but he still did it. He wrote me, told me that none of us had the choices others thought we did. I'm still not sure if he was right—or if I shouldn't have done something then."

"They would have found out, and killed you, and then I'd have lost you, and Kerial wouldn't be."

"They didn't find out other—"

"Lorn . . . he's the Second Magus. The Magi'i would never stop looking."

"It doesn't matter. I didn't. I didn't even try." He does not look at Ryalth, instead looks nowhere.

"Lorn . . ."

"What?"

"You won't solve this by looking into space. You can try to sleep. You can talk to me. You can try to find a verse in the book that helps. You can use the chaos-glass . . . seek out something . . . I know you . . ."

He turns, opens his mouth as if to speak, then closes it. He shakes his head. "That's not fair."

She raises her eyebrows.

"Nothing."

After a long silence, he finally reaches for the silver-covered volume that has remained on the bedside table since he returned from Assyadt. He looks at the cover, the green-tinged silver that almost holds a rainbow in the lamplight, before he turns the pages. After a time, he reads.

Should I again listen to which song?
We have listened oh so long.
Should I again fly on learning wings?
We have learned what yearning brings.

"That's sad," Ryalth says. "It is like Myryan in a way."

Lorn swallows. "I know. That's why I read it." He continues to turn pages. Then he begins again, more slowly, until he comes to a verse which, strangely, he does not quite recall, not really, yet now the words seem all too clear.

The sages honor the chains of duty, pride,
how they uplift those who live, those who died.

What think they of the death of love and care?
Of the children women will never bear,
a dry-eyed consort too bereft to cry,
a mother who will see her sons but die,
a consorting suit that never will be worn—
these weapons of the forgotten and forlorn
pierce bright cupridium and chaos fire,
flaming honor to ashes of desire.

Speak not of honor, you who command hold,
nor bright ballads write of your days of old,

> when, in age, you put your pen upon the page
> and claim that all you did was meet and sage.
>
> I have claimed the same, and yet well I know
> that to that chaos I created will I go.

Lorn shakes his head. After a while, he begins to speak. "That's the problem. No matter how great the ideal, no matter how noble the cause, the innocent suffer. Anything I do for Myryan—that I know how to do—will hurt others worse. All I can do is listen, and try to cheer her up. And it's not enough."

"Sometimes . . . sometimes listening is all anyone can do. And sometimes it is enough." Ryalth offers a kind smile. "She knows you care. That helps."

As he sets down the book, and finally turns down the lamp wick until the flame gutters out, Lorn wonders: Will his caring help enough?

CXX

IT IS NEAR midday when Lorn walks into the Majer-Commander's study, uncertain of the reason for his summons, since he has submitted all the reports that are required. Has the Majer-Commander finally decided to discuss his draft report on the Jeranyi strategy?

He bows. "Ser?"

"Please have a seat, Majer." Rynst leans back in his armchair, the one behind the wide table desk. Behind him, bathed in warm fall light, the Palace of Eternal Light is once more framed in the large and ancient windows.

Lorn sits, comfortably, but neither fully into the seat, nor on the front edge.

"Majer . . . you are considered a good commander of lancers, by every commander who has supervised you. Most are wary of you, but all recommend you. Would you care to explain?"

"Ser, I honestly cannot say I know why this is so."

Rynst laughs. "Well and carefully said. Then I will ask you to guess why such might be so."

Lorn considers what and how much he should say. Finally, he begins. "I would guess, and this is but a guess, that my approach to tactics differs initially, although my goals have always been to accomplish any task with the greatest gain and fewest losses for the Mirror Lancers and for Cyador."

"Perhaps the last few words explain it all," suggests Rynst.

"Ser?" Lorn immediately wishes he had not said those three words, safe though they had sounded.

" ' . . . and for Cyador.' You do believe in the Empire of Perpetual Light."

"Yes, ser."

"Why? Please do not provide the words of the Lancers' Code or some such."

"Because, ser, for all its faults, from what I have seen, Cyador offers more than any other land in which people live. There is less hatred, and people live better lives in less fear."

"A practical answer from a very practical lancer officer." Rynst nods. "Majer . . . why were you successful in subverting Majer Dettaur's attempts to have you removed from your position?"

Lorn does not try to hide the frown, knowing that Rynst is looking for something other than the obvious. "I recognized that was his goal from the beginning."

The Majer-Commander smiles coldly. "That is the first element of dealing with a problem. One must recognize the problem. What did you do then?"

"I did my best to train and upgrade the forces at Inividra and to use the most effective tactics I could develop."

"Again . . . a simple application of well-known maxims, enhanced by your ability to develop and use tactics others had not considered . . . for various reasons." Rynst fingers his chin. "Yet . . . when you returned to Inividra, whether you will acknowledge it or not, and I do not intend to press the matter, Majer Dettaur had arranged for you to be relieved in disgrace. You took six companies to Assyadt. Why? And why was that successful?"

Lorn smiles coolly, managing not to swallow, and gambling that he faces a time when only truth will suffice. "Because there is never more than a company of lancers at Assyadt and because, once I held the compound, I knew that I could use the reports and the materials there to prove that Majer Dettaur was acting contrary to the best interests of the Mirror Lancers."

"As you did." Rynst nods once more. "Most carefully, and most meticulously. You were right about the records. You were right about the tactics, and you were right about Majer Dettaur's goals. For all that, you would have failed, except for six companies of lancers."

"Yes, ser."

"Sometimes, one must have his forces where they can be noticed."

Lorn nods, silently wondering exactly where the Majer-Commander is leading the strange discussion—and why.

"We have but four fireships now. What are the most effective forces remaining that can still draw upon chaos?"

"The Mirror Lancers—and the firelances that remain."

"And where are they?"

"Stationed around the Accursed Forest, and mostly along the Grass Hills."

"And where do the outland traders port most often?" presses the gray-haired Rynst.

"In Cyad." Lorn pauses. "You are suggesting that it might be advisable to have some of the Mirror Lancers here? Or perhaps at times, with maneuvers that the outlanders could watch—with firelances while we still have such?"

"What do you think of that proposition, Majer?"

"It could not but help." Lorn frowns. "We would have to set up a maneuver area near the piers, perhaps where some of the older warehouses now stand. If the Mirror Engineers used something like their firecannon to level the structures . . . that might also create an impression."

"Hmmm . . . that is also a good idea. Commander Muyro would like that."

Lorn waits.

"There remains one significant problem with that proposition."

"Ser?"

"I have no field commanders here with recent experience, and those in the field now do not understand the delicacy of the situation. I trust you can understand that."

Lorn fears that he does. "You would like me to help a commander with these, as your aide?"

"No." Rynst's denial is firm and cold.

"If you wish a recommendation," Lorn says slowly, "perhaps Majer Brevyl—"

"I think it best that you command the two companies— and that one of them be a company you know already. You have a reputation. I intend to ensure that the outlanders know of that reputation." Rynst pauses. "Do you understand, Majer?"

"Yes, ser."

"I believe you do. I believe you honestly do." The Majer-Commander leans forward. "Before the afternoon is out, you will submit a list of companies that you would wish— with the company officer you desire. You will command them as if Cyad were a standard outpost. That is, your duties

will remain as they are here, except that you will plan and
direct the training and maneuver schedules, based on the
port schedules of the outland traders. And you will offer in-
vitations—in person, if necessary—to those traders and
ships' masters as I direct. Also, much as you dislike it, you
will, as you can, suggest that it is past time that Cyad should
take over ports in Candar that are unfriendly. Then, you will
stress that, of course, those are but your own ideas."

Lorn conceals—he hopes—the wince he feels.

"Do you understand the importance of that, Majer? Can
you explain it back to me?"

"Yes, ser. I believe I am to be regarded as an example of
the bloody-minded lancer officer who would sack every
trading port in Candar for Cyador, were I not kept under
tight rein by my commanders."

Rynst laughs. "You can be *slightly* less direct than that. Just
allow them to guess such from your carriage and actions."

"Yes, ser."

"And, Majer . . ." Rynst's voice hardens.

"Yes, ser."

"You and those two companies are under my direct command . . . and no one else's. Should anything happen to me,
you are under the Emperor's direct command, and no one
else's. And this you are to tell no one. No one."

Lorn does swallow before responding. "Yes, ser."

"I am very glad you understand that." A smile follows. "I
doubt anything will ever come to that, but it is best to have
that clear. That is also another reason why this command is
yours."

Lorn waits again.

"You are a scion of Cyador, not of the Mirror Lancers, no
matter how well you serve. At times, we need such, and this
is one of those times." Rynst nods. "You may go."

"By your leave, ser?"

"By my leave."

Lorn stands, bows, and then walks from the study. No matter how matters are couched, the idea of two companies of Mirror Lancers in Cyad, pledged to the Majer-Commander directly, and then to the Emperor, is a frightening thought.

A faint smile crosses his lips as he descends the stairs from the foyer to his own study, a smile not of humor, but of irony. More frightening than that is the realization that Rynst understands Lorn well enough to know that Lorn will indeed regard himself as bound to the Emperor and Cyador and not to the Captain-Commander or any other commander.

CXXI

THE TRIM AND muscular man who wears shimmercloth blues, with a deep-blue slash across each sleeve of his tunic, steps into the second office on the second floor of the clan building. He bows. "I was looking for Vyanat'mer."

"Alas, his office is the larger one to the right," offers the black-haired and younger merchanter who rises from behind the stack of invoices he has been perusing.

"He is not there," says Tasjan. "I thought he might be here, Vyel'mer."

"You honor me, most honored Tasjan'mer, and the House of Hyshrah."

"You come from a most honorable house, Vyel'mer. You should be honored." Tasjan smiles politely.

"You are kind." Vyel smiles, and the brief smile reveals that one of his upper front teeth is of gold.

"I was hoping to find your brother." The slender Tasjan shrugs, as if in disappointment. "He is often hard to find. Perhaps you could assist me?"

"I am only privy to the workings of Hyshrah House and

Clan," replies Vyel. "What Vyanat does as Merchanter Advisor, I know but what all know, I fear."

"Ah, were I Merchanter Advisor . . . but . . . No, one must not venture judgment before one has walked many kays in another's boots. Many kays." Tasjan smiles. "I would have you pass a message to your honored elder brother, if you would. For you are most trustworthy, and that is clear in that Vyanat has made you privy to all that the House does."

"He has."

"He may know that the Mirror Lancers are bringing two companies into Cyad. These lancers will be conducting maneuvers near the trading piers. They will be inviting outlander traders and ships' masters to show them the power of the firelances and the Mirror Lancers. With so few fireships remaining, I am sure we all agree that something must be done to instill respect in the outlanders. Do you not agree?"

"Of course."

"And it is prudent to have an experienced field commander for these lancers." Tasjan frowns. "Yet I have a concern which, if you will convey to your brother, I would most appreciate. This concern should not be committed to paper."

Vyel nods, waiting.

"You may recall . . . there was some talk, when your brother's name was put forth, of the head of Ryalor House being one of those also put forth."

"There was." Vyel's voice is even. "I recall that."

"Naught came of that, and that was for the best, for successful as the young house has been in most recent years, the lady who heads it has less experience than . . . many. You have far greater experience. So do others. Now . . . this is my concern. The majer who will command the lancers in Cyad is the consort of the head of Ryalor House. Moreover, he was brought to Cyad before his previous tour of duty in the Grass Hills was properly over. And . . . there are rumors, and these rumors cannot be discounted, that there were several loyal officers who would have reprimanded the majer for his bloodthirsty tactics. They . . . vanished, and none know where they went or where they are."

"That is most strange," Vyel admits.

"You will tell your brother?"

"I will indeed."

"You are a good man, Vyel, and a better trader than many. One would wonder how you might do. . . . were you given your own house. Even a small one, such as the size of say . . . Ryalor House." Tasjan smiles.

Vyel shrugs. "I am most happy here."

"I am certain you are. You do your brother's bidding, and none but he will question your authority. Still . . ." Tasjan pauses. "There is one other matter I had forgotten."

"Oh?"

"It is not a matter of great import. I did run across an odd bill of lading, one dealing with, shall we say, dun cotton from Hamor, carried on a ship—the *Hypolya*, that was it. Quite a lot of dun cotton, as I recall, near-on three hundred bolts. That would have been a quite a tariff if it had been true white Hamorian fine cotton—some fifteenscore golds. That is the sort of tariff that would interest the Emperor's Enumerators—even after a year or so."

Vyel looks up. "It well might."

"Do keep it in mind, Vyel. Please do." Tasjan smiles politely. "And do convey my concerns to your brother. He would not be pleased if he found out about the majer from another source."

Vyel smiles, politely. "You can be most assured that I will, most honored Tasjan, and that I will keep your interests in mind. So long as they do not harm Hyshrah House."

"I do appreciate your support, Vyel. I always will. And I would never ask a man to go against his house, or even against another merchanter." Tasjan bows and departs.

CXXII

LORN STANDS BEHIND the desk in his study. Then he walks to the door, pauses with his fingers on the handle. After a moment, he turns and walks back to the desk, putting his hands on the back of the chair.

Lorn does not know if what he will try will work. It is a skill practiced only by first-level adepts. . . . and he can ask no one in the Magi'i—not even Tyrsal—to assist. According to what he remembers . . . the idea is simple. The practice is hard, and it is one skill he cannot judge whether he has learned.

Finally, he shakes his head, walks to the study door, opens it, and walks down the short upper hall to the main bedchamber. Again . . . he remembers to slide the iron latch closed when he closes the door.

Ryalth is propped into a sitting position with pillows on the bed, and is perusing a stack of papers—invoices, Lorn suspects. A faint snore emanates from the small bed against the wall.

"I still need to read through these," Ryalth says. "I can't do it when Kerial's awake."

"I cannot imagine why," Lorn says dryly. "I will have a favor to ask in a bit, but just go on reading. I need the long mirror here."

"Magi'i things you'd best not be caught doing?" Her mouth curls into a momentary smile.

"Something like that. Except this might help my not getting caught."

With a half-nod, Ryalth turns her eyes to the next sheet in the stack in her lap.

Lorn looks in the bedchamber mirror, then concentrates

on what he recalls, the idea that vision is the interpretation of chaos reflected from all objects in a more ordered pattern and gathered by the eyes. If that pattern is modified, so that the reflected order is changed into a less ordered pattern or one that moves the secondary chaos away from one object . . . then most onlookers will find their vision averted from that object, while not even sensing why.

Lorn attempts to repattern his image, but nothing happens and the full-length mirror continues to show a brown-haired and amber-eyed lancer officer in his undertunic.

Perhaps . . . repatterning creates too much order and actually enhances his reflection. He frowns, then tries to direct the secondary chaos away from himself.

Abruptly, the entire room seems to go black, and while Lorn can sense objects around him, he can see nothing. Ryalth says not a word, and that means that his vision is affected—not the light from the lamp. With a swallow, he stops trying to divert the chaos of the light from himself. While that approach might make him invisible, he cannot see himself groping his way along a street where everyone else can see—even if they cannot see him.

He blinks and glances at Ryalth, watching for a moment as she lays aside another invoice or bill of lading.

He rubs his forehead, then takes a slow and silent deep breath. What if he just nudges the chaos, blurring it, or breaking up the sense of order emanating from himself? He concentrates, but chaos does not blur . . . not as he feels it, and his image remains fully in the mirror.

After taking more slow deep breaths and massaging the back of his neck, and ignoring the speculative glance from Ryalth, he tries again, this time trying to disrupt just little portions of the chaos.

His image in the full-length mirror ripples, but it is still recognizably a lancer officer. His lips twist. That kind of image will call more attention to him, not less.

He recalls the word *aversion*—can he somehow nudge or blur the chaos so that people do not wish to look at him, without knowing why?

He tries one combination, then another.

Ryalth is more than two-thirds of the way through the stack of parchment and paper, and Lorn still sweats, trying to discover—or rediscover—the technique he knows exists, if but mastered by a few.

For a moment, the mirror appears not quite blank, as if an image made of fog or smoke is there, before Lorn the lancer officer reappears.

Still . . . there is a hint of something there. Lorn takes another deep slow breath, ignoring a faint whimper from Kerial and the rustling of pages from his consort.

He finds his eyes wandering away from the full-length mirror, and he concentrates on trying to hold his image . . . then laughs softly.

"What is it?" Ryalth looks up, as if slightly annoyed at the noise.

"I'm sorry," Lorn says softly. "I'll ask for my favor. It won't take but a moment, and then I'll leave you to the reading."

"What is it?" Suspicion mixed with amusement clouds her voice.

"I want you to read for a moment or two, then look up at me, and tell me what you see."

"Is that all?" A faint frown furrows her brows.

"That's all." Lorn grins at her. "Really."

"I start reading now . . ."

"Exactly." Lorn concentrates once more on the sense of aversion, of nudging the order-reflected chaos of light just slightly so that the pattern makes Ryalth, or anyone, wish to look away from himself.

"Lorn! Don't do that."

Lorn drops the blurring shield. Perhaps that is not what it is called, but that is what it feels like. "Do what? What did you see?"

"I wanted to look at you, and it was as though I couldn't. My eyes kept drifting away from you as though you weren't there."

"Good."

After a moment, Ryalth nods soberly. "I can see that, but be careful when you do that."

"I will, but from what I recall, it's hard to detect, even by a lector, because it's such a gentle and delicate manipulation of order and chaos."

She shakes her head, then smiles. "There are times when not being seen could be useful, especially when some Austran trader wants to know why you won't sell him a quarter-case of golden brandy."

"Because most others won't buy a broken case?"

Ryalth nods.

"That's my favor, dearest. I need to practice some more so I don't forget how I did it."

"Just don't expect me to watch."

"I won't." After his smile fades away, and Ryalth picks up the next invoice, Lorn tries once more . . . and then again.

After a mere halfscore of attempts, he finds his whole body is shaking, and his vision is blurring. Faint stars seem to appear wherever he looks. His lips curl. Another skill that takes much energy, and even more practice.

He wipes his brow. "I need to get some bread or cheese or something. Do you want anything?" He looks at the trader who is more than halfway through the invoices.

"Just some more quiet."

Lorn nods. "I'll be in the study. If you let me know when you're done?"

"I will."

He unlatches the bedchamber door, steps out into the dark corridor, and starts down the stairs to the kitchen to see what he can find to eat, placing each foot carefully, and trying to ignore his wavering vision.

CXXIII

THE OLDER MAGUS looks at the unconscious healer lying on the bed. He concentrates, and the slightest shimmering of chaos enfolds the young woman for a moment, then vanishes. The younger magus, broad-shouldered and with dark red hair, breathes a gentle sigh.

After a moment, the two step from the bedchamber.

"You see?" asks the red-haired and green-eyed older magus. "That was her sister's doing, and she will not remember this . . . not for a time, if ever. The suroyen will make her feel ill, as if a minor flux . . . but she will not have her order powers fully back for a day or so. Best you ensure you have an heir by then."

"Yes, ser. Was there no other way?" Ciesrt wrinkles his forehead, then purses his lips.

"Have you found any such, my first-level adept?" Kharl's eyebrows lift. "You have been consorted now for, what, four years?"

"Almost five," Ciesrt replies.

"And have you an heir?"

"No. But I worry. In her own way, she is fragile."

Kharl shakes his head. "She is a healer. She will love the child, and it will make it easier in time for you two to have another. Be kind and gentle, and you will see. Healers always love children. You have seen her with her brother's son, have you not?"

Ciesrt nods.

"All would have been well, had her elder sister not become involved. Yet . . . one can say nothing, not now, for she is most effective as a healer, even if she chooses to dally with a dissolute merchanter."

"None know much of him, save he provides her lodging and gambles much."

"He gambles well," Kharl says, "well enough to hold a dwelling in the merchanter quarter, and to do little else. It is sad that a daughter of such a once-great line will have neither consort nor heirs." He frowns, momentarily. "But you and Myryan will continue that heritage, and you may prosper far more than any would have dreamed."

"She'll be all right, won't she?"

"She will be fine." Kharl coughs gently. "She will not even recall anything until tomorrow morning, I would judge. Do what you must, and tell her that she has the flux when she wakes."

Ciesrt frowns, then nods.

"I will be going." Kharl steps toward the doorway of the bedchamber. "I can let myself out."

Ciesrt looks at Myryan, then at the doorway, but it is empty, and shortly there is the sound of another door closing.

CXXIV

THE RECORDING HALL in the Quarter of the Magi'i is of polished white marble, like that of the small hall in Jakaafra where Lorn and Ryalth were consorted. The tall and narrow windows are also of ancient blue glass, and there are no furnishings in the hall save a single white sunstone pedestal. There, the resemblance ends. The white granite walls soar high overhead, into an arch whose highest point is nearly thirty cubits directly above the pedestal. The windows are more than ten cubits high, and their casements are of green marble.

Among the halfscore couples standing at the back of the hall before those windows, all are in total shimmercloth white—except for Lorn and Ryalth. He wears the green-and-cream formal Mirror Lancer uniform, and she the green-trimmed formal blue shimmercloth tunic and trousers of a merchanter clan head consorted to a Mirror Lancer.

To their right stand the parents of Aleyar—Liataphi and Lleya—and to their left, Tyrsal's mother.

Behind the sunstone pedestal stands a senior lector—Hyrist'elth. Hyrist looks down at the massive open book that rests on the stand of white sunstone. Each page of the book is a cubit-and-a-half in height and two-thirds that in width. The senior lector wears a sashlike white shimmercloth scarf that barely stands out against his white shimmercloth tunic and trousers.

"I am Hyrist'elth, senior lector, and recorder of consortings for all the Magi'i. Approach . . . you who wish to record your consortship here in Cyad, the city of Eternal Light, and home of the Magi'i." The lector and recorder inclines his head to the couple.

Tyrsal and Aleyar walk slowly toward the book and sash-wearer until they stop and stand two cubits back from the sunstone pedestal and the book upon it. Both look to the recorder.

"Do you two—Tyrsal'elth of the Magi'i and Lady Aleyar, healer of Cyad—declare your intention to take each other as consorts?"

"I do," Tyrsal replies.

"I do," affirms Aleyar.

"Would you each inscribe your name in the book before you, signifying that such is your choice of your own free will, in the prosperity of chaos and light and under the oversight of the Emperor of Light?" With a smile, Hyrist extends a shimmering white pen to the slender healer.

After taking the cupridium-tipped pen, Aleyar bends forward and writes her name. She straightens and hands the pen to Tyrsal. He leans forward and writes his name.

Hyrist takes the pen and replaces it in the ceremonial cupridium holder, then clears his throat before declaiming, "As entered in the book of the Quarter, in Cyad, the City of Eternal Light, you are hereafter consorts." Hyrist looks at the couple and declaims sonorously, "May you always be fulfilled in the light and in the fullness of time."

Tyrsal slips the shiny silver onto the pages of the book, according to custom, then steps back, standing before the sunstone pedestal almost awkwardly.

Aleyar whispers something, and Tyrsal turns and kisses her, flushing slightly.

Beside Lorn, Ryalth sighs. Lorn can hear more than one gentle sigh from the back of the hall where the halfscore of couples stand as witnesses and family.

Then, Tyrsal and Aleyar turn and walk back toward the double doors that are opened by two junior Magi'i.

As the just-consorted couple nears Lorn and Ryalth, Tyrsal smiles broadly and happily at his friend. Lorn smiles back. After the two pass, Lorn and Ryalth turn and follow the others out of the hall and down the wide white-granite steps.

A line of carriages waits outside the hall, and Lorn and Ryalth share a carriage with Syreal and Aleyar's youngest sister, Nyarl. Like all of Liataphi's daughters, Nyarl and Syreal are blonde, although Nyarl barely looks old enough for the healer pin she wears in the collar of her white tunic.

"They both looked very happy," Ryalth says.

"So did Father," suggests Syreal. "Aleyar is happy, and he has a magus in the family at last."

"Having the head of a trading house in the family is also good," Lorn observes.

"From you, Lorn, I will accept that gratefully." Syreal smiles. "From others, it would be condescension. I wish Veljan would have come to the ceremony," she adds. "He will be at the consorting dinner."

Lorn notes the absolute lack of doubt in Syreal's voice, and represses a smile.

Syreal glances at Ryalth. "I hope you don't mind, but he insisted that we be seated next to you. He wasn't sure there would be anyone else he could talk to."

"I do understand," Ryalth replies. "It felt strange being the only ones not in white."

"I wanted to wear my greens," Nyarl said, "but Father and Mother insisted on white. When I get consorted, I will wear green."

Lorn smiles.

"You were a magus, once, weren't you?" Nyarl asks Lorn.

"I was a student magus," Lorn admits.

"I thought so. I'll wager—"

"Nyarl . . ." cautions Syreal.

"Yes, sister dear."

"I've been a lancer officer for many years now."

"Tyrsal says that you're the best field officer in the lancers. Are you?"

Syreal rolls her eyes.

Lorn laughs. "Tyrsal is kind, and he's my best friend. He may rate me higher for that reason." He inclines his head to Ryalth. "My consort, the lady trader, has accomplished far more than I have."

"He says you're the most accomplished lady trader in the history of Cyad—"

Syreal sighs.

Ryalth bursts out laughing, shaking her head. "That may . . . be true . . . but only because there have been so few."

The carriage slows, then stops, then creeps, then stops, the pattern repeating for several times until it halts before the stone floral gateway to Liataphi's dwelling. Lorn slips out of the carriage and holds the door for the three women.

"Thank you . . ." murmurs Syreal.

Lorn and Ryalth follow the sisters into the house and up the circular staircase to the second-level foyer, where several groups of people are already gathered and talking. As Lorn surveys the small crowd, again he notes that virtually all are clad in white shimmercloth.

He frowns as he senses the brief chill of a chaos-glass, and he glances at Ryalth, who responds to his glance with a nod. Syreal catches the exchange. A slightly puzzled look vanishes almost immediately as she says in a low voice. "Terrible manners . . . and less point, except to be rude. Probably Rustyl. I told Father and Tyrsal he could not be invited."

"You're not exactly fond of him?" Ryalth asks.

"He tried to insist Father allow Aleyar to be his consort, and even got Chyenfel to put in a good word. Father, for once, listened to the rest of us."

"Even were he not my friend, I would find Tyrsal far better for your sister," Lorn says.

"Rustyl is a finely-formed dungball," suggests Nyarl brightly.

"Nyarl . . ."

"He is, but I'll be still."

"Thank you," answers Syreal.

Lorn and Ryalth smile, then watch as Syreal turns.

Veljan—wearing pure blue shimmercloth, not the blue-and-green of Ryalth's tunic, is blocky, clean-shaven, and square-faced. He makes his way from the circular staircase toward the foyer outside the dining area, and his brown eyes sparkle when he catches sight of Syreal standing beside Ryalth.

As he approaches, Veljan bows to Ryalth and then to Lorn.

"You have heard of Lorn and the Lady Ryalth, Veljan," offers Syreal.

"I am most pleased to see you both here, and especially you, Lady Ryalth."

"And I, you, honored trader." Ryalth smiles warmly.

Lorn inclines his head politely.

Veljan laughs. "I can only lay claim to seeking to be honest and fair and listening to two of the best advisors a trader could ever have." His head inclines to Syreal.

"Lorn! Ryalth!" Two dark-haired figures make their way through the growing crowd.

Lorn smiles as Jerial and Myryan approach. "I was looking for you."

"We just got here," Myryan explains. "Ciesrt was late, and now he's stopped downstairs to talk to someone."

"These are my sisters, Jerial and Myryan." Lorn looks the other merchanter couple. "And Veljan and Syreal. Syreal, you may recall, was a favorite of Father's."

Syreal flushes slightly as she bows. "Aleyar has talked about you both so much. I am so pleased to meet you."

Veljan bows. "And I, also."

A handbell rings, and Liataphi's voice rises above the conversations taking place around the foyer. "If you would all find your placards and seat yourselves . . ."

"We'd better find Ciesrt," Myryan says, then looks at Veljan. "It was good to meet you." She turns to Lorn and Ryalth. "We'll talk to you after dinner."

"And you, too," replies Syreal.

"Please find your placards," Liataphi's voice rises again.

"Father . . . always organizing everyone," says Syreal good-naturedly.

"There's one in every family," Veljan says. "My sister Elnya is that way."

"Yes, she is," agrees Syreal, "nice as she is."

"Chyla looks like her," interjects Nyarl. "Perhaps she'll be like Lady Ryalth."

Syreal rolls her eyes. "Nyarl . . . you need to find your place."

"So do you." But Nyarl bows and turns.

"I love her," Syreal says as the younger healer slips past several Magi'i and consorts Lorn does not know, "but she has the healing skills of one twice her age, and the tact of people of one-half her age." After a pause, she adds, "We're over on the left side of the first table."

"At the bottom, I imagine," suggests Veljan, withholding a grin for a moment.

Syreal flushes, if briefly, then shakes her head, moving toward the table. The other three follow, and seat themselves before the simple white cards with their names. Lorn is seated farthest to the right and from the head of the table, jointly shared by the newly-consorted couple. Above him on the same side are Aleyar's parents, so that Lorn sits beside Lleya. Ryalth is seated on Lorn's left, with Veljan beside her, and Syreal at the bottom corner.

Serving girls come down the tables, offering either Fhynyco or redberry juice. Lorn, Ryalth, and Veljan take the wine, Syreal the juice.

Somewhere the bell rings, and silence finally reigns in the dining area that holds three tables. At the head table, Tyrsal rises and surveys the party.

"Thank you all for coming," Tyrsal says. "I'm supposed to make a few light remarks and then let everyone enjoy the food. So I will. First, we thank our parents, for being the first ones in making this happy event possible. Second, I would like to thank Lorn, and only say that you and your father were absolutely correct about Aleyar, and I wish I'd listened sooner." Tyrsal grins. "Except I probably wouldn't have appreciated her half so much then. And lastly, I'd like to say how much it means to us both for you all to be here." With another broad smile, Tyrsal sits down.

"He was brief," offers Veljan.

"Tyrsal never speaks long unless he has something of worth to say," Lorn says. "Unlike some of us who are more wordy."

"You are more like Tyrsal than you would admit," suggests Syreal, "else you would not be friends."

Lorn shrugs. Both Syreal and Ryalth nod at each other, then lean back as a serving girl offers the braised lamb in lemon sauce, followed by buttered and nutted beans, and grass-rice.

After the servers pass on, Veljan clears his throat and

turns to Ryalth. "I hope you will pardon me, but we haven't had the pleasure of meeting before, and I would like your thoughts on some matters." He smiles boyishly. "I have to confess that I like to get opinions from everyone I respect, because I know that I know very little."

"That alone means you know a great deal," Ryalth parries.

Syreal laughs. "She knows what you want, dear."

"I make no secrets of it," Veljan admits. "I am not like Tasjan, sneaking around with all his informers, and Sasyk and all his guards. Nor like Vyanat'mer, who must study every invoice in his house each time before he decides on a venture. I prefer to listen to people, not spies or papers."

"And you listen very well," suggests Lorn.

Syreal nods.

"What think you of the cochina dyes from Hamor?" Veljan asks Ryalth.

"They are good dyes, especially for wool, but at ten golds an amphora?" Ryalth shakes her head. "Besides, most folk in Candar, except the Hydlenese, are not partial to red. The Kyphran green is a better buy, and there are more customers for it."

Veljan laughs. "So . . . you have already sold all you have?"

"Of course." Ryalth grins. "Not that I didn't buy and sell an amphora or two of the cochina red as well—as you did, I recall."

Veljan shakes his head, ruefully. "What of the yellow of Suthya?"

"I would not sell it."

"Tasjan buys much there," Veljan points out, adding after a moment, "but he will only sell it to outland traders."

"What does he receive for buying it?" Lorn asks.

Veljan frowns.

Syreal nods and answers. "The right to hire armsmen for his vessels."

"So . . . most of his guards . . . are outlanders?" Lorn pursues.

"Many, I have heard," Veljan admits.

"Are they just guards?" asks Ryalth. "Does he not have them wear uniforms that are the same, no matter what ship they serve?"

"He says he is preparing for when the fireships are no more," Syreal says flatly. "But some few vessels of smaller traders have vanished when no other ships were near save his."

"Wouldn't someone notice the cargoes?" questions Lorn.

"Not if they are sold to outlanders," Ryalth points out.

"It is true that Tasjan has cultivated many outland traders," Veljan says slowly, "but one cannot accuse another merchanter or bring a charge before Vyanat without some proof. Tasjan is most careful."

Lorn nods.

"Aleyar has said that you and Lorn met long years before you were consorted," Syreal says. "And that you were not consorted in Cyad."

Both Lorn and Ryalth understand the meaning of the question. Lorn looks at Ryalth. "Best you answer."

"Yes, let us hear the lady's version," suggests Veljan.

Ryalth smiles, then takes a brief sip of the Fhynyco before speaking. "I was a very junior merchanter, and he was still a student magus . . ."

Lorn watches as his consort speaks, marveling once more at how fortunate he has been that she had been so patient with him. Around them, various conversations ebb and flow as he listens to Ryalth's voice.

CXXV

LORN STANDS BY Fayrken's desk in the fourth-floor foyer of Mirror Lancer Court. He extends several sheets of paper to the senior squad leader. "Here's the report of the oneday meeting. I'll need two copies."

"Yes, ser." Fayrken nods as he takes the sheets. "Short meeting."

"It was this time." Lorn smiles. "Thank you." He turns, and as he sees the curly-haired and narrow-faced commander nearing, he says, "Good day, Commander."

"Good day, Majer." Shykt slows, frowns, then adds, "Might you have a moment?"

"Yes, ser."

Shykt inclines his head toward the door to Lorn's study.

Lorn holds the door to the study and allows Shykt to enter first, then steps into the room, closing the door behind him. The study is dim on a fall midafternoon when the rain, occasionally heavy, slides down the ancient windowpanes. Lorn waits for the senior officer to seat himself before he takes his own seat behind the desk.

"Majer . . . I have heard certain rumors, and I will not put you in the difficult position of denying them falsely or betraying confidences . . ."

"Thank you, ser."

"So I will phrase what I have to say as suggestions about an event that has yet to take place and that may indeed never take place." Shykt purses his lips and tilts his head, then focuses his eyes directly on Lorn. "If it should come to pass that several companies of Mirror Lancers are indeed transferred to Cyad, under the command of a field commander . . . whoever that field commander is might well be advised to be most careful in how he views his orders."

Lorn nods. "Any Mirror Lancer officer must be most careful in such."

Shykt's smile is perfunctory. "We claim to serve chaos and prosperity for the benefit of all Cyador. That can never be, because there are as many Cyadors, in a way, as there are people within our land. Each man, each woman, has a vision of Cyador."

Lorn offers a smile in return. "That is true, and I have pondered that."

"Unhappily, the greater the position a man holds, the more likely he is to feel that what is good for him is good for Cyador. Unless he is the Emperor, or one who can see all of Cyador selflessly, and such are rare, and, I fear, becoming more rare."

With an interested look upon his face, Lorn waits for Shykt to continue.

"It is no secret that the Emperor looks well beyond himself. So does the Empress, and they have been good for Cyador. Less well-known is the fact that this time of change may last longer than the Emperor, and all around Cyad are those positioning themselves for what may occur." Shykt's smile is hard, bright, forced. "Even you, I suspect, Majer."

"Like all men, I have a vision of Cyador, ser, but I am not one to force that vision on the people of this land, and I am a lancer, bound to my duty, and to the Majer-Commander and the Emperor."

Shykt raises his eyebrows. "Those are fine words, if careful."

Lorn laughs, gently. "Ser . . . what would you? If I offered less, you would not be pleased. If I offered more, you would not believe me."

Shykt purses his lips. "Were there . . . Only speculation, you understand, but were there lancers armed with firelances in Cyad, what sort of officer should command them?"

"I was asked that once," Lorn says reflectively. "I recommended Majer Brevyl."

For a moment Shykt is silent, as if Lorn has offered words he had not expected.

"And I say this not in flattery," Lorn says, "even though it might come out as such, that you also would do well in such command. As would Commander Sypcal."

"Flattery indeed, nonetheless." Shykt laughs, more harshly than Lorn would have expected.

"Perhaps," Lorn allows, "but true. You are concerned about what happens to Cyador more than what happens to you."

"Are you, Majer?"

"I hope so," Lorn answers truthfully, adding with a wry expression, "but words are but that until one has to choose."

"That, too, is true." Shykt stands. "I trust you understand why I offered my thoughts on something that might never occur." The commander's voice is neutral.

"You have great concerns for the future of Cyador, as might any man of vision in these times," Lorn replies. "You wish to preserve that which is best about our land at a time when few even consider what things have made it a great land."

"And, I would like my son to have the chances that I did. And his children as well." Shykt nods. "Thank you, Majer."

"Thank you, ser."

Lorn watches as the curly-haired commander closes the door. Then he sits down slowly, wondering who else has read the orders sent by the Majer-Commander, and what others, if any will visit.

After a time, he shakes his head. Speculation will avail him little . . . yet, and he has reports to read, and to summarize for the Majer-Commander. He picks up the first sheet and begins to read. When he finishes the first report, he writes three lines on a separate sheet, then picks up the next one.

He finishes three reports, ignoring the heavier beat of rain on the panes of the closed window.

Thrap.

At the knock on his study door, Lorn looks up. "Yes? Come in." He stands even before he has finished speaking.

The swarthy and dark-browed Luss steps into Lorn's study, and closes the door firmly. "Did you know I was coming, Majer?" asks the Captain-Commander with a frown.

"No, ser. But in the season-and-a-half I've been here, I've yet to meet an officer junior to me, and the messengers and rankers are always announced."

Luss laughs. "Every time I talk with you, I discover more

why the Majer-Commander ordered you here. You see too much too quickly at too young a rank to be left in the field without understanding headquarters."

"I appreciate your compliment, ser, but I am sure there are others who see more."

Luss waves off Lorn's demurral and sits down opposite the table desk.

Lorn sits slowly and waits.

"The Mirror Lancers have always served Cyador, Majer. I'm certain that you understand that."

"Yes, ser."

"And every company, wherever it may be, is in the end under the command of the Majer-Commander."

Lorn nods, understanding all too well the impact of the phrases yet unuttered, but keeping his expression politely interested.

"The duty of the Majer-Commander, whoever he may be," Luss continues, "is to use the Mirror Lancers to preserve Cyador, just as the duty of the First Magus is to use his powers to preserve the Land of Eternal Light."

"Yes, ser."

"Those who serve the Majer-Commander cannot question the Majer-Commander's orders, not and carry out their duties as Mirror Lancer officers."

"No, ser, they cannot."

Luss smiles, almost lazily. "Are you a Mirror Lancer officer, Majer?"

"Yes, ser. My duty is to the Majer-Commander, and to serve Cyador under his command."

Luss frowns, ever so slightly. "Would that be your answer were you still in Invidra?"

"Not quite, ser. My duty would still be to the Majer-Commander, but I would serve Cyador through his orders to the commander at Assyadt."

"As I recall, Majer . . . you had some difficulties there."

"No, ser." His eyes hard, Lorn faces Luss. "I always served Cyador, and the Majer-Commander. I did not serve Majer Dettaur."

"He was in the chain of command, Majer."

Lorn smiles. "He failed to protect Cyador, or the lancers, and I brought this to the attention of both Commander Ikynd and you, and the Majer-Commander. Had I been wrong, I would have been disgraced or executed. I put my life and belief in the Majer-Commander, the Mirror Lancers, and Cyador in the hands of the Majer-Commander."

"You did indeed." Luss smiles genially—and falsely, Lorn knows. "But the Majer-Commander is not a person, but a position of trust."

"Yes, ser, and had you been Majer-Commander, I would have done the same." Lorn hopes Luss will accept the words, because, true as they are, Lorn would have done the same, had Luss been Majer-Commander, for most different reasons.

"You do believe that, don't you?"

"Yes, ser," Lorn replies truthfully.

"Would that others had such devotion to the Mirror Lancers and the Majer-Commander as you." Luss stands.

Lorn stands quickly. "I feel that most officers feel as I do."

"One would hope so, Majer." Luss inclines his head. "Good day." He leaves as abruptly as he has entered.

Lorn feels like taking a deep breath, but does not. Instead, he sits slowly and looks at the heavy raindrops striking the ancient glass. He feels like the name in the ancient poem—whoever Sampson might have been.

After gathering himself together, Lorn has just turned back to his reading and summarizing the stack of reports from Syadtar, when there is another knock at the door, and Fayrken peers in. "Ser, Tygyl sent down word that the Majer-Commander expects you in his study soon as you can get there."

Replacing the two reports he has just read on the stack, Lorn stands. "I'm on my way."

He walks quickly up the stairs. At the upper desk, Tygyl motions for him to enter the Majer-Commander's study.

Lorn does so, closing the door, and bowing. "You requested my presence, ser."

Sitting at his desk, Rynst gestures to the chairs, barely waiting for Lorn to sit before he asks, "How many visitors have you had about your coming assignment, Majer—besides the Captain-Commander and Commander Shykt? Has Commander Inylt contacted you?

"No, ser. And there were no others . . . so far, ser."

"Another cautious answer. I wondered about Commander Inylt, since he is charged with converting part of one of the unused Mirror Lancer warehouses into a barracks and a stable." Rynst leans forward in his chair, seeming larger-than-life framed in the ancient windows that show the backdrop of heavy gray clouds and rain that sleets across Cyad, almost obscuring the Palace of Eternal Light. "I assume that Commander Shykt warned you—most obliquely—against the machinations of others, most probably those of Commander Muyro and the Captain-Commander—and that the Captain-Commander reminded you of the chain of command. Luss doubtless tried to make the point that all companies of the Mirror Lancers are ultimately commanded by the Majer-Commander—whoever he may be—on behalf of Cyador." Rynst pauses.

Lorn waits.

"Yes . . . or no?" Rynst's voice is cold.

"Commander Shykt was far more cautious, ser. He merely suggested that I think through my actions in light of their probable results and remember that, in a way, the fate of Cyad and Cyador rests on the soundness of every officer, no matter how junior. He also asked—if companies of Mirror Lancers were stationed in Cyad—what kind of officer should command them. I suggested that the officer should believe in Cyador above himself."

Rynst laughs. "Ah . . . Shykt knows you. He knows you far better than Luss." Laugh and smile vanish. "How would *you* interpret these visits?"

"Commander Shykt worries that I may hold power greater than I realize if given command of two full companies of Mirror Lancers in Cyad."

"Do you think so?"

"Ser . . . as my father said many years ago, neither the Magi'i nor the Mirror Lancers nor even the merchanters can stand against the will of the people." Lorn offers a shrug he does not feel. "If I do my duty, and my senior officers uphold Cyad, then I will have little power except to uphold what is. If I do not do my duty or my senior officers do not, I will also have little power, for two companies are of little use against a city."

Rynst frowns. "You do not think your senior officers know their duty?"

"You know your duty, ser, and you will die, I believe, before you would betray it. The others know it. Some may not have your strength of will."

Rynst laughs. "You seek to flatter me."

"No, ser. I tell you what I see, and I fear to do so. Honestly is seldom well-regarded, despite all that is said for it."

"That indeed is true." The Majer-Commander shakes his head. "So . . . what will you do if you are tested?"

"My duty is to Cyador, ser."

"An ambiguous answer, Majer."

"It must be, ser. If I answer that my duty is to you, then I could betray all that Cyador is. If I say that it is to the Majer-Commander, then I would be bound to support whoever held the position, no matter if he would destroy Cyador . . ." Lorn shrugs helplessly.

Rynst nods slowly. "You will command those companies, Majer, and your duty remains as it always has been. You may go."

"Yes, ser."

Lorn stands, bows, and turns, wondering if Rynst has any parting comments.

The Majer-Commander does not, and Lorn leaves the study silently, walking steadily to the steps and back down to his study, holding a faint and pleasant smile in place. Yet he worries, knowing that he has been too honest, too direct, careful as he has been. Yet, if he says what others wish to hear, how long before he will do what they wish done, even when such actions are not right or for the good of Cyador?

He smiles grimly. Fine thoughts, when anything can be claimed to be for the good of the Mirror Lancers and Cyador. Everything in Cyador is mirrored in everything else, and some reflections are true, and some of those true reflections are yet false, for they portray true images reflecting onto and concealing deception.

CXXVI

LORN STANDS IN the middle of the bedchamber and concentrates again.

Ryalth looks up from where she sits on the bed and nurses Kerial. "I can see you, in a way, but perhaps that's because I'm getting used to working around it, and because I *know* you're there."

"What if we go downstairs, and I'll follow you," Lorn says. "You ask, say, Kysia, if she's seen me. Since I'll be behind you, she won't think you'd see me, and if she does, just turn and ask me where I was."

The red-haired trader shakes her head. "Is your daily life in Mirror Lancer Court this convoluted?"

"Not yet, but I fear it will be. Word is out, among some of the senior officers, that I will be commanding the two companies of Mirror Lancers."

"And they seek to curry favor? Or threaten you indirectly?"

"More threatening and warning." He frowns. "I can feel all the currents, but there is nothing that anyone could really call proof. The Captain-Commander suggests that loyalty is to the position of Majer-Commander, not the person. The senior commanders try to make sure that they are seen as friendly to those who appear to have power. Eightday after eightday, it continues, because all know power will shift in Cyad. The Emperor will die in the seasons or few years ahead. Chyenfel and Rynst are old." He pauses. "Vyanat'mer is not, but Tasjan still schemes, and Veljan does his best, if with the help of Syreal and Liataphi."

"I like Aleyar and her father," Ryalth says, patting Kerial on the back to burp him. "Veljan would be a better successor to Vyanat than Tasjan, but it would be best if Vyanat remained the Merchanter Advisor. Then, there are those such as Denys and Kernys who would support Tasjan."

"Why? Vyanat has been good for the merchanters, has he not?"

"He has, but they are more interested in their own good or the good of their clan and not the good of all merchanters, or of Cyador."

"You sound worried."

"Many within the merchanters clamor against the tariffs. They claim that Vyanat does little for them but make it harder to prosper."

"What do you think?"

"Vyanat cannot lower the tariffs. He knows this, but some would rather have blood on the sunstones than try to persuade the Magi'i and the Mirror Lancers to change." Ryalth gives Kerial a last pat on the back, then lowers Kerial slightly on her shoulder, before easing off the bed and to her feet. "Let us try what you suggested. It seems silly, in a way, but I know it's not."

"Gaa . . . maamaaa . . ." Kerial offers sleepily.

"In a moment, sweetheart. In a moment." Ryalth nods to Lorn.

He opens the bedchamber door and follows her down the stairs.

Kysia is standing beside Ayleha in the kitchen, and both are hanging the pots used in fixing supper on the rack to the left of the stove. Lorn lets Ryalth get far enough ahead as she enters the kitchen so that he could not be seen even if his effort fails.

"Lady?" asks Kysia, turning.

"Have you seen Lorn?" Ryalth asks. "He's not in his study. I wondered if he'd come down here for something else to eat."

Both women shake their heads.

Lorn eases farther into the kitchen, standing just behind Ryalth's shoulder.

Kysia blinks. "I thought for a moment . . . No, Lady, I haven't seen him."

Lorn eases back out through the archway and releases the blurring effect. "Were you looking for me?" he asks, again stepping into the archway. "I was just walking around, thinking. I should have told you."

Ryalth offers an exasperated glance at her consort.

"I'm sorry," Lorn says apologetically.

Kysia smiles.

"Have you finished your thinking, my dear?" Ryalth asks. "It is time to put Kerial to bed."

"I'm done for now," Lorn admits.

"Good." Ryalth turns back to Kysia and Ayleha. "I'm sorry to have bothered you."

"It was not a problem or a bother, Lady."

"I'm sorry, too," Lorn adds, before he turns to follow Ryalth back up the stairs.

Neither speaks until Lorn closes the bedchamber door.

"I don't know which was more frightening," Ryalth says.

"Which?" Lorn's brows furrow.

"I could feel you behind me, and they couldn't see you. That was frightening. But the way you looked so innocent . . . in saying you were walking around. That was frightening, too."

"It was the truth," Lorn says.

"Dearest . . . you and your family . . . you all can tell the truth . . . words that are what is, and yet convey something else entirely. That is one reason why I am glad you are not a magus." She slips toward Kerial's bed and slips him into it, stepping back.

"Gaa! Maamaaa . . . gaa . . ."

Ryalth shrugs. "He will be awake for a time." Her eyes stray to the stack of papers on the bedside table.

"I'll play with him. You have to read those, don't you?"

"I would appreciate some time," she says.

"You shall have it." With a smile, Lorn walks toward the small bed and his son.

CXXVII

THE TWO MEN approach the shoreward end of the pier nearly simultaneously. Both wear merchanter blue, with similar blue wool cloaks to protect them against the cold wind that blows off the harbor. One, unlike the other, is trailed by two guards in green-and-gold uniforms. The guards stand back as he moves toward the unaccompanied merchanter.

"Oh, Vyel," calls Tasjan, "how good to see you. I was going to stop by after I finished with my tasks on the *Intryg*."

"She is a marvel, like all your vessels," Vyel says pleasantly.

"I would hope so. We have spent enough golds on her." Tasjan laughs. "I have been considering our last conversation, Vyel."

The younger man raises his eyebrows.

The slender Tasjan smiles. "You know that a merchanter

house cannot go to one who is not of the merchanter clan. Even the Emperor cannot change that."

"That is true." Vyel frowns slightly. "All know that."

"And I have found some other interesting invoices." Tasjan extends a sheet that appears from under his cloak. "This is a copy, of course. The one with the seals is in a very safe place."

Vyel reads for a moment, then hands the sheet back. "An interesting invoice." His eyes are dark.

"I thought you would think so." Tasjan smiles. "I would not like to see Hyshrah Clan ... disturbed by such ... were they to become public. Oh ... and if anything were to happen to me, some of them will appear in the hands of the Emperor's Enumerators. Now ... we had discussed the possibility of your obtaining a house of your own, and in a manner that would not harm the interests of Hyshrah Clan."

Vyel nods. "I believe you had mentioned something about that."

"I am certain you know those ... who can arrange disappearances or perhaps those who are less fastidious but can obtain the same results. In these days ... you understand that times are troubled, and it appears as though the majer who is the consort of the trader heading Ryalor House has made some enemies. More than a few." Tasjan shrugs. "He is not likely to survive, one way or another, and right now should anything happen to him ... well, all fingers would point somewhere in Mirror Lancer Court, or even toward the Quarter of the Magi'i. These things happen. One would not want an heir to revenge such an unpleasantness. One would not wish a consort with power, either, who might purchase such revenge." A smile follows. "I am certain you understand."

"I believe I do," says Vyel.

"I would hate to see such invoices as these appear publicly. I do have a soft spot in my heart for you and your elder brother." Tasjan shrugs. "Yet ... in these troubled times, one must do as one can."

"Most honored Tasjan ... ?" Vyel inclines his head.

"You wish to know why I cannot deal with this myself?" Tasjan smiles. "Because the Magi'i follow my every movement with their chaos-glasses, and not being a magus, I know not when I am watched. So I can talk to other merchanters, my family, shopkeepers, and the like. I cannot act on my own behalf, not at the moment, much as I would prefer it, for there is less chance of failure when I can." The smile fades. "My limits are your opportunity. The opportunity may not exist that long. And while you have good contacts, Vyel, my others are also good, and could accomplish . . . other ends, if indirectly. I would prefer to use a man who has much to gain, and who wishes to avoid disgrace, rather than one merely paid in golds. I'm sure you understand."

"I understand. You must realize that matters such as you have suggested cannot occur overnight."

"Not overnight. No. But these invoices will be either burned or public within the eightday. The choice is yours, Vyel." Tasjan offers a last smile, and wraps his cloak about him. "Good day."

The younger man stares along the stone pier, out toward the oncoming storm, for a time before he turns.

CXXVIII

As LORN PASSES the fountain, its cold spray drifting around him, he wonders if they should shut off the water to it before long. Then he smiles as he sees Ryalth standing on the veranda, waiting for him. She is not smiling.

"What's the matter?" he asks.

"Mryran sent a messenger, saying that she wasn't feeling that well, and asking if she could come another time," says the red-haired trader. "It doesn't feel right."

"I worry about her," Lorn replies, stepping forward and hugging his consort.

Ryalth hugs him back, warmly, but for a moment. "She also sent word that she must have dinner with Ciesrt's parents tomorrow, and that she will need to be strong for that." She shakes her head. "I would not wish to wear her boots."

"We're all different. I doubt she'd wish to wear yours." He glances around. "Where's Kerial?"

"Sleeping. He was awake all afternoon. I didn't have to meet with any outlanders, and that was fine. I just hope he isn't awake all night."

"Two of us share that wish," Lorn affirms, following her into the foyer from the chill of the veranda.

"Don't you think it's strange?" Ryalth asks, turning as they stand in the sitting room just off the front foyer. "We've never met Ciesrt's family. Vernt and Mycela have, but we haven't."

"We're not Magi'i," Lorn points out. "The honorable Kharl'elth appears to count that of great importance. Even to encouraging Ceyla to consort to Rustyl."

"That was last eightday, Myryan said."

Lorn shrugs. "You see. We weren't considered important enough to invite."

"I'm glad we're not. I'm glad you're not. You're better than they are."

"So are you," Lorn replies with a smile. "So are you." He embraces her again.

CXXIX

THE ONLY FOUR sitting around the Majer-Commander's conference table are Commander Muyro, Commander Shykt, Rynst, and Lorn. Although the morning sun streams through the windows behind the Majer-Commander, a cold wind whistles outside the closed windows.

"You had three of the large portable firecannon around the

Accursed Forest, and three smaller cannon, did you not?" Rynst looks at the dark-faced Muyro.

"Yes, ser. Two remain there. One of each has been stored in one of the Mirror Engineer warehouses in Fyrad, as you requested."

"I would like you to make arrangements to bring those two now in Fyrad here to Cyad, as soon as you can."

The faintest of nods comes from Shykt.

"Ser?" Muyro looks puzzled. "That will bring them farther from the Accursed Forest."

"The Accursed Forest is not the problem it once was." Rynst pauses, then goes on, almost wearily. "As you know, Commander, we now have four fireships, and perhaps we will have but three in the eightdays or seasons to come. But the firecannon will work so long as the Magi'i operate even a single chaos-tower. The Emperor has suggested that a firecannon or two might well provide greater protection for Cyad—and, upon occasion, its power could be demonstrated for the benefit of the outland traders."

"Ah . . . yes, ser . . . but it could easily destroy . . . many things . . . here in Cyad."

"In fact," Rynst replies, "it may be used for such. We will be needing it . . . for a number of practical reasons here."

Muyro glances across the table at Shykt, who shrugs to indicate he has no words to add.

"How soon could you arrange for the two to be transported here, Commander Shykt?"

"I would have to talk to Commander Inylt, ser, but it is no more than three days by fireship, if we could use one to bring them here. If we use a merchanter vessel, it will take an eightday, perhaps longer, if there are none with cargo space for something that large. And it will cost quite a few golds if we use a merchanter vessel."

"You have permission to request a fireship . . . if that is what you were seeking." Rynst's smile is cold.

"Thank you, ser. We will work to have the two firecannon

here as quickly as possible. Do you wish them kept in the Mirror Lancer supply warehouse?"

"Is there adequate space there—where they will be safe?" asks the Majer-Commander.

"Yes, ser. We can have an iron gate in place on the empty side in the time it will take to bring them here."

"Good." Rynst looks at Muyro. "You and Shykt work with Commander Inylt. I'll expect the firecannon in less than two eightdays."

"Yes, ser."

"You all may go." Rynst stands.

In the foyer outside the study, the bearded Muyro turns to Lorn. "You would not know what this is all about, would you, Majer?"

"I understand that the Emperor has asked the Majer-Commander to find a way to show the outlanders the power of Cyador," Lorn replies. "I imagine, although no one has said anything to me, that a firecannon could be most impressive. Those used by the Mirror Engineers when I had a company at Jakaafra were extremely effective."

Muyro shakes his head and turns, muttering to the curly-haired Shykt, "A firecannon, in Cyad. What order-fired good will that do?"

"We are not here to question the Majer-Commander, Muyro," Shykt responds. "We are to make sure his orders are carried out. We should find Inylt before the Majer-Commander contacts him directly . . ."

Lorn turns toward the steps that will take him down to his study, and the short report he must write on the meeting.

CXXX

SIX PEOPLE SIT around the long table that could easily hold twice that number. The three men all wear the white shimmercloth of the Magi'i, and two of the women wear white tunics and trousers, trimmed in pale green. The third woman—the one with curly black hair—wears the green of a healer.

The light cast from the shimmering cupridium reflectors of the wall lamps blankets the formal dining room with a warm glow, and turns the white linen into a pale gold. The golden-oak backs of the carved dining chairs are sculpted into smoothly interlocking arcs, none quite forming a complete circle.

The older magus who sits at the head of the table is the only one of the three with the crossed lightning bolts glimmering on the breast of his shimmercloth tunic. The others wear but a single such lightning bolt. After taking another small sip of the maroon Fhynyco, the older magus turns his eyes to the healer who sits to his left.

"Your brother Vernt . . . he is most dedicated to the Magi'i."

"He always has been," replies Myryan.

"And your older sister?" asks Kharl'elth politely.

"She remains a healer. As you know, she has found healing to be her calling."

"Without a consort, alas."

"There is a need for some healers who remain without consort." Myryan smiles politely, lifting her glass of redberry, but barely sipping any of the juice.

Kharl inclines his head to the thin-faced healer. "Your ability to assist the . . . lower . . . healers, and your aid to the officers of the Mirror Lancers, are most remarkable,

Myryan. And your actions have bestowed much honor upon your consort and this house."

Myryan bows her head. "What little I do but is but a trifle in the light that already shines forth from this house."

"Modest, she is, as well." Kharl turns his eyes from Myryan to the tall and broad-shouldered Ciesrt. "Yet she is talented in healing, and in teaching her craft, and from a most distinguished lineage, and with a garden with which few compare."

Myryan lowers her eyes.

"She is most remarkable as a consort." Ciesrt beams. "In so very many ways. I look forward to coming home each day."

"And you are most fortunate, my son," adds the white-haired woman who sits at the end of the table opposite Kharl. "Remember that in years to come."

Myryan covers her mouth and swallows quietly, her eyes remaining downcast.

In the dimness of the dining room, and against the distant lightning of the fall storm over the harbor, the vague unseen luminescence of chaos perceived by four of those around the table, and with the flickering of the lamps in wall sconces, none remark upon the faint and also unseen mist of darkness that lifts away from Kharl.

Nor do any note the sudden pallor that crosses Myryan's face. The healer takes a slow sip of wine, and steadies herself beneath the level of the table with her left hand—the one that had been resting in her lap. Her eyes remain demurely downcast, not meeting those around the table for some time.

When she does raise her head, ever so slightly, an enigmatic smile plays across her lips momentarily.

CXXXI

SSssssssss. . . . ssss . . . sssss . . .

Lorn is wide-awake even before the second hiss of the watchgeese, and the Brystan sabre is in his hand, even as he sends out his perceptions. The corridor outside the door is empty.

"What . . . ?" Ryalth sits bolt upright almost as quickly as Lorn has.

"Bolt the door after me," he whispers to Ryalth as he holds the Brystan sabre ready and pads toward the bedchamber door.

She follows him to the door, wordlessly.

He pauses, letting his senses recheck the hall, but it is empty, and he steps out, blade ready. The door closes behind him, Ryalth sliding the latch into place. Step by quiet step, he descends to the main level, but the house remains empty, and he moves toward the foyer and the steps up to the veranda.

Rrrrr . . . eeeekkk. . . . The dull squeaking, straining sound comes from the door from the veranda to the foyer.

Abruptly there is a single *clang*ing sound, as if a long iron bar has fallen on the stone tiles of the veranda. Lorn's perceptions tell him that two figures are beyond the heavy oak door. After waiting until his senses tell him that the two have turned from the door, he slides the latch-bar open and slips out, trying to use the blurring shield, then dropping it as he can sense it will distract him far too much.

Both intruders have blades in position and are moving toward the gray-haired form of Pheryk, who holds a lancer sabre at the ready.

Lorn steps forward silently, and from behind the two, his chaos-aided blade severs the taller man's torso from his head.

The second figure glances sideways, momentarily, and both Lorn and Pheryk strike.

Pheryk's blade cuts into the bravo's sword arm, and the double-edged Austran blade clanks on the stones.

Lorn slashes through the man's knee, using chaos as much as cupridium. "Don't kill him."

Two geese still hiss loudly—Lorn can see two other white shapes lying on the grass beside the walk.

As three other men in black appear on the edge of the veranda, longer blades flickering toward Lorn, he eases himself well around the fallen bravo, careful not to step on the fallen blade, and very glad of his ability to see in the darkness.

Two of the men attack Lorn, and the third goes for Pheryk.

Lorn parries the heavier Austran blade of the first to attack him, then steps back, mustering chaos, and flinging a crude firebolt in the face of the second.

"Aeeiii . . ." The man screams, dropping his blade.

The first bravo cannot help but gape, if but momentarily, at the chaos-fire, and that gaping is enough for Lorn's chaos-aided sabre to slash up through gut and ribs. As the man staggers, trying to turn his blade, Lorn's second cut takes his wrist.

Clunnnggg. The sound of the Austran blade echoes dully across the veranda.

The chaos-fire–ravaged figure staggers, then collapses, and the sound of yet another fallen blade reverberates through the night.

Lorn turns, just in time to see Pheryk's blade slash through the neck of the third bravo. Lorn then glances around quickly, sending his perceptions out past the now-silent fountain, but he can sense no movement, hears no sounds but those of the geese hissing, and the moaning of the fallen bravo who lies on the stones of the veranda. He looks at Pheryk, who cleans his blade on the black cloth of the tunic of the man he has dispatched.

Pheryk looks at Lorn. "Fine bladework, ser. Just blade-work."

"Just bladework, Pheryk," Lorn agrees. "From what I can tell, there aren't any more, and the geese are quieting." He turns back to the one living figure lying on the stones, but addresses his words to the old lancer. "You watch the garden, just in case, please. I want some answers."

"Yes, ser." Pheryk, who, like Lorn, is barefoot, but who wears a pair of trousers, steps out to the edge of the veranda.

Lorn edges the fallen blade well out of reach of the badly wounded man. "Who sent you?"

The bravo grimaces and tries to spit. Lorn slashes his cheek.

"Was it Tasjan?"

The truth-reading tells him that the man doesn't know.

"Bluyet House? . . . Hyshrah House . . . ?"

". . . don't know . . . frig you . . . chaoser . . ."

"Assassins?"

In the end, Lorn leans forward and cuts the man's throat. He stands and turns to Pheryk.

"No one else around, ser. Did you learn anything?"

"He doesn't know who sent him. He was probably hired by someone acting for yet someone else."

"That's oft the way they work. So I've been told."

Lorn looks at Pheryk. "I'd like four of these five to be found—but in the street away from here."

"That be easy, ser. And the one who looked to have stuck his head in a stove?"

Lorn pauses. While he could use more chaos, that does not feel right. He pauses as the chill of a chaos-glass sweeps across him, then he looks at Pheryk. "He needs to vanish."

"The harbor's not that far, ser." Pheryk smiles grimly. "I have my cart. I often carry refuse down there."

"Can you manage it?"

"If I wait till just before dawn, no one will think odd of it. The others . . . you and I . . ."

Pheryk glances at Lorn. "Best you wear a cloak."

Lorn laughs softly. "And boots and trousers."

"A mite easier that way."

"I'll be back in a few moments." Lorn walks back through the foyer door, sliding the iron latch in place behind him, then makes his way through the darkness up the stairs. The sense of a chaos-glass fades, but Lorn knows the watcher could return again at any moment.

He taps on the door. "It's me," he says loudly. "The fellow who went off with a blade in his smallclothes."

"Do I know you?" comes the answer.

"Far better than a fellow by the name of Halthor," Lorn replies.

The door slides open, and Lorn slips inside. With a nod, he notes that Ryalth has a sharp dagger poised. "You're a careful lady." He slides the bolt-latch into place.

"I shouldn't be? What happened?" She smiles. "How did you remember Halthor's name?"

"I just did." Lorn moistens his lips. "Someone hired some bravos. There were five. They're dead. Pheryk got one. We need to move the bodies. It would be better that they just turned up dead in the street." Lorn sets the Brystan blade against the wall and pulls on a pair of trousers, an undertunic, and his boots.

"Do you know who sent them?"

"I tried to get answers from one of them. He didn't know. Hired in the darkness, I'd guess. Probably through someone else."

"Tasjan," Ryalth says.

"Why?"

"The Magi'i don't work that way," she points out in a low voice. "The Mirror Lancers don't, either. They were after all of us. Otherwise you would have been attacked alone somewhere. Vyanat needs me. I don't think Veljan would do this, and Bluyet House, much as they hate you, wouldn't dare, because it could mean they would lose clan status."

Lorn stands and takes up the blade again. "I can't imagine Tasjan risking that directly."

"He didn't. It was done by someone who owes him or someone he can force to act. There's no way to prove it, but I know it as surely as I'm standing here."

Lorn nods briskly. "We'll talk more after we deal with the refuse. It's probably better if you stay here until I get back. It won't be long."

"Be careful. They could have others beyond the wall."

"I will . . . but I can tell if they're there."

"Make sure of it."

That . . . that, Lorn will certainly do. He slips from the bedchamber, listens to make sure Ryalth slides the iron latch shut, and heads down the steps to rejoin Pheryk. Even if the dead man with the burned face is found, so long as he is not found near Lorn, people can surmise that he was struck with a lantern or attacked a magus. But . . . with whoever was watching through a chaos-glass, Lorn does not wish to reveal how much chaos he can muster until he must.

CXXXII

IN THE EARLY-MORNING light, Lorn stands in the door to the bedchamber, his eyes going to his consort and son. "Pheryk and I are walking with you to Ryalor House. You were right about last night, but if Tasjan is behind this, he may not be quite so indirect the next time. And you aren't exactly in the best position to defend yourself or run if you're holding Kerial. I'll either come by and walk back with you, or you hire a pair of guards to accompany you and Pheryk."

Ryalth nods as she wraps a small woolen cloak around Kerial, who is trying to crawl away from his mother so that he can plunge off the bed. Ryalth scoops him up. "No." She turns to Lorn. "I would have suggested that, had you not. I think this morning might be safe, but from this afternoon on, it will not be." She frowns. "Yet. . . . if you escort me, and all know that . . ."

"Pheryk was out early this morning, and heard the news about the dead bravos," Lorn says. "You've heard word that certain merchanter rivals have made threats. If merchanters are beginning to kill merchanters, a little care is warranted." Lorn smiles. "After all, it is not as though you have a half-score of guards—merely your consort and a pensioned old lancer."

"The two of you are worth a halfscore," Ryalth snorts.

"Perhaps a quarter-score," Lorn concedes, "but none need to know that. An escort of two for a lady trader and her heir are scarcely excessive."

"True." Ryalth nods.

"There is one other thing, once you reach Ryalor House," Lorn says.

"Besides finding out everything that Tasjan is doing, and if he is hiring more guards, or building ships with cannon?" asks Ryalth.

Lorn shrugs sheepishly. "You're ahead of me."

"I will know more by this evening—and even more by to-morrow evening." Ryalth hoists Kerial to her shoulder. "We need to go. If we do not, you will be late, and that will raise questions. And one of the senior Austran traders will be coming by. He has suggested by his request to meet me, that all is less than desirable with his current merchanting house in Cyad."

"Tasjan's, I imagine," Lorn says lightly.

"Tasjan's or one of the smaller houses like Ryalor." She starts for the bedchamber door, and Lorn follows.

Pheryk is waiting downstairs, and he nods to Ryalth. "A sunny morn, but chill, Lady. Saw but few when I was dumping refuse this morning."

"The others?" asks Lorn.

Pheryk shrugs. "I saw nothing. Perhaps none will."

The three and Kerial make their way through the dwelling, across the veranda, now without bloodstains, Lorn notes, and along the dew-slicked marble walk past the fountain that has been turned off for the winter.

Lorn lets his senses range beyond the gate, but the narrow way is empty, and he unlocks the iron gate. Pheryk steps out first, then Ryalth, and Lorn follows and locks the gate.

The walk to the Traders' Plaza and up to Ryalor House is uneventful. Ryalth exchanges greetings with a handful of others as she crosses the Plaza to the stairs.

Eileyt is waiting inside the door of Ryalor House, holding several sheets of parchment. "Once you are ready . . . Lady . . ."

Lorn smiles and bows to Ryalth. "Until this evening. Should I come by here?"

"I would guess you should. It will be a long day." Ryalth returns his smile warmly.

Lorn and Pheryk turn and walk down the steps.

Halfway down, Lorn says in a low voice, "I think we should have goose tonight."

"Ah . . . a good idea, ser, and I will tell Kysia and Ghrety. My consort has a wonderful way of fixing it . . ."

Lorn laughs. "That would be fine. Perhaps you should also inquire about some more geese or goslings."

"I had thought to do so, ser." Pheryk inclines his head.

At the edge of the Traders' Plaza, the two men part. While Lorn is more cautious than usual, he notes nothing strange on the rest of the walk to Mirror Lancer Court.

He has no more than entered his study when Senior Squad Leader Tygyl is knocking at his door.

"Ser?"

"Yes, Tygyl?"

"The Majer-Commander would like to see you for a moment."

"I'll be right there." Lorn turns and follows Tygyl up the last flight of stairs to the fifth floor and waits for the senior squad leader to announce him, then steps into the long study as Tygyl motions for him to enter.

Lorn closes the door and steps forward, seating himself at Rynst's behest.

The gray-haired Majer-Commander studies Lorn. Finally, he speaks. "I will be announcing your appointment as maneuvers coordinator for the two squads of Mirror Lancers that will be arriving in the next few days. You will be their commander, and the company officers will be told such, but there is little need to state directly that we are assigning two fully armed companies under the command of a field commander. Especially one with a record such as yours."

Lorn nods.

"You do not seem surprised, Majer. Why not?"

"Because, ser, as you know, a number of officers have already approached me indirectly. If they know, many in power know. They will have contacted you, or others who contacted you, and none will be pleased, except the Emperor. The Emperor will care little for titles, and if you can employ a name to placate others, then it is for the best."

"You don't sound as though you think much of the idea." Rynst's eyes are cold as he studies Lorn.

"I doubt it will change anything, ser. Those with something to gain will not be deceived. Those who do not understand how dangerous the times are will not understand, whatever title is used, and few of the senior commanders will be happy with my being in charge, for whatever reason you give."

"You are most cynical, Majer." Rynst offers a dry laugh.

"You have few illusions about your fellow officers, perhaps too few illusions for a majer."

"Perhaps."

"What if I made you a commander?"

"They would be even more angry, and I would advise against that, ser."

"So would I, and I am glad you see that." Rynst shakes his head. "In truth, Majer, all you have said, I understand, yet there is a reason why I will do what I told you. Can you suggest why I might?"

"It implies a weakness in your position, which will allow others the luxury of thinking they have time to plot, when you but wish to ensure that the Mirror Lancer companies arrive and are firmly in my command." Lorn does not say more, although there is much he could say.

"You could say more, Majer."

"Anything beyond what I have said would be a wager based upon a guess, ser." Again, Lorn forces himself not to volunteer more.

"I wished you to know." Rynst nods. "You may go."

After Lorn has risen, bowed, and turned, and has taken several steps toward the door, Rynst says, "Majer . . ."

Lorn turns.

"I would not travel Cyad without your sabre and great care."

"Yes, ser."

As he heads back down to his study, Lorn questions how much Rynst *knows* and how much of what the Majer-Commander has implied is based on his understanding of human nature.

"Does it matter?" Lorn murmurs to himself as he stands and looks out the ancient windows of his study.

The only things that are clear are that the times are about to change, and are dangerous, and that Lorn must be ready to act when the time comes—if he can even recognize when that will be.

CXXXIII

LORN LOOKS ACROSS the dining table at Ryalth, over the large sections of goose they have not touched. The nearly a third of a goose remaining does not include more than half the bird which was already eaten by the other four in the household. Ryalth eats one-handed, occasionally feeding small morsels to the active boy in her lap.

"What else have you discovered about Tasjan?" asks Lorn.

Ryalth takes a sip of the ale, then answers. "He has been careful. So far as any know, he has met with no one except those of his own house in the past eightday or so. He continues to seek more guards with experience as armsmen or lancers. You remember Sasyk, his head of guards?"

Lorn nods.

"Sasyk is also a cousin of one of your schoolmates, I think. Allyrn'alt is the cousin."

"Anything else about Tasjan? What about your Austran trader? Did he have anything to add?"

"The trader was hoping I had still had grain."

"I thought you did," Lorn says, breaking off a small morsel of bread. "You talked about it earlier because of the poor harvests in Hydlen."

"I do, but not at the prices he was willing to pay. He would pay but a tenth-part above what was asked last eightday in the exchange, and but a fraction over the day's bid. Prices will be half again what they are now by midwinter." The redhead sips her ale before continuing. "So I told him that it appeared I might have some grain by midwinter, if my shipments came in as paid for, and that he should see me then if he still needed such."

"Will he?"

Ryalth nods, easing Kerial's hand away from the goblet. "The goblet is for Mother, not for Kerial."

"Did he have anything to say about Tasjan?"

"He was forthright. I must doubt his accuracy, but he said that Tasjan had whole granaries, and would sell to none."

"Tasjan's doing what you are."

Ryalth shakes her head. "No. It might seem so, but it is not. I have perchance a hundredscore measures. Tasjan has that a hundredfold. Had I what he does, some I would sell, for one needs goodwill as much as golds."

"Why would he hold so much—" Lorn purses his lips for a moment before he speaks. "We need to watch him closely."

"My thought, as well . . . If grain prices and that of flour rise in the winter, then many in Cyador will grow hungry."

"And Tasjan will make golds, and use the discontent to blame Vyanat and the Emperor. How many merchanters will support him?" asks Lorn.

"The Yuryan will not, nor the Hyshrah, not so long as Vyanat is clan head."

"Who would become clan head if something were to happen to Vyanat?"

"His younger brother Vyel is next in line." Ryalth frowns. "He has cost Vyanat much, and there are rumors that Vyanat has had to pay the Emperor's Enumerators for tariffs Vyel lied about more than once."

"So Tasjan will try to remove Vyanat."

"That is why Vyanat cannot take clan status from Bluyet House," Ryalth points out. "He needs their support, and why Tasjan spread rumors about Vyanat stripping their status."

Lorn shakes his head. "Bring our little friend up to the study. Let us see what we can discover." He stands, then moves around the table and lifts Kerial from Ryalth's lap. "Come on. Your father will carry up upstairs."

"Maa . . ."

"Daaa . . . this time," Lorn says. "Daaa . . ."

"Waaaa . . ."

Lorn shakes his head, mock-ruefully, and then shifts his son into his left arm and turns toward the stairs.

"Maaa . . ." Kerial repeats.

"I'm coming, dear. I'm coming," Ryalth reassures him, following Lorn up the steps and along the upper corridor and into the study.

Once he has closed the study door—one-handed—Lorn transfers Kerial back to Ryalth and seats himself before the desk, sliding out the glass from the drawer. He concentrates on the image of the slender Tasjan.

As the silver mists dissipate, Lorn studies the glass, and Ryalth and Kerial watch over his shoulder.

Although he is alone, Tasjan paces back and forth in a capacious study, before a large carved desk that is of a style Lorn has never seen, with wooden flowers and garlands forming the legs.

When Tasjan continues to pace, Lorn lets the image lapse. "In a while, I'll try again. Perhaps we'll find him in a more compromising situation. I'll try a few more people."

The next image is that of the Captain-Commander. Once again, Luss is dining with the blond commander Lhary. Lorn releases that image almost as soon as it forms.

"Those two are far too close for my liking."

"Lhary commands all the outposts in the west, does he not, all those close to Cyad?" asks Ryalth.

Lorn nods.

"That is why you report to the Majer-Commander and will hold the two companies."

"One reason, certainly."

Lorn tries yet another image, and finds Commander Muyro and a woman in green, presumably his consort, dining with a mage—Rustyl—and a young-faced, but red-haired and large-boned young woman, probably Rustyl's consort Ceyla, although Lorn has never met the woman, but she looks much like a womanly version of Ciesrt.

The narrow-faced Rustyl glances up, and tilts his head, almost as if listening. Lorn releases the image, shaking his head.

"Everyone is tied to another, and all circle, waiting to see what will happen." Ryalth laughs.

After letting the image in the glass lapse, Lorn leans forward and rubs the back of his neck with his left hand. He feels very much like the times are deciding what will occur, the times and not the men, for he can see nothing he dares do—not yet, anyway.

CXXXIV

IN THE MIDMORNING of fourday, Lorn has just finished summarizing another meeting—this one between the Majer-Commander and Commander Muyro about the last details of installing the Mirror Lancer firecannon.

There is a knock on his study door, and, even before waiting for Lorn's response, Fayrken steps inside. "Two lancer captains reporting to you, ser." The senior squad leader's eyebrows lift.

"They should be the captains for the two companies—the ones I'm the maneuvers coordinator for. That's the latest official title." After a wry smile, Lorn asks, "Do you know who they are?"

"Cheryk and Esfayl, I believe, were the names, ser." Fayrken smiles. "They seemed to know you."

"Have them come right in." Lorn stands and waits for the two to enter. The older captain is thin-faced, gray-eyed, long-chinned, and has brown hair tinged with gray; the second has dark curly hair, and a boyish look to his features.

The long-chinned Cheryk sees Lorn and smiles. "Ser. Might have known it was you."

"Ser." Esfayl barely refrains from shaking his head.

"It's good to see you both." Lorn pauses, then asks, "Your orders didn't say who your commander would be?"

"No, ser. We got here, and climbed up to the top floor, and the senior squad leader said that you were our commander. Here . . ." The veteran with the pale gray eyes extends the scroll.

Lorn takes the scroll and reads it.

. . . report to the Majer-Commander, lancer headquarters, for further assignment in Cyad as determined by the needs of the Mirror Lancers . . .

Then he hands the scroll back, wondering exactly how much to tell the two.

"Ser . . . before I forget . . . Majer Brevyl sent a message," Cheryk offers.

"Majer Brevyl?" Lorn cannot help but frown. "He was at Biehl. What's he doing in Inividra?"

"They sent him from Biehl for a season, ser. Something about making sure that everything was the way it was supposed to be."

After a moment, Lorn asks, "The message?" He would wager that he knows the sort of message Brevyl would send.

Esfayl smiles, his expression confirming Lorn's suspicions.

"He said, ser, that he still didn't care for you personally, but that if you ever made commander, or higher rank, he'd accept serving under you just to see if you have the same nerve when you had power as when you didn't."

Lorn bursts into laughter. "He hasn't changed a bit. How did you find him?"

Cheryk and Esfayl exchange glances. Finally, Cheryk speaks. "His words are rougher than yours, but no one noticed much difference, except that he seldom commands patrols. Gyraet does."

"Did that work out?"

"Yes, ser. Good man. He's a permanent overcaptain now." Cheryk looks around the small study before speaking again. "The majer also said, ser, that we'd be the first Mirror Lancers stationed in Cyad in generations."

"That's true. One reason for that is that the Empire is losing its fireships, and that leaves the Mirror Lancers as the most powerful weapon remaining."

"What about the Magi'i?" asks Esfayl.

"Individually, a number of them are very powerful, but there aren't that many. That means you have a task to do. It's necessary, and if everything goes right, unless someone's really careless, it won't get anyone killed." Lorn smiles. "Call it a reward of sorts."

"Ser?"

Lorn laughs at the dubious tone in Cheryk's voice. "It's simple enough. The outlanders have never seen any of the Morror Lancers' powers, except the fireships, and most outlanders generally only port in places like Cyad, Fyrad, or Summerdock, where there aren't many lancers, even though much of Cyador's strength lies in the lancers. We will be conducting maneuvers—almost on a parade ground—with firelances, whenever the Majer-Commander thinks an important trader is around. Some will even be invited to watch."

Cheryk nods. "Sort of following up on what we did in Jerans?"

"In a way. To show the outlanders that, whether we have the fireships or not, the Mirror Lancers are to be reckoned with."

"Is that why the Majer-Commander brought you here, ser?" asks Esfayl.

"I don't think so, but I wouldn't presume to guess about what the Majer-Commander plans and how far he thinks into the future." Lorn clears his throat before continuing.

"Now . . . you'll be billeted in a warehouse that they've converted into a barracks with officers' quarters. I've seen it, and the quarters are not bad. If you have family here, or find a place to live . . . you can do that, but one of you has to be able to be reached by messenger at all times . . ."

Lorn goes on to explain the details, finally ending with, ". . . if you can't find me, Fayrken can." He pauses. "Oh . . . and the only one who can countermand my orders is the Majer-Commander or the Emperor."

Cheryk looks hard at Lorn.

"Those are the near-exact words of the Majer-Commander," Lorn answers.

"Ser . . ."

"I know . . . they're strange orders, but that's the way it is."

Cheryk looks at Esfayl, then at Lorn. "You report directly to the Majer-Commander, ser?"

Lorn nods.

A slow smile fills the older captain's face. "We'll be having an interesting year, ser."

"I hope not, but it could be." Lorn waits for a moment, and then asks, "Any other questions?"

"No, ser. Both companies are supposed to be here day after tomorrow. When do you want us to start running drills?"

"How about the next day?" Lorn pauses. "Give it some thought. Why don't you both come by after midday tomorrow? Then we'll discuss the kind of drills that might serve our needs."

"We'll be here, ser." Both captains bow.

After the two leave, Lorn goes to the doorway and looks into the foyer. Fayrken is alone at the central desk, and Lorn steps out to talk to the senior squad leader.

"Yes, ser?"

"I'll need two copies of this for the Majer-Commander. It's another meeting report, on firecannon transport to

Cyad." Lorn pauses for a moment. "Were you ever able to find anyone who'd heard of a lancer named Sasyk?"

"Yes, ser. Much easier—real sour pearapple, ser. He was a captain at one of the small outposts—Tyert . . . that's one that used to report to Assyadt, but they closed it. Anyway, about ten years ago, he took his company and killed an entire settlement in the Grass Hills. He claimed they were barbarians posing as settlers. The Majer-Commander sent several commanders to look into it. They found barbarian weapons and some Jeranyi golds, and not much was said. Then, something else happened—no one seems to know what, except that he got cashiered there. He disappeared for a year or two and then came back to Cyad. He is the head of guards for one of the trading houses—someone said Dyjani. None of the senior squad leaders I could talk to knew much more, except that he was supposed to be very good with both a firelance and a sabre."

"Thank you."

"Not a problem, ser."

Lorn does not frown until he returns to his study. Outside the ancient panes, although the sky is clear, the wind has begun to whistle as if heralding a storm.

CXXXV

AS THE CARRIAGE comes to a halt in the circular drive, Lorn opens the door from inside and steps out, extending a hand to Ryalth. She descends onto a white marble mounting block and looks over a halfscore of wide white marble steps that climb to a columned entrance portico. Behind the portico rises a two-story villa that stretches more than a hundred cubits north and south of the portico. Each level of the long dwelling is surrounded by shaded and columned porticos, and on the east side of the circular drive is a garden, enclosed by a hedge with a single entrance—and that entrance is a topiary gate.

Lorn steps down off the mounting block and around to the gray-haired coachman with the kindly and wrinkled face. He looks up and extends a half-silver. "If you could come back at around the eighth bell . . . ?"

"Be pleased to, ser."

The carriage draws away and Ryalth turns to Lorn. "You said that golds ran in Tyrsal's family. This is grander than any of the dwellings of the major clan heads."

"I know," Lorn says. "Tyrsal doesn't like to talk about it. He feels it's really still his mother's dwelling, and he's embarrassed that it's his. Now that he's consorted . . ." He looks up as Tyrsal hurries out of the portico and down the steps.

"Lorn, Ryalth! I was talking to Mother and Aleyar and didn't hear the carriage at the gate. It's good to see you both again."

"Since three days ago?" asks Lorn.

"You know what I meant. Besides, this is the first time we've been able to have you for dinner." Tyrsal leads them up the entry stairs, then through a blue marble-tiled entry foyer to another set of steps. At the top of the wide marble staircase, he turns right along another corridor to the first archway.

Aleyar rises from an old blue-upholstered armchair as the three step through an archway into a sitting room that is alone half the size of the entire first floor of Ryalth's and Lorn's dwelling. The healer smiles warmly. "I'm so glad you could come."

"We are glad to be here," replies Ryalth.

Tyrsal's mother remains seated in the other upholstered armchair, adjoining the one where Aleyar had been sitting.

Tyrsal steps forward. "This is my mother, Ensra. Mother, you remember Ryalth."

"She looks as charming and beautiful as before."

Lorn inclines his head to the white-haired Ensra. "It's good to see you again."

Ensra smiles. "It's good to have younger folk back in the house. The next time, perhaps you could bring your young one."

"Mother Ensra. . . ." Aleyar shakes her head gently. "Let the poor woman have a few moments to enjoy herself away from her son."

"He must be a good child . . . with such parents."

"Good, but he does keep her busy," Lorn says.

"And Lorn, as well, at times," Ryalth adds.

Aleyar gestures. "Please sit down."

Lorn and Ryalth take the settee across from the armchair where Ensra sits. Tyrsal sits on the other settee.

"This dwelling . . . it is quite something." Ryalth gestures around the sitting room, with the dozen or so blue-upholstered armchairs, the matching set of blue velvet settees, and the thick blue-and-gold carpet centered in the middle of the blue-tinged marble tiles.

"It should be," replies Tyrsal with a grin. "My grandsire was the head of Dyjani House. My father was his only heir, and he was a magus." Tyrsal shrugs. "You can imagine how the merchanters felt about that."

"They felt that any merchanter who had the talents of a magus would have an unfair advantage, I'm sure," Ryalth replies.

"He was not given that much of a choice," adds Ensra. "Tasjan's grandsire threatened to bring the matter before the Merchanter Advisor and the Traders' Council."

"You don't hear much of Tasjan's sire," Lorn ventures.

"He died at sea when Tasjan was young," replies Ensra. "Tasjan's grandsire lived to be almost fourscore."

"So the grandsire pushed your father into the Magi'i and became the head of Dyjani clan?" asks Lorn.

"Pretty much," admits Tyrsal with a glance at his mother.

"Exactly so," confirms Ensra.

"Your friend Husdryt . . . what does he think of Tasjan?" Lorn asks.

"Husdryt says very little," Tyrsal replies.

"That alone suggests he has his concerns," says Ensra. "Husdryt was never close-mouthed about that which he likes."

"... uhhh ..." Aleyar clears her throat. "If we do not begin dinner ..."

"It will be cold," Tyrsal says with a grin.

The five rise.

As they follow Tyrsal and Aleyar from the sitting room, Lorn wonders how matters might have turned out had Tyrsal's father remained a merchanter.

CXXXVI

IN THE NEAR-BLACK purple of night, Lorn and Ryalth walk down the wide marble steps of Tyrsal's dwelling to the waiting carriage, followed by Tyrsal and Aleyar. The driver sitting on the coach box is younger, harder-faced than the gray-haired man who had brought them to Tyrsal's.

Lorn stares at the man for a moment, then asks, quietly, "What happened to the other driver?"

"He had a touch of the flux, ser ... asked if I'd spell him, ser."

Lorn can sense the lie. "Oh ... I see." He casts his chaos-senses around the carriage, but can sense no one hiding within. He turns to Tyrsal, still standing on the white marble steps behind the mounting block. "Do you sense it?"

Tyrsal nods.

The coachman looks puzzled, and leans forward slightly. The pose is a lie, as well, one which Lorn ignores.

"Here ..." Lorn points to the rear wheel. "Best you come look. The axle-post is splitting in half."

"Ser?"

"Come look for yourself." Lorn motions to Ryalth. "You'd better step back ... if that fails here ..."

"Yes, dearest." While the redhead's voice is demure, her eyes are hard as she steps back from the mounting block.

The driver clambers down, clearly puzzled. As he steps toward the rear wheel, the Brystan sabre is at his neck.

"One move and you're dead," Lorn says pleasantly.

"Ser . . ." The driver freezes.

Tyrsal appears, and his cupridium sabre is also bared.

"You're lying, and you're not very smart," Lorn continues. "My friend there is a first-level magus. No one told you that, I am sure, but he could tell you were lying. Now . . . you can tell the truth, or you can die."

The man's eyes widen. "They . . . just told me that all I had to do was drive you back to your dwelling except stop short of the gate . . . maybe a hundred cubits . . . and look the other way."

"That's the truth," Tyrsal says quietly. "But there's more."

The driver's eyes flick down toward the shimmering blade at his neck. He swallows.

"Who hired you?" asks Lorn.

"Benylt . . . does work for. . . . for whoever has the golds . . ."

"Who hired him?"

"Ser . . . I don't know . . ."

"You know more than that," Tyrsal says.

"Which merchanter?" Lorn questions.

"Ser . . . I can't say. . . . I mean . . . he's been around . . . His name . . . No one said . . ."

"Benylt didn't tell you . . . but you'd seen the merchanter before?"

"Yes, ser."

"And you weren't supposed to know?"

The hard-faced man swallows. "No, ser."

"What does he look like?"

"Dark-haired, like, but he wore a cloak . . . only remembered him 'cause one of his front teeth be gold . . . Seen him once 'afore when I was first on the piers . . . as a loader . . . came two, three times to the same ship. Wore one of those blue cloaks with a hood all the time, same as when he hired Benylt."

"What ship?

"The *Hippo*—something."

Lorn can sense both Tyrsal and Ryalth stiffening. "How tall was he?"

"Middling, ser . . . not too tall, not too short."

"Did you hear him speak?"

"No, ser."

"How many men will Benylt have?" Lorn's eyes flick to Aleyar, who watches the bravo as closely as Tyrsal does, then back to the pseudo coachman.

"Six, perchance eight. Be not calling more than that, not Benylt."

Lorn looks at Tyrsal, who nods. "Can you handle four or five?" Lorn asks his friend in a low voice.

"If they don't know it."

"What about a shield? Can you sit next to the driver?"

"Be easier if I sat up on the roof, in the baggage rack," Tyrsal points out. "Then I'm behind him."

"Good idea."

Aleyar's mouth opens, then closes, as Tyrsal turns to her and says, "It's more than just Lorn's problem, dear."

Ryalth offers the smallest of nods to her consort.

"You're going to drive us home," Lorn tells the would-be driver. "Just the way you were told."

The man swallows. "Ser . . . ?"

"Unless you'd prefer I use this sabre here and now."

"I'll drive, ser. I'll drive."

"And the magus will be behind you. He's very good with both a sabre and a firebolt."

"I'll drive right careful, ser. I will."

Lorn addresses Tyrsal, his eyes still on the bravo. "Can Ryalth stay here?"

"Of course," the magus replies. Behind him, Aleyar nods.

"What about Kerial?" asks Ryalth.

"I'll bring him back . . . after we deal with this difficulty. We can't get there any sooner."

The redhead clamps her lips together. "You'll be careful. Both of you."

"Very careful." Lorn motions to the driver. "Back up to your seat."

"Ah . . . yes, ser."

As the driver mounts and Tyrsal climbs up on top from the footman's station, Lorn steps back toward Ryalth and lowers his voice. "That ship . . . it's a Hyshrah vessel, isn't it?"

"How did you know?"

"Because it wouldn't have made sense any other way. No other house is a threat to Tasjan, except you. See if you can think about who or how Tasjan would use that to hurt both us and Vyanat."

She nods.

Lorn looks up at Tyrsal, sitting in the baggage rack.

"I'm ready. I'm glad it's not that long a drive."

After a last glance at Ryalth, Lorn climbs into the carriage, his sabre still unsheathed.

The carriage lurches forward, then settles into a even motion. Lorn continues to hold the unsheathed sabre, if loosely, as the driver follows the roads that lead northward and east into the merchanter quarter.

"Just drive up exactly as you're supposed to," Tyrsal orders the driver as the carriage turns off the main way.

"Yes, ser."

The carriage halts beside a torch set in a bracket in the dark low wall more than a hundred cubits east of the iron gate to his own dwelling. Lorn can sense a number of figures, on both sides of the carriage, concealed in the shadows. With several on the wall to the right, Lorn opens the right door from inside. He does not exit, instead, sensing the four men in the shadows, he slides back to the other side, holding the blur-shield for long enough to step clear of the carriage.

Thunk! Thunk!

Two arrows go through the driver's chest.

"Bast . . ." the man gurgles as he slumps.

Hssstt! Hssstt! Two quick firebolts from Tyrsal incinerate the pair of archers who stand in the darkness atop the flat wall adjoining the wall that surrounds Ryalth and Lorn's dwelling.

Lorn does not drop the vision-blurring shield until his chaos-aided sabre slices through the neck of the bravo who steps out of the deeper shadows on the left side of the lane. He then pivots, and steps back toward the second assailant—the one approaching from the rear.

"Where are they?" mutters someone.

Hssstt! A scream begins and dies almost immediately after Tyrsal's firebolt.

Lorn parries a lancerlike slash by a figure nearly a head taller than he is, and then a second, and several more before he has an opening—but the one is all he needs.

Another firebolt hisses through the night as Lorn turns from the second fallen bravo.

"Got a fire-magus there!"

Lorn hurries around the back of the carriage and steps silently behind the rearmost bravo, the one he suspects is Benylt. The chaos-aided Brystan sabre slides through bone and muscle like a red-hot poker through water, sizzling and steaming.

"Got Benylt! Run!"

Two sets of boots begin to run.

Neither makes it a dozen cubits before Tyrsal's firebolts bring them down.

Lorn casts his chaos-senses around, but can find no hint of anyone besides the chaos-shimmering figure of Tyrsal. "There isn't anyone else, is there?"

"Not alive," Tyrsal replies dryly. He slowly climbs down from the carriage box, holding a sabre he has not used.

Lorn studies the figure of Benylt sprawled on the stones.

Tyrsal looks from one sprawled figure to another, shaking his head. "I don't know as I could do what you do all the time."

"I could do it with types like these every day." Lorn snorts, bending and wiping his blade clean on Benylt's cloak.

"What do we do with all these bodies?" asks Tyrsal, blotting his forehead.

"I don't think there ought to be any," Lorn suggests. "If bravos just vanish every time they take on Ryalor House . . . in time . . . perchance . . ."

"You are an optimist, my friend, but I can muster enough chaos, I think."

"Good. After that we'll check on Kerial, and go back to your house, if you don't mind." Lorn smiles grimly.

"You're welcome . . . Can you put a stop to this?"

"I have some ideas." Lorn begins to gather up the fallen blades. "They might even work."

CXXXVII

LORN CLOSES THE door of the guest bedchamber in Tyrsal's dwelling and turns to Ryalth. She is propped up on the bed and is already nursing Kerial. He unclips the sabre scabbard from his belt and leans weapon and sheath against the wall.

"How was he?" she asks.

"He was sleeping—a bit fussy when I woke him up, but he liked the carriage ride. Pheryk's a better driver than most." Lorn takes a deep breath. "I think everything would have been all right at home, but there wasn't much point in risking it, and then traveling out to get you and then coming back again and worrying."

"What did you do with the carriage?"

"Pheryk drove us back and then said he would leave it tied at the carriage station that serves Hyshrah Clan. There's no one there at this time of night."

"You're being more indirect thàn usual," the redhead says.

"I want Vyanat to have something to think about." Lorn shrugs

"You acted as if you *knew* the *Hypolya* were one of Vyanat's vessels. Is there something you haven't told me?" Ryalth looks at Lorn. "I cannot believe that he would wish either of us dead—or that any thinking member of his house would."

"It would depend on the thoughts." Lorn sits down on the side of the bed and gestures to the bag beside the armoire. "I brought daywear for the two of us, and three sets of clothes for Kerial." He bends to pull off his boots. "I also brought my chaos-glass."

"You dòn't think Vyanat—"

"While I trust no one, I do trust your feelings, especially on that. But there are enemies and relatives within every large house, and their goals may not be at all the same as Vyanat's. Perhaps you should pay Vyanat'mer a visit—tomorrow—and bring me along. Tell him that I wanted to meet him because he had appreciated my report on Biehl so much. I'll send a messenger in, saying that I'll be slightly late to Mirror Lancer Court."

"You think Vyanat will see me if I just show up?"

"With me beside you? I think so." Lorn grunts and pulls off the other boot. "At the very least he will wish to know why you want to make such a call."

"How many did you kill tonight?"

"They killed the coachman with archers. We killed eight plus the leader. Tyrsal used chaos-fire to incinerate the bodies. He has a headache, and he's not going to feel wonderful in the morning."

"Aleyar will help."

"That's true. I also asked him if he would request she not tell Liataphi for a day or so."

"Just a day or so?"

"Until after we meet with Vyanat."

Ryalth lifts Kerial to her shoulder and burps him gently.

Lorn stands and walks to the corner by the armoire, setting his boots almost against the wall, then bending again and easing the chaos-glass case from the bag. He carries the case to the table under the window and eases back the vase with the spray of cut flowers to make room for the glass.

Lorn concentrates, and, as the silver mists form and then dissipate, the image of Tasjan appears in the glass, sitting at a long table, clearly enjoying what seems to be a family gathering of sorts. Lorn shrugs and releases the image.

The next image is that of Luss—in his bedchamber. Lorn also releases that image quickly. Rustyl, too, is in bed, apparently sleeping, although the magus turns in his sleep. Lorn lets the image vanish.

"Did you find anything?" Ryalth asks, yawning.

"No. I would have been surprised if I had."

"Because Tasjan worked through someone else?"

Lorn nods as he replaces the glass in its case. "We do need to see Vyanat in the morning."

"If he is in Cyad."

"He will be. Tasjan needs him to be."

Ryalth offers a sad smile.

CXXXVIII

RYALTH BOWS AS she steps into the square room that is Vyanat's office. Lorn bows as well, before straightening and taking in the muscular but trim Merchanter Advisor. Behind the merchanter's table desk is a wall that is entirely bookshelves, and almost every shelf is filled with leather-bound volumes.

Lorn notes two volumes on one of the higher shelves, volumes bound in the same shimmering silver as Ryalth's book of verse, but the majer does not let his eyes dwell on them.

"I do appreciate your seeing me with so little notice." Ryalth smiles.

Vyanat bows. His perfectly combed black-and-silver hair moves not a fraction of a cubit. "When a house head so successful as you asks for a moment, I am more than pleased to grant it." His head inclines toward Lorn. "This, I presume, is your consort, the redoubtable Majer Lorn."

Lorn bows politely once more. "I have heard much of you from Ryalth—much good." He smiles. "I have also heard that you believe directness and honesty to be necessary for the merchanters of Cyador to flourish."

Vyanat laughs. "You must wish to be direct."

"I may in the future," Lorn counters.

"Lorn had wished to meet you and to see Hyshrah House," Ryalth says.

"It appears as though much of what affects Hyshrah House and other merchanter houses also bears upon Mirror Lancer Court, and I have but seen my consort's house," Lorn admits.

The faintest frown flickers across Vyanat's brow.

"I see you have rather a large number of volumes here." Lorn gestures to the shelves behind the Merchanter Advisor.

"Most were gathered by my sire. He insisted that I read and learn certain of them."

"One can learn much from the past," Ryalth suggests. "The hearts of men change seldom from generation to generation."

Another faint frown appears on Vyanat's face, then vanishes.

"I would not take too great a portion of your day," Lorn says. "But if you would indulge me slightly, and just walk us around your house."

"There is little one would not see in many houses, I am certain." Vyanat glances at Ryalth, then looks back at Lorn and offers a quick laugh. "Still, seeing is believing, and since you do assist the Majer-Commander, I am pleased to indulge your curiosity." The Merchanter Advisor steps from behind his table desk.

Lorn and Ryalth stand back and then follow the muscular merchanter out the office door and along the corridor.

"This study is that of my brother Vyel." Vyanat gestures toward the open door, a gesture that is not meant to suggest entry.

Lorn ignores the body language and steps into the office, smiling.

The slender and dark-haired man behind the table filled with stacks of papers rises, his brows briefly knitting in puzzlement, his eyes going from Lorn to Vyanat and then back to Lorn.

"Ah . . . Vyel . . . this is Majer Lorn. Majer, my brother Vyel."

Vyel smiles pleasantly.

Lorn notes the single gold front tooth. He feels that Ryalth does, as well, although nothing changes in her expression or posture.

Lorn smiles at Vyel. "You had much to do with the . . . difficulties with the *Hypolya*, did you not?"

Vyanat glances at Ryalth, who shrugs.

"Honored ser . . . I fear I do not understand."

Lorn smiles. "I must have been mistaken." Lorn smiles. "But could you tell me why you chose Benylt?" He pauses long enough to get the internal reaction he seeks, then adds, "Was that because of your respect for Tasjan? Or because of his promises?"

"I fear, ser, that you are gravely mistaken, and were you not a consort—"

Lorn looks hard at Vyel. "You do not have to answer to

me, Vyel. I suggest you answer to your brother and your house." He smiles again, and then turns to Vyanat. "I fear, most honorable Merchanter Advisor, that I have trespassed upon your hospitality, and upon your forbearance, but well you should know that there have been two attempts on my consort's life in the past eightday. I would not intrude upon merchanter matters, but for her safety, and for the fact that I fear the devious Tasjan would put his green-clad guards against Mirror Lancer Court, after he has destroyed your reputation for honor, and that is something none of us would wish." Lorn inclines his head toward Vyel. "I fear your younger brother has had the misfortune to be indebted in some fashion to Tasjan, and, if it is not handled discreetly, you will find matters most difficult. So . . . as is most unlike my usual fashion, I will leave the matter in your hands."

Vyanat looks at Lorn. "What you say is a charge most serious, and you have presented no evidence."

"There is little evidence, honored Vyanat, save two attempts on my consort, and the word of a would-be assassin, who died later of his wounds, that he was hired by a merchanter involved with the *Hypolya* who also had a gold front tooth." Lorn shrugs. "I am certain, that with your skills, you can determine the truth of the matter far better than I. As for me, I would prefer that you do." He offers a last smile. "But should anything else along this line occur, you will understand fully that I will be far, far less forbearing."

"Majer . . ." Vyanat's voice is low and almost threatening. "You come into my house, on my sufferance of your consort's position . . ."

Lorn's eyes are hard, like frozen fire, as he faces Vyanat. "Honored Merchanter Advisor—and you are honored— were my consort not convinced absolutely of your personal honesty and worthiness, I would not be here, and neither would your brother. You have read of my devotion to Cyador. I am even more devoted to my consort. Your brother's actions endanger both. Because of your honor, I offer you the chance to address the matter. Only because of your honor."

After a long stillness, Vyanat nods slowly. "Were I in your boots, I would feel much the same—"

"I am glad you understand." Lorn pauses. "When I was at Assyadt, Commander Ikynd observed that, while I was born in Cyad, I would never be a city lancer, for I loved all of Cyador too much . . ." His eyes go to Vyel. "I hope you have the wisdom to offer the truth and throw yourself on your brother's mercy. I have no mercy for those who would have blood flow across the sunstones of Cyad." Lorn looks back at Vyanat. "I would have you know, also, that I did not tell my consort the precise reason for my wish to see you this morning, only that it concerned last evening's attack." He bows. "I have troubled you long enough, honored Merchanter Advisor. We can find our way back to Ryalor House. Good day."

A slight smile crosses Vyanat's mouth, although his eyes are cold as he looks to Ryalth. "He is devoted, Lady, and you are fortunate. The rest of us may not be so."

Ryalth returns the smile with one equally cool. "We are most fortunate that Lorn is most temperate, and most farseeing, honored Vyanat, you in particular. You have the first opportunity to avoid what might well be seen as a sign of weakness in a time when weakness is less than acceptable." She bows and turns.

Lorn takes her arm, and they walk down the corridor and then down the steps to the main Traders' Plaza.

Outside, Ryalth raises her eyebrows as she looks at her consort. "You came perilously close to insulting his house, dearest."

"I have no quarrel with him or with Hyshrah Clan, but I want him to act."

"So that the Mirror Lancers cannot be said to become involved in merchanter affairs? Or to make Vyanat seem stronger and more perceptive to Tasjan?"

"The wisest of leaders can be less perceptive when they must judge those close to themselves." Lorn shrugs. "You can do no wrong in my eyes. At least, I know such." He offers a wry smile. "Now . . . I must repair to Mirror Lancer Court, after escorting you across the Plaza to Ryalor House."

"You expect me to conduct trade after this?" Ryalth raises her eyebrows.

"I expect you will do so well." Lorn grins.

She shakes her head and smiles back.

CXXXIX

VYANAT STEPS INTO Vyel's office, leaving the door open behind him.

"I wondered where you had gone," offers Vyel. "You disappeared this morning after that Mirror Lancer officer left. I thought you were remarkably pleasant, given his insolence, but I suppose you have to deal with the lady trader too often to say what you felt."

"She is most astute, and one ignores her at one's peril," Vyanat replies. "She says little, and often seems demure. She is not." Vyanat laughs once, but the laugh is forced.

"Where were you?"

"I needed to attend to a few matters," returns the older brother. He pauses, then asks, almost casually, "What in chaos were you thinking?"

"You believe that magus-descended butcher who thinks with his blade?" questions Vyel. "He wouldn't know an invoice from a bill of lading or a weight-and-balance form."

"Actually, Vyel, I do believe him. I wish I did not. First, the Lady Ryalth was with him. Her bearing and her presence mean she believes him. Second, I did check on a few matters. Almost a score of bravos that do the sort of 'work' that Majer Lorn mentioned, have either appeared dead on the streets or vanished. Yet, no other merchanter houses report any problems. I am not stupid. The Magi'i do not use bravos. They don't have to. The Palace does not. Nor do the Mirror Lancers, except for perhaps the Captain-Commander. Third, Majer Lorn could have turned you into a corpse without even raising a sweat, and without your body ever being found. He's done it to far better and more talented men than you. Fourth, he was right about the *Hypolya*. I've known that for years, but Father asked me to forbear unless you made another error such as that. This is worse than he could have foreseen, and he had few illusions about you. Oh . . . and you seem to forget that Majer Lorn was bright enough about trade to figure out what Bluoyel and his cousin had done in Biehl, and he did so in a matter of days."

"So . . . why didn't Majer Lorn just remove me the way you say he did the others?"

"You are stupid, dear brother. Because he wanted me to know, and to act against Tasjan. I will not. Not now, but I cannot fail to act against you, because you have jeopardized Hyshrah House. Again."

"You don't have the guts, for all your talk, Vyanat. Or you would have dumped me overboard years ago."

"I thought there was a chance you would learn—and I gave my word to Father. All you have learned is that deception and deceit bring quick returns." Vyanat gestures behind him and three archers appear, and step into the smaller study nearly silently. They have shafts ready to nock.

"What you—and Tasjan—have failed to learn," Vyanat continues, "is that any merchanting built on deception will fail in the end, and at a far higher cost. One of the matters I attended to was meeting with others in the house."

Vyel looks at the archers. "You don't even have the guts to act yourself."

"I have no intention of soiling my hands further. My heart and spirit, perhaps, but not my hands." Vyanat looks at the middle archer. "Make it quick."

The small study is filled with the muted sounds of bow-strings and arrows striking.

Vyanat stands, impassive, and remains in the study, alone, long after the archers have departed. His eyes are reddened and bleak.

CXL

IN THE LATE afternoon, Lorn sits behind his desk, looking out into a fall day that has gotten grayer and colder with each passing moment. The wind whistles intermittently around the ancient panes of his study, and the sky continues to darken.

The simplest course of action would be to remove Tasjan, but that is a solution that may lead to more difficulties than it resolves, since Lorn does not know how many others may be involved with Tasjan and whether removing the merchanter would merely result in someone else taking over as head of Dyjani House, and carrying out the same schemes with different names.

There is a knock on the study door.

Lorn turns in his chair. "Yes?"

"Ser?" Tygyl steps just inside the doorway. "The Majer-Commander would like to see you, as soon as you can get there."

"I'll be right behind you."

As he follows the senior squad leader up the stairs to the fifth level, Lorn wonders. Rynst's informers seem to know everything. Is it about the attack of the night before—or his visit to see Vyanat?

Tygyl closes the door behind Lorn, leaving Lorn alone in the oversized study with the Majer-Commander.

Lorn bows. When he straightens, he can see that a thunderstorm is moving across the city from the east. A lightning bolt flashes to the northeast, and after a few moments, a rumbling crash rolls over Mirror Lancer Court.

Rynst remains standing beside his desk and gestures for Lorn to step closer. Lorn halts three cubits short of his superior. "Ser . . . as you requested."

"You were somewhat delayed this morning, Majer," observes Rynst, ignoring the oncoming storm.

"Yes, ser."

"Would you care to explain?"

"Ser . . . last night, when we were returning from dinner at a friend's, some bravos attacked our carriage outside our very door. "

"You were late this morning, not last night."

Lorn smiles apologetically. "One of the bravos mentioned that he had been hired by someone associated with a ship— and the ship was one of those of Hyshrah Clan. I persuaded my consort to introduce me to Vyanat'mer so that I could bring the matter to his attention. I did, and then I came to Mirror Lancer Court."

Rynst's smile is frosty. "How many bravos were there, Majer?"

"A halfscore, ser."

"They are all dead, I presume."

"Yes, ser."

"You killed them all?"

"No, ser. We were fortunate that my friend Tyrsal was with us. He is a most capable magus."

"Majer . . . could you attempt to explain why bodies always appear around you, or if they do not, why people vanish, never to be seen again?"

"I do not believe the attack was on me, ser. I have heard a number of rumors dealing with those who are less than pleased with the success of my consort as a merchanter. Were there some concern about me, I believe that the attacks would have taken place at the many times when I have been alone."

"Although you did not answer my question, I am forced to agree with your conclusion—at least publicly." Rynst nods. "I received a message from the Merchanter Advisor just a few moments ago. His younger brother confessed to the attempt on your consort. Vyanat appreciates your tact in informing him and in not taking matters onto your own blade. He assures me, in my capacity as advisor to His Mightiness, that this unfortunate event is not a matter which involves the Mirror Lancers or the Magi'i."

"Yes, ser."

"Unhappily, anything which involves my staff also involves the Mirror Lancers. Such is life in Cyad."

Lorn waits.

"You are the commander of the two companies of Mirror Lancers. You are known to be an excellent field commander. You are also noted as an officer capable of taking no captives, should the necessity arise for such. And you report directly to me. By tomorrow, everyone will know there was an attempt made on your life by a highly placed merchanter. Tongues will suggest that Vyanat killed his brother as a convenient scapegoat, and that the merchanters were foiled in their attempt to halt the growth of the power of the Mirror Lancers in Cyad. Vyanat will find himself being considered as one plotting to place a merchanter as the heir to the Emperor. The Emperor will have to deny that there was a plot, and affirm that the Malachite Throne will not fall to any known in power in either the Magi'i, the Mirror Lancers, or the merchanters."

Lorn continues to wait.

"Majer . . . Vyanat is too smart to attempt anything like this. He could not possibly benefit from it. We both know this. Thankfully, so do most of those in power in Cyad, but it is too good an opportunity for those who dislike Vyanat's honesty not to use it against him. You should have known that forcing him to act would cause this sort of problem. You are too intelligent not to know. Why did you do so?"

"Because it was not the first attempt," Lorn admits. "I kept everything quiet after the first attempt."

"How many attempted the first time?"

"Six."

Rynst shakes his head. "I suppose I should congratulate you on your forbearance. Still . . . it creates a problem."

"Yes, ser."

"Could you explain why you did not bring the matter to my attention?"

"The attacks appeared to be upon my consort. If I brought them to the formal attention of the Mirror Lancers, then you would have been placed in the position of either ignoring an attempt to bring down the only merchanter house headed by a woman, or worse, using your authority to support a non-traditional house."

"Why should I care?"

"Because, as you know, someone is trying to use the attacks to discredit both the Mirror Lancers, and to stir up support for a merchanter heir to the Emperor."

"Do you think you should have made such a decision?" Curiosity, rather than coldness, tinges the voice of the Majer-Commander.

"If I run to you, ser, then I am seen as being in Cyad only to further your ambition. That will make the merchanters even more determined that the Imperial succession should change, and will boost their claims that I am here but to suppress them."

"They can charge that now," Rynst points out.

"They can charge that, ser, but it will not be believed by near so many folk as it could have been."

"What do you plan now, Majer?"

"As I always have, ser. To do my duty."

"It will be interesting to see how you view that duty, Majer." Rynst offers a faint smile. "When do your lancers begin their exercises?"

"The day after tomorrow, ser."

"Do you plan to lead them?"

"Yes, ser. Unless you wish otherwise."

"You had best lead them often, Majer." Rynst nods. "Good day."

Lorn bows, then turns, walking toward the study doors and waiting for some last parting comment. There is none, and he leaves and makes his way down to his own fourth-floor study.

CXLI

IN THE MIDAFTERNOON of late fall, at least fivescore citizens of Cyad, and more than twoscore sailors and traders from the Hamorian and Spidlarian vessels tied at the stone piers of the harbor, line the walls that surround the maneuver grounds created by the Mirror Engineers. Among the sailors are more than a handful of curious outland factors and traders. The expansive grounds are almost half a kay long and a quarter-kay wide. The newly-erected granite walls stand slightly less than three cubits high, low enough so that bystanders can easily watch.

Lorn glances at the walls, built by the Mirror Lancers in half a season at a cost Ryalth has estimated at enough to provision and supply all the Mirror Lancer companies for more than a year, had the construction been attempted by a merchanter house. And Lorn's maneuvers are supposed to justify all such costs.

After riding along the rows of lancers, inspecting them, if briefly, Lorn reins up before them. "The first drill will be a single-burst attack on the target. One short burst only for each lancer. Senior squad leaders will keep track of who strikes the target and where, and who does not."

Allowing each lancer to fire multiple chaos-bolts would have been flashier, Lorn knows, but he also wants the maneuvers to keep the lancers' aim sharp, for those who will go back to the Grass Hills will need those skills. He also knows that sooner or later, the more sharp-eyed outland observers will be more impressed by accuracy.

Lorn begins the first drill by urging the white gelding into a brief gallop at an angle past the straw figure that is clad in captured barbarian clothes and weapons—and more armor than the barbarians usually don. Lorn's closest approach is forty cubits, where he triggers a single chaos-bolt from the four-cubit-long firelance.

Hsssttt! The brief flash of chaos burns into the wooden target, right at the neck, leaving a black, fist-sized circular hole.

Lorn reins up on the south side of the grounds, watching as each of the lancers makes a pass. There are four targets—one for each squad.

From what he can tell, the chaos-bolts of two out of three of the lancer rankers strike the their targets.

He has his chaos-senses out, trying to pick up comments from the bystanders watching from the wall fifty cubits behind him.

". . . never seen a Mirror Lancer mounted . . ."

". . . hit you . . . won't leave much . . ."

". . . don't all hit, though . . . See . . . second one over missed . . ."

". . . they do this before barbarians get close . . ."

". . . good archer do as much . . . well . . . almost as much . . ."

Lorn continues to listen until the companies begin to reform at the eastern end of the maneuver grounds. Then he urges the white gelding toward the formation as several supernumerary lancers remove the four wooden targets.

Once the two companies are arrayed, Lorn nods at Cheryk, then Esfayl. Both nod that their lancers are ready.

"First Company, first squad! On the oblique! Attack!" Lorn orders.

The drill is a variation on the formation he used at Inividra, the glancing attack at an angle with firelances alone, one of the few formations that he has used or developed that will be, and will look, effective in a mass drill with firelances.

While there will be one-on-one blade drills, those are for the benefit of the lancers, and have little visual appeal to the traders or those citizens of Cyad who have never seen the Mirror Lancers fight.

"On the oblique! Attack!" echoes Cheryk, and then the senior squad leader of the first squad.

The twenty white mounts of the first squad charge forward, for all the mounts of the two companies in Cyad are white, at Rynst's orders. After less than a dozen paces, the riders turn leftward at a forty-five-degree angle toward the twenty half-figures set up on the cubit-and-a-half-high stone wall that had once been the foundation of a warehouse.

Lorn catches sight of several figures in green-and-gold uniforms, watching from the corner of the Second Harbor Way West. Although he cannot be sure, one wears gold epaulets—the only such figure Lorn has seen, either around the piers or in his chaos-glass. He guesses that it is probably Sasyk, although the man is not close enough for Lorn to ascertain that accurately.

The guard leader's presence, on the first day of Mirror Lancer public maneuvers, confirms for Lorn that he must continue to watch Tasjan and his greenshirt guards.

Lorn suspects the next attack from the merchanter will not be direct, nor at Ryalth, but that, in time, there will be another attack of some sort.

He can only hope he can anticipate it.

CXLII

HIS MIGHTINESS TOZIEL, Emperor of Perpetual Light, Heir to the Rational Stars, and Protector of the Steps to Paradise, lies under a light shimmercloth cover on the high bed in his private bedchamber in the Palace of Eternal Light. His face is flushed, yet pale under the flush. Ryenyel's hand rests lightly on his forehead.

"Every audience . . . like this . . ." Toziel's form shivers. "We . . . still . . . should not tell . . ."

"Just rest . . ." Ryenyel says gently. "You'll be better in a bit."

"Will you . . . though?" he murmurs.

"We do this together." She squeezes his hand gently, but firmly. "You must rest now. We can talk when you are stronger."

". . . can't rest . . . Tell me . . ."

"About what, dearest?"

". . . ever have an heir? . . . Cyador ever have a true scion?"

"Majer Lorn has foiled two or possibly three attempts on his life or on that of his consort," Ryenyel says. "As you know, yesterday he conducted an impressive display of Mirror Lancer power on the new parade grounds off Second Harbor Way. Rustyl is now consorted to Ceyla, the daughter of the Second Magus, and is convinced that he indeed should be First Magus, but I imagine he would settle for being your successor. Tasjan has made public certain papers that show Vyanat's brother evaded Imperial tariffs. Tasjan has had others suggest that Vyel was killed to cover up Vyanat's own tariff violations."

"Poor Vyanat . . . acted quickly because he is an honorable man, and now he faces dishonor." The Emperor pauses to gather breath. ". . . Because he wished to show that he would punish the unjust were they even his brother." A lop-sided smile appears on Toziel's face and vanishes.

"The most honorable head of Dyjani House continues to maneuver to incite the merchanters, particularly the weaker large houses, like Kysan and Bluyet—against the Mirror Lancers, and to add more armsmen to the green-suited guards—"

"What of Sasyk?"

"As self-centered as ever. His second consort vanished on a short voyage from Cyad to Summerdock. After a time, he will find another young blonde woman."

"You dislike him." Toziel smiles.

"No more than you. He makes Tasjan seem principled." Ryenyel's fingers touch Toziel's forehead. "You must rest. You must."

"Can Lorn or Rustyl deal with Tasjan?"

"We will see, and before all that long."

"That . . . I hope . . ." Toziel's words break off into a fit of coughing. When the coughs cease wracking his tall and slender form, his eyes close.

Ryenyel's hand remains lightly on his forehead, even as she also shivers, and her own complexion pales.

CXLIII

LORN LOOKS OUT through the small side window of the sitting room into the darkness, watching the white forms of the geese. After a long moment, he turns back to Ryalth.

"What are you thinking, dear?" She has Kerial seated in her lap, and the two play finger games. " 'One little hare, and he goes there . . . second little hare, and he goes there . . . ' " Despite the bright tone of her rhyme to Kerial, her eyes are dark as they look to Lorn.

"Geese, iron locks and bolts, more and more use of the

chaos-glass . . . your use of information from Ryalor House, armed guards to escort you . . ."

"All because an Emperor is dying and will not name an heir," she says.

Lorn smiles tightly. "He cannot name an heir. The heir must name himself and be recognized as the sole scion by enough of the Quarter, Mirror Lancer Court, and the Plaza. Now . . . they see no one."

"And . . . you cannot see . . ."

"I can see, but not without blood across the sunstones, and more bloodshed after that, and Emperors are not anointed in blood in Cyad itself. Alyiakal was the only one to shed blood on the sunstones . . . and recall how he is remembered?"

"I understand," she says slowly, her fingers still playing with those of Kerial. "For reasons very clear to all—and we have talked about this for seasons—the Mirror Lancers have not kept any armed companies in Cyad. Now there are two companies—fourscore with firelances." She looks up from the settee toward her brown-haired consort and smiles softly. "All my sources tell me Tasjan has gathered more than ten-score armed guards, and they have been trained by Sasyk and by other former lancers. Pheryk knows some of them. That's like five lancer companies, is it not?"

"They have no firelances, but if they moved on the Palace in support of Tasjan, we would have to use ours, and most of his guards would die. I cannot see the merchanters being pleased with such, or with anyone who commanded or ordered such." Lorn shrugs.

"Waiting may not help, dearest," Ryalth points out. "Tasjan has now begun to suggest that Vyel was killed to keep anyone from finding out the extent of Vyanat's corruption. And when your companies began maneuvers the day before yesterday, Tasjan again sent out word that he was looking for additional guards for his vessels, another twoscore."

"Six companies—does he plan to turn the sunstones red with blood?"

"You can handle them," Ryalth says.

"That I know, but what will happen to Cyad? Will there be blood in the streets?"

"What if Tasjan is not there to call them forth?" she asks.

Lorn raises his eyebrows.

"Sasyk wishes to seize the Palace. Few know this, but Pheryk was able to talk to some of Sasyk's guards he knows. Tasjan may suspect Sasyk's ambition, for he will meet with Sasyk only when Sasyk could not leave without encountering those guards who are loyal to Tasjan. Yet Tasjan needs Sasyk, because he cannot train or command armsmen. So the two contest silently. Many merchanters will not support Sasyk—not if Tasjan were to die now. Sasyk wishes conflict and unrest, and he would have it last long eightdays, until all would settle on any heir, and he would either be that heir, or the right hand of that heir. If Tasjan were to die or vanish . . . now," Ryalth says slowly, "the Dyjani would either select Tyrsal's friend Husdryt or Tasjan's nephew Torvyl as clan head. Neither would support Sasyk, and either would not oppose the Mirror Lancers, were they needed to destroy the green-suited guards."

Lorn shakes his head. "I would be bringing firelances and death into every way and road in Cyad. Would you have me do this?"

"I would have you as a merchanter or a lancer captain still in Isahl." Ryalth leans forward and nuzzles Kerial. "Good. . . . good boy." Then she looks back up at Lorn. "I have supported all you have done. Would you like less than my judgment on what will happen?"

"No." Lorn purses his lips. "Yet . . ."

"You do not wish to be the lancer majer who loosed the firelances in Cyad."

"No. I do not."

"Did you encourage Tasjan to bring in guards? Did you tell the Emperor to have no heirs and to name no one? Were you the one to raise the tariffs on merchanters and trade?"

"No . . . but . . . firelances in Cyad?"

For a time, there is silence in the sitting room.

"Lorn, dearest . . . why do you think that the people of Cyad are any different from those of Jera?"

"Because . . . because . . . do you remember the poem about Cyad . . . the one in the book?"

"Not really," she confesses.

"The lines . . . I don't remember them all, but there are some that go like this . . .

. . . for Cyad holds the fate of all this earth,
and all of soul and skill that is of worth.
So shine forth both in sun and into night
bright city of prosperity and light."

He clears his throat, then looks at her. "How can I be the one to bring firelances into Cyad?"

"You do not have to be that one. You can be the one who stands by and lets Tasjan and Sasyk destroy Cyad, and spill other blood on the stones. If you do nothing, Tasjan will order out his guards within an eightday of the Emperor's death. What will the Majer-Commander order you to do?"

"Bring the firelances to the streets of Cyad," Lorn admits.

"You did not hesitate to attack Jera, because you felt it was the right thing to do for Cyador. You did not hesitate to kill scores to protect what you believe in. You have killed, and rightly, I believe, those who are corrupt and evil, like Dettaur. Yet Cyad is beginning to fall apart, and you question whether you should use the weapons at hand to prevent it."

Lorn's amber eyes meet her blue eyes. He sees neither greed, nor guile, nor ambition. He senses no untruth. After a long time, broken only by Kerial's murmurings, he takes a deep breath. "You have the right of it." He offers a crooked smile. "I must do what is right, though it will cost me all I have sought, for if I bring the Mirror Lancers to the street, I may well be respected, but once more it will be the respect for a skillful butcher."

He shrugs, then takes a deep breath. After a moment, he shakes his head. "Still. . . ."

"I know," she says. "Yet . . . how would you feel if you stood by?"

"Worse than I do, I would wager." He walks to the window once more, looking out into the darkness yet again. It is some time before he turns. "So . . . where do you think I can best dispatch Tasjan?"

"There must be somewhere that the guards do not follow," Ryalth says, "somewhere where you can wait, and he will come to you."

Lorn nods. "Where he will come to me . . ."

"He knows he is followed in the glass. Will that not cause him to be more careful?"

"I'm sure it will, but I'm certain he thinks that the Magi'i are tracking him, not a poor and unknown majer."

"You are not poor or unknown. Not any longer. You must be careful, for any blade mark will be tracked to you."

"I know." Lorn smiles coldly. "But if there are no blade marks . . . it could be a paid assassin—no honorable Mirror Lancer would stoop to that."

"Lorn . . . although I can see no other course, not with all that is poised to fall into chaos, this is most dangerous . . . dearest one."

"But you are right. Now . . . now . . . to do nothing is even more dangerous." Lorn sighs once more. "Can you bring Kerial up to the study? I would that you look at the glass with me."

Ryalth rises, gracefully, despite the burden of Kerial, who tries to lurch from her arms toward his father. "Careful now . . . you're not ready to jump that far . . ." She laughs. "He is like I imagine you were."

Lorn shrugs helplessly, but he smiles before turning and heading up the stairs.

Once settled at his table desk in the study, Lorn concentrates on the glass.

As the silver mists swirl away, the glass shows Tasjan. He is standing in a corridor with Sasyk, who wears the gold-trimmed green uniform and the golden shoulder epaulets. Behind the pair are other guards, all dressed in blue—not the green-and-gold of the guards recruited by Sasyk. Lorn studies Sasyk more than Tasjan, noting his trim figure and the well-worn and functional sabre scabbard. He also notes that Sasyk offers no deference to Tasjan, and that the two are clearly not agreeing on some matter.

He motions for Ryalth to study the images.

He has much to do, and far too little time in which to accomplish it, for he has waited longer than is wise . . . perhaps because he has been trapped by a reflection, a reflection of what he has wanted Cyad to be, just as the unknown Sampson had been trapped in reflections.

He takes another deep breath.

CXLIV

VYANAT DOES NOT bother to seat himself after he enters Tasjan's office.

Neither does the slender Tasjan bother to rise from his chair behind his desk, but nods for the Merchanter Advisor to speak.

A faint smile crosses Vyanat's face. "I will be brief, honored clan head. My brother Vyel confessed to planning the killing of the head of another trading house. The plot was unsuccessful, and he has been executed under merchanter justice."

"Ah . . . such a terrible thing to happen to you . . ." Tasjan says mildly. "To be betrayed so, and by one's own brother."

Vyanat shrugs, sadly. "It is almost as sad to be betrayed by the head of another trading house. Vyel was weak, and he wanted more. He did not seem to understand that he could not obtain it because the very weaknesses that tempted him led to his failure. There are those who have the largest fleets, the grandest warehouses and dwellings, and yet they are not satisfied. Wanting more than can be obtained in an honest and open manner is always a weakness. So is spreading untruths when justice has been done."

"You seem to have someone in mind."

"I do . . . and if you know him, I offer advice, and a warning."

"Oh . . . ?" Tasjan

"A merchanter who heads a great house has more freedom, more luxury, and more power than any who have ever held the Palace of Eternal Light. Likewise, a true lancer can crush such a merchanter before that merchanter could lift a blade for a single stroke."

"But . . . the question is, Vyanat . . . are there any true lancers in these decaying times?" Tasjan's smile is as cold as his eyes.

"I know of three, and there may be more, Tasjan. You could have been the greatest of all merchanters. If you have the skill, you may yet survive. If you attempt to be more than you are, you will fail."

"That is true of all of us, is it not, Vyanat'mer?"

"Yes, it is. Some of us understand that." Vyanat's last smile is both cold and somehow sad. "Good day, honored Tasjan."

Once the door closes, Tasjan laughs.

CXLV

LORN LOOKS UP from the glass.

Ryalth steps inside the study, carrying Kerial. "Myryan and Ciesrt should be here before long."

"I was going to use the glass to follow Tasjan and some others before it got too late." Lorn nods toward the blank glass before him. "Tasjan always travels with guards—his own—the ones garbed in blue. I thought that if I kept trying I might find somewhere that he doesn't. He walks a different route to the Plaza each morning and night."

"There is one thing I found out today," Ryalth says. "I was going to tell you later, but I was late because of the Suthyan who arrived at Ryalor House so late . . ."

Lorn raises his eyebrows, waiting.

"Tasjan dines at Ayadyr often, usually on fiveday evening." Ryalth shifts Kerial from one shoulder to the other.

"So he might not take his guards to the table?"

"I do not know," Ryalth admits, "but when he dines with family in his dwelling there are no guards in the dining chamber—that, your glass has shown."

Lorn nods. "We will follow him tomorrow and see . . . If so . . ." He shrugs. "I can but hope that naught else occurs in the few days it will take to see what can be done."

Ryalth glances over her shoulder. "They should be here soon."

Lorn looks at the blank glass. "Would you mind if I studied the glass for a few moments?"

"No." She smiles. "If it is but for a few moments. I will check on dinner with Kysia and Ayleha."

"A few moments," Lorn confirms.

Even before she leaves the study, he focuses on the glass, and upon the first image.

Sasyk is in an exercise hall Lorn does not recognize, sparring with another man. Both are larger than Lorn, and both appear accomplished. There are other figures in green, sparring as well. As Lorn lets the image fade, he frowns. Sasyk is clearly trying to ensure his greensuits are well-trained with the blade, and despite the rumors, since piracy has not increased, that training bespeaks an interest in more than protecting trade.

The next image Lorn calls up is that of Tasjan, but the merchanter merely walks along a white paved street, followed by four large and muscular blue-clad guards. Tasjan looks up, and smiles, as if to tell any magus who follows him that he is aware of the scrutiny. Lorn lets the image of Tasjan fade.

At the sound of women's voices drifting up the stairs, Lorn slides the chaos-glass into its case, and glass and case into the drawer of the table desk. Then he stands and stretches before heading down the stairs to greet his sister.

As Lorn enters the sitting room, from where she sits on the far side of Myryan, Ryalth mouths, *Thank you.*

"I'm sorry," Lorn says to his sister, "I was working on something that took a bit longer than I had thought." Lorn looks closely at Myryan. She is frail, thinner than he recalls, and yet her amber eyes glow. "I'm glad you could come tonight. Where's Ciesrt? I thought he was coming."

The dark-haired healer shrugs. "As I was telling Ryalth, he came back from the Quarter and told me I'd have to come alone. He's over at his father's. Kharl wanted to talk to him." She sighs. "He's been spending a great deal of time with Kharl lately. I cannot say I like it."

Lorn looks at his sister. "Is anything the matter?" He seats himself beside Ryalth on the settee.

Myryan offers a sad smile in return. "Nothing that is any

different from before, Lorn. Ciesrt is centered on himself, like most of the Magi'i, but he is kind enough, and gentle enough."

"What about his parents?"

"I detest them." Myryan's words are level.

Lorn can sense near-fury, and absolute truth in the three words.

"Because of the children thing?" asks Ryalth.

"That . . . and because, to them, I'm an ornament. No . . . I'm a tool to be used. I'm a thing that is valuable because of who my parents were."

"Doesn't Ciesrt . . . ?" Ryalth ventures.

"He tries . . . but Kharl is strong, and will have his way. Ciesrt can't stand up to him." A wry smile crosses her face as she brushes back unruly black curls from her forehead and looks at Ryalth. "Lorn could. Lorn stood up to Father, and to senior officers. Ciesrt isn't that strong. I knew that. I didn't think that his father . . . though . . ." She shakes her head. "I have decided something, though," she adds, as if it were an afterthought.

"What?"

"Too much order, even in healing, is worse than too much chaos."

"Is there any doubt of that?" Lorn says with a laugh.

"Ah. . . ." Myryan draws the word out with exaggerated slowness, "but do you know why?"

Ryalth frowns, her blue eyes flicking between her consort and his sister.

"I don't see where you're going," Lorn admits.

"Order's greatest cruelty is that it denies chaos," Myryan declares, her eyes glowing even brighter. "I see that now."

Lorn nods slowly, trying to make sense out of all the words, and find the meaning behind them. "Why do you say that?" he temporizes, trying to draw her out.

"Lorn . . . perfect order is perfect memory. Would you truly wish to remember every unkindness done to you, every cruelty you dispensed? Would you wish to live in a world where every chamver is perfect, yet without heat? Where fire does not exist . . . because it changes, and order denies change? Where children are never born, and no one dies? Where each person is unchanging . . . ?"

Lorn finds himself shivering at the image.

"The kindness of time is that it passes . . ." Myryan murmurs. Then she smiles abruptly. "I didn't come here to mope about things. I came because I like to be around you two." She smiles at Kerial, and the boy tries to lurch from Ryalth's lap.

Ryalth stands and carries her son to his aunt.

"He's *so* good," the healer says, taking the Kerial into her arms. "And he feels so good to hold."

"Most of the time," Lorn suggests, "unless he's wet."

"We should probably begin dinner," Ryalth ventures, "or it will get overcooked, and I do not care much for overcooked fowl. Also, Kerial is being good, and how long that will last . . ."

Lorn laughs.

As the three enter the dining area, Kysia appears and takes Kerial.

The three sit, and Ayleha begins to bring in the serving platters, starting with a gold-rimmed blue platter holding slices of fowl covered in a golden cream sauce.

"When I'm here, everything is so elegant," Myryan says.

"You deserve elegance," Lorn says, laughing and adding, "and so do we, but we only get it when we have company."

"Elegance and grown-up company," Ryalth adds, passing the tray to Lorn, who takes but one slice of sun-nut bread, before holding it for Myryan.

"You have been busy lately," Myryan says. "Even Ciesrt is talking about how effective your demonstrations of the firelances have been. Are you the one who developed those drills?"

"They're just variations on what I've used in the field,"

Lorn says, holding the platter to allow Myryan to take several slices of the sauce-covered chicken. "No drill really shows what it's like."

"We were at Kharl's several nights ago, and Ciesrt suggested that perhaps some of the Magi'i should put on a display." Myryan laughs, if with a note of sadness. "Kharl was not amused. He said that the use of chaos was for what needed to be done to preserve Cyad, not to provide entertainment for outland traders and ignorant . . . folk."

"He said 'ignorant merchanters,' I would wager," Ryalth responds.

"He did. I sometimes forget how sharp you two are . . . until I come here. I think that's another reason why Ciesrt feels uncomfortable with our family. Everyone sees things he doesn't, and he has trouble accepting that." She shrugs. "Then, Kharl sees what Ciesrt doesn't, and I suppose Ciesrt doesn't wish to be someplace else that reminds him of that."

"I'm sorry for him," Ryalth says. "I felt that way at first, I think, but your father and mother helped so much."

"I miss them," Myryan says simply.

"We all do."

For a time, the three eat, near-silently.

Lorn takes the last sip of the Alafraan in his goblet. "I think this is even better than usual. What do you think?" He inclines his head to Myryan.

"Brother dear, how would I know? Your wine is the only one I drink, and I can take little enough of that."

"It is good," Ryalth says. "Is there anything left in your garden?"

"After last eightday's frost?" Myryan shakes her head. "Just some of the root vegetables, the late carrots, potatoes . . . I did get all the rest of the pearapples pickled or stewed."

"Stewed pearapples . . . waste of a good fruit," Lorn grumbles.

"Letting them rot on the tree or the ground is the waste."

Ayleha appears, silently as always, and begins to clear away the dishes.

"How much did you put up?" Ryalth asks.

"I don't know. It seemed like scores and scores of jars. But they'll all be gone before midwinter, I'd guess."

As the serving woman places a dish of egg custard before her, Ryalth smiles. "I might actually finish a dinner by myself." She frowns. "That's really not fair to Kerial. He deserves a more regular schedule, but I never know when I can leave Ryalor House or when I'll be late."

"Or when I will be," Lorn adds.

"Part of that is because you both want to spent time with him and each other," Myryan suggests.

"Until this year, we haven't spent that much time together," Lorn agrees.

"It has been good to see him every night." Ryalth smiles.

"Sometimes, it amazes me," the healer says. "You two belong together, and I've heard the story so many times, yet it doesn't quite seem real."

Lorn and Ryalth share a glance.

"That's what I mean. Neither of you are Magi'i, yet you know so much about each other."

"Names are not everything," Lorn observes, taking a last mouthful of the egg custard and adding, "That was good."

"Almost as good as pearapple tarts?" asks Myryan, with an innocent-looking smile.

"It was very good," Lorn grins back, "better than anything except the best of pearapple tarts."

Myryan tries to cover a yawn.

"Are you getting enough rest?" asks Lorn.

"Always the big brother. It's been a long day. I spent the morning in the garden and then went to the infirmary."

"I have a carriage waiting to take you home. Pheryk will go with you," Lorn says.

"I can make my own way," Myryan insists.

"I am sure you can," Ryalth says, "but Lorn and I would feel better if you accepted the offer."

"Besides," Lorn adds with a laugh, "you'd waste my coins. I've already paid for the carriage."

"I would not do that. Not to either of you." Myryan smiles the extra-bright smile once more. "It has been a long day, and I will not insist."

The three rise and make their way out of the dining area and then to the foyer off the veranda.

"You have to come more often," Ryalth says, opening the door.

"With or without Ciesrt," Lorn adds. "We like to see you."

"I like to see you two," Myryan replies.

The three walk out to the iron gate, the area lit by a single lamp Pheryk had obviously hung and lit sometime during dinner.

Myryan smiles a last time before entering the carriage.

Pheryk nods to Lorn and Ryalth. "Be back shortly, ser, Lady."

Once the sound of the carriage dies away, Lorn closes the iron gate and locks it, then looks at the redhead beside him.

She looks back at him. "There's something wrong."

"There's a lot wrong," Lorn says. "But there's no flux chaos around her, and no excessive order."

They walk slowly through the cold darkness, past the still fountain.

"You think she and Ciesrt are having problems?" asks Ryalth.

"I don't know. I was truth-reading her. There are things she doesn't want me to know. That, I could sense, but they center on Kharl, I feel. There's just . . . a sadness . . . around her when she mentions Ciesrt. I don't feel I could use the glass . . ." Lorn shakes his head.

"Even for her safety?"

"Dearest . . . you see how often I use the glass to follow

Tasjan, and how little I discover from each attempt. Myryan would know my screeing, and how would she feel seeing me watch over her every other moment?"

"She is your sister, but I worry."

"So do I." Lorn opens the door from the veranda to the foyer. "So do I."

CXLVI

TOZIEL LEANS FORWARD in the smaller version of the malachite-and-silver throne that dominates the Lesser Audience Hall. "For the past two eightdays, the Mirror Lancers have held their maneuvers on the new parade grounds above the harbor. I would have each of you provide his thoughts on the effectiveness of such." With a faint smile, the Emperor straightens. "Perhaps you should begin, honored Majer-Commander, since the lancers are under your command."

Rynst bows, then looks directly at the slender figure with the dark-rimmed eyes within the silver robes. "Your Mightiness . . . as you suggested, the Mirror Lancers have transferred two companies from the Grass Hills to provide . . . as it were . . . a portrait of their abilities where those abilities could be viewed by outlanders. During the first days, nearly tenscore watched each day, but, as we suspected, the numbers of those who watched have declined. Yesterday, there were but twoscore. Most of those were outlanders. If but twoscore outlanders each day watch the lancers and are dissuaded from thinking to take advantage of Cyador, the golds spent to provide such . . . edifying . . . entertainment may be well spent."

Toziel nods to the First Magus. "Honored Chyenfel?"

"I must confess, Your Mightiness, that I was among the

tenscore, for I did wish to see for myself the effect of such a demonstration. And I would agree with the most honorable Majer-Commander that the display of firelances and the skill of those who employed them created a most desirable effect. I do have concerns about the wisdom of maintaining such for long periods of time here in Cyad. I would ask that I be given leave to advance those concerns after hearing what the honored Merchanter Advisor may have to add."

"All will heed your concerns, First Magus." Toziel looks to Vyanat. "Your thoughts, honored Merchanter Advisor?"

"I am more than somewhat puzzled," says the Merchanter Advisor. "I cannot recall when one of the Magi'i expressed concern over the Mirror Lancers being more effective. Certainly, most of us who are merchanters are pleased, for the obvious power of the firelances has left many outlanders shaking their heads. They are indeed chastened. They are so taken aback that one would wish that this stratagem had been adopted earlier." Vyanat looks to his right at the First Magus. "Or is the First Magus concerned about the additional authority that such lancers invest in the Majer-Commander?"

"Majer-Commander Rynst has always used his authority and the Mirror Lancers for the good of Cyad and Cyador, and I have no doubts that he will continue to do so. In years to come, his successors may not be so astute, and what we do must serve the future as well as the present." Chyenfel bows to Vyanat. "My concerns lie not in having such demonstrations by the Mirror Lancers, but in their frequency. I would suggest that Your Mightiness could obtain the same or greater impact by merely bringing in a different set of companies twice a year for two eightdays, or four times a year for a single eightday. In this fashion, all would see with fresh eyes the power of the Mirror Lancers. Likewise, we would not see the development of what might be called city lancers, as opposed to those lancers who must face and fight the barbarians." The First Magus bows to the Emperor.

"You raise some matters of concern to us all," Toziel says deliberately.

Behind him, Ryenyel coughs, once.

The Emperor turns and smiles. "Is it chill in here, my dear?"

"I caught something in my throat. I beg your pardon for interrupting." Ryenyel smiles at her consort. "I truly do."

"Sire?" asks Vyanat.

"Yes, Vyanat'mer?"

"I would ask that we see how matters progress for another three eightdays," suggests the Merchanter Advisor, "before any decision is considered. Even should the most honorable Chyenfel prove correct in his assessment, I would argue that for the first appearance of the Mirror Lancers in Cyad, a longer period might well prove necessary, and would not prove detrimental. After all, we are in a time of change, and at this time, as many outland traders as possible should see the true power of the Mirror Lancers." With only the slightest of pauses, the merchanter adds, "And the First Magus has noted that in this time, while Majer-Commander Rynst serves the Empire of Light, all will be well with such lancers."

"That would seem reasonable," suggests Toziel. "At our normal audience three eightdays from now, we will revisit the matter."

Chyenfel nods. "I will defer as His Mightiness suggests."

"And I, also," adds Rynst.

"Although I retain grave doubts about relying upon the mere occasional appearance of the Mirror Lancers," counters Vyanat, "in three eightdays, the matter may well become more clear as to how Cyador may best show the outlanders its might."

The shadow of a frown crosses Ryenyel's face, although no eyes are upon her.

CXLVII

RYNST MOTIONS FOR Lorn to take one of the chairs set before the Majer-Commander's study desk. Lorn does so, and waits, watching the Majer-Commander and listening to the moan of the early-winter wind that lows around the ancient blue windowpanes, a cold wind, despite the bright sunlight that falls on Cyad.

"Yesterday, I attended the regular audience with the Emperor," Rynst begins, conversationally. "There I heard that your maneuvers have been successful in giving some of the outland traders a few matters to think about."

"I understand that such was the intent, as you told me, ser. The maneuvers are but exercises and are at best a limited way of showing what the Mirror Lancers can do."

"They are indeed, but they are effective." Rynst purses his lips, and then tilts his head to the side. "Perhaps too effective. The First Magus raised a most interesting point. He suggested that perhaps it would not be wise to maintain the lancers in Cyad for any great period, but for perhaps two or three eightdays twice a year. Or one eightday every season, with a different set of lancer companies each period."

Lorn waits once more.

"He fears that any companies remaining in the City of Light will become city lancers, and, although he did not say such directly, another tool of the Majer-Commander. He also feels that their presence, in daily maneuvers, will jade all those who watch, and the impact on outlanders will fade, while the citizens of Cyad will come to believe the Mirror Lancers are unmatched."

"They are unmatched, but they can be outnumbered, ser, as we know."

"We know that, but those in Cyad do not understand what lies beyond its borders. They do not see the hatred of our land, our roads, our cities, our prosperity. If the First Magus is correct, and correct he may well be," Rynst continues with a wry smile, "we of the Mirror Lancers may find it even more difficult to obtain the golds required to equip and maintain the forces necessary to repel the barbarians in the years to come. And should any within the city raise arms, in years to come, there will be few Magi'i to stand against such a mob, and no firelances to bring. It will be a far different land, yet few wish to contemplate that."

Lorn nods slowly.

"You will live in that time and land, Majer. And so will your son." Rynst pauses momentarily. "As you are the commander of the lancer companies in Cyad, I felt you should know this. I would not pass this on to them at this moment. If you are asked, I would suggest that you tell the truth, and that is that the role of Mirror Lancer companies in Cyad is being considered by the Emperor."

"Yes, ser."

"That is all, Majer. I expect a copy of the report on the latest fireship replacement meeting by midmorning tomorrow."

"Yes, ser." Lorn stands.

Rynst does not seem to look up as Lorn departs the study.

As Lorn descends the stairs to his study, he considers what Rynst has said. Everything that the Majer-Commander has relayed makes sense, far too much sense, in some ways. One thing does not. That is why Rynst has told Lorn before any decision is made, and why Lorn has been told when a decision will be made.

Lorn fears he understands that, as well. Rynst wants the lancers used—somehow—before they must leave Cyad. Yet the Majer-Commander cannot order such, or will not, and if they are used, he will not be the one to give the order—unless there is a danger obvious to all.

CXLVIII

IN THE LATE evening, with but a single lamp lit, Lorn sits at the study desk, squinting at the chaos-glass, and drawing out the rooms in Tasjan's dwelling on sheets of paper beside the glass. With each image, he draws what he needs to know, then checks what he has drawn, and finally lets the image fade. Then he closes his eyes and rubs his neck before he calls forth the next image from the glass.

The lower levels of Tasjan's dwelling have no windows that are not barred, and all the doors are iron-bound, bolted, and guarded at all times. The outside guards, and those that patrol the gardens and porticoes, wear green. Those inside wear blue.

Lorn looks at what he has drawn, shifting from sheet to sheet.

Tasjan's private study opens onto a balcony, and that balcony can be reached easily enough by climbing up a stepped chimney from the second-level portico. There are two guard posts along the portico flanking the upper gardens, but if the guards see no one . . .

All Lorn has to do is figure out how to get to the second-level portico.

With a deep breath, he looks down at the glass yet another time.

A dozen or more glimpses of Tasjan's dwelling, and he thinks he has a way. If he can climb a particular tree. If he can hold his blur shield long enough. If it works.

He shakes his head and puts away the glass, ignoring the burning in his eyes, and the headache that seems as though someone is trying to cleave his skull with a very dull and heavy ax. Then he turns down the wick and puts out the single lamp in the study.

He walks quietly along the upper corridor to the bed-chamber, where he slides the iron bolt shut.

"You were using the glass late," Ryalth says sleepily.

"Later than I would have liked. I was studying Tasjan's dwelling and how he enters and leaves it." Lorn sits on the end of the bed and pulls off his boots, then stands and begins to disrobe.

"Will you check Kerial?" she murmurs.

"I will." After he pulls off his undertunic, he steps to the small bed and glances down, listening as much as looking. The small figure breathes evenly, regularly. Lorn smiles and steps away to hang his clothes in the armoire, then returns and slides under the covers next to his sleepy redhead.

"He's fine."

"Good." She snuggles against him and seems to relax.

Lorn slips one arm around her, enjoying her closeness. But he stares through the darkness, and it is some time before he finally drops into sleep.

CXLIX

IN THE LATE afternoon, almost upon returning from Mirror Lancer Court, Lorn pulls the merchanter blues—those normally worn by a senior enumerator—from the back of the armoire. Then come the blue boots, stiff, but usable.

"It might yet be wiser to wait," Ryalth says from the doorway, before stepping into the bedchamber.

"No . . . it would be safer for me to wait, but what if Tasjan does not dine at Ayadar next eightday . . . or the eightday after, then what? Rynst has indicated that, in no more than three eightdays, they will decide when the Mirror Lancers will leave Cyad, and that it is likely to be immediately. Then who will oppose Tasjan and the greensuits? If I wait until then, there will be no lancers, and then how could I oppose Tasjan, knowing that Sasyk would leave even more blood across all the sunstones?"

"So you will act sooner, rather than later, for fewer will suspect you now?"

"Most expect less action before decisions are made—especially in Cyad, where acting wrongly and early can be most dangerous." Lorn offers a crooked smile.

Ryalth nods. "How will you do this?"

"With the blurring shield I showed you." Lorn sits on the edge of the bed and pulls off his white lancer boots. "And some tree-climbing . . ."

"Will he not sense it?"

"I think not. That is why only the upper-level adepts are taught such, because it is an aversion, not the use of order to bend the chaos of light away from one. Use of much order or chaos creates a disruption that any sensitive to chaos or order may sense. This uses less chaos than that from the sun during the heat of the day."

Ryalth frowns. "Will you wait until it is full dark?"

"No. I leave shortly—in merchanter blue." He smiles. "These Jerial had made for me years ago still fit well enough." The cream-and-green uniform comes off next, to be hung in the armoire, and Lorn pulls on the blue trousers, then the tunic.

"You would have the merchanters torn by strife?"

"They already are," Lorn points out dryly as he sits to pull on the blue leather boots. "Tasjan is trying to overthrow Vyanat. Blouyal was using his position to gain unfair advantage for his house. Vyel wanted to kill you to take over Ryalor House. I suspect other problems have occurred with Kysan House, from what you have said, and Denys, you said, schemes to redeem Bluyet House." He pauses. "My plan is to have it clear that one of Sasyk's guards murdered Tasjan. I do not want the cream-and-green seen near Tasjan's."

"See that you do that." She nods slowly. "Still . . . I do not like that you must act so quickly."

"I like it not that I should have to act at all. Yet . . . I can sense far more is taking place than I know."

"That is always so," Ryalth responds.

Lorn holds a frown. She is not telling all she knows. "What else should I know?"

Ryalth shrugs, almost helplessly. "I fear that Sasyk holds more power in the Dyjani House than any realize, but that I do not know. Like you, I can feel currents beneath the surface of a harbor that seems calm. Yet I can see nothing."

"As can I. And if we wait until we can . . ."

"Then it may be too late," Ryalth concludes.

Lorn nods, then stands. "Best I be going." He fastens the Brystan sabre to his blue belt. While most enumerators do not wear blades, some do, and there is no standard for what type of blade they wear, save that it can be worn off a belt.

"Be most careful, my love."

"I intend such. Since I will not follow Alyiakal . . . I must be most careful so that you can support me when I am stipended off as an old, old majer."

"Were it to happen so, that would be only fair. You have made possible all that is Ryalor House." She smiles, then leans forward and embraces him, brushing his cheek with her lips. "Be most careful."

"I will."

They walk down the stairs and out onto the veranda. With a single backward glance, Lorn walks from the veranda, past the fountain, and out the gate, locking it behind him. His blues should not be remarked, for most know that the dwelling belongs to a trader.

In the twilight, Lorn walks westward down the lane and then up the Fifth Harbor Way. At the next corner, he turns westward once more until he reaches the Eighth Harbor

Way, although, like all ways and roads outside of the central trading quarter of Cyad, it is unmarked.

Tasjan's dwelling occupies a small block of its own, and at the first level, the building walls are blank stone and offer no windows or entrance except for the carriage gate and a service door, and both are guarded inside and out. There are no other guards outside the dwelling. The tall trees—Lorn has no idea what they are—grow outside the walls and arch over the upper-level porticos. They are still shedding second-year leaves and turning the first-year leaves gray for winter, but all those on the main ways have been trimmed of lower branches.

Lorn continues westward on the unnamed lane at the back of the dwelling until he reaches the gnarled tree that stands perhaps fifty cubits east of the west corner. He thinks the tree is a lorken, whose dark wood resists most axes and all but the sharpest saws. The tree is far shorter than the others, and its topmost branches barely reach the top of the second-level portico columns. Those short branches are sturdy, and the remaining leaves barely move despite the cold wind blowing northward off the harbor.

Lorn eases the blurring shield around himself. He has to jump to grasp the lowermost branch, and then levers himself into the tree. His scabbard slams against his leg, hard enough that it will probably leave a bruise, and he sits on the branch in the fading light, catching his breath for a moment.

Then he begins to climb, testing each branch. The wind that rustles the branches of the taller trees will help, both in disguising any movement of the leaves of the lorken, and in concealing any sounds he may make.

When he stands as high as he can safely go, he is three cubits from the stone railing. To reach the railing will take a leap—one that must be successful or he will fall close to twenty cubits onto hard stone.

He extends his chaos-senses, and listens closely, as well. A single guard walks past. Once the man is more than fifteen cubits away, still pacing eastward, Lorn takes a deep breath, then leaps.

Again he must lever himself up and over the railing, and he stands in the shadows of the portico pillars, catching his breath, while he waits for the return of the single guard in green who patrols the corner post of the second-level covered portico that encloses the garden

As the man passes, Lorn steps out, and using his chaos-enhanced Brystan blade, takes a single cut. There is little more than a muted cry, a gurgle, and the sound of a body falling on pebbles.

Lorn wipes his blade on the green tunic of the dead guard, then eases the shortsword from the man's scabbard. He glances around, letting his chaos-senses scan the area, but no one is near.

He concentrates, and chaos flares across the body.

All that remain are some coins, some iron nails, and a few metal studs. Using his kerchief to protect his fingers from the lingering heat, Lorn scoops up the items and tosses them out and over the railing. The faint clink of the coins on the stones below cannot even be heard.

The use of chaos leaves him with a headache—not as bad as some, but one that is more than a mere dull ache. He slips the shortsword through his belt and eases his way along the railing and past one pillar and then another until he reaches the east side of the garden. Then, concealed by his blur-shield, he waits until the next green-clad guard passes before he climbs onto the railing and lifts himself onto the brick step of the chimney. He makes his way up the three huge stepped sides of the chimney.

Tasjan should still be dining. Above him, the study windows are dark yet. While using the blur-shield, Lorn could still follow the trader, anywhere in the dwelling, until he has an opportunity—but the study would be best.

There are three windows. He can reach two from where he stands. The first is shut firmly. The second is closed, but there is a crack there. Slowly, with the back edge of the shortsword, Lorn wiggles it wider, and then wider, until he can pull it open.

Then he jumps and grabs the sill, and slowly drags himself up and into the empty study. He closes the window, slowly and gently, then makes his way to a corner behind the carved desk, a corner where the built-in bookshelves meet.

While there is a temptation to look at the papers and folders on the desk, Lorn refrains and merely stands in the corner. He lets the blur-shield down while he waits. There is little sense in using the effort when none are around to see him.

He waits for some time—so long that he has begun to debate whether he should strike out with his chaos-senses and try to locate Tasjan. Then, he reflects, waiting in another's dwelling to murder someone may well slow time.

The sound of steps, and a *click*, alerts Lorn, and he cloaks himself in aversion and waits.

The door opens, and dim light from the corridor oozes into the study. A slender figure stands in the door, looking across the study. With the door still open, Tasjan takes the striker from his belt, and clicks it, once, twice, before light creeps from the lamp set in the sconce beside the doorway.

Tasjan glances around the study, once, then again. His brow furrows, and he looks almost directly at Lorn, but his eyes pass by the lancer in blue.

Finally, the merchanter closes the door and slides the bolt. He steps toward the table desk.

Lorn moves from the corner, and with the borrowed blade, slashes across the left side of the merchanter's unprotected neck.

Tasjan barely has the time to look surprised.

Lorn manages to grab part of the merchanter's tunic and swings the body so that it falls onto the carpet, rather than into the desk or the chair before it. Then he lowers the shortsword with the green leather grip to the carpet beside the dead merchanter.

Standing quickly, he slides the window back open. Then, regathering the blur-shield back around him, he slides out, lowering himself down to the first ledge. He leaves the window wide open. Slowly, in the growing twilight, he makes his way down the stepped sections of the chimney to the portico roof. There he freezes, blur-shield around him.

Two guards have stopped on the far side of the railing, and are talking.

"You see Wyst?"

"No. You're on his post. Thought he got the flux or something."

". . . just disappeared . . . Gyan's asking all the guards . . . be not happy . . ."

". . . something up . . . don't know what . . . calling in the guards off the ships . . ."

"Double guards at the Plaza building, too."

"Sasyk whipped someone in the second squad . . . doesn't do that 'less he's frettin'."

"Look up there . . . he's at it again. Light still on in the study."

"Not that warm . . . he's got the window open . . ."

"Where he sits these days, it's warm enough." The first guard laughs.

"Funny, though. Cold out here, and it'll be colder 'afore Vansyn comes on relief. Give anything to be inside and warm, and he's inside and warm, and trying to get cooler."

"Life is like that, friend. Better keep moving. Don't want to get on Gyan's bad side."

"Nor Sasyk's."

The two part and walk back along their separate posts, away from the corner. Lorn slips from the deeper shadows and with one hand holding the stone rail, he leaps across the emptiness, and slides through greenery, finally managing to clutch a branch. He can feel the scratches on his hands and on his neck. He keeps clutching the branch, letting stretched muscles rest, and breathing deeply.

Even after he reaches the base of the tree, he holds the blurring shield until he is two blocks away, despite the pain in his eyes that has grown into sharp daggers jabbing into his skull, intensifying the headache he already suffers. He uses a kerchief from his belt wallet to blot the blood from the scratches on his neck.

It feels as though every eye is on him as he walks back down Eighth Harbor Way West, yet the streets are almost empty, and, so far as he can tell, neither eyes nor screeing glasses are upon him.

As he turns onto the narrow way that holds their dwelling, he can sense the chill of a chaos-glass. There is little he can do but continue walking, and the feeling passes even before he reaches the iron gate.

He can but wonder what magus was screeing him—wonder and hope. At least he was not observed by a glass while near Tasjan's dwelling.

He double-checks the locking on the iron gate before he makes his way along the marble walk toward the veranda.

"Ser?" calls a voice.

"It's me, Pheryk. I'm back."

"The lady asked me to watch for you, and to let the geese out of the pen once you returned."

"Thank you. You can do that. I'm not going out again. It's been a long day."

"Good night, ser."

"Good night." Lorn opens the veranda door, then slides the bolt behind him and steps down into the foyer.

"Is that you, Lorn?"

"It's me."

Ryalth waits in the sitting room, a goblet of Alafraan in her hand, a second goblet on the table.

Lorn looks at the goblet.

"I thought you might need it. You look like it was harder than you planned."

"You didn't ask how it went."

"I could tell that when you entered. There's a coldness about you. It was there after Shevelt, but I didn't recognize it as such then. You've got some cuts, and your eyes are watering. Are any . . ."

"No . . . the cuts are from a lorken tree I was climbing. I got them climbing down. They're just scratches." Lorn takes up the goblet. "Thank you."

"And you used enough chaos that your head is splitting and your eyes water?"

"That, too." He sits on the front edge of the chair across from Ryalth, who leans forward on the settee. "It's all a mess." After the smallest sip of Alafraan, he adds, "Tasjan blackmails Vyel to kill you. He releases papers so that all would believe Vyanat murdered his own brother to save himself, when Vyanat had killed his brother to show he would not countenance favoritism and ill-doing by his brother. Now I act so that Tasjan cannot create a cause . . ."

". . . and Sasyk will use it as such in some way?"

"Possibly," Lorn admits. "Or someone else."

"Did you leave something to tie the death to Sasyk?"

"A green-wrapped blade and an open window—and one guard is missing."

Ryalth nods. "That will suffice." Her blue eyes are as sad and hard as Lorn's amber orbs.

They each take another sip of the Alafraan.

CL

THE BLOND AND broad-shouldered first-level adept magus steps into the study in the private dwelling. He bows to the older magus who stands by the window, looking down across Cyad itself at the gray winter waters of the harbor.

"You suggested we talk before dinner, ser?" asks the tall and blond first-level adept.

"It would be opportune," answers Kharl as he turns. "How is Ceyla?"

"Your daughter is in good health, and talks with your consort in the sitting room." Rustyl smiles politely.

"A magnificent harbor, is it not?" Kharl gestures to the scene framed in the window. "It is a pity that, unless some action is taken soon, it will fall to the outlanders, and within your life, Rustyl, perhaps sooner."

"The First Magus has suggested such can be averted if the Magi'i gain greater control of Cyad."

"It is rather late for Chyenfel to think of such," Kharl snorts. "He is the one who buried the chaos-towers of the Accursed Forest in the mists of time, and now we have too few towers to power the firewagons, or to charge the firelances of the Mirror Lancers when we need them most. We have no tow-wagons on the Great Canal, and soon will have no fireships."

"But . . . would not the Accursed Forest—"

"The Accursed Forest . . . what was it? A place that bred large animals that occasionally killed livestock and a few peasants? A place whose name was used to frighten children? There were twelve chaos-towers there. And ten still functioned. We have but three left in Cyad, and the tower that serves the Quarter is failing. And Chyenfel gave away years of good use of the towers so that a few peasants might live? He gave away much of the power of the Magi'i." The second snort is far louder. "Did he not keep you from that project? Why? I wonder. Or was it because you might see that Chyenfel wanted to be known for a great deed—a deed that for its greatness would cost Cyador and those of the Magi'i who follow him dearly? And now he says that the Magi'i should seek greater control?" After a moment of silence, the Second Magus adds, "I fear that it will take the Magi'i far greater control than Chyenfel believes, for us to redeem Cyad. You know the Emperor will not last a half a season, do you not?" Kharl's green eyes focus upon the younger magus.

"Who does not know that?" Rustyl laughs.

"Most outside the Magi'i do not. Do not assume others know what you do." Kharl's warm smile returns. "Now that you have a consort . . . you could have heirs."

"We do so hope."

"I know you do, and they will be welcome. Most welcome." The Second Magus smiles warmly. "You have been favored by Chyenfel—to the point that there has been talk about your becoming First Magus." Kharl holds up his hand. "No . . . do not deny such. Chyenfel has made his favoritism clear within the Magi'i." He frowns. "There is a problem with that."

"Oh . . . ?"

"Chyenfel remains First Magus."

"He cannot do so forever." Rustyl smiles, the twisting of his lips providing an ironic edge to his words.

"If he remains First Magus long enough, his support of you can only harm you. If he is First Magus when the Emperor's heir takes the Malachite Throne . . ." Kharl shrugs. "Then . . . it may be that the new Emperor will also favor Chyenfel, as Toziel has."

"Who do you favor for the successor?" asks Rustyl. "Or think it may be?"

"The most honorable Tasjan was playing for that, and the word is that a former lancer named Sasyk is rallying the tenscore armed guards he trained for Tasjan—as well as others within the merchanters—to force a merchanter upon the Malachite Throne."

"A merchanter emperor?" Rustyl sneers.

"That is why the Majer-Commander has two companies of trained lancers in Cyad, under his best and bloodiest field commander."

"What is to prevent Lorn from seeking the throne? His lancers will support him." Rustyl watches the older magus.

"Majer Lorn has removed himself from serious consideration as the Mirror Lancer heir," Kharl says.

"Removed himself? He is yet on duty." Rustyl frowns.

"No. I found him entering his dwelling—wearing merchanter blues. Two nights ago. The very night that Tasjan was murdered by one of his guards. That is . . . a guard is missing, and his weapon murdered Tasjan within his own study."

"One could scarcely advance a charge such as that against the majer and expect many to believe it," Rustyl points out. "Not after all he is perceived to have done for Cyador over the years."

"One need not prove such, only point out that such an action benefits Ryalor House and Majer Lorn. Vyanat can offer no support to any, not after all that has occurred with Hyshrah Clan, and if one were to point out that he has specially favored Ryalor House . . . and Rynst were persuaded to step aside . . . and if all the Magi'i opposed Lorn . . ."

"I count three *if*'s, honored ser." Rustyl's voice is polite.

"Only two. Vyanat is truly powerless. I have strong reasons to believe that the present Captain-Commander will shortly succeed the Majer-Commander . . . and if you become First Magus, and I am Second . . ." Kharl smiles. "You see . . . it is most simple. Nothing need be said or done, unless Rynst steps aside. And if he does . . . why then, you can decide whether you will be First Magus, or whether Lorn may be Emperor. The choice is in your hands."

"My hands? What of yours?"

"All know me as Second Magus, as clever, as scheming. Who indeed would accept me as First Magus?" Kharl offers a self-deprecating smile. "But . . . it is of no matter, yet. We can only see what may occur."

"That is true."

"We should join the others." The Second Magus starts for the study door, then pauses. "There is also something you should know. Should you lack sufficient chaos to accomplish a task, a first-level adept can indeed draw upon the power of the chaos-towers directly—that is, from their very core. One must do so with care, but I should explain how this may be done, in the event that you find yourself threatened. . . ."

Rustyl nods as Kharl continues to explain.

CLI

IT IS ALMOST midafternoon in Cyad, and Lorn finds himself once more before the Majer-Commander, not knowing exactly what Rynst may have in mind. He bows. "Ser?"

Rynst looks up from his desk, surprisingly less cluttered with papers than is normally the case. "Yes, Majer. There are some things I thought you should know. Several matters." The Majer-Commander does not smile. "A number of old bills of lading and other papers have appeared at the Traders' Plaza."

"Ser?" Lorn does not have to counterfeit puzzlement.

"They appear to be authentic, according to the First Magus. They are records showing that the recently murdered Dyjani clan head was receiving additional golds from cargoes and goods he was selling in Swartheld. There were also shipments of iron shortswords, for which he paid nothing. Shortly thereafter, other documents appeared. The accuracy of these is more in doubt, but they would indicate that the Emperor's Merchanter Advisor had his brother killed to ensure that his own failings were not made public."

Lorn nods to hear what he already knows.

"I would trust that you will hold your lancers in readiness, Majer, and that all drills you hold for the next few days be without firelances, so that, should they be needed, full charges will remain in all lances."

"Yes, ser."

"And I expect you to be where you can be reached by messenger."

"I'll either be here, ser, or at home, or at the harbor barracks or grounds."

"Good. You should be here early tomorrow, and the morning after."

"Yes, ser."

"That will be all, Majer."

"Yes, ser."

Before Lorn can turn, Rynst adds, "And I trust you recall your orders and chain of command, Majer."

"Yes, ser."

Lorn manages to retain a pleasant smile on his face as he makes his way out of the Majer-Commander's study and down the stairs to the fourth-floor foyer.

The thin-faced commander Shykt is standing outside his study door. "Fayrken said you would not be long, and he was right."

Lorn nods. "Yes, ser."

"I've been dispatched to Dellash with Commander Dhynt and Commander Muyro to study the disabled fireships, and we're to make a firsthand report." Shykt smiles, if nervously. "I thought you might like to know, in case it applies to any reports you are doing."

"Thank you, ser. I appreciate the notice."

"You are most welcome, Majer." The thin-faced commander pauses. "Did you hear about Commander Sypcal?"

Lorn's stomach tightens even more. "No, ser."

"Quite ill, I understand. Some sort of flux. If he recovers, it will be eightdays before he's himself again." Shykt offers another strained smile. "I'd guess that would leave you, the Majer-Commander, the Captain-Commander, and Commander Lhary at the next twoday meeting."

"I suppose it would, ser. I appreciate knowing that, as well."

"I thought you might." Shykt nods.

"Have a good trip, ser."

"I'm sure it will do us good."

Lorn walks back into his study—but only long enough to gather his personal items, before he walks back out.

He stops by Fayrken's desk station. "I'll be down at the harbor barracks. There are some things I need to discuss with the officers and rankers."

"Yes, ser. Will you be back this afternoon?"

"I don't know." Lorn shrugs. "If I can be."

As he walks down toward the harbor, he can again sense a chaos-glass being focused on him, and whatever magus follows him holds the image until he enters the end of the converted warehouse that holds the studies of the two Mirror Lancer captains.

He finds both Cheryk and Esfayl in the slightly larger space—Cheryk's study.

"Ser!" Both officers stand.

"Matters here in Cyad are getting . . . shall we say . . . unsettled."

Cheryk and Esfayl exchange glances.

"I can see you have heard something along those lines," Lorn says with a faint smile. "What, might I ask?"

"Well . . . there's word that the merchanters are gathering together the greensuit guards," Cheryk ventures. "Some are saying the Palace had that Tasjan fellow killed."

"And others say that the Emperor is ailing," adds Esfayl.

"I don't know that the Emperor is any more ill than he has been," Lorn says, "but the guards of Dyjani House could be a real problem. You are to restrict tomorrow's maneuvers to light one-on-one drills with padded blades. You are to keep all firelances ready, but under your personal control, and no one is to leave the area without my orders or those of Majer-Commander Rynst—and the only Majer-Commander to whom you answer is Rynst. Otherwise, you answer to the Emperor. If none of those can offer you orders, you are to protect the Palace of Eternal Light."

"Those are grim orders, ser."

"I doubt it will come to that, but those are the orders I received."

"Ser . . . ?" offers Esfayl.

"Yes." Lorn's voice is level.

"Majer Brevyl said one other thing. He said never to wager against you, and never to ignore your orders." Esfayl smiles ruefully. "Tell us what to do, and we'll do it."

Cheryk nods.

"What we want to do is hold Cyad together," Lorn admits. "I can't tell you how, for sure, but it's likely we'll have to take on the greensuits, and even with firelances, it won't be easy. They've been trained by a renegade lancer officer, and I'd wager they have mirror shields somewhere. You might think about how to attack a squad with a mirror shield wall on foot in the streets where they can't easily be flanked."

"Too bad we can't use the firecannon," mutters Cheryk. "That'd do it."

Lorn smiles. "Why don't you find out who can operate it? Let me know by messenger. I'll see if the Majer-Commander will put them under my command for a while."

Cheryk smiles. "That . . . that we'll do."

"Now . . . I'm headed back to the Mirror Lancer Court . . ."

"Ser . . . best you take your mount, and take him to your dwelling," suggests Cheryk.

Lorn nods. He may indeed need speed.

CLII

His Mightiness Toziel'elth'alt'mer looks up from the high bed. His head does not move as he murmurs. "Ryenyel . . . my dearest . . . you can do no more. There are so few shreds of order left in this frail form, that any strength you give me . . . it will destroy me yet sooner. I would . . . have liked . . . to have spent . . . another spring . . ."

"So . . . so would I." The redhead whose hair whitens even as she holds his hand, kneels on the chair beside the bed, her head almost beside his.

"I would . . . not . . . have left Cyador . . . so." He takes several wheezing shallow breaths before he speaks again. "We tried so hard to find one who could hold . . . our Land of Eternal Light . . ."

"We did as we could, dear one." She squeezes his hand, offering the slightest hint of order.

"Your touch . . . good . . . as always."

"I am here, dearest."

"You must . . . write out the documents—one for each, naming him as heir—hold as you can . . . and choose as you must." He forces a smile that lapses as he struggles for another breath. "How . . . Which . . . ?"

"Lorn—he may yet surmount what faces him. I would have him over Kharl or any merchanter, but either Kharl or Lorn will keep Cyador strong."

"Cyador . . . Cyad . . . there is no other . . . no other."

Once she has completed her task, and he his, as the night darkens, the Empress-Consort continues to hold Toziel's hand, long past that time when she can offer strength or warmth.

CLIII

IN THE DARKNESS just after dusk, Lorn sits at the small study desk in his dwelling. He looks into the chaos-glass as the silver mists slip away. Ryalth stands behind him, holding Kerial. The image in the glass is clear enough. Five men sit around a table. Lorn recognizes but one of the five, and that is Sasyk.

"Daaa!" Kerial tries to lurch from Ryalth's arms toward the chaos-glass. "Gaaa . . ."

"Kerial! Hold still!"

At the sharpness of Ryalth's tone, tears begin to form at the corners of the boy's eyes.

"Hush . . . be quiet, dearest." Ryalth cuddles him even as she strains to make out the faces in the lamplit glass. "Sasyk is the one in the middle . . . I don't know the two others in green . . . that's Kernys on the right, and Denys on the left."

"That is Denys?" For some reason Lorn has pictured Denys like his predecessor, large and bulky, but Bluoyal's successor as the head of Bluyet House is a handsome man of modest proportion.

"For all his looks, dearest, he is less trustworthy than Bluoyal was."

Lorn lets the image lapse. He closes his eyes and massages his forehead for a moment before turning and looking at his consort. "I do not see others from Dyjani Clan. You had said that the clan would most likely support others."

"Nor do I see those who should be there." Ryalth sighs. "That bodes ill for Husdryt and Torvyl."

"Could Sasyk be plotting with Kernys and Denys? To hold Dyjani House?"

"It would appear that he already does. So Sasyk has the Dyjani, Bluyet House, and Kysan House behind him? Most merchanters do not trust Vyanat that much because of the death of his brother."

"What about Yuryan House?" Lorn asks.

"Veljan will not support Sasyk, but the strength of Yuryan House lies in its vessels and outland warehouses and factors." As she stands beside Lorn, Ryalth rocks Kerial back and forth in the dimness of the study, lit by the single lamp on corner of the desk. "Sasyk is telling all that the Magi'i killed Tasjan, for only a magus could enter a locked and guarded dwelling and vanish so. He says that is because they wish to take more of the merchanters' golds for themselves."

Lorn gestures at the blank glass. "Some believe him."

"They are the ones who wish to believe."

"Were you the one who had the old bills of lading and other papers showing Tasjan's treachery appear in the Plaza?" Lorn raises his eyebrows. "Rynst told me this had happened."

"I did not do such." Ryalth smiles. "But it would not have happened had I not requested a favor."

"It may help. I hope that it does." Lorn frowns. "Rynst ordered Shykt, Dhynt, and Muyro to Dellash. They're all his supporters, after a fashion. Why would he order them away from Cyad right now? Sypcal's been poisoned, or something, and he's the only tactical commander besides me who supports Rynst. That leaves the Captain-Commander and Commander Lhary, and they oppose Rynst."

"The Majer-Commander left you in Cyad," Ryalth points out. "And you command the only Mirror Lancers around. Could the others do anything—except have their loyalty tried and risk being killed?"

"Rynst truly expects bloodshed."

"He expects you to shed it."

"How soon?"

"Sasyk does not have all the guards yet in Cyad, but he will have what he needs in the days ahead, perhaps less than half an eightday."

"Will some come by ship?"

"I would think so."

"Good." Lorn pauses. "I do not favor what we see." He shakes his head. "Once I had hoped . . ."

"Like Alyiakal? It still might happen."

"I think not, for to preserve Cyad, I will have to shed blood, far too much blood, it would appear from what the glass shows."

"One can hope otherwise," Ryalth suggests.

"I will hope, but we must plan for what will come." Lorn looks back at the glass to call forth another image.

CLIV

THE TWO FIGURES in shimmering white stand at opposite sides of the corridor that adjoins the Quarter chaos-tower of the Magi'i.

"You requested I join you here for a demonstration, Rustyl," Chyenfel says slowly. "Have you found some way in which to prolong the life of the failing chaos-tower?"

"Were you ever interested in such? Really?" asks the younger adept. "If you were so interested, why did you bury so many chaos-towers within the mists of time, so that now we must struggle to charge firewagons and firelances but from a pair of chaos-towers beyond this one?"

Chyenfel frowns. "I thought you understood. What use would a handful of chaos-towers be, surrounded by a resurgent Accursed Forest? How would one even reach them?"

"What does the safety of a handful of peasants matter, when Cyador struggles to defend herself because you gave away the greatest of the chaos-towers?"

"You are mistaken, Rustyl. Gravely mistaken. That is not the case—"

"It is the case. You do not wish me to succeed you as First Magus. Or even Kharl."

Chyenfel's mouth opens. "Dear Rustyl. I had never, ever expected that. I had thought more of you—both in ability, and in common sense. Why did I expose you to all of the facets of Magi'i operations? Yet why do few outside the Magi'i know of you? Surely you can understand that now?"

"You only wished to use me a counter to Kharl . . . nothing more." Chaos flares around the younger mage as his shield forms.

"That is not so . . . but were it such, is that not an honorable duty—to counter one who would destroy all for which the Magi'i stand?" A paler, deeper shield forms around the slightly bent form of the First Magus.

"He would have the Magi'i strong. You merely wished to be recalled for a great deed, and care little for what happens to those who follow you." The taller mage casts a bolt of chaos at the older man.

The older magus merely stands and lets the firebolt splatter into nothingness across his order-chaos shield. "You *were* the Magi'i candidate to be Toziel's heir. I can see my hopes exceeded my reason."

"You tell me that now to save yourself." Rustyl sneers. Another firebolt begins to form.

"I need no words to save myself from an ungrateful whelp such as you." A searing white-red flame rips the air in the corridor, throwing Rustyl against the granite wall, his shield diminished to a mere shadow of that which he had raised but moments before.

"You are a demented old man, who would ruin Cyad for your own glory," Rustyl snaps as he straightens, frowning. His body begins to glow, even as the shimmer that filters through the black glass portal to the chaos-tower chamber begins to diminish.

Chyenfel's mouth opens, but momentarily. "No . . . you must not. You will destroy yourself as well."

"Again . . . you throw words to save yourself. I will do as I must!" Rustyl returns, a broad smile crossing his face.

A massive bolt of blue-white chaos appears before Rustyl, and incandescence fills the corridor, expanding in all directions as elemental chaos sears the corridor and further whitens the granite.

In the granite structure behind the now-empty corridor, the chaos-tower glows blue, if momentarily, before it begins to melt into itself.

At the far end of the Quarter of the Magi'i, the Second

Magus smiles, then nods to himself, murmuring in words that do not leave his study, "If Chyenfel can use a halfscore failing towers, then one is a fair price to save Cyad from weakness."

CLV

RYNST STANDS BY the study window, half-turned toward the Palace of Light, its white walls seeming less crisp than normal in the hazy midmorning light of a day in early winter. His eyes ease to Lorn, but the Majer-Commander does not move from the window.

"Ser?" Lorn bows after closing the door to the Majer-Commander's study. Then he steps past the conference table and halts before the desk, waiting.

"One of the chaos-towers of the Magi'i failed last night," Rynst begins, without looking at Lorn. "The First Magus was killed, as was another magus. They were attempting to stabilize the chaos-tower, according to the Second Magus, but something went astray. So . . . now there are but two chaos-towers operating in all of Cyador, save the three on the remaining fireships."

Lorn swallows silently, waiting.

Finally, Rynst turns from the closed and ancient glass panes. He does not step toward the desk. "That is not the worst. The Emperor has canceled all audiences. It is unlikely he will survive the eightday. The Empress has announced that the heir has been decided and will be named shortly. That could be before or after the Emperor's death. It may not matter. You should have your lancers in readiness, Majer."

Lorn nods his acknowledgment.

"I have not heard how the Magi'i will choose a successor to Chyenfel, but it is likely that the Second Magus will become the First Magus, and the Third the Second, and that a

Third Magus will be named at a later time." Rynst smiles, briefly, and without meaning. "For these reasons, and others, I have approved your request to put the Mirror Engineers operating the firecannon directly under your command. That order is good for three eightdays. That should be sufficient." The Majer-Commander offers a cold smile. "I have also informed Majer Hrenk and Captain Ghyrat that you are their superior in the chain of command, and that whatever orders you give regarding the use and placement of the firecannon are to be obeyed and carried out without delay."

"I hope it is not necessary, ser."

"So do I, but it is appearing more so. Former captain Sasyk appears to have seized control of the guards of Dyjani House. Word is that he has killed the two most notable candidates to succeed Tasjan." Rynst's lips curl. "That is a merchanter matter, and one in which neither the Magi'i nor the Mirror Lancers can intervene without the order of the Emperor. The Emperor is unlikely to give any more orders."

"And until the merchanters strike, you can do nothing?" Lorn asks.

"Unless the merchanters threaten the city or the Palace, the Mirror Lancers will not shed blood. What the merchanters do within their houses is their affair."

Lorn nods.

"Once it leaves the merchanters, it is our affair. *Your* affair, Majer, and I will not second-guess your actions or decisions. I only order you to make sure that whatever heir the Emperor names does take the Malachite Throne." Rynst's voice hardens. "Whomever the Emperor names. No matter what that name may be."

"Yes, ser."

"You are known as an officer whose word has always remained unbroken. Will it be so in this, Majer?"

"Yes, ser."

Rynst nods abruptly. "Good. Best you see to your companies and to the engineers. I would judge that little will occur before tomorrow, but that is but a wager in a game whose rules are unannounced and changing with each passing moment."

Lorn bows.

"And Majer . . ."

"Ser?"

"Without honor, without duty, you have nothing. Nor do I. The Majer-Commander of Mirror Lancers must *never* be a candidate for the Malachite Throne. Nor the Captain-Commander. Were that to happen . . . then none could trust the Mirror Lancers. I would hope the Magi'i would feel that way as well. I know Chyenfel did."

"Yes, ser."

"Good day, Majer." Rynst turns back to the window, his eyes on the Palace of Eternal Light.

As he leaves the Majer-Commander, Lorn's face is impassive, but the combination of duty and near-fatality in Rynst's words chills him within. Rynst has as much as ordered him not to allow Luss to claim the Malachite Throne. Yet it is an unspoken order.

The white gelding remains where Lorn had tied him earlier in the morning, in the third stall in the small stable for visiting officers. Lorn gives the gelding a pat, then leads the horse out into a day that remains chill and hazy. As he rides the white gelding from Mirror Lancer Court down Third Harbor Way West, his eyes scan the streets. They seem almost as normal, although there may be a touch fewer souls about. Then, that may be because of the chill wind out of the northeast. He rides past the warehouse barracks to the next building, the one housing the Mirror Engineers and their large and small firecannon. He has barely dismounted and tied the gelding to the bronze ring of the innermost hitching post, before a ginger-bearded, balding, and young-faced captain steps out of the narrow doorway and toward Lorn.

"Ser." Ghyrat bows. "I have received the Majer-Commander's orders. What can we do for you?"

"Nothing . . . I hope, but I fear we will need both your cannon."

"So do I." Ghyrat fingers his pointed goatee. "The Majer-Commander would scarce order such were he not concerned. Yet he offered no reasons."

Lorn nods. "I doubt he would wish any placed in ink. It appears likely that the Dyjani merchanters may use the piers to land ships and more of their greensuited guards, to require a merchanter heir to the Palace."

"A merchanter heir?"

"The current head of Dyjani House has assembled more than tenscore of the armed greensuited guards. He is a former Mirror Lancer officer and has trained them to the same degree as are lancer rankers."

"Tenscore?" Ghyrat swallows.

"Also, the First Magus was killed in an accident with a chaos-tower last night. How that may impact us . . . I am uncertain."

"I would not guess, ser, save that it might make the merchanters more quick to act."

"If any vessels appear with the Dyjani ensign or any that appear unknown or otherwise suspicious, can you move the firecannon quickly to the base of the pier? The large one?"

The engineer officer nods. "We can have it set to move."

"Then do so, if you would. As quickly as you can."

"We will. But you will have to give the orders to fire and upon whom."

"If it comes to that, then I will." Lorn holds back a frown. Rynst has given Lorn a clear chain of command, but to whom can Lorn turn? For he is not invincible, as he knows all too well.

"Ser?"

Lorn glances toward the harbor and the piers, empty except for a Sligan deepwater vessel and a Gallosian coaster. "I hope an heir is named soon, one that all accept, and that it does not come to the use of lances and cannon."

"We all hope such, Majer," replies Ghyrat. "But who is the man whom all will accept as heir and Emperor in these times?"

Who indeed?

"The Emperor has decided," Lorn replies. "We are to support whatever that decision may be." In chaos and in blood—the chaos and the blood Lorn has never wished upon Cyad, City of Eternal Light.

CLVI

IN THE DARKNESS after dusk, Rynst turns from the window, away from the myriad lamps that illumine the Palace of Eternal Light, and sits down behind his table desk. He looks at the blank sheet of parchment before him and shakes his head.

Then, in the glow cast from the lamps on his desk, he looks up as the faintest *click* comes from the latch to his study door. The ancient golden-oak door to the Majer-Commander's study opens, then closes.

A faint breeze wafts from the door and then fades.

Deliberately, slowly, Rynst eases back his chair. The fingers of his left hand ease the black iron throwing knife from the slit pocket in his belt.

"I cannot say I am surprised, Kharl," the Majer-Commander says slowly, though his eyes search the space between the door and his desk for any sign of the unusual. "Managing to get Rustyl to remove Chyenfel showed your touch."

There is the slightest whisper of leather on the sunstone tiles of the study floor.

"I suppose Luss has no idea of this. That way you can have the Third Magus truth-read him, and Luss can answer honestly that he has no idea what happened."

The figure of the Second Magus appears at the end of the conference table closest to the Majer-Commander. Kharl smiles ironically. "You say you would not be surprised, yet you still underestimate me."

Rynst shakes his head as he eases his chair slightly farther back from the desk, his right hand visible on the edge of the wood. "No, honored Second Magus, I underestimated Chyenfel. I thought he would hold you more in check, and I thought you had some vestige of honor. I thought you would stop at becoming First Magus, and I did not realize you would sacrifice a chaos-tower to your endless ambition. Do you really think you can seize the Malachite Throne?"

"That depends on what the Empress announces as the Emperor's decision, does it not? For now, I am First Magus, at least in practice, if not in title." Kharl's green eyes dance.

"For the moment." Rynst shrugs, and then his left hand blurs, and the iron throwing knife flashes toward the red-haired magus.

Hssssst!

Firebolt and knife meet, but the chaos-flames and iron droplets splash back across Kharl's left shoulder.

As the magus steps back, Rynst quickly slides out the cupridium-plated and iron-cored sabre from the scabbard fastened to the underside of his table desk, and leaps forward with the iron-cored blade in his right hand.

Kharl steps back, silently, giving ground.

Rynst holds the blade high, his eyes flicking between the midsection of the magus and his eyes, moving closer to Kharl.

Abruptly, firebolts flash toward the Majer-Commander from the left and then the right.

Rynst's sabre flicks to the left, parrying one firebolt. His blade is slow on the return, and the second firebolt slams into his right shoulder. His blade drops from his numbed fingers. Another firebolt catches him full in the chest, and he topples forward.

For a long time, there is silence and the sound of one man's heavy breathing.

Then there is another series of flashes of chaos.

After a time, Kharl slowly opens one of the doors to the balcony outside the study, then flings a few metal items into the night. He leaves the door open, and walks unsteadily toward the closed door leading to the fifth-floor foyer, and the empty stone staircase. One hand holds his left shoulder.

Just before the door opens, he appears to vanish, and the study of the Majer-Commander is empty.

CLVII

IN THE DINING area Lorn and Ryalth sit alone, eating, in the reflected glow of a pair of lamps set in wall sconces.

"You were late tonight. You were preparing for an attack by Sasyk's guards." Ryalth nibbles on the crust of the dark bread.

"I think they will attack, but the Majer-Commander is not sure whether it will be tomorrow or the day after." Lorn eats the lamb stew slowly, methodically, hardly tasting what passes his lips.

"Noon or afternoon tomorrow, I would guess," Ryalth says.

"Why do you think that?"

"The winds in the morning will make a swift approach difficult, and there were no vessels standing off the harbor."

"That is good to know." Lorn takes a sip of wine he scarcely tastes. "Rynst told me that the Majer-Commander can never be Emperor. Nor the Captain-Commander. He said it would destroy Cyador. He believes his own words."

"He's telling you to kill Luss, if anything happens to him, isn't he?"

"I fear he's suggesting that Luss will reach for the Malachite Throne."

"What will you do?"

"What I must. If I must." Lorn shrugs wearily. After a moment, he asks, "Did you hear anything about Husdryt and Torvyl?"

Ryalth shakes her head. "None knows anything, and there were a score of greensuited guards around Dyjani House today."

"That's all? Sasyk just kills the heirs and walks in?"

"What would you have them do?" asks Ryalth. "Traders are not lancers, and all those with arms owe their allegiance to Sasyk. Why have the Mirror Lancers not acted, I could well ask."

Lorn takes a sip of the Fhynyco before responding. "I asked the Majer-Commander about that. Lancers aren't supposed to interfere in the internal doings of merchanter houses. We only act if a house threatens other houses, or the Palace. Or, I suppose, the Mirror Lancers."

"You were right to deal with Tasjan silently. None would lift arms until it would bloody all Cyad."

"That could still happen," Lorn says. "Perhaps you should stay here tomorrow."

"In the afternoon . . ."

"What is so important that you would risk yourself in the morning?" he finally asks Ryalth.

"If I shy from the Plaza when others do not . . . then who will trade with me? I have spent years, dear lancer, getting folk to understand that I am no frail woman." Ryalth raises her eyebrows.

Lorn sighs. He recognizes the cupridium in her voice. "Promise me this. If other houses close . . . you close as well, even if it is morning. And take Pheryk and the hired guards. There is a difference between prudence and faintheartedness."

"I will—but I will not be the first to close."

Lorn holds back a frown. Ryalth's words are not quite true. "You don't have to be the very last."

"I will not be so, not if I can help it."

Lorn relaxes slightly. Those words are clearly truth-felt.

He takes another sip of the wine. Then he stiffens, shaking his head. "Did you hear about the First Magus?"

Ryalth frowns. "I cannot said that I did, save that some ask why the Magi'i have not stepped forward to press for an heir."

"A chaos-tower failed yesterday, and the First Magus was killed. Rynst said that he was trying to stabilize it because there are but two towers remaining in all Cyad. Except for three on fireships."

"That does not ring fair."

"No, and that means Kharl will be First Magus. I do not like that at all."

"Could he have . . . ?"

"Tyrsal says that, old as he is, Chyenfel is . . . was . . . far stronger than Kharl in handling chaos." Lorn frowns.

"Should you talk to Tyrsal?" Ryalth asks.

"I should . . . but I do not dare take the time to seek him, nor compromise him, not tomorrow, not when we know not what Sasyk plans." Lorn shrugs. "All the glass shows is Sasyk plotting and guards upon ships." He laughs once. "We know both almost without a glass, and a glass does not tell when something will happen until it does."

Ryalth looks at Lorn. "You had not planned for this."

He shakes his head slowly. "No. I had thought . . ." He breaks off with a sad and wistful smile. "One doesn't think . . . life changes . . . I had not thought my parents would die so soon . . ." He smiles. "At least they saw Kerial . . . and you. Your parents didn't get to see any of that."

Her smile is sad. "When one wishes . . . the costs are far greater than mere golds."

"Is Ryalor House worth it?"

"It is. My mother would be pleased. My father would be astonished. Yet . . . there is always something more to be done. There is always another cargo lost, another factor who distrusts a woman . . ."

"And a consort who is often never around?"

"I cannot ask you to be what you are not, dear one, and you have loved me more than any could hope or ask. I would that I could give you half of what you have given me." Her hand reaches across the table and takes his. "It is just . . . in these times . . . we do what we must . . . and never know if it is what should be done . . . or what may come of it."

Lorn squeezes her hand, half wondering, half dreading, just what the morrow may bring.

CLVIII

CIESRT HOLDS MYRYAN'S arm as they climb the steps to the second level of the dwelling. His steps are so quick he is almost dragging her slight frame. "Please hurry. . . . please . . ."

"I won't be much help . . . not if I can't breathe when I get there." Myryan's voice is low.

"I told you. Don't you understand?" Ciesrt slows his climb to match her steps. "Father needs a healer . . . and you are one of the best."

"You told me that."

"A bravo attacked him coming back from the Quarter tonight," Ciesrt explains. "He must have had an iron blade . . . or something." He says nothing more, and they walk, silently, the last cubits up the steps and across the portico to the study.

Slightly behind her consort, Myryan follows Ciesrt into the lamplit study.

Kharl is half seated, half slumped, lying back in an armchair, his feet on a stool. His face is flour-white, and his breathing is fast and shallow, almost panting. His tunic and undertunic have been removed, and his chest would be bare, saving that it is covered with a blanket, except for his left shoulder and arm. His green eyes are open, and fierce, even as his form convulses into another shudder.

A woman in white, Kharl's consort, places a damp cloth across the forehead of the magus, and another across the shoulder and the arm.

"The iron . . . Mother removed it as soon as he got here, but she has not your skill," Ciesrt explains.

The new First Magus says nothing as Myryan bends and moves the cold damp cloth to inspect the wound. Her fingers brush his skin momentarily. Red lines spread from a small wound, no larger than a thumb, in his left upper arm just below the top of his shoulder. Heat radiates from the entire arm and shoulder.

"Well . . ." The normally smooth and modulated voice is raw.

"It is ferric poisoning." Myryan's face is drawn. "It is well along, but I *think* I can do something about it."

"If you would . . ." Ciesrt says.

"Quickly," rasps Kharl.

Myryan touches the skin of the magus once more, lightly. She winces, murmuring. "Order-spelled iron."

". . . would be . . ." mutters Kharl.

Myryan seats herself on the stool that Ciesrt has drawn from somewhere for her. A cloud of unseen darkness rises from the healer and gathers about the wound. The air within a quarter of a cubit of the center of the wound sparkles, as if tiny points of order and chaos collide in miniature firebolts.

All eyes in the study are upon the sparkling, and none notice the second veil of darkness that wells from the healer and slips into the ailing magus.

Myryan shivers on the stool, and Ciesrt must steady her.

"Better . . ." says the First Magus. ". . . can feel it already."

"You're wonderful," Ciesrt tells Myryan. "No one could do that but you."

The faintest of smiles appears and vanishes before she speaks. "I'm sorry." Her head turns slowly to Ciesrt, as if it is a tremendous effort. "I can do no more, and . . . I must rest."

"She is a good consort, son. Have her rest." Kharl says.

She offers a wan smile in return. Her face is pale, and she leans on Ciesrt, as she steps from the study.

Behind her, the green eyes of the Second Magus are cold on her back.

CLIX

MIRROR LANCER COURT is almost empty when Lorn walks into the lower foyer not all that long after dawn and starts up the staircase to his study. Even the whispered impact of his light steps echoes in the vault of the open staircase.

"Ser?" calls Fayrken, even before Lorn's foot touches the first tile of the fourth-floor foyer.

"What is it, Fayrken?" Lorn moves toward the senior squad leader.

"The Captain-Commander . . . he was already asking for you."

"So early?"

"He said he needed to see you. As soon as you arrived. He had me send a messenger down to the warehouse barracks in case you went there first."

A faint smile crosses Lorn's face. "Do you know if the Majer-Commander is in yet?"

"Tygyl hasn't seen him. He left the door to the portico open last night."

The smile leaves Lorn's face.

Fayrken steps back, almost involuntarily. "Ser?"

"I'd best see the Captain-Commander. Thank you, Fayrken. Thank you very much." Lorn's fingers brush the hilt of the Brystan sabre as he turns back toward the staircase. He takes his time ascending the last flight.

Once he reaches the open fifth-floor foyer, Lorn pauses by Tygyl's open desk. "Tygyl . . . could I trouble you to have a messenger sent to Captain Cheryk? If you would, just tell him to have the men ready to ride. I should be there shortly, but I didn't expect to be meeting with anyone this early."

"Yes, ser. We can do that." The senior-most of the senior squad leaders raises his eyebrows.

"It appears that the Dyjani usurper will be bringing in close to fifteenscore armed guards today . . . most likely by ship."

"Yes, ser. I'll send that message."

"The Captain-Commander?"

"He's in his study, ser. Commander Lhary is with him. They expect you."

"I'm sure that they do. Thank you, Tygyl." Lorn turns to the right and steps toward the door to Luss's study.

As he steps inside the study, he closes the door, but keeps his eyes on the two men standing before Luss's table desk. "Ser. You requested my presence."

Luss looks at Lorn. Lhary stands behind the Captain-Commander's right shoulder.

"Yes . . . I did, Majer." Luss offers the warm and open smile of the type that Lorn distrusts. "You always do your duty, and in these times, we are grateful for officers such as you." Luss pauses. "The Majer-Commander has vanished. He is not in his dwelling. Nor is he in his study. nor have any seen him. Have you any knowledge of this? You have been . . . familiar . . . with the disappearance of officers, it is said."

Lorn smiles, lazily. "No, ser. I have not seen the Majer-Commander. Nor do I know aught about his disappearance. His disappearance would scarce benefit Cyador, and it would benefit me even less."

"Yet you smile, Majer," offers Lhary.

"I am a loyal Mirror Lancer officer, and I stand ready to

carry out my duties to protect the Emperor and Cyador."
Lorn's eyes continue to watch Luss.

"What do you intend, Majer?" Luss's blue eyes seem to focus into the distance for a moment, even as he studies Lorn.

"My last orders from the Majer-Commander were to ensure that the merchanters did not threaten either the Emperor or the Palace of Light. I will carry them out."

"The Emperor has died. There is no Emperor to protect. And there is no Majer-Commander." After the briefest of pauses, Luss adds, "Not that can be found."

"Yes, ser."

"I believe we discussed this earlier, Majer."

"We did, ser. There is still duty, ser." Lorn ostentatiously touches the hilt of the Brystan sabre.

Lhary's eyes tighten, and a frown begins.

Lorn's sabre is in his hand, even before either man starts to react. The first chaos-aided cut goes through Luss's throat. Luss tries to speak, then slowly crumples.

"No!" Lhary yells as he reaches for his sabre. He has his blade clear of his scabbard, if barely, when Lorn's chaos-aided iron and cupridium runs through his chest.

Lorn looks at both bodies, then wipes his blade on Lhary's tunic, even before the commander's eyes turn dull. In turn, he takes Lhary's blade from the dying man's hand and runs the edge across Luss's throat, before replacing it beside Lhary's outstretched hand.

Then he stands and sheathes the Brystan sabre, wondering how Luss could ever have bested Rynst and disposed of the Majer-Commander's body. Then, Lhary could have done it.

For a long moment, Lorn looks at the two bodies on the sunstone tiles. Then he steps out into the foyer.

Tygyl stands outside the door, sabre in hand, face blank. Behind him is Fayrken.

Lorn shakes his head. "Commander Lhary attacked the Captain-Commander. I was a shade too slow to save

Captain-Commander Luss. I was fast enough not to allow Commander Lhary to succeed in his treachery."

"Ser . . . treachery?"

"The Majer-Commander is missing. Commander Lhary is the senior commander in the Mirror Lancers. I believe the idea was to insist I attacked the Captain-Commander. Commander Lhary would dispatch me for my treachery. After all, I am the Butcher. Then, as senior commander, he would be acting Majer-Commander, and a hero to all the traditional officers for removing me."

Fayrken and Tygyl look at each other, but hold their sabres ready.

"According to the chain of command, I believe Commander Sypcal is now acting Majer-Commander."

Lorn freezes for a moment as the chill of a chaos-glass sweeps across him, but forces himself to wait calmly for Tygyl's response.

"He be ill still, ser." Tygyl's face remains blank, and he does not lower his sabre. "Are you not better fitted?"

"Tygyl . . . I am under the command of the Emperor, but I am not Majer-Commander of Mirror Lancers. Nor should I be. Sypcal is a good officer, and a good man, and he was probably poisoned by Lhary . . . just because he is a good and loyal officer. If you and the other senior squad leaders would ensure his protection . . . I'm sure the Emperor—or his heir—will confirm Commander Sypcal. If they do not, there are other senior commanders of talent. Perhaps someday I might be one of them." Lorn smiles grimly, half relieved as the sense of being observed in the chaos-glass vanishes. He wonders if the magus who has screed him is Kharl or Rustyl. "I need to get to the harbor before the ships carrying the merchanter guards arrive."

Tygyl lowers his sabre. So does Fayrken.

"Best we get to Commander Sypcal, then . . ." Tygyl says.

"And perhaps you should sent a message to Commander

Shykt in Dellash, as well." Lorn frowns. "Would you ask Commander Sypcal if he would consider bringing Majer Brevyl to Cyad to serve? As my suggestion. A suggestion only."

"Ah . . . yes, ser."

"That's the commander's choice, but with a commander and the Captain-Commander dead, and the Majer-Commander missing, and probably dead through some plotting of Commander Lhary . . . Commander Sypcal and the Emperor may need some talented and loyal officers."

"Yes, ser."

Lorn turns and hurries down the steps.

"Not one officer in a score . . . turn down that . . ."

". . . meant what he said . . ."

". . . always does . . ."

Lorn only hopes that he can continue to keep his word, both to Rynst, and to himself.

CLX

LORN GLANCES AT the cold blue sky to the south, above the harbor, as he rides downhill toward the maneuver grounds and the warehouse barracks beyond. He thinks he sees two ships under sail on the horizon, but that could be because he expects to see them. He looks again, standing in the stirrups, but still is not sure.

Cheryk is standing outside the barracks as Lorn reins up the gelding and dismounts.

"Ser . . . there was a messenger for you . . ."

"I already got it. The Captain-Commander wanted to see me. That's why I'm late."

"The messenger said we'd be posted to protect the Mirror Lancer Court," Cheryk says in a level tone.

Lorn shakes his head. "Matters...The Majer-Commander has disappeared. Commander Lhary killed the Captain-Commander, and tried to kill me. Commander Sypcal is acting Majer-Commander."

"Commander Lhary? Ser? They say he's most excellent with a blade."

"Not quite excellent enough. He's dead." Lorn's voice is weary. "We're still to protect access to the Palace."

"After all that, ser?"

"Especially after all that. Our duty, and our orders from the Majer-Commander and the Emperor, were to protect the Palace and the city. That doesn't change." Lorn pauses. "And if anything happens to me, those are your orders, Captain." Lorn's voice is like cold ordered iron.

"Yes, ser."

Esfayl steps out of the barracks. "Everyone's mounted out back and ready to ride, ser."

Lorn motions for Esfayl to join him and Cheryk, waiting until the younger captain steps closer. "Cheryk, I'd like you to take your company and Esfayl's second squad to Second Harbor Way West—I'd say the corner of Benevolent Commerce. That's above the Dyjani compound where they're mustering the greensuits already here in Cyad. That way, you'll be between the greensuits and the Palace."

"How do you want it handled?" asks the older captain.

"Have them lay down their arms and turn back or they get killed." Lorn frowns. "Can your men aim the lances low enough to hit their legs if they use mirrorlike shields?"

"We practiced that last eightday. With short bursts. Ought to be good enough to tear holes in their shield wall somewhere. Then we'll fire on the open sides of the gap."

"Do what you can. If you can rout them quickly, try not to leave many survivors. We don't want them re-forming later in the eightday. If you can't hold them, fall back and send me a messenger. Esfayl and I will be supporting the firecannon to stop reinforcements from being landed on the piers. If

we can stop them, then we'll rejoin you. If you can stop the
greensuits there, hold your position, but send Esfayl's squad
here to the piers." Lorn glances from Cheryk to Esfayl, then
back. "Is that clear?"

"Yes, ser," the two reply.

"Then we'd better start. Esfayl, have your first squad meet
me at the Mirror Engineer building."

Esfayl nods, then turns and hurries into the barracks.

Lorn remounts and rides the gelding the quarter-kay to the
Mirror Engineer building, where Ghyrat, as Cheryk was, is
waiting for Lorn. His breath steams in the cool morning air.

"Majer, we're ready to move the cannon up to Mirror
Lancer Court."

Lorn does not dismount as he replies. "The Majer-
Commander is missing, and the Captain-Commander was
killed by Commander Lhary. Commander Sypcal is acting
Majer-Commander, and our original orders stand, Captain.
There are two ships coming into the piers. I'd guess the outermost deepwater pier. You'll need to set up at the foot of the
pier so that you can sweep it clear of any armsmen. We may
have to fire the ships as well."

"Cyadoran ships?"

"Cyadoran ships carrying armed guards to reinforce those
already trying to storm the Palace. They would put a merchanter on the Malachite Throne."

"You know this?"

"So did the Majer-Commander and the Captain-
Commander. Our job is to hold Cyad for the Emperor."
Whoever he may be. "So . . . move the cannon to the foot of
the outermost pier, but leave it ready to be moved again, if
necessary."

"Yes, ser." Ghyrat bows and reenters the engineer building.

Lorn turns in the saddle, waiting as Esfayl and his squad
of lancers ride toward him.

As they near, Lorn calls, "To the outermost pier." Without
looking back, he urges the gelding past the engineer build-

ing, and then along the paved seawall road from which the piers jut into the water.

Just short of the foot of the outermost pier, Lorn reins up and again studies the harbor—and the Great Western Ocean to the south. The blue-gray water of the harbor itself bears a slight chop, with a scattered small whitecap here and there. Farther out are indeed the sails of two large trading vessels.

"Coming in for sure, ser," Esfayl says from where he has reined up beside Lorn. "Not with the best wind, either."

Lorn turns to Esfayl. "Once the firecannon is set up here, I don't want your first squad in sight of the piers."

"You want the guards on shore before we attack," Esfayl suggests.

"I'd rather not have you attack at all. You're here in case the cannon can't destroy them. If necessary, I'll have Ghyrat turn the cannon on the masts, or even the hulls, but I'd prefer to sweep the pier and save the ship."

The black-haired captain nods. "Treat them just like the Jeranyi."

"These are worse," Lorn says slowly. "The Jeranyi had no understanding of Cyador and did not know what it offers. These guards would destroy it for a handful of golds."

"We can stand down behind the sheds between the piers," Esfayl suggests.

Lorn nods. "If you would also take my mount . . . but you need to be the one who can watch for my orders, if we need you."

"Yes, ser."

Behind him, Lorn can hear the rumbling and whining of a small firewagon as it tows the cannon—like those once used against the Accursed Forest—along the seawall road. The small firewagon is but four-wheeled, and armored in cupridium plate. It tows an armored two-wheeled device with a tubular projection. When the firewagon halts, several engineers step from a hatch in the side, and unhitch the cannon, and slowly wheel it toward the pier.

Lorn turns the gelding and gestures as to where he wants the cannon placed. "Here . . . on a straight shot along the pier."

"Yes, ser," replies Ghyrat.

Once the cannon is positioned, one of the engineer rankers brings a crank out and inserts it into a fitting on the side of the cannon. He turns it rapidly, and, slowly, a small hatch opens on the side of the cannon. The engineer slips into the hatch. Another ranker rolls a long cable from the firewagon that has towed the cannon, to an assembly on the rear of the cannon. There, he fits the sheathed cupridium cable into a square bracket.

When Ghyrat has the cannon set up and positioned as Lorn desires, the majer waits until Ghyrat steps forward and looks up at the mounted lancer officer.

"You can hit anything on the pier, can you not?" Lorn asks, seeking a confirmation of what he has seen years earlier.

"Ah . . . yes, ser."

"Stand by for a moment." Lorn looks out from the foot of the outermost deepwater pier. The wind has shifted, and now blows from the south, much as Ryalth has predicted. The two vessels bearing no ensigns or banners make their way toward Cyad, along the wide main channel, under more than half-canvas, far more than most vessels coming into the piers.

Lorn looks at the engineer captain, then points to the ships. "Those will be Dyjani vessels. Or they will carry Dyjani guards. We will see." Then he turns to Esfayl. "Best you pull the lancers back." He dismounts and hands the gelding's reins to the young curly-haired captain.

"Yes, ser. We'll await your orders." Esfayl eases both mounts back toward the still-mounted squad. "Back behind those sheds."

"How long will it take to fire the cannon after I give the order?" Lorn asks Ghyrat.

"A few moments, no more."

"So, if I said to fire now . . ."

"One . . . two . . . three . . . now," Ghyrat says. "That long."

"Can you widen the chaos-bolt so that it is as wide as the pier?"

"Ah . . . we could . . . but it wouldn't be as strong."

"Would it be strong enough to kill men in light armor?"

"Oh . . . yes."

"How long would it take to change the bolt back?"

"Not much longer than to fire the cannon."

"Then have them widen the bolt and have it centered on the middle of the pier for now."

"Yes, ser." Ghyrat turns and walks back to open cannon hatch where he leans partway inside. Shortly, he returns. "It is as you ordered, ser."

"Good. Now we wait."

The wind has risen somewhat, but gotten warmer, when the first vessel swings in toward the pier, and two seamen jump from the slowly moving ship, carrying light lines. As soon as they have planted themselves by bollards, each pulls in, hand over hand, the heavier hawser, and with practiced movements, use hawser and bollard to kill the vessel's momentum. On the ship itself windlasses creak, and the lines are drawn tighter, easing the vessel up to the pier.

"We'll wait as long as we can," Lorn says. "I'd really like them both to be tied up at the pier."

"Will they?"

"I hope so. All that they can see is a vehicle and few souls. I'm trusting that won't put them off. I doubt any have seen a firecannon that is not on a ship."

The second vessel swings in farther along the outer pier than the first has, and, again, linemen leap onto the pier.

Two gangways drop onto the stone surface of the pier from the first vessel, to tie up, and almost as quickly from the second.

"Now?" asks Ghyrat.

"Not yet. Wait until they have armsmen formed up." Lorn hopes that they will have such.

His hopes, or fears, are well-founded, for green-clad armsmen scurry down the gangways and form into ranks. Lorn frowns as he sees the shimmering, near–body-length shields in the first rank, and the long cupridium-sheathed pikes being passed down.

"Almost fourscore already . . ." he murmurs, noting that the two groups of twoscore each appear almost ready to march down the pier. He turns. "Now."

Ghyrat runs forward to the firecannon, thrusting his head inside, then turns and runs back to stand behind Lorn.

The two wait.

HHHSSSTTT! With a whooshing hiss, the narrow flame sprays along the pier. Even from fifty cubits behind the cannon, Lorn can feel the intense heat. The mirrorlike shields have provided no protection, and the fourscore or so green-clad armsmen stand momentarily like charred posts before slowly toppling onto the stone of the piers.

Lorn can see nearly as many armsmen on the open decks of the ships.

Then, suddenly, seamen are scrambling up the rigging. Lorn can see that someone is using an ax to cut the hawser on the rearmost vessel—the one closest to him and the cannon.

"Chaos!" Lorn turns to Ghyrat. "Rake the ships. First one, then the other. Use the wide flame. Then tighten it and cut the masts! Now!"

Ghyrat hurries to the cannon, issues an order, then hurries back toward Lorn.

HHHSSSTTT! With another loud hiss, the narrow flame sprays the nearer ship. Almost immediately, the sails— which had just begun to billow—are half flames, half charred canvas. Some of the spars have caught flame.

The second blast is not as well-aligned, and the forward

mast of the more distant vessel escapes part of the flame discharge.

"Ghyrat!" Lorn bellows. "Take the masts of the far ship first! The far one first!"

The engineer officer sprints back to the cannon.

Hssst! Hsst! It takes two blasts, but the ship farthest out on the pier is demasted and a mass of flames even before the cannon turns slightly and shears all three masts of the inner-most vessel, reducing it to a flaming pyre.

Lorn turns, and gestures. "Esfayl! My mount!" He hopes his voice carries, but Esfayl either hears or guesses correctly, for the captain appears from behind the shed, riding toward the base of the pier, leading the white gelding.

Ghyrat walks from the cannon toward Lorn. His face is white.

"Thank you, Captain," Lorn says. "You and your men did a good job."

"Yes . . . ser."

Lorn looks back at the burning hulls, then at Esfayl, who has just reined up a halfscore of cubits away. "Have we heard from Cheryk?"

"Yes, ser. They have mirror shields. He's giving ground . . . as slowly as he can."

Lorn turns back to the Mirror Engineer captain. "We need to reinforce Cheryk as fast as we can get there. Captain— hold your position here. If any of the green guards attack from the city, use the cannon on them. If another ship appears, do what I did here." Lorn mounts the gelding.

"Those are your orders, ser." Ghyrat swallows.

From astride the white gelding, Lorn looks hard at the young-faced and goateed captain. "They are the orders of the Majer-Commander and the Emperor."

"Yes, ser."

Lorn turns the gelding. For perhaps the first time, he truly understands, with both feelings and mind, why the loss of the fireships is such a blow to Cyador.

"Ser . . . there's little left . . ." Esfayl notes. "If we had one of those in the streets . . ."

"With one of those in the city, I'm not sure we'd have a city left to hold," Lorn says.

"Oh . . . hadn't thought that way."

"What else did Cheryk's messenger say?"

"Sasyk has his force moving up Second Harbor Way, where the shops are wall-to-wall. They have pikes and mirror shields, and except at the infrequent intersections, there is little way for the lancers to strike them."

"We'll try an attack from the rear, then," Lorn says.

Esfayl's squad rides behind him as he leads them along the seawall road and then to the west, and then onto the lower section of Second Harbor Way West near the harbor. Even from there, he can hear the *hss*ing of firelances, the occasional dull sound of metal on metal, and men yelling, both orders and imprecations.

"Firelances at the ready!" he orders. "Four-abreast."

"At the ready," Esfayl echoes. "Four-abreast."

As the small column nears the fighting from the south, Lorn can see his fears have indeed been realized. Not only has Sasyk developed a shield wall, but behind the shields, and protruding forward, are long cupridium pikes, the cupridium untouched by the chaos-bolts of the firelances.

Cheryk has his lancers firing their lances at legs well enough, but the shields are long, and for each man that falls, another appears with a shimmering shield, and step by step the phalanx is pushing the lancers back uphill toward the Palace of Eternal Light.

From behind the shield wall come arrows, arching over the ranks and into the lancers. Those arrows have taken a toll, for Cheryk looks to have lost almost a squad.

Lorn watches for a long moment, but only for that. There are no pikes left on the back side of the phalanx and the shields there are few and spread.

"Ser?" asks Esfayl.

"First, we're going to charge and try to flame down the archers from behind. If they don't have any pikes, we'll run right up their backsides. They can't be that well trained."

"Ah . . . ser . . ."

"I'm leading the charge, and I expect everyone to be with me."

"Yes, ser." Esfayl smiles.

"Six-abreast, and three trailers," Lorn orders.

"Six-abreast. Move up as needed! Lances ready!" Esfayl's voice is tight, but clear above the muted din coming from the gently sloping way ahead.

The lancers' mounts pick their way over and around perhaps a score of fallen greensuits, but the rear of the ever more swiftly moving phalanx is almost open. Lorn can see that Cheryk is retreating more quickly uphill and toward the Palace. Has the older captain seen Lorn's force, and is he trying to lure Sasyk forward so that the former lancer will not check his rear? Lorn hopes so.

The halfscore of archers stands behind large mirror shields that require both arms for the guards who shield them. The archers continue to loft shafts toward the retreating lancers.

"Charge!" Lorn orders.

"Discharge at will! Short bursts!"

So occupied are the archers in lofting arrows toward the retreating lancers under Cheryk, that only two look up, initially, as Lorn and Esfayl's single squad bears down on them.

Hssst! Hssst!

"Last rank to the rear! Last rank to the rear!" comes an order from somewhere among the green figures.

Hssst!

One archer turns and tries to loose a shaft, but is transfixed by a firebolt from one of Esfayl's lancers.

Lorn directs one burst, then two, with his own personal chaos, felling two archers immediately, then a third.

Within moments, most of the archers are down, but almost a halfscore of the green-suited shieldmen have banded together, and Lorn can see some of the pikemen trying to swing the polelike weapons to fend off Lorn's attack.

"Now!" He digs his heels into the gelding's flank. If they do not break the shield wall while it is forming, they will not break it at all.

"Follow the majer!"

Lorn lays chaos in all directions before him, slashing with the sabre that cuts as no blade should, and firing power-bolts from the lance. The gelding lurches, and Lorn has to fight to hold his seat even as he slashes down with the chaos-aided sabre to cut aside one shield-bearer, and then another.

"Major's through! Widen the gap!"

The words seem to float past him as sabre and lance flare. Behind him a mount screams.

Every green tunic he sees that moves gets a bolt of chaos or a cut from the sabre, and he knows he must cut through the green tunics ahead. The tightness of Sasyk's formation now helps, because the green-clad guards have nowhere to go, except to break formation and face the firelances and sabres before them, or risk being cut down from behind.

Lorn wheels the gelding short of the first line of pikemen still facing uphill, and begins to chaos-slash and hack his way eastward.

The disciplined phalanx has begun to disintegrate.

"Charge!" comes the command from Cheryk, and a full company of lancers sweeps downward, chaos-bolts flaring.

Then pikes fall and the green-clad guards begin to run.

Lorn charges after three, cutting one down with his firelance, the second with the sabre, and the third with the lance.

He turns the gelding, using the short lance to knock aside a single pike, then aims it and dispatches the pikeman. He knows, somewhere, that he has no charges left in the lance, and that he is drawing chaos from where he can find it. He will pay for that—but pay he will . . . later . . . for if he does not use chaos now, there will be no "later" for him to consider.

So he rides one lane, then another, then a road, then a way, leading perhaps three lancers, perhaps four, although he does not turn to count, using sabre or chaos or both, as necessary, on fleeing forms in green.

It is midafternoon, or later, when Lorn reins up in the white stone street. He glances around, finally recognizing that he is still on Second Harbor Way West. The white granite is red-and-pink most places, those where it is not covered with blood-smeared silver shields or green tunics. Black splotches appear in places on the walls of the shops lining the street. Bodies—those of men and mounts—lie everywhere, but most are clad in green.

"Ser!"

Lorn wheels the gelding, sabre and firelance ready, but the call comes from Cheryk. The veteran rides toward Lorn slowly.

"It's over, ser."

Lorn blinks. His eyes water, and he realizes that he can barely see, so bright are the flashes of after-chaos that flare before his eyes. His head throbs, and that will get worse, he knows. Or, rather, he will feel it more.

"Maybe a halfscore escaped. Once you broke their back . . . they had nowhere to go."

Lorn nods, slowly. "You'd better send out a few men as scouts . . . down to the Plaza . . . and to the west piers. Make sure there aren't any more armsmen forming up."

"Yes, ser."

Lorn doubts his forces could fight more than a handful of armed men after the carnage and the cost of the street battle. He winces inside, thinking about the mirror shields and pikes. How could he have missed those? On an open field, the lancers would have an advantage, but not in the streets of Cyad, and Sasyk had known that. Then, Sasyk had been a lancer, a corrupt one, but corrupt did not mean stupid. And Sasyk knew he would be working against the

Magi'i and had doubtless kept himself away from the shields and pikes so that their presence would not have been detected.

Cheryk turns his mount, and Lorn just sits on the gelding, trying to watch, his eyes watering, his head splitting, letting the remaining squad leaders supervise the collecting of weapons and the stacking of bodies in the wagons someone has commandeered.

After a time, shivering in the afternoon chill, he eases his mount into the full sun as the wind rises.

"Ser . . ." Cheryk rides back to Lorn and reins up. "No sign of any trouble anywhere. City is quiet everywhere."

"Everyone's in shock," Lorn says. "The first time ever, or since Alyiakal, when there's been blood on the streets here."

"Was there any other way, ser?"

"No one seemed to know it. I didn't." Lorn pauses. "I haven't seen Esfayl . . . Did he . . . ?"

"Yes, ser." Cheryk looks at Lorn. "Only six of you broke through. You slaughtered close to fourscore, but . . ."

"There wasn't anything else we could do. At least, I couldn't think of anything that would work in time."

"Ser . . . you made something work that no one else could."

"We haven't done the task as well as any would like." Lorn smiles raggedly. "How many of them . . . ?"

"Our count is rough, but the men say we took down almost twentyscore here on the streets."

Lorn shakes his head.

"Ser . . . could be more."

"Cheryk . . . I'd guess your count was right. There were close to tenscore on the piers, and that doesn't count the sailors we fired with the cannon."

"Chaos-fire, ser . . ." Cheryk is the one to shake his head.

"Sasyk?" Lorn asks.

"You cut him down, ser. Don't you remember?"

"There were so many. I just went for whoever was giving the orders. It was a bloody mess breaking that phalanx."

They both look down at the stones that are no longer white.

Lorn straightens in the saddle, conscious that his entire body aches, that his eyes water, that he has trouble seeing, and that his head is being cleft with a dull ax. "I need to report to the Majer-Commander."

Cheryk gestures, and two pair of mounted lancers ride toward them. "Escort the majer . . . wherever he goes."

"Yes, ser."

Lorn rides slowly back up to Mirror Lancer Court, the four lancers he does not even know by his side. There, he dismounts by the front entrance, and hands the gelding's reins to one of them. "If you would wait . . ."

"Yes, ser."

Lorn turns and trudges up the steps, ignoring the squad leaders who step away from him as he walks into the lower foyer and starts up the staircase that seems all too long.

"Ser?" Tygyl looks at Lorn as the majer reaches the topmost level and takes several deep breaths.

Lorn looks down. His uniform is stained everywhere with blood and other, less-sightly remnants of the battle. "We won. If you consider the loss of a company, the slaughter of nearly thirtyscore greensuits, and the total destruction of two good merchant vessels a victory." He takes a deep breath. "Is the acting Majer-Commander here?"

"Yes, ser. He's pretty weak, but he said he'd see you when you returned." Tygyl offers a tight smile. "He said you would."

Lorn nods slightly and turns toward the fifth-floor study that had been Rynst's. He opens the door and steps inside.

"You can close it, Majer." Sypcal sits in one of the armchairs in front of the desk. His feet are propped on a stool. He still wears a commander's insignia, and the uniform collar is not tight. "You will pardon me if I do not stand."

"I doubt you should, ser." Lorn stops five paces back from the senior officer, and bows. "For now, we hold Cyad, and Sasyk is dead. So are almost all of his armsmen."

Sypcal takes a long look at Lorn. "When I heard the first reports and how many armsmen Sasyk had gathered . . . I wasn't sure even you could break them."

"We almost didn't. According to a rough count, they had thirtyscore under arms with mirror shield men, archers, and pikes."

Sypcal smiles. "Vyanat'mer has already been here. He said that all the merchanters would accept whoever the Emperor's testament named as heir." Sypcal's laugh is weak, but his eyes are bright. "He said that, thanks to the Mirror Lancers and Ryalor House, there were no dissidents left. The Traders' Council will pick the heir to Dyjani Clan. Sasyk murdered all those next in line."

Ryalor House? Lorn will discover that later, he fears. He decides against raising that question on a day that has raised all too many. "What about the Magi'i?"

Sypcal shakes his head once. "We have heard nothing. I doubt we will anytime soon. Possibly not until the heir is officially announced."

"Is there any word on who that might be?"

"None. It may be that the heir named by Toziel is already dead."

Lorn winces. "Then what?"

"Then . . . Then, matters will become more interesting." Sypcal coughs before speaking, and Lorn can sense the weakness in the man. "I suggest, Majer, that a half-squad of your lancers . . . no . . . I am ordering a full-squad to guard your dwelling. Go to it, and rest. We may need you and your skills again." There is another smile. "I doubt it will be again today, and probably not tomorrow. After that . . . who knows?"

"Yes, ser." Lorn bows.

"And Majer . . . the Mirror Lancers owe you more than

they can ever repay. I tell you this because I cannot afford to have all of what you did made known. But we pay our debts. Now . . . get some rest."

"Yes, ser." Lorn turns and walks slowly from the study of the Majer-Commander.

Hoping that Sypcal can hold himself and Mirror Lancer Court together, Lorn slowly makes his way down the stairs. Several of the senior rankers make their way to the balcony railings and watch. Lorn can hear the murmurs.

". . . see why . . . Rynst brought him here . . ."

". . . talking to the lancers came with him . . . said he broke a shield wall himself . . . killed nearly twoscore himself, giving orders and directions the whole time . . . none of 'em ever saw anything like it . . ."

". . . don't take on the Butcher . . ."

". . . Butcher . . . maybe . . . but none more honest . . ."

Lorn winces but keeps descending the white stone stairs, feeling that every eye around the open foyers is upon him.

Is that what it takes to keep Cyador from falling into anarchy? Lorn asks himself. The ability to butcher mercilessly? He laughs once, harshly. Who is he to judge, with the blood on his hands and spirit?

He mounts slowly for the ride back to the barracks . . . for he still has much to do before he can rest.

The sun dips below the dwellings and the hills in the west as he rides slowly back down to the harbor. Behind him, the four lancers are silent.

CLXI

OUTLINED IN THE green-maroon sky of dusk, Lorn steps down from the veranda door and into the foyer. Ryalth hurries through the archway from the sitting room, then stops, relief flooding her face.

"Thank chaos . . . you're all right," Lorn says.

"I'm so glad to see you," she says almost at the same moment. "You're . . . you're not wounded . . . are you?" Ryalth looks at him, at the blood on his uniform and the tiredness in his eyes.

"Not in body." He sees the blackness in her eyes. "I heard that there are no dissidents among the merchanters, thanks to Ryalor House. Kernys and Denys?"

She nods slowly.

"Are you sure you're all right?" he asks.

"I'm fine. What I did was easy."

Again . . . her words are not fully true, yet he can sense the concern behind what she says . . . and the tiredness. "I'm not sure about that. That was why you were worried last night."

"And about you."

"I'm fine. Mostly," he adds.

"You can barely stand or see, and your head is splitting."

"How do you know?" he asks.

"I can sense that, remember?"

"Kernys and Denys?" he asks again.

"I had them over to Ryalor House, on the promise to ask for your support. Brinn and tyacl in wine. It takes about a half-day, and it is tasteless." She takes a deep breath. "They had promised another fivescore armsmen to support Sasyk and the Dyjani Clan." She pauses. "You look exhausted. At least come into the sitting room and sit down."

"Where dare I sit?" Lorn glances down at his uniform. "Kerial? Is he all right?"

"He's fine. Ayleha is feeding him mashed pearapples in the kitchen." Her lips curl into a semblance of a smile, if but momentarily. "He does take after you in that."

"Let me get out of this uniform. I want it burned."

She but nods once more as he walks heavily toward the stairs, and up to the bedchamber, and then into the washroom, where he begins to peel off the stained and bloody tu-

698 ◇ L. E. Modesitt, Jr.

nic. "Sasyk murdered all the heirs to Dyjani House, Sypcal told me. I assume that means Husdryt and Torvyl."

"Yes." She frowns. "Sypcal? Why Sypcal?"

Lorn sits on the washstool and pulls off his boots, one at a time. His hands come away dull red. His once-white boots are mottled pink and dull red. He sighs. "Someone killed Rynst. I think. He vanished last night. It's likely it was Luss and Lhary, but if they were the ones, I won't know." Lorn looks down. Even his undertunic is splotched with blood in several places. He pulls it off, and his trousers as well, and begins to wash.

"You won't know?"

"I told the lancers that Lhary killed Luss, and tried to set me up as the killer. They believed me, maybe because I insisted that Sypcal be acting Majer-Commander. He's capable and honest. That was even before the piers or the street battles."

"I think you'd better tell me more," the redhead says.

As he washes, Lorn recounts the day, ending with his meeting with Sypcal: ". . . then I checked with Cheryk at the barracks and rode home. Oh . . . as Sypcal said, we are guarded by a squad of lancers tonight." He looks down. The basin water is pinkish. "A squad will stop any armed men left in Cyad. Nothing might stop the Magi'i, but I don't see why they would come after me."

She shakes her head. "Half the merchanter heirs gone, one way or another, most of the high command of the Mirror Lancers gone, the First Magus dead, the Second Magus attacked, and the Emperor dead. It's stupid."

"People are stupid when it comes to power." He pauses. "The Second Magus attacked? Someone attacked Kharl? I suppose he deserves it . . . but who?"

"I don't know. No one seems to."

Lorn steps into the bedchamber, where he pulls trousers and undertunic from the armoire, then fumbles on his second pair of boots. "I want to see Kerial."

"He is fine."

Lorn stops in the chamber doorway. "What aren't you telling me? What's happened? What's wrong?"

"Lorn . . . there's more," Ryalth says softly, her eyes dark not just with fatigue, but with concern. "I wanted you to have a few moments . . ."

"Who . . . What . . . ? It's not Kerial? You said he was all right."

"He's just fine," she repeats. "Jerial came to Ryalor House this morning. She brought this." Ryalth hands Lorn a scroll, apparently unsealed. But within the unsealed scroll—parchment, not paper—is a second sealed scroll, of a paper fine but faintly tinted with green. "She is waiting in the kitchen with Kerial."

Lorn frowns. "Myryan. It can only be Myryan." He swallows as he opens and reads the inner scroll. He holds in a shiver at the familiar script and the few words written there.

For the partners of the house . . .

"Such an odd phrasing . . ." he murmurs.

Ryalth returns his look of inquiry with open blue eyes that do not flinch from the pain in his.

Lorn continues, reading deliberately.

The absence of order within the heart of those who hold chaos second-most dear will lead to the ultimate order, whether for those thought far higher than merchanters or lancers . . . or for a consort without understanding.

A healer cannot heal the absence of understanding, and healers cannot heal their own wounds or hold their own deaths at bay. A healer can use skills to allow chaos to unbalance those already unbalanced, whether through hatred of happier households, boundless ambition, or petty jealousy . . .

All a healer can do is but use her skills to allow a soul or a land to heal, and hope that those who follow to complete the healing . . . if they but will.

I have done what I must . . . for I cannot be held captive to the desires of others, whether for heirs or power . . . I have done what I can for you, and I have done so gladly.

Lorn just looks at the scroll, written so precisely, and yet it seems to make almost no sense except for the last paragraph.

"Jerial is waiting downstairs," Ryalth says gently. "She can tell you, far better than I, what happened."

His fingers clench about the scroll and he walks toward the bedchamber door. Ryalth follows silently.

Jerial is waiting at the foot of the stairs, as if she has sensed or heard his approach. Her eyes are red-rimmed.

Lorn holds out the scroll. "What happened to her? Is she ill?" As he asks the question and looks at Jerial, he knows. "How? She was fine. Who . . . ? Did that . . . Kharl? Ciesrt?"

"Let her tell you, dearest." Ryalth touches Lorn's shoulder, gently.

Lorn moistens his lips. His eyes rest on Jerial.

"I got a message, and I hurried to her dwelling. Late last night." Jerial shakes her head. "She was just lying there. She just waited . . . until I was there, and then she pressed the scroll into my hands, and she . . . said . . . it was better . . . this way . . ." Jerial's voice trembles, and her reddened eyes tear again; Lorn has never seen either from his sister the competent healer.

"Better . . . ?" he asks. "Better?" His voice is rough.

Jerial's face hardens. "She was with child."

"What?"

"It was hard to find . . . but . . . someone had removed what we had done . . . only . . . a first-level adept . . ."

"Ciesrt?" blurts Ryalth.

"Kharl," Lorn says. "He wanted heirs. The bastard wanted heirs . . . Myryan worried about that. I didn't think he'd go that far . . . I didn't think . . ." He looks down at the shimmering and spotless stone tiles of the floor. "I didn't think . . ."

After a moment, he raises his head and looks at his sister. "I don't understand." He lifts the scroll he still clenches in his hand. He looks at the parchment, almost as if he has not seen it. "She says she did what she could . . ."

"She said she'd just come back from Kharl's," Jerial explains. "He needed healing. Ciesrt said he'd been attacked on his way back from the quarter. So Ciesrt took her to heal his father. Ciesrt had brought her home, and helped her to bed, then he went back to his father's when I came."

"Why? If she was so ill . . . ?" asks Lorn.

"She didn't let him know. She just got him to send a messenger and a carriage for me. As soon as I arrived, he left."

"Did you tell him?"

"I waited. I sent a message for Kharl's consort, and Liataphi's as well. This morning I also sent a message to Tyrsal. I thought he should know, and I didn't want you to have to do it, not after I heard about the fighting in the streets." Jerial's smile is cold, even as the tears ooze from her eyes, slowly, as if she has few tears left to give. "Lleya came immediately; Kharl's consort—I don't even know her name—she came later. We all agreed that somehow she had overextended herself in healing, possibly at the infirmary, and not understood that the child would take what little chaos and strength she had left. Ciesrt is distraught . . . truly so."

"It is not enough," Lorn whispers. "Distraught . . . merely distraught." He stands rigid until he can see again. "She healed Kharl . . . after all he had done? I don't understand."

"I don't, either, Lorn," Jerial says softly. "But you know Myryan and I have never looked at things quite from the same window."

Abruptly, Lorn extends the scroll to Ryalth. "Do you know what she means?"

Lorn sees her eyes go back over the words . . . once, twice. Abruptly, her eyes shimmer, and tears course from her eyes, silently, but the only word she offers is, "No."

"I should have done more," Lorn finally whispers. "I should have acted all those years back. I should have. Father was wrong."

But the protest changes nothing, and Lorn gazes across the dining area, his eyes blank.

Ryalth shudders.

Jerial stands there mute.

Kysia appears at the edge of the room. "Ser, Ladies . . . there is a magus at the gate."

"If it's Ciesrt . . . I don't want to see him," Lorn says.

"This late?" asks Jerial.

"Did he say who he is?" asks Ryalth.

"His name is Tyrsal. He has red hair . . ."

Lorn turns. "I'll go.

Tyrsal stands beside the gate. He has tethered his mount to the single bronze ring set in the wall. Behind him the lancers watch.

"It's all right," Lorn calls to them. "I'm sorry," he apologizes as he unlocks the gate and motions for the redheaded magus to enter.

"There's nothing to be sorry about. I should be the one apologizing for coming this late and intruding." Tyrsal steps inside the iron gate, and gestures back at the mounted lancers. "Your idea?"

"The new Majer-Commander's." Lorn locks the gate, steps around the privacy screen, and turns back along the darkened marble way.

"Rynst? What happened? He wasn't in the fighting, was he?" Tyrsal steps up beside Lorn as they circle the silent fountain.

"He vanished last night. Then Commander Lhary killed the Captain-Commander, and I killed Lhary." Lorn shrugs as he walks.

"That isn't everything," Tyrsal says.

"You're too good with truth-reading. No . . . it's not," Lorn admits, "but that's the way it will be."

"It's interesting that Kharl was wounded last night, badly enough to need a healer," Tyrsal says. "I doubt a common bravo would have the skill . . ."

"It could be," Lorn says tiredly. "But there's not much I can do except watch Kharl now . . . is there?" He opens the veranda door once more.

Tyrsal stops, and looks at Lorn. "Before we go inside, you need to know something."

Lorn waits.

"Ciesrt died in all the turmoil."

"Ciesrt?"

The redheaded magus offers a sad smile. "I killed him. I followed your example. No one will ever find him."

"Because of Myryan?"

"After Jerial's message, I decided." The redhead nods. "There's not much else I can say, Lorn. I'm not asking for forgiveness or praise. Ciesrt was weak, and he let his weakness destroy Myryan. He would have let it happen again, and keep letting it happen."

"I know." Lorn looks down. "I should have taken care of the problem when I could. I didn't, and I'll always regret that."

"I don't need to come in," Tyrsal says. "Aleyar is worried. She didn't want me out at all, but I wanted you to know before tomorrow."

"I'm glad you came." Lorn claps Tyrsal's arm and hand. ". . . Thank you . . . for caring . . . for being a friend."

Tyrsal smiles wanly. "Sometimes . . . that's not enough. I know that."

"It is enough." Lorn says, meaning it fully. "Thank you."

"I'll talk to you later." Tyrsal turns.

Lorn and Tyrsal walk silently back to the gate, where Lorn unlocks it and lets Tyrsal out. He watches until the sound of hoofs dies away. Then Lorn walks back into the house.

"Where is Tyrsal?" asks Jerial.

"Tyrsal just wanted to say he was sorry. He didn't want stay or to come in. Aleyar is worried."

"He must have wanted to let you know that a great deal," Jerial says, "to be out on a night like this."

"He did. He is . . . He's always been a true friend." Lorn looks at Jerial. "You'll stay here tonight."

"I'd thought I would."

Then he looks at Ryalth. "I'm going upstairs. I just need to be alone for a little bit."

She nods and smiles softly, sadly. "Kerial and I will be waiting in the bedchamber. Whenever . . ."

"I won't be long."

Lorn walks up the steps, slowly, heavily. He puts a hand to the railing to steady himself. Once on the second level, he slips into the bedchamber, where he picks up the silver-covered book. He carries it to his study, where he uses a striker to light the lamp. Even the thought of using chaos for as little as that intensifies the headache that has yet to show any signs of subsiding.

After looking for long moments at the silver-covered book, he slowly leafs through it until he finds the page he recalls. He reads the words slowly.

Ashes to ashes
and dust to dust
will not bring back the dance
nor the dancer.
Chaos to order and back to flame
brings back no songs without name.

For the lesson that I have learned
is that there is none.
No one else will sing those songs,

nor dance, nor smile that smile.
because one less one is none.

In her own way, Myryan had been a dancer, a dancer of the soul . . . Had he and Ryalth—and Tyrsal—been the only ones to see that?

For a long time, he studies the lines in the book. Finally, he closes it and gazes out the window into the darkness.

A man can change the times—sometimes—and the times may make one man, but they destroy many others in the process.

There is a rustle behind him, and he turns.

Ryalth stands there. "I was worried."

"I'm all right," he lies. Then he opens the book and hands it to her, open to the verse he has read again and again. "I was thinking about Myryan."

She nods and twin lines of silver streak her cheeks. In time, she closes the book, and he turns down the lamp wick, and they walk to the bedchamber, where Kerial sleeps, restlessly.

They watch their son, silently, as the night deepens.

CLXII

LORN STANDS BEFORE the acting Majer-Commander of the Mirror Lancers. Behind Sypcal, cold droplets of water bead on the antique panes of the study windows, droplets from the cold drizzle that blankets Cyad and the Palace of Light.

"You report that all is calm in Cyad, Majer. Can you be sure of such?" asks Sypcal, leaning forward slightly over the table desk that had been Rynst's.

Lorn nods. "Since the street battles, I have taken the liberty of having squads ride the roads and ways, ser. They have seen no signs of others bearing arms." Lorn does not report that he has also used his chaos-glass, if sparingly, because of the headache that has not yet fully left him, and asked Tyrsal to do the same. "The rain may aid in keeping the calm."

"And your presence, I am certain, has a certain restraining effect."

"They're afraid I'll slaughter them?" Lorn smiles mirthlessly. "I only slew those who rose against the Emperor."

"Exactly. If they do not rise, then you will not slaughter them." Sypcal's smile is almost as mirthless as Lorn's. The acting Majer-Commander remains seated behind the table desk. His red hair seems dull, although his eyes are alert as he looks at Lorn. "There is one more matter, Majer."

"Ser?"

"Your presence has been requested at the Palace. By the Empress. Immediately."

Lorn swallows.

"She wishes to convey her gratitude to you for saving Cyad from Sasyk. In person." Sypcal frowns slightly. "She is less than perfectly well, I understand, but she insisted that I bring you in person."

"Yes, ser."

"I will meet you at the entrance shortly."

"Yes, ser," Lorn responds a last time. He bows, then makes his way out of the Majer-Commander's study.

CLXIII

LORN'S WHITE BOOTS whisper on the polished sunstone and granite floors of the Palace of Eternal Light as he and Sypcal follow the two guards along the high-ceilinged and pillared corridor. To the right, between the columns, are narrow windows stretching nearly fifteen cubits from the polished floor to the buttresses that connect the columns. Outside of Palace

Guards dressed in green uniforms with silver trim, the Palace seems eerily empty, and Lorn glances at Sypcal.

A faint smile crosses the face of the acting Majer-Commander as he looks back at Lorn. "Don't ask me. I've been here but a handful of times, and only to the Great and Lesser Audience Halls. Like you, I'm following orders."

Lorn laughs to himself.

The two green-clad Palace Guards lead them down a smaller corridor—ten cubits wide, and then to a set of double doors, guarded by yet another pair in green. One opens the right-hand door, and Lorn follows Sypcal into a foyer a good twenty cubits square. There are several golden-oak chairs set against the paneled walls, and a single guard in silver stands by the inner door.

The guard in silver looks at Sypcal. "Ser . . . the Empress has requested that you remain here until the other advisors arrive. She will see you all together. She wishes to see Majer Lorn first, alone, and she wishes that he bring the special sabre at his side."

Lorn moistens his lips. *"The special sabre"?* How does the Empress know it is special?

Sypcal smiles. "Best of luck, Majer."

"Thank you, ser." Lorn steps through the door. He finds himself at the end of a bedchamber—one comparatively modest for what he has seen in the Palace of Light so far, perhaps thirty cubits long, and fifteen wide. The left side of the chamber is comprised of alternating panels of polished green marble and green tinted glass, that somehow seem to diminish the light pouring in from the south. Still, Lorn can see the harbor, and the two hulks that were once Dyjani trading vessels.

The high bed is wide enough for four people, and the headboard is almost plain, but of a wood that might have once been white oak, but which now bears a green stain that allows the grain to show through despite the darkness of the color. The Empress is propped up on the window side of the overlarge bed, the white counterpane folded back at her waist. She wears a plain dark-green velvet gown with long sleeves. Her hair is half mahogany, half snow-white.

"Majer . . . please do not delay. Step forward, if you will." The voice is firm, and almost melodic. In her left hand is a scroll, sealed with green-and-silver wax, and wrapped with green ribbon.

As he steps forward, finally halting at the foot of the bed, just a cubit from the green-and-cream velvet coverlet, Lorn studies her and nods, almost to himself, in spite of his resolve to betray nothing until he truly knows why he has been summoned.

"Why do you nod, Majer?"

"You are a healer. The Emperor would have died years earlier, would he not?"

"It is most likely, but that concerns you not." A faint smile creases the wrinkled face. "You are both healer and magus, lancer and merchanter. But you will not be Emperor unless you act quickly and decisively."

"Why would I be Emperor?"

"Who else could there be now?" she counters, a wry twist to her lips. "Your actions have left very few with any ability."

"I did not slay any for that reason," Lorn says quietly.

"Had you, you would not be here." She pauses, as if gathering herself together. "In a few moments, the advisors will enter, and I will to announce you as heir . . . you must be prepared for all manner of trial. Nothing may occur, and then it may."

Lorn bows. What is there to say?

"What indeed?" Ryenyel pauses. "You have trusted your consort, have you not?"

"You must know I have."

"You will need to trust her even more, for if you become Emperor, all save her will seek to flatter you and deceive you, and many will be skilled enough to deceive you with only the truth." A small smile precedes her next words. "As you yourself have often done."

Lorn returns her smile with a slight one of his own.

"Oh . . . the Palace thanks you for your efforts in saving Cyad from the depredations of Sasyk. I should have said that first, but I have little time, and it is an effort to continue to think clearly." Ryenyel clears her throat. "Why did you have the sabre plated with cupridium so many years ago?"

"I could not say, Lady Empress, save that it seemed like a good idea, and that it has proven so over the years."

She laughs. "If you only knew how much consternation that act created for how many people for years . . ." She reaches up with her right hand and tugs the bellpull.

The door behind Lorn opens, and the silver-clad guard enters and bows.

"Norgyn . . . are the advisors here?"

"Yes, Lady Empress."

"Send in the guards for Majer Lorn, then . . . after they are here, bid the advisors enter."

Lorn frowns, but does not move.

"You will stand at the side, Majer, between the windows there. The guards are required when any bring a weapon into the Emperor's or Empress's presence. They will convey another impression, which will be . . . useful." She smiles. "They would be no match for you, but I trust you will not test them so."

"Not unless necessary, Lady."

"Good."

A second door, one so flush to the inner paneled wall that Lorn had not noticed it, opens, and two of the regular Palace Guards in green appear. They walk around the bed and station themselves on each side of Lorn. They bear the short firelances in scabbards fastened to their silver belts.

The hidden door closes, and the door through which Lorn has entered opens. First comes a magus, broad-shouldered, tall, red-haired and green-eyed. Although Lorn has never met him, Lorn knows the magus must be Kharl, both from the resemblance to Ciesrt and from the crossed lightning-bolts on the breast of his white shimmercloth tunic.

After Kharl comes Commander Sypcal, his face expressionless, and after Sypcal comes Vyanat, who avoids looking in Lorn's direction.

The three line up at the foot of the massive bed, looking at the Empress.

"I have summoned you, in the name and memory of Toziel." Ryenyel lifts the beribboned scroll slightly. "He has named his heir."

"This is not a proper audience, Lady Empress," states the new First Magus.

"How can it not be proper? The three Advisors are present. His widow is present. There are witnesses." Ryenyel smiles serenely. "And . . . as you can see . . . I doubt I will survive to what you might term a proper audience."

"Might I ask why a mere majer is present, Lady?" asks Kharl, inclining his head toward Lorn.

"He was the one who saved Cyad from being turned over to flux chaos and who kept the Palace of Eternal Light inviolate, most honored First Magus. For his reward, do you not think he should be among the first to know the heir?"

Kharl bows slightly.

"Have any of you words on this before I break the seal?"

"Lady Empress," Kharl says smoothly, "I would but say that the people of Cyad would wish to see the father figure of the Emperor . . . one who has known their pain and their grief . . ."

Ryenyel nods. "You mean that you wish to fulfill that image? Would you recall that folk outside of Cyad itself only wish to live their lives in prosperity and be left alone, and that they would prefer one who would guarantee such?"

"The two can be one," Kharl points out, "and I am certain that the Emperor understood such . . . at least before his last illness."

Ryenyel's voice strengthens. "What does the house of a

crafter in Jakaafra look like, First Magus? You have such wide experience . . . would you describe it to me?"

Kharl looks at the Empress as if she is mad.

"Does it not have thick and sturdy shutters—and a strong ceramic screen built so as to allow air to flow yet so none can see directly into the dwelling—with yet a second screen inside the dwelling so that any welcomed at the door can scarce see the interior?"

"That may be," Kharl admits.

The hint of smile plays across Vyanat's lips. Sypcal merely watches.

"Are not most houses built so?" questions Ryenyel.

"I would not attempt to guess what the common folk built or how they dwell."

"Yet you would be their father figure?" A lilting laugh follows the words. "Come now . . . does not the very structure of such a dwelling tell you that those who live there wish their lives to be hidden from the Emperor, the Mirror Lancers, and the Magi'i . . . and your chaos-glasses?" Ryenyel turns her head to Sypcal, then back to Kharl. "Do you, First Magus . . . do you think it a whim or a coincidence that no streets are named in the cities beyond Cyad and Fyrad? That the common folk guard their names jealously?"

"They are as children," Kharl offers gently. "They must be protected."

"That they must be protected . . . on that we all agree, I am certain," the Empress responds.

Lorn looks at her countenance. He is certain that far more of her hair is white than when he first entered the chamber, and there are more wrinkles and creases upon her face.

"Here is the will of the Emperor," Ryenyel states. "Majer-Commander . . . I would have you break the seal and read what is written thereon."

"As you command, Lady Empress." Sypcal bows, and steps forward. He takes the still-sealed scroll from her and turns. He breaks the seal and slowly unrolls the short parchment. Then he reads:

> I, Toziel'elth'alt'mer, Emperor of Cyador, in the fullness of time, and in the wisdom of experience, hereby declare that the heir to the Malachite Throne, the man who shall succeed me when I am gone, and my spirit returned to the Steps of Paradise, on the path to the Rational Stars, shall be Lorn'alt, Majer of the Mirror Lancers, of elthage birth, Mirror Lancer through ability, and merchanter through consortship, fulfilling all the needs and requirements of Emperor. Let it be so.

Sypcal smiles, if slightly.

"Lorn'elth'alt'mer *will* be the son and heir of Toziel," Ryenyel orders.

Lorn bows his head, but his eyes watch Kharl.

"This is a travesty . . . Lorn is but a butcher and a pup without the ability to rule his own dwelling, let alone Cyad or Cyador." Kharl steps away from Vyanat.

Lorn can sense the massive amount of chaos swirling up and infusing itself around Kharl. At the same time, he can sense a pit of darkness within the other, one he doubts Kharl can even sense. Lorn lifts his own shields, knowing he must strike, and strike quickly. The Brystan sabre is in his hand, and he steps away from the guards.

"Let them be!" cracks Ryenyel's voice. "What will be, will be."

Sypcal and Vyanat back away from Kharl, as do the two guards from Lorn.

Lorn has the Brystan sabre in a guard position even before the chaos-firebolt reaches him.

Hsssst!

With a lazy smile, Lorn uses the order of the iron blade to turn and fling the firebolt back at the First Magus . . . and then lets the blade follow the firebolt, its iron-cored length slashing into the older magus—and linking with that dark order within the First Magus.

Kharl opens his mouth, and suddenly his eyes widen in shock, and the font of chaos that Kharl has summoned collapses back in upon him, drawn by that well of dark order. The iron-cored blade—momentarily halted, as if in midair, slashes even deeper into Kharl. Sparkles of light flare into the air of the bedchamber.

Lorn blinks. So do the others.

When he can see again, there is little on the chamber floor—except a few cupridium items, a melted pin that had once been an emblem of crossed lightning, some buckles, and cupridium boot-nails—and a shimmering sabre.

Lorn bows to the Empress. "I beg your mercy."

"I should beg yours, Lorn, for I see that you have mastered more than would appear." The Empress's words are dry. Her eyes travel to Sypcal, and then to Vyanat. "Have either of you, for yourself, or those you represent, any objections?"

"No, Lady Empress," offers Sypcal. He turns and bows to Lorn. "Your Mightiness."

A broad smile crosses Vyanat's face. "If we cannot have a merchanter, we will have an Emperor whose consort has proven herself as among the best of merchanters, and all will be pleased with that." He, too, bows to Lorn. "Your Mightiness."

Ryenyel clears her throat, as if with difficulty. She looks at Lorn. "Before you go, and prepare to ascend the Malachite Throne . . . take the book here on the table—and read it well."

Lorn steps forward toward the Empress and the table on the window side of the bed.

"There," she says. "It is yours, to read and to pass on in your time."

"Yes, Lady." He picks up the volume with the green-

sheened silver cover—so like the book of verse with which
Ryalth had entrusted him so many years before.

"Read it well." Ryenyel pauses and turns toward the two
men at the foot of the bed. "None of you will see me again.
That is as I wish it. Now . . . please . . . depart while I retain
some dignity." When Lorn and the two advisors do not move,
she adds, "I do mean that. Honor that as my last request."

The three bow and slip from the chamber, followed by the
pair of guards.

Lorn realizes, absently, that he has the answer to his father's
final question, an answer he has known all along: The world is
based on power. Power is simple. It is the ability to get others
to do one's will. Nothing more, nothing less—but its complexity lies in how one obtains the compliance of others.

As Lorn stands in the foyer outside the bedchamber, half
pondering what he has so belatedly recognized, Sypcal steps
up and hands Lorn the Brystan blade. "I trust you will not
need this, but you might wish to keep it. I would that you not
leave the Palace to inform your consort until your lancers
can escort you."

"I will wait," Lorn says.

"You will find you will wait more than you ever wished,
Your Mightiness," Sypcal says, as they leave the foyer outside the bedchamber of the dying Empress.

Lorn suspects Sypcal's words are all too true.

CLXIV

LORN SHAKES HIS head as he reins up outside his dwelling,
followed by Palace Guards, and a company of Mirror
Lancers commanded by Cheryk. At Sypcal's insistence,
Lorn has earlier sent a messenger to Ryalor House request-
ing Ryalth meet him at their dwelling. He glances at the

clear green-blue sky, a winter day's sky somehow . . . austere. Or perhaps that is the way he feels.

"Your Mightiness . . . while it is an imposing dwelling, I do not think you will see much of it," suggests Cheryk as Lorn dismounts.

The title sounds strange to Lorn, but he offers a smile to the captain. "There's likely much I will not see as I did." He turns and unlocks the iron gate. He is barely inside the walls, followed by two of the Palace Guards in the green-and-silver, when Ryalth comes running from the veranda.

She slows a good dozen paces short of Lorn, and her eyes go from Lorn to the guards, then back to him. "What's the matter? Are you in trouble?"

"I think," he begins with a smile, "we are both in trouble." After a slight pause, he adds, "I have the stone . . . or it has me. Toziel named me his heir. That makes you Empress-Consort."

Her eyes widen. For a moment they both stand in the chill and sunny day, beside a fountain that does not flow.

"Truly?" the redhead murmurs.

"Truly."

Another silence falls between them.

"What of the Magi'i?" she finally asks. "Most would oppose you."

"Kharl . . . he tried to kill me when the advisors were read the declaration. I was fortunate enough to prevail."

"There is no one else left, then?"

"Liataphi will be First Magus. Rustyl was the magus who died with Chyenfel. Sypcal will be Majer-Commander. Vyanat declares he is pleased, that in these days the merchanters are most gratified that you are Empress-Consort, for they will have a voice." Lorn grins. "And that they will have a voice is certain."

Abruptly, Ryalth shivers. "It's cold out here."

Lorn takes her arm, and the two turn toward the veranda.

One of the Palace Guards slips ahead of them and into the house. The other holds the door.

Lorn and Ryalth descend the steps and cross the foyer into the sitting room. Lorn looks at Ryalth. "Where's Kerial?"

"Kysia's feeding him in the kitchen."

"Good. I just worry." Lorn nods.

"What are you holding?" she asks.

He lifts the silver-covered volume. "Something of great interest." He extends the book to her. "The Empress gave it to me. It was the Emperor's. There's a note. Go ahead . . . read it."

Lorn looks over her shoulder, seeing the words again, as Ryalth reads the angular and shaky script of the note.

To the Emperor-to-come:

These are the words of His Mightiness Kiedral'elth'alt'mer, the Second Emperor of Light, as he wrote them. So far as is known, this is the only remaining copy.

He has much to say. Read them all, if you dare, before you sit in the Malachite Throne.

There is a verse marked . . . *for the Emperor Toziel.* . . .

At the bottom is a single, spiraled initial *R*.

"Have you opened it?" Ryalth asks.

Rather than answer, the man who is not sure he is either Mirror Lancer majer or Emperor opens the silver cover, holding it open to the first page, a page with but a title in large letters: *Meditations Upon the Land of Light.* When he is certain Ryalth has read it, he turns to the second page, and a dedication: *To those of the Towers, to those of the Land, and to those who endured.* Below the dedication is a name, and a title Lorn has never seen nor heard before: *Kiedral Daloren, Vice Marshal, Anglorian Unity.*

Then he turns to the page with the green leather marker, and reads the lines there slowly, aloud.

I would be remembered in the morning breeze,
in a single daffodil above late snow,
in slanting sun through trees,
and distant hills where cold winds blow.

Do not wear mourning green;
you have seen what I have seen.

Is that the way Toziel would like to be remembered—or as the father figure that the Emperor always must be?

Ryalth's eyes are bright, and her blue eyes meet Lorn's. "I wonder."

He closes the book, then takes the note from her hand and slips it inside the front cover, before he hands her the book. "We each have a copy." He smiles. "Since you have entrusted yours to me these long years, I will entrust mine to you."

CLXV

JERIAL STEPS INTO the green-walled salon of the Empress. Her eyes circle the room, then come to rest on the man in the silver-trimmed green tunic and trousers who stands from where he has been sitting on the white divan, beside a red-haired woman in formal blue tunic, trimmed in both green and silver.

A small boy in green trousers and tunic turns. "Jehwhal!" His legs pump, carrying him toward the healer in green.

Jerial bends and scoops him up, hugging him.

Lorn and Ryalth follow their son.

"This is all . . . hard to believe," Jerial says, shifting Kerial to her left shoulder.

"It's hard to believe you won't be staying in Cyad," Ryalth says. "I worry about Kerial . . . with you gone."

"You and Aleyar can do all that I could." Jerial turns to her younger brother. "You know it's better this way. All I've ever really wanted was to be free and to help you as I could, and with you on the Malachite Throne . . ."

"I know," Lorn says heavily. "We still worry."

"I'll be fine. Ryalth has arranged a villa for me in Lydiar . . . and a position as the healer for Ryalor House there."

"Eileyt will ensure that we know if you need anything," Ryalth confirms.

"It was good you gave him Ryalor House."

"Besides Lorn, he worked the hardest to build it. But he didn't get everything," Ryalth says. "You're getting the two thousand golds, and we did keep a little, in an account with the Trader's Exchange. It has to be mine. Lorn cannot own anything." She smiles. "If anyone had thought about a lady trader as Empress-Consort . . . they would have forbidden that, too, and someone will probably make sure it does not happen again." She laughs gently.

"I wish you could be here for the ceremony," Lorn says.

"The longer I stay, the harder it will be to leave, and if I try to be free here, I'll always be looking over my shoulder. And you will worry about me, and then I will be caged by your concerns." Jerial eases Kerial back to Ryalth.

The healer and the heir embrace, and then Ryalth and Jerial embrace.

After a time, Jerial looks back once, at the door, before she steps from the salon.

CLXVI

DO TIMES MAKE the man? Or does the man make the times?

His Mightiness, Lorn'elth'alt'mer, looks at the malachite-and-silver throne, then at the Empress-Consort who follows him, their son in her arms, as he walks slowly from the doors of the Great Audience Chamber toward the Malachite Throne.

On the immediate left side of the Great Hall are the Magi'i of Cyador, and their families. In the group of Magi'i stands Tyrsal, who will be the Hand of the Emperor, and knows it not, and Aleyar, who doubtless does. Beside Tyrsal stands Vernt, who believes he is there solely because he is Lorn's brother. The First Magus, the sad-faced Liataphi, stands to the left at the base of the dais.

Also to the left is the newly-promoted Majer-Commander Sypcal, who will never fully recover from his poisoning, and who is slowly dying and knows it, and behind him, Captain-Commander Brevyl, who yet protests his triple promotion and who still does not care personally for Lorn, but for whom honesty and duty remain more important than personal tastes. Behind them are the remaining senior commanders, and the newly-promoted overcaptain Cheryk.

On the right side of the hall are the heads of the merchanter houses, and those who head the trading firms too small to be houses.

Lorn steps toward the Malachite Throne, each step measured.

Do times make the man? Or man the times?

Does it matter? Except to acknowledge that, either way, the costs are high?

Lorn bows his head as he approaches the Malachite Throne, not in respect for the throne, but in homage to all those who have paid those costs, one way or another, from the innocent grower's daughter who still at times haunts his

dreams, to Myryan, and to Tyrsal, who will pay more than
he knows for Ciesrt's death. He bows, too, in respect for all
those who have paid whom he does not know and may
never know.

. . . and in respect to the ancient Emperor whose words
helped in ways the writer could never have imagined.

. . . and the new becomes the old,
with the way the story's told . . .
So shine forth both in sun and into night
bright city of prosperity and light.